Demons of Astlan Volume II: The Heavenly Host

By
Jerry Langland
Copyright 2015

Special Thanks and Dedication to:

Michael Begal, Jay Haesly, Sean Jones, Bob Bingham, Jeff Hodapp, Rick Szekeres, Don Meyer

Edited By: http://www.5starediting.com
Cover Art By: Jacob Atienza (http://jacobarts.weebly.com)
Visit http://www.Astlan.Net for Maps, History, Details and Artwork.
Special thanks to all the Beta Demons who helped get the story into shape:

Beta Demons				
ackior	Dan C	James	Myzifer	SomethingSomething
aden	Daoed	jameshanky	Naberius	spacer
Aditya	Darkenmal	jameshanky	Napalm222	Stahel
AJOswell	dave	jamison	Netter	SwiftGifts
akira44513	David Warren	Jamisont	Nick	tannim
angakok	Davids	JasperBloodstone	NickD	technitium
Anskier	Demonsyc	jmtxam	Nightmares	TheOtherGuy
Arad an-BÃis	Dirk Flamberge	JMX	nilrem	Threefinger
archit	dobby175	Joe	NinjaKittens	trinter
Arean	DogmaPiece	john	nobahde	Uuvini
Arkon86	Draelith	Jonnyboi	NocandlE	vinfrost
Arthur	Eric	JPranna	noi	Vladimir Privman
Astra19	eugene2k	jumpmage	Nuromir	WarmCocaCola
Attolis	EyeDeKay	Jürgen Christoph Affenzeller	Ogbebaba	wendy
AussieKid	Finaltheorem47	Kellysdec	ookami	whomightub3
Azazail	Flakes	kieta	Pandemonius	wolfy0118
Azpen	Flinx	Killblah	Pat	xenofixus
baochou	Fox12	Kingskunk	Pathologic	YoshiA
battlezoid	Fralur	KnightofAbyss	Puck	Zelosh
bearit	franco	Kuryuu	Punic	Zieggenfus
BetaDemon	galeblaze	kyler	puri	ziipoo
big19817	GameGraphix	Lafoia	Quibbler	Zombie
Bludflag	Gardock	Laith	Racue	Zutrak
bob	Gehlert	Lhans	ragnok	
Bobby	Gelcube	Liam	ronag	
boomstick3000	George	lothlaine	Rosver	
boy toy satan	GhastlyFire	Lucifer	ryorka	
Broken	gjarboni	Lyndrek	sdhanju105	
Burien	Goblyn	MaddHatter	Sea of Tranqility	
cairol2	goldenz	Madfox11	ShadowFerret	
Cali'x	Grant	Malahadiel	shakez	
CAN07	Guthan	malidhor	Shakez	
Carson Gabbard	Heartfrost	Maou	shakez4	
castleguard	hose45	mask19	Silverpest	
CelticLord	Iblees	masozrava palma	Sir Isaac	
chestnevsky	Icanrememberpito68decimalplaces	MatCauthon15	SixFeetUnder	
Corey	iume	Mesmerizing Suggestion	Skepti	
Corum	Ivan	mhh	Skrekert	
CrispyMouse	-J-	Mikey	smw	
Crying Tiger	Jago	Mithalraman	socal24	

Contents

Prolegomenon: Dates, Time, Calendar and "Previously On"

Reminder from Volume I: The planet of Astlan has two moons, Uropia, the closer moon orbits Astlan around the axis of rotation from East to West (like Earth's moon) and Anuropia, the further out moon orbits Astlan over the poles of rotation from North to South and then South to North.

http://www.astlan.net/Home/AstrometryAstrology/TheMoonsandTheirCycles.aspx

Uropia, the moon with a feminine aspect has 10 months per Astlanian year, Anuropia has 5 months per year and thus for every one Uropian month, there are two Anuropian months. The five months of Anuropia conveniently correspond to the five seasons: Hearth, Winter, Spring, Summer, Harvest.

Anuropian months are not specifically named, given that they also correspond to the seasons which are reversed in the Northern and Southern hemispheres. Anuropian quarter months are however named, each named quarter month has two ten day weeks that correspond to the relative positions of the two moons.

While timekeeping does vary across Astlan, the dates are fairly standardized for trade purposes. Typically, dates are given as Anuropian Quarter Month/Day of Quarter Month/Year. In texts, the quarter month is denoted by either a number 1 to 20 or the name of the month.

http://www.astlan.net/Home/AstrometryAstrology/AstlanianCalendar.aspx

There are multiple calendars that designate the current year depending on specific events; over the last few centuries, those calendars that do not start and stop at the same time have fallen out of favor so that currently the major calendars in use have years that are only offsets of each other.

http://www.astlan.net/Home/History/Timeline.aspx

The Council States, where most of the humans in Demons of Astlan live, officially uses the Post-Vargosian Calendar which dates from the fall of the Vargosite Empire 424 years ago.

To understand time tracking during the day, please refer to this Appendix on Time of Day.

As a reminder, here are some recent historical points.

- Approximately 10 years ago, Lenamare the Great learns of a book of immeasurable value to both conjurors and demons alike. Lenamare's nemesis, Exador and his allies Ramses and Bess were already aware of the book and had been trying to locate it for many years.

- A few years ago, Lenamare ascertained a very likely location for the book and hired a band of interdimensional rogues and bounty hunters to retrieve the book from ruins inside of Oorstemoth.
- Lenamare's agents acquired the book but were captured; Lenamare, however, had planted magic items on his agents that caused them to blame Exador for the robbery.
- Exador spent nearly a year clearing himself of the charges, and determined that Lenamare had the book that he and his allies wanted.
- Exador and his allies plot to seize Lenamare's Academy of Wizardry and more specifically the book. Lenamare discovers the plot by Exador and begins planning his defense.
- On Cyclos 7th 440 PV during a training session with students, Lenamare and his partner Jehenna discover what they thought was an unbound lesser demon. Upon trying to summon the demon for the first time they realize it was actually a Greater Demon. With great risk to themselves and the students Lenamare succeeds in binding the demon to his will.
  - Cyclos 7, 440 is Day Zero for the events detailed here. It is the day that the Demon Tom is first summoned.
- 14 days later (DZ+14), Lenamare blows up his own school and takes out the majority of Exador's forces.
- The following evening (DZ+15) Verigas, the High Priest of Tiernon in Gizzor Del has his own demon summoning hijacked by a Demon Lord with a party of humans. This begins the Rod's involvement
- A few days later, an Oorstemothian ship attempts to apprehend a smuggler and is illegally destroyed by one Lord Edwyrd, a powerful animage that also controls demons. This begins Oorstemoth's involvement
- 30 days later (DZ+30), on Electh 17th 440 PV the Greater Demon Tom battles Talarius, Knight Rampant of Tiernon, Tom defeats Talarius by subverting the mana links between Tiernon and his priests, and using it to take control of the Rod of Tiernon, the holy army. Further, he reverses the holy dagger, Excrathadorus Mortis, and tosses Talarius "Into the Abyss."
  - Electh 17th 440 PV is known as the "Day of Fight" or DOF.

This volume begins on DOF, mere seconds after Talarius is tossed "Into the Abyss."

Chapter 80

"…Thpp" Ramses made a tongue-sucking noise on his teeth. "Did you, my dear compatriots, witness what I think I witnessed?"

Bess and Exador were silent. Everything around them was quiet; one could hear the tassels on their flying carpet fluttering in the wind.

Or at least, it was quiet to persons of typical human hearing; if they'd so chosen, the three archdemons could have heard what was going on down on the ground below them and in the sky behind them and to their left. Chaos, insanity, slaughter, you name it—that's what was going on all around them.

In the air behind them, the Oorstemothian Sky Fleet was eradicating the last of a horde of several hundred to a thousand lower-level demons that had just been expelled, forcibly, from the city of Freehold. Demons that had been under orders from Exador, one of the three occupants of this flying carpet floating about a thousand feet above the encampment of the Holy Rod of Tiernon, the military arm of the Holy Church of Tiernon.

"Is there anyone on this carpet who does *not* think that an, *ahem*, fourth-order demon just started Armageddon?" Exador asked.

"It's going to take a bit of work to avoid it," Bess commented sourly.

"I think we should adjourn to the Abyss to discuss this. Agreed?" Ramses said quietly. "My place?"

"Yes." Exador agreed.

"I don't want to be here when Tiernon's flunkies show up," Bess stated. "After getting kicked out of Freehold on my ass this morning, I'm not up to dealing with a bunch of avatars."

"Particularly not his," Ramses agreed. He shook his head and opened a demonic gateway in front of the carpet, and Exador flew them through into Ramses' estate in the Abyss. Once through, Ramses closed the gate behind them.

~

"This is very inconvenient," Exador complained as they sat around a table in a smaller, cozier chamber of Ramses' palace. One of the servants had brought them cups of Denubian Choco-Coffee™, the extremely caffeinated beverage with a great mocha taste at 132 degrees centigrade. Among other effects, it was quite intoxicating to demons. Completely lethal to humans, even if served chilled—meaning any temperature below the boiling point of water.

"We shouldn't be drinking this early in the day, but hell, if you can't drink at a time like this, when can you drink?" Bess complained.

"That so called fourth-order of Lenamare's somehow tapped into the link between a god and a high priest. I had no idea that was even possible!" Ramses complained.

"Who the hell would be dumb enough to even try?" Exador exclaimed, shaking his head. "Who doesn't think that a god or their avatar is going to notice when their incoming mana levels start dipping? Or when there are huge, non-authorized drains on the reserves?"

"Or when you kidnap one of their highest ranking, most Graced agents on the plane and haul him off to the Abyss?" Bess asked.

"As soon as Lilith or Sammael hear about this, they are going to work to secure this so-called fourth-order demon," Exador pointed out.

"That should be a fun scramble," Bess said drily.

"I am so glad we don't mess with Court politics," Ramses added.

"However, politics aside," Ramses interjected, "it is a given that Tiernon's avatars are going to show up to investigate, and there is not much we can do about that. They will probably interrogate everyone in the city as well as in the surrounding armies." The others shrugged in agreement. "Therefore, our primary concern is ensuring they don't find out about the book."

The sound of cups being set down in saucers was very clear in the silence as they contemplated what would happen if Tiernon or his avatars got hold of the book. It is very hard for archdemons to get chills running down their spines, but it can happen, and at that moment, it did.

~

Arch-Diocate Iskerus was in shock, as was Arch-Vicar General Barabus. Barabus was staring at the spot where a flaming hole in the ground had opened up and swallowed the greatest knight of Tiernon into the Abyss. The only thing Barabus appeared capable of doing was to blink repeatedly.

Arch-Diocate Iskerus, on the other hand, was staring at a point a few feet away, where a holy, albeit very dark, artifact of his god had been, apparently, repurposed. He reached down to hold his hand over it, feeling its aura. He had only ever examined the dagger once before and even though he had sensed his god's presence in it, the darkness in it had terrified him. Now that darkness was gone, and in fact, he felt the normal radiance of a healing artifact of Tiernon. It was as if the blade had been reversed.

Reversed by a demon. A demon! Iskerus shuddered all the way down to the roots of his soul. How could this be? It was not possible. His mind boggled at the very idea! He felt a gentle touch on his shoulder; a priest. He could not remember the man's name.

"Arch-Diocate, what should we do with the high priests who have collapsed, and Verigas?" someone asked.

"Take them to a quarantine tent; give them all the healing we safely can, but ensure every precaution is taken. Apply to them every purification you can find or imagine. I'll provide more instructions later."

"And the Rod members who were also possessed?" the same someone asked Iskerus.

"The same, different tent; disarm them, remove their armor and station guards," Arch-Vicar General Barabus said, walking over. He extended his hand to Iskerus and the man took it, getting up slowly, suddenly feeling far older than his current age.

"Any thoughts?" Barabus asked as he led the Arch-Diocate back to his tent.

Iskarus gestured for a nearby high priest to secure the dagger. "Not yet. I'm numb." That was the only word he could come up with.

"As am I, but I'm slowly waking. We need to put on a very brave face for the troops and the junior priests. A lot of faith has been shaken today; we must work to restore it." Iskerus nodded in agreement. "For now, we must put aside our own doubts, fears, insecurities and not think too deeply upon our own questions. We must think of the souls in our care."

"Agreed. So which of us gets to report this to the Supreme Temple?" Iskerus asked.

Barabus chuckled. "I hope that's as far as this goes—I pray—but I am not convinced."

~

"What an Abyssal disaster!" Jenn exclaimed as she walked around the palace with Maelen and Gastropé. "Did no one think through the consequences of this?" Jenn waved her hands angrily towards a pile of rubble. "You've got hundreds of demons trapped in a palace, many with no way out, and then on short notice, with no real planning, you cast the most powerful banishment spell anyone has ever used?" She shook her head in exasperation. "How could these supposedly brilliant master wizards not even think to open the doors and windows?"

The palace looked like a war zone; windows were smashed everywhere, and the walls had holes in them, surrounded by rubble where demons had blasted through to escape the city.

"Seems like another detail beneath the bother of your friends Lenamare and Jehenna," Maelen observed in his humorously sardonic manner. Jenn just shook her head.

Gastropé was scanning the area as they walked. "No demons, none. They are all gone. Amazing; I can't believe it."

"You would think they would tell people first, though," Maelen said, noting more than a few people reclining near fountains, having previously fainted or soiled themselves when hundreds and hundreds of invisible demons had started popping up and desperately trying to flee via any means possible.

"This is so like men!" Jenn exclaimed. "Were there any women involved in this crazy scheme?"

"Jehenna," Gastropé replied.

Jenn glared at him. "You know that icicle doesn't count. She needs a bigger codpiece than most of the men I know." Gastropé glared at her. "Yes, that includes you." Jenn snapped and then suddenly realized what she was saying and softened. "I'm sorry, I'm just frustrated." She grabbed his forearm and gave it a squeeze before releasing it.

"Where are Edwyrd and Rupert? I went to check on them, but they apparently didn't return to their room after breakfast," Jenn asked. Maelen shrugged and Gastropé went pale, which actually was not that unusual for him.

"Uhm," Gastropé hedged, "they're probably running around with Damien trying to clean things up. My understanding is that he didn't know about this until this morning when they dragged him down to the wards."

Jenn nodded. "He was with me all day yesterday. I am sure he was beat and went straight to bed last night."

~

Damien shook his head as he gazed downward at the mess in the palace from his balcony. Seriously, he had to wonder at his fellow council members. Abyss, he had to wonder about himself. He had allowed himself to be dragged into this undertaking at the last minute and then had been so overwhelmed by the complexity and ingenuity of the spell that he'd just gone along with it.

He had not stopped to think about all the consequences, nor had the others. This seemed to be emblematic of many of Lenamare's actions. Like blowing up his own school along with the besieging army. He wasn't sure if Lenamare was all there. Perhaps he was more ego than wisdom. He wished he could talk this over with Antefalken, but the bard would have been expelled from the city, as would Tom/Edwyrd and Rupert. He had gotten quite used to strategizing with them in the last several days. He needed someone to vent to.

Well, better to find out what was going on, or had gone on, outside. He would go see Gandros about leading a team outside to see what had transpired and to reopen negotiations with the Rod and Oorstemoth. That was sufficiently unpleasant enough that he didn't expect to get much opposition from Gandros.

[Appendix: Clerics, Priests, Monks, Nuns and Holy Warriors]
[Appendix: The Church of Tiernon]

Chapter 81

Not-Edwyrd changed into Tom as he closed the gateway above him. The human form he had been using had no wings and he was hurtling toward the ground like a rock from this high altitude. Assuming his true form (it still gave him twinges to think of it as such), he swooped down to make sure that someone had caught Talarius in his free fall.

Fortunately, Tizzy had the knight securely in all four of his hands. Clearly, there were times when it would be convenient to be an octopod like Tizzy. Talarius had put his helmet back on; probably a good idea, as the magical suit of armor apparently acted as some sort of environmental, or space suit. The knight had said it kept him safe from all hostile environments. Tom was not sure about vacuum, but fortunately one only had to worry about an air temperature near the boiling point of water, acid-like mist and spontaneously exploding giant balls of fire. Well, that and a rather extreme lack of humidity, if what the two humans he had talked to about it with were correct.

Tizzy brought the knight down onto a plateau jutting out from the side of one of the rather gravitationally impossible cylindrical stone pillars that rose a mile or more out of a seemingly barren plane. Tom really had to wonder who designed this place. Obviously it was some really demented science fiction writer or something.

The plateau was about twenty feet in diameter, just sufficiently big that they could all land on it: Tizzy with Talarius, Rupert, Tom and Antefalken the bard. Tom looked over at the bard, who was putting his harp away; he had been using it to bat away arrows when they had been banished from the city.

"How do you keep the wood from drying out?" Tom suddenly asked. "I'd think this place would literally be *Hell* on it." Immediately, he bit his tongue. What exactly was it he had told Antefalken? Was he showing ignorance? Crap, these lies just kept piling up and now, he was so exhausted he couldn't keep up with them.

The bard smiled mischievously. "It's Denubian wyrmwood. It is quite at home in this environment. Takes a bit of Denubian worm slime now and then, but that's it," the demon said, either not noticing or purposefully ignoring the slip.

"Same place as the Choco-Coffee?" Rupert asked.

Antefalken shook his head. "You forgot the TM. Denubian Choco-Coffee™," Antefalken corrected. "The Denubians get very picky about their trademarks."

"Sorry," Rupert said.

"No problem, it's no biggie out here, but if you were in the city and one of their lawyers heard you…" Antefalken shook his head. "I think the Denubians must somehow be related to the Oorstemothians. They have similar perspectives when it comes to the law." Antefalken stroked his beard in thought. "Although, come to think of it, most Denubians I've met have more than one mouth—so I'm sure they're even better at double speak and triple speak than the Oorstemothians." He frowned, thinking about it, and then grinned and winked at Rupert.

Talarius was swiveling his head, and thus his helmet, back and forth between the two demons, trying to follow their absurd conversation. Tom smiled; he was sure the knight didn't expect demons to talk like normal people.

"How long are you planning on holding me hostage here?" the knight suddenly demanded.

"Until Fierd sets in the sky," Tizzy replied.

"At the end of the day then? That soon?"

Antefalken grinned broadly at Tizzy and Rupert.

The knight made a gesture of frustration. "And when is that?"

Antefalken shook his head in mild surprise and looked at the knight. "It doesn't; there is no Fierd here, so it never sets in the Abyss. I would have thought you knew that."

The knight groaned. "You seriously can't expect to keep me here forever!"

"Why not?" Tizzy asked, turning to more directly face the knight.

The knight simply stared at him. "Why would you? Either you will ransom me, or you will kill me."

Tizzy shook his head as if not understanding. "Why couldn't we just keep you here and torture you for eternity? It is kind of what we demons do, you know."

The knight shuddered slightly, but had nothing to say.

"That is what you believe, isn't it?" Tom asked the knight.

The knight turned and sighed. "Yes, it is. Get on with it then."

"You really are as nutty as a wizard," Tom told him. "We are not going to torture you."

"We aren't?" Tizzy whined loudly. "But Tooohhhmmm!" The shrill demon started pouting.

Tom shook his head with a big grin on his face, but seeing the knight blanch under his helmet, he stopped grinning. To be fair, he was not completely sure Tizzy was joking. "No, I'm sorry Tizzy; we've just brought Talarius here so he could find out what the Abyss is really like. What demons are really like."

"Like a field trip!" Rupert exclaimed.

"Exactly." Tom gave the boy a pat on the shoulder.

"Okay, I've seen it." The knight gestured around. "It's a lovely place. Can I go now?"

"Hah, hah," Antefalken said. "You aren't getting off that easy. It is a big plane with lots of places to go and you haven't seen anything yet. Wait until you see the salt mines!"

"So, back to my original question. How long, demon?" The knight was getting rather imperious again.

"As long as it takes; maybe two or three centuries, maybe a thousand years or more," Tom snapped.

The knight dropped his hands at that. "Well, the joke is on you then. I'm a human; I won't live that long."

Tizzy laughed hilariously, and the knight turned to glare at him. "Joke's on you, lad. Humans don't age or die here, not if they are kept at a reasonable temperature and in a less toxic region where their flesh won't dissolve, or unless they get evaporated by a really big demon or similar, but that's a risk we all take. That's how we can torture them for so long. They regenerate, just like demons!"

The knight blanched within his helmet.

"Actually, Sir Talarius," Antefalken said to the knight, "Given that you are here—and you have to obey the same rules as us—to all intents and purposes, you are a demon now."

The knight stared at the bard. And stared. And then stared some more. He finally shook his head. "Your lies are pathetic."

"Well, I don't know," Tom said. "Most humans would expire and decay in this environment, which is how they would die here, but your armor keeps you alive and fairly invulnerable. I am thinking Antefalken is correct."

"Well then, I'll just take my armor off," the knight stated.

"You can try, but you won't," Antefalken told him.

"You don't think I can stand the pain?" the knight sneered at him.

"No, I think you could; but if you do that then you abandon hope."

"What need have I of hope? I am cursed in this wretched place."

"I don't know, but what does your god tell you? If you die here, your soul ends here, and you will never join those you love in the afterlife with Tiernon. On the other hand, if you keep your armor on, stay alive, you will always have the hope of returning to Astlan to die there and ascend to the heaven you have been promised. Correct?" Antefalken asked the knight.

The knight stared at the small demon. He was silent for a long time. "You know, I think you are the most devious of all these demons." He gestured to the others.

"Why, thank you!" The bard took a bow.

Chapter 82

Damien came to their doors and gathered Jenn, Gastropé and Maelen. "I have to show the council something that I think you are going to want to see." The wizard was looking visibly shaken.

"What's up?" Gastropé asked.

"You'll see. What I'm showing everyone will speak for itself; I'll answer what questions I can afterwards."

Damien led the three to a mid-sized auditorium, where the rest of the council was arriving. They took seats and Damien pointed out various council members as they arrived. "I believe you have met Lord Gandros?" They nodded. "Beside him is Alexandros Mien." Gastropé sucked in his breath, impressed by the legend. "The gentlemen near them are various associates of theirs."

Damien pointed a little ways over. "Obviously, you know Lenamare, Jehenna and Zilquar and their associates," he said as he gestured at Hortwell, Elrose and Zilquar's people. There was no sign of Master Trisfelt.

"That is Sier Bavron of Yorkton and his closest advisors. Next is Tureledor, Archimage of Tureledor."

Jenn looked askance at Damien. "His given name is the same as his title name?"

Damien grinned. "Hereditary tradition. I don't know how fathers and sons refer to each other." He pointed down further and went on, "Davron of Markforton with two of his people, and now entering the room is Randolf of Turelane, with whom you are probably both familiar." Gastropé nodded. Jenn shrugged; she had heard of him. Exador theoretically worked for him.

"And behind him and his two aides is Trevin D'Vils, Enchantress of the Grove, and her maidens." Jenn frowned; the woman was way too old to be wearing that sort of outfit.

Randolf spoke to Lord Gandros, but did so in such a loud voice that everyone could hear. "I fear, my Chancellor Arcane, Councilor Exador is indisposed at the moment and won't be able to attend." There were a number of murmurs at this.

Sir Bastion, the Lord Chairman of the Council of Magistrates, who was there on behalf of the magistrates, spoke up. "This is a very critical meeting, My Lord Archimage; we have requested all to attend."

Randolf nodded, acknowledging the point. "Unfortunately, he's been called off to handle some issues for me in Turelane."

"I thought you said he was indisposed," Trevin D'Vils snapped as she seated herself.

Randolf turned gingerly to face her and sort of grimaced or simpered or something at her. "My apologies, Enchantress... a poor word choice on my behalf. I had hoped to avoid bringing up my issues at home and so chose words that added to the confusion. My sincerest apologies."

Jenn whispered into Gastropé's ear, "Is it just me, or is he slimy?"

Gastropé shook his head and whispered back, "No, he's very slimy. I think he is actually a toad that Exador turned into an Archimage. He's done the reverse often enough, so why not?"

Jenn giggled softly to herself. Damien overheard them and gave them a rueful grin.

Gandros stood to address the gathering. "Very well, then, I think we are all here. Due to its sensitivity and arcane nature, Lord Chairman Bastion is going to view this on behalf of the Council of Magistrates and will decide whether to show it to them. What you are about to see is, well, rather disturbing."

He gestured to Damien, who stood up. "Damien ventured out today after the purge to reopen discussions with the Oorstemothians and the Rod, and to ascertain the state of affairs after we dumped a demon horde on them," Lord Gandros explained.

Lenamare spoke up. "I do hope you know we appreciate your fortitude in your willingness to deal with these groups." He made a small shudder.

Jenn raised her eyebrow; that statement seemed very uncharacteristic of Lenamare. However, he was probably feeling very magnanimous after having pulled off a rather unthinkable level of wizardry, of which everyone in the room was aware.

"Thank you, Councilor." Damien bowed his head to Lenamare. Damien proceeded down the steps to a pedestal at the base of the auditorium, lifting a small bag from his waist. "Before I go into too much detail, I want to show you a balling that was made for distribution by the Oorstemothians. This," he held up a crystal ball from the small bag, "contains a copy of a Viewing recorded by Wing Arms Master Heron's personal sorcerer." He set the ball down on a mount in the pedestal.

"Now, first, some background. Lord Alexandros ventured out yesterday to negotiate us more time and to alert the Rod and the Sky Fleet of our plans. They devised a scheme to deal with the demons fleeing the city."

"You mean kill or dispose of them," Davron interjected.

Damien shook his head. "As best they could."

"Better than them heading down the road to our cities," Sier Barvon of Yorktown stated emphatically.

"Indeed," Damien concurred.

"As we know, we were inadvertently playing host to several archdemons and likely a few greater demons." There were a few gasps from around the room from those who hadn't realized how severe the problem had been.

"Did we drive out the archdemons?" Trevin asked.

"We believe so; but that's complicated."

"Can't Talarius fly over and look again?" Tureledor asked. "That's what he did before, right?"

"I think it best if we watch the ball, and then I'll tell you what else I know." Damien gestured and the room lights went down. He waved his hand over the ball and the air above it lit up with a frozen vision of the Rod's encampment.

"As I said, this was taken by Heron's personal sorcerer. Given what we all know of the Oorstemothians, I have no doubts as to its authenticity." Damien made some gestures to zoom in on the scene.

"My demon!" Lenamare exclaimed, nearly standing up and pointing to the demon currently frozen in the air.

"What's with that miniature version of him over there?" Jehenna wondered.

"Isn't that your demon, Damien?" Bastion asked Damien, referring to the smallest demon.

"I'm afraid so. As you see, this affects many of us in the room personally."

"Gastropé!" Jehenna suddenly spoke up. "Isn't that your ugly demon there as well?"

"Apparently," said Gastropé, looking extra-pale in the dark of the room.

"As I said, let's proceed; we can go back and watch it over again as much as needed afterward, but I think we want to get the full event shown first," Damien said.

"Very well, proceed," Gandros ordered. Damien waved his hand. The knight Talarius was speaking to the smaller version of Lenamare's demon. Jenn had no idea where the small demon had come from. She had wondered where that Tom demon had been; apparently he was in the palace all along.

As the video started, the smaller demon was saying, "...I'll be able to put up a fight."

"I don't think it will be that much of a fight; I've taken your measure once before, demon," Talarius told the smaller demon.

Lenamare's greater demon came in for a landing. He still gave Jenn a queasy feeling. "Well then," the big demon boomed, "How about fighting an adult? Man to man, rather than slaughtering children for sport?" There was some consternation in the room; it sounded like others found this statement as disturbing as Jenn.

[Appendix: Greater Demon vs. Knight Rampant of Tiernon; Freehold]

Jenn soon ceased to think or question; all she could do was watch in horrified fascination along with the rest of the room as the scene played out as it had that morning. As the events unfolded, there were various gasps and an occasional cheer, but mostly *ahhhs* and indrawn breaths, particularly towards the end.

The viewing ended and everyone sat there in silence. It was beyond shocking; Jenn wondered if the entire Council of Wizardry had ever been rendered speechless before.

"So, Lenamare," Davron spoke up. "How sure are you that you summoned a type IV demon?"

"Uhm..." Lenamare said, sweat visible on his brow. "Uh..." Jenn nearly choked; she had never seen Lenamare so speechless.

Trevin snapped, "Stop teasing Lenamare, Davron." She shook her head. "Are we in any way agreed on what we might have seen? Obviously, we have no wizard's sight view of the event—it is just a visual recording—but given the behavior of the priests, it appears that Lenamare's demon linked up with... what, five high priests and hijacked their divine links? The links between themselves and their flocks? And then at the end, the healing mana and the artifact... Was it pulling mana from the heavens? From Tiernon's own infrastructure? Is that what we saw?"

The room suddenly burst into pandemonium as people tried to voice their opinions on what they saw. "Excuse me. Excuse me!" Alexandros Mien spoke up, and everyone else quieted down. "I'm sorry, but before we debate that, could I have you back up to the point shortly after Lenamare's demon hit the ground with its limbs chopped off?"

Damien nodded.

"Thank you, dear boy," the elderly wizard said. Damien backed up to the point when the type IV hit the ground. "Now, stop—good. I want you to zoom out and scroll up and to the right. See there up in the air, above the fight, over the camp." There were whispers; no one seemed to know what the old wizard wanted to see.

"Zoom in if you can." Damien zoomed in as the wizard nodded in confirmation of what he had seen. The small object in the sky was a flying carpet with people on it—three people.

"Oh, shit," Gandros stated slowly. The rest of the room gasped as well. On the flying carpet, apparently having a picnic, were Councilor Exador, an extremely dark-skinned woman in a revealing dress, and a man wearing leather straps with two straight-edged, single-sided blades over his shoulders.

There were gasps in the room.

Maelen said aloud, "Ramses the Damned."

"Bastet, Defender of Home," Trevin D'Vils stated equally loudly.

Maelen suddenly made a noise like he'd just swallowed wrong. Jenn glanced over at him; he was staring straight ahead and was looking extremely pale for some reason. She hoped he was okay.

"Exador?" Randolf exclaimed. Chatter broke out again.

"Silence, one at a time!" Lord Gandros exclaimed, and everyone quieted down. "Very well, first things first. Thanks to Maelen here"—he pointed to Maelen, who seemed to be pulling himself back together quickly—"we were suspicious that Ramses the Damned might be wandering in the Palace. Now we have that confirmed." There was a lot of talk among various associates with their Council members confirming this. Randolf, of course, had heard none of this and was looking particularly flustered.

"Enough, let us continue," Gandros stated. "It is becoming clear who our archdemons are, or were." Randolf sputtered, but Gandros waved him down.

"Trevin, what was the name you mentioned?" Gandros asked.

"Bastet, Defender of Home," Trevin D'Vils stated. "She is, or rather was, a goddess worshipped on the continent of Natoor, on the far side of Eton, more than a thousand years ago. She is from the forgotten Nyjyr Ennead pantheon. She was a defender of house and home, a protector of her people. She was considered a good goddess, not evil. She is definitely not an archdemon. The Etonians displaced them; their troops and knights drove the religion underground. As far as I know, no one has worshipped them in close to a thousand years."

"So how do you know this?" Davron asked.

"I travel. Archaeology is a hobby of mine, and I'm always fascinated by powerful female goddesses." Trevin shrugged. "I've seen her likeness on many old scrolls and stone carvings. She often appears like this, and sometimes with the head of a cat. A black cat."

"Cat? Why a cat?" Randolf asked.

"The original Natoorians believed that cats brought good luck; they defended the home from mice and rodents, who would eat grain and damaged goods. And, given the cat's affinity for magic, I can't say I disagree with their judgment."

Randolf shook his head.

"Now I'm getting confused," Tureledor said. "We have a flying carpet floating above this battle with a reborn Anilord Time Warrior, or maybe he's an archdemon; an ancient forgotten deity who was a protector of life but now appears up to no good; and one of our own Council members who seems to have gone rogue, or who at least has conveniently disappeared"—here he glared at Randolf—"when we banished all the demons from the city.

"Is anyone else having any trouble figuring this out?" Tureledor asked. The room erupted in a flurry of discussion again.

"Folks!" Maelen rose to his feet. "Esteemed wizards, please let me speak." He spoke with an air of authority and at a volume and timbre to quickly quiet the room. "I apologize for interrupting—"

"Who are you again?" Randolf asked.

"I am Maelen Serenanus, Doctor of Animastery and Animagic and Senior Fellow of the Society of Learned Fellows."

A new round of discussion suddenly erupted. Sier Barvon spoke up the loudest. "Are you telling us that the Society is still around?" That quieted the room.

Maelen bowed slightly. "Yes, that is what my presence is informing you. However, that is not why I am speaking; the continued existence of the Society is not relevant to the point I wish to make."

"Then what might be?" Alexandros Mein asked knowingly. He appeared to know what Maelen was going to say.

"On our very doorstep, a being, a demon that had been hiding here in the palace, has somehow managed to interrupt a link between several high priests of Tiernon and their god."

"Yes, yes, I brought that up early on," Trevin sputtered.

"Wisely so, My Lady." Maelen nodded. "But what you did not ask is this: how long before Tiernon sends his emissaries down to enquire as to who has been tampering with his supply line?"

There was shocked silence for a moment. "And by emissaries," Sier Barvon stated, "you do not mean the Rod or any priests. You mean…"

"His avatars." Maelen nodded.

Gandros moaned and put his head in his hands. The room once more broke into chaos.

~

"I seriously need a drink." Lenamare said as he entered his office followed by Jehenna, Elrose and Hortwell. He headed directly to the glass cart with the brandy decanter on it and began pouring brandy for everyone. No one said anything as he passed the glasses around.

Lenamare nodded as Elrose took a glass; normally the sorcerer did not imbibe, as he felt that alcohol dulled his senses. He was making an exception tonight.

Jehenna took a sip and closed her eyes for a moment before opening them and observing, "So, as we suspected, our fourth-order was in Astlan all along, which was why we couldn't summon him."

"And in this palace," Hortwell added. "Under our noses."

Jehenna grimaced. "Embarrassing."

"Well, he's in the Abyss now," Elrose observed.

Jehenna allowed a grim smile to cross her lips as she glanced at Lenamare. "Unfortunately, the wards around the city will prevent us from summoning it any time soon." She gave a dark chuckle.

"Yes, how *unfortunate* that is." Elrose shook his head, chuckling as well; Jehenna's sense of humor was a bit dark.

Lenamare glanced at Jehenna half irritated, obviously not sensing her irony. "I may have a high opinion of myself, but I'm not stupid. We are not going to be summoning that thing any time soon."

"I do not understand how it could have fooled us so well." Hortwell shook his head.

"Clearly, it wanted into Astlan and we were a convenient portal," Elrose stated.

Lenamare had closed his eyes, keeping them shut he took another sip of brandy, remaining silent.

Jehenna shook her head and then seemed to realize something and looked around. "Where is Master Trisfelt? I thought he and his students came in just before the wards went up?"

Lenamare nodded. "He did, but I sent him back outside to be our eyes and ears out there."

"Elrose," Lenamare turned to look at the other master, "I took over the keystone position for the wards this morning from Trevin. I can have them tuned to let you teleport out and back in to resupply Trisfelt. He may have a longer tour of duty ahead of him."

"Longer?" Jehenna asked.

"More than ever, we need an observer outside that we can trust. If any avatars show up, I want advance warning." Lenamare finished his brandy. "I have the wards set to allow telemirrors, and he still has his. Therefore, Elrose, coordinate a location and what supplies he needs and I'll open the wards to let you out and back in. I only want to have them open for a few minutes at most."

Elrose nodded. "Sounds wise. I am pretty sure I know what he's going to need. I'll go tap a few wine kegs." Elrose and Hortwell chuckled, and even Jehenna made a small grin. At this point, any amount of levity helped.

~

"This is most distressing!" Randolf whined to his two lords as they walked back to the archimage's chambers.

"It is, My Lord, most certainly," Lord Rothgart agreed.

"Indubitably, my illustrious lord," Bartholomew agreed, adding extra color to his words to make up for answering second.

As they reached the doors to his chambers, Randolf stepped aside to let his lord chamberlain go forward and open the doors for him. Once opened, he slunk through the entranceway as was his habit. Randolf could tell by the sour expression on Bartholomew's face as the man looked into the suite that Crispin must have returned and was most likely draping himself over a divan in the parlor.

As Rothgart shut the door behind them, Randolf marched through the rear doors of the entrance hall into the parlor, where Crispin was indeed lying on the gold divan. As was his custom, the boy was scantily clad and provocatively posed to arouse maximum discomfort in the two lords. Randolf stopped in the middle of the room, standing up straight and holding his arms out from his sides to allow the lord chamberlain to remove his robe. The chamberlain snapped his fingers and two young men in livery emerged from the sides of the entry hall and flowed into the parlor to remove the Archimage's robes.

Randolf coughed slightly. Bartholomew raised his eyebrows in sudden understanding of the oversight. Clearly, the crystal ball playback had rattled his wits. The lord chamberlain produced a mint chocolate and placed it in Randolf's mouth, which opened as the chamberlain's fingers approached.

Randolf savored the mint as the two valets removed and folded his robe and then removed his boots and replaced them with slippers. A rather tricky feat, considering that the Archimage insisted on remaining standing. Randolf appeared to be contemplating as he savored the mint.

"As I was saying," Randolf suddenly continued as the valets backed away and began to leave. "This is most distressing. The fact that Exador would so depart without telling me, on a flying carpet no less, and with a bunch of hooligans." Randolf began pacing. "And to think he gave me no word of his departure before leaving, I am summoned to this council meeting, which he knows I hate attending, and I have to make excuses for his absence—off the cuff, even!" Randolf continued pacing silently.

The two lords looked back and forth at each other. Finally Rothgart spoke up. "My Lord?"

Randolf paused and looked at the lord chancellor, raising an eyebrow, awaiting the chancellor's question. "Are you not at all concerned with the fact that he was seen on the carpet with two archdemons?" Rothgart asked.

"And that the Council now suspects, nay, believes Exador to be an archdemon?" Bartholomew asked.

Randolf stopped where he was, his face going slightly pale. "Hmm, interesting point. I hadn't considered that in great detail." He tilted his head from side to side, then glanced at Crispin, who was smiling brightly. "Yes, this is most awkward. I mean, it would look bad to have an archdemon in one's employ, yes?"

The two lords gave the archimage slightly horrified stares. "My Lord, I think that may be the least of our problems?"

Randolf seemed puzzled. "Well, what? You think he would do us harm? I've known Exador since I was a child, just as my father knew his father. They've served us loyally for over a hundred years! If he meant any harm to us, don't you think we'd know it by now?"

The two lords were looking extremely pale. "I'm not sure, My Lord; I'm not an expert on the machinations of demon lords," Rothgart replied. "However, I am not sure I would trust one."

Randolf tried to smile, but the smile broke down and he grabbed himself. "I know, I know! But what choice do we have? Are you willing to call him out on it?" He looked around worriedly. "I know I certainly don't want to walk up to someone who might be an archdemon and tell them that they've been lying to me!" He raised his hands up and out. "You know the man! He was scary enough when we thought he was a human!" Randolf shook his head and began pacing. "I think we have no choice. I have no choice! I must continue as if nothing has changed! If he returns, we pretend nothing has changed, that we do not suspect him, or anything! Am I clear?" He glared at his two lords; both of whom gulped and nodded.

"And furthermore, spread the word that I, the archimage, do not believe such scurrilous lies and have the utmost confidence in Lord Exador!" Randolf nodded at the two lords, trying to get them to nod back.

"Yes, Milord," Rothgart and Bartholomew murmured.

"Also, he's got an army camped in the basement somewhere. Locate his generals and make sure they have whatever they need now that Exador has gone missing. Technically, they march under the banner of Turelane, so I probably need to keep them fed."

He paused and added, "Oh, and don't bring the archdemon thing up, unless you hear people grumbling, or whatever. We don't want to make them nervous if they haven't heard anything!"

Chapter 83

DOF
Night 15-17-440

Saint Hilda of Rivenrock trudged through the brambles in the dark, in the middle of the night, scanning the terrain for any demonic manifestations. It was quite tedious. If only she had not been so diligent, she could be home enjoying a good book and a fine glass of wine this evening.

This morning one of her illuminaries had suddenly gone dark and then, not long after, had started drawing mana at a rather large rate for several minutes before dropping to a very dark level. A single illuminary might not have been noticed by some of the more famous avatars; but frankly, Hilda didn't have a huge number of illuminaries, so she was sensitive to each one.

She had reported it to her supervising archon, who probably would have ignored it, except that another avatar reported a similar experience shortly thereafter. Both were identified to be in the same area, and after a few more enquiries to avatars with illuminaries in the area, it was learned there was a total of five illuminaries in the same state in Astlan, all in close physical proximity and all stationed with most of the Rod. All currently dark.

Clearly, something had happened. Unfortunately, the bureaucratic nature of these things slowed down their ability to synthesize all the relevant information. Thus it wasn't until late in the evening, relative time for Hilda, that she'd been notified that she was to join the advance team to do the ground work preparation for a Visitation from the archon currently overseeing this project. She had been chosen, as one of her illuminaries had been affected and she had been the first to report the problem. Joy.

Naturally, to the uninitiated, being part of an advance team sounded like a high honor; but having been at this now for just over two hundred years since her canonization, Hilda knew better. This was her fourth recon job, and they all sucked. They had to do a complete perimeter scan and interior scan for the region, which meant manually checking the area for any sign of anything that could potentially disrupt the archon and his or her Host.

If only she had a decent singing voice, maybe she could have gotten into a Host. Just show up and sing praises to Tiernon and whichever archon needed to announce their presence. Unfortunately, she couldn't carry a tune, so that wasn't going to happen. Not to mention that the body fascists in the Hosts would have made her afterlife miserable.

Squelch. Hilda stopped and rubbed the bridge of her nose. She had just stuck one of her golden-slippered feet into a six-inch-deep puddle of mud. Great. It would probably get stuck in there. Boots would have been so much better, but no; avatars could not wear boots while in the field. Not unless it was specifically mentioned in their canonization and subsequent depictions that they wore boots.

Seriously, was it really this big of a deal? There was a battle, a few priests got taken out, so they went dark. Priests die. If the Afterlife Receiving Department was a little quicker on reporting deaths, they could have had the explanation already, with no need of a Visitation. However, there were no reported dead priests from the area. Of course, everyone knew the department was a day or two behind on reporting.

[Appendix: Gods and Their Agents]

~

"So, what are your plans for him?" Antefalken asked Tom as they sat on a ledge a few hundred feet from the mouth of Tom's cave. They had taken the knight there as a first staging location. The knight would need to sleep and the cave was far safer and cooler, a dark place for him to rest. The man was extremely beat up. Tom guessed he was about as close to dead as a human could get in the Abyss, without actually being dead.

"I have no idea." Tom shook his head. "It was one of those ideas I had in the middle of combat that sounded a lot better then, than it does in reality now." His wings twitched; he was still feeling rather wired from the battle, which was surprising given the time that had passed.

Antefalken smiled and shrugged. "Yeah, I've made more than a few of those decisions in my life. Usually involving a pretty maid."

"After the crap he was pulling during the battle, I figured he'd try one last time to cheat, kill me. I was thinking if he finally showed some honor, I would just grab you guys and we'd leave. However, if he wanted to try and cheat one more time, I'd give him a lesson he would never forget." Tom shook his head again. "Of course, what I didn't realize at the time was that that meant I'd get a lesson too: what to do with a hostage."

"Killing him would have been a lot easier. He would probably be happier up there in the heavens with his god. Who knows, they might have made him a saint," Antefalken replied.

"Easier, yes, but I'd like to put an end to these stereotypes of demons being pure evil killing machines—basically all the bullshit he represents," Tom said, gesturing to Talarius back in the cave. Tom grimaced and emitted a small belch, rubbing his stomach.

Antefalken chuckled. "Good luck with that; it's pretty much what his religion is about. Tiernon is a warrior god, dedicated to expunging evil. It is their raison d'étre. You get rid of the stereotypes about evil, you get rid of their religion."

"But evil isn't a thing. It is a point of view, a perspective. It's how one behaves and interacts with others that determines good versus evil," Tom complained.

"Well, I might argue that it's not that simple. From a practical point of view, it is political, or societal. People form groups, align with others for their common good. Oftentimes, what is good for one group is bad for another. Think of it as a competition for resources. So in that sense good and evil become relative, depending on which group you are in," Antefalken said.

"Yes, but I think there has to be a higher level of arbitration or justice that can define intergroup good and evil," Tom said, grimacing again as his stomach continued to rebel. Rather odd, since he had not eaten anything.

Antefalken shook his head. "That can only happen when everyone agrees on the same ultimate authority to decide that." He rolled his eyes back a bit. "And even then, you have groups that say they worship the same god, but have almost entirely opposite views of that god or goddess, and then you get intragroup schisms and warfare."

Antefalken chuckled. "I'd be careful of taking that too far; you might get lumped in with the followers of the archdemon Anselm."

"Who?"

"Anselm, he was, or I suppose is, an archdemon popular about 1700 years ago. He was probably the only religious demon ever. He was also a masterful logistician who provided to his followers a logical proof that basically required the belief in the existence of a one true god, of which nothing greater could be conceived," Antefalken said.

Tom grinned. "I think I've heard of such a being."

"Indubitably, the omniscient, omnipotent single creator god," Antefalken agreed. "Not a preferred concept on the Outer Planes." He raised his arms in an amused shrug. "Go figure."

He sighed and then continued. "In essence, Anselm argued that as a mental exercise, if one could comprehend or conceive of a being of such infinite magnitude that it was the best and most of everything, that it had every virtue, power and grace conceivable, such that no being could possibly be greater, then the existence of such a being in the physical world must be true, and one could not possibly deny such an existence."

Tom shook his head. "That doesn't make sense."

Antefalken smiled. "His construct was to have one conceive of a being so vast, so omnipotent, omniscient and omnipresent that one could not possibly imagine anything greater than that construct existing. This is because if you came up with some other property that a being could possess that would make it greater than the being of your concept, on any front, then the being of your concept would automatically possess it, in order to become the greatest thing you could conceive of."

Tom shook his head again, still not following.

"Here is the clincher: existence, the actual physical existence of something is and must be a higher state of being. It must be greater than the simple concept of such a thing." Antefalken looked him in the eye. "The existence of something is greater than the concept of that same thing. It is more real," he said.

"Yes. I agree," Tom said.

"So if your imaginary being was actually real, tangible, then it would be greater than your imaginary being. Yes?"

"Yes," Tom said, starting to see where this was going.

"Thus, if you took your imaginary being, of which nothing greater could be conceived, and it actually were physically real, that real being would be greater than the imaginary being that wasn't real. Thus, in order to complete your imaginary construct, your imaginary being must be real. Because true reality is greater than a mental construct. Thus, you must believe that your mental construct is real in order for it to be the greatest thing you can conceive of. Thus, if you *can* believe in such a being, then you *must* believe it exists in order to be logically consistent with yourself." Antefalken smiled brightly at Tom as the demon tried to digest this mental bender.

"So," Antefalken summed up, "Anselm held that if a sentient being could go through this exercise of conceiving of such a being, they had to believe in its existence. Therefore, one would also have to believe that there were no greater gods than this single god. That all other gods were simply false gods." He laughed. "As you can imagine, he wasn't too popular among the priests of any religion."

Tom tilted his head; Anselm's god sort of sounded like the one he was familiar with. "I'm not sure I'm going that far. I am really just looking at good vs. evil and stereotypes. I'm not trying to define what a god is or isn't. I think people are entitled to their own beliefs as long as they don't try to impose them on others. I see Talarius as trying to impose his beliefs on me and other demons."

Antefalken shrugged. "They do tend to evangelize via the sword."

Tom smiled. "Even so, I want to try, however futilely, to change a few of his crazy beliefs. Who knows, maybe he can then help convince others in his religion."

Antefalken turned to look at him strangely. "Hmm, you are from one of those monotheistic deist type cultures then?"

"What do you mean?"

"A world with a single god, one who is all powerful and stays above the fray?"

"I guess. I mean, there is no proof that God exists. People just have to have faith. If they choose." Tom said.

"Yeah, well... that's why your plan might work in your world, but not here," the bard told Tom. "The gods are not hands-off in Astlan. In fact, they tend to be very hands-on. They are egotistical, power hungry, vain people who bicker and fight among each other and who stir up considerable trouble in the worlds of men."

Tom felt the other sick feeling in his stomach return from this morning. The one he had felt when he had first seen the umbilical cords to the sky. "Yeah, those links went somewhere. The gods, so to speak, aren't real in my world. But apparently they are very real here?" Antefalken nodded; Tom was getting his point. Tom continued his observation. "The mana stream coming from the heavens, or wherever, was extremely purified; possibly flavored, you might even say." Tom paused for a moment, thinking. "So then Tiernon is an actual person that you can, at least in theory, talk to?" Tom asked.

Antefalken grinned grimly. "Yeah, Tiernon is very real, as are his avatars; we are probably going to find that out soon enough."

Tom got an even worse feeling. "What exactly do you mean?" His stomach was now a total mess. Actually, he wasn't even sure he had a stomach, but something inside him was upset. He was getting a very sick feeling from this conversation, beyond the feeling of indigestion and of being too wired he had been dealing with.

Antefalken snorted. "Are you telling me you don't understand what you did?"

"Apparently not. At least not completely."

Antefalken sighed. "Well, you stole mana dedicated to and destined for Tiernon; and then you actually started using his already collected mana in a way that only very powerful priests are permitted to do." Tom grimaced. "He is not going to be happy and he'll most likely send some avatars to investigate."

"What are avatars?"

"Saints, angels, lesser divine beings. Sort of counterparts to demons, I guess. I'm not an expert, but from what I understand, they are sort of like demons in the service of the gods."

"Oh. I'm thinking that's not good," Tom said. "I suppose they aren't going to be happy about me abducting their champion either?"

Antefalken simply flashed him a grin.

Tom belched, his indigestion starting to turn to nausea.

~

Hilda was close to completing her circumference of the city and the two encampments. She was tired, dirty and sweaty. Her feet were killing her. She could have done a cleaning ritual, but that would have only lasted so long before the forest soiled it again; it simply did not seem worth the bother.

White silk was just a ridiculous fabric for marching through a forest; Hilda far preferred wool or cotton fleece, but no… avatars of Tiernon had to maintain an appropriate level of graceful appearance. Which, considering she was under the aspects of an invisibility ritual and a silence ritual made no sense whatsoever. Who was going to see it? No one. Who was going to have to clean or repair it? Her, that was who. Argh.

Hilda was distracted by a rather curious light ahead and to her right, a bit further away from the Rod's camp. There was the typical sort of flickering of a fire, but also a strange, pale glow. Moreover, there was something else seeming to distort both lights. Clearly something to investigate. Hilda moved cautiously up on the small clearing.

Okay, that is a bit odd, Hilda thought. As she got closer, the first thing she realized was that there was some sort of light refraction spell around the lights. An invisibility shield, apparently. She'd been using her divine sight and so had not been tricked by the spell. Clearly, something worth investigating. It felt like something a bit beyond the typical sort of spell, something more complex, most likely harder for an ordinary practitioner to see through. Being an avatar, however lowly, did provide some benefits.

It appeared to be the camp of a single man. He was a rather portly gentleman possibly a few years older than Hilda appeared to be. He was dressed either as a monk or a very unkempt wizard. He was sitting in a hammock chair next to a rather nice folding camp table that held a selection of meats and cheeses, along with a very interesting-looking bottle of wine. The man was reading a book underneath a glowing ball of light. However, what was far more interesting was the fact that the wine was actually labeled and not one's typical refillable bottle.

She zoomed in on the bottle with her divine sight: *House Darryne: Old Vine Meryst; 405 PV.* Hilda sighed; it was an excellent vintage. This man had taste and money. The meats and cheeses also looked delicious. Technically, being an avatar and thus "dead," she did not need to eat or drink, but old loves were very hard to give up. There was a second chair on the other side of the table.

Hilda closed her eyes. There was nothing she wanted—no, needed—more at this moment than a place to sit, a bite to eat and a glass of that intoxicating wine. Surely, after her long, fruitless trek around the camp, she was entitled to a small bit of time off? Further, this odd man must clearly be somehow affiliated with the local goings-on. Perhaps a bit of inquiry would not be out of order? Technically, that wasn't within the scope of her assignment, but how could anyone criticize her for taking the initiative to go beyond her minimal duties?

Hilda's divine scent suddenly picked up the aroma of the meats, cheeses and yes, that refreshing hint that could only come from an Old Vine Meryst grape, sacrificed at its most luscious. That settled it. She quickly ran through a series of Seeings and the standard detection rituals.

There was no hint of the supernatural about him, no demonic influence, no ghosts, undead or other evil stigmata. Actually no darkness beyond normal, forgivable human vices that she could detect. His aura was quite earthy; most likely he was a thaumaturge. He was not of a clerical persuasion; she detected no real sign of excess piety , thus no significant religious affiliation. He seemed safe. Time to introduce herself.

~

Trisfelt looked up from his novel, a book about a young wizard whose parents had been slain when he was a babe by an evil wizard but whose innate talent had shielded him from the blast that killed his parents, leaving only a scar on his forehead. Trisfelt had a passion for "true crime" stories. His passion however, was being interrupted; something wasn't quite right. There was a disturbance in one of his wards.

"Ouch!" someone exclaimed as he felt them bounce up against the low-range repulsion barrier he had set up to keep animals from sneaking in to steal his dinner. "That's odd, who would put up an invisible wall in the middle of the forest?" a decidedly female voice said.

Trisfelt put his book down. How could someone have run into his wards? The aversion spells should have subtly caused the person to walk around this area. He shook his head and peered through the trees towards where the noise had come from. It was quite dark outside his camp, and the spells somewhat obscured his vision, but it appeared to be a good-sized woman in a white dress. Trisfelt made gestures and muttered the incantation to temporarily lower the wards.

"Oh! A campsite!" the voice said. "How unusual." A woman proceeded forward into the camp, apparently completely fearless. What an odd woman, Trisfelt thought. "Well, hello there!" The oddly bright-eyed and beaming blonde woman smiled cheerfully upon seeing Trisfelt. She was looking around at his camp. "Sorry to barge in; I was in the neighborhood trying to get back to my own camp when I bumped into your invisible wall!"

Trisfelt blinked. The woman seemed to have an effervescent charm about her, almost radiating joy. Definitely not a normal quality of any of the women around the school. Jehenna, for example, seemed to impose a rather dark cloud on those around her. This woman was wearing a layered white silk dress, only slightly muddied around the hem from tromping through the forest. Her gold-trimmed white slippers, clearly not designed for hiking, were coated with mud. As he'd noted, she was full-bodied; rather voluptuous actually, Trisfelt thought. She had brilliant golden hair that he swore almost glowed on its own and seemed to match her beaming eyes and wide smile.

"I'm Hilda!" The woman introduced herself, extending a hand to Trisfelt.

"Uhm, Trisfelt," he said, shaking her hand after a momentary bit of confusion. "What brings you out into the woods at night?"

"Well, I'd been at this wedding," she said, gesturing at her white dress. "Not mine though—I was just a handmaiden and was returning to Freehold, and what do you know? There's an army around it!"

"Uh, yes… it's been there for a while now," Trisfelt said, puzzled but still a bit flustered by her intensely brilliant smile.

"Well, it was an alvaren wedding party and as I'm sure you know, those can go on for weeks!" She shook her head, still smiling brightly. "I think it has something to do with them living for thousands of years. Time doesn't seem to move the same for them as it does for the rest of us.

"So anyway, not knowing who the army was, and why they seem to have brought a bunch of ships and parked them on the ground hundreds of leagues from the sea, well… it just seemed a bit odd and so I was out scouting around the city to try and figure out what was going on."

"Ah, yes." Trisfelt was at a bit of a loss for words. "Sensible. Yes, sensible indeed. I myself have been keeping an eye on them as well. Very curious."

Hilda shook her head smiling. Her eyes moved to his left and widened. "Is that a bottle of Old Vine Meryst? If I'm not mistaken, the label is House Darryne?" Trisfelt blinked. Given the distance to the table, she either had very good eyesight or was very familiar with the house and label.

"Uhm, yes," Trisfelt confirmed. "A 405, in fact."

"A 405 you say?" Hilda's mouth twitched in an appreciating manner. "An excellent year. The next three years were much too wet and the wine was a bit mineral-heavy. Not bad, mind you, but nothing like the 405 or the 402. The 396 was possibly the best, but the 405 does give it a good run for the money."

Trisfelt felt a strange, indescribable feeling in his gut. A woman who knew her wine as well as he did? He smiled back at her brightly. "My dear… where are my manners? You've been trudging through this dark nasty forest all night. Perhaps you would like to have a rest and enjoy a glass with me? I have a few snacks as well…"

Hilda grinned even more brightly than before. "Master Trisfelt, aren't you the gentleman? I would be most grateful to sit for a bit and share your company."

~

A knock came on Elrose's door, as he had been expecting. The sorcerer rose from his chair and went to answer it. The seer Maelen was there, arriving per his request. "Thank you for joining me," Elrose said. He stepped back and gestured for Maelen to enter.

Maelen smiled. "My pleasure. After all, before things went crazy, it was you I was coming to see. We finally get to confer."

Elrose shook his head and smiled grimly as he shut the door. "I apologize; I haven't had much time since I finally made it into the city, with your assistance."

"No need, no need. I've been here the whole time and have seen the very… er… I have no words to describe what it is that's been going on." Maelen threw up his hands.

Elrose chuckled. "Can I get you some wine?" he asked. "Normally, I don't drink alcohol, but I started again after today's screening, and I'm not quite ready to stop."

Now it was Maelen's turn to chuckle. "I could certainly use a glass for my nerves," he replied.

Elrose smiled and gestured the seer to an overstuffed chair next to a small table, adjacent to the sorcerer's own overstuffed chair, where a glass of wine had been already poured. Elrose retrieved another wine glass and the wine bottle from a small cart.

Maelen sat down as Elrose began to speak while pouring the seer a glass of wine. "Well, it appears that the visions of battle I had, which I wanted to discuss with you, are already upon us." Maelen nodded in agreement with the obvious. "I also noted," the sorcerer continued, setting the wine bottle down on the table between their chairs, "that your reaction to the name of the third occupant of the magic carpet was similar to my own."

Maelen shook his head in consternation, remembering his reaction. Elrose sat down in his chair. "I had never heard that name before, but as soon as I did, I was struck by a series of very intense visions," Maelen said.

Elrose raised an eyebrow. "Really? My shock was that I had heard the name, and seen her face... or at least her aspect with the head of a cat, in my prior scrying."

Maelen moved his head from side to side, thinking. "Clearly she is critical. Apparently more critical than Ramses the Damned. Which, in and of itself, is disturbing. I was shocked when I first heard the name Ramses mentioned in the hallway with Exador for us, but I received no strong sense of dread or prescient visions with his name. With her name, though..." the seer trailed off uncertainly.

"What exactly did you see?" Elrose asked.

Maelen shook his head. "I'm not sure yet. It was extremely intense. There was a rapid series of images—her face, a sphinx, incredibly verdant valleys, blood everywhere, and massacres. People dying, murdered perhaps, I would say. I saw the Rod, although with very different uniforms than they wear today. It didn't make a lot of sense."

Elrose stared at the seer, intent on his words. Maelen continued, "I don't know, the uniforms may indicate the Rod some time ago. I can't imagine they'd be changing their uniforms in the same time frame your visions seem to be occurring in."

"What about demons?" Elrose asked.

Maelen twisted his mouth around a bit, thinking. "Yes, I got the feeling of demons, but not connected to the Rod directly, at least not in those scenes. But again, there were lots of demons, perhaps an army. However, they were more like thought than reality. It was rather tenuous. Perhaps a side possibility?" He shook his head in frustration. "It was very odd, extremely intense. And lots of anger. Actually, that might be part of what struck me; the sheer fury associated with the images."

Maelen looked thoughtfully at Elrose. "What did it spur in your memory?"

"In my original scrying, she had been there as a background figure. Her presence did seem to get stronger in some visions after Lenamare summoned the greater demon. As did images, or rather symbols, of the various Etonian gods."

"Symbols or images?" Maelen asked, puzzled.

Elrose shrugged. "Not clear. Whenever I deal with the actions of the gods or get close to them, I seem to see their key symbols or flashes of pictures I've seen from paintings of their exploits and teachings. I never seem to get a direct lock on a deity in the way I would a person, or even a demon. It's very hazy and inexact."

Maelen nodded. "I typically see various colored clouds with a strong sense or feeling of the deity, and it's as if the deity is blurry or cloudy."

"I suppose one wouldn't want to actually look upon the face of a god." Elrose took a good swallow of wine.

Maelen frowned at this and picked up his glass, taking a large sip himself before nodding in agreement. He sighed as he set his wine glass down again. "I think it's beyond time that you and I go over what you've seen in detail, and I'll fill you in on what some of our seers have seen as well."

"Agreed. I also think we should make some enquiries of Trevin tomorrow about this Bastet person."

"Agreed." Maelen nodded.

"While I have never heard of her, Trevin says she's from Natoor. As you may know, my family came to Norelon from there a few generations back. My first instructor in sorcery, his father was from Natoor. Thankfully he's still alive, albeit quite old; he might be of some assistance on this as well," Elrose told Maelen.

At that moment, a knock came at the door.

"Who could that be?" Elrose asked puzzled, getting up.

"It seems a bit late for surprise visitors," Maelen greed.

Elrose opened the door to find the Councilor Trevin D'Vils standing in the hall. Elrose blinked. "Well, speaking of the enchantress..." Elrose said to Maelen.

"Master Elrose, and is that our guest from the Society that I see in there?" Trevin asked.

"Councilor, please come in." Elrose stepped aside and gestured for her to enter.

"Sorry to intrude so late, but a little bird noticed Maelen heading this way, so I thought it would be a great opportunity to speak with both of you together!"

Elrose stared at Maelen from behind the councilor, giving him a very puzzled glance. He had only met the councilor on a few occasions, mostly formal, and she had never met Maelen before, but here she was.

Trevin entered with a smile. "I know it's odd, but I was so struck by both of your expressions when I mentioned Bastet's name that I felt it important to speak with you while things were still fresh in your minds."

Maelen nodded and gave her a pleasant smile. "That is often the best course with visions."

"Would you like some wine?" Elrose asked the councilor.

"That would be so kind of you!" Trevin said as Maelen gestured to the nearby sofa.

Trevin moved to the sofa. "So my sources tell me that you, Dr. Serenanus, came to Freehold to discuss visions that both you and Master Elrose have been privy to?"

"Indeed, My Lady Councilor," Maelen agreed with a polite nod.

"Well, good then, I would love to hear all about both the prior visions you two have had and the ones you had today," Trevin said.

Maelen glanced at Elrose, who was behind Trevin at this point. The sorcerer shrugged. The woman was clearly determined, and they'd planned to talk with her about this in any event.

~

Bess arrived in a flash of light on the telepad outside the main gates.

Jeshbella approached, smelling her and looking at her with her True Sight. She finally nodded and smiled. "Greetings, mistress! I was not expecting you to return to New Nyjyr so soon." The sphinx gave Bess a concerned look.

Bess sighed, shaking her head. "My precious, you know me only too well." She placed her right hand on Jeshbella's shoulder. "We have a slight complication; a new player, in fact. The dynamics on the ground are changing rapidly, and our plans may get accelerated."

Jeshbella shook her head in dismay and moved forward to rest her head on Bess's shoulder to comfort her mistress. Bess hugged the sphinx and purred in rhythm with her. After a few moments, Bess pulled back and smiled. "I need to discuss this with Anup. Is he in his quarters?"

Jeshbella stared off into the dark, star-filled sky above the horizon behind Bess. "He is. Shall I let him know you are coming?"

"Thank you, my dear," Bess replied.

Jeshbella simply nodded and looked through the gateway for a few moments. "He will meet you on the veranda between your quarters," she informed Bess.

Bess nodded her thanks and proceeded to the giant archway. She pulled her sistrum from her pocket and played the required notes. As she did this, Jeshbella sang her song, both vocally and mentally. As their small duet ended, the previously empty gateway held two large stone doors. Bess moved forward and traced an invisible inscription on them while Jeshbella mentally performed her part of the ritual as well. The two stone doors opened and Bess walked through them into New Nyjyr. She waited briefly for the doors to shut behind her and then headed down the path, where a chariot was just pulling up.

Bess stepped up into the chariot, taking a position in the rear passenger seat. She glanced at the driver, who appeared to be a young man in a silk kilt. While she had not seen him since his last reincarnation, Bess had no trouble recognizing Bakari, who had driven her through many incarnations, along with several other members of his family. "Bakari, it is good to see you. How long have you been driving in this incarnation? I haven't seen you since your last birth, and I doubt you remember that."

Bakari had turned to bow at Bess, and he straightened, smiling. "My mistress, you honor me with your remembrance. I turned sixteen last month, and so have rejoined the service. The work the soothsayers have accomplished since my previous reincarnation is remarkable. It only took four years for me to regain the memories of my last three incarnations. They believe that I will be able to recall my lives back to Old Nyjyr within a few more years, hopefully by my twenty-first birthday."

Bess clapped her hands. "That's incredible! In your previous incarnation, your memories were not at this level until your early twenties. I shall remember to thank the soothsayers for the work they've done to improve the process." She looked at him with a touch of sadness. "I am so sorry we have to do it this way, but I thank you for all you and your family have gone through."

Bakari shook his head. "No, my queen, do not thank me. It is you to whom we must all be grateful, you and all the Ennead, for all the sacrifices you've made to protect us."

Bess shook her head in turn. "I must not forget how hard it is to thank you or compliment you, Bakari. I remember now; this is my most serious criticism of you." She smiled brightly at the young man, and he returned her smile. This was a joke going back many lifetimes for Bakari.

~

Anup was on the veranda as promised, leaning against the ivy-covered marble balustrade when Bess arrived. She could see the concern in his eyes as she approached. They gave each other short kisses on each cheek and then grasped each other's elbows in greeting. "You've returned unexpectedly. pêTah is out. He's working on the slow diplomacy we've settled on."

Bess nodded; she had assumed as much. "I assumed so, but I needed to get word back while I could. There's been a complication," she said.

"The book being lost and playing musical owners wasn't complicated enough?" Anup asked with a smile.

Bess shook her head. "I think we should sit down. I know you will find what I have to tell you as unsettling as I did, when I witnessed it."

[Appendix: Select Pantheons with a Presence in Astlan]

~

Trevin made her way deep into the depths of the palace's underground towards one of her most private workrooms. She needed to discuss these visions of Elrose and Maelen with Elraith. She winced slightly at her own brusqueness in barging in on them as she had, but their reactions today to her mention of Bastet had gnawed at her.

Unfortunately, speaking with them about their visions had only succeeded in making things worse. Much worse. She sighed. This would likely be tricky. Those wards were quite effective at cutting off all outside contact. It was for this reason she was going deep, very deep, down to the very bedrock upon which the palace and Freehold stood.

Waving her hand to open the last of the sealed doors on her journey, she entered the cavern she needed. Technically, it was more of a cave than a cavern; it was not that large. The air pressure on the other side of the door shut it behind her, as she had willed. The room was pitch-black and absolutely silent, but she needed neither wizard sight nor light to find the small throne that had been shaped from the bedrock floor.

She sat on the throne and willed herself to relax. The stone throne, part of the bedrock itself, was rather antithetical to her own preferred element of air, but Duranor had fashioned it for her for just such situations. She only hoped the Grove's chief geomancer and representative to the Grove of the Modgriensofarthgonosefren would not be listening in.

She allowed herself to sink into the stone as she began chanting the ancient phrases that would virtually transport her to the Grove's own similar chamber. She closed her eyes as she felt herself sink deeper into the bedrock, becoming one with it. Concentrating on the Grove's version of the throne, she worked to juxtapose her current Freehold self with a simulacrum of herself in the Grove's throne.

Trevin heard the gasp of the gnome on duty to monitor the throne chamber in the Grove. She opened her imaginary eyes in the dark chamber. Being one with the rock, she could sense the presence of the gnome, although she could not see him in the dark. She was actually rather surprised she had made it through the wards. However, she had been fairly sure this form of sympathetic geomancy was not something Lenamare would have ever considered.

"Monitor, it is I, Trevin D'Vils. Is Elraith awake?" Trevin asked. The deep bass of her stone simulacrum surprised even her. She had not used this method in several centuries.

"Mistress, he meditates," the gnome replied.

"We must wake him," Trevin said.

"Very well. This may take some time."

One pleasant thing about being stone was that time passed quite quickly comparatively, Trevin reflected. She had no idea how long it was before the very old, formerly human Senior Elder of the Grove arrived in the chamber.

"My dear. So sorry to keep you waiting," the ancient druid said.

"Not a problem, love," Trevin told him. She could sense no other presence in the chamber; he was alone and they were in private, as she needed.

"So what brings you to use this rather drastic form of communication?" Elraith asked curiously.

"And wake you from your meditation?" Trevin asked with a smile.

"I was not going to mention that, but since you brought it up… I am going to sit down; it takes me a while to recover from being so deep." He sat down on a ledge facing her stone throne and simulacrum.

"We have had exceedingly portentous events, the details of which will have to be revealed to the Council of Elders. But I needed to speak with you first, in private," Trevin said.

"Go ahead," Elraith said, listening intently.

"First, Freehold is surrounded by both the Rod and the Sky Fleet of Oorstemoth."

"That is an issue, but I think the Council of Wizardry can handle that."

"We are," Trevin said, "but we also discovered that the city was overrun with about a thousand lesser demons and two or more archdemons, something else and someone else."

She could sense Elraith nodding. "Now things are seeming a bit more interesting."

"We expelled the demons, but in so doing revealed the identities of what we thought were three archdemons." She sensed a raised eyebrow. "I believe one of the beings we had thought was an archdemon is actually Bastet of the Nyjyr Ennead."

She could sense Elraith pausing on that point. "That would be quite interesting. Why would she be posing as an archdemon? I did not even realize she was anywhere near the localverse." Elraith shook his head. "And the others?"

"The second archdemon is Ramses the Damned, formerly of the Time Warriors; the third, our neighbor Exador," Trevin said.

"Exador, son of Exador, etcetera. That actually makes quite a bit of sense, and helps explain Abancia." Elraith shook his head. "I still regret not doing more then. They were next door, so to speak."

He paused. "Ramses the Damned, also a demon. Never liked any of the Ramses. I can assume they were all the same, like the Exadors?"

Trevin shrugged. "At the moment, you know what I know. But that would be likely."

"He is a threat to us. The Anilords were a threat to us, and the various Ramses were particularly annoying," Elraith noted.

"Well, it gets more complicated yet. And I still have not gotten to the point that concerns me the most, and I am sure will concern you," Trevin said. It was exhausting to talk this way. Stone was not the best method for rapid communication. "We also have what we thought was a greater demon who possessed a bunch of priests and then somehow broke into Tiernon's illumination stream."

That made Elraith gasp. "That should not be possible!" the druid said.

"It should not, and it's going to annoy Tiernon very much," Trevin said.

"So that is what you are concerned about? Tiernon's people coming to Astlan and interacting with the Nyjyr Ennead again, and various demons that have apparently been sitting on our doorstep and making threatening noises?" Elraith asked.

"I am, but again, not so much," Trevin said.

"My dear, you are drawing this out too much. I am an old man. I can't take too many more interesting things, each of which is worse than the last."

"This is it, then. A sorcerer who works for Councilor Lenamare and a senior fellow from the Society have both had visions of a great war, perhaps several."

"That sounds probable, given what you've said," Elraith pointed out drily.

"Yes, and that's the level I am working with them on, or plan to. It is certainly dire enough. However, in more offhand remarks they mentioned a few other visions, which they made less of than I do. The first was of armies of orcs and armies of alvfar." Trevin could sense Elraith's shoulders sinking. "Further, visions of smiths—two smithies, in fact. At least one located under a volcano with large channels and floes of metal. However, they could see only one of the two smiths; the other was hidden from their Sight."

"Oh, dear," Elraith breathed to himself.

"And one odd note: this was not clear to them, but they mentioned having a sense of orcs attacking from the skies," Trevin said.

"Orcs attacking from the sky? They don't have that kind of magic; at least, not on any large scale," Elraith stated.

"I know. It means a very sophisticated orc army," Trevin said.

"And the smiths? The volcano, a smith hidden from the Sight? You think this portends the god Hephaestus?" Elraith paused and added, "Who, as I recall, is also known as pêTah among the Nyjyr Ennead."

"And one of the preeminent gods of the Modgriensofarthgonosefren," Trevin said.

"I don't suppose they saw Hephaestus making alvaren steel by any chance?" Elraith asked.

Trevin could not shake her head in this form. "They did not See that."

"We have orcs versus alvar, and Hephaestus involved." Elraith sighed.

"That may mean a bit of tension between the alvar and the dwarves," Trevin said.

"It is a peace that is not easy to keep," Elraith said.

"This is why I want to keep this quiet. I want to take the Nimbus near to Jotungard and see if the orcs are rising, see if there is any sign of these visions, or if we can trigger more visions. We will head to Murgandy and Ferundy and see what the situation is."

"A sizeable portion of your crew is alvaren," Elraith noted.

"Hence I intend to say we are hunting Bastet," Trevin explained. "Our visit to the border regions will be but to survey the territory around Najaar; our first stop in looking for signs of Bastet. We have had no major ventures in that region for nearly a century or more. It has been very quiet."

"Too quiet." Elraith shook his head. "I don't know. It seems rather risky. You will have both dwarves and alvar on the ship with you."

"I know, but can you think of a better plan? The sorcerer and seer are confident that their visions are imminent."

"You will be bringing the sorcerer and seer with you?" Elraith asked.

"Unquestionably. I will also discreetly ask them to not mention the orc or alvaren armies," Trevin said.

Elraith snorted, shaking his head. "I think that may get taken from your hands by fate."

Chapter 84

DOF +1
Predawn 15-18-440

Hilda was running late, but she figured it was worth it. There was a meeting scheduled two Etonian hours before local dawn in Freehold. She'd spent so much time with Master Trisfelt that she barely had time to get home and take a nice long bath, get into some clean clothes and whip up a sugar-and-cinnamon breakfast cake and stick it in the oven for a slow bake before the meeting. It had been worth it, though, in so many ways.

First, the Old Vine Meryst had been exquisite, and when that was gone, Master Trisfelt speedily pulled out a bottle of House Zyrkoft Kabdorgh PV 407, which was really one of the most underappreciated years the house had ever produced. She herself had never previously tried that year, but she'd read about it, of course. The meats and cheeses were both excellent accompaniments; the man was clearly a gourmand after her own heart. He was also witty and a lively conversationalist. It really had to have been one of the most enjoyable evenings she had had in the last century; possibly since her canonization even. Oh, sure, a feast in the Great Hall of Tierhallon was a spectacle most would die to attend, and in fact, she had done just that—but that was beside the point. It was great spectacle, but really not that relaxing and enjoyable on any level.

Hilda was not much for politics. The official dinners were always crammed with people trying to get a witty word in edgewise with one of the higher-ups, honored guests or someone at the political heights of Tiernon himself. It was really too much pressure. Not to mention the effort in terms of wardrobe and makeup, the fear of the wrong word or slip of the tongue. Some of the Host were terribly catty; one small faux pas and they would hold it against you for decades.

Hilda shook her head as she took a seat at the back of the briefing room. Archon Moradel had just finished consulting with a few of his lieutenants and had stepped up to the podium.

"First order of business: the Pool monitors report that the net draw down yesterday morning was equivalent to about two and half miracles, nearly on par with a greater miracle in terms of overall withdrawal," Moradel stated. There were gasps around the room.

Someone asked, "Clearly not authorized?"

Moradel nodded. "Definitely not. However, the true oddity is that it wasn't from a single illuminary. The drain was spread out over several illuminaries." There was a lot of mumbling. "Five in total," Moradel added and looked around the room. "The Holy Ciphers guarding the illumination streams were hacked. Someone, or something, pierced the illumination streams and first diverted mana intended for the Pool, and then a bit later pulled mana from our avatars, masquerading as legitimate illuminaries. Once the cyphers were broken, they had the authority of the high priests whose illumination streams were intercepted. While none of these high priests would have been able to withdraw a greater miracle's worth of mana without explicit permission, the individual stream requests were within the limits allowed to the infiltrated high priests. In all, a very complex and sophisticated effort that took us completely by surprise."

The room was abuzz with amazed chatter among the other members of the advance party, but also among the assembled Host and the various other bureaucrats in the room. This was old news to Hilda. Of course, finding an inebriated wizard who had actually helped conjure the culprit was something of a small coup on her part. She suppressed a grin of triumph. Hubris was a sin, after all.

"Now, further," Moradel continued, "we've been investigating prayer reports for the senior Rod leadership and we believe they were in Freehold investigating demonic activity." Some of the beings present, who had not been in the advance party and were hearing this for the first time, made shocked noises. Moradel nodded. "So, in addition to standard checks, we had the advance team check for the presence of demons in the vicinity." Numerous individuals nodded in agreement with this decision.

"So, advance party?" Moradel glanced around the room, momentarily locking eyes with each of the advanced team, including Hilda. "Any signs of significant demonic presence?" the archon asked.

"None detected by Team Alpha," Seralina stood and stated. *Team Alpha?* Really, is that what Seralina was calling her coterie of hens? She had managed to wrangle her four "minions" into the advance party. Meaning everyone except Hilda.

"There is some evidence of demon mana in the area, but we observed no demons currently in or around the city," Seralina stated with military smugness.

"No demons in the city?" An older archon leaning against a sidewall asked, sounding puzzled. "This is Freehold, a city with more wizards per square foot than anywhere else on the plane." He shook his head in disbelief. "And you are telling me you found no demons in the city? There have always been demons in that cursed city. Wizards really can't stop themselves from summoning and trying to foolishly control demons. It's a genetic abnormality or something." Several people in the room laughed at this.

Seralina looked a bit taken off guard. Apparently, she really hadn't known much about the city. "Uhm, yes, we flew over the city and scanned it for demons. There were none in the city. We could detect the residue of demon summoning, and various protective spells, but there were no demons in or around the city." She looked to her clique, who all nodded in agreement.

"I have to admit, that sounds very odd," Moradel added, looking suspicious.

"How could there not be demons in Freehold? We were simply wanting to check the area around the Rod and the Oorstemothians. We expected demons in the city," another avatar sitting in the room stated.

"Yes, and why are the Oorstemothians camped right near the Rod? While we have no current hostilities with them, this seems a bit odd," Beragamos

Antidelles stated. Everyone looked towards the archon. Beragamos was one of the oldest still active archons. He had been with Tiernon even before the Etonians' arrival in Astlan.

"We haven't ascertained that yet, either, I fear," Moradel answered, shaking his head. "It is another mystery, along with the missing demons."

Hilda hunched her shoulders a little. It all made sense to her, thanks to Master Trisfelt. She tried to suppress another grin. Her face muscles wanted to smile so much, she had to fake a small cough to hide her grin. "Uhhm hem," she coughed into her hand. Hilda suddenly went cold, realizing that the room had been completely silent, taking in Moradel's response. Everyone had heard her cough and were now turning to look at her.

"Hilda?" Moradel asked her in surprise. "Do you know something?"

Hilda closed her eyes for a moment; now she had done it. Slowly she stood; she had not done any real public speaking since her death, so was not really comfortable doing so. "Uhm, yes, I did discover a fair amount of information in my explorations." She heard Katassa, one of Seralina's minions, snort in disbelief.

Moradel seemed pleasantly surprised. "Proceed, if you will."

"Uhm, certainly." Hilda was not really sure how to proceed, but glancing over at "Team Alpha," she decided to take a terse, more military style than her normal style. She would leave out how she knew until someone asked. She did not want to go into that. She cleared her throat and looked around. "I can confirm the findings of Seralina and her team," she began. This seemed to please "Team Alpha." "However," Hilda continued, "I can also confirm that up until yesterday morning there were well over a thousand demons in Freehold." There were gasps, and she decided to speed up to get the big news out before she lost them to excited gossiping. "The thousand demons also included at least three, perhaps four archdemons and multiple greater demons who were directing the thousand demons." Now there were multiple gasps of disbelief.

"Further, both the Rod and the Oorstemothians were drawn to Freehold following the trail of at least one of the archdemons and his entourage. Apparently, the Oorstemothians had experienced numerous casualties from this archdemon. The Rod had detected him in Gizzor Dell and followed him here. Sir Talarius was called on site and had discovered Freehold to be completely infested with more archdemons and a thousand lesser demons."

People were suddenly talking back and forth in amazement. Moradel brought down a gavel on the podium to silence people. "So where are they now?" he asked sternly.

"Well, as I understand it, the wizards in the city hadn't been aware of the demon infestations—"

"Likely story," someone snorted.

Hilda shrugged, and Moradel motioned her to continue. "Be that as it may, the Council devised a scheme to expel all the demons from the city. To drive them out."

"Ludicrous!" "Impossible!" and "Suspicious" were some of the words Hilda heard from around the room.

Hilda cleared her throat and continued. "In any event, they arranged with the Rod and the Oorstemothians to slay the demons as they came fleeing over the city walls."

"This worked?" Moradel asked incredulously.

"Apparently," said Hilda, nodding. "That's why there is still a strong demonic residue; most of the demons were killed."

"Including the archdemons?" Beragamos asked.

"No, apparently three of the archdemons escaped using a flying carpet." More gasps from around the room. Why would archdemons use a flying carpet?

"And..." Hilda said, waiting for the crowd to quiet. Moradel motioned for her to continue.

"And in this process, apparently Sir Talarius encountered a greater demon he'd dispatched previously, and was about to do so again, when what everyone believed to be a *greater* greater demon showed up and challenged Talarius to a duel."

"Talarius killed a greater greater demon?" someone asked, sounding awed.

"Not exactly," Hilda said. The room fell silent.

"So what happened? Surely the Rod helped?" Moradel asked.

"Yes, well, apparently—and I am getting this secondhand—the two fought and the Rod helped with lots of rituals and archers. It was tough fight, and Talarius succeeded in dismembering the demon and was preparing to perform a Ritual of True Death on the greater greater demon and several of his minions, when— pardon the expression—all hell broke loose." The room lit up again with chatter and Moradel slammed his gavel to quiet people.

"All hell?" the archon asked Hilda.

"Yes, well, apparently the demon didn't really die; it simply dissipated and then possessed a number of high priests and Rod members." People were gasping in shock and horror. It took Moradel five minutes to quiet the room.

"Possessed? Are you sure?" Moradel asked her.

"That is what is being reported by observers and the Rod itself. Apparently, several high priests suddenly collapsed and then one began acting strangely and claimed to be the fallen greater demon. The high priest then collapsed, whereupon the previously dismembered demon re-formed out of fire and ordered the Rod to attack Talarius. From the reports I have, somewhat under a third of the Rod members obeyed the demon and attacked Talarius." There were more gasps and another minute for Moradel to quiet the room.

"I don't want to ask, but continue."

Hilda nodded. "Well, the demon then proceeded to beat Talarius nearly to death before Talarius surrendered." There were more gasps at the thought of the Knight Rampant surrendering. Hilda continued, "Talarius pleaded for mercy, and oddly, the demon granted it." This caused another huge stir and more gavel thumps.

"A demon granting mercy?" Moradel sounded incredulous.

Hilda had been as well, but Trisfelt had had a logical explanation, so she used it. "Well, the demon *tried* to grant Talarius mercy; it allowed him to surrender, whereupon the demon shape-changed into a human male." This evoked some discussion, but not as much as she would have expected. "He then walked over and was apparently accepting the knight's surrender when Talarius pulled Excrathadorus Mortis on the demon and stabbed him." The room broke into a loud round of cheers. They were all, of course, familiar with the ancient Excrathadorus Mortis dagger. It was legendary and over four thousand years old.

Hilda coughed again, loudly. The room went silent, realizing she was not done. Hilda grimaced. "Okay, this is where the Pool drain comes in…" The room was deathly silent. "Apparently, at this point, the human-shaped demon began pulling mana from the priests he'd compromised and used divine mana to cleanse the wound and heal himself." Pandemonium broke out as people began arguing about the obvious impossibility of this.

Moradel had to let this rage on for ten minutes before he got them to quiet down. "Anything more, Hilda? Where did the demon go?"

Hilda grimaced, preparing to give more bad news. "Well, that wasn't the totality of the mana drain…" The room stayed silent. "Apparently, the demon then used the divine mana to reverse Excrathadorus Mortis." People began yelling at this point, since this was beyond impossible.

"Enough!" Moradel shouted at the room after another ten minutes. "Hilda, we all find this hard to believe, but fine for now… Please explain why things seem so calm on the battlefield now."

"Well, apparently after doing this, the demon opened a portal to the Abyss under Talarius and dropped him through it." People gasped and Hilda continued quickly, "The demon then sent his minions through before leaping through himself and sealing it behind him." She gestured that she was finished, then added, "Which is why I say the demon tried to grant Talarius mercy; Talarius refused it." The room once again became pandemonium.

~

Not surprisingly, the morning's planned intercession was canceled. For one thing, the predawn meeting that was supposed to last for less than an hour went nearly two hours. Afterwards, Moradel, Beragamos and Sentir Fallon, the older archon against the wall, had taken Hilda back to a private conference room to delve into more details of what she knew.

It was, Hilda sighed to herself afterwards, exhausting. She had spent four hours with the three archons peering at her with every form of Sight they could come up with as they quizzed her on all the details of what she had told them and how she knew it.

"So," Beragamos asked for at least the third time. "This wizard, Trisfelt, he didn't know who he was talking to? He just thought you were a mortal woman?"

Hilda nodded, tired. "Yes, my cover was quite good. We had a very relaxed conversation over wine, meats and cheese. How many humans, wizard or otherwise, are going to have a relaxed conversation with an avatar who shows up on their doorstep?"

Sentir shrugged. "She does have a good point. Most people go slack jawed."

"He could be extremely skilled; he is a Master Thaumaturge at this fellow Lenamare's school," Beragamos noted.

"Well, his cover was very good then, because he certainly knew his food and wine. Further, he was clearly intoxicated in my presence; would someone trying to fool an avatar allow themselves to get intoxicated?"

"Admittedly, someone capable of that level of power and deception is unlikely to be posted as an observer in the woods," Beragamos admitted.

"This is all quite interesting. I have to admit, Hilda, I'm very impressed with your surveillance skills."

"Thank you, Archon." Hilda smiled at the compliment.

Moradel smiled a bit more grimly. "Give it a moment, and you may not be thanking me." Hilda arched an eyebrow in question. Moradel looked at the other two archons. "I assume we can agree that there is too much unknown, and too many unknown parties here, to do a straightforward intercession?"

"I think it's too dangerous to tip our hand at this point," Beragamos agreed.

"Clearly, this is a very dangerous situation with archdemons all over the place, demons stealing mana from us, Oorstemothians and who knows what else. We need to understand the players better, and if we just show up in all our divine glory, the other players will know we are on to them."

"But they will assume as much anyway, correct? How are we supposed to ignore this?" Beragamos asked.

Moradel chuckled. "Was it not you who told me that it is often better to remain silent and to be thought incompetent rather than reveal yourself through action to be incompetent?"

Beragamos twisted his mouth into a dark smile. "That sounds like me. I agree with the assessment in any case; I simply want to point out that without some reaction, we might be thought weak. We need to be aware of that."

Sentir rubbed his chin. "I am not so sure. I suspect the Arch-Vicar of the Rod and the local Arch-Diocate are worried we are going to show up. Perhaps letting that fear build might be to our advantage. This is a major screw-up on their part, and the more we can learn about how it happened without disturbing the scene of the crime, so to speak, the better.

"Further, the reversal of Excrathadorus Mortis gives me great pause. You know my history with it, before I brought it to Astlan?" Sentir looked at the other avatars. Hilda had no idea what he meant, but she was certainly not going to ask. Beragamos nodded solemnly. Moradel looked puzzled for a moment before opening his eyes wide in some realization and then closing them for a moment of silence.

Beragamos became resolute. "Clearly we must engage in this delicate situation with the utmost caution."

Moradel nodded. "My thoughts exactly. Sentir?" Moradel looked at the elder archon.

"I think it seems eminently reasonable given the opportunity that has fallen into our laps, so to speak." Sentir beamed, somewhat bemusedly, at Hilda, which in turn made her a bit nervous.

"Hilda? Do you agree with this plan, that we do more recon on the situation before an intercession?" Moradel asked.

Hilda had a queasy feeling in her stomach. Why was an attendant archon asking her opinion? "Um, yes. Forewarned is forearmed, as they say."

"Excellent!" Moradel slapped the palm of his hand on the conference table. "We thank you for your service in this. Undercover work is not something we do well in Tierhallon, but you've done an outstanding job and I can only imagine what more information you'll retrieve for us!"

Hilda blinked. "I'm not sure I follow."

Moradel smiled. "Why, your generosity in volunteering to continue undercover, posing as a mortal. It's perfect; this Trisfelt fellow is obviously intimately connected with the source of this entire incident! Let's get you set up and in the field immediately."

"Uhh..." Hilda was struck speechless. She'd left her cinnamon-and-sugar breakfast cake baking in the oven. She couldn't go under cover this morning —it was already over-baked as it was!

~

"I'm thinking I should go into the Courts and gauge the reactions," Antefalken said to Tom as the greater demon exited his cave after checking on his sleeping guest.

"Huh?" Tom looked at him, puzzled. "What reaction?"

"The reaction to your little display yesterday. Don't tell me you've forgotten already?" Antefalken snorted.

"How would anyone in the Courts even know about yesterday?" Tom asked. That other sick feeling, the one he'd had after his last conversation with Antefalken, was coming back. It felt like indigestion, as if he had eaten way too much food, rich food full of butter, fat, sugar and caffeine. It had kept him pacing all night, unable to feel comfortable sitting still. Now the queasiness that he had felt thinking about avatars was creeping back into the fray.

Antefalken shook his head, not understanding how Tom could not see the obvious. "Hel-*lo*... there were at least a few hundred demon witnesses to your battle, that are now back in the Abyss, having been evicted."

"Ugh." Tom seemed shocked. "I didn't think about that. The demons were fighting for their lives. Are you saying they stopped to watch?"

Antefalken shook his head in... well, Tom wasn't sure if it was admiration or exasperation, but certainly some form of -ation. "When you and Talarius started fighting, not only did the entire Rod stop to watch, so did all the demons they'd been battling. Hell, even the Oorstemothians stopped slaying demons to watch once they figured out what was going on. Everyone outside the city, and a huge horde of people on the walls of the city watched the fight. This was like a classic grudge match, greater demon versus Knight Rampant of Tiernon. No one in their right mind would miss that."

Tom looked stunned. "So you're saying that all the demons that watched came back and told people here?"

Antefalken slapped his thighs and started laughing. "I am sure every bar in the Abyss was packed with demons hearing a blow-by-blow account from witnesses last night." Antefalken shook his head. "Ignore for the moment the trick with stealing a deity's mana; you defeated and then kidnapped one of the greatest knights in the Rod's history, on several planes. That is big, my friend. Toss in the mana trick and you're going to be the stuff of legends!"

Tizzy buzzed up and into the conversation. "Yep! I am thinking you're going to be mobbed by people asking for autographs next time you hit the courts. And the paparazzi are going to be jumping out around every corner!"

"Paparazzi? You mean like tabloid photographers?" How could there be paparazzi in the Abyss?

"Photographer? Not familiar with the word," Antefalken said, "but mirrographers, and tabloid ballers, definitely. The Courts thrive on gossip, so tabloids and gossipmongers do great business!"

Tizzy shook his head. "I only wish you'd told me in advance you were planning all this; I'd have figured out some way to set up a mirror feed to the Abyss and then charge admission at bars for demons to watch it." The octopod shook a couple of index fingers at Tom. "Remember that next time and I'll cut you in for a share!"

Tom grabbed his horns with his hands and just shook his head back and forth. "Argh!"

~

Bess purred as the gentle warm air of the fur dryer cascaded over her body from all directions, gently whipping the water from her body. She really missed the luxuries of home. The Abyss was so damn hot that it was impossible to get a decent bath, let alone a blow-dry. The Outpost, as they called it, did have air dryers but they were principally used for cool air on extra-hot days. Of course, that was every day in the Abyss; there were no seasons in that hellhole.

She had no idea how that place had come about. It had just always been there, certainly as long as she could remember, which was an incredibly long time. Like any normal deity, she had ignored it until they'd hatched this scheme about a hundred years ago, or no more like a hundred and fifty years ago—time flew. That's when they'd built the Outpost and she'd "revealed" herself to the "Court." Since then, she had had to spend the vast majority of her time there schmoozing demon princes and archdemons.

What morons. All of them, running around pretending to be evil. The evil of the demons was nothing compared to the evil of the Etonians. Now there was true evil with a capital "E." It was hard to imagine she could hate any pantheon more than the Demi-Urge, but somehow the Etonians had managed to one up the biggest Ego in the multiverse. The Demi-Urge was just a crazed greedy narcissist, and not that bright; not bright enough to understand the concept of hypocrisy. The Etonians were a different story. They seemed to revel in hypocrisy.

Further, at least the Demi-Urge had the Adversary to oppose him. No one seriously opposed the Etonians and their massive land and soul grab. For one thing, their PR teams would quickly brand anyone standing in their way as "evil." The joke of that!

"Enough!" Bess said aloud to herself. She could not allow herself to go down this path again. Too much anger was a distraction. It made her boil inside, and she needed to be cold. As cold as the Abyss was hot. Bess exited the dryer chamber into the poolroom. Anup was still in the pool. She admired his trim muscular form, his firm muzzle and sharpened canines, his silky long ears pointing straight up. The jackal had to be one of the most beautiful creatures after the cat, Bess thought idly, smiling to herself.

"Do you have to go so soon?" Anup asked, licking his maw with a lustful stare.

"Three times is enough for one morning." Bess smiled playfully at him.

"Yes, but when I only get one morning every decade, I should be entitled to make-up sex for all the missed mornings!"

Bess arched her eyebrow. "Men. You are all the same. You confuse a man's entitlement with a woman's gifts. Two things that only occasionally coincide." Anup chuckled. "Besides, I must meet with General Thuti to assess the recovery of the troops we lost when Lenamare blew up his castle."

"That was painful; you could literally hear a roar as the Wheel of Life sped up to unprecedented levels to hold the lost souls until they can be reborn. I'm still amazed it was able to handle that large of an influx so incredibly fast."

"Usiris is good. You have to admit that," Bess stated.

"That I will give him." Anup gave her a grim smile. "It's not his skill that annoys me."

Bess laughed.

~

Vaselle dropped his backpack in the clearing. It was midmorning and he was finally outside the city. He had tried to get out yesterday, but they were still under lockdown. As of this morning, however, the city guard were finally letting people leave the city, and letting them back in, but with significant inspections and long lines. However, he would worry about that later. For now, he was outside of the city and outside those damn wards that had driven all the demons out, and which completely prevented him from conjuring his demon back.

It was seriously annoying, but given the power he had witnessed from the walls yesterday, the council's precautions certainly made sense. It was just inconvenient that sensible precautions were keeping him from realizing his dreams. Although, he supposed, the fact that such sensible inconveniences were impeding him might be an indication that he should heed them.

But how could he? What he had seen yesterday, what that demon lord had done to the priests... Was that not his dream? To be filled with the divine spirit? Okay, maybe a negatively divine spirit in this case, but... seriously, to be the servant of a being capable of standing toe-to-toe against the forces of Tiernon and winning? A being capable of subverting, infiltrating and manipulating those same priests and soldiers that had rejected him?

Vaselle was off the road by a half-hour walk, surely far enough to avoid attention. He began pulling his components from his backpack to set up his pentacles. Vaselle smiled to remember the tales of Myrion, the old priest of Hendel who had spent hours tutoring him when he was a young boy. His stories of how the spirit of his god, Hendel, would enter him to perform healings and miracles. The peace and joy that came from being filled with the divine spirit, to be the willing tool of a greater power, a greater good.

He had dreamed of being a priest and letting a god fill him, use him to work the god's will upon Astlan. He had first entered the seminary of Hendel as an aspirant spending a year learning the ins and outs of the religion, but when it came time to dedicate himself, the priests had informed him that he did not have the calling. His nature was not a good fit for the god; he was not really priestly material. The bitterness, the disillusionment had hurt. To this day, this memory brought tears to his eyes.

He had then thought maybe a different god, a different Etonian. There were no proscriptions against changing one's devotion between the different

Etonian gods. He tried to get accepted as an initiate of Tiernon with again the same answer. Okay, fine. He could dedicate himself to the Rod. Be a soldier for Tiernon. That had lasted about two months when they gave up on him as being a failure at most traditional weapons skills, and again, not a great spiritual fit. Either liability was forgivable, but not both.

Thus, Vaselle had decided that if he could not be a servant of a higher power, he'd *be* the higher power. He had gotten accepted at Master Yeltsin's School of Conjury; and while starting very late, it proved to be something he was actually talented at. He often mused that perhaps it was his very talent for summoning and controlling others, particularly demons, that made him not a great fit for the priesthood.

He laughed as he sketched out the pentacles in the area he had cleared of forest debris and grass. Clearly being talented in demonology would be contraindicated for Etonian priesthood. So perhaps that had been for the best. The priests must have known or Seen something in his future. It might have been nice for them to explain or mention it to him; it would have saved him a lot of pain. However, given that Etonian priests did not like conjurors, pointing him in that direction would not have been something they would have wanted to do.

There; the pentacle was complete, the brazier set. He lit the fire and began his chant. It was the standard conjuring for a bound fiend. A type II demon that he knew well. At home, he had permanent pentacles set up and inscribed for conjuring this particular demon, but that was not working now, thanks to the Council's anti-demon wards. It had certainly been a shocker when Estrebrius had suddenly jumped up and slammed the door open and fled Vaselle's house with no warning. Vaselle had followed, yelling and screaming at the demon to return, but it just made a beeline over the city walls. Vaselle had quickly cast a flying spell and took off after the demon as it flew over the city, but had been stopped at the wall.

As he chanted the summoning spell for Estrebrius, he reflected on what he had seen going on outside. It was hard to see through the wards, but he had eventually adjusted his wizard sight for a clear view of the events that were about to occur. He had been floored , could not believe what he was seeing. Fortunately, by the end of the evening, the black market had bootlegged scryings of the event for sale and he had been able to watch it over and over again throughout the night. And thus, in the wee hours of the night, he formed his plan.

"Estrebrius, I command you come forth!" He released a handful of sulfur into the brazier, causing a large flash. And there the demon was, standing in the pentacle as usual, although he was looking a bit sickly, Vaselle thought.

"Master," the demon bowed slightly unsteadily.

"Why are you so wobbly, Estrebrius?" Vaselle asked, rather concerned. It was odd to be concerned about a demon's health, but Estrebrius had always been a very reliable demon. He clearly was not well.

"I am sorry, Master. Yesterday I was overcome by a compulsion to flee the city." Vaselle nodded and waved to the demon that he understood and was not mad. "And once outside the city, I was overtaken by some scoundrels on a flying boat who shot me out of the sky and proceeded to turn me into a pincushion, forcing me back to the Abyss." The fiend shrugged. "Unfortunately, I'm still recovering."

"Hmm, sorry to hear about that. Very unfortunate. I won't keep you long, but I do need your assistance." Estrebrius looked at him, a bit confused by the apparent contradiction. "Are you aware of the battle yesterday between Sir Talarius of the Rod and an extremely powerful demon, who in the end defeated the knight?"

Estrebrius blinked in surprise at the question and then nodded. "I saw a bit of it, and naturally everyone in the Abyss is talking about it."

Vaselle nodded, pleased. "Are you familiar with the demon champion? Do you know him?"

Estrebrius looked at his accursed master in surprise. "Uhm, no, no one really knows who he is. No one had seen him before yesterday, or very few. There are lots of liars in the Abyss, so it's hard to know for sure."

Vaselle frowned; that was inconvenient. "Hmm, so this may take you a while. I need you to locate this demon, reach out to him and get me in contact with him."

Estrebrius made a choking noise and seemed to almost jump in his pentacles. "Master, are you serious?"

"Very," Vaselle confirmed.

"You understand this demon must be at least an archdemon, if not a Prince. It's really not a good idea to attract the attention of such a being." Estrebrius sounded incredulous, as if Vaselle had lost his mind. Perhaps he had, the conjuror thought to himself. However, after yesterday, he knew in his bones that this was the right course.

"I understand that, but I need to meet with this demon. I believe I can offer him something of great interest and it would be most worth his while to grant me an audience."

Estrebrius stared at his accursed master. "My Lord, master," he finally said, "I really must advise against this. It can only lead to pain and death for both of us. This demon is thousands of years old and has remained a complete mystery over all that time. That requires a tremendous amount of cunning and almost unimaginable shielding power. Plus, he's tied to a number of other archdemons, the Rod, the Oorstemothians; you'd be safer to walk into the very Abyss than to have so much as a whisper with this demon!"

Vaselle took his demon's warnings very seriously; they were thoughts he had had himself. However, he had steeled himself for this. He would be strong. He shook his head. "I'm afraid I must do this, Estrebrius. I command you by your true name to obey me and locate, contact and act as my emissary to this demon."

Estrebrius looked almost desperate. "Please master, don't do this. You are a very great master, wise and powerful, and I am honored to be your humble servant, but this is a most dangerous course of action. Please reconsider!"

Vaselle shook his head again. "No, demon. Obey me. Locate this demon for me, and arrange contact!"

Estrebrius bowed his head, feeling the wizard's spells urging him to obey. "Very well, master."

~

Randolf rolled over on his side and caressed Crispin's face in the late morning light. Their morning love session had been as magical as ever, perhaps even sweeter now that Exador's undoing seemed to be underway. He mentally reached out to his wardings around the room, ensuring they were still secure. He was not concerned about the privacy of making love with his catamite; that was an open secret. It was their conversations that needed to be secure.

"New day, new perspective!" Randolf grinned at Crispin.

The youth grinned back. "Don't get your hopes up yet. It's too early," he said, massaging Randolf's side. "I know how you want this charade to end, but until we are sure Exador is completely exposed and discredited as a human, the masquerade must continue."

Randolf rolled onto his back and sighed. "I know, I know. But I've lived my entire life as someone I am not. I want to be me and not Randolf the Second, Exador's Arch-Toady!"

"Well, unlike your father or grandfather, you may get a chance to escape the role your line has been forced to play to protect Turelane," Crispin said, rolling onto his own back.

"It's a shame you couldn't see the balling," Randolf noted, "It was fantastic. It totally upended the playing field. I have to believe Exador was near shitting himself on that carpet near the end."

"You may thank your esteemed fellow councilors for my hasty departure yesterday morning. I was almost blasted back to Djinnistan!" Crispin shook his head. "Fortunately, their spell was directed at demons and other extra-planar individuals. The *other extra-planar* part is what saved me, I think. I would hate to have been a demon subject to that spell! Even after they turned off the overt expulsion part, the general compulsion gave me a headache until I eventually figured out how to counter it."

"And I assume that's why you weren't back when I had to leave for the meeting?" Randolf asked.

Crispin raised his arm to give Randolf a thumbs-up from beside him on the large pillow-topped bed. "My master's wisdom is as deep as the waters in the sea!" Crispin giggled.

Randolf rolled over on top of Crispin, his forearms propping him up above the lad. "You boy, need to quit with the sarcasm before I stuff you back in your bottle!" Randolf pretended to snarl before breaking down into laughter.

Crispin laughed as well. "How many times do I have to tell you, it's a lamp! Not a stupid bottle! Men have lamps, women have bottles!"

"Bottle this!" Randolf's mouth covered Crispin's and their laughter was lost to their lust.

Chapter 85

DOF +1
Late Morning 15-18-449

Hilda stood at the edge of the still dewy clearing, gnawing on her burnt, crusty and cold breakfast cake, about four hours after dawn. Not that she needed to eat the damaged baked good; she never *needed* to eat, it was really more stress relief. She could not actually gain or lose weight as a saint. Saints generally looked exactly the same for all eternity, short of some strange event. In some ways this was convenient in that she had never had much luck losing weight when she was alive; she had been on what seemed like a lifelong diet. Now she could eat whatever she wanted and not gain any weight. However, that also took a lot of the pleasure out of it. No more sense of being "bad" and cheating on her diet.

Actually, it was pretty dang hard to be "bad" as a saint. It certainly put a damper on getting dates. She would be at a party or a bar, and someone would ask her what she did. "Oh, I'm a saint." Suddenly, the other person would make pleasant excuses and move on. And that was at an avatar bar; she was sure a human party or bar would be even worse.

That was one nice thing about this undercover work; she could pretend to be someone else. She could lie and do it for the cause of Good. She shook her head and put the rest of the burnt cake into her belt pouch. The other nice thing about this whole adventure was wearing street clothes. She had been given an account at the quartermaster's to be outfitted in Astlanian garb and tools.

Unfortunately, they had no "normal" horses to complete the masquerade, so she would have to get some from the Rod. She had also been advised to locate a follower of hers and use him or her as a guide to current customs and appropriate behavior. Further, as a lady in the city, she would need to have a man-at-arms or squire. Technically, she should also have a maid, but that would start to get really complicated. They needed to keep this quiet.

The question had been, who? She had scanned her followers in the area and finally decided on a young man named Danyel. Danyel had been born not too far from Rivenrock and was in fact a descendant of the children Hilda had died to protect. He had also been possessed by the demon, and then had the stuffing beaten out of him by other Rod members, who had to take him down to protect Talarius.

At the moment he was unconscious from his wounds. He'd been going in and out as far as she could tell, but she hadn't been monitoring that actively. Given that he would almost certainly feel great contrition for allowing himself to be possessed and attacking Sir Talarius, she was fairly certain she could get him to agree to assist her quietly as part of his penance. Naturally, he would help her in any circumstances, but her thought was that his guilt, undeserved in her opinion, would help assuage his concerns in performing surreptitious services. Not something the Rod was famous for conducting.

Hilda was currently dressed in a modern version her old habit as a Sister of Tiernon, and had surrounded herself in her most subtle misdirection and anti-noticeability rituals. Being invisible was too risky in this camp, so simply being unnoticed would be far better.

She made her way through the camp towards the guarded area where the possessed soldiers were being kept. At least, that's what she assumed the guards were for. She was actually just following her link to Danyel. She paused near the tent to allow some guards to look the other way before sneaking into the tent.

There were three soldiers in the tent, unconscious and heavily bandaged. They also appeared to be loosely chained to their cots. She was going to need to heal Danyel so he could help her, but she could not ignore the other two. So, first things first. She went to each cot and said a prayer of sleep over each man to keep them sleeping, and then she set about examining and healing their wounds.

It took her a few minutes per patient, as she had to make sure she had caught everything, but as she had often noted, saintly healing was a heck of a lot faster than priestly healing and definitely faster than what she'd been able to do as a Sister of Tiernon.

She healed Danyel last. When she was finished, she sat back on her stool for a moment and took a deep breath, preparing to wake him. Hilda grimaced and then put a silence spell around the tent. She did not want Danyel waking up and screaming when he saw her. With the ritual in place, they would be able to talk, but no one outside would hear them.

~

"I have to admit, you do have a nice view," Ramses said, looking out the French doors of Exador's breakfast room. They were at Exador's tower in Astlan enjoying a late breakfast, Astlanian time.

"Thank you. I've spent centuries perfecting these gardens," Exador said, setting his coffee down. They were having human beverages this morning, playing the necessary role for the servants and staff.

As Ramses picked up his cup, the room suddenly dimmed considerably and a deep, damp chill came over the room. "The air conditioning kicking into overdrive and dimming the lights?" Ramses asked, raising an eyebrow. That did not seem too likely, given that they were in a brightly fierdlit room.

The chill was bone deep, oddly palpable even to archdemons. Ramses gave Exador a concerned look. Exador glanced around the suddenly dim room and smiled. "Greetings, Morthador!" he exclaimed to the room.

A deep bass whisper reverberated from the darkness. It was felt more in the inner bones of the ear than in the air itself. "Greetings, master. I have news to report."

Ramses relaxed slightly, realizing that Exador was in control of whatever this was. He was still on edge, of course; they were archdemons and treachery could never be ruled out.

Exador grinned over at Ramses, fully understanding his associate's disquiet. "Ramses, allow me to introduce my most trusted spy, Morthador." Exador gestured at the room.

Ramses looked around the room, trying to locate the source of darkness.

Exador chuckled. "Morthador is a greater shadow," he explained.

"A greater shadow?" Ramses asked uncertainly.

"A type IV Shadow."

Ramses shook his head. "A shadow that is a greater demon?" His brows furrowed. "I don't believe I've heard of such a demon before."

"They are rare, but not as rare as one might think," Exador said. "For obvious reasons, they are often hard to find."

"So this is a demon that has chosen to advance its skills, but not morph to an imp, sprite or fiend along the traditional paths?" Ramses asked.

"Exactly. There are a few who find true and lasting comfort in the darkness of the Shadow," Exador said with a grin. "Morthador is one such. He has been quite invaluable in many ways. For the last thousand years or so, he has been stationed deep in the under-chasms of Astlan, in particular between Freehold and the Grove."

Ramses furrowed his brow again, not understanding. "I see." He clearly did not.

"As you may or may not recall, the Grove in Astlan is located due east of this tower, about three hundred plus leagues. Their ridiculously high mountains and more importantly, sizable military resources have been a thorn in my ability to deal with Cal Crestor on the other side of the Grove." Exador shook his head.

Ramses nodded. "I recall they were a pain for us on the Council of Anilords. We never were able to conquer them."

Exador nodded. "And as you may recall, going south one crosses the United Federation, whose general anarchy is something of a nuisance, and is also loosely Grove aligned. They were not organized back when you were here. One then has Jotungard to deal with, as you recall? Clearly, not Grove aligned, but still unpleasant."

"Indeed, I recall," Ramses said drily.

"Going north through Turelane, I am blocked by Kel Femaer, which is purely alvaren territory and also closely aligned with the Grove." Exador waved his hand.

"Yes, I get your point on the alfar. Never have liked the sanctimonious bastards," Ramses said.

"In short, the Grove has been a thorn in my side for my entire time in Astlan. Both before my adventures with the Rod and you, and since." Exador took a breath. "So, I like to keep an eye on my fellow Councilor Trevin D'Vils and her Grove."

"And Morthador fits in how?" Ramses asked.

"The Grove has a very secure communication line that runs through all of Norelon and, in fact, to all continents that rely on very deep rock veins and geological plates," Exador said.

"Ahh," Ramses said, suddenly understanding.

Exador smiled. "Exactly. Morthador enjoys the really deep, dark caverns and has no trouble spending time underground. He can intercept those communication lines."

Ramses chuckled. "Quite clever."

Exador smiled. "Thank you." He rotated slightly toward the darker part of the room. "Morthador, what news do you bring?"

"The enchantress shall be journeying very shortly to the Grove with an entourage and shall then be taking the Nimbus out to investigate urgent Seeings of orc uprisings in Murgandy and Jotungard," The bass voice reverberated in their ears.

"How soon?" Exador asked.

"From what I gathered, she plans to depart on the Nimbus to Murgandy within a day or two," the shadow informed them.

"The Nimbus?" Ramses asked.

Exador sighed quietly. "One of their military vessels. Trevin's flagship." He stroked his chin in thought. "I have allies in Nysegard who will want to know about this." He looked up towards the darkness. "Excellent work, Morthador. Thank you."

~

Danyel was having horrible dreams. He dreamt of imminent evil attacking his companions. He tried to stop it, and then his fellow soldiers turned on him, apparently possessed by the evil. The next thing he knew, he was in some weird location, some sort of leather-padded seat in the back of something like an enclosed chariot, hurtling down a stone road at an ungodly speed with no sign of horses; and then he was back on the battlefield watching Talarius slay the demon. In the dreams, a giant fireball would suddenly expand, then his legs would ache as if he had jumped off the top of a mountain and landed on stone feet first.

He remembered coming to between dreams and seeing nurses bandaging him, and feeling bruised and battered all over. But now, on waking, he found himself feeling better; quite refreshed, in fact. Actually, thinking about it with his eyes closed, he felt better than he had in some time. He smiled and opened his eyes to see his patron saint, Hilda of Rivenrock, dressed in her Sister of Tiernon habit, beaming down at him.

"Fuck, I'm dead!" Danyel cried out in dismay.

Saint Hilda frowned momentarily.

Crap! He had cursed in the presence of a holy saint! Some start to his afterlife. Danyel closed his eyes and gulped. "Forgive me, Saint Hilda! I beg you to forgive my ingratitude for your generous presence in greeting me at the gateway to Tierhallon."

His patron saint seemed to snort and then chuckle. "Okay, not the reaction I'd been expecting," she said, "but then I really wasn't sure what to expect."

Danyel felt the holy saint pat his hands, just like any Sister of Tiernon might do to a patient in her care.

"Sorry to disappoint you," Saint Hilda continued, "but you're going to have to wait a bit longer to feast in Tierhallon." Danyel cracked his eyes open again to peer at her. She beamed back at him, her radiant smile making him feel warm and safe for some reason. "You're very much alive, and chained to this bed after being possessed by a demon."

Danyel blinked. Possessed by a demon? What was she talking about? "I'm sorry, Your Holiness, but…"

"You don't remember?" She moved her head from side to side. "I am not really surprised. You were under the complete control of the demon, so you probably didn't have much conscious thought." Danyel just stared at her in shock. "Okay, we need to make this short. You remember the battle between Talarius and the big demon?"

Danyel nodded.

"Well, Talarius apparently defeated the demon, but not really. It somehow took possession of a good number of high priests and about a third of the Rod's nearby archers and some others , including you. He then used those he had possessed to battle Talarius and defeat him. A few details later, and the demon hightailed it back to the Abyss with Talarius as a hostage."

Danyel gasped in shock at this information. How could this be? He did not remember any of this, at least nothing after seeing the demon crumble to ashes on the battlefield. After that, things got blurry and he really only remembered a bunch of chaotic and weird dreams.

"Long story getting shorter still," Saint Hilda continued. "Because you were possessed, they locked you and the others up in these tents while working to heal you." She pulled on his arm to show him that he was, indeed, chained to the cot.

"Uhh…" Danyel was at a loss for words. "What? Uhm, I'm not dead?"

"Not at all!" The saint beamed at him. "In fact, I just healed you and purged any lingering demonic influences in you and your tent mates!" She gestured around the tent. Danyel noted that there were two other Rod members in here with him. He had seen them around, but did not know their names.

"If I may, Your Holiness?" Danyel was shaking his head, and the saint nodded for him to go on. "To what do I owe this great honor? For a great and holy saint like yourself to so intercede on my behalf in this manner is…" Danyel had no idea what to call it.

The Saint of Rivenrock smiled again and patted his shoulder. "Well, you are one of my most loyal devotees, so of course I want to help you." Hilda paused and tilted her head a bit. "And you can help me in return."

Danyel tried to bow his head, which was hard since he was lying down. "How can I possibly help you Your Holiness?"

"Well for one, don't call me 'Your Holiness' in public!" The saint laughed good-naturedly. "I am trying to put together a solid understanding of the events that transpired here yesterday, and the events that led up to it." Danyel nodded. "And I don't want to alert too many people to what I am doing."

Danyel shook his head, puzzled. "But certainly, you could just appear to the arch-diocate and vicar general and ask for a Holy Accounting?"

Saint Hilda made a small grimace. "Well, you see, that's the thing. We—or rather, I—am concerned that we might not get a full and accurate accounting." Danyel looked shocked, and Hilda patted his arm. "No, not like that. I fully trust our people on the ground. It's just that when saints and archons appear, people sort of, well… misremember things, or sometimes just go numb and can't remember anything. Further, I need to investigate outside the Rod. I need to go into Freehold and investigate what led to this incident and gather information about this demon and the plots surrounding it."

Danyel looked at his patron saint, trying to understand. "You mean like a secret inquisition?"

The saint moved her head from shoulder to shoulder, thinking. "Yes, I suppose that's a good way of phrasing it. A secret inquisition. I don't want the identity of the questioner influencing the answers she receives."

"So you aren't going to tell people who you are?"

"Exactly!" Hilda beamed at Danyel, again making him feel warm and relaxed, even though intellectually he knew he should be freaking out.

"So how can I help you, Your Holiness?" Danyel asked, shaking his head. "I'm but a simple Rod member."

The saint smiled. "My dear, you are no simple Rod member. You are a loyal devotee of mine. Not only were you a witness to these events, you were a participant. And…"

"And?" Danyel asked when she paused.

"I need you to get us a couple of horses from the Rod's quartermaster along with tack, and then for you to pose as my squire—my man-at-arms if you will—while I pretend to be a resident of Freehold returning from an alvaren wedding."

Danyel blinked in shock at this completely unexpected request.

~

"Very interesting, Madam Councilor," Elrose said to Trevin D'Vils in her guest parlor as a knock came on the door. He and Maelen were continuing their discussions with her from last night.

"My, this is a busy morning!" Trevin exclaimed from the divan, upon which she was sitting upright and sipping a cup of tea. She set the cup back in its saucer and nodded to one of her serving boys to answer the door. "I beg your pardon for the interruption." She nodded to her two guests, Elrose and Maelen.

The boy opened the door to reveal Damien as her newest visitor. "Master Damien!" Trevin greeted her fellow councilor and gestured for him to come in. "To what do I owe this unexpected visit?"

"I beg your pardon, Councilor, but at the request of our Archimage, I've come seeking one of your visitors: the good seer, Maelen." Damien gestured to the seer.

Trevin shook her head in surprise. "And what does Gandros want with the good seer?" Maelen and Elrose both looked curiously at Damien.

Damien coughed slightly and glanced to make sure the servant had closed the door. "Well, it's more like where he'd like our visitor to be."

Trevin raised her right eyebrow in question, motioning for the inquisitor to continue.

"Well"—he looked back and forth between Elrose and Maelen —"as you are aware, we have an army still sitting outside the walls."

"And an air fleet as well," Trevin observed.

Damien smiled grimly and nodded. "And both are looking for Maelen, Gastropé, Edwyrd, Rupert and Jen."

"Aaahh," said Trevin with a nod, understanding.

"So," Maelen said, smiling, "I'm guessing we are being invited to leave?"

Damien shrugged, slightly uncomfortable. "I'm afraid so. However, obviously, I will unofficially assist in your departure."

"And where do you, or rather Gandros, want them to go?" Elrose asked.

"We haven't figured that out yet, but we do know the Rod and the Oorstemothians will want to try and verify that you all departed with the demons," Damien said. "Yes, the whole thing is going to look awkward, but if you are all verifiably gone, they won't have much choice but to leave."

"I think you underestimate the logic of the Oorstemothians," Maelen stated drily.

"And the fervor of the Rod," Elrose added.

"Actually," Trevin interrupted, "my colleagues here and I have been discussing an idea that may help with this situation." Maelen and Elrose chuckled; Damien looked at her, puzzled.

"The three of us were just discussing the option of visiting some of Bastet's old temples to see if we can: one, pick up any residue of recent activity and two, try and use these once holy sites to see if we can scry her current activities. If she has been in Astlan recently, as we are starting to suspect, we should get some sympathetic residual emanations from the shrine and any artifacts left in it, and they could provide us a link to her that we can follow. We had thus been discussing mounting an expedition to investigate. We could easily bring your friends along with us," she said, gesturing to Maelen.

Damien shook his head. "An expedition?"

"Well, we would have to go to Natoor, on the other side of Eton. It is not a quick trip. The lady councilor is the only person we know to have been there, and even so, that was long ago. Thus, we are blind for more instantaneous forms of magical transport. Therefore, we shall have to travel conventionally. It would be an expedition," Elrose explained.

Damien shook his head again. "I like the idea, but unfortunately, we don't have time to mount a full expedition from here, and that would be a bit too obvious."

Trevin waved her hand. "Nonsense. We won't mount it from here, we'll mount it from the Grove. I've got reasonable transportation there and I can get us to the Grove quickly and without anyone knowing."

~

"Master Trisfelt!" Hilda called out as she and Danyel approached his encampment. It had taken a bit more effort than she had expected. The local quartermaster had been not entirely helpful to Danyel, so she had had to add a bit of her own persuasion and then a rather high-powered forget ritual. She had not dared to use the standard forget ritual, which was, of course, a proscribed spell. The Rod had plenty of priests with them, so they would have been able to detect the standard ritual, and so she had had to get slightly "miraculous."

In any event, they had acquired two horses and a mule; she had then had to zap back to the quartermaster at Tierhallon and get a non-Rod set of man-at-arms clothing for Danyel. She had her own clothing already packed, which was why they had needed a mule. Of course, due to modesty, she had stopped by home and changed to her city clothes. A Sister of Tiernon was a good disguise for the Rod, but would be completely at odds with her "Hilda" persona that Trisfelt had met. She and Danyel were leading their animals as they approached the wizard's encampment.

Trisfelt looked up from a mirror he was staring at intently. His face split into a broad smile as he saw her. "My dear lady, what a pleasure to see you again!" he said, beaming. He glanced curiously at Danyel.

"And good to see you as well," Hilda replied. She gestured to Danyel. "This is my man-at-arms, Danyel." Trisfelt nodded at Danyel, smiling in greeting. "Apparently, it's not seemly for a lady to go unaccompanied to a wedding." She shook her head in pretend exasperation.

Hilda waved her hand, brushing away the annoyance. "In any event, I noted people coming and going from the city gate again."

"Yes," Trisfelt agreed, slipping his mirror into a large pocket in his robe. "They just opened it this morning. The city guard is inspecting everyone going in, and the Rod and the Oorstemothians are inspecting everyone coming out."

Hilda shook her head. "My, they are paranoid." Trisfelt chuckled and made a face that implied she was making an understatement.

"I don't suppose you are going into the city?" Hilda enquired.

"Well, actually I am. My friend Master Elrose has some issues he wants to discuss with me in person, so I am temporarily leaving my post. I also need to restock a few supplies." He winked at her.

Hilda laughed. "I am so sorry to have depleted your supplies!"

Trisfelt laughed. "Not at all! Supply depletion is always better with good company!"

"Well, I do have a very nice bottle of House Tregorian 912 that we might enjoy." Hilda frowned slightly. "Although, if they are being picky about whom they let back in, it might be best to not be intoxicated. Perhaps we can try it after you meet with your friend?"

"Excellent!" Trisfelt beamed. "I am packed. I simply need to hook up my horse and wagon."

Hilda handed Danyel her reins. "Will you hobble the animals, dear? I'll help Master Trisfelt with his horse and wagon."

~

"So, we're being carted off to a distant continent now?" Jenn asked rhetorically of Gastropé. The two were walking back towards their apartments from a meeting with Lenamare, Jehenna, Elrose and Damien.

"Would you prefer they hand us over to the Oorstemothians?" Gastropé asked. "Or the Rod?"

Jenn sent a small glare in his direction. "You know what I mean. We don't get a lot of say in this."

"And Jehenna normally gives you a lot of say?" the conjuror asked.

Jenn gave a disgusted sigh. "Gastropé? I'm guessing you don't have any sisters?"

"No." Gastropé gave her a puzzled look.

"Because if you did, then you would know that you are supposed to be agreeing with me right now. I am not in the mood to be reasonable!" Jenn shook her head in exasperation.

Gastropé chuckled. "Think of it as a field trip!" He smiled at her. "We are going to the Grove. The Grove! Do you know how many humans get to see the inside of the Grove?"

Jenn shrugged, not knowing.

"Other than some druids, none! That's how many. It's a place filled with Sidhe, satyrs, centaurs and all sorts of exotic races that most of us only hear about in stories! It is said that alvaren princes dine there! The noblest of the fey!"

"Are you sure you aren't just looking to meet a cute nymph?" Jenn asked.

"You really are a curmudgeon!" Gastropé shook his head.

"Jenn!" came a booming voice from down the corridor ahead of them. Jenn's mood lightened immediately and she took off down the hall to embrace Master Trisfelt. Gastropé caught up with them. Jenn's wizard friend was being followed by a good-sized woman with a very bright smile, and a young man about Gastropé's age, dressed as a guard of some sort.

"Oh, it's so good to see you! It seems like forever!" Jenn gushed.

"It's been completely crazy, my dear!" Trisfelt laughed and pulled back to look at her. "You seem to be doing well, though!"

Jenn shrugged. "To be honest, I've been through hell, literally, a couple times now... but I'm getting used to it."

Trisfelt shook his head in amazement. "I did hear something about you traveling through the Abyss, but not much more than that." He looked to Gastropé. "Is this one of your new friends? Rupert's cousin, maybe?"

Jenn shook her head and gave an exasperated look. "No, Rupert's cousin is Edwyrd and he and Rupert apparently departed shortly after the demons to make sure they all went back to the Abyss."

Trisfelt glanced at Gastropé as the wizard made a rather weird face. "Isn't that a bit dangerous for little Rupert? I mean he is only ten. Are we that hard up for wizards?"

"Tell me!" Jenn almost shouted, raising her hands. "However, he's infatuated with his cousin, who apparently is fairly powerful!" She was shaking her head. Gastropé coughed. Jenn's eyes went wide for a second. "Oh, yeah—this is Gastropé. We, uhm, met him shortly after our caravan ambush."

"Really?" Trisfelt looked curiously at Gastropé. He stuck out his hand and the two shook.

Neither Jenn nor Gastropé had a great desire to explain how they met, so Jenn quickly tried to change the conversation. "So, who are your new friends?"

Trisfelt blinked for a moment and then suddenly seemed to remember his company. "My apologies! This is my friend, Hilda, and her man-at-arms, Danyel!" Trisfelt stepped back to allow the four to have a clear view of each other.

"My dear girl!" Hilda moved forward and gave Jenn a great big hug. "I've heard so much about you from Trisfelt, I feel like we've been friends for ever!" She pulled back and gave Jenn the biggest, brightest smile Jenn could ever recall seeing. The large woman seemed to have a very calming and welcoming manner.

"And Gastropé, a pleasure to meet you as well!" Hilda gave the wizard a very hearty handshake and another brilliant smile. Gastropé blinked, slightly taken back by her overwhelming presence.

"So, Hilda..." Jenn struggled to recover from the woman's strong presence. "How did you and Trisfelt meet? Are you a thaumaturge?"

Hilda beamed; Trisfelt got a puzzled look on his face, as if trying to remember what Hilda did for a living. "Oh no, dear," she replied, "I'm no good at memorizing all those spells and such. I'm a healer, an animage!" Hilda smiled at her and then at Gastropé.

Jenn shook her head and glanced at Gastropé, looking for agreement as she exclaimed, "An animage? I had never met an animage in my life—I was not even sure they existed until all this craziness started—and now you are the third in the last few weeks! All completely independent of each other!" Gastropé shrugged, equally puzzled.

Hilda chuckled. "Well, I find that when 'craziness starts,' people in my profession do start to pop up, so to speak. Most of the time we like to keep a very low profile. Who are the other animages you've met?"

"Uhm, Maelen the seer, whom you may meet shortly, depending on schedules, and then Edwyrd, Rupert's cousin."

"A seer?" Hilda asked curiously and, it seemed, somewhat cautiously.

"Yes, an actual member of the Society of Learned Fellows. No one even knew the Society still existed!" Gastropé chimed in.

Hilda smiled, a bit more formally, perhaps. "Oh, they certainly still exist. They have a definite presence on Eton; not so much on Norelon." She shook her head. "And this Edwyrd? He is chasing demons with a ten-year-old?" Hilda seemed rightfully puzzled by this.

Jenn somehow managed to nod her head in agreement and shake her head in disbelief in a single motion. "Yes, we met him in Gizzor Del. He is apparently, according to Maelen at least, a very powerful animage. A pyromaster and a couple other terms I'm not familiar with." Gastropé was nodding in agreement.

"Well. Interesting, very interesting." Hilda nodded. She looked at Gastropé. "You are, if I am not mistaken, a pyromancer? And also a conjuror, perhaps?"

Gastropé blushed slightly under Hilda's observation. "I try my best."

"Excellent." Hilda gave his shoulder a firm squeeze. "That's what is important. Always strive to do your best—that is how you grow in strength and talent. I can tell you are young, but I can See you've got great promise!"

Hilda beamed in admiration at Jenn and Gastropé. "Clearly you've been through so much, far more than wizards three times your age ever have to deal with. I'm dying to hear of your adventures, if you have time at some point?" She turned to Trisfelt suddenly. "You know, I do happen to have a couple of bottles of note with me, and a few alvaren delicacies? Perhaps we could all have dinner this evening?" She gestured to Gastropé and Jenn.

Trisfelt started nodding and Jenn was grinning but then suddenly frowned. "Oh, I'm sorry. Dang it! I completely forgot!" She grimaced in frustration, and Gastropé also groaned.

"What is it, my dear?" Hilda asked.

"We are leaving this evening for the Grove, on an expedition."

"An expedition?" Trisfelt asked, puzzled.

"To the Grove?" Hilda's eyes widened. "That is quite an undertaking. Surely, my dear, you've had enough adventures for a while?" Hilda asked, giving Jenn a reassuring pat on her forearm.

"Yes, well, the two armies outside are looking for Gastropé, Maelen and me, as well as Edwyrd and Rupert, and the Council wants us out of Freehold as of about a week ago," Jenn explained.

"So the three of us are going with Elrose and Councilor D'Vils to the Grove and then on to Natoor," Gastropé informed them.

Hilda blinked. "You are going with Trevin D'Vils to the Grove and then on to Natoor?" She blinked a few more times. "Surely there are... less remote places you could go to get away from the Rod? They have a bigger presence on Natoor than on Norelon. In fact, given the route to get there, you are passing through the heart of the Rod's operations. Unless you've got a gateway?"

Jenn shook her head. "No, we are going conventionally, whatever that means. Given that Trevin D'Vils appears to be about 300 years old, I can't imagine she actually intends to go on horseback and sailing ship, but you never know."

Hilda looked slightly puzzled. She mused out loud, "Trevin D'Vils? I'm surprised she's not dust at this point." Jenn did not think they were supposed to hear that, but they all did. Hilda seemed to suddenly realize she was thinking aloud and blushed.

Jenn grinned at Hilda and whispered, "She's ancient, and wears the most inappropriate clothing!"

Hilda laughed, glad not to have offended anyone. Gastropé laughed as well.

Trisfelt just shook his head in amusement. "But why Natoor?" he asked.

Jenn looked around. "My room is just around the corner; let's go there and discuss this in a bit more privacy."

[Appendix: Animus and Mana Wielders]

~

Hilda put down her glass of wine and reached for a piece of H'skallen cheese. They had gone back to Jenn's room and decided that since they could not have dinner together, they should at least have a late lunch; that way Jenn and Gastropé could try some of the alvaren delicacies she'd gotten from the quartermaster's pantry. She had to be able to back up her wedding cover story, and clearly anyone who knew Hilda would naturally have assumed she would have raided a few of the buffet tables at an alvaren wedding.

However, as enticing as the wine was, with this rather insane story of Jenn's, she had to keep a grip. As it was, she was fighting a splitting headache from the stupid wards blanketing the city. When she and Trisfelt had entered the city, she had nearly fallen off her horse. She had to pretend to have nausea from some stale travel cake at breakfast. Not very convincing, but better than the truth. She had had to quickly work out a ritual to damp down the expulsion symptoms, so she could enter. Technically, the ward was supposed to have been for demons, but clearly, it was aimed at general extra-planar beings. Fortunately, being a saint, she had a mortal background and was not a pure spirit. An archon would have had a lot more trouble with the wards. They would need to keep that in mind if the Host needed to enter the city.

Once she was settled, she could come up with something better. The best thing would probably be to anoint an amulet with its own mana pool so she would not have to maintain the ritual herself. If she got seriously distracted, say fending off a wizard who had caught on to her, she wanted the expulsion repulsion, or whatever she was going to call it, to stay on. Otherwise, the wards would send her packing.

"So, let me see if I have this right," Hilda tried to clarify. "Trevin thinks that one of the archdemons might actually be an old goddess named Bastet, from Natoor?"

"Exactly," Gastropé confirmed rather tipsily. Hilda had to smile; these youngsters were so much easier to loosen up than Trisfelt. That man was a professional imbiber. She had needed a few divine tricks to keep her head about her last night and get him inebriated. It really would have been nice if she had been able to let go and truly enjoy the wine's effects. However, she had had a job to do. Moreover, today, with her headache, she was more than happy to just do her job.

A clock in the courtyard gonged that the afternoon was halfway done. "Oh, dear lord!" Trisfelt exclaimed in dismay. "I need to meet with Elrose! He needed to meet with me privately and in person!"

Gastropé nodded. "Yeah, he's going to tell you about the expedition."

"And," Jenn hiccupped, "that since both he and I are going, Lenamare and Jehenna need you inside the city for their project."

"Project?" Hilda asked. "Surely the wards are stable and the city secure?"

"No," Jenn shook her head, "the other project, the one that got Exador to attack the castle."

Hilda thought back for a moment. "I don't recall what you said that was—some dispute about an artifact of some sort?"

"A stupid magic spell book they can't figure out how to open," Jenn said. Gastropé was nodding up and down in rather excessive agreement.

"Okay, yes, I remember now. I'd sort of forgotten that in all the other crazy adventures you've been through." Hilda shook her head in sympathy at Jenn.

"I fear I must take my leave to go and see Master Elrose then, before he leaves." Trisfelt stood.

Hilda nodded. "Danyel and I should be getting home. I am pretty clear on our route in, so we should be able to get ourselves back to the stables." She glanced a bit skeptically over at Danyel, who was also inexperienced when it came to libations. She shook her head and gave Trisfelt a glance, as she noted that he had noticed her look to Danyel.

"Youth," he said and chuckled softly, shaking his head in agreement as well. He seemed quite fine. Hilda was not surprised; the man had true fortitude when it came to libations. She briefly wondered if he had a similar fortitude in the romance department. Hilda blushed; clearly, the wine and headache were getting to her, for that thought to pop up!

[Appendix: Mana Pools and Anima Jars]

Chapter 86

Estrebrius handed the waiter demon another coin for his second mug of Denubian Choco-Coffee™. This was really a crapper of a day —actually, the last two days. He had been hanging out in his penta-cage at his accursed master's laboratory when that damned crazy expulsion spell had hit him. He had nearly puked out his non-existent guts and released his non-existent bowels. He had headed out of the city as fast as possible and seen the last half of the fateful battle before being dispatched by those bastards in the flying boat after the battle.

Then, still recovering, his accursed master had summoned him! That had been very painful, although the magic of the summoning did help accelerate his healing. However, his accursed master had apparently become completely unhinged. This stunk! Master Vaselle was the best accursed master he had ever had. He never wantonly tortured and only did modest and appropriate punishments when warranted. Plus he let Estrebrius hang out in Freehold with him, which was a much more interesting place than the outlands of the Abyss, and safer than the Courts.

He was not a huge fan of the Courts, but when you needed a drink there weren't a lot of other options. Estrebrius sighed; he wished he could cry. He felt so despondent! How would he ever find this new demon lord? Everyone in the Abyss was trying to figure out who he was and what he was up to, and no one knew anything! In addition, there were plenty of others trying to find the demon lord. What chance did he have?

Even if he did find the demon lord, what then? Assuming the demon lord did not eat him for lunch, he would never agree to see Vaselle. He was going to fail in his task and likely die in it. The only thing worse would probably be to succeed. Well, maybe that would not be worse than dying, unless he died in that option too. The point was, if the demon lord did agree to meet with Vaselle, he would surely kill the wizard and then he would be out a particularly good master. Not that it was such a bad thing, but he had never had much luck staying free, so it was better to be bound to a decent master.

"Hoy, Estrebrius! Why so glum, dear chap?" Estrebrius looked up to see Boggy joining him at the table. He was happy to see that Boggy had recovered from his post-master-slaying drinking binge. Estrebrius had checked out early from that party. He had not wanted a hangover when Vaselle summoned him to work the next day.

"I am up the Styx without a paddle," Estrebrius whined despondently.

"Why, what happened?" Boggy asked.

"You know that big demon that kidnapped the knight of Tiernon?"

Boggy beamed extremely brightly. "I certainly do!"

Estrebrius shook his head, not understanding why Boggy was so enthusiastic about it; but of course, if he had been in the Courts he could not not know about the demon. "Anyway, my master, Vaselle—"

"The one you keep telling me is a decent fellow? The one I insist can't be?" Boggy interrupted.

"Yes, him. He has gone over the edge. Bonkers! And he's set me to an impossible task!" Estrebrius ground his eyes into the palms of his hands.

"Ahh, finally tortured you. I told you, they all do it eventually!" Boggy patted his arm.

"No... If only!" Estrebrius looked up, dropping his arms to the table. "It's worse than that. He is completely insane! And he's given me an insane task that I can't possibly complete!"

Boggy nodded. "Cor blimey, I hate it when they do that. We aren't djinns, for the Concordenax's sake!" Boggy sighed. "So what does he want you to do?"

"He wants me to locate that demon lord that kidnapped the knight yesterday and set up a meeting between himself and the demon lord!" Estrebrius raised his hands in the air and shook them, as if crying out to a heaven that certainly was not there for him or any demon.

"Oh, is that all?" Boggy shrugged. "Well, I'd have to admit that does seem sort of stupid, even for an accursed master. However, if that is all you need , my lad, I can set it up."

Estrebrius dropped his arms to the table and stared at Boggy as if Boggy had just gone insane as well.

~

Tom, Rupert and Tizzy were sitting outside the cave while Tizzy regaled them with tales of his accursed masters. Suddenly Tizzy stopped his nearly continuous monologue, and his nose started twitching. In fact, it started twitching up, down, right, left, and then his face began scrunching and contorting in all sorts of weird and vaguely disturbing ways.

"Tizzy? Are you okay?" Rupert asked, putting his hand on Tizzy's upper shoulder.

"IT'S LIKE BUTTAH!" Tizzy suddenly shrieked in his yenta voice. Rupert, having never heard this voice so up close and personal before, jumped so high he fell off the ledge and it took him a few seconds to fly back onto it. At that point, Tizzy had reared up on his rear legs and was sniffing in all sorts of directions as if trying to locate a scent. He really was quite tall when he stood all the way up, Tom reflected.

"What is it?" Tom asked.

"Well, it ain't popcorn, but it's gotta lotta buttah!" Tizzy said again in his yenta voice. Rupert looked at Tom with concern.

Tom shrugged, and then he thought back to his own arrival. "Tizzy, are you saying that you smell a new arrival?" he asked, suppressing a belch. Even talking about butter made his indigestion act up.

"Yes! Very strange… I did not see this one coming. New arrivals aren't usually this frequent." Tizzy shook his head, still sniffing. "I think you will want to come with me, Tom!" he said, sounding something like a yenta matchmaker.

"We'll all go!" Rupert said with excitement. "What's a new arrival?" He was looking back and forth between the two demons.

"Can't you handle this on your own, Tizzy?" Tom asked. He did not want to take Rupert and have to explain what a new arrival was. That would complicate his own story.

Tizzy scrunched his eyes and looked at Tom, then looked away and made other weird facial expressions. "Nope, think you need to come with me. Boggy's not here and he normally goes with me."

Tom sighed, and then remembered Talarius sleeping in the cave. "Rupert, we can't leave Talarius alone. If he wakes up and no one is around, he's liable to do something crazy."

"So?" Rupert asked, realizing he was about to be stuck babysitting.

"So I don't need him freaking out any worse than he probably already is." He really was not sure what the knight's mental state was.

"But I want to come with you guys!" Rupert complained.

"I know, but we are getting stretched too thin. We have commitments to honor, which sort of happens when you kidnap someone. You become responsible for them and their safety. Plus other demons are probably looking for him; I need you to defend him if any of them show up!"

"But he tried to kill you, and he did kill me!" Rupert complained. "Why do we care about his safety?"

"Because we are the better people. We have honor and integrity. It's what *we* do," Tom told him sternly.

Rupert frowned and made an annoyed face. "Okay, but don't be gone too long! If a demon army shows up, I'm not going to be able to protect him."

Tom shook his head. "We shouldn't be more than a couple hours, I hope." He had no idea, but this would force them to limit the time. He really did not expect any demons to come looking for Talarius; only Antefalken, Boggy and Tizzy knew where he lived. It was not like any of them would be playing tour guide.

~

Tizzy had taken off at nearly warp speed and Tom really had to work to keep up. It was amazing how fast that little demon could move when he was in a hurry. They quickly left the mountain range and then headed south, or at least what Tom thought of as south, over the giant plain with the pillars and fireballs. Within about fifteen minutes, they were crossing the Styx and continuing on. Tom really had no good sense of direction and was not quite sure how Tizzy knew where he was going. It was also odd that Tizzy could smell a new arrival from this many miles away.

Within about half an hour of leaving the mountains, they were heading towards a somewhat squat, very wide pillar. It was more of a mesa, Tom guessed. The mesa was roughly three to four thousand feet above the ground and maybe half a mile to a mile across, depending on which direction you measured and where you were. It was not particularly oval or round in shape; it was more like a series of adjacent mountains that all had their tops sliced off at the level where they were still merged.

On that mesa was a demon running around in circles, wildly swinging its arms and periodically yelling or making weird gestures. As his long-distance vision focused on the creature, Tom noted that it was a rather handsome demon. Mostly humanoid with dark burgundy skin, goat hooves of course, rather hairy lower legs. A tail more like a monkey's; it seemed rather weirdly animated. Large bat wings, four arms with absolutely massive pectorals and tight abs. Holy crap —the demon's junk was huge! The demon itself was probably no more than seven feet tall, but its male equipment was nearly as large as Tom's. Which made it appear really big on the much-thinner demon.

The demon also had a Van Dyke goatee and moustache, and a rather human face, albeit very chiseled, and rather interesting dreadlocks for hair. Overall quite handsome in some odd manner. As Tizzy and Tom landed, the demon had begun shouting again. He was marching the other way and had not noticed them.

"Wake up, man! Wake up!" The demon was shouting, apparently to himself. "I want this trip to end. Now!" The demon pinched itself, and from where they were behind him, Tom guessed the demon had pinched one of its four nipples. "Aaaahhh... Fuck! Gotta not do that. Shit, I'm hard again. What's up with that! Stop it, stop it... Goddamnit, this crazy-ass nightmare needs to end!"

Tizzy gestured at Tom to interrupt the ranting demon. Tom shrugged and coughed loudly. The gesticulating demon stopped in its tracks and then slowly turned to face them. It then shrieked extremely loudly and fell over backwards. Tom frowned at the bizarre behavior.

Tizzy shook his head. "Surprisingly, not an uncommon reaction." He walked over to the demon and bent over at his lower waist to peer at his face. "He's a pretty one, gotta give him that!" Tizzy stroked the demon's chiseled jaw line with his upper right thumb. His lower right index finger had started tracing the outline of the demon's lower left pectoral.

"Are you going to wake him up or just stand there molesting him?" Tom asked.

Tizzy shook his head suddenly and stood up. "Sorry... he's an incubus. Has that sort of effect on people. Men, women, doesn't matter." Tizzy waved all four of his hands as if trying to shake off the spell. "I'm normally into the ladies, myself, but these incubi are something else."

"What is an incubus?" Tom asked.

Tizzy shifted around to stare back at Tom. "You ever heard of a succubus?"

"Uhm, yeah, a female demon who has sex with men and steals their strength, or their soul," Tom replied.

"Exactly. Succubi steal animus from men, typically, and sometimes from women so that they can combine it with the seed of a male demon and produce a child," Tizzy explained.

"Okay, and an incubus is like the male version?" Tom asked.

"Exactly. They take the seed of a male demon and deposit in a female host to create a child," Tizzy said.

"They take the seed of a male demon? They don't use their own?" Tom was puzzled.

"Incubi and succubi are pure instruments of delivery and pleasure. Or well, actually, the succubi bear the children too, but they don't use their own eggs or sperm; they are infertile. They use those of another demoness. Same for incubi," Tizzy stated, staring down at the incubus again.

"Okay, I know I'm going to regret asking this." Tom knew he was, but hell... "Why wouldn't a demon who wanted a baby just do it themselves? What's with the middleman? Or middlewoman?"

Tizzy turned back to Tom and beamed a bright smile at him while raising and lowering his eyebrows. "Many reasons: anonymity, size differences between the two parents, but the two most important ones are one, succubi and incubi are experts at pleasure and are really fun to play with; and two, more important from a political point of view, they are capable of having trans-planar sex!"

Tom had to shake his head at that. "Trans-planar sex? You mean extradimensional sex?"

Tizzy was grinning from ear to ear. "An even better way of putting it, they can receive or deliver their packages, so to speak, to the Planes of Men from the Astral Plane." Tizzy was still making those crazy eyebrow motions as if he were revealing some wondrous surprise.

"But why would you want to do that?" Tom asked.

Tizzy shook his head and made a tisking noise at Tom. "Because the host demon can have a child with a human and not have to materialize or incarnate on that plane! In the case of an incubus, this results in a virgin birth, which is always impressive to mortals. They also do not have to kill a bunch of people to get at their target. They can find and make love to their target in the target's sleep, while they are dreaming. Very few humans have any defense from an attack like that!"

Tizzy started pacing as he talked. "In particular, if a demoness wants a baby with a powerful king or a wizard, there's not a lot that can stop a succubus. Their magical seduction spells are highly sophisticated and work between the Astral Plane and the Planes of Men, and are very strong against sleeping targets. Same with an incubus and a virgin bride!" He was going around in circles waving his arms and looking more than a little lecherous, if Tom thought about it. "Most kings protect their daughters' virginity as a precious treasure. An incubus can easily screw over plans for a royal wedding by impregnating a virgin locked in a tower!"

"Okay, you've convinced me," Tom said, laughing. "You have convinced me."

Tizzy stopped and raised his index finger. "Plus! And this is big— it takes a lot of mana for a demon to incarnate on a plane or to open a gateway. On mana-poor planes, like many of the technology planes—the 'Earths' for example —getting the mana together for demons to incarnate on the plane requires a lot of work and effort. However, if you can impregnate people on Earth with half-demon babies, then you have a foothold on those planes. You can create a new demon on a low-mana plane by letting nature do all the work. And your half-demon babies, once grown, can collect the necessary animus and mana to open a gateway or summon their parents."

"Whoa." Tom shook his head. This explained a lot. Or at least it explained *Rosemary's Baby* and similar stories and legends.

"Uggh... would you figments shut up? I'm trying to wake up and you keep babbling on about crazy shit!" the incubus complained from the ground. His eyes were still closed; he brought his right upper arm up and covered his eyes with his forearm. His lower left hand reached down and scratched underneath his privates. Tom frowned at the crude behavior and grimaced even more when the demon started stroking itself.

"Do you mind not playing with your junk in public?" Tom asked. He supposed it was a bit hypocritical, since he ran around with his junk hanging out all the time, but he did not play with it or anything like that.

"Shit!" The demon pulled his lower hand away and sat up, his eyes going up and down to take in Tom's height. He then looked over to Tizzy. "Sorry, I just can't help myself." He kept glancing back and forth between Tom and Tizzy.

Tizzy was nodding. "They can't help themselves, they've got the equivalent hormones of a fifteen-year-old boy, and then some." The incubus frowned at Tizzy.

"Are you talking about me?" he asked Tizzy.

"You are the only incubus around here." Tizzy gestured in various directions around the mesa.

"An incubus? What's an incubus?"

Tizzy shook his head. "I don't think you were asleep, you had to hear my explanation. Do I have to repeat myself?"

"No!" Tom interjected a bit loudly. The whole idea rather creeped him out; he did not want to rehash it.

"You mean some sort of demon sex fiend? Me?" the incubus asked. Tom nodded.

"Yes, you." Tizzy folded his upper arms across his chest. "Although I don't think you're a fiend. I'm guessing you're more of a class three, which would make you a major demon." Tizzy unfolded his arms and tilted his head to the sky, closing one eye and staring upward. The incubus was just staring at the octopodal demon.

Tizzy grimaced, then put his pipe in his mouth and inhaled. Where did the pipe come from? Tom suddenly wondered. It was in his upper right hand, which had been empty not two seconds ago. Now it was lit and Tizzy was puffing out smoke clouds.

The incubus's nose twitched. "Hey, I know that smell!"

Tizzy turned and glared at him. "No, you don't."

"I sure as hell do. That's that same funky shit I was smoking just before this whole dream started!"

Tom raised his left eyebrow. Tizzy was smoking pot? He inhaled some of the smoke from the pipe; there was a definite smell to it, one he had smelled before. Had it been pot? He really did not know what weed smelled like. He had only tried it the one time, and what with all the craziness that ensued, he'd sort of forgotten what it smelled like.

Tom turned back to the incubus. "Tell me what happened, what started this thing you think is a dream."

The incubus shook his head. "Well, it probably would help to talk it out. Maybe that will help me sort things out and wake up."

"You ain't ever waking up, bud!" Tizzy snorted. "This is, was and always will be. Alpha, omega, beta and zeta. Done deal, no going back. You've been given the gift of eternal damnation! Live it up!" Tizzy stuck his pipe back in his mouth and started puffing heavily. He seemed very upset for some reason.

"What's his dysfunction?" the incubus asked.

Tom shook his head. "We don't have enough time to go into that. We're only immortal."

The incubus shook his head again. "This is one crazy fucking trip!"

"Okay, just tell us your story and then we'll explain what's going on," Tom told the demon.

"Shit, man, I just wanted to take a break from the hell of the last few weeks. I have been up shit creek with lawyers and police and all sorts of crazy crap. I finally got the DA off my back and not pressing charges. So while my parents went out to dinner, I headed up to my room and decided to relieve some tension."

"Relieve some tension?" Tom asked.

"Yeah, you know." He gestured to his privates. Tom grimaced and nodded. The guy had been going to jack off. The incubus shrugged. "Anyway, when I got into my secret stash box for my porn SD card, I found I still had one of those damn joints that had started this whole shit storm. So I decided, what the hell. I lit up, got mellow and started having some fun downtown."

Tom shook his head and rubbed his eyebrows. He was pretty sure where this was going.

The incubus continued, "Well, the next thing you know I'm riding these incredible waves of pleasure, more intense than any previous session with pot or with myself. I sort of lose track of things and then there's this big-ass sista with a huge set of badongas calling me to come make love to her."

Okay, Tom thought, this wasn't quite what he had been expecting.

"So I came over, and it was like a dream, you know, all clouds and funky colored lights and such, and anyway we started, you know, getting it on." The incubus had started fondling itself again.

Tom coughed and it stopped.

"Yeah, sorry. Well anyway, I like, well, entered her and then the next thing you know there's this searing pain and she's shouting this crazy shit at the top of her lungs. I thought she was calling for the cops or about to go all voodoo on me or some shit, and then the next thing I know there's this incredible, monstrous, all-consuming agony." The incubus shuddered remembering it. "And this creepy blackish-red dude with wings and four arms sort of jumps me or... I don't know, it was weird."

The incubus stood up and started pacing. "Anyway, all I know is I'm lying in some strange-ass bed with all sorts of candles surrounding it and these weird glowing symbols on the floor and on the sheets. She hops out of bed to the other side of these symbols and starts shouting crazy stuff like: 'You are mine Reginaldjacksonaustinkincaid!' I bind you by you true name!"

Tom stopped listening when the incubus said its true name. He could not believe it! What a fucking coincidence! What sweet, sweet justice!

"And then"—the demon had kept going, not noticing Tom's expression — "I'm here on this crazy mountain and like *I am* the freaky four-armed blackish-red guy."

"Reggie, you jackass, I'm going to kick your butt into the next plane!" Tom launched himself at Reggie, tackled him and started hitting him as fast as he could.

"Ow... Ow... What the fuck man... What the fuck, that hurts! Stop it...." The demon was crying.

Tom stopped, realizing what he was doing; the smaller demon did not have a chance. Tom shook his head and stood up, getting off Reggie.

"I'm sorry, I've just been so pissed at you that I couldn't help myself." Tom reached down to help pull Reggie up.

"What the fuck, man? I just met you." The incubus wiped tears from its eyes. Apparently, incubi could cry. Tom felt like crap suddenly. What an asshole he was being. None of this was really Reggie's fault, and now he was stuck just like Tom.

Tom leaned in and gave Reggie a big hug. "I'm sorry man, it wasn't cool of me. I was just so angry at you and then you show up, and I sort of went postal."

Reggie struggled to get free. Tom quickly released him as he suddenly realized that the incubus had been extremely aroused by his hug. Tom stepped back and Reggie, realizing he was at full mast, tried to shield himself with his four hands. He was staring at Tom as if Tom was insane.

"Reggie. It's me, Tom, Tom Perkinje." He waved at Reggie.

Reggie blinked. "Tom?"

"Yeah!"

"Tom who I gave the joint to and then he went and died on me?"

"That's me!"

Reggie's eyes rolled back and he crumpled to the ground in shock.

Tizzy started coughing. Coughing and laughing and clutching his guts with all four arms, rocking back and forth. "That's gotta be the greatest reunion scene of all time!" Tizzy was laughing and somehow wiping tears from his eyes—tears of blood, it appeared, but tears still. "See, I told you! I knew you'd want to come with me!"

~

Talarius woke to darkness. He hurt all over. Every joint, every muscle, every pore seemed to ooze pain. However, none of it hurt as much as the pain in his heart, in his soul. He had failed. As his mind cleared, the events of the day before came rushing back in. He had failed Tiernon. He had failed the Rod. He had failed himself. His hubris had been his downfall.

He should have been more thorough in dispatching the damn demon and its minions. He should not have been so lenient. The damned monster had turned the tables. It had stolen mana from his god; it had possessed priests and the members of the Rod. It had used the Holy Church of Tiernon against him, and then it had survived an impossible death stroke and destroyed a Holy Artifact of Tiernon. It had then abducted him to the Abyss.

He was now here and damned for… well, a very long time. He was not quite sure. All he knew was that his immortal soul was possibly lost. That damned clothed demon had been right. If he died here, his soul would die here. He would never…

"Stop," the knight ordered himself aloud. He did not have time for this line of thought. He was in enemy territory. Deeper enemy territory than he had ever been in before. Furthermore, he was unarmed, or mostly unarmed. A few small blades inset into his armor, a couple of flash bombs, a Rod of Smiting along with a Rod of Holy Lightning, both also part of his armor. Like the blades, they were designed into the armor to appear as part of it. He also had a garroting wire, lock picks, two vials of healing, and three vials of holy water. But other than that, and his impenetrable armor, he was completely defenseless!

He did have his Sash of Heavenly Flight as well, under his armor, so he could fly away if he needed. He had been in too much shock to use it when he fell through the hole. That multi-limbed nightmare had grabbed him before he had invoked it. The problem, of course, was where would he fly? He had absolutely no means of extradimensional travel. No way to get home.

However, if he was going to count the sash as part of his defense, then he'd have to also count his Grefalgar's Girdle of Grace for the agility and dexterity it provided him, as well as his Gauntlets of Grappling, and his Undergarments of Cleansing. While all useful on a crusade and okay in combat, they were not particularly offensive or defensive devices.

Of course, the Ring of Invisibility on his left hand was theoretically defensive, but hiding was always a last resort. A coward's resort. And the pendant he wore with its mana pool did nothing in and of itself; it was just reserve mana for any of the holy rituals he might need to cast. Certainly, his Flask of Holy Refreshment with its unending supply of icy cold water could not be counted as offensive or defensive. Unless he needed to put out a fire —there seemed to be a fair amount of fire around this place.

And since demons were not undead, his bracelets were useless and thus not to be counted. He supposed the Ring of Blessing on his right hand was equally useless. Normally he used it to bless his allies. He had never tried it on himself, but it seemed just a bit self-serving to bless oneself. A Blessing of Tiernon might, however, have some negative effects on a demon. He just was not sure. It did cause problems for undead; skeletons and zombies in particular.

He shook his head and sat up. It was no use lying on the ground wallowing in his weakened state and the minimal resources he currently had at his command. He had not planned on coming, so he really had not packed. The floor of this cave was miserable for sleeping, particularly while in full plate armor , but he had been so exhausted that it had not mattered. He did have to admit that, aside from the initial discomfort, he did feel better now, after his nap. How long had he slept? Three, four hours at least.

There was a scratching noise from across the room, the sound of demon hooves on the stone. Someone was approaching. He needed to adjust his helm's visor to see in the dark. "So, finally awake?" The Rupert demon said.

"Yes, fiend."

The Rupert demon sighed. "I'm not a fiend. Tizzy and Boggy are fiends. I'm at least a third order, maybe a greater demon." He actually sounded a bit whiny and defensive, almost like the young boy he had pretended to be. These demons took their deceptions to ridiculous levels, Talarius sighed to himself. Why they were continuing such nonsense when he was clearly at their mercy was a mystery.

"As you will," Talarius acknowledged. No need to pick a fight at this point.

"I was beginning to think you'd gotten a concussion and weren't going to ever wake up!"

Talarius frowned in the dark. "What do you mean by that?"

"Well, you've been out cold for almost a solid day. Or something like that; there's no Fierd in the Abyss. But I'm pretty sure it's been a full day since you fell asleep."

A day? He had been out for twenty hours? He shook his head. Argh, headache. "You cannot be serious, demon!"

"Uhm, yeah. Why would I lie about that?"

"Because you are a demon?" Talarius retorted as if stating the obvious.

Rupert sighed. "You really are a nut job." Talarius had the feeling the demon was shaking its head. "Believe what you will, it's been a solid day for the rest of us."

Talarius sighed to himself. The demon probably was not lying; he was just so tired still. However, he had been in a lot of pain, so recovery would be slow. Further, the demons had said he would regenerate here. He had no idea how that would work, but he was a bit better now. "I'm going to light my armor so I can see. I'm not attacking, demon," he told Rupert. Really not a good idea to accidentally start a fight at this moment. He could have used his visor, but felt that the fewer strengths he revealed now, the better his advantage later.

"Sure," Rupert replied.

Talarius willed his armor to light the room dimly. He did not want to turn it to full power, lest he blind himself with the unaccustomed light. He looked around the cave he and Rupert were standing in. It was large, quite large, but very sparsely decorated. A giant throne crudely carved of stone, a horribly shoddy stone table; and a few objects that he guessed were carved shelves high up. There did not seem to be much on them. Hmm. Was that a dragon tooth on the top shelf? Odd. Of course, it could just be another demon's tooth. It was higher than his reach, so he frankly did not care.

Talarius started walking stiffly towards the entrance. "If you don't mind, I'd like to take a look at where you're holding me prisoner." He glanced at Rupert.

The demon shrugged. "Not like you can go anywhere; we're very high up and in a rather empty part of the Abyss."

Talarius nodded and continued up the long, winding tunnel. He barely remembered coming down, he had been so beat. Eventually he reached the cave mouth. There was a reasonably-sized ledge outside the mouth. The demon had been correct. There was a very nasty precipice at the end of the ledge, and no easy route to climb down or up. He would not be leaving here without the sash. Praise Tiernon he had had it on. Of course, he nearly always wore it in full combat gear. One only needed to fall off a flying horse once to realize the need for a reliable backup plan.

Talarius shook his head. War Arrow would be nearly frantic at this point. He imagined Ruiden, his sword, would also be quite bothered. The sword would be very annoyed he had gone off to the Abyss without taking it. Ruiden enjoyed cleaving demons more than nearly anything else.

The knight sighed and looked around. They were very high up on the side of a mountain in what had to be one of the most rugged mountain ranges he had ever seen. Between that and the oppressive, omnipresent red light from the disturbingly surreal sky, the landscape was almost intimidating. He tried to rub the bridge of his nose, an old habit, but that didn't work well when wearing a great helm.

"Ahoy there! Rupert!" A loud, accented voice came from the sky over his right shoulder. He turned to see a man-sized demon with large bat wings and an extremely craggy face coming in for a landing. Talarius backed up to the other side of the ledge. There was a very short, pudgy and hideous fiend behind this one.

Rupert came out, scowled horribly and then clapped his hands as if happy. "Boggy! Great to see you!" These demons had seriously weird emotional responses. He would have never guessed that that horrendous scowl was meant to be welcoming.

"I see you've got the prize!" The first demon landed on the ledge and patted Rupert on the shoulder.

"Unholy miracles!" The short, ugly little demon screeched, staring at Talarius. "Are you sure it's safe to have that thing running around unbound? I've heard that Paladins are extremely dangerous."

"I'm not a Paladin; I'm a Knight Rampant!" Talarius glared at the annoying demon.

"Who is this, Boggy?" Rupert asked, gesturing to the ugly demon.

"Oh, right-o! Sorry about that. Where are my manners?" The demon that Rupert had called "Boggy" shook its head. "This is an old friend of mine, Estrebrius. His accursed master has some sort of business proposal for Tom."

Rupert looked at the demon named Boggy as if he did not understand; he then turned his gaze to Estrebrius, who was suddenly looking very uncomfortable. "You mean his accursed master, as in the wizard he is bound to, wants a deal with Tom?" Rupert seemed rather incredulous.

Talarius found it extremely odd himself; however, everything at the moment was odd. It was widely suspected that wizards had secret deals with these demons. This would of course, prove it. If he ever got out of here, the Rod would have good cause to take out all wizards when they were located. Although, thinking on it , taking out the entire city of wizards might be difficult. Clearly, they would have to plan carefully.

"I've never heard of wizards wanting 'deals' with demons before. Usually, it's just do this or suffer!" Rupert said.

Estrebrius bowed deeply. "I assure you, Great One, my master has no ill intentions. He simply seeks to assist Your Lordship in his endeavors!"

Talarius raised an eyebrow under his helmet at that. Interesting, he had never been so privy to the direct machinations of the forces of evil. Intellectually, he supposed that it was interesting, but frankly, it was the sort of information that he had no need to know. Evil was evil; the how and why was not important. In the end, only the what, where and when mattered, so that one could be there with the right tools to defeat it.

"So anyway," Boggy said to Rupert, "I told Estrebrius that I'd introduce him to Tom and at least let him pitch the idea."

Rupert nodded and shrugged. "Sounds crazy to me, but what do I know?" Rupert said.

"Is he inside?" Boggy asked.

Rupert seemed to do a double take. "Oh, sorry—wasn't thinking. No, he and Tizzy went zooming off that way." He pointed over Talarius's shoulder. "Tizzy started making all these weird faces and said something about buttah and a new arrival and that Tom would want to meet it. Whatever that is. What's a new arrival?" Rupert asked.

"A new arrival?" Boggy frowned; this was very clearly a frown, Talarius thought as he suppressed a small discomfort in his spine. "Damn, I like to be with him for those!" Boggy shook his head in annoyance. "Really strange to have another one so soon."

"That's what Tizzy said," Rupert told Boggy. "What's a new arrival?"

"It's a new demon," Estrebrius told him.

"A new demon? You mean like a baby?" Rupert asked.

Estrebrius shook his head and looked at Rupert as if he were insane. "No, a freshly captured and enslaved demon."

Rupert blinked. "I'm not sure I understand. You mean like a demon that wasn't enslaved but now is? Just captured?" Rupert was twisting his head in thought, "so how do you tell that?"

Estrebrius started to open his mouth but Boggy interrupted him while staring at Talarius. "I'll let Tom explain that to you. It gets complicated."

"Why are you staring at me, demon?" Talarius asked.

"No reason. I just see no need to bore you with the details," Boggy said.

Talarius squinted through the eye slit in his helmet. There was something this demon did not want him to know about these new arrival demons. Perhaps some secret in how to bind demons? Something that if he knew, he might be able to sabotage? A way to keep demons from being conjured to Astlan? That would be valuable. Although if they were talking about binding demons, was not a bound demon better than an unbound demon? Hmm, clearly more investigation might be warranted.

Talarius suddenly opened his eyes wide. Was this why he was here? Did Tiernon have a plan for him? Perhaps to uncover something that would allow them to defeat these evil creatures once and for all… Could it be that his downfall was the will of Tiernon? The start of a most holy of crusades? Dared he hope?

~

Antefalken made his way to the bar. He needed a drink. He had come to the Courts to hear the local gossip and ended up with more than he wanted. He had not been more than a few blocks into the city when these big goons surrounded him and provided him an invitation to see Lilith. They were friendly enough, but it was clear they were not taking no for an answer.

Admittedly, he had thought of visiting Lilith, depending on what the word on the street was. He just had not planned on it being his first stop. The goons had ushered him in to her quarters and then quickly left.

"My dear, sweet Anty!" Lilith cooed as she emerged from behind a curtain. Antefalken felt his shoulders slump. She was in her see-through form. That was never good. It was a very dramatic form where you could see her skeleton and a few select organs, while her body itself was a currently purple, translucent shell. You could see her skin normally; it was simply see-through. On top of that she wore a rather diaphanous skirt and back cape, along with numerous articles of jewelry.

Fortunately, she had not eaten anyone recently. That was always disconcerting: to see her digesting some poor sap that had gotten on her bad side. Unless she was hungry? Antefalken shuddered slightly and bowed to her. "My Lady, so good to see you again." He smiled brightly.

"And you." She smiled, coming closer and wrapping an arm around his shoulder, drawing him over to her divan. "So, it seems you've had a near-final death experience?"

"My Lady, as always, is well informed." Antefalken kissed her hand.

"It must have been very nerve-racking," Lilith said as she wrapped herself around Antefalken on the couch.

He really did not find this form attractive. "It was indeed," he said.

"Fortunately, this Tom friend of yours was a bit more than he seemed?" She smiled at the bard.

He could not determine what sort of smile it was, and that made him more nervous. "Very fortunate, my love." He kissed her left breast , closing his eyes to avoid looking at her beating, glowing red translucent heart.

"So, I assume he has returned to the Abyss?"

"Yes, My Lady, along with the rest of his entourage and his hostage. I simply left them to come report to you," Antefalken murmured around her nipple. He doubted he could distract her, but he would give it a try.

"So he's at his cave?"

"He has nowhere else."

"Well, that's a shame!" She pulled back from him suddenly and gave him a wide smile.

"He's bound to be hounded by who knows how many lickspittles trying to curry his favor! And the paparazzi will be insane. A cave just won't do!" Lilith stood, marched seductively over to her diamond drink cart and poured two glasses of some blood-red beverage that did not look too much like blood.

She pivoted with the two glasses and came back towards Antefalken. "He must come visit me! I will provide him, his entourage and his hostage with appropriate accommodations!"

Antefalken smiled as best he could, taking one of the glasses. This was exactly what he had been afraid of. "My love! As always you are so wonderfully generous!" He raised his glass to hers in a toast.

She smiled sweetly. "So, when can we expect his presence? I shall have a feast prepared!"

"Ah..." Antefalken twisted his head slightly. "I will relay your invitation immediately upon my return. I am sure he will be... delighted." He took a drink. "I can't, of course, promise that he'll accept—"

"Oh, Anty! Do not be so dismissive of your charms! You are the most persuasive demon I know. I am *sure* you can convince him to enjoy my hospitality." Lilith sipped her drink.

"You flatter me, My Lady. I will do everything in my power to persuade him." She smiled at this. "However, he is a greater demon and I'm simply me..."

Lilith's eyes were steel. "Again, I am sure you will succeed. I have every confidence in you."

Antefalken ordered a second cup of Denubian Choco-Coffee™. This was not something he would be able to get out of easily. One did not turn Lilith down. No one did. Antefalken was sure that even Asmodeus would hesitate. However, he really did not think it a good idea for Lilith to host Tom and friends. For one thing, she hated Tizzy with a passion. He needed to get them out of the Abyss. But how?

~

"So, do you think he'll succeed?" a tall, reddish-skinned gentleman asked as he stepped through a wall that had simply appeared in Lilith's parlor. He had black, slicked-back hair with only a touch of gray at the temples along with two small, dark, pointy horns, and a Van Dyke beard and mustache. He wore a somewhat theatrical suit and cloak with large pauldrons. As soon as he had stepped through, the wall vanished.

"I give it fifty-fifty." Lilith refilled her glass and poured a new one for her eavesdropping colleague.

"You did seem to incentivize the bard," Asmodeus observed, taking the glass. He grimaced slightly as he watched the blood wine flow down Lilith's clear esophagus. "Would you mind changing into something less see-through? You know I dislike that form."

Lilith frowned at him in annoyance and allowed her skin to return to its normal porcelain white. A black full-length dress and cape formed around her previously nearly naked body. "I am not sure why I take fashion advice from a man whose own form for the last few decades has been taken from some book he found in the outer realms."

"It was an encyclopedia of various legendary beings, and I happened to be in it. While the likeness was completely wrong, I found it quite flattering to be included, so I took the form of the drawing."

"I think it was a children's book or something." Lilith shook her head at his silliness.

"I doubt that; it was written by an obviously astute and knowledgeable author."

"An obviously knowledgeable author?" Lilith arched an eyebrow and took another swig of blood wine.

"Yes, one Egary Gygax, clearly a name of distinction and good breeding. There were numerous other books of his in the library," Asmodeus protested. Lilith rolled her eyes.

"I think the sage you had translating the book was probably drunk."

"He was not. He was, actually *is*, quite trustworthy and knowledgeable. He has been with me for the last three thousand years or so. Further, this tome described me as the Law of Evil. And if there is anyone that applies to, certainly it is I." He swept his arms around as if gesturing to his domain.

Lilith took another swig of blood wine. "Seriously? Have you cleared that with any of your colleagues? They all think *they* are the Law of Evil."

Asmodeus gave her a small snarl and glare.

"Back to the issue at hand. Do you think the bard will bring this demon to us? We need to know how he managed to tap into Tiernon's private mana stream. It is clearly the biggest breakthrough and most exciting development in the Eternal Conflict in at least six or seven thousand years! It could tip the balance in our favor once and for all!"

"Yes, and you want to know how to do it before any of the other princes find out," Lilith observed.

"Well, at least before Tiernon comes down and obliterates this demon and sends the secret to the grave."

Lilith laughed. "Yes, that's quite likely, I'm afraid. Maybe I should not have invited him to stay with me. Not if he is going to have unexpected visitors."

"Assuming he comes, which you do say you aren't sure of. Of course, I do not blame you. If this demon is smart, he won't accept your hospitality." Lilith glared at him. "Not that you are a bad host, but that you clearly have ulterior motives. Everyone who has ever met you knows that." Asmodeus took another sip of wine.

"In any event, I've assigned two of my best to secretly follow Antefalken to find out where this Tom's cave is," Lilith told him.

"Again, a cave. This must be a safe house, a ruse location to distract us from his true seat of power, the location of which would clue us in as to his background and allies." Asmodeus paced around the carpet. "But if it is a rendezvous point, still good to know. Your minions will be discreet?"

"I sent Rosencrantz and Guildenstern," Lilith replied.

Asmodeus nodded. "Excellent. Those two are exceedingly loyal, as I recall. You've had them for almost as long as I've known you." The demon prince paused for a moment. "Wait, weren't they disintegrated a century or so ago in that whole

Dark Shibboleth affair on the moon of that gas giant orbiting Tau Ceti in the Alderen universe?"

Lilith thought for a moment. "Yes, that's right. No mind, I had them re-imprinted on two other demons I decided to repurpose. It is not the first time I have had to do it. None of my Rosencrantzes and Gildensterns have lasted more than a few centuries. Being in my service can be dangerous. I make no secret of it." She tilted her head back to swallow the last drops from her glass.

"More blood wine?" Lilith asked as she moved back to the wine cart.

"Certainly, my dear. It is an excellent vintage; it has a nice blend of male agnostic virgin and female atheist slut. A very hard combination to blend, but your winemaker is clearly a genius."

~

They were finally getting close to home, such as it was. Reggie was a slow flyer. He also kept falling out of the sky, so they had to fly low. This had made the journey much longer once they reached the mountains. Tom did have to admit that Reggie's first attempt, in which he fell like a stone and landed up to his thighs in rock, had been amusing. That probably would not get old, even though it did cause his legs to ache in sympathy.

Of course, before that he had had to run through the same Q & A session that Boggy had provided him on the nature of demons and the Abyss. Not to mention his own story, or at least an exceedingly abbreviated version of it. He really only told Reggie the parts about the Abyss and sort of skipped most of the stuff in Astlan because he wanted to get them moving, figuring once they were back at the cave, there would be time for the rest of the story.

Surprisingly, Reggie initially was not that appalled by the thought of being a demonic sex slave. He did like sex. He had not really gotten much in Harding, which Tom interpreted as being none. Of course, his enthusiasm changed quickly when they got to the part about his body on Earth being dead, like Tom. Reggie had suddenly gone pale, or at least as pale as he could get.

"You mean my folks are going to find me in bed with my pants around my ankles and my hand around my junk, in flagrante, and dead from a pot overdose?" Reggie had asked incredulously.

"You can't really die from a pot overdose," Tizzy commented. "It's the batty wizards slicing your silver cord that kills you."

"Afraid so," Tom had replied, ignoring Tizzy.

At that point, Reggie had made a bawling noise, dropped to the ground, curled up into a fetal position and cried. It was definitely embarrassing for the poor incubus, Tom mused. Oddly, he felt bad for Reggie. He had tried to keep thoughts of Reggie out of his head since he had arrived, but he'd been really pissed at the guy for giving him the weed. On occasions, he had had some revenge fantasies very similar to this, but the real thing was a letdown. To be fair, it was a horribly embarrassing way to go, much worse than Tom's demise.

However, on the other hand, for some reason, Reggie had tear ducts and could cry. Although, where the water was coming from was a mystery, and why it did not evaporate in the super-heated air was also a mystery. How many times had Tom wanted a good cry?

In any event, they, or rather Tom, eventually got him up and convinced him to come back to his cave. Tizzy was not particularly helpful. He did not seem to like Reggie too much. Tom wondered if Tizzy was jealous; it was hard to tell with the octopodal demon. He was rather insane, after all.

They stopped at the top of the last mountaintop before the cave to wait for Reggie to catch up after his latest fall.

"This is spoiled buttah," Tizzy ranted in his yenta voice.

"What is?" Tom asked. Tizzy pointed to Reggie. "Why don't you like him?"

"Don't trust him. I think he is crazy. I think he lies too."

"What would he lie about? It is clearly Reggie, he even rather sounds like the old Reggie, and his account of the party and my death match what I recall. Everything is logically consistent. I can certainly believe his story. It sounds like something he would do."

Tizzy scrunched up his face. "How much can you trust him? After all, he gave you the drug that got you high and then trapped by Lenamare. Are you sure he's not one of Lenamare's minions?"

Tom shook his head in disbelief; that was a pretty out-there conspiracy theory. "Yes he gave me the joint, but he ended up using one himself and got enslaved. If he had been working for Lenamare, he would not have been so stupid as to smoke the joint. Further, Lenamare does not know anything about Earth or humans beings getting enslaved as demons. He and all of the wizards are convinced demons are primordial evil. You and Boggy said so yourselves!"

Tizzy made a pouty motion and harrumphed, turning to look towards the cave as Reggie finally flew up to them. "I'm about dead, guys," Reggie told them. He was clearly sagging.

"Sorry," Tom shook his head. "I forgot that I took a nap on the plains before heading to find a cave. The initial materialization and binding takes a lot out of you. We really should have let you rest, but I felt it best we get home as soon as possible. I've got a guest to deal with."

Reggie looked at him quizzically. "A guest? Do demons entertain?"

"I don't, normally. It's a long story, but the short version of the story is that I sort of have a hostage."

"A hostage?" Reggie asked in surprise.

"I'm not sure if he's really a hostage; I guess more of a prisoner of war."

"A prisoner of war? Are you at war?" Reggie was looking back and forth between the two demons. Tizzy just ignored him.

Tom sighed. "Well, like I said, it's a long story. However, the Wikipedia version is that I and a bunch of other demons, including some friends of mine"—he gestured to Tizzy—"got driven out of this city that was surrounded by a bunch of religious fanatics. The religious fanatics started shooting demons out of the sky and managed to bring down one of my friends, and this super-powered knight was trying to kill that friend, who happens to be a ten-year-old boy, so I challenged the knight to a duel."

Reggie's eyes were as wide as saucers at this point.

"Anyway, it was a nasty fight; he cheated, a lot, and his army helped him. It was supposed to just be the two of us, but as I said, he cheated." Tom launched himself back into the air. "So, yada yada, I kicked his ass, gave him the opportunity to surrender, he reneged and tried to kill me again, so I sort of dropped him through a portal to the Abyss and am holding him captive."

"Shit!"

"You don't need to do that anymore! It's like breathing. So don't do it!" Tizzy retorted.

Tom looked at Tizzy, who just shrugged and took off back towards the cave.

"What exactly is his problem?" Reggie asked.

"Aside from being insane, I don't know. I don't think he likes you for some reason."

Reggie shrugged. "So I don't have to shit? What about eat?"

"Not unless you want to." Tom said. "The plumbing seems to work okay, but it's not required, and we don't get hungry." Tom pointed to the mountaintop with the cave. "We're just heading over now. You can sleep safely there. I'll make sure Talarius doesn't try to kill you in your sleep."

"Great!" Reggie said sourly.

"Actually, that's another thing we usually don't have to do: sleep. We only sleep after expending a lot of energy, or getting hurt badly, while we regenerate."

"We regenerate?" Reggie asked in surprise.

"We are remarkably hard to kill. In fact, if we are on some plane other than the Abyss and we get killed, we just end up here and regenerate."

"Like in a video game?"

Tom had not thought of it that way. "Yeah, like in a video game."

Talarius noted some motion in the sky to his left. He tapped his helm to adjust the long-range focus on his visor, zooming in on the flying objects. There were three demons approaching: his captor, that annoying octopod thing, and what appeared to be a humanoid with four arms flying rather drunkenly. They had probably gone to celebrate his capture and gotten inebriated. It was well known that demons had no self-control when it came to overindulgence.

"Your friends are returning, apparently with another demon in tow," Talarius told Rupert, Boggy and Estrebrius. He pointed to the approaching demons.

Boggy looked, blinked and then turned towards Talarius. "You have uncommonly good eyesight for a human."

Talarius shrugged, giving no response. The squat demon, Estrebrius, seemed to be hyperventilating or something; Talarius noticed he was making some rather odd huffing noises.

"What's wrong with you?" Talarius asked, forgetting for the moment that he had no interest in the odd behavior of demons.

"Nothing," Estrebrius huffed. Talarius squinted; if he did not know better, he would have said the demon was nervous. Perhaps having an anxiety attack? He had to talk many a man down from such feelings before a battle. Interesting; he would never have thought demons to have such issues.

Talarius backed up closer to the cave's entrance so the three demons could land. There was plenty of room, but no reason to get too close. Estrebrius slid back to join him in the entrance. Talarius frowned, hoping his own motion had not implied any fear or anxiety on his part. It had simply been pragmatism, nothing more.

His captor landed and quickly stepped forward as the drunk demon came in a bit fast and somewhat clumsily behind him. Talarius's captor had to reach out and steady the drunk demon before it fell over the precipice.

The octopod thing just sort of hovered over the ledge. It seemed to do that a lot, Talarius noted. Perhaps it felt too ungainly on the ground. It was certainly an awkward demon. It was equipped for twice as much sinning as any normal being. Thinking of which, and he should not be, he could not help but notice that the new demon began to fondle itself once it was steady. It seemed to be slightly aroused.

"Boggy!" His captor thundered. Did demons ever speak in a normal tone of voice? "Good to see you!" The Boggy demon stepped forward and gave his captor a hug.

"Good to see you, lad! To think, I knew you before you were famous!"

His captor laughed. "Famous?"

"Oh, yeah, you're the talk of the town. Several hundred demons saw you kick this bloke's arse!" Boggy pointed to Talarius. Talarius frowned inside his helmet; he would need to get used to this sort of shame. Boggy pulled back. "So! You and Tizzy went out to collect a neophyte?"

His captor laughed again. "You will not believe this. You remember my friend Reggie, the one who gave me the joint?"

"Uhm, yeah?"

"This is him!" His captor pointed at the new demon. "This is my buddy, Reggie! Turns out he had an extra joint and tried it himself and got bound as an incubus!" Talarius frowned. An incubus? He turned his gaze back on the demon that was fondling itself. Well, that at least explained its perverted nature. However, the rest of this discussion was lost on him. Apparently, after ripping limbs from their victims, they liked to pass around the joints to eat and this made them susceptible to binding spells? It made no sense, but that was what it sounded like his captor was saying.

"Holy smokes!" Boggy stared at the new demon.

"You mean unholy smokes, don't you?" His captor laughed uproariously. Boggy laughed along while the new demon frowned, looking back and forth between Boggy and Talarius's captor. Rupert seemed about as puzzled as Talarius was, Estrebrius was looking nervous, and the octopod was looking very peeved for some reason. It probably did not like the attention that the new demon was getting. That thing seemed to like to be the center of attention.

His captor suddenly noticed Estrebrius. "Who's your friend?" The short demon visibly swallowed.

Boggy lightly smacked his forehead, avoiding his horns. "Dearie me, where are my manners? This is my longtime chum, Estrebrius!"

His captor stuck out a giant claw towards the little demon, who cautiously shook it.

"Uhm, pleasure to meet you, Your Lordship!" the little demon piped up, sounding a bit more high-pitched than it had earlier.

His captor laughed. "Just call me Tom."

Talarius shook his head slightly inside his helmet. His captor's behavior was quite bizarre. He did not act like a demon should. Talarius wished he could figure out the demon's ruse. For one thing, what sort of name was "Tom" for a demon? It was excessively informal. He had heard his captor referred to by that name but had been ignoring it. The ignobility of being captured by a demon named simply "Tom" was rather galling. It sounded like some sort of peasant demon, not an archfiend capable of defeating a Knight Rampant of Tiernon!

Talarius gritted his teeth; he needed to get his pride in check. A *failed* Knight Rampant of Tiernon, he corrected himself. Clearly, his defeat was a sign of his own moral failings. If he had only been more virtuous, more devoted, he would surely have prevailed. His downfall was of his own doing. Perhaps it was his hubris? That was often the downfall of a knight. Hubris, vanity, greed, lust, any of the cardinal sins could have been responsible. He needed to take inventory of his failings and determine which had caused his defeat. He shook his head. Now was not the time for this; the demons were discussing their plans and he was not paying attention. Perhaps inattentiveness had been his failing?

~

"So let me get this straight," Tom asked Estrebrius, "your accursed master wants to meet me? He says he has something of value to offer me? And you are tasked with arranging a meeting?"

"Yes, My Lord." The small chubby demon bowed.

"Again, just Tom. I'm no lord of anything or anyone." Tom shook his head. "So is this some sort of weird trap or is your master simply insane?"

Estrebrius shook violently and fell down on his knees. "I swear it is no trap, My Lord. He is a good, honest accursed master, as they go. He is also nowhere near skilled enough to trap someone of your power. He just wants to make a deal with you. I have no idea what it is, or why. I really do think he may have taken leave of his senses, but this is what he's commanded me."

Tom shook his head and looked to Boggy. "What do you think?"

Boggy scratched his chin. "Well, I've known Estrebrius for several centuries; he's certainly honest and reliable." Talarius made a choking noise; Tom gave him a quick glare. "He's spoken quite highly of this accursed master on numerous occasions. Honestly, I've tried to dissuade Estrebrius on his master's apparent decency, but he's stuck by it for several years now."

"How long have you had this accursed master?" Tom asked Estrebrius.

"Only about six years, sir. I was his first bound demon out of conjury school."

"So he's not super-experienced? Compared with say, the Council of Wizardry?"

Estrebrius shook his head. "Not at all. He's a very competent wizard, but he's not involved in politics. He's not famous or renowned; he's just out to make a living in the city."

"Thoughts?" Tom looked around at his companions. It might have been nice to have Antefalken around, but the bard was still in the Courts. Tom glanced at Tizzy, who was apparently picking his nose and examining the results; no help there. Reggie shrugged; of course he wouldn't know anything.

"What else do we have to do?" Rupert asked when Tom looked at him.

Tom shrugged. That was a very compelling point. He turned to Estrebrius. "When is your master next summoning you?"

"He said he'd summon me the next morning, which would be in maybe another twelve Astlanian hours or so."

Tom nodded. "That will work. Reggie is going to want to sleep for most of that time. I am thinking that in the event your master pulls any funny business, we want everyone at full strength. I'm not sure I want to take any more chances on Astlanians not doing stupid stuff."

Chapter 87

Hilda collapsed in the overstuffed chair in the suite she had rented at the Havestan Gardens Inn. The rates were completely ridiculous, but she needed someplace decent to stay in the event anyone came calling. Technically, according to her story, she lived in the city; however, she was not about to go house shopping at this point. Not to mention furnishing, staff and all the rest. For one thing, it would be way over budget and hard to justify. So she had settled on a story of her home being repaired and updated while she was at the wedding and the contractors had not finished on time, so she had been forced to rent rooms at this inn.

Since she was supposed to be an animage and healer, perhaps she was adding an improved hospital ward to her house, better medical facilities. That sounded better than simply redecorating or personal improvements. That sort of story seemed just too self-centered to fit with her assumed persona. It was also against her real nature. While she undeniably enjoyed the small comforts of life, and afterlife, she really was not hung up on frilly or fancy trappings. Quality was important, but so was pragmatic value, utility and durability.

Yes, perhaps this suite might seem a bit much, with a bedroom for her, a small bedroom for Danyel, a parlor and a private bath with running hot water. However, she could claim need of the parlor for seeing patients; similarly for the bath; and clearly, Danyel would need his own room for propriety's sake. The fact that the Inn's tavern was rumored to have the best wine cellar in the city? Well, that was simply a nice coincidence. And that being rumored and not proven, she would add it to her list of things to investigate.

She had paid for a week in advance with an option to renew. She was not sure how long she needed, but better safe than sorry. A week seemed reasonable, in particular due to the fact that she would need to go back to the quartermaster to get more coins for a second week. They had stopped by a jewelry shop and she had bought a small sapphire pendant that she felt suitable for enchantment. Between that rather expensive purchase and the room at the inn, her coin purse was left feeling hungry.

One did not need coins in Tierhallon; everyone used credit rings linked to their bank account. It had been a bit odd to discover that one needed a bank account in the afterlife, but that was how one was rewarded. No one really had "living expenses," of course, since no one was technically living, but she did get a small token payment for her services on behalf of Tiernon, and with that she could acquire the luxuries she needed to make after life more comfortable.

Danyel had finally finished unpacking her bags. She had been about to unpack them herself, but the lad had insisted that he should do it. Normally, she would have politely refused, but her head was nearing an explosion point. She needed to come up with something to provide extra shielding.

"Danyel, I'm thinking a few small sandwiches for the evening, perhaps a cup of soup as well if they have something interesting? Unless you want something more? If so, feel free to order what you would like. Could you perhaps go down and arrange something for later this evening, and also if they have a list of wines that they could recommend with the sandwiches, could you bring that back for us to go over? We'll then choose something appropriate that we'll both enjoy."

"Yes, Your Holiness." Danyel nodded.

"Danyel?" Hilda gave a disapproving look. "Do not use that term, simply call me Hilda. Understand?"

Danyel blushed and grimaced, bowing slightly. "I'm sorry... Hilda."

Hilda beamed at him and his own smile returned of its own accord. Much better. While you're gone, I'm going to enjoy a nice bath and try to get rid of this headache!" She stood and made her way to the bathing room.

~

"Ugh," Jenn moaned to herself as she collected the last of her belongings. She had taken a nap after Hilda had left. The wine had gone straight to her head. Now, a few hours later, she was coming down, and not gracefully. Jenn was quite cross with herself; she normally did not imbibe like that, but that Hilda was just so charming and warm and confiding. What a truly likable woman! She had noted that Trisfelt and Hilda seemed to really hit it off. Who knew , perhaps there were sparks of romance?

Trisfelt could certainly do far worse. Hilda was so kind and sympathetic, and she had given both Jenn and Gastropé the warmest hugs, wishing them all the best for a demon-free journey. Hilda was just so reassuring; she simply had a way of making people feel good. Jenn was curious as to what would happen if Hilda unleashed her charms on Jehenna. Which would win? Now that would be an interesting conversation to observe.

Gastropé knocked on her door. "You set?" he asked as he stuck his head in.

Jenn smiled weakly at him. "Other than the start of a hangover, I'm good. One nice thing about evacuating every few weeks: you don't end up with much to pack!" She shouldered the new backpack that Damien had given her. It was really quite roomy, and at least this time there would be no confusion over whose book was whose. The council had been more than helpful in restocking their spell components. She was far better prepared for this adventure than her last one—evacuating Lenamare's school. Gastropé was already wearing his backpack and had a new walking staff in his hand.

"I assume that's just a normal staff , not a wizard's staff?" Jenn asked.

"I bought top quality with the intention of wizardizing it, but I just haven't had the time. I'm thinking that with a long journey, I might get the time. As we were discussing this afternoon, I assume we won't be on foot or horseback."

"There you folks are!" Maelen exclaimed as he came down the hallway. He too seemed loaded with additional equipment in a new backpack. "We are going to Elrose's chambers to fetch him and then we are off to Councilor D'Vils suite."

They took off down the hall towards Elrose's apartments. "So, I get that this is a 'get out of town' sort of thing for Gastropé and me, but what is this expedition you and Elrose have planned with Councilor D'Vils?" Jenn asked.

Maelen chuckled. "I probably should wait until we are all together, but being the friendly sort"—he laughed at himself—"I'll go ahead and tell you. We are hunting down a goddess." He laughed slightly evilly.

Jenn looked at him askance, noting from the corner of her eye that, as expected, Gastropé had just gotten paler. "You are kidding, of course," she stated.

"Not at all!" Maelen smiled. "As you may recall, Trevin noted that the dark-skinned woman on the flying carpet with Exador and Ramses looked exactly like images she'd seen of the now vanquished goddess, Bastet. Both Elrose and I have had visions linked to her name, and the goddess appears to be involved in some way. We are therefore going to seek out some of her old temples to see if we can get some sort of linkage to determine if she's actually involved, and what she might be up to."

"Seriously?" Gastropé was shaking his head in disbelief. "We just managed to evict a giant horde of demons and a party of archdemons, and now we're going to try to track down and spy on a goddess?"

"Is there something they don't teach us in school? Does too much mana use cause one to go insane?" Jenn asked, half rhetorically.

Maelen chuckled. "I understand, and trust me; my chuckling as we speak is a defense mechanism to hide my own unease." He smiled brightly at both of them. "However, from the visions we've had, I think I'd be more nervous not knowing and just sitting around waiting for things to get worse, than trying to get a handle on what's going on so that we can prepare for it, and maybe even try and nudge things in a less disastrous manner."

"Less disastrous manner?" Gastropé asked in shock.

"Yes." Maelen suddenly turned very somber. "The visions that we are seeing imply a rather massive conflict between gods, demons, several armies and us. And by us, I mean in general, Astlanian wizards and animages, and since we seem to be in the heart of the maelstrom, if you will, it appears specifically the Council and the three of us plus Edwyrd and Rupert."

"Rupert? He's still out being stupid with his cousin!" Jenn exclaimed. How had that slipped her mind? That wine was evil. "What's going to happen to them once they return?"

"They need to be gone from Freehold as well, I'd assume," Gastropé added.

Maelen nodded. "Trevin has assured us she'll have a large, long-distance mirror on our vessel. When they return, Damien can contact us, and depending on the distance, hopefully be able to teleport them to us."

Gastropé frowned. "We are going to the Southern Hemisphere. That's thousands of leagues away. That would have to be one huge teleport spell."

"I'm not even sure that's possible," Jenn said, worried.

"I know very little of teleportation. Personally, I prefer to walk or ride a horse as a rule; however, Damien seems to feel it should be no problem for them to join us," Maelen replied.

"Agh, of course. I wasn't thinking." Gastropé shook his head.

Jenn looked at him askance. "What do you mean, 'of course?' You make it sound obvious. I don't think you know that much more than me about teleportation. That distance is clearly out of range of any standard teleportation spell."

Gastropé got an awkward look on his face but then recovered. "Yeah, but remember, there are other ways besides just a teleport spell. According to the maps I studied here, we jumped nearly 500 leagues from Exador's camp to Gizzor Del."

Jenn blinked and looked back at him angrily. "That wasn't jumping, that was traveling through the Abyss and then back to a random location in Astlan."

Gastropé nodded. "Exactly my point, and we did it again in a more controlled manner to get to Freehold." He nodded at Maelen to get the seer's agreement. Maelen shrugged.

"Yes, but that means going through the demon Tom's cave, the only place we know in the Abyss. Given what happened out there"—she gestured vaguely beyond the walls of the city—"what we saw that demon do, do you seriously think it's safe for Edwyrd and Rupert to travel through that demon's cave? For one thing, the demon probably has a very angry knight held hostage in his cave!" Jenn waved her hands in the air. "You seriously want Edwyrd and Rupert to walk right in on that scene?"

That seemed to stop Gastropé's arguments. He sputtered and made all sorts of weird expressions trying to figure out something to say, but finally just remained silent, granting the wisdom of Jenn's argument.

"I thought so." Jenn nodded decisively, her point made. Maelen simply shook his head and shrugged.

"There you are!" Elrose's voice came from up ahead. The wizard was backing out of his apartments pulling a very large wooden trunk that had wheels on one end and a large handle on the other. Quite interesting, Jenn thought, she had never seen anything like it. The wizard was also wearing a backpack like the rest of them.

"I see you're traveling light." Maelen chuckled.

Elrose did not seem to get the joke; he just looked down at the trunk and shook his head. "These are just my personal things; I've sent my larger apparatuses on ahead to Trevin's lab with some valets."

Jenn frowned. "Where did you get so much equipment? You certainly didn't haul it with you from the school."

Elrose smiled. "No, no, I've had these quarters for the last four years since I joined the Committee on Sorcery. As you know, I've been seeing troubling things for several months, which is why Maelen was coming to visit me, so I've been stockpiling things here in readiness."

"Wait." Jenn turned to Maelen. "You were coming to visit Master Elrose?"

Maelen smiled. "I know, very small world. I had no idea when we met that you and Elrose worked together. I must confess, my failure to See that on the ship is a bit embarrassing."

Elrose laughed at Maelen's admission. "That makes me feel better," Elrose told the seer. "The way you can simply See things without going through rituals or using devices makes me quite jealous."

Maelen grinned but shook his head. "No, trust me; it is nothing to be jealous of. It leads to a lot of bad dreams."

Elrose chuckled as he shut his door and made the necessary gestures to magically lock it. "So, we are off to Trevin's lab." He grabbed the handle on his trunk and rotated it so he could pull it behind him, then gestured forward for the others to lead the way.

"Isn't fierdset an odd time to start a journey?" Jenn asked.

Maelen laughed. "I would say so, but Trevin has her reasons. We are heading to the Grove and from what I've read, getting in and out of that place is non-trivial."

"Other than Trevin, of course, Trisfelt is the only person I know of who has been there," Elrose remarked as they walked down the hall.

"The surrounding mountains are a bit overwhelming," Gastropé stated.

"Yes," Elrose noted, "you're from Turelane, which is adjacent to the Grove."

"Yes, I'm from Freelane. I studied at Master al Bastante's Academy, which is located about seventy leagues east and south of Freelane, nearly up against the mountain ranges. The outer range is about the same height as the mountains around Freehold, so about half a league in height; the next range in, which you can easily see at a distance, is probably twice that, and the innermost ranges are said to be another two to three times as high."

"What? Are you saying there are mountains that are two or three leagues high?" Jenn asked incredulously.

"And roughly fifteen leagues wide at their base, if you could measure such a thing." Gastropé nodded in agreement. "According to our school's Geomancer. However, that is taking in the rapid rise in overall altitude; ground level would be a third to half of a league to start with there. So they are only going maybe two leagues higher than whatever you want to call ground."

Maelen looked at him askance. "That's a rather incredible height. I know that they are said to be unimaginably tall, but a 48,000-foot-tall mountain seems a bit more than unbelievable. I'm not sure there is enough air at the height to breathe."

"There would be air at that height, but it would be quite thin," Elrose stated. He was also a Master of Enchantment, so was quite familiar with airflow and density.

"According to the masters at my school, only the aetós can breathe at that altitude, and even they have trouble and can't exert themselves too much," Gastropé said.

"So, you are saying the Grove is basically surrounded by an impenetrable range of mountains?"

"I don't know if your young and handsome friend is saying that, but I will," Trevin D'Vils said, appearing from a side corridor leading into the foyer they had just entered. This foyer let onto a spiral ramp leading up and down, rather than the more traditional spiral staircase. The ramp was built for hauling furniture and equipment between the various suites and the labs. Elrose had quietly directed them this way to use the ramp to get down to the labs due to his large-wheeled trunk.

Jenn noted that the councilor was once again seriously underdressed in blousy sheer silk pants that went only halfway down her calves, and a vest made out of the same material that left way too much cleavage and midriff exposed for her seriously advanced age. She was also wearing an insane amount of jewelry: several diamond necklaces, bracelets, armbands, ankle rings, toe rings and finger rings. Jenn shook her head.

Elrose and Maelen nodded in respect to the enchantress, as did Gastropé. "The mountains are very high, higher than Oorstemoth's ships can sail, in fact. Of course, mountains are peaks, so there are gaps and valleys, but the mountains are concentric and those valleys have extremely complex and dangerous currents. Only the aetós know them, and they patrol them diligently."

"So how did the first residents ever make their way in?" Gastropé asked curiously.

"Hmm," Trevin murmured, apparently really seeing Gastropé for the first time. She walked up very close to him and ran her right hand gently down his left bicep and forearm. "A fellow Turelanean, and as I mentioned, such a strong, young, handsome one. This trip is suddenly looking much more interesting." Trevin smiled very brightly and more than a little disquietingly. Gastropé coughed uncomfortably.

Trevin chuckled and spun away, moving slightly apart again. "When the first residents of the Grove arrived, the mountain ranges were a bit more normal-sized. Let's just say they've been fortified over the last several thousand years by the residents." She smiled back at them as she started down the spiral ramp. "Our residents are quite good at erecting things." She chuckled.

"Several thousand years?" Maelen asked. "How long has the Grove been there, as we know it today?"

Trevin shrugged. "A very, very long time, longer than even I've been alive." She glanced sharply at Jenn for some reason. Jenn could not help but blush, feeling guilty about her internal fashion commentary despite the fact that there was no way the enchantress could know what she'd been thinking.

"As you probably know, the Grove is a refuge and migration center for beings fleeing other realms. There are numerous Sidhe there, along with nymphs, dryads, satyrs, centaurs, minotaurs and various related species. In particular, followers of the gods Cernunnos, Artemis Agrotera, Pan and Dionysus."

Jenn had never heard of any of those gods, except perhaps Pan. Trisfelt might have mentioned him, a satyr god if she remembered correctly. She was so busy pondering this she almost missed Tevin's final remarks. "It is also unique in that it is multidimensional." This last bit of information Trevin imparted as if an afterthought.

"Multidimensional?" Elrose asked, puzzled.

"Yes, meaning it exists simultaneously and well, I guess you could say contiguously, on multiple planes at once. Dimensionally transcendent is the term some of our druids use. One nice feature for us, but I'm afraid most likely disturbing for you two visionaries, is that this nature makes scrying and Seeing very difficult there, both in and out, since multiple realities collide/coexist in the Grove."

Maelen gave her a very odd look. "And how exactly is that stable? It seems to me that it would extremely volatile and dangerous."

Elrose had a rather disturbed look on his face and seemed to be in agreement with Maelen.

"One might think." Trevin shrugged.

Jenn noted that Gastropé's pallor had increased at this, predictably.

They continued down the winding ramp and then down a long corridor before arriving at Councilor D'Vils' laboratories. There were guards in Turelanean style uniforms and turbans guarding the main entrance to the labs, which seemed a bit unusual to Jenn. Lenamare just kept his magically locked. They had gone through the main entrance to the councilor's space and then down a long corridor with doors on each side before coming to a set of very large doors that were currently open wide into a very large, domed room.

Given the fact that there had been multiple armies with horses and a multitude of demons hiding in the nether regions of the palace, all the various wizards' labs, the storage rooms and now this large room, Jenn was starting to wonder if the Council dungeons were not larger than the palace proper. The underground warren was full surprises. This room was definitely one of them.

The room was a large rotunda with a domed roof with what appeared to be a large glass window at the apex. However, given how deep underground they were, Jenn doubted that it was an actual window. The walls were lined with ivy, particularly dense over long fluted columns spaced evenly every ten feet or so around the rotunda. The center of the room was dominated completely by a large dais with a circular ramp surrounding it. The ramp's path led directly to two large round columns inscribed with runes and connected by a rune-carved arch, all of marble.

It was definitely one of the most ornate and beautiful runic gateways Jenn had ever seen, which admittedly was not that many. Currently the gateway was off and the other side of the room was visible through it. In the room already were Lenamare, Jehenna, Damien and Lord Gandros, who were chatting as they entered. Several other people in Turelanean garb were in the room, securing three wagons' worth of equipment and tending to the horses pulling the wagons.

Damien came over to Jenn and Gastropé, smiling apologetically. "Sorry we have to basically kick you out of the city, but I'm not seeing many alternatives. We need the two armies to leave."

Gastropé shrugged. "I agree; I'm just happy you aren't tossing us out the front gate and into their arms."

Damien chuckled. "A couple of members of the Council of Magistrates have suggested as much, but rest assured, neither council had any particular love of either the Rod or Oorstemoth before they decided to surround the city."

"However, and more important," Gandros said, coming up on their small group, "what Elrose and Maelen have told us is quite troubling, and the city may be in for much worse than these two armies. We need to know what we are up against and this seems like the best investigative path available at the moment. I'm not sure what, if anything, this expedition will be able to find, but we need as much information as we can get to prepare."

"You're sure"—Jenn looked at Damien directly—"that you'll be able to get Rupert and his cousin to us once they return?"

Damien looked a bit awkward for a moment and finally said, "At the moment, they are safely outside the city and a very long way from here. As soon as I am able to reestablish contact with them, we will coordinate. I am sure that if joining you is the safest course of action for them, then we can make that happen."

Jenn nodded. "Okay. It's just that Rupert's sort of been my personal charge lately and I'm just very worried about him out there basically on his own with Edwyrd. He has something of a knack for getting in trouble." Gastropé suddenly coughed for some reason.

Damien smiled. "I understand. We established a means of communication before they left, but the wards are blocking them. Once we can open up those lines of communication, I will have information on Rupert and will relay it to you."

"Thanks." Jenn smiled, as relieved as she could be at this point. Gandros was now talking to Elrose and Maelen.

Jehenna walked over to Jenn with Lenamare following. "You do understand this is very inconvenient for us?" she asked Jenn in her usual bitchy tone of voice.

"Sorry, just obeying orders," Jenn apologized, trying not to smile at being able to inconvenience the woman.

Jehenna frowned. "Here, take this with you; keep it on your person at all times." She thrust a small, smooth, rectangular metal box at Jenn. The box was made of some sort of black metal, about the size of a small jewelry box. It had a good-sized gem embedded on one side, with a gold rim holding it in the box lid. Well, not really a lid; there were no seams on the box. It was smooth with rounded edges and no discernable means of opening it.

"What is it?" Jenn asked.

"It contains a variety of sensors and recording equipment for monitoring power levels, fluctuations, locations and time," Lenamare stated.

"Yes. If you are going to go off hunting a goddess, we decided you might as well collect some useful information about deities while you are at it," Jehenna stated.

Jenn was puzzled. "But isn't that exactly what Master Elrose is doing with all his gear?"

Jehenna shook her head. "He's trying to detect a goddess and solve the mystery of his visions; he's going to be too focused on that purpose to record background and ambient information."

"Or power manifestation levels of the deity," Lenamare added.

"Power manifestations?" Gastropé, who had been standing beside Jenn, asked.

"Yes. If she uses her power on or around you, we want to measure it so we can learn more about god magic," Jehenna said, nodding.

"So what do I have to do?" Jenn asked.

"Nothing. Just keep it on you at all times," Lenamare said.

"Unlike your diary," Jehenna added.

"So then I just bring it back to you and you can extract the measurements?" Jenn asked.

"That would be the preferred option," Lenamare agreed.

"Preferred option?" Gastropé asked.

Lenamare shrugged. "I've got links to it, so I can always find it. The box is constructed of adamantite with mithral circuitry. It is as close to indestructible as I can make it. In the event that one of the goddess's power manifestations incapacitates or otherwise vaporizes you, we should still be able to recover the box."

"And it would provide a great deal of useful information on the nature of a deity's destructive magic, so we can prepare defenses," Jehenna stated.

Gastropé made a gulping noise, and Jenn frowned. "Great," she said without a lot of enthusiasm.

Lenamare nodded. "You are correct. It is a great piece of work, given how little time I had to prepare it. I do think it is one of my best arcane devices. And, again, on such short notice."

"Everyone!" Trevin was up on the dais. "Let me have your attention. We are almost ready to depart for the Grove." She smiled brightly. "This will be quite an adventure for you, my young friends, and I include the two of you in that comment." She gestured to Maelen and Elrose. "Master Lenamare will, in a few moments, order the wards to be adjusted to allow my runic gateway to open."

Trevin gestured to the gate behind her. "The gate will take us to the Western Outer Grove, which is about thirty-three leagues from the previous Abancian border. We'll then have about a half hour's journey, on foot, to the fortress at Fierd's Rest." Jenn had never heard of either of these places. Abancia, of course, she knew about; it was a long-defunct kingdom south of Turelane.

The Enchantress continued, "We'll have a nice, if slightly late, dinner there and then spend the night. We'll need to resume our journey before fierdrise, which will mean taking the lift to nearly the top of Widow's Peak." She looked to Maelen. "Which, you'll be happy to hear, only has an elevation of 1.2 leagues." She chuckled. "From there we shall go through a tunnel to the eastern slope. With Fierd's first rays of light, we will open the Fierdal Bridge to Grove Home. We'll spend the day and a night in Grove Home as my crew finishes preparing the Nimbus for our journey, and then we'll begin that at fierdrise the next day."

~

Wing Arms Master Heron sighed with exhaustion as he covered the crystal ball on his desk. He leaned back in his chair and closed his eyes.

"A positively productive series of both post-active and pro-active discussions, if I do say so, My Lord?" Wylan questioningly stated to the arms master.

Heron opened one eye and just stared at the protectator. Eventually he said, "As you say, Protectator, as you say; I am heartened that you are able to recognize this." He opened his other eye and sat up. "Now, Protectator Wylan, I need to write a few things up from our meeting. Since we missed dinner, please notify Cook that I am ready for my supper, and have his people bring it up. Also, ensure he serves you food as well. I know he's a stickler for people eating on time, but you were working with me."

"Thank you, Arms Master." Wylan smiled, bowed his head and quickly departed.

"Youth," Heron muttered, leaning back in his chair and closing his eyes again. He was not sure whether he meant the phrase enviously or as a curse. Perhaps both. He rubbed the bridge of his nose, trying to rub out the pain centered between his eyes. The last two days had nearly been too much.

The demon wave and cleanup, yes; that had been quite remarkable and unprecedented, but that was battle. He understood that; it was everything that had come after. Not the least of which was the contents of the crystal balling they had done. Followed by endless discussions with the Council, the Rod and finally, but certainly not least by any possible or conceivable means, the endlessly tedious and sublimely ridiculous sessions with his superiors in Keeper City.

Heron wanted to pound his head on his desk in order to knock the memories of those insane, ridiculous, alarmist and never-ending discussions out of his head. Chancellor Alighieri, not unexpectedly, Heron had to admit, had been one of the primary troublemakers. Alighieri along with Chancellors Ain and Sagramn had led the arguments for taking the prosecution of the law not only to, but also *through* the very Gates of the Abyss!

The insanity of this proposal was nearly impossible for Heron to grasp. The Abyss was the fulcrum of Chaos! How could one possibly seek to impose Law upon pure, raw, unadulterated Chaos? The Chancellors literally wanted to pursue the prosecution of justice into the Abyss! He could, at least intellectually, understand Alighieri's desire; the man had spent how many tax dollars and how many years on that boondoggle of his? This situation was nearly perfect for that overpriced project; this was what it had been built for. Heron had not believed, however, that anyone had ever seriously thought they would have need or cause to use it. The very thought of pursuing demons into the Abyss and forcibly extraditing them to face justice seemed simply ludicrous!

If only, Heron thought, he had retired before this engagement. He was old enough. He could have gracefully bowed out a year ago, or any time up until this moment. He had accepted this command, and he could not back out now, not even if the Chancellors of Law determined he needed to pursue his warrant through the Gates of the Abyss and to the very Courts of Chaos themselves. Well, then... but... seriously? Serving legal warrants to the Courts of Chaos? Did these fools even listen to themselves talk, or did they, like the majority of their audience, simply tune the sound of their own voices out? Heron sighed. If the Chancellors so determined, then so must he prosecute the law.

~

A knock came upon the front post of the tent in which Arch-Vicar General Barabus and Arch-Diocate Iskerus were sharing a late night glass of wine. "Come in," Barabus called. The tent flap pulled back and in walked Sir Gadius, who had arrived midday on Peace Bringer, his rather large, iridescent unicorn. Frankly, Barabus found the unicorn more disturbing than Talarius's flying horse, War Arrow. At least he did not feel the winged horse was staring at him in judgment all the time.

The knight bowed his head to the arch-vicar general and the arch-diocate. "My Lords, no luck on the missing Rod member. We have gone over the entire area outside the city a league in radius and found no sign of him. Further, intense questioning under truth sight has yielded no additional information as to what happened to the two horses and tack that have disappeared."

Barabus shook his head; this was all very disquieting. Apparently, at some point around midmorning, one of the possessed soldiers, still seriously wounded and recuperating, had disappeared without a trace. Vanished from a guarded tent in the middle of the Rod! Further, his tentmates, who had also been recovering from wounds— healing resources and spells had been devoted to the non-possessed wounded first—had all been completely healed and all signs of possession gone. Subsequently, two mounts, a mule and their gear had simply vanished from the stockade. Again, no one saw a thing.

Iskerus sighed. "I do not like this."

Gadius nodded. "We have also interrogated, probed, Seen, scried, done everything imaginable to get information from the other soldiers in the tent. None, however, remembers a thing. All they can report is that they had been having horrible dreams, which they no longer remember, and then suddenly they felt peace, warmth and what they describe as the warm embrace of Tiernon. After that, they report peaceful slumber until we awakened them."

"The peaceful embrace of Tiernon—a healing spell of some form?" Barabus looked to Iskerus.

The Arch-Diocate shrugged. "A very powerful one, by that description and given the level of healing that was done, particularly to the one named Mikael Rhys Barton."

"So it doesn't sound like demonic influence then," Barabus stated.

Gadius made a snorting noise, "True, but then my examination of Excrathadorus Mortis shows no sign of demonic influence either. Quite the contrary." Iskerus nodded in agreement.

"Damn it," Barabus muttered aloud. "That damnable demon has turned the world upside down!"

Gadius nodded. "If only I had arrived sooner."

Iskerus chuckled, but not pleasantly. "No offense, my good knight, but from what we've seen or witnessed, I'm afraid if you'd been here, you would be sharing a torture chamber with Sir Talarius. That demon was not at all what we thought initially. It was clearly an archdemon, at a minimum."

"A minimum?" Gadius was too shocked by this admission to take umbrage at the observation of the value of his assistance. "I thought the energy requirements for a demon prince to materialize on the Planes of Men was too great—that all seers and those sensitive to mana and the supernatural would be instantly alerted? How could a demon prince have been on this plane and everyone not known?"

"Perhaps because it's been here for a very long time?" A voice from outside the tent observed. The flap parted and Sir Sorel entered. "Perhaps it came during a period of great strife and upheaval, when no one would have noticed the power surge?"

"Aren't you supposed to be the cheerful one?" Iskerus asked Sorel as he entered, the Arch-Diocate smiling and rising to welcome the newly arrived knight. Sorel laughed ruefully and the two embraced as old friends.

Gadius saluted Sorel, who returned it. "It's good to have you with us, Sorel. It's been a long time since we were able to do battle together."

"It has indeed." Sorel smiled warmly and clasped Gadius's arm. "I only wish I'd been here sooner. I dare say the two of us working with Talarius could have tamed this beast."

Barabus stood and Sorel saluted him as the arch-vicar general returned the salute. "Good to have you, Sorel," the arch-vicar said solemnly. "We need all the expertise we can get. The level of infamy has risen to new heights on this battlefield."

"So I hear." Sorel nodded, looking concerned. "What's this I hear about negotiations for an alliance with Oorstemoth?" Gadius shuddered, Iskerus frowned.

"Very preliminary at this point. We had good success working with them in eliminating demons fleeing the city, and their sorcerers managed to capture the battle on crystal ball, which has been immensely useful in dissecting what happened. You will definitely want to see it, and we should probably watch it again ourselves. However, first things first... have you eaten?"

CRASH! BOOM! SCREECH! SCREEEECH!

The extremely loud sound of a lightning strike followed instantaneously by massive thunder shook the entire camp. That was followed by a horrendous shrieking and screeching of metal wrenching that caused all within the tent to cover their ears.

"What the—?" Barabus bolted from the tent, followed by the others.

Upon exiting the tent, a large plume of smoke could be seen from several tents over. Barabus shouted, "Talarius's tent!" They all charged towards the smoke plume where the tent had been.

Gadius and Sorel, swords drawn, had to push Rod members out of the way to allow Barabus and Iskerus through the circle of soldiers surrounding the former tent. A huge cloud of smoke and steam as well as the very distinct smell of a smithy permeated the area where Talarius's tent had been.

The tent was gone. A few flaming pieces of canvas were all that remained, other than a few magically secured chests which were smoking. As the smoke and steam cleared, a figure about seven feet tall could be seen within the remains of the tent.

Several soldiers and priests made gestures of faith at the sight of the individual within the tent. Barabus blinked to see a seven-foot-tall metallic knight standing vengefully within the tent.

"Is he in plate mail?" Gadius asked, puzzled.

"I have never seen such a massive, complete set of plate mail." Sorel shook his head in disbelief. The large figure seemed to be solid metal of sharp planes and angles. The outer edges of his armor's arms and legs were razor-sharp edged metal.

Barabus shook his head. "I think he's made out of metal?"

"A metal golem?" Sorel asked the vicar general.

"More like a sword golem," Iskerus said, frowning.

"I have never heard of a sword golem," Gadius stated flatly.

"This looks like no metal golem I have ever seen," Iskerus said.

"You there, in Talarius's tent!" Sorel shouted. "Identify yourself."

A deep baritone voice spoke in a monotone. "The Knight Rampant Talarius has been abducted by a demon. He has been gone thirty hours. He has not returned. You have failed to rescue him. I shall retrieve him."

"Okay." Gadius smiled grimly at the golem. "Again, identify yourself, golem!"

"I am not a golem," the metal man said.

"Who are you then?" Barabus yelled.

"I am Ruiden."

The two knights blinked and stared at each other. Sorel then turned back to face Ruiden. "You mean like Talarius's sword?"

"Not like. Am. I am Ruiden, Sword of Talarius. You have failed to retrieve him. I shall succeed."

~

Gastropé sat down on the bed in the small chamber he had been assigned to at Fierd's Rest. It was similar in size to his room at school, so while cramped, was comfortable. Fierd's Rest was a surprisingly robust keep dating back about six hundred years. It was fairly utilitarian, and military in nature. The most striking aspect of the fortress was that it was situated at the base of a giant mountain; one with, from what he could see in the dark, an unscalable cliff face. That cliff face seemed to be the back wall of the keep.

He had not been able to see much in the dark. They had arrived in what he would have called a sylvan glade in the middle of dense trees. The glade had been lit both by the light from the runic gateway and the palace dungeon behind it, as well as the brightly lit torch stands around the glade. Not unexpectedly, based on what Trevin had said earlier, this end of the gateway was manned by short elves. He guessed they must be forest alfar; they were all between four and five feet tall and generally had brown hair with various colored streaks. Gastropé was not sure he'd ever seen any forial alfar, as they were called before. He had seen and even briefly met a few rialto alfar, the so called "royal elves," all of whom were at least six feet tall and incredibly thin.

From a distance, he had seen a few races of Dok Alvar in Exador's army. He had no idea what the various races were, though. He had also had no desire to make their acquaintance. He was not xenophobic; it was simply that some races were better left alone. In hindsight, if he had continued working with Exador's army, he probably would have had to deal with some of those more "evil" races.

Fortunately, or maybe unfortunately, he had switched sides and was now aligned with three demons from the Abyss. Gastropé shook his head; his career trajectory was not moving in a positive direction. He had started out working for an "evil" overlord, who apparently was actually an archdemon allied with a previously dead Anilord; also an archdemon. He was now keeping secrets for the most-wanted demon lord on the planet, the demon lord's son, and a loud-mouthed octopodal demon, while working for room and board for an egomaniacal wizard who had slaughtered the entire army he had just deserted in a single blast. To top it all off, he was now tracking down what was probably a goddess who may or may not have gone rogue.

Gastropé sat down on his cot and put his head in his hands. This was not where he saw his life going at the beginning of the year. After graduation, he had thought he would settle down to a nice job in a city, earn a good living, hopefully meet a nice girl and get married. Instead, he was mired in tuition debt to the school and had had to take the only job he could find so he could make his first loan payment, and that job was with Exador. He had known full well the reason Exador was always hiring wizards; he went through them very quickly.

Sure, he had lived through Exador, unlike most of the wizards that had started with him. Gastropé figured that should, in fairness, be counted as a plus. If only he could have done that and avoided being at the epicenter of an upcoming war between demons and gods! He was literally "trapped between Heaven and the Abyss." Everyone knew what happened to mortals who meddled with demons and gods. They had an even worse record than Exador's wizards did!

"Could things get worse?" Gastropé muttered to himself, just before a knock came at his door. He shook his head and called out, "Come in!"

"I hope you're still decent," Trevin's voice called as the door swung open, her eyes immediately landing on Gastropé on the bed. She made a small pout. "Apparently, you are," she muttered to herself, but still audible to Gastropé.

"Just checking in to make sure you found your quarters and are getting settled," Trevin said, smiling at Gastropé.

"I am, thank you," Gastropé politely replied.

"You had enough to eat at dinner, I trust?" Trevin asked.

"It was very good." Gastropé nodded with a smile. They had been served beef stew, cheese and bread in the great hall shortly after arriving.

Trevin nodded, apparently satisfied. "It was nothing fancy, just keep food. Tomorrow night, though, we shall have a true meal. We are going to have a combined welcome and farewell feast to celebrate this rather ad hoc adventure." She smiled. "There will be a number of delicacies humans rarely get to sample, along with satyr beer and honey wine, as well as alvaren frost wine. You'll want to eat and drink fully; it may be the last feast we get for quite some time."

"Sounds good." Gastropé nodded to her, his eyes trying to keep contact with hers as she slid into the room to rest her hand on his shoulder. "I'm looking forward to seeing the Grove," Gastropé said nervously, trying to eye her hand.

She gave his shoulder a squeeze. I'm sure you'll find it quite... provocative." The enchantress was really standing a bit too close for comfort; Gastropé was getting a very strong dose of her perfume. He smiled and tried to scoot away slightly. This only caused the councilor's gnarled hand to slide down over his right deltoid and grasp his bicep firmly. He felt a small bit of panic as he realized that his movement could have been interpreted as making room for her to sit down beside him. He glanced to the bed beside him and then back to her, hoping she was not taking the wrong kind of hint.

She simply grinned at him, sliding her hand down his bare bicep a bit more. Her gaze moved to what appeared to be a few inches in front of his chest, or was it his lap she was looking at? She got a slightly puzzled look for a moment and then a bright smile as she tightened her grip slightly on his bicep.

"Very impressive," she said.

Gastropé got a panicked look on his face and turned pale, glancing down to make sure he was not showing anything in his lap. The old woman could not be that crude, could she?

"I imagine that very few young wizards your age, fairly fresh out of school, have the skill and ability to locate and bind a fiend. A rather powerful one at that, it appears. That binding could probably hold a major demon," the enchantress said, still staring in front of him.

What was she talking about? Gastropé wondered if she had lost her mind. He was at a loss for words until he remembered that he had told people in Freehold that Tizzy was his bound demon. She must be referring to that. He relaxed a bit.

"Ah, so you saw my demon in Freehold?" Gastropé asked.

Trevin blinked and shook her head, looking him in the eyes again. "Uhm, no, afraid I didn't. I was just noticing the binding link you had extending off into the nether regions and into the Abyss. Very skillfully crafted, I must say. I can honestly say, I am impressed." She grinned at him. "In any event, sleep well tonight. We'll be rising early, before dawn. A servant will wake you in time to do your morning ablutions before we break our fast with some fruit and bread. We will then take the lift up the cliff side. Unfortunately, the view won't be ideal in the predawn light, particularly on this side of the mountains, but for some that's a blessing." She tilted her head. "Being a fellow Turelanean, however, I'm sure you are comfortable on carpets, so heights won't be a problem?"

"Uhm, no, no problem," Gastropé replied, still quite nervous and reeling from her statement about a binding link extending from him to the Abyss. What was she talking about? He had never, would never, put any sort of binding spell on Tizzy!

"Excellent then." Trevin let go of his bicep and patted his shoulder again, before spinning away to exit the room. "Sleep well!" she said as she glided from the room.

Gastropé shook his head slightly as if to clear it. He quickly spoke the words necessary to invoke his wizard sight and stared down to his chest. He had to focus it a bit, but the enchantress had been right! There was some sort of link spell emanating from his chest and extending off into the aether.

He probed it, trying to determine what exactly it was and where it was going. He frowned; it was clearly a binding spell, from him to someone else. He was on the controlling end and the link clearly went off plane. Gently touching the translucent black cord, he suddenly got a whiff of unusual smoke. A very identifiable smoke; it was the same smoke he smelled when Tizzy was puffing on his pipe. He did not recognize the exact binding—it seemed a bit archaic—but it was very clearly a lower third-order binding from a conjuror to an enslaved demon.

Where the hell had it came from? He knew for a fact he had never cast any spell on Tizzy. There was no way he could have —he didn't even know the demon's true name. How long had it been there? Who had put it there? Was it even possible for a third party to create a binding linking between a conjuror and a demon? He had never heard of such a thing. It really should not be possible. Something very strange was going on, and once again it felt like things were spinning out of his control.

Chapter 88

DOF +2
Predawn 15-19-440

Hilda glided unnoticed down the street in the dark predawn hours, Danyel softly sleeping back at the Inn, no one the wiser that she had even left the building. She was more than happy to not be wearing her normal saint attire on these muck-filled streets. One would think that such a modern city of such learning and wealth could have cleaner streets. Clearly, she had been spoiled by her afterlife and the tidiness of the Outer Realms. Objectively, Freehold was nicer than the villages and cities she had known during her mortal existence, but once one had seen the lights of Heaven, it was hard to settle back into the mundane world.

Nonetheless, she had her duty. During her bath, she had finally gotten enough relief from the headache to get a feel for the city. There had been no temple of Tiernon in Freehold for centuries, but there was a chapel, and that would have to do. Actually, it was probably better for her purposes. Security at a true temple would be much higher. She needed to get in and out unnoticed; hence, the after-hours visit.

"Alms… alms for a poor blind beggar!" A hand suddenly shot out from a doorway to brush her own hand. Hilda stopped in shock; it was amazing that a beggar could pierce her spells. She glanced at the beggar, a man of about thirty years with a pockmarked face and the milky gaze of a blind man. His hands were dirty, dry and scaly and covered in rather nasty boils and pockmarks.

Hilda did a quick reading of the man. Yes, definitely blind, rather lice ridden, some nasty skin conditions and some fluid congestion in his lungs, but otherwise able-bodied. He was also, she noted, of Etonian faith; weak faith admittedly, but he had been dedicated to Namora at some point, most likely as a sailor.

"Thank you, mistress. Thank you for stopping. Can you spare a few coins so that I might get some soup?" the beggar pleaded with a strong whiff of cheap beer on his breath. Hilda shook her head. She had no problem with drinking beer, but drinking cheap beer was pretty much the definition of a sin. However, she supposed beggars could not afford anything else.

Hilda thought for a moment. She knew most beggars in large cities were actually professionals, and there were, in fact, beggar guilds. Perhaps his ability to spot her was a sign that his life was at a turning point. "I shall do better than that!" Hilda beamed at the blind man, who of course could not see her smile, but his head did tilt, perhaps at the melodic sound of her voice as she ramped her aura up.

"Take my hands," Hilda instructed, sticking both hands out towards his, practically in his face. Uncertain and puzzled, the beggar lifted his hands upward and Hilda grasped them. The man flinched at her touch, clearly sensing something unusual. He started to pull away, but Hilda would not let go.

"Sorry for bothering you, mistress. I should go now," the beggar pleaded with her.

"Nonsense, my good man. I can sense the spirit of Namora on you. Clearly, you have fallen on hard times in this distant land. Namora's brother, Tiernon, believes in helping all true Etonian kin. Allow the power and might of Tiernon to lift you and guide you!" Hilda began pulling from her illuminaries; she would not need to go upstream for this. "May the power and blessing of Tiernon be upon you now and for all your days!" Hilda sent the power of Tiernon's healing blessing down her hands and into the beggar's.

The man gasped as the divine rapture of Tiernon filled his body. Given that she could see fine in the dark, she could easily see the milky film fade from the man's eyes and the corrupted skin peel from the man's hands and face as fresh new skin replaced it.

The man suddenly went rigid and then limp as the healing finished. He collapsed back into the doorway gasping for breath, inhaling more deeply than he had probably been able to in a few years. He stared at her, seeing another face for the first time in who knew how long.

Hilda gave him her most beatific smile. "May the blessings of Tiernon and his sister Namora be upon you as we part in peace!"

She turned abruptly, releasing her built-up aura, and started down the street once more. "Wait! Wait!" The beggar called out from behind her. "I can see! I'm healthy!" Hilda smiled to herself, pleased. "You just took away my livelihood! Do you have any idea how hard it is out here for a healthy beggar?" The man sounded almost angry.

Hilda shook her head. "What am I supposed to do?"

The beggar whined some more.

Frustrated, Hilda called back, "I don't care, How about getting another job and earning your money from work? Return to the sea—you were a sailor at some point, yes?"

"Uh, yeah... uh..." the beggar spluttered. Hilda simply shook her head. Whatever happened to people wanting to get a miracle? Seriously, this current generation; never satisfied with what they had. She laughed softly. Yes, it was annoying, but she had pretty much expected something like this. He had been a professional guild beggar; she was now certain of that.

She supposed it would be awkward to return to the guildhall both empty-handed and healed. Not her problem though; as a saint, it was her job to help people, whether they wanted it or not. Tiernon would also be pleased. While he certainly believed in charity and assistance to those in need, he had no patience for slackers and societal parasites. She laughed to herself once more, pleased with her side mission tonight.

~

The chapel priest had been sound asleep in his bed. His assistant, sleeping near the chapel's front door to assist with late night supplicants, was asleep as well. Both as Hilda had hoped. She had deepened their sleep and then magically barred the doors to the chapel to keep any other late-night visitors from intruding.

It felt so nice in the chapel. The consecrated space acted as a buffer to the unpleasant sensation of the wards. As she had hoped, it allowed her to focus and concentrate better than at any point since she had entered the city. She headed to the altar, noting the bowl of holy water nearby. Excellent—she would need both to complete the ritual. She pulled the small sapphire amulet from her pocket. Calling it a sapphire amulet was a bit strong; it was more of a small sapphire pendant on a silver chain. However, it should do just fine.

She needed to fashion something to hold the spells to keep the wards at bay so she did not have to actively keep the ritual going herself. This would be only her third holy artifact since she had graduated from saint school, but she felt confident that she would have no problems. Once the necklace was working, she could, with luck, also use the chapel's sanctity to boost her ability to contact the archons off plane and file her report. These stupid wards were a huge pain in the butt.

~

"Decisions, too many decisions!" Tom complained. He was sitting on his chair. He felt bad that he did not have furniture for anyone else, but he had never expected to have so much company. Nor had he really had time to build more. He had offered to let anyone who wanted to sit in his single chair, but it was really too big for anyone, including Reggie and Boggy.

"That's not a common demon problem," Boggy observed.

Tizzy nodded emphatically up and down while chewing on the stem of his pipe.

"Well, let's see," Antefalken mused. The bard had returned a few hours ago from the Courts and brought them up to speed on the reactions there. Tom had introduced him to Reggie as an old friend who had shown up when he had heard about the commotion in Astlan. Boggy then introduced Estrebrius to Antefalken and explained Vaselle's request for a meeting.

"We've got an invitation from Lilith to stay with her at the Courts, and you've got a business proposal from Estrebrius's accursed master, but we don't yet know what that proposal is. Further, as I said, I think half the Abyss is looking for you and your guest," Antefalken said, pointing to Talarius.

"I suspect a lot of people will be coming out of the woodwork to be your friend," Boggy noted.

"Or to kill him permanently," Tizzy added. Tom glared at the octopodal demon.

"Clearly, Lilith wants you to come to her, and she can protect you from other demons, but she'll also have you all to herself at that point," Antefalken said.

"This Lilith, who exactly is she?" asked Tom. "From what you have said, and what I read in Freehold, she sounds like she's pretty important. I know the name, but they cannot be the same person. Different mythologies." He made a shrugging motion.

Talarius seemed to shuffle in his armor over in the corner, where he was sitting and listening to them. Tom assumed the knight had also heard her name. Antefalken gave him a puzzled look, apparently wondering if Tom had been living in a cave, given that he did not know who Lilith was. Fortunately, Tom felt their current environment was sufficient evidence that he had, in fact, been living in a cave. Tom would just have to live with that lapse; he was not up to revealing his story to everyone today. Not with Rupert here, in particular.

"Well, don't be too sure of that." Tizzy chuckled. "She's multiversally famous. Nearly every religion features some version of her."

"Bad breakups will do that." Boggy nodded.

"Yeah, and this one was bad." Tizzy puffed out some smoke. "Really an epic breakup."

"And of course, she came out looking bad," Boggy said. "Women often do. Even if it's the man's fault, the ex-wife always ends up with the bad reputation."

"I will refrain from joining this discussion," Antefalken said.

"Are you still sleeping with her?" Boggy asked.

Antefalken gave him a surly look. "I'm not joining this discussion, and not discussing my love life."

"Okay, I'm not that interested in her past. I am more concerned about the present. Who exactly is she today? If she's so powerful that everyone knows who she is, is it safe to turn down her invitation?" Tom asked.

Antefalken shrugged. "To be completely honest, I don't know which is more dangerous: accepting her invitation or declining it."

"So who is she?" Reggie interrupted.

Tizzy shook his head. "She's the Empress of the Damned, of course."

"The Empress of the Damned?" Tom asked.

"She is about as close to being a ruler as the Abyss gets." Boggy shrugged.

Antefalken continued, "She is one of the two Co-Factors, she and her consort, Sammael. They are the two most powerful demons in the Abyss, after the Concordenax."

Reggie asked, "The Concordenax?"

"The Demon Father, the creator of all demons," Estrebrius chimed in.

Tizzy suddenly started coughing loudly, pulling the pipe from his mouth and billowing out clouds of smoke. He looked up, realizing everyone was staring at him. "Sorry, inhaled the wrong way!"

"And where is he in all this?" Tom asked. "I read about him in a treatise, but it says he's been missing for some time."

Antefalken shrugged. "No one knows. Other than Lilith and Sammael, I do not know anyone who has ever claimed to have met him, or so much as seen him. And Lilith has no idea where he went, but he's been gone for an extremely long time, even by demon standards."

"This is all getting much more complicated than I'd expected." Tom sighed.

Tizzy made a harrumphing sound.

"You think this is complicated, wait until Tiernon's folks show up on your ledge with an arrest warrant!" Talarius chuckled, apparently with glee.

"I don't think they're going to come down into the Abyss." Antefalken shook his head.

"That would be considered a broach of détente." Boggy was nodding.

"But it would be kinda interesting," Tizzy whined.

Estrebrius was shaking his head, clearly wanting no part of such an invasion.

"Yes, but more important, I'm not sure if they'd have access to all their resources here," Antefalken said.

"What do you mean?" Tom asked.

"Well, look at our friend over there." He pointed to Talarius. "You can't feel your deity right now, can you?" Antefalken asked.

The knight simply glared at the bard. Antefalken continued after a moment of the knight's silence. "I mentioned this earlier; clerics tend to get disconnected from their gods here, and no souls can escape without being intentionally released somehow. From what I have seen, and what Lilith has said, clerics can only do minor rituals here that draw on their own mana, or the mana from any followers in their immediate party. Those links they have to the higher planes don't work here."

"So his agents would be cut off from him?" Tom asked.

Antefalken shrugged. "That's what I'm thinking."

"And that's why it would be interesting!" Tizzy exclaimed, pounding one of his fists into its opposing palm. "We could capture them, torture them, eat them!" He got a slightly wild look in his eye. "All that super-sweet angel mana!" He closed his eyes. "I bet their souls are really tasty!"

"You foul beast!" Talarius spat at Tizzy.

Tizzy turned and grinned at him. "I bet they're even tastier than Paladins!"

The knight shrugged. "I'm not a Paladin, I'm a Knight Rampant, and so your ignorant point is wasted."

"Enough!" Tom said. "No one is eating anyone, and we aren't going to worry yet about Tiernon's people coming for a visit. We take this one day at a time!" Tom was really starting to stress out. He was definitely in over his head. He sighed. "I think we need to consider this Lilith thing a bit more. How about Estrebrius's accursed master? Do I take this meeting?"

Estrebrius grinned rather oddly and wrung his hands. "Great One, do as you please. I'm just so grateful you are considering it. I swear, my master is no threat to you. He does not have that much power, and as humans go, he is a good man. He's never tried to screw me over; he's really the best master I've ever had!"

Tom nodded. "Boggy?"

"Estrebrius has talked about this master with me before, and he sounds pretty reasonable. Moreover, I am pretty sure he can't hurt you in any way. You've been dealing with far greater wizards than Vaselle."

"Antefalken?" Tom turned his head to the bard.

Antefalken shrugged. "I don't know the man, but my guess is that he's an average wizard, certainly not on par with any of the Council members. Lenamare and his crew are far more dangerous and you have taken their measure. He'll be stronger than Gastropé, I'd bet, but probably not that much stronger."

"And you don't think it's a trap?" Tom asked.

Estrebrius shook his head from side to side, vehemently indicating it was not.

Antefalken responded, "Not this soon. Given what everyone in Freehold has probably heard or seen, anyone thinking of setting a trap would want more time for preparation. Quite a bit more time."

"Did you hear something?" Reggie suddenly asked, turning around in circles as if looking for the source of something he had just heard.

Tom glanced at him, but continued, "Okay, so let's agree to that, then. See what he wants; otherwise, such an insane request is probably going to bug me until I find out." Estrebrius was looking very ecstatic. Or something—Tom couldn't tell what, sort of pleased and terrified at the same time. Tom did not know, but everyone on both of these planes was simply too strange to understand.

"There she is!" Reggie was pointing to a blank wall. Everyone else looked at him in puzzlement. Tom realized suddenly that he could see through Reggie, that he had become translucent and then quickly transparent, and then had vanished. Interesting, Tom thought to himself. He had wondered what his fading looked like to people around him.

"Time to get to work!" Tizzy chuckled.

"So, Estrebrius?" Tom asked, and the little demon turned back to him. "When did your master say he'd contact you again?"

"Shortly after dawn in Freehold. He has to wait for the gates to open and then go a ways out into the woods away from the two armies."

"Anyone got a watch?" Tom asked.

Antefalken laughed. "It gets hard to tell time between the realms, but it shouldn't be that long; maybe a few hours by the time he gets out of the city. That's the same time Damien would normally summon me."

"Have you heard anything more from him?" Tom asked.

"No. My guess is that the city is still sealed off from extra-planar forces and communication. Well, actually, we know that from Estrebrius here." Antefalken shrugged. "I have to admit to some curiosity in knowing how much the Council knows about what happened outside the wall. If they got reports, they are probably freaking out pretty badly at this point."

Tizzy and Boggy both laughed.

"I wonder what Jenn is thinking?" Rupert asked.

Tom shook his head. "I am sure she's not worried about Edwyrd, but she will be a basket case about you."

"We have a good idea what the demonic response is; we can guess what the Rod and Tiernon's church's response might be; but we don't have any idea about what the Council knows or what the next move will be for Oorstemoth."

"I am sure my master can give you a good report about what people in Freehold know," Estrebrius chimed in. Antefalken nodded.

Chapter 89

DOF +2
Still Predawn 15-19-440

Gastropé woke to a knock on his door. "I'm up!" he yelled to the knocker. He wearily conjured a mage light to illuminate the dark little chamber; it was still quite some time before dawn. He had barely slept; he had tossed and turned all night worrying about how the binding had become attached to him. He had not even noticed it! He had run every scenario over in his head, and nothing made any sense.

He used the chamber pot and then washed his hands and face with the cold water in the bowl on a stand in one corner. He had no mirror, and it was rather dark even with the mage light, so he decided not to try and shave—not that he had that much to shave. He shrugged and got dressed, then packed up what little he had taken out last night. Finally he seated his turban on his head. That was one nice advantage to prewound, sewn turbans; you did not have to worry about combing your hair. Traditional wrapped turbans made a mess of anything other than short hair; the prewound type, which his father insisted was an abomination, were more like a hat and not as bad.

Gastropé had taken to wearing a prewound turban during wizard school, when a friend had introduced him to a turban winder who could sew small secret compartments into the bands of the turban, where one could then secretly store spell components, money or small tools. This convenience, plus the convenience of not having to wind it every day had driven him to the dark side, as his father called it. Gastropé had to chuckle. His father had no problem with his wanting to learn how to summon demons, but wearing a prewound turban—that was where he drew the line. Fortunately his father, while a traditionalist, was pretty soft hearted for a shopkeeper.

Gastropé made his way down to the main hall where they were to meet. Jenn and Maelen were already there eating some meats, cheeses, fruits and bread that had been laid out by even earlier-rising servants for them to break their fast on.

Jenn frowned as he approached. "Did you get attacked by a necromancer in your sleep? You look like a barely risen corpse!"

Maelen chuckled as he popped a yellow piece of melon in his mouth.

"I didn't sleep very well." Gastropé looked around the room. There was a servant over by the fireplace, tending it, but no one else was around yet. "Take a look at me with your wizard sight," he said to them, "and whatever it is you do similarly. Do you notice anything odd? Say, around here?" He gestured to his chest.

Jenn frowned again and shook her head, but muttered the incantation for her wizard sight and stared at him. Maelen simply looked at him intently. "I don't know," Jenn said slowly. "Is there some sort of string or cord coming off of you?"

"It appears to be some form of link extending"—Maelen's eyes traced a path up into the air—"somewhere off plane perhaps?"

"Yeah, Trevin noticed it last night and complimented me on it," Gastropé replied sourly.

"What is it?" Jenn asked curiously.

"It's a demon binding going off to the Abyss," Gastropé told them.

"A demon binding? You mean like a conjuror would use to bind a demon?" Jenn looked at him, puzzled. "I didn't know you had any bound demons; you've never mentioned it. You know that's sort of a big deal, given what's been going on." She sounded like she was starting to get annoyed.

"I didn't! I have never actually cast a demon binding, ever! I've studied them and practiced them, but I've never actually bound a demon to myself before!" Gastropé waved his arms to emphasize his point. "I didn't even know it was there until last night when Trevin pointed it out. That's why I couldn't sleep; I was trying to figure out how it got there!"

"So what or who is on the other end?" Maelen asked.

Gastropé frowned. "Well, it appears to be an older-style link for a second to third-order demon. Sort of like they used to do a hundred to two hundred years ago."

"And it goes to…" Jenn prompted.

"I'll give you one guess…it smells like funky pipe smoke!" Gastropé exclaimed.

"Tizzy?" Jenn asked in shock. "How could that be? Demons cannot bind themselves to wizards, it's the other way around, and even then, a fiend like Tizzy could not. He's said he doesn't have any magical abilities, unlike Tom."

"I know," Gastropé gestured broadly. "That's why I have no idea how it would have got there. I have never heard of a demon able to bind itself, and it is a traditional one way binding with me as the master, let alone one of that order. Have you?" Gastropé looked at Maelen.

Maelen was still staring at the link, apparently. "No, never heard of that, but following it, I am pretty sure you are right and that Tizzy's on the other end of it. When did it appear?"

Gastropé shrugged. "I have no idea. I don't usually go looking at myself with wizard sight. So it could have been there for quite some time."

"Do you suppose the demon Tom did it?" Jenn asked.

"When? You've been with me whenever he's been around." That was a lie, of course; he and Edwyrd had spent a lot of time together, but neither Maelen nor Jenn knew that Tom and Edwyrd were the same person. However, Gastropé had never seen Edwyrd casting any spells. Besides, Edwyrd was an animage, and this was definitely a classic wizard spell in structure; not something an animage would do. At least, he did not think so.

Further discussion was cut off as Elrose and Trevin entered the hall. "Good morning, everyone!" Trevin greeted them. She was wearing what appeared to be a leather and fur-lined version of her normal attire. Much warmer, more rustic but still way too revealing for her age, Gastropé noted. That was one thing he and Jenn could completely agree on. Particularly when the enchantress started running her eyes up and down his torso while looking at him.

The two wizards took some wooden plates and began filling them, and Gastropé decided to do the same.

"Jenn and Maelen, I think your travel clothes for today are fine, but my dear Gastropé, as much as I love your outfit, I fear you may get a bit cold this morning," Trevin said as she speared a large chunk of melon to put on her plate.

"I've got a jacket in my backpack I can put on," Gastropé said.

"Good, you'll want it. We are taking the lift up to the western landing, which is about a league straight up!" She smiled and looked at all of them. "We will then enter the western gate and take the tunnel through the mountain to the eastern front. From there, I will open the Fierdal Bridge at dawn, which will transport us into the Grove."

"The Fierdal Bridge?" Maelen asked.

"Yes, it's not dissimilar to a Prismatic Bridge, except that it only works when Fierd is at certain positions in the sky, and those positions determine where the bridge goes. At different points during the day, opening it will take you to different locations within the Grove." She paused and smiled. "Some of those locations aren't particularly pleasant, so you are all advised not to try to force the gate's guardians to open it, or you may find yourself in a less than ideal spot." She chuckled. "Like inside of Fierd herself!"

Gastropé made a sour face at that thought. Jenn was not looking exactly comfortable either. They were definitely going to be at the mercy of the wizard.

~

"What are we going to do?" Iskerus asked Barabus.

"I don't know about you, but I plan to try to get some sleep before Fierd rises. Perhaps an hour or two?" Barabus put his head in his hands, elbows on the table. They and the two knights had spent the night being debriefed by a sword. A sword, for Tiernon's sake!

Ruiden had gone out to personally inspect the battle scene and the site of the former hole through which Talarius had been dropped. Swords, logically enough, did not sleep. Ruiden had informed them that he would be working around the clock to find Talarius.

"I'm concerned this Ruiden—golem—whatever it is could be a problem." Iskerus said.

"Do you have any idea how to stop him—it?" Barabus asked. "Its arms and legs are razor-edged blades, as are its fingers! Hell, almost every part of him is sharp. And he's an animated inanimate object! How do you kill a sword?"

"By melting it?" Iskerus shrugged, depressed.

"Yeah, and who exactly is going to catch it to toss it in a volcano?" Barabus asked through his hands.

"Swords aren't supposed to move on their own," Iskerus moaned. "Sure, we all know about swords that can fly to their owner's hand and such, but walk around and talk? Take notes?"

"Where is a heavenly host of avatars when you need one?" Barabus looked up from his hands. "I am reasonably certain an avatar could force him to change back into a sword."

"Really?" Iskerus asked skeptically. "How many demons has Talarius slain? That we know of? Consider what Talarius did with Ruiden to that super-demon right here in this camp. You think the sword couldn't at least slow an avatar down to get away?"

Barabus stood up to go to his cot. "Then we shall just have to try and reason with it, I suppose."

"Yes, because words so often win out over swords," Iskerus said sarcastically.

~

Jenn clutched her cloak tightly about her shoulders; the wind was wicked. Given their current location, she was extremely glad for the predawn darkness on the western side of this very large mountain. Their party was a tight fit in the lift and she had gotten pushed up against the side. Fortunately, the lift had cross-hatched metal wire walls; more like a cage or fence, actually. The walls were completely open to the wind, but they ran from floor to ceiling to keep people in with small enough openings between the metal wires that nothing very large could fall out. It was a tight fit with all of them and their backpacks; thankfully, Trevin had sent both her and Elrose's extra trunks up earlier.

The darkness hid their true height as the lift barreled along up the cliff face. She had made the mistake of looking down as they'd left the keep, which was fairly well lit for their departure. The dizzying speed at which the lights of the keep had shrunk made it very clear how high they were rising.

The lift was basically two platforms, a roof and floor, with support posts between in each corner, wrapped in the linked fencing. It was attached—or guided by, she guessed was the word—twin metal rails that scaled the mountain cliff. The vertical rails were at each corner and on each of the longer sides of the lift cage. The rails were I-shaped and the cage sides each had a double set of wheels that ran along the inside and outside of the rails. Sort of like mechanical sliding drawers, except with wheels on both side of the guide rail.

According to Trevin, the roof and floor were inscribed with runes and gems that controlled high and low pressure zones below and above the lift. The floor generated a region of high pressure below it and the roof generated a low pressure region above the cage; the combination when activated caused the lift to rise quickly, or conversely to descend at a controlled pace by balancing the pull of gravity. The metal rails kept the lift cage on a direct path up the mountainside. At first the rails provided a gentle rocking, but by the time the cage reached its full climbing speed, Jenn felt like she was inside a dice cup.

Trevin had explained that the mountain's abrupt height created extremely high winds which made it unsafe for winged creatures and flying carpets to ascend the mountainside; hence, the lift. Jenn could attest firsthand to the winds. She was feeling battered herself, between the wind and the shaking on the rails, but she was reaching her limits. If it had been light out, she was pretty sure vertigo would have conspired with the wind and rails to relieve her of her breakfast and the previous night's dinner.

They were going a league straight up into the air. Jenn had never been that high before. Very few carpets flew at that height, unless they were crossing mountain peaks, but even then, most people would just fly through valleys to avoid going so high. Trevin had warned them that as they got higher in altitude, the air would become thinner and thus they should pace themselves once they got to the top, since they would not be used to the altitude and thin air. Jenn could attest to the enchantress's accuracy. Her ears kept plugging up and then she would have to move her jaw to get them to "pop," as Trevin had called it.

It was also getting quite a bit colder as they rose. She was sure Gastropé was glad to be wearing his jacket, but his silk pants could not have provided much warmth for his legs. She shook her head at the young man; he put his fashion sense ahead of common sense clothing. Worrying about clothes and one's appearance was not something she normally associated with men, but doing stupid, impractical things was, so she figured it balanced out.

The lift suddenly lurched to a stop, sending Jenn slamming into the metal caging. "Ouch!" Jenn muttered to herself as her nose got squashed on the metal wiring exactly at the wrong spot. There were a bunch of shuffling noises, and Trevin was talking to someone outside the lift.

"We are here!" Trevin called out more loudly, apparently having turned to face into the lift. "Hethfar will place a ramp with railings between the lift and the deck for us to safely get out; however, I suggest you take his or one of his men's hands to help you out rather than using the railing. "They are very strong," she added, suddenly much closer to Jenn. She then bent her head to Jenn's ear, eyes closed, and advised her softly, "And really gorgeous, my dear. I recommend fainting and letting one of them catch you in his brawny arms so you can get up close to his chiseled bare chest. Their scent is intoxicating." Trevin opened her eyes again. "They use scent to attract their partners, but it works on other races as well."

Jenn simply nodded in agreement; she really had no desire to engage in girl talk with someone old enough to be her grandmother's grandmother. However, she felt she should be polite. Trevin turned and began ushering the others out. Elrose went first, followed by Maelen, who was peering over the edge of the small bridge and clutching his staff a bit tighter than usual.

Gastropé went next, looking especially pale, his Adam's apple bobbing in his neck. As he reached the midpoint he somehow managed to trip—on what, Jenn couldn't imagine—but he managed to fall into one of the guard's arms. Jenn could not see the guards that well in the dark. The torches were all behind them. About all she could see was that they were indeed bare chested, but wearing what appeared to be very large capes.

Trevin turned to Jenn with an arched eyebrow. "Interesting! I did not even suggest that to him, I thought it would make him too uncomfortable. However, it turns out I was wrong. Your young friend is far more adventurous than I thought. This is quite the pleasant surprise."

Jenn blinked, trying to understand what Trevin meant. Was that a purring noise that the enchantress was making? She shook her head, suddenly realizing what Trevin meant. "No, no, it's nothing like that, he's just being Gastropé. I'm sure that was an honest trip, not a ruse to get closer."

Trevin smiled and patted her shoulder. "Don't worry, dear. If he does prefer the same, or even both sexes, no one in the Grove will care. Quite the opposite, in fact! If he does like both men and women, he can have twice or even thrice the fun!"

Jenn had no idea what she meant by *thrice the fun*, and she was also certain she did not want to know.

Trevin continued, "A very large percentage of our patron deities are extremely interested in fertility, virility, lust, free love, you name it. Every form of mating, productive or not, is celebrated in the Grove!" She raised both eyebrows at Jenn, as if letting her in on a delightful secret.

Jenn grinned a bit stiffly, trying to be polite and mask her own reaction. Trevin had said there were a lot of satyrs and nymphs in the Grove, and Trevin's words just now brought back childhood warnings about satyrs and nymphs.

"Your turn, dear!" Trevin told her, waking her from her thoughts. Trevin grinned as if they shared a secret and leaned in conspiratorially. "I can see I've caught your imagination. You are going to really love the Grove!" She patted Jenn on her shoulder and practically shoved her towards the bridge. Jenn was so caught off guard that she stumbled onto the bridge a bit off balance, and before she knew it, she was tripping on whatever had tripped Gastropé, landing in the arms of the guard at the other end of the bridge.

The guard's strong arms caught her and pulled her up close, and immediately Jenn noticed the scent. Trevin had not been lying; the man's scent was intoxicating. She could not describe it. She was lost for a few seconds and suddenly realized that her right hand was resting on—no, cupping the man's extremely large, bare pectoral muscle. Jenn pulled back slightly in shock, still held tightly by the guard's right arm. She stared up into the guard's face.

The man's large golden eyes suddenly caught her. So entranced was she that she barely noticed the mischievous grin on his face. She only noticed the extremely chiseled jaw with perhaps a day's worth of stubble. The stubble extended to most of his head, and Jenn blinked to realize that the man's head had been shaven on both sides, leaving a single stripe of long hair running down the center, almost like a horse's mane. The hair was black at the base, tapering up to a brilliant gold at the tips. It was breathtaking, Jenn realized.

If she thought his face took her breath, that was before her eyes drifted beyond his face. What she had thought was a dark cloak was not a cloak at all, but large, black, feathered wings rising up from his back. They were slightly unfurled to assist in his balance. The wings were lined with a gorgeous shiny black down on top, along with deep black coverts, while the lower primary and secondary pinions changed to the same gold as his hair.

The guard was an aetós or aetón or… she really did not know the word. "Aetós…" Jenn managed to whisper in surprise. She had heard of the legendary beings, but had never seen one, nor expected to.

The guard smiled broadly and then chuckled, apparently familiar with the reaction he was having on her. "Aetóên," he corrected gently. "I am an aetóên in the common tongue. *Aetós* is equivalent to humans; aetóên corresponds to the singular human. But in particular, I am named Danfaêr." He effortlessly lifted her and her heavy pack and spun them around from the ledge and onto the large landing pad at the top of the mountain. He released her gently, ensuring she was stable, and then turned back to where Trevin had apparently fainted into Hethfar's arms, as planned.

"Whoo." Gastropé let his breath out, shaking his head. "I guess that bridge really is treacherous if three of us tripped and fell."

"You tripped, I was shoved, and she planned her faint so she could cuddle," Jenn said while internally scolding herself over her reaction to Danfaêr.

"What are you talking about?" Gastropé asked, looking at her as if she were crazy.

"Never mind; it's just ridiculous." Jenn shook her head.

Gastropé frowned for a minute and then his eyes widened. "Oh, I see why she would do that." He stopped and thought for a moment. "I have to admit, Treyfoêr smelled really good. If I was into guys…"

"Please!" Jenn said, wanting him to shut up.

"We're ready to load up!" Maelen called over to them. He gestured for them to join him, so Jenn and Gastropé headed over to where the seer was standing near a wagon. Actually, Jenn realized, it was a rather odd wagon; it had large iron wheels that were sitting on parallel iron rails. The wagon had sides about four feet high.

Maelen pointed at his own pack in the wagon. "We put our gear here and then ride in the next cart." He gestured to a platform on wheels closer to the mountain. The platform had several wooden bench seats with backs and end panels, sort of like Jenn had seen in churches. There were metal bars running along the backs of the benches so that people in the following bench could hold on.

In all, there were four carts. The wagon cart and bench carts were in the middle. On the ends were more bench carts, but those bench seats had no backs, and it appeared, in the dark, that they had leather handholds for each position on the benches.

"Elrose," Trevin said, walking up with the sorcerer, "we sent your large gear through on a previous trip, so it's already on the other side near the bridge gateway. Everyone load your stuff in this cart; we will then tie it down with a tarp. Maelen"—she turned toward the seer—"I'd suggest you and Gastropé put your staves in the cart as well. The ride through the mountain is a bit bumpy and you'll probably want to hang on in the cart."

"Do we go all the way through the mountain?" Jenn asked.

Trevin smiled and nodded. "Almost straight through at this altitude. It's about two leagues."

"I thought we had to be at the bridge at fierdrise? I don't think we can make that," Gastropé said.

Trevin just chuckled. "Oh, we'll make it; it's only about a ten-minute journey."

Gastropé looked at the wooden carts on metal rails. "We're going to be traveling at twelve leagues an hour on this contraption?"

Trevin chuckled and nodded. "Up and down numerous inclines and through several large caverns and over a couple of large chasm bridges. So, as I said, you may want to hang on tight."

Maelen and Gastropé secured their staves quickly in the cart. It was hard to say, but Jenn thought Maelen may have turned a shade of Gastropé gray. Elrose shrugged and put his pack in, his dark skin color hiding any signs of nervousness. Jenn and Gastropé placed their packs in the cart and one of the aetóên she did not know began covering the loaded cart with a tarp.

"We recommend those new to this trip sit in the seats with backs and sides." Trevin gestured to the second cart with the pews. "The aetós, of course, use the backless benches for their wings. I sit up front next to Gnorman, our engineer." She gestured to rather short, rotund fellow who suddenly appeared beside her.

He was about half her height, had a huge head in proportion to his body and an even larger nose. He was dressed in a weird single-piece outfit that appeared to be pants with a large bib covering his chest, with suspenders over his shoulders holding them up. The outfit was vertically striped with grey and white bars. He had a nicely fit bright red shirt on under the bib, tucked into the pants. On his head, he wore a cap with a large front brim made of the same grey and white striped material as the pants.

Jenn suddenly realized that this Gnorman must be a gnome. She had heard of the legendary engineers and craftsmen, but had never actually seen one in person. Gnorman the gnome? That seemed just a bit trite, but she knew it was not polite to question other cultures and their traditions.

"If any of you, say Gastropé, want a more exciting ride, you can sit up next to me in the front," Trevin continued. "You are more than welcome to grab and hold on tight to me." She grinned mischievously, "And I, of course, will hold on to you in return!"

"Uhh…" Gastropé was not sure how to respond and it took him a few seconds. "Thanks, but maybe on the return trip or something. I'm thinking I'd better follow your advice for newcomers."

Trevin smiled and shrugged. "Have it your way, then. It would have been a lot of fun—for me, at least." She turned and headed toward the front cart. "Everyone aboard! Anyone with motion sickness issues should take the sides and aim outward with your breakfast!"

They climbed aboard the cart. There was plenty of room; the benches could easily sit three to four people across. Jenn and Gastropé took the second-row pews and Maelen and Elrose took the one behind them. Hethfar and Danfaêr took the benches behind Trevin and Gnorman; only two aetós could fit on a bench given their large, gorgeous wings. Treyfoêr and four other aetós, including the two that had assisted Elrose and Maelen, filled the back cart.

"Everyone seated and ready?" Trevin called back to the party. Jenn and Gastropé nodded towards Maelen, who called out, "Middle car ready!" From the rear car there was a loud hooting noise and what sounded like a cheer. Jenn took that to mean they were ready.

Trevin looked back and smiled before shouting, "Gnorman, power up! Ahoy, gates! By the order of Niall, open the mountain to our train!" Suddenly the sides of the train lit up as previously dark crystals lining the edges of the carts began to glow with yellow and white lights. Ahead of them in the new light, Jenn saw a large portcullis in the side of the mountain start to rise with a loud rumbling noise. Not squeaky, though; the portcullis was surprisingly well oiled.

Suddenly the carts rocked slightly as the magic powering it hit the wheels—or something like that, Jenn decided. Gnorman pushed forward on a lever between him and Trevin and the cart slowly started lurching forward. *Clack, clack, clack* went the iron wheels on the iron tracks. Rather amazing, Jenn reflected, how they were using magic to propel iron wheels on iron tracks. Iron was notoriously resistant to magic.

As the portcullis locked into place above them, the carts lumbered through into the side of the mountain. A few feet into the tunnel, they saw a side room off the tunnel with a group of gnomes in armor waving at them. Trevin waved back, and feeling the mood, Jenn and the rest in the middle cart did as well. The aetós in the rear car made hooting noises as they passed the gnome guardroom. As they moved into the tunnel it got darker, the guard room having apparently lit up the opening quite a bit. Within a minute, the only light came from the carts themselves. The dark stone walls with timber shoring were rather eerie, Jenn thought.

"All systems ready, mistress!" Gnorman stated loudly over the clacking of the wheels.

"Then give our metal mount her head, Master Engineer!" Trevin yelled back. Gnorman grinned at her and shoved the lever further forward. Suddenly the carts lurched forward, accelerating to what could only be called a breakneck speed, slamming Jenn back into her seat and forcing her to quickly grab for the metal bars in front of her.

"Shit!" Gastropé shouted beside her as the carts began careening madly down the tunnel. Jenn was just starting to get her breath back when suddenly she was thrown forward as the carts dipped and headed down a very sharp incline. It had to be at least sixty degrees. Jenn and Gastropé both yelled in fright as the carts plunged down the dark tunnel. *Wham*! They were thrown to the left, Gastropé slamming into her, and then they tilted the other way as the cart started turning in the other direction. The hooting from the aetós behind her and ahead of her rose to a higher level, echoing eerily in the tunnels. She was going to lose her lunch, she knew it.

"Ahoy, gates! By the grace of Niall, we have arrived in good order!" Trevin shouted ahead. Jenn blinked. What had happened? The carts had been diving downward at an impossible descent rate and she remembered thinking she was going to lose it, and now suddenly they were exiting. She was leaning closely against Gastropé, his arm around her holding her tight.

In shock, Jenn took a deep breath as they entered the light. She could feel fresh, cold mountain air in her lungs as they emerged from the tunnel, the carts veering hard to the left as they exited. What had happened? Why was she in Gastropé's arms?

"Well, what do you know? That was only ten minutes!" Maelen stated.

Jenn sat up quickly, looking back to see the seer peering at a pocket chronometer.

"You mean ten hours!" groaned Gastropé, removing his arm from around Jenn, but saying nothing to her.

Elrose laughed. "I have to admit, that was one of the longest ten minutes of my life!"

Several aetós laughed loudly behind them. "If you thought that was an experience, just wait for the Fierdal bridge! Treyfoêr exclaimed. "Grounders never enjoy that!"

"Joy." Gastropé quipped sarcastically.

The carts came to a halt near a large, flat area on the side of the mountain. There was a wagon there, which was equipped with poles out the front and rear, as if to be pulled and pushed by people. On the wagon were the multiple chests and trunks belonging to Elrose. Beyond the cart at the end of a path was a large frame with what appeared to be an unbelievably large crystal lens. It had to be fourteen feet in diameter, if not more. The path ended in a small bridge leading up to the middle of it.

"Out we go!" Trevin called. "Fierd's approaching; we need to move!"

Jenn slid to the left to exit, Gastropé sliding along behind her to exit on the same side. He still hadn't said anything about her being in his arms. As she stepped down to the ground, a wave of dizziness swept over her and she nearly collapsed. She grabbed the side of the cart for support, and Gastropé also reached to steady her.

Trevin nodded. "The ride does have a tendency to throw off one's balance, but you will be fine in a bit."

The others also seemed wobbly as they unloaded their gear. "Everyone load your gear up. Each of you will be accompanied by an aetóên on the bridge to help you keep your balance. The remaining aetós will bring the wagon with the equipment. Everyone line up side by side!"

Danfaêr came up beside her. "I think you're going to want to hold my hand until you get used to the bridge," he stated. Jenn was once again caught up in his incredible scent and magnificent torso in the predawn light. She could only nod. Goddess, these beings were gorgeous, Jenn thought to herself.

The group took their positions: Trevin was at the gate to the bridge, preparing to open it, Hethfar just behind her. Elrose and his aetóên companion were next, followed by Gastropé and Treyfoêr, and then Jenn and Danfaêr. Maelen and his companion were behind them, and last came the wagon.

Trevin began chanting and arranging crystals on a pedestal beside the giant lens. The wind direction was such that Jenn could not make out the words of the incantation. Probably just as well; she was not much with enchantment. Or was this pyromancy? It was a Fierdal bridge, and Fierd was by definition the source of fire. Or with the crystals, was it some form of runic magic? She had read once of something called crystal magic, but she did not know anything about it. Anyway, it seemed better to speculate on this rather than how she had gotten in Gastropé's arms.

While she was thinking about this, Fierd rose above the horizon and the lens lit up like a thousand candles, showering a rainbow of colors around them.

"Time to go!" Trevin shouted and walked forward right through the lens! Jenn blinked and realized that there was no longer a lens; there was instead a bridge of fierdshine on the other side of the portal.

Hethfar followed her and Treyfoêr started forward, gently pulling Gastropé with him. As they moved forward, Danfaêr started pulling Jenn forward as well. As Gastropé stepped through the portal, Jenn heard him curse and halt briefly, but Treyfoêr dragged him forward saying, "You really don't want to stop and look down. Trust me; this is disconcerting even for the aetós."

"I will agree." Danfaêr looked down and smiled at Jenn. "Just look forward and concentrate on following those in front of us." They stepped through and Jenn was hit with the worst case of vertigo she had ever experienced. There was nothing below her feet and a one-league drop other than sparkling, shifting rays of light.

It was very disconcerting. She had no idea what light rays were supposed to look like, but what was below her feet looked like the bright streaks of light you saw when looking at Fierd through squinted eyes. It was insanely dizzying. "Look forward. It gets worse as you walk," Jenn heard Danfaêr say.

Holy mother goddess! Did it ever! With every step she took, the ground far below her seemed to telescope and stretch. "What the Abyss?" Jenn gasped.

"Every stride on the Fierdal Bridge covers a league. It's a very fast way of traveling, but it's also very disturbing." Jenn decided to stop fighting the advice she had been given and she focused on Gastropé ahead of her, locking her gaze only on him. As she did, she realized that he was walking rather rigidly, his sight apparently locked on Elrose ahead of him.

They had been on the bridge for maybe two dozen strides when she suddenly heard Trevin caterwauling from the front: "We're walking on fierdshine—whoa oh! Walking on fierdshine—and don't it feel good!" No, Jenn decided, Trevin's off-key singing did not feel good! She hoped the woman did not use that voice to try and enchant people! Fortunately, the enchantress stopped singing and laughed as she picked up her stride, swinging her arms briskly as she marched along the bridge.

"This, my friends, must be the manner in which the gods of old used to tread the lands of men!" Trevin shouted over her shoulder at the rest of the party. "Sure, teleportation is quicker if you know where you are going, but this is far more liberating and exciting!"

Jenn closed her eyes for a bit to allow Danfaêr to lead her. She was nearing her limits on keeping her breakfast from leaving. And she had thought the cart ride was stomach wrenching; she'd had no idea what was to come.

They continued to march for several minutes or more—Jenn had lost track of time—and she simply let Danfaêr lead her. After some time she finally opened her eyes to see they had left the mountains and were striding over a huge forest that stretched for leagues in each direction. She had not realized with her eyes closed, but they were actually heading downward towards the ground at this point. It probably was not three or four minutes before she saw a large glade in the middle of the forest that the bridge seemed to be leading to.

Down they marched at a dizzying pace, and suddenly they were stepping through another lens portal and into the glade itself. Jenn was not sure she had ever felt anything as wonderful as the soft dirt and grass beneath her boots as she stepped into the glade. The light from the bridge was still quite dazzling in the glade and it took her eyes a few minutes to realize that they were surrounded by naked, overly endowed women and short, brown, hairy wingless demons!

Chapter 90

Vaselle stepped back from the pentagram he had constructed in the dirt in the clearing outside the city. He was now ready to summon Estrebrius. He had to admit to being nervous. After he had sent his demon on the quest to find the super-demon, he had had second thoughts. It was really rather ridiculous to think that his little demon would be able to find and contact such a powerful force of evil. Moreover, if somehow Estrebrius ever did, the demon would surely slaughter his poor servant. It was just stupid and selfish of him. He had put at risk his good and faithful demon.

Estrebrius had served him faithfully with no tricks or games for the last few years; he had also been a great companion around the lab. He really hoped he had not sent the poor fiend to his death. That was probably the main reason for his anxiety this morning. Being honest, he had a good idea how many demons there were and what a big place the Abyss was, and there was no realistic way Estrebrius could have found the demon, nor would it have agreed to meet him. Yet he could not resist a nagging guilt that he might have seen the last of his faithful demon.

He shook his head and began the summoning. It was his standard summoning spell for Estrebrius. He probably should use something stronger in the unlikely event that Estrebrius had found the demon lord; however, Vaselle didn't think he knew anything powerful enough to protect him from a demon capable of defeating a Knight Rampant of Tiernon and possessing hundreds of Rod members and priests. In addition, such bindings would be antithetical to his proposal in the first place.

He finished the summons and waited for Estrebrius to appear. His stomach twisted slightly, as it seemed to be taking the demon an unusually long time to appear. Finally the fire began to glow very brightly, higher and higher, and the familiar form of Estrebrius appeared.

"Master, I have come at your summons." Estrebrius bowed.

"Thank goodness! I was a bit worried. I realized after I sent you on your task that it was unrealistic of me to expect you to succeed, and I was putting you at great risk. I'm so sorry." Vaselle shook his head in apology.

Estrebrius coughed, and Vaselle looked at him oddly. "Well, I have to admit, I agreed with that assessment when you sent me off, but, well… I've had some luck."

"Luck?" Vaselle asked, shocked. "You've found out something about the demon lord? A trail to follow?"

"Uhm, well, a bit more than that, master." Estrebrius grinned.

Suddenly Vaselle could feel a disturbance in his spell and the fire that had summoned Estrebrius suddenly burst higher, rising far over the short demon's head. The small brazier fire was now a giant bonfire and Vaselle could feel the link expanding on its own. It should not do that—that was not possible! There wasn't fuel for a fire that big!

"To your left, Estrebrius," a thunderous voice ordered from the fire. Vaselle felt his stomach drop. Estrebrius stepped to his left and a monstrously huge, gigantic hoof came through fire. Vaselle backed up hurriedly. A huge, scaly digitigrade leg followed the hoof, and then the largest set of male genitalia Vaselle had ever seen! The testicles were nearly the size of his own skull ; the male member a one-eyed serpent of terror! Vaselle made a croaking noise and fell to his knees, unable even to think.

Next he saw individual abdominal muscles larger than his entire abdominal region, clawed hands capable of engulfing his entire body, forearms larger than his thighs, and biceps and triceps the size of his waist. Vaselle was simultaneously in awe and terror. He gasped as huge slabs of pectoral muscle came through the flames, with giant spiked nipples on giant aureoles.

And then the maw… the fangs, the jaws of death, above which were fiercely penetrating black eyes that were already staring into the depths of his soul to render and encompass his entire being. Humongous ebony horns rose above those life-stealing eyes, suitable for disemboweling him with a simple head shake of "no."

Vaselle was hyperventilating by the time the entire magnificent demon emerged from the flames in its most awe-inspiring, dark glory. He was in the presence of a god among demons! Clearly a demon prince; Vaselle was sure of this. Coming to his senses somewhat, he prostrated himself before the one he had inadvertently called into this glade.

"Wizard!" The voice of Lassalle's personal god thundered. "Your servant claims you have a proposition for me?"

"My... aghhk!" Vaselle choked on the saliva swarming down his throat in his terror. "Master, Lord High Prince of the Abyss! Forgive this foolish mortal's temerity! It is not so much a proposition as an offer, a gift!"

There was silence for a moment and Vaselle feared he had angered the mighty demon.

"A gift?" The demon lord sounded puzzled, or maybe it was intrigued? Could it be?

"Yes, My Lord. The only gift I have worthy of your eminence!" Vaselle wailed. He was nearing panic at this point.

"And what would that be?" the demon asked.

"My Lord, as insignificant as it is, as unworthy as it is, I humbly offer you my immortal soul and would beg to be your agent in this world, to be taken and possessed by you, to do your bidding in Astlan! To be your slave, your puppet, your plaything, your devoted sycophant!"

There was complete silence. Vaselle felt his bowels begin to loosen. Had he angered the demon? Was he about to be rendered limb from limb in ecstatic agony and suffering?

After what seemed to be an eternity, he dared to glance up towards his prospective master to see the demon lord peering down at him, apparently lost in thought. He was not sure.

"Uhm, yes, well, I need to think about this," the demon lord stated. "I'll get back to you." He suddenly backed up into the flames, disappearing.

Estrebrius was staring at Vaselle in shock.

"Estrebrius, get your butt through the gateway!" A new voice hollered through the flames. Was the demon's entourage on the other side of the gateway?

Estrebrius shook his head and hurriedly entered the flames, disappearing into the nether regions. The flames then suddenly shrank down to nothing, leaving only a few burning embers and finally only cold ash. Birds chirped in the forest around him as if nothing had happened. Vaselle planted his face in the grass and wept with a mixture of fear, relief and frustration.

~

"Thank you for joining me for breakfast, Archimage," Damien said, gesturing to a seat at his patio breakfast table. Damien's third-year apprentice, Gemma, had shown the Archimage of Turelane to the patio where Damien was waiting for him.

As the archimage sat, Damien sat as well. "Well, thank you for this most unexpected invitation, Inquisitor." His use of Damien's alternate title indicated that he knew full well why he'd been invited for breakfast. Randolf looked around the balcony. " I do not believe I have ever been to your quarters before. What a magnificent view of the city!"

"Thank you. To be fully honest, the fact that I had no idea that you had an archdemon in your employ may have contributed to my tardiness in entertaining you," Damien said drily.

Randolf chuckled softly. "Surely you flatter me, Inquisitor. I myself had no idea I had an archdemon as an employee. While I appreciate the thought that I might be capable of commanding the service of an archdemon, I fear that, assuming Exador actually *is* an archdemon, I am but a dupe of his; as is, of course, the Council for admitting him as a member."

"Obviously, although was it not you who recommended him?" Damien smiled and lifted a cup of tea to his lips.

Randolf chuckled again. "Not precisely. As I recall, this was about ten years before your tenure began and Lenamare was nominated, and given their rather high-pressure rivalry, it was almost obligatory that Exador also be nominated. There were many on the Council who thought it best to elevate both of them at the same time," Randolf reminisced as he poured himself a cup of tea.

Damien nodded in concession. "Yes, I can certainly understand that logic." He set his tea down and took a bite of sweet cake before continuing. "Yet, two years later you chose Exador to be Mage of Turelane over Lenamare. No thought of having co-mages?"

Randolf sighed. "It was a difficult choice. As we've seen, Lenamare is a truly exceptional wizard. However, there is no legal precedent for co-mages, and there is historical precedent for an Exador holding the title."

"Your great-grandfather, I believe, created the title for him?" Damien enquired.

Randolf shrugged. "Well, this was not that long after the rather destructive events in Abancia. He felt that a solid alliance with the Exadors would be advantageous to Turelane."

"Yes, that seems reasonable, given that it was that Exador's father who toppled Abancia," Damien noted taking another sip of tea.

"Exactly."

"Or perhaps the same Exador, if he is an archdemon?" Damien asked.

Randolf nodded in acceptance of Damien's point. "Of course, a rather convoluted ruse, since I can assure you that according to my own observance of the current Exador, and the accounts of others whom I trust, he does age and die, and he does produce heirs to succeed him."

"Is it true," Damien asked, setting his cup down, "that the Lady Exadors have particularly hard labors?"

Randolf chuckled. "I know the rumors—that they all mysteriously die in childbirth—but that's not actually true." He smiled. "At least not every time. It has happened that several of them have become pregnant quickly after marriage and then died in childbirth, and several others died within months due to delayed effects, vapors or something. However, the current Exador's mother was alive until he was five years old."

"So these men simply have a predisposition for wives with poor constitutions?" Damien asked.

"It would seem so; further, they all come from the other side of Norelon, from distant lands. Never from local nobility. To be perfectly candid, if I had a daughter, I would not marry her to Exador."

"Even though he's been your most trusted advisor?" Damien asked curiously.

"Even so." Randolf took a long drink of tea.

"Well, fortunately, you have a son , yes?" Damien asked.

Randolf shrugged. "I have an heir with my wife, Lady Magret, and I have a bastard with an old friend of mine. I have acknowledged both."

Damien nodded. "Ardashir, who is eleven, and Darien, who is seven."

Randolf smiled. "Exactly."

"I am unclear as to what your position is on Exador. Do you believe he is an archdemon?" Damien asked.

"I have known the man for a very long time, and dealt with him quite closely. I assure you, he has never manifested any demonic traits that I can detect. I have, in fact, seen him conjure and control demons of multiple orders. By every measure listed in the Council library that I have ever tested, he is not a demon. None of the normal traits apply. That being said, the number of demons in the palace would be very hard for a wizard of even Exador's caliber to control. Further, this Ramses fellow is quite an anomaly. I know no more of him than you. As to the woman, I again have no idea."

"Well." Damien sat back, slightly surprised. That was the clearest answer he had ever heard from the Archimage of Turelane. "That was very…"

"Direct?" Randolf said with a smile.

"My fellow councilor," Randolf continued, "I want to assure you that whatever past relationships between Turelane, the Council, Exador and myself have been, I want to understand what is going on as much as anyone on the Council, and even more so. If Exador is an archdemon, it paints a very different picture of the history of both Turelane and Abancia."

Damien nodded. "I understand. It would help explain a lot of things in your land's past."

"Exactly, and if he is not an archdemon, and/or he manages to clear his name, I'm going to have to continue working with him, as will my people."

"The way you phrase that implies that clearing his name is not the same as not being an archdemon," Damien observed.

"Well, if that's how you choose to interpret my words, then so be it. However, in such case, it would be no different from the previous status quo, before the expulsion. He is a powerful influence in the region, archdemon or not, as he and his family have been for a very long time."

~

Bess purred and rolled over to stroke Exador's chest hair as the faux light of the Court's simulated dawn streamed through the bedroom's floor-to-ceiling window. "So, as of last night Lenamare's wards were still around Freehold. This, naturally—and very inconveniently—protects the book, as well as causing the very sudden disappearance of one of the councilors in the middle of a siege."

Exador snorted. "Yes, inconvenient would be the correct word." He chuckled as he stared thoughtfully at the ceiling. "I spent a good amount of time venting my frustration yesterday."

"Hmm," Bess mused. "I assume someone, or ones, found that unpleasant."

Exador laughed aloud at this, tilting his head up from the pillow to give her a gentle kiss. "Indeed. Unfortunately, nearly everyone here in the Abyss is a demon and for them, fireballs, lightning bolts and explosions are everyday occurrences. Anyway, they all regenerate." He shook his head in half-mock sorrow. "It really takes the fun out of venting one's wrath if there is no permanent destruction or loss of life."

Bess grinned. "So is this why you've spent the last millennia or two living in Astlan? I've always thought it was such a strange choice of venue." She made a mock shudder. "The climate there is so cold. The average temperature is less than a third that of boiling water."

He gave her a gentle, mocking expression. "Says the woman who ups the power to my runic coolers every time she comes here."

Bess laughed softly and lay back on the pillow. "What I love is the change in temperatures, from hot to cold and then back. It causes goose bumps, which is very erotically pleasurable in my fur."

"Ehh." Exador grimaced. "I hate that feeling of hair standing on end."

"Yes," she retorted, "but you are not a cat!"

"True."

Bess frowned slightly for a moment. "But back to what we were discussing. How will you explain your disappearance to the Council? Are you going to tell them you were trapped by demon-caused debris in one of the lower chambers?" Bess shook her head. "But then, why wouldn't you have just teleported out?"

Exador chuckled. "Yes, covering one's tracks gets tricky at times; however, for that I have Randolf."

"Randolf?" Bess asked, trying to remember who Randolf was.

"The Archimage of Turelane. If ever there was a more pusillanimous sycophant, I have never met them in my thousands of years of life. He will loyally cover for me. He'll make up an excuse about my being called away on business in Turelane or something similar."

"You have an archimage as fawning sycophant? That's rather impressive," Bess murmured, impressed.

Exador snorted. "Not as much as you might think. Remember, archimage is a title for a ruler; it is not an indication of mage ability. Not for over a thousand years. Randolf is completely inept as a mage. He's lucky to keep a mage light following him."

"So he's more of a bureaucrat for you then? Administering things?"

Exador shrugged again. "One might think, but he outsources a lot of his governing duties to others. He mainly runs errands for me with the Council and others I don't care to deal with." Exador shrugged. "And spends hours locked in his room with his catamite." He rolled his eyes.

Bess gestured to themselves in the bed. "I don't think you're in a position to criticize people for spending time in bed with a lover."

Exador laughed, suddenly moving on top of her. "You are correct, so let's make me an even bigger hypocrite!"

~

"Has your master lost his marbles?" Tom asked Estrebrius, raising his hands over his head in disbelief. The gateway had just snapped shut as Tom turned to face the little demon, causing a big change in the light level of the room. Estrebrius blinked.

"I, uh—I have no idea." Estrebrius shook his head, completely befuddled and shocked.

"So you had no idea of his proposal?" Antefalken asked.

"No. I mean, obviously he was going to bargain for something, but I figured it would be a fixed transaction of some sort, not a full-scale plunge into insanity!" Estrebrius began pacing back and forth, trying to understand what his accursed master was thinking of.

"Every time I think these wizards can't get any crazier, they prove they can!" Tom shook his head and took his seat. "He basically wants to be a demon slave? Like the reverse of the normal relationship?" Tom looked between Boggy and Antefalken. Tizzy was busy puffing on his pipe, strangely quiet. "So he's just unhinged then?"

Antefalken shrugged. "Not necessarily; it's been known to happen."

"You mean it's a real thing?" Tom asked.

"Such wizards are called warlocks. Actually, they do not have to be wizards. About any mana user can become a warlock. I suppose anyone could."

"Why would someone subject themselves to the whims of a demon? We are evil and untrustworthy, and all that other bullshit!" Tom waved his forearms in circles in frustration.

"Well, yes. But as you know, it is complex. I am not sure that all do it willingly. There are many legends of wizards being overpowered by demons and forced into slavery. I think that is the more likely scenario. However, there have been tales told of those who seek out demon lords for this purpose."

"Why would anyone do that?" Rupert asked.

" 'Cause they're daft!" Boggy harrumphed.

Antefalken shrugged and raised his eyebrows in consideration of Boggy's point. "I can't completely disagree; however, there are advantages for both parties."

"Like what?" Rupert asked as Tom nodded in agreement.

"Well, obviously the demon gets an agent—a spy in the mortal realms. One who can summon its master whenever the master desires." Tom adjusted his head in thought at that. Given the past few weeks, that could be useful. He had used his friends in much the same way —to both their benefit.

"The demon master can also easily possess the warlock and work through him or her," Antefalken continued.

"Yeah, but if I'm in Astlan, I'll just shift to my human form and go around that way." Tom shrugged, not impressed.

"But can you be in two places at once, as needed?" Antefalken retorted.

Tom twisted his mouth, implicitly admitting that Antefalken had a point.

"So what's the warlock get?" Rupert asked.

"Protection," Antefalken replied, "and power. Or at a minimum, the appearance of power."

Tom gestured for Antefalken to continue.

"Well, the demon master will typically protect his warlocks in most cases. Perhaps not all; it depends on the demon. Orcus apparently wasn't very good at that." Antefalken made an unpleasant grimace.

"Orcus?" Boggy asked. "He was real?"

"Very much so." Antefalken caught Tom's and Rupert's puzzled glances. Tom noted that Talarius suddenly seemed much more interested; he had gotten very still.

"At some point, I could play the Balladae Orcusae for you, but it takes a bit over thirty-four hours. So I'll just give you a quick overview." Antefalken sighed, apparently trying to summarize in his mind. "About four thousand years ago, the demon prince Orcus established a cadre of warlocks in Etterdam, who in turn raised a giant army of evil."

"Etterdam?" Rupert asked.

"It's another world that was frequently visited by Astlanians. Fairly similar, perhaps identical laws of magic." Antefalken gestured slightly dismissively. "It's still there, but people in Eton and Norelon don't travel there much. I think some others do, maybe the Natoorians? Anyway, this is all somewhat ancillary to the point I was trying to make."

"Why did he raise this big army?" Tom asked.

Antefalken shrugged. "The ballads don't go into that. It's assumed—or I and everyone I know assumes—he wanted to take over Etterdam and make it a playground for his people. Maybe he wanted an unending supply of virgins. It's not really important." He began to walk back and forth as he spoke. "According to the ballad, Orcus raised a great army, in fact. The army was led by the Seven Great Warlocks of Despair. In any event, it was your typical dark horde: wizards, lesser warlocks, necromancers, undead of all sorts. Lots of jötnar: orcs, ogres, giants, you know the type. And naturally, the Dok Sidhe joined in, as did all the typical unsavory types you'd expect to be involved in an 'Army of Darkness.' "

"I think they must get package deals," Tizzy interjected suddenly.

Antefalken stopped and looked at Tizzy in puzzlement.

"Well, they're always the same. You've seen one Army of Darkness, you've seen them all. It's just who you put at the top: warlocks, Dark Queen, Eternal Emperor, Necromancer of the Night, etcetera." Tizzy waved his pipe and suddenly went silent again.

Antefalken turned his head slowly back to the rest of the cave's occupants. "So... as I was saying, Orcus had a great unstoppable army that swept through the land—"

"Until a reluctant band of young heroes rose to the occasion?" Tom asked suddenly with a smile.

"What?" Antefalken gestured. "Are you trying to channel Tizzy?"

"Well, they always are," Tizzy stated.

"Always are what?" Rupert asked.

"Reluctant, innocent, inexperienced heroes." Tizzy shrugged. "They always are in the bard's tales. They overcome a bunch of obstacles and defeat the unstoppable evil that people with ten times the power and experience had been unable to defeat."

Antefalken sighed in exasperation.

"Except!" Tizzy suddenly moved forward, raising his pipe dramatically. "In the real world, they usually end up on a spit or at the bottom of a deep pit!"

"Or corrupted," Boggy observed.

Tizzy twisted and pointed a finger at Boggy. "Right you are, partner! I forgot that one. Yeah, most of these folks can be bought off with promises of power, eternal life, and of course, virgins!"

"Yeah, and then they accept the offer, relinquish their values, turn on their former allies, and in the end get totally screwed by the Supreme Evil!" Estrebrius clapped his hands and made jumping motions.

Antefalken rubbed the base of his horns. "I've been too long in Astlan; I forget what crappy audiences demons are!"

"So is that what happened?" Tom asked.

Antefalken shifted his eyes to look up at Tom under his brows. "To avoid the peanut gallery, that was basically where I was going. He promised his warlocks, both the seven and the lesser ones, great power, but when the chips were down, he sacrificed them in a heartbeat. So, yes, he would protect them up to a point, but he was quick to dispose of them when their usefulness was over."

"So do you know Orcus?" Rupert asked.

Antefalken chuckled. "No. Not to spoil the Balladae, but Orcus dies at the end..."

"At the HAND OF TIERNON!" Talarius shouted triumphantly from the back of the cave. Everyone jumped.

Antefalken chuckled at how startled they all were by the outburst and the knight's enthusiasm. "At a hand of Tiernon, one of his senior archons," the bard admitted.

"The Holy Sentir Fallon! The Hand of Tiernon in Etterdam!" Talarius added, nodding proudly.

Antefalken smiled. "He is correct. The high priests of Tiernon in Etterdam were getting desperate after years of war, and in an act of desperation, somehow managed to summon a supreme archon onto Etterdam. Then, well... things got very bloody. No one alive today, that I'm aware of, knows all the actual details, but after about four hours of battle in the Balladae, Sentir Fallon slays Orcus permanently."

"The End!" Talarius was shaking a mailed fist in triumph. "As always, the forces of Goodness and Light prevailed!"

"Just a second. This Sentir guy, the archon you called him, is he one of these avatars of Tiernon you were talking about?" Tom asked. Antefalken nodded. "The ones you said were likely to show up in Astlan to investigate?"

Antefalken gave Tom a worried grin. "If it makes you feel any better, I'm sure no one on the level of a Supreme Archon, like the legendary Sentir Fallon in the Balladae, will have any interest in this."

~

"Thank you, lad!" Hilda beamed at Danyel as he handed her a Bloody Tatania. It was still breakfast time, much too early for wine, but a Bloody Tatania was perfect. Tomato juice, hot peppers and spices, and Corswyn Extra Dry 7 Times Distilled Vadter along with a skewer of celery, cheese and sausage. That and a fresh-baked hard biscuit ring with spread. Who said you could not enjoy life in the boonies?

Of course, she had always loved Bloody Tatanias. Particularly when she had been alive. Admittedly, in her afterlife, meeting the drink's namesake saint and learning firsthand of her grisly martyrdom and thus the source of the drink's name, had put her off them for a few decades. Really, poor girl—what a ghastly way to go. Hilda shuddered at the thought.

The important thing was to start collecting her wits, now that she could think. Her homemade relic was working fantastically, if she did say so herself. It was such a relief. She was quite pleased with her success with it.

Unfortunately, her link meeting with Moradel, Sentir Fallon and Supreme Archon Beragamos had been of very poor quality, as well quite taxing and unsatisfying, thanks to those stupid wards.

She had managed to let them know that she was in the city, had made contact with Trisfelt, and had interviewed several people with direct knowledge of the greater greater demon, and would be interviewing others over the next couple of days. The key point she had wanted to get across, and she felt she had, was the nature of those wards and how detrimental they were to her, and likely far more so to archons.

They had all agreed that she would try to get out of the city for their meetings if she could. The links from inside the city were just too much of a pain. Once outside, she could physically go to Tierhallon, which would make things far simpler. However, of course, there were days where that might not be possible without blowing her cover, so they agreed not to assume the worst if she missed a day. No need for a Tierhalloc Invasion on her behalf! She chuckled to herself.

"So"—Hilda handed the plate of biscuit rings to Danyel as he sat down at the table with her—"with all that damage in the palace, I am thinking that as a healer and responsible citizen of Freehold, we should go volunteer to help with any remaining wounded. Wizards are not noted for being great healers. We can be of assistance and can insinuate ourselves more into the life of the palace and the Council to gather more information."

"As you advise, Your Holiness!" Danyel smiled at her as he reached for the orange juice.

"You don't need to call me that. I'm just Hilda here in our rooms." She shook her head and smiled. "If you wish, among the wizards you may call me mistress, since you are pretending to be my valet."

~

Tom sat back in his chair as they all paused for a bit. They had spent the last who knew how long discussing the insane wizard's proposal. Oddly, Talarius seemed to be feeling better, or at least slightly more talkative after discussing Orcus and Etterdam. He supposed that hearing demons admit to the defeat of one of their own at the hand of one of his own gave him more self-confidence. It was as if the knight had needed that.

Talarius, naturally, felt that Vaselle deserved to burn in the Abyss for even thinking of offering himself to a demon as a slave. Such a bargain was obviously unholy, a sin and abomination, thus requiring the person committing it to be sentenced to eternal damnation. Perversely, Tom thought, the knight did not seem to understand that that was exactly what Vaselle was asking for. The wizard had just volunteered his eternal soul to a demon, and for nothing in return. That seemed very odd.

Boggy, of course, was all for it. He loved the idea of turnabout, and Tom was sure he would love to tell other demons that he was friends with someone who had a warlock. Boggy seemed to be quite the gossip. Estrebrius was mainly pacing, worried about his master's mental state. Tizzy was not saying much, just smoking on his pipe. Rupert was excited by the idea. He was a kid, after all; he probably thought it would be cool and in fact, had probably started plotting how to get one of his own. Admittedly, if Tom had been reading this in a book or playing a video game, he would have wanted to see the protagonist get himself a wizard slave. Seriously, who would not want a wizard slave?

It was just that things were a little more complex in reality, even as insane as it currently was. Vaselle was a real person, with hopes, dreams and feelings. Taking such a person and 'enslaving' him just seemed extremely wrong. In addition, the whole possession thing that Vaselle seemed to want was not something Tom felt that comfortable with. He had not spent a whole lot of time reliving or rethinking his experience on the battlefield. But when he did, it had all just been rather uncomfortable, too intimate. During the battle, if he had had the time or desire, he could have easily accessed those people's memories, their thoughts and feelings. He had felt their fear, their adrenaline; he had even harnessed it and redirected it. Redirected the fear and hatred from himself to Talarius.

Such power was frightening. Tom had to admit that that was a big part of it. When he was possessing those men, he had felt rather splintered. He felt like he was a whole bunch of different people at the same time. He was not really himself, but more of an amalgam or something. He could not really describe it to himself in words. Nevertheless, it had been unsettling. Even as the subject of the possession lost themselves to the possessor, so the possessor lost a part of themselves. More precisely, Tom corrected himself, they opened themselves to the possessed, let the possessed in and made the possessed part of themselves.

The air in the cave suddenly shifted slightly and there was a loud *thunk* as Reggie suddenly appeared and fell to his knees. "Holy fucking fuck!" the Incubus gasped.

Boggy rushed over to give Reggie a hand up. "Are you all right, lad? Were you beaten mercilessly by your master?"

Reggie chuckled with what seemed a large dose of irony. "Mistress. And well, yeah, there was a bit of whipping, but not the bad kind."

"What kind of whipping is not the bad kind?" Rupert asked.

"The sexy kind." Reggie shook his head as he stood up. Tom got up from his chair and offered it to Reggie. "I have never, ever dreamed of having that much sex in that short a time!"

"Sex?" Rupert asked, shocked.

"Shit man, the woman was insatiable. We were going at it continuously from the moment I got there, and I had to have shot my load thirty to forty times. I cannot believe it! I'm exhausted."

"Sounds like hell," Tizzy commented drily.

"It sort of was." Reggie nodded. Antefalken chuckled.

"Seriously!" Boggy yelled. "Why can't I get an accursed mistress like this? It simply is not fair!" The demon stormed around the room furiously, presumably for dramatic effect. "One bloody summons and he gets his brains screwed silly! It simply is not just!"

Talarius was shaking his head. "A wizardess summoned a demon to use as a sex toy? Clearly, Astlan has fallen into the hands of sin and debauchery. Wizards are a pox on humanity!"

"Okay, finally! That's something we can agree on!" Tizzy smiled and tried to pat the knight on the shoulder, but Talarius dodged out of the way, frowning through his visor. Tizzy just shook his head in mild annoyance. "Just trying to be nice! See what it gets me?" He took a big puff of his pipe.

Estrebrius was frowning as well. "It really does not seem fair. I hope she's ugly."

Reggie chuckled. "Not at all. My chocolate mistress is gorgeous with junk in all the right places . She is totally fine!"

"Yeah, yeah, yeah… like huckleberry wine. Yes, we get it. You got yourself a hot accursed mistress who tortures you with endless sex. Boo hoo!" Boggy said, harrumphing and crossing his arms in front of him.

Antefalken chuckled. "Well, actually, the prolonged bonking is actually part of the bonding process for an incubus. So she was not doing it just for pleasure; it was also binding Reggie much closer to his mistress. Am I not right, Reggie?"

"Uhm, yeah," Reggie stuttered, nearly forgetting that Antefalken did not realize he and Tom were recent arrivals in the Abyss. Tom nodded at him in approval. He still needed to explain things better to Reggie so he did not screw anything up. The lies were starting to get tricky; he was afraid they were only going to get worse.

[Appendix: Druids and Shamans]

Chapter 91

"Holy…" Gastropé breathed out, staring at the naked women surrounding them. Jenn closed her eyes tightly as they accidentally drifted across the hairy crotch of one of the brown, wingless demons. Satyrs—she knew they were satyrs, she had read about them and Trisfelt had told her stories about his travels among them—but they looked so much like wingless demons!

"So!" Trevin said loudly, drawing the group's attention back to her. Opening her eyes, she noted that even Maelen was forcing his gaze to return to Trevin from the nymphs. "Welcome to the Grove!" A cheer rose up, followed by shouts of welcome and cheers from the assembled forest dwellers. Jenn nodded politely and tried very hard not to look at all the naked individuals.

"We will be spending the day here resting up, bathing and getting ready for launch shortly after fierdrise tomorrow. It's timed with first tide, interestingly enough." Trevin chuckled. "So I'm afraid that means we'll be taking the skiffs at a very early hour, or perhaps very late hour depending on your nocturnal plans!" She winked at Maelen.

"On that note"—here she looked each of the outsiders in the eyes—"you may be aware that people here are extremely friendly, and even more curious. They love new experiences, new friends, etcetera. Thus you are all likely to receive invitations for fun and games." Cheers rose from the local denizens. "Do not feel pressured into accepting; a polite 'no thanks' will always be respected, if grudgingly by some." She glared at an older satyr standing nearby, who suddenly looked at the ground.

"But if you do accept, you need not fear the normal consequences." Trevin smiled brightly. "Gentlemen, in case you were not aware, nymphs and dryads only get pregnant when they desire it, and the other ladies have their own precautions."

Trevin smiled at Jenn, looking directly at her. "And while, yes, it is true that satyrs can breed with nearly every living species everywhere, it generally takes quite a bit of effort to prepare the host." She paused for a moment as if thinking. "Typically for a human female, you'd need to have intercourse at least two dozen, if not three dozen times. So do not worry about a few rounds! Given the time we have, I doubt there'll be time for more than a dozen attempts." She smiled at Jenn, who found herself blushing furiously and somewhat angrily.

Trevin turned and smiled even wider at Gastropé. "It takes almost twice as much to prepare a male host, so feel free to have at it!" Gastropé blanched and adjusted his turban nervously. Trevin spun. "I have to go make a few arrangements. Allow the welcome committee to show you to a breakfast buffet and some bathing ponds so you can freshen up. We shall reconvene at lunch!" The enchantress waved and strode off quickly, disappearing into the throng of nymphs and satyrs.

Barabus entered the command tent where Iskerus was eating a late breakfast, presumably having tried to get a little sleep in himself. "Rested?" Barabus asked the Arch-Diocate.

"No," Iskerus said rather irately—unusual for him. "Ruiden woke me this morning with a demand to watch the balling."

"He was there! What does he need the balling for?" Barabus asked, puzzled.

"I have no idea. I did not ask. I am running at near capacity. I have been running back and forth between Oorstemoth and High Chamberlain Mericas in Justicia. I have finally gotten him to send church lawyers to work directly with these crazy people. Then, trying to provide hope and guidance to those who have been shaken, not to mention worrying myself as to why no Host has appeared to interrogate us as to this rather huge screw-up..." Iskerus was definitely looking frayed.

Iskerus looked at Barabus. "I need you to deal with the dagger and maybe work on some recommendations as to what to do with the priests who were possessed, along the lines of what you are doing for Rod members."

Barabus nodded. "Not a problem."

A knock came on the tent pole.

"Yes?" Barabus said, turning to the doorway.

"Sirs?" A Rod member stuck his head in. "I have the High Chaplain of Freehold here, along with another... gentleman."

Iskerus sighed and closed his eyes for a moment. "Very well, show them in."

The Rod member held the tent flap aside and in came the High Chaplain of Freehold, a man whose name Barabus could not recall. They had never met, but he had been told the man's name in a briefing. Following the high chaplain was another man, a beggar—a very rank and gamy smelling beggar. Barabus backed up; the beggar appeared to be more a collection of festering wounds than a man.

The high chaplain bowed deeply to Iskerus and said, "Your Holiness."

Iskerus nodded and gestured for him to arise.

"How may I help you, Uripes? Can I get a healer for your friend?" Iskerus asked.

The beggar seemed to take offense at this suggestion but before he could say anything, the high chaplain put a calming hand on the man's forearm, which was luckily clothed in a very dirty robe.

"Actually, Your Holiness, I am afraid that is precisely the problem. This is Delapodos, our city's beggar meister." Iskerus nodded in greeting to the man. "It seems a high priestess of yours has been roaming the city healing beggars and depriving them of their livelihoods."

"I would highly doubt that. The city is still under wards and I have not given permission to any of our people to enter it," Iskerus said.

"Well, someone healed Rathbert up. Cured his blindness, got rid of his snotlung, all his boils and various other ailments, and claimed to do it in the name of Tiernon!" The beggar meister retorted angrily.

Barabus frowned. "Exactly how long did he lie there for this healer to do all of this? Could he not have escaped?"

Delapados looked at him suspiciously. "She just grabbed him while he stood there. It took but a few moments and he was all healed! He had no time to run; she was holding his hands mighty tight!"

"He was fully blind? Had snotlung, boils like your own?" Iskerus paused and Delapodos nodded. "And she cured all of this within moments from simply grasping his hands?"

"That's what I said," the beggar meister retorted, apparently angry that they did not seem to believe him.

Iskerus glanced at Barabus, who shrugged. "Well, I thank you both for reporting this! None of our people were authorized to be in the city; however, we shall certainly investigate."

"What about reparations? He lost his livelihood! You need to order that priestess to put him back the way he was!" Delapodos demanded.

Iskerus grimaced. "I am afraid 'putting him back' is not something we can do. All of our priests and priestesses are sworn not to harm or cause disease. As far as other reparations: as I've said, we will investigate and get back to the high chaplain."

"That's not enough! She needs to make amends," Delapodos demanded.

"We will work on that." Iskerus was trying to get rid of the beggar. "High Chaplain, take down a description of the priestess from Master Delapodos and get it to me as soon as possible."

The high chaplain nodded and began trying to drag the beggar meister from the tent. The man did not want to go and was most upset.

"Trust us, Master Delapodos, we shall get to the bottom of this and justice shall be done!" Barabus said as he closed the tent flap behind the high chaplain and the beggar meister.

They waited in silence for the two get out of hearing range. Given the loud complaints of the beggar meister, this was not hard to judge. Once they left, Barabus asked, "So do you have a high priestess who can heal that fast?"

Iskerus snorted. "Not likely. I could not heal someone with that man's issues that fast. Disease is far more pernicious and harder to root out than simple flesh wounds."

"So who is this woman?" Barabus asked.

Iskerus shrugged. "I have no idea who, or even what profession could heal that fast."

"And would do so in the name of Tiernon," Barabus added.

Iskerus sighed. "Only an avatar could heal that fast."

"So you think there is an avatar of Tiernon in Freehold?" Barabus asked.

"Why would an avatar of Tiernon be in there?" Iskerus pointed to the warded city. "We are out here! Any avatar would come to speak with us first. Plus, no demons can get into that city; how would an avatar get in?"

"Then what?" Barabus asked.

"I have no idea. I may have just reached my limit," Iskerus stated sadly before finishing his tea.

~

Elraith Castegones took his seat in the central kiva. His bones ached; he was getting way too old for these duties. He had been awakened from meditation by Trevin but a few days ago and was still groggy and perhaps a bit cranky. One did not come out of three years of deep meditation and harmony easily, not at his age. The ramps down into the kiva groaned as Taergon Thunderhoof made his way down the wooden incline. The representative of the centaurs was large, and like most centaurs, claustrophobic and hated the kiva.

Taergon took up his position near the eastern edge and slowly knelt down on all fours. Uncomfortable, yes, but better than being bent over. As Elraith watched his friend take his seat, he smelled Satyricus walking down the ramp. Not that it was a bad smell, far from it, but it was a very strong and nearly intoxicating musk. The high priest of the god Pan nodded to Taergon and Elraith.

Daphne and Chloe, as usual, came bounding down the ramp with great energy. Elraith shook his head slightly at their energy; those two were older than he, yet the nymph and dryad elders had their eternally youthful energy to propel them.

Elraith felt an odd disturbance to his right and turned his head slightly to see that Ariel ap Auberon had taken his place. Even after all these years of knowing them, the highest of the alvaren could arrive and depart with barely his notice. Elraith nodded to the alvaren prince, it had been at least four years since they had seen each other; barely a moment in an elf's life, yet still some time for Elraith. By the creaking of the ramp and the slight, barely noticeable motion of Ariel's eyelid, Elraith surmised that Duranor had arrived. Elraith turned his head to nod at the Grove's Geomancer. Duranor nodded back, but naturally ignored Ariel's presence.

After all his years, Elraith still marveled at the ability of the Los Alfar and the Modgriensofarthgonosefren to hold grudges. Grudge after grudge, dimension after dimension, and century after century. It was actually rather ridiculous and beneath both races if you asked Elraith, which none of them ever did.

This grudge is what he and Trevin sought to keep under control. The Grove depended on harmonious relations between the various races. A war between the alvar and any of the jötnar races would be tense at best; if Hephaestus himself was involved, then the Modgriensofarthgonosefren could easily become directly involved.

As Duranor took his seat, Elraith felt the air of the dark and rather damp kiva lighten. A feeling of tranquility and safety filled the room as the most gorgeous woman Elraith had ever met entered the kiva. He had no idea how old she was, but her appearance—and as far as his powers could discern, her reality—was that of an extremely well-endowed twenty-something human. A woman who could put nymphs to shame, and if one did not believe that, one only needed to see the glances that Daphne and Chloe gave the enchantress as she entered.

Ariel rose and took her hand to bestow a kiss on it, gallant as ever. Duranor simply shrugged at the alfar's actions. Satyricus saluted her in a typical satyr manner and gave her a very lascivious leer. Taergon nearly matched the satyr's leer as he shifted uncomfortably, clearly adjusting his hindquarters.

Trevin smiled as Ariel released her hand, turning her magnificent gaze to Elraith. Trevin somehow bowed and curtsied to him at the same time. "My Lord Castigones, thank you for breaking your meditation; we are truly honored by your presence.

Elraith chuckled. "My dear, you get more charming by the decade."

"As do you, My Lord!" She smiled seductively at him.

"Nice try, my dear, but I fear at my age there is little wood left in the tree." Elraith smiled at her, enjoying the sparkle in her eye. Perhaps no wood, but certainly a small spark remained within his heart. "Sit, and let us speak of these issues that have summoned us. It's been years since all of us have gathered in person."

Trevin took her seat, a small wooden armchair much like Ariel's and Duranor's. "Bad tidings. I have brought with me a seer and sorcerer who both have had dire visions that seem to be coming to pass. Freehold was overrun by a horde of demons, at least three archdemons were in residence, undetected, and now Oorstemoth and the Rod surround the city."

Ariel frowned. "Clearly a problem for Freehold, but what matters this to us?"

Trevin smiled. "That, My Lord Ariel, is but the appetizer. I have here"—in Trevin's hand a crystal ball seemed to simply appear—"a copy of a balling made by Oorstemoth of events that transpired when the Council evicted the demon horde from the city. I think you need to watch it, and then we shall dive deeper into what we must discuss. Our past inactions may be coming back to haunt us."

"Great. I love it when that happens," Duranor groused.

"No, you love scolding us when we don't heed your call to action." Satyricus chuckled.

~

Tom flew over the mountain range near his cave. He needed to get out and stretch his wings. He also needed to get away from the incessant discussions in the cave. By this point, all the arguments were going in circles and none of them were giving him any better idea of what to do.

He should have left Talarius alive on the battlefield. He really did not have the resources or patience to deal with a hostage. The guy was also very bullheaded; it seemed unlikely that he would change his mind in regards to demons. Yes, it was a great finish to a life-and-death battle. Way too close to death, actually; he really should avoid such battles in the future. Even so, the aftermath? They never talked about that in the fantasy books.

No one ever talked about what happens after you ride into the sunset and then the sun sets. Or, as in this case, Fierd sets. Did the happy couple find a cozy inn and settle down to a nice stew and some bread? Or did they end up slogging through a marshy swampland or, worse maybe, a desert.

That was basically how he felt. He had had the triumphant victory and now he felt like there should be more. But more what? He had now dug himself into a situation where he had avatars of Tiernon hunting him down, and probably a few archdemons hunting him down as well. Well, certainly there was Lilith; she was more than an archdemon, and she was not so much hunting him as inviting him over.

He had pretty much ruled out her invitation. He was fairly sure he would simply end up being her hostage. He had to assume he could not really trust any of the old-guard demons here. They had been around too long and were too used to playing games with others. He needed to keep his independence; he actually needed to get a team together, some sort of Scooby gang or similar.

Technically, he supposed he had that with Rupert, Reggie, Boggy, Tizzy, Antefalken, Estrebrius and maybe even Vaselle. Of course, he had to laugh because they were a demonic Scooby gang fighting off both the Forces of Good and the Forces of Evil. What was that then? The Forces Of Other?

Tom blinked. He had been so lost in his own thoughts, he had almost missed seeing a figure sitting on a nearby mountaintop. Actually, it was very close, since he did not need to use demon sight to see the person. Tom turned in midair to look at the person again, circling the mountaintop.

What he was seeing was quite odd indeed. On the top of this mountain peak was a relatively flat, rocky space about thirty feet by ten feet, from which a smaller outcropping of rock about eight feet high and three foot in diameter projected at an angle. On top of that outcropping of rock sat a young man in hiking gear, wearing a Swiss hiker's hat. He appeared to be eating a sandwich.

While something one might expect to see in the Alps, or even the Appalachians, Tom supposed, in the Abyss this was definitely odd. The hiker appeared to be completely human, in his early twenties, with red hair and what might have been a nicely trimmed beard that had not been groomed in several days. Exactly what one would expect from someone hiking in mountains on Earth. Puzzled, Tom flew in closer.

"Hello?" Tom called to the hiker.

The hiker, who oddly had not seemed to have noticed Tom fly by, looked up at his call and after a moment or two, waved at him in greeting.

Tom flew in closer and finally landed on the main summit of the mountain. Indeed, the hiker was wearing something very similar to Alpen hiking gear. Corduroy shorts, white striped socks, hiking boots on his lower body and a light tan polo with suspenders on his upper body. He also had quite a bit of gear—ropes, pitons and climbing gloves—attached to him. There was also a rope on the main summit leading down over the edge. It was as if this rather odd, and very human person had actually climbed the peak.

"Greetings!" the hiker said with a friendly smile.

"Hello," Tom said uncertainly. "So you are doing a bit of mountain climbing, I see?"

"Indeed." The hiker smiled and took another bite of what appeared to be a baloney sandwich. From beside him he then brought up a can of Mountain Dew and took a sip to wash his sandwich down. That made Tom raise an eyebrow. Yes, the mountaintop was cool, but how would one get a can of soda even to this point in the Abyss, short of magic?

"I'm Tom." Tom said. He was not sure if he should stick out his hand or not. Given their size differences, he figured not doing so would be best.

The hiker nodded and grinned. "Nice to meet you. I am Sam."

"So did you climb all the way up the mountain?" Tom gestured to the rope. Sam nodded. "I did."

"Well, that would be good exercise. I guess," Tom said. This was extremely weird; Tom was not sure how to proceed.

"So, are you from around here?" Tom asked, gesturing around the mountains.

"I have a getaway cave a few leagues over." Sam made a motion with his chin in a direction roughly opposite of Tom's cave. "I work in the Courts most of the time, but I like to get away now and then, do some hiking and climbing. I also go skiing now and then." Sam had set his can of soda down and could now gesture freely, and he waved towards the distant, snowcapped mountains.

"Really?" Tom asked, surprised.

"Yes, it is pretty cold up there, and the snow is rather acidic. It is not water based. You need to have appropriate clothing or demon hide."

"That sounds fun, though," Tom said, nodding. It did sound fun.

"It is, and no lift lines, if you have wings." Sam smiled and nodded to Tom's large wings. "Although I don't know if they make ski bindings for hooves." He looked down at Tom's hooves. "I ski down in this form with a protective suit and then change and fly up in my winged form."

"I'll have to go sometime. Is there a skiing store in the Courts?" Tom asked.

"There are exactly two places with ski equipment. Von Trapp is a general outdoor and mountaineering store, and the Slippery Slope is a climbing and skiing store," Sam said.

"So, were you just passing through or do you live around here?" Sam asked Tom.

"I live a few valleys over." Tom gestured towards his cave. "I was just out stretching my wings; I've got a lot of company and needed to get away for a bit."

Sam grinned. "I know how that goes. That is why I have my getaway cave. At work, I'm surrounded by clamoring demons always full of crazy ideas, plans for world domination; you know, the usual."

"People at your work plan on world domination?" Tom asked.

"Well, they are demons, after all. It is really just talk; they never actually specify which world they are planning to dominate. If they did that, they would actually have to explain exactly how they intended to do it in concrete terms. Thus, such ideas never make it past the office acid cooler."

"Put up or shut up, then?" Tom asked.

Sam grinned. "Exactly. And since they will do neither, I like to get away have some old-fashioned fun."

"I should think of that. It would probably be a good way to get rid of stress," Tom said.

Sam smiled. "You know it! That is why I do it, and in a close-to-human form, where I have to actually work to climb, no giant muscles or anything. I want to feel the strain, the pain of aching muscles afterwards. While climbing, I can focus only on climbing and when I'm finished, my aching muscles tell me I have accomplished something."

"That really does sound good," Tom said, nodding.

"Well then, Tom. Perhaps the next time I go climbing I will stop by and see if you want to join me." Sam tilted his head and looked inquiringly at Tom.

"That would be great. I think I'd like that!" Tom said with a grin.

~

"Well, Trevin, I grant you this is worth our discussion." Ariel shook his head in disbelief.

"Which part? The demon stealing god magic, reversing a holy artifact and taking an Etonian knight hostage? Or the fact that the Nyjyr Ennead are not only back, but apparently forming alliances with demons? Or the fact that the deity whose mana was stolen is also the one most responsible for evicting the Nyjyr Ennead from this and other nearby planes?" Duranor asked.

"I'm not completely up on the history here; some of us do not live forever," Taergon said.

"Dwarves don't live forever, just a few hundred years," Ariel noted disdainfully.

Duranor gave the alfar a glare. "Some people know to not outstay their welcome."

"Enough, you two," Elraith chastised them. "Ariel, you were a seated elder when the Nyjyr Ennead were driven off, correct?" Elraith asked.

"Yes. My sister and I take turns, as you know. I was seated at that time. As was Trevin," Ariel said.

Trevin gave him a small glare for revealing her age.

Elraith chuckled. "No need to hide it, my dear. While I was not seated at that point, I do remember that you were."

"Helspaeth, your mentor was the senior elder at the time," Trevin noted.

Elraith nodded. "She was as old then as I am now. So I suppose there is some justice."

"We should have done more when their priests asked for aid. You know gods don't forgive easily," Trevin said.

"I find it curious that Bastet herself would be involved. Gods never involve themselves," Ariel noted.

"Could it be an avatar that simply looks like her mistress?" Duranor asked.

"Weird choice. Did you notice how hairy she was?" Daphne asked.

"I know, eeesh! Someone get the poor girl a razor!" Chloe replied.

Satyricus shrugged. "Personally, I find all the fur intriguing."

"Since you aren't being forthcoming, I'll get to my point. When was this?" Taergon asked.

"About the same time the Vargosite Empire formed," Duranor told him.

"How exactly do you know that? You could not have been alive then; that was a thousand years ago," Satyricus asked, puzzled. "Even I had not been born yet, and I'm pretty sure I am older than you."

Duranor shrugged. "My people have long memories and even longer tales." He stroked his long beard.

Taergon laughed and replied, "You mean face tails!"

Duranor smiled at the joke and nodded. "Precisely. However, there is a bit more to it. Many of my people are miners, as you know, and metalworkers and artisans. Many of us, myself included, worship Hephaestus, god of the forge, craftsmen and our people."

"I'm familiar with your god." Taergon shrugged. "I don't see the connection."

"Hephaestus is, or was, a member of the Triad of Memphis. In that manifestation he was known as pêTah and one of the Nyjyr Ennead."

"So Hephaestus, who is still actively worshipped by your people, was actually also one of the Nyjyr Ennead? I had thought them all driven from Astlan, Etterdam, Nysegard and Romdan?" Elraith asked the dwarf.

Duranor chuckled. "The Etonians and their clerics aren't the brightest, and they've never really paid my people much heed or respect. In short, they never bothered to investigate. For which my people are, I suppose, grateful. But I can assure you, the Etonian clergy can be even more grateful, as it would have been a bloody battle and their casualties far greater than those of the Natoorians and the Najaarans."

Ariel remained silent but his left eyebrow rose slightly as if in doubt. Elraith supposed the eyebrow twitch was required whenever an alvaren prince heard one of the Modgriensofarthgonosefren boast of their people's prowess in battle, particularly given that such legendary prowess was well deserved and something the alvar did not like to acknowledge. He hoped it would not be tested.

"So then, the Nyjyr Ennead still have a foothold in Astlan?" Satyricus asked.

"One must think; although none of our lore discusses them much." Duranor shrugged.

"Fine enough," Taergon said, "but I'm still trying to piece this together. I gather the Nyjyr Ennead are, or were, the gods of the people of Natoor and Najaar?"

"And a few other adjacent regions." Trevin nodded. "As well as having strong bases in what we would call the localverse: Astlan, Etterdam, Nysegard, Avalon, Targella and Romdan. I believe they may have been on many other planes as well, but I can really only speak the worlds we here intersect with." Trevin gestured to their surroundings, meaning the Grove and the planes to which it was permanently attached.

"They were on Earth at one point as well, before the bridge was destroyed," Ariel said.

"Then they were widespread," Elraith observed.

"Earth?" Taergon asked.

"A very distant set of planes that we used to be able to get to indirectly through Avalon. However, that connection was lost during Ragnarök," Trevin said.

"So this relates to the Nyjyr Ennead and the god-mana wielding demon how?" Taergon asked.

"In no way that I'm aware of." Ariel shrugged. "You just wanted context on the Nyjyr Ennead. They were a large, widespread religion that basically made some bonehead moves and began dying out as a religion, and the Etonians moved in and started destroying their temples, killing their priests and converting their worshipers."

Trevin shrugged and nodded. "That's basically it. Their priests came to us, asking for our help. The elders at the time, Ariel and myself included, thought it was simply a normal turf war."

Ariel made a rather sour expression. "We did not anticipate the level of brutality and the thoroughness at the time. The Etonians had been making inroads for quite some time and setting up a long-term game plan that essentially drove Nyjyr Ennead from the localverse completely. I thought they had gone extinct."

Taergon shuddered at such a thought. "What happens to gods with no worshipers?"

"I have no idea." Trevin shrugged. "However, the balling we just watched seems to imply that at least a few of them are still around and they are aligning with demons, one of which is able to steal mana from Tiernon himself."

"Which brings us, I suppose, to your guests?" Elraith asked Trevin.

"Yes, the two seers have independently seen an epic conflict coming between the gods, demons and everyone else caught in the middle."

"If the Nyjyr Ennead can turn Tiernon's own magic against him, then that would completely change the landscape," Duranor noted.

"Given that there was a demon army hidden inside Freehold, undetected, where else could they have a second demon army stationed?" Ariel asked. He looked slightly perturbed for an alfar, Elraith thought.

Chapter 92

Bess rematerialized in an alley three blocks over from Exador's high-rise. She had no desire to let anyone see her shape-change and suspect what she was up to; better to fake a teleportation and change form during translocation. She looked down at her scaly, digitigrade, clawed feet and long serpent's tail. Her finger claws were about four inches long. She had a svelte yet full-figured female form with reflective green and dark red scales, long black hair on top of a relatively normal-looking human face, albeit finely scaled as well , all topped by two pointy, slightly curved, dark green horns.

She knew the form well; it was her succubus disguise. Of all her non-cat forms, this was probably her favorite. It was ideal when she wanted to slum it as a type III demon. Hmm, that reminded her: she needed to concentrate on making sure her aura was appropriate to her assumed station. After a few self-inspections of her aura, she was satisfied and headed to the bar.

She had arranged to meet her favorite avatar there. Admittedly, they were meeting where he was working undercover. Through the swinging wooden doors she strode, noting that a few demons did eye her lasciviously, which was nice. However, none paid her to too much attention. At least none beyond what her current disguise warranted.

Where was he? Ah, there he was. A young, slim demon with a human torso of ebony and the thighs, legs and tail of a horse. His head was human except for some very large incisors and curly horns twisting from the sides of his temples. His black, tightly curled hair was neatly trimmed on his head. He was lugging a basket filled with mugs to the back of the bar. Bess sauntered over and sat down at the bar as he set his load down.

"What does a demoness have to do to get a drink around here?" Bess asked playfully.

Tut looked up in surprise, having not recognized his mistress in this form. He quickly started to bow and Bess slapped her claw down on his arm in a warning not to do so in public. She shook her head.

"Mistress, I'm sorry; I didn't recognize you," Tut said softly and nervously.

"Obviously not." Bess grinned and looked down to the demon's groin, which was reacting to her succubus disguise. Tut quickly moved to cover himself.

"Mistress, I'm so sorry. I meant no disrespect," Tut murmured, embarrassed.

"Tut, tut, my lad." Bess tilted her head, she loved saying that. "It's all part of the disguise." Maybe she should incorporate that feature into some of her other forms. It could be useful. She looked around the room to ensure they were not being overheard. Thinking better of it, she quickly ringed them in a veil of silence. If no one was staring directly at them, they probably would not notice the veil.

"So, I assume you are aware of the duel in Astlan between the Etonian knight and the greater demon?" Bess asked.

"Everyone is talking about it; a great victory!" Tut said, smiling. Like his mistress, he held only a divine fury in his heart for the Etonians.

"It was indeed. But what do people know about this greater demon and his entourage?"

Tut shrugged. "Unfortunately, not a great deal. Although Marfaenel claims the greater demon has actually been here, in this bar, no one really believes him."

Bess shrugged. It was kind of a dive bar for someone that powerful, but it was clear this demon was playing a deep game, as was she. "Nothing more?"

"Well, some demons have said that Tizzy was in the demon's entourage, and others claim the bard Antefalken."

"Tisdale? The octopodal basket case?" Tut nodded.

Bess thought back to the fight. She had not paid much attention to the demon's followers. They had spent much of the fight under that net. However, it was quite likely; that pest was everywhere. They had not had the outpost completed but a day when he showed up there, in the highly secret middle of nowhere Abyss location… with a giant batch of cookies to welcome them to the neighborhood! Bess shook her head.

"Who is this bard you mentioned?" she asked.

"Antefalken. I gather he's a rather famous demon bard," Tut said. "I have seen him in here on occasion, but I have never spoken with him."

"Well known, you say?" Bess asked. Tut simply nodded. Bess twisted her mouth, thinking. "Does he have any particular allegiances, patrons?"

Tut grimaced slightly. "He is well known in the cathedral, apparently, and it's rumored that he is on very personal terms with Lilith."

Bess's right eyebrow shot up. "You mean…?"

Tut nodded. "Yeah, very personal."

Bess sighed; this was starting to look bad. If this greater demon was one of Lilith's pets, things were going to be very difficult. She really did not need demon princesses, and particularly not Lilith, getting their noses into this. She would need to talk some more with her demon partners.

~

"So that was weird," Tom said as he entered the cave.

"What was weird?" Rupert asked.

"I was out flying around, stretching a bit, and I encountered a demon in human form wearing alpine climbing gear and shorts, eating a baloney sandwich on a mountaintop. He had climbed it in human form," Tom said.

"Well, that is one way to kill an infinite amount of time." Tizzy shrugged, not particularly interested. He had been muttering to himself, having one of his odd internal conversations.

"He also likes to ski on the really high mountains," Tom said.

Antefalken frowned. "There are several that do that in the courts, your new friend must be rather wealthy; skiing is not cheap unless you can form your own skis."

"He says he goes to Von Trapp or Slippery Slope," Tom said.

"Hmm, very nice stores. Popular among greater demons and a few archdemons," Boggy said. "Never been, myself. Haven't got that kind of money."

"What does your friend do?" Antefalken asked.

"Sam just said he worked in the Courts," Tom replied.

"Sam?" Tizzy perked up.

"Yes, his name is Sam. He works in the Courts and has a getaway cave not too far from here," Tom confirmed.

"Human-shaped demon you said?" Tizzy asked. Tom nodded. "Red hair, beard, drinks carbonated beverages?"

"Yes." Tom said, frowning. "I take it you know him?"

"Tizzy seems to know everyone," Estrebrius commented.

"I know him. Haven't seen him in a while; he must spend a lot of time in that cave. Don't trust him," Tizzy said.

"Why don't you trust him?" Antefalken asked.

"I did not say I don't trust him, although I don't. I said, do not trust him, meaning Tom should not trust him," Tizzy said.

"Why?" Tom shook his head. "You've been getting rather paranoid recently. You've been rude to my friend Reggie, and now you don't like Sam."

"I didn't say I did not like Sam," Tizzy said. "As his type goes, he's quite pleasant and can sometimes be fun to be around."

Boggy was now staring at Tizzy and shaking his head. "So you don't trust him, and you don't think Tom should trust him, but he's fun to be around?"

"Yep." Tizzy nodded and stuck his pipe back in his mouth.

Boggy shrugged and shook his head, looking back to Tom.

~

Hilda was enjoying herself. One did not get to do much hands-on work as a saint. Pretty much by definition, you just sat there on a pedestal. This was like her mortal days, going from patient to patient, examining them and treating them. The nice part was that she had a lot more healing power as a saint than as a human.

Initial triage had been done, and many of the worst issues dealt with, but there was only so much healing to go around, at least when it came to thaumaturgy. It was relatively inefficient healing to begin with, and being mortal, the wizards had limited mana reserves and needed to sleep. Neither were a problem for a saint.

Of course, technically, one was really supposed to focus on healing the faithful and there were not a lot of those here, but they had been working in concert with the Rod to drive the demons out, so they were allies. There was no proscription against helping non-believers; it was really more of a prioritization sort of thing. If there were more believers here, she obviously would prioritize them.

Anyway, it was mainly broken bones from falling masonry, a few concussions, and some cuts and bruises. A lot of trauma, understandably. A lot of her focus today had been on the servants and apprentices that had been bowled over by fleeing demons and their paths of destruction. Like clerics, the thaumaturgists had their priorities: the city elite, meaning other wizards and their families; plus, of course, the very seriously wounded. Therefore, she was doing a lot of work with the lower classes, which suited her fine. As a saint and a former Sister of Tiernon, caring for the disadvantaged was a critical component to her ministry.

She and Danyel had come by after breakfast and gone to the reception desk and advised them of her skills and willingness to help; they had been quickly led to the main infirmary and from there assigned a young page with a list of people to visit. Currently she was in a courtyard area tending to staff who generally lived in the city proper and came for help. They had had some people from the city itself, who had been wounded by fleeing demons, held in laboratories outside the palace as well.

Technically, she supposed, as a healer, she should have been doing this yesterday, but as a spy, she had had other priorities. Hilda shook her head. The higher one rose in the ranks, the more priorities one had to manage. Danyel, who had been holding a man's foot as she healed his broken thigh, suddenly stared over her shoulder and made a coughing noise before quickly looking down, as if hiding his face. What was his problem?

"Arch-Diocate, Vicar General, here you see a courtyard where we have healers tending to the wounded from all over the city," a voice behind her said. She did not recognize the voice, but the titles were rather obvious. She quickly tried to adjust her healing to be more precise and focused. She had been a bit lazy and had allowed for some aura leakage. She could not let them see her doing a healing ritual. Even as she finished healing the leg, she felt the presence of a group of people behind her.

Hilda finished as quickly as was prudent and then stood and turned to face the group of people behind her. Sure enough, there was a high-ranking wizard in his mid-thirties along with someone dressed as an arch-diocate and another as a vicar general of the Rod, along with a few other Rod members. Hilda clamped down on her aura, gave a low-wattage smile and curtsied. "Holy Sirrahs," she addressed the two senior members, "Rod members, my pleasure. I am Hilda the Healer."

The vicar general beamed in what seemed genuine pleasure. "Amazing, My Lady." He bowed slightly. "I hardly expected to find someone in Freehold who knew the plural protocol for addressing a senior church official and a senior Rod official in a single greeting."

Hilda blushed slightly, both to appear natural and out of embarrassment for that slip-up. "Thank you, Vicar General. I spent my youth in Eton, where, of course, we are all familiar with the good works of both the Church and the Rod."

"Are you of the faithful per chance?" the arch-diocate asked.

Was that a loaded question? Hilda thought to herself. She made a small grimace. "In my youth, I fear that since moving to Norelon and Freehold, I may not have attended chapel as often as I should." She tried to look appropriately ashamed. Technically it was true; she did not actually go to chapel, although her day job was listening to prayers and entreaties from people in chapel, and for collecting mana and animus from worshipers and dispensing mana to priests engaged in higher-level rituals, typically in a chapel or other setting.

The arch-diocate smiled and shook his head. "An all too common problem when we get caught up in our daily lives. But remember, prayer and celebrating Tiernon can be revitalizing and useful for everyday life."

Hilda nodded. "There is a chapel here in town, and I have been already; I will work on going more often."

"Excellent, and I must say your healing is very good as well, very fluid and relaxed. You are not a thaumaturge though, correct?" the arch-diocate asked.

"Ah, no. I'm an animage, actually," Hilda admitted. Alright—lied.

"Ah, an old-school healer. Excellent work, excellent work. Well, keep up the good work." The arch-diocate patted her shoulder. Hilda tried not to tense as she worked to suppress any hint of her true nature. "The grace of Tiernon be with you."

"And with you, Your Grace." Hilda bowed her head as the party moved on. She followed them visually until they left the courtyard. She had not dared to use any Sight on them. She had no idea if they too were lying; if they had discovered her or not. If so, they were silent about it.

Danyel suddenly let his breath out loudly. "That was tense."

Hilda smiled and gave him a pat on the back for reassurance. "Yes, rather unexpected. Definitely awkward."

"I would have a word with you, healer," a rather odd-sounding voice said behind her. Danyel glanced behind her and his mouth went wide. She noticed that all of the patients and aides in the courtyard were also looking behind her in shock.

~

"So you are off then?" Randolf asked Crispin.

"I fear so," Crispin said with a smile. "The calyphs must be brought up to speed and with these wards in place, I can't just zap to Djinnistan. I have to physically leave the city, wander off somewhere into the woods and then zap myself."

"I'm not used to seeing you in non-Turelanean garb. Or non-djinn garb, as the case may be." Randolf smiled.

"Or non-ungarbed?" Crispin winked at him playfully.

"So when are you coming back?"

"I am sure this copy of the ball will cause every bit the consternation in Djinnistan as it has here. I'll get besieged by an unending stream of questions, to which I'll have little answer other than this." Crispin held up his left hand containing a crystal ball with a copy of the battle. "I probably won't escape tonight, so hopefully sometime tomorrow. What will you be up to?"

"I hope to get a copy of the plans that Lenamare gave his team for modifying the wards. My messenger should be by later this afternoon."

"Those wards are impressive, and the information on how he was able to expel archdemons could be critical for the 'thing.'" Crispin made air quotes as best he could with a crystal ball in one hand.

"What pushes one out, should be able to keep one in," Randolf stated, and Crispin nodded.

~

Hilda turned to see one of the most unusual, if not *the* most unusual individual she had ever encountered. Her first thought was that it was a metal golem. However, closer inspection revealed a being of such amazing artisanship that, if a golem, it was a true masterpiece beyond the scope of any normal priest or wizard. This golem-like creature was pure metal, and almost every edge was razor sharp. Its arms and legs were curved with trailing razor edges along what would be the outer edge of a human arm or leg. Its fingers seemed to have retractable blades, as did the edge of the golem's palms.

"Hello!" Hilda beamed at the golem.

"I would interview you," the golem said.

"Very well. Why don't we go somewhere more private?" Hilda asked, gesturing to a nearby exiting corridor.

"As you wish," the golem stated.

Hilda motioned for Danyel to stay put; this golem appeared exceedingly dangerous for living creatures. She shepherded it along the corridor to a small storage room, currently commandeered for bandages and other medical supplies. She opened the door and let it in, then entered and closed the door behind her.

"So, who might you be, and how can I help you?" Hilda asked.

"I am Ruiden, Sword of Talarius," the golem stated. "I wish to interview you about his kidnapping."

Hilda blinked. She had never been interviewed by a sword. She had never actually spoken to a sword. In fact, while not an expert she was reasonably confident that swords were not normally ambulatory. "Well, I'm afraid I can't help you much. I was out of town when he was kidnapped and did not return until later."

"You are an avatar of Tiernon. You are here investigating the demon that kidnapped Talarius," Ruiden stated rather than asked.

"Again, I am afraid I don't know what you are talking about." Hilda did not like this. This golem saw right through her.

"Lies do not become a servant of Tiernon." Ruiden said.

Hilda sighed. "Okay, I am Hilda of Rivenrock and yes, I have been sent here to gather information as to the very strange goings-on here." She put her hands on her hips. "So how did you find me?"

"I followed Iskerus and Barabus into the city and saw them talking to you," Ruiden said.

"So you are working with them?" Hilda asked.

"I am working to find and retrieve Talarius, as they were proving inefficient. I have started my own investigation."

"So you do not report to them?"

"I do not. I am autonomous. My only loyalty is to Talarius," Ruiden said.

"Do they know that I am an avatar?" Hilda asked.

"They did not seem aware of it. However, they are aware of healers of Tiernon who are in the city accosting beggars," Ruiden said.

"Dung beetles," Hilda cursed. "If I agree to help you, will you agree not to tell them I am an avatar?"

Ruiden paused for a moment. "I do not lie. However, if I am not directly asked, I do not have to volunteer information."

Hilda shrugged. "Well, I suppose that is good enough." She shook her head. "My investigation is still quite preliminary; I am working undercover among the wizards to understand how the situation that resulted in Talarius's loss came about. In particular, I am seeking information about the demon that has kidnapped Talarius. I hope to interview multiple individuals directly responsible for the demons that were in the city."

"But you have not done so yet?" Ruiden asked.

"Not yet, but subterfuge is not something those of us from Tierhallon are experienced with. I am moving carefully."

"Every day that Talarius is in the Abyss is a day of agonizing torture for him. He must be rescued soon." Ruiden said. "Humans have a very low threshold for agonizing pain."

Hilda nodded. "I understand. I will tell you what I know so far, and will keep you up to date with everything I discover. Is that acceptable?"

Ruiden nodded. "As long as you do not take too much time; otherwise I will need to escalate."

Hilda sighed.

Every moment I sit here listening to these insane demons is pure torture, Talarius thought to himself. He was, of course, being melodramatic. True demonic torture would be far worse; he had been well schooled in their foul techniques. He had read stories of demons peeling the flesh from their victims, rubbing salt on the muscle tissue and then replacing the skin and massaging them. Talarius shuddered. Only the foulest of dark fiends would even think of such things.

Yet the whiny rantings of the unstable octopod were grating. His captor seemed to seek way too much advice from his ineffectual toadies. True, the bard demon did seem to have good information, but the others? Their obtuse and pointless discourse, atrocious non-sequiturs, unhinged speculation and absolutely asinine assertions were infuriating.

Talarius stood up to go out on the ledge; he needed to get away for a few minutes. Even his captor had needed to seek some solitude a short while ago.

"Where you off to?" Rupert asked.

"Where do you think? The ledge. I can't go anywhere else without more contusions," Talarius replied, heading up the tunnel.

"I'll come too," Rupert said.

Talarius just shook his head inside his helmet. So much for some solitude. He went out, stood on the edge of the ledge, and sighed.

Rupert came up behind him and took a position to his left. "The cave is pretty boring, isn't it?" he asked.

"It is, but such is the lot of a hostage," Talarius replied.

Rupert shrugged. "In some ways, we are all hostages here."

"I am the hostage; you demons are free to go about your business."

"What business do you think I have? I'm a kid. I have only been here a few times. This is the longest I have ever been in the Abyss. Trust me, I enjoy listening to Tizzy talk to himself no more than you do."

"You have only been to this cave a few times? Where do you normally live in the Abyss?" Talarius asked. Perhaps he could get better insight into the true nature of his captor.

Rupert shook his head. "No, I've only been to the Abyss a few times, and never for very long. I grew up in Astlan."

It was Talarius's turn to shake his head. "What do you mean, you grew up in Astlan? Demons do not live naturally in Astlan."

Rupert frowned, or Talarius assumed that was what he was doing. "They do if they were born there. I am a half demon. Tom is my father; my mother was human."

Talarius blinked and stared at Rupert. "Your mother was human? Tom raped your mother, who then begat you?"

"Well, it wasn't rape. They were lovers, but he had to flee before I was born," Rupert explained.

"So then you were born and your mother died in child birth—"

Rupert shook his head. "No. What's up with you?"

Talarius gestured at Rupert. "You think a mortal woman could survive giving birth to you?"

Rupert rolled his eyes and shook his head from side to side, and suddenly there was a naked human boy standing before Talarius.

"I looked like this my entire life—well, smaller and younger, of course—up until my father rescued me from Exador's troops," Rupert said.

"You are saying you looked like that, or younger versions of that?" Talarius said.

"Yes," Rupert said firmly, as if talking to an idiot. "I looked like a normal human, and grew up like one until I was about ten, when I started growing horns and such. I suppressed them to stay looking like this. However, I was exposed and the others in the village stoned and killed my mother, so I fled."

Talarius was silent, staring at Rupert. "So then how did you meet your father?"

Rupert shrugged and looked out over the valley. "I made my way to Lenamare's Academy, where I passed the entrance exams and enrolled as a student. My potential for conjury was sufficiently high that Lenamare granted me a scholarship."

"You enrolled to be a conjuror? To summon and bind demons?" Talarius said, shaking his head. "Yet you knew you were a demon?"

Rupert looked back at him for a moment and then said, "I know it sounds weird, but I wanted to learn to conjure my father. However, Lenamare managed to do that for me. So all is well and good."

"Uh huh," Talarius said. What a bizarre story. It was however, consistent with other things the boy and his captor had said. It was strange; why would these demons make up such a convoluted and implausible set of lies?

Talarius suppressed a chuckle. He had to admit, their crazy background lies at least fit well with the rest of the nonsensical discussions they had. Again, consistency was the key to good lies. This demon captor of his had spun one amazing story.

Talarius frowned, noting motion on the side of a mountain across the valley. He quickly adjusted his visor to telescope in on it. There was a man standing on the side of the mountain. A human man in hiking gear with red hair and a short beard. This would be that Sam character that his captor had met. He was on the far side of the valley and appeared to be surveilling the cave.

Why would a demon that Tom had just met be spying on them? "Let's go inside. I think I've had enough fresh air." Talarius gestured for Rupert to go first. Rupert looked at him oddly and headed inside. Talarius did not like this red-haired demon. Something about him seemed off. He seemed like a stalker or a spy. Perhaps the insane octopod had been correct. Perhaps his captor should not trust this Sam demon.

~

"Hilda! What a surprise!"

Hilda looked up from her most recent client to see Trisfelt coming across the large hall with three rather sour-looking wizards in tow. She gestured to Danyel to finish cleaning up the dried blood on the now healed patient as she stood, wiping her hands. She was glad the sword had gone off elsewhere in its investigation; a walking, talking sword would be quite hard to explain.

"Master Trisfelt! As always, a true pleasure!" Hilda beamed as Trisfelt made his way over. Following him were two men, one bald with only a small beard and mustache, the other rather pale and slightly greying at the temples. The third wizard was a woman dressed rather extravagantly for daytime and who seemed to be trying to stay as far away from away from the cots of wounded as she could.

The two shook hands and Trisfelt stepped sideways to reveal his colleagues and introduce them. "This is my employer, Councilor Lenamare"—he gestured to the greying wizard, who nodded slightly in response to Hilda's nod—"and this is Councilor Jehenna."

The woman gave her an appraising gaze as Hilda nodded at her.

"And this," continued Trisfelt, "is Master Hortwell of our school."

"An honor to meet you all," said Hilda, beaming at them. "I've heard so much about you from Master Trisfelt. And of course, the entire city owes an incredible debt of gratitude to Councilor Lenamare. Everyone in the city is talking about his singular historic achievement." Hilda made a gesture indicating her amazement. "To single-handedly drive three archdemons and thousands of lesser demons from the city with a single spell, is… is… truly awe inspiring." Hilda shook her head and gave Lenamare a gaze full of such admiration that he could not help but stand up straighter and work to suppress a smile.

"It is a pleasure to meet you… Hilda, is it?" Lenamare reached out a hand in greeting.

Hilda smiled and curtsied slightly as she shook his hand. "The honor is mine. I am but a local healer here in the city, and I was simply offering my assistance to those here in the palace."

"Well, it is quite nice to meet you," Lenamare said. "Isn't it, Jehenna?"

The woman looked at Lenamare out the side of her eyes and finally said, "Yes, a pleasure."

Hilda laughed self-consciously. "Well, it certainly is for me. I am but an animage and unschooled in conjury and the traditional wizardly arts, but every time I look at those wards, I am amazed by their complexity and skill. I should think if the Rod were to send Tiernon's own Host against them, they would surely give it pause and likely stop it in its tracks. The strand weaving is so intricate, the power channels so strong and deep, well, it's beyond my ability to follow, but clearly it is an unparalleled work of warding in the history of wizardry." Hilda squinted and tilted her head as if looking through the ceiling at the wards. "I swear, a work of art as much as work of engineering." She sighed and then shook her head as if coming to. "I'm sorry. I know you must get tired of fawning admiration like this, but I just get a bit overtaken when I see great works of mana manipulation."

Lenamare chuckled. "Not at all, my dear. I am always happy when people appreciate my efforts."

"Well, the city certainly does. You are the talk of the town," Hilda told him.

"Really?" Jehenna asked.

Hilda nodded. "Certainly no one has ever commanded so many demons so thoroughly before; not to mention the fact that Councilor Lenamare here commanded the demon that beat the Rod's champion. In a city dedicated to wizardry, how could they not talk about such amazing achievements? Although, to be honest," Hilda lowered her voice a bit, "I have noticed a rather large amount of envy and jealousy along with the admiration."

Lenamare chuckled again. "My dear, it goes with the trade. Envy and jealousy are so often the traits of those who are unable to find fulfillment in their own craftsmanship."

Hilda noticed Trisfelt rolling his eyes; she gave him a wink as Lenamare looked to Jehenna and Hortwell for confirmation of his opinion.

"So Trisfelt tells me you both have a passion for good wine?" Lenamare asked, turning back to Hilda.

Hilda grinned and said, "I fear we both may be a bit susceptible to a good bottle now and then."

"Excellent; then you should join us for dinner this evening. I have a very rare House Trefalgaereon PV392 Meridel that I was wanting to bring out to relax with."

Hilda's eyes lit up with joy. "A truly rare bottle indeed. I would be greatly honored!" She looked to Trisfelt to ensure he was happy with the invitation. He clearly was; the House Trefalgaereon PV392 was a very expensive bottle of wine.

~

"You know, I think coups were a lot simpler in the old days," Ramses observed just before sticking a large forkful of triceratops sirloin into his mouth. He closed his eyes to savor the flavor.

"Coups are never easy," Bess told him as she took a drink of Denubian Choco-Coffee™.

"Yes, but do new players have to keep getting involved?" Exador asked. "I think that is Ramses' point."

"Well, technically this mana-draining demon isn't a totally new player; remember, he was playing around at Lenamare's Academy before you managed to lose my army," Bess reminded him.

"I lost troops as well," Ramses said around another chunk of steak in his mouth.

"We all lost people." Exador shook his head in frustration. "Those Dok Alvar of mine are particularly hard to replace. Being relatively long-lived, alvar of both sides are particularly averse to being vaporized. Once word gets out that you've had one alvaren legion reduced to ashes, it is damn difficult to get another." He cut another piece of steak and promptly ate it.

"Okay, I am sorry I brought it up," Bess said. "We have already agreed to move on from that incident. We should focus on the current issue, and whether or not Lilith is involved with this demon."

"I find it hard to believe," Ramses said, sipping on his blood wine. "This demon actually had the book. It took it from Exador's camp with Lenamare's student. If the demon had been working for Lilith, would it not have gone directly back to her, given her the book and then game over?"

"One would think." Exador shook his head in frustration.

"So then, are we back to the demon being Lenamare's?" Bess asked.

No one had an answer for that. It was a theory the three felt they had discredited. They ate in silence for a few moments. Exador poured himself some more blood wine. Ramses had a very nice wine cellar; they should dine here more often. He had not had triceratops in decades. It was a difficult import even to the Abyss, let alone hauling it to Astlan and finding a human chef that could adequately prepare it. One would almost need a jötunn chef to butcher it properly.

"What if," Ramses began before taking a bite of his mashed parsnips, "we've got it backward? What if Lenamare is working for the demon?"

Bess simply stared at him.

Exador frowned and said, "You mean like a warlock?"

Ramses shrugged. "It might explain how Lenamare has been able to give you such a difficult time. We've often remarked on how unusually gifted the man is for a human."

"So, you think he's had help?" Bess nodded at the idea.

"It is a possibility. Isn't it?" Ramses asked.

Exador was silent, thinking about it. "I suppose it's possible. We just know so little about this demon. As we have discussed, he is clearly not newly bound as we had thought, nor is he simply a greater demon. He is at least an archdemon, if not a prince. Although how he could have remained hidden all this time is very odd."

"Really?" Bess asked. "How long have you known me?"

"She has a point," Ramses said around another giant piece of steak.

Bess shook her head. "The Abyss is huge; infinite, in fact. After I had my falling out with Orcus, I took my minions and we headed to the far side of the Abyss for six thousand years or so. I'm still rather pissed that none of my contacts bothered to tell me he'd been offed four thousand years ago and that I could have come back sooner."

"What was it you did again that got you on his wrong side?" Ramses asked as he took another drink of blood wine.

Bess shrugged. "I messed with his wand."

The other two archdemons started laughing. "Ahh, so you had an affair that ended badly."

Bess threw her napkin on the table. "Not that wand, you lecherous old perverts." She shook her head in disgust, although she was obviously not that mad. "His magic wand—you know, the legendary Wand of Orcus.'"

Exador swallowed a bit hard and asked, "Whatever happened to that?"

Ramses shrugged. "I assume that Tiernon's people took it. I had not yet arrived at that point. Never met the man. I only know what they say in the Balladae Orcusae." He paused for a moment, a puzzled frown coming over his face. "Of course! I knew I'd heard that bard's name somewhere."

Bess looked at him, puzzled. "You mean the one in the demon's entourage that provides the link to Lilith?"

Ramses nodded. "Exactly. It had a familiar ring to it, and that is why. He has played before the Triumvirate and their guests on a number of occasions. The only time I've heard the entire Baladae Orcusae was from him." Ramses closed his eyes and rolled his head. "Concordenax, did that thing go on and on. The Triumvirate insisted on having the entire ballad played. I think they like savoring their former compatriot's defeat."

Exador shrugged. "I am sure Mephistopheles does. If Orcus hadn't bit the dust, he wouldn't be in the Triumvirate today."

"Well, apparently those Etonians have some use." Bess shook her head. Her dislike of the Etonians was not unknown to Exador or Ramses. It was something of a hobby of hers, apparently.

"Would an avatar of Tiernon even be able to pick up the wand?" Exador asked hypothetically as he took another bite of steak.

Bess grimaced. "I'm sure, if he or she were properly shielded. Look what Lenamare's demon did with that artifact the Paladin had."

Exador shook his head. "He's not a paladin, he is a Knight Rampant. If you call him a Paladin, which is a lower rank, he will get rather peeved. They all do. You don't get to be a Knight Rampant without having hubris issues."

Exador shook his head, smiling. "It is so nice to see weakness in such otherwise insufferable people."

Bess rolled her eyes; Ramses noticed and smirked in agreement. Exador was not one to talk about being insufferable. Although to be fair, none of them were.

Jenn watched Maelen and Elrose dancing with various denizens of the Grove around the large bonfire. Everyone was more than a little tipsy, including Jenn. Ugh, Jenn groaned to herself, she was so incredibly stuffed. She had no idea how those two could move, let alone dance. Furthermore, the world was spinning around her. Gastropé was reclining drunkenly in the embrace of two large-breasted nymphs, barely able to move himself.

Jenn was feeling so incredibly good and relaxed at the moment, she didn't even mind Gastropé's lascivious behavior. This afternoon, when he had gone off bathing with a bunch of nymphs and dryads, she had been quite peeved for some reason. She was not exactly sure why now, but she had been. She herself had turned down multiple invitations for carnal relations. She had to admit, now in her current state, that that might have been a mistake, but what was the point of staying chaste for that special someone, if you gave it up at the first real opportunity?

Oh, and what an opportunity. She glanced over to see the aetós sitting around in a group with various nymphs and dryads on their laps. She would not mind being the nymph on Danfaêr's lap. Snuggled in his strong arms, his rock-hard chest pressed against her back, his rigid—Jenn shook her head, trying to clear it of such thoughts.

She needed to remind herself what a very productive day this had been. The Grove was a thaumaturge's paradise. There were plants here, in this single location, from all over Astlan, and apparently several other planes because there were quite a large number she did not recognize. Moreover, they were almost all in season. It was very odd, actually. However, she was not one to turn down the opportunity to stock up on esoteric and nearly impossible-to-find spell components. She had ended up having to ask Danfaêr if he could find her some spare sacks she could use, as her backpack was getting too full. He cheerfully complied and she now had an extremely large sack filled with smaller sacks of precious ingredients for spells and some potions and remedies. Today had literally been a field day!

She had to admit, this place could be mistaken for heaven. Clearly, Gastropé was mistaking it for such. She glanced over at him as the nymphs were taking turns kissing him. Jenn shook her head, disgusted, yet feeling oddly disconnected and removed. She poured herself some more alvaren ice wine. It was so incredible!

Even the normally staid Elrose was enjoying himself out there dancing. He really was an incredible dancer. Maelen looked a bit shaky in comparison, although Jenn doubted she could have done any better, and Maelen was an old man. Not as old as Trevin, of course—and where was she? Jenn glanced around. Oh, there she was. The enchantress was giving this insanely huge satyr a lap dance, her fleshy, full, yet firm thighs undulating obscenely in the satyr's lap. Her taut back with its supple skin was exposed by her too-tight, revealing outfit. She arched her back, bending over backward in his lap, revealing her large, firm breasts to the clearing. Her youthful cheeks were glowing red with warmth, her full, pouting lips smiling with lascivious delight.

Jenn fuzzily wondered why she had ever thought this young enchantress was old. The woman more than held her own against the nymphs and dryads. She had pitied Maelen and Elrose for being locked up in that underground meeting room with the enchantress and other elders of the Grove, but seeing her now, Jenn realized the two men might have enjoyed the close confines with the enchantress.

~

Tom and Antefalken sat on a boulder outside Tom's cave. Reggie, Rupert and Talarius had all wanted to sleep. Talarius was still healing, Reggie was new and, Tom was sure, exhausted. Rupert just had bad habits; hopefully he would grow out of them. Although to be fair, Tom reflected, just going unconscious and letting the world go by without him sometimes seemed appealing.

Tizzy, Estrebrius and Boggy were about a thousand feet away, arguing about where to take Rupert sightseeing tomorrow. They were all going a bit stir crazy, stuck in the cave endlessly rehashing things, so they had decided to take Rupert and Talarius sightseeing. It would also be good for Reggie and Tom.

"So you think I should take this crazy wizard up on his offer?" Tom asked Antefalken.

The bard sighed. "I am conflicted, but I think it could be useful. You may need to get out of the Abyss in a hurry at some point, and having a warlock that you can directly contact via link and have summon you could be extremely useful. It is also a lot more reliable than hijacking random summoning spells."

Tom gave a short laugh. "Yes, and it's far less likely to scare the crap out of someone and get another army after me."

"Exactly," Antefalken agreed.

"However, why do you think I might need to get out of the Abyss in a hurry?"

Antefalken grimaced. "Well, it may be nothing, but Lilith was pretty insistent on your coming to stay with her. If she were to somehow locate you, fleeing to Astlan would be one of the best ways to avoid her." He shrugged. "Of course, by that logic, you would probably want to find warlocks in multiple planes, make yourself even harder to find."

"If that's such a good idea, why don't more demons have hidden warlocks?" Tom asked.

Antefalken shrugged again. "I don't know that they don't; not if they are hidden as you say. However, my suspicion is that the princes and archdemons have more reliable ways to get where they want to go on the Planes of Men than depending on warlocks."

"I don't suppose you have any idea how one links to a wizard to make them a warlock?" Tom asked.

Antefalken shook his head and laughed. "You are our resident expert on possession and such things."

"Argh. I was afraid you were going to say that."

"If it helps," Antefalken said, "from what I've read and heard, a warlock is to a demon not unlike a familiar is to a wizard. So that might be one route."

"A familiar—you mean a black cat or something?" Tom asked.

Antefalken nodded. "That is a common one, but a familiar can be any animal, and sometimes even an imp or other small demon."

"But I'm guessing you don't know the familiar spell?" Tom asked.

Antefalken held his hands open in front of him. "Sorry. I'm a bard, not a wizard. I can read some runes and do a few small tricks to entertain people, but wizardry is not one of my skills."

"You don't suppose I can get him to cast a familiar binding spell on himself, do you?" Tom asked jokingly.

Antefalken looked thoughtful for a moment. "You know, there might be some logic in that."

Tom shook his head. "Huh? What do you mean?"

"Well, think about it. He is subjecting himself to your will, giving himself up to be your warlock. It seems only fitting that he should be the one who does the binding, so that there is no question of his doing it of his own free will. It is an unusual sort of thing, but you can also frame it as a test for him. Have him do this; it will test his resolve to see if he is serious. He would probably have to go away and figure out how to do it; this would give him plenty of time to reconsider his actions. You could also make it clear that there will be no punishment if he changes his mind."

Tom thought for a moment. That did make a lot of sense. The wizard would have to be really committed to wanting to do this. He would need to do the act of binding himself; he would thus be forced to feel the pressure of what he was doing and maybe rethink things. It would make the man's decision and Tom's acceptance of the bargain much more real.

"I think you are right. It would also make me feel better about this. He would have to really want to do it, and this would give him a way out." Tom nodded his head, liking this decision a lot better.

~

Hilda helped Danyel get into bed; the poor lad was extremely deep in his cups, as they used to say. She smiled as she tucked the lad in. When they had arrived he had been led off to join the servants for dinner, and apparently, they were celebrating as well.

The evening had been quite taxing; she had really had to play the part. Lenamare and Jehenna were truly a handful, but the information had been quite worthwhile. She wished she understood wizardry better so she could have gotten a better handle on the wards; but hopefully she would be able to recall enough details to be useful.

She had gotten Lenamare and Jehenna's side of the story about what happened at the school, and the summoning of the demon that eventually captured Talarius. A very odd story, yet while she had had to work to sift out Lenamare's braggadocio, she was fairly certain that the base story was correct. It corroborated with what Trisfelt had said and he had not significantly objected to Lenamare's telling, other than the occasional rolled eye or raised eyebrow.

She still had no clear idea of why Exador had decided to lay siege to the school; they were keeping that a secret. She did not buy the story of professional jealousy, unless this Exador was an even bigger egomaniac than Lenamare, which would be a feat.

This business about Exador and the two others on the flying carpet was quite interesting. Ramses the Damned? Obviously, she had heard about him and the Time Warriors, but they were well before her time, and had proved more problematic on Norelon than Eton. Nonetheless, his reputation was enough to make anyone nervous. As to this suspicion that the third was some defunct goddess? Hilda shrugged as she made her way to the bathroom to prepare her evening soak. Well, she would run it by the archons, but it seemed far more likely that it was just another archdemon that looked similar.

Hilda did not know much about the Nyjyr Ennead, other than they were a pagan religion that had been evicted from Astlan, as well as Etterdam and other surrounding planes. It just seemed inconceivable that any deity, no matter how down on their luck, would sink to slumming with demons, let alone pretend to be a simple archdemon. Pagan deities had even bigger egos than Lenamare; that was what made them and their avatars so difficult to deal with.

Chapter 93

Gastropé tried to carefully untangle himself from Ashea and Eshea, the two nymph sisters who had fallen asleep on top of him last night. As he stumbled out of the sleeping alcove, he fumbled with adjusting his clothes. He really wished he remembered more of last night. He gave the buxom, nude young women in his bed another look in the dim light of the fairy globe that had been lit by the youthful-looking alfar who had awoken him. He really, truly, wished he remembered more. Amazingly, his head did not hurt as much as he would have expected, given his lack of concrete memories of the night before.

He managed to get his turban in place and tied up his backpack. Fortunately, Trevin had suggested he pack it before the feast so he would not have to deal with it this morning. Gastropé was thankful she knew what she was talking about. It was excessively early in the morning to be thinking about packing, not after last night's bacchanalia. Bacchanalia: that had been a new word for him. It was the word the people of the Grove used to describe feasts like last night. Apparently tied to one of the gods of the Grove. Gastropé grinned to himself. If that was a religious feast, he might need to consider getting a bit more religious.

He put his pack on and headed out through the curtains closing off his chamber and made his way to the small glade where Trevin had said they would meet. As he entered the glade, Trevin was just lifting a large kettle off a campfire grill. There was an enticing smell coming from the kettle. Maelen was sitting on bench next to a table, quietly eating some melon. Elrose and Jen had yet to arrive.

"Good morning!" Trevin smiled as she turned to face Gastropé. She was in a different colored outfit today: principally red silk, but still every bit as age inappropriate as her other clothes. "I just took the coffee off the fire."

"Coffee?" Gastropé asked. He was not familiar with it.

"Yes, it's made from the ground-up pit of a fruit similar to a cherry. They look like little half beans, so people often call the coffee beans, although they are really just seeds." Trevin poured a good-sized cup from her kettle and offered it to Gastropé. "You might want to put a bit of milk, honey, or both in it to taste." She gestured toward the table where there was pitcher of milk and a jar of honey.

"Ahh! Do I smell coffee?" Elrose boomed from the edge of the clearing as he came towards them. "It has been years since I've had a good cup of coffee. Very hard to get in Norelon." He walked over to Trevin, who was in the process of pouring him a cup.

Gastropé took a sip. "Huh…" He made a face. It was hot and bitter. Honey would be good; he made his way to the table. Maybe some milk too. Maelen smiled at him.

"How are you this morning?" Maelen asked.

Gastropé grimaced slightly then said, "Amazingly, not as bad as I think I should feel." Maelen chuckled. Gastropé took a drink of his adulterated coffee. Much better; surprisingly good, in fact. A loud shuffling noise came from the edge of the clearing; Jenn was coming in backward, dragging a very large sack.

"It looks like someone's been shopping!" Trevin chuckled.

Jenn looked over her shoulder and grinned. "This place is amazing! I hope this doesn't look as bad as I'm now realizing it probably does…"

Trevin chuckled. "Not at all, dear. We've had thaumaturgists here before; we are used to them going a little bit bonkers with their collecting things." She tugged Jenn. "Come, place that here, along with all your backpacks. The aetós will put them on the cargo carpet."

As people moved to pile their belongings, Maelen asked Trevin, "So, we are going by carpet?"

Trevin shook her head. "No, no, the carpets will just take us to the Nimbus. No way am I going to be cooped up on a carpet for thousands of leagues."

"So the Nimbus is a ship?" Jenn asked.

Trevin rocked her head from side to side in a sort of yes-or-no way. "You can call it that—we do. You'll see soon enough."

"The Grove is landlocked. Is it an airship, like the Oorstemothians have?" Elrose asked.

Trevin shook her head. "No, no, nothing so primitive. I do not want to spoil the surprise. Come now, sit down and have some breakfast and coffee. Although if you have trouble with air sickness, I advise eating lightly."

After finishing their breakfast, the group followed Trevin down to a larger clearing near a lake. On the shores of the lake were half a dozen large carpets. Two of them were piled high with baggage that had been tarped down tightly. Gastropé assumed this is where their packs had gone. Their group of aetós was standing nearby talking amongst themselves. There were a few other groups on the shores as well.

"Alright, time to meet people," Trevin said. "You already know Hethfar, Danfaêr, Treyfoêr, Lythdaér, Raêfaér and Foéren." She gestured to the six aetós. "This is Gnorbert," she said, gesturing to a young-looking gnome coming up beside her. "He's the Nimbus's chief engineer." Although *young* was an odd term for any gnome; they all looked old by human standards.

"Hulloo!" Gnorbert said.

"You met his father yesterday, Gnorman," Trevin said. "Standing behind him is his apprentice, Gnermin." A smallish, apparently shy gnome peeked out from behind Gnorbert and waved hello at them.

A very tall, thin alfar with long, brilliantly white hair walked up behind Gnorbert. He was dressed in a rather ornate long coat with a frilly mauve shirt underneath.

Trevin turned towards the alfar and smiled. "This is our guide, Chief Navigator Bealach." The alfar—Gastropé guessed he was a nuren alfar, or mountain alfar—bowed to them and nodded politely.

Trevin gestured to a group of six dwarves laughing and joking about thirty feet away. "Cumberlin, Darowin, Farswath, Molche, Tevyn and Carnwath are over there, you'll have time to get to meet them on the Nimbus, particularly if you play cards." Trevin grinned. "They are my personal ground detail, even as the aetós are my personal aerial detail."

"You see over there"—she pointed to one of the four rugs—"Tibault, our procurer." That seemed like an odd title for the short, barefoot fellow, Gastropé thought to himself. And why was he barefoot on this rocky shore? Yes, he had disproportionately large feet but… oh. Gastropé finally realized that Tibault was a hearthean. *Never mind*, he thought, shaking his head and laughing at himself. "Procurer" made a lot more sense now.

Trevin was continuing, "Maude is our ship's healer. I am sure the two of you will have a lot to talk about." Trevin smiled at Maelen, who nodded back. "Beside her is Alicia, our combat aeromancer." Trevin looked around, and suddenly pointed a short distance away, where a young human lad appeared to be relieving himself near the forest. "That's Peter, one of our combat pilots." Combat pilot? Gastropé wondered.

"There at the final passenger carpet is Trolg." Trevin gestured to a rather ugly green fellow in leather armor. Was he an orc? Gastropé wondered. That would be rather odd. "Sylenea, who is inspecting the rug right now"—Trevin obviously meant the alfar woman inspecting the edges of the rug—"is another of our combat pilots. That is Tereth sneaking up behind her, unwisely." Trevin chuckled as the short, brown-haired forest alfar made his way quietly up to Sylenea. "He is a combat geomancer."

Gastropé shook his head. He had never heard of a combat geomancer; that did not make much sense. Unless maybe you were laying siege to a castle?

"Abbey, who has just pointed Tereth out to Sylenea, is our aquamaster."

"Aquamaster?" Maelen asked. "So an animage rather than a wizard?" Trevin smiled and nodded. "I've never met an aquamaster; I will have to compare some notes with her, most certainly." Maelen seemed much more interested in this person than any of the others.

Gastropé grinned to himself. He was pretty sure that in Maelen's case it was the desire to compare notes and learn new information, and not the young lady's very nice form that had the animage interested.

"Securing the cargo carpets are Marin and Faelen." Trevin gestured to two other forial alvar who were busy making sure the cargo was stored and secured.

Trevin began looking around the lake, apparently searching for missing people. As she did, a loud huffing noise came from the clearing entrance they had came through. Coming down the path towards them was another hearthean, this one with a backpack twice his height. "Sorry I'm late, so sorry, just had to get a few last minute supplies!" the hearthean huffed as he came up to them.

Trevin shook her in mock disapproval. "Everyone, this is Bernaud, the Nimbus's galley master."

"Hello, hello, glad you're all coming aboard!" Bernaud huffed, still out of breath as he gave a brief salute to each of them.

"You do know they've already tarped the cargo carpets?" Trevin asked.

"Hurry, hurry, why is everyone always in such a hurry!" Bernaud shook his head in exasperation. "If the peaberry soup is bland tonight, you'll wish you hadn't hurried so much, I can tell you that!" Bernaud marched off towards the carpet with Sylenea on it. "I'll just strap it down next to me. Won't be the first time everyone was in a rush..."

Trevin shook her head in amusement at the hearthean. Suddenly a second mountain alfar appeared beside her. Gastropé had not seen him approach. "Area is secure, ma'am," the alfar said softly. "We are clear for liftoff."

Trevin smiled and nodded. "Thank you, Seamach." She looked to the rest of the immediate party. "This is Seamach, our scout and Bealach's closest confidant. Between the two of them, we always know where we are and what, or who, is nearby." The nuren alfar gave them a nod and then hurried over to the carpet with Beranud.

"Everyone!" Trevin called out to those around the lake. "It is time—saddle up!" Everyone cheered and Trevin turned back to their group and motioned them towards the closest carpet. "Gnorbert is in front as the pilot, I'm taking the rear as backup. You four in the middle as you like."

"What's with all the ropes?" Jenn asked as they approached the large carpet. It was an extremely unusual carpet; most carpets were simply large, flat rugs with some sort of pattern. One just sat or stood wherever one pleased. This one, on the other hand, had seats, or rather pillows in six positions. Those pillows seemed to be woven into the carpet along with a series of ropes, loops and pockets.

As Gnorbert sat down and started moving the ropes around him, Gastropé realized the ropes were really harnesses to keep one locked onto the carpet. That was very strange; normally carpets had their own magical field that kept people stable on the carpet, and you did not need straps to hold on.

Trevin smiled and answered Jenn's question. "These are combat carpets. We do not have the normal stabilization spells on them that consumer-grade carpets use. Obviously we do have some, but not to the point that they interfere with maneuverability. Combat carpets have to be very agile and so we have harnesses and handholds for people to hang on to." Trevin chuckled. "You will also notice a number of pockets and tie loops in front of each position. These pockets are for material components, wands and other paraphernalia that the occupants might need during battle."

"You mean wizards are strapped to this thing casting spells and blasting lightning bolts?" Gastropé asked in wonder.

"Exactly!" She shrugged. "Casting from a carpet isn't that uncommon, but in those cases the carpet is being used more as a floating platform. In this case, we are diving in, striking and then pulling out fast."

"And this is a common occurrence?" Maelen asked with concern in his voice as he tried to figure out the harness.

"In Astlan? Not since the days of the Anilords, with some of the other adjacent planes, on occasion. In particular, some jötunn tribes can be problematic." She paused. "Here, let me help you with that." She came over and helped Maelen adjust his harness; she then went around and ensured everyone was secure.

Trevin sat down in the rear seat and fastened her harness. "Very well, Gnorbert. Take us away!"

Gnorbert waved his right hand in acknowledgement and then made some gestures in front of himself. Suddenly the carpet was rising in the air, straight up, very fast.

"So, where are we headed? Where is the Nimbus?" Elrose asked Trevin. Gastropé and Jenn twisted in their seats to look back at Trevin.

She pointed up and grinned. "Straight up."

They looked up into the grey predawn light. The sky over the Grove was generally clear, with the stars fading as the morning began to light the sky. There was only a single large cloud hovering directly over the lake. Thinking about it now, Gastropé realized the weather had been essentially identical yesterday. Clear skies except for the one cloud right over the lake. The Grove must have very odd weather patterns, what with the giant mountains; maybe the cloud did not have much of anywhere to go.

"Straight up?" Jenn asked. "So the Nimbus is up above the cloud?" That would be a very high-flying ship, Gastropé thought to himself.

Trevin simply grinned and flashed her eyebrows mischievously. "Not exactly," was all she said.

As the light grew with the dawn, Gastropé suddenly realized that the aetós were not on any of the four carpets; they were flying on their own. He had never seen an aetóen in flight before. Since flying straight up would be quite taxing, the aetós were circling the carpets at about a forty-foot radius, spiraling upward.

Jenn gasped as the first rays of Fierd came over the vast mountains, lighting up the multicolored wings and mohawks of the aetós. It was breathtaking to watch their mighty wings beat rhythmically, lifting them higher and higher in a spiral around the carpets. As they rose, the chill morning air of the higher altitude caused their breath to become visible. Gastropé was at a loss for words as he looked out over the sylvan beauty of the Grove, nestled inside its circle of oversized, rugged mountains, the light beginning to sparkle on its thousands of ponds and small lakes.

They were at a truly dizzying height, Gastropé realized looking down; higher than he could remember ever being on a carpet before. So high, in fact, wisps of the giant white cloud above the lake were starting to mix in with their chilled breaths. They were now rising through the very outer edges of the large cloud. He wondered when they'd be able to see the Nimbus above the cloud.

For a few moments, they were enveloped in the soft whiteness of the edge of the cloud, and then it began clearing as they rose out of the edge of the cloud, revealing the top of the cloud like a giant snow-covered hill.

Jenn, sitting beside Gastropé, begun looking around, presumably for the ship. Oddly, there did not appear to be a ship above the clouds. *Where could it be?* Gastropé wondered.

As they cleared the cloud top, the aetós shifted their motion and began flying toward the center of the cloud. Gnorbert made some different gestures and their carpet began following the aetós. They had floated over the cloud for perhaps a minute when Gastropé spotted what appeared to be a man in a long coat and large hat waving at them. He was standing in the middle of the cloud!

"Ahoy!" The man called.

"Ahoy, Nimbus!" Gnorbert yelled back.

"Chief Engineer Gnorbert and her ladyship, the Enchantress of the Grove, with her entourage. Permission to come aboard?" Gnorbert called out.

"Ahoy, Gnorbert! Second Mate Trefalger here. By the Captain's leave, permission granted! Welcome, her ladyship!"

Gastropé blinked as other figures began appearing on top of the cloud with the first officer. Jenn gasped as the aetós began landing on the cloud beside the first officer.

Gnorbert made more gestures and their carpet started rotating sideways; as Gastropé looked to the other carpets, he realized they were all in a long line, side by side, also rotating.

"Ahoy, Nimbus! Battle carpets preparing to dock."

"Battle carpets, docking stations ready," said one of several men walking out to meet the carpets. "All carpets aligned, prepare for touchdown!" The sailors?—Gastropé did not know what to call them—walked right up to the edge of the carpets and were suddenly pulling ropes out of the cloud and fastening them to loops on the corners of the carpets.

"Carpet down," Gnorbert said at normal volume.

Gastropé felt the carpet touch down as if on solid ground, but he could see only fluffy cloud at the edge of the carpet. What were they standing on?

Trevin was standing up free from her harness. She stepped off the carpet and onto the cloud.

"Welcome to the Nimbus, my friends! It's my home away from home, and I've been gone way too long!" The crew of the Nimbus, including the riders on the other carpets, all cheered. Jenn and Gastropé and even Maelen and Elrose were peering suspiciously at the cloud beneath her feet.

Trevin saw them all looking and laughed. "Have no fear—look at the Modgriensofarthgonosefren." She gestured to the dwarves getting off the carpet with no qualms. "Do you think one of them would be getting off the carpet if the deck beneath their feet was not solid?"

The one named Molche heard and replied loudly, "Aye, but it's damn unnatural. Dwarves don't belong in no cloud. If my ancestors could see me doing this, they'd shave my beard for sure!" The other dwarves laughed, and a couple exchanged hand slaps.

"If Hephaestus had meant dwarves to travel in the clouds, he would have forged us some metal wings!" Farswath griped loudly.

Trevin laughed. "Well, you may just get the chance to ask him why he didn't then! Our quest is to track down one of his good friends and fellow god."

Carnwath shouted back good-naturedly, "And that's supposed to make us feel better? Hunting gods in the clouds? Aye, you overdwellers have all been driven nuts by too much fierdshine!" The other dwarves all laughed.

Gnorbert had finished helping the sailors secure their carpet. "During tonight's card game, I will certainly drink to that!" the gnome shouted to Carnwath.

"We all will!" Trevin shouted in return.

"I have to admit," Elrose said, cautiously stepping off the carpet, "getting the Modgriensofarthgonosefren out from under a mountain and onto a cloud is nothing short of a miracle."

Trevin grinned at him. "They're a good and loyal band. I could not ask for better. Although to be honest, it did take some convincing."

"And a fair amount of braich!" Carnwath added as he walked by heading for the cargo carpets.

"Braich?" Maelen asked curiously.

"A favorite among the underground peoples," Trevin told him. "A fermented grain, similar to a whisky." She turned to the others. "So, are you planning on staying on the carpets for the entire trip, or would you like to see your staterooms?"

~

"Very interesting indeed," Moradel said as Hilda finished her report.

"An incredible wealth of information!" Beragamos exclaimed. "We really should have been using our own field agents sooner—far better information than we get out of the Rod or the priests."

Sentir Fallon was shaking his head. "I find it amazing, Hilda, how you get those people to just open up and tell you this." He looked to the other avatars. "This is far better than traditional interviews and interrogations."

Hilda shrugged, happy with their response. "Well, there is that old saying: in wine there is truth."

Moradel chuckled. "Keep this up, Hilda, and we may have to change your title to Patron Saint of Loose Lips!" They all laughed at this as they sat around a table in the small meeting room.

"Unfortunately, while an incredible amount of information, it still doesn't make a lot of sense," Beragamos complained.

"Well, clearly Lenamare was tricked by this so-called greater demon; it must be an archdemon, if not a prince," Sentir Fallon stated.

"What about this Bastet?" Hilda asked. "Could she be a pagan god up to no good?"

Moradel shrugged. Beragamos grimaced and said, "I doubt it. The Nyjyr Ennead have been gone from all the local planes of reality for nearly a thousand years. I'll need to confirm, but I believe I read a report that their outer realms had collapsed."

"That would mean they would have no power base, no place for their god pool or for their dead," Sentir Fallon stated. "At which point they would be defunct as a pantheon."

"Could they have survived as individuals, reduced in stature to demon level?" Moradel asked.

Beragamos shrugged. "I suppose anything is possible, but the level of humiliation that would entail is more than I can imagine any of them could deal with."

Sentir Fallon nodded. "I think it far better to assume that this woman is, as she appears to her compatriots, an archdemoness who just happens to take on a form favored by Bastet."

Beragamos was making odd faces as if trying to recall something. "As I recall, she was particularly moral. I can't see her consorting with demons. Killing demons, as a cat would kill vermin? Yes. Consorting with them? No."

"Now, on the other hand, this sword could be a problem," Beragamos said.

Sentir Fallon sighed. "Talarius bore Excrathadorus Mortis by right of being the most senior Knight Rampant. Does anyone know where he acquired this Ruiden? Is it a holy artifact of Tiernon? I have never heard of one of our swords being able to shapeshift."

Beragamos snorted. "You know how old I am—I have never heard of any sword being able to shapeshift and walk around looking for its owner. This is completely unprecedented."

Moradel asked, "Are we sure it is actually a sword? It sounds more like some sort of being that shape shifted into the form of a sword."

"All good questions, to which we have no answers." Sentir Fallon shook his head from side to side in puzzlement. "It just strikes me as unnatural. Metal—pure metal is inhospitable to animatic creatures as far as we know. When forging a blade, spirits are generally attached to an anima jar linked to and embedded in the blade. Did you see any crystals?"

Hilda shook her head. "It is possible that its two black eyes might have been some sort of stone or crystal, but they struck me more as being like polished hematite or similar shiny black metal."

"And you say it did not attract much attention?" Beragamos asked.

"Well, it did when it approached me; everyone was staring at it. How it got through the city without being accosted, or for that matter left, is something of a mystery. I left it in the hallway off the storage room," Hilda said.

"One would think the city guards and various wizards would have stopped it to question it. They can't be that jaded," Moradel said.

"One would hope." Beragamos shook his head in wonderment.

"I will make inquiries with those of our people who have worked the most with Talarius to find out where this sword came from. But it does not sound like a holy artifact dedicated to Tiernon," Moradel said.

"One would think we would have heard of something so wondrous and unusual," Beragamos said.

~

Vaselle was nearly beside himself; however, he could not decide if it was from fear, joy, excitement, terror, anxiety, love or exactly what. With great trepidation and more than a little fear, he had ventured out of the city this morning to summon Estrebrius to see if the dark master had come to any conclusions regarding his fate.

Much to Vaselle's joy and fear, the dark master himself had come forth to instruct him. He had told Vaselle that he had to be sure of Vaselle's devotion. The dark master would only take him and his soul if it was freely given and Vaselle was totally committed. In his infinite generosity, the dark master had also told him that should he change his mind, or be unable to complete his task, the dark master would not hold it against him and he would be free to go. Could one ask for anything better from such an awe-inspiring being?

The task? Vaselle had to figure out how to cast a familiar binding on himself and then hand the ownership of the binding over to the dark master. It was inspired, Vaselle had to admit. He had had no idea of how demons bound their wizards; clearly, it was a closely guarded secret of the demon lords. However, this made so much sense he could not believe he had not thought about it. A warlock was to all intents and purposes a demon lord's familiar!

It was so logical, so ingenious—and by requiring Vaselle to enslave himself, to debase himself to the level of a familiar, it was perfect! Of course, the problem was, he had no real idea of how to reengineer the spell. The dark master had told him he could have time to figure it out, and he was certainly grateful. He would need to spend some serious study time at the palace library. While obviously there were plenty of books on binding demons to oneself, he was reasonably certain there would be no books on binding oneself to a demon. However, he was sure he could piece something together.

~

Jenn poked the milky-white wall of her stateroom aboard the Nimbus with her forefinger. It was surprisingly solid, for a cloud. To say the… uh, *ship* was a bit odd was an understatement. Apparently, the entire cloud they had seen from the ground was the ship. Unlike a normal ship, however, the passengers were all inside the cloud rather than on top. The top deck was mainly for launching and landing flying carpets.

The interior of the cloud was composed of hallways and rooms that had been "carved" out of the cloud, or so it appeared. The halls and rooms were all lined with carpets and rugs to give people a more secure feeling and to add to perspective. Left with a solid white ceiling, floors and walls, it would be extremely difficult to tell where one was going or where the walls actually were.

To ease navigation around the ship, there were tapestries hanging from the walls here and there, particularly at corners and intersections. Her room was not huge, but was still good sized compared to an actual sailing ship's cabin. She had a normal-sized single bed, a nightstand, a dresser and a small writing desk and chair. There was no door, only a solid blue, heavy curtain. All the doors were solid curtains; their color indicated whether they were common areas, private cabins, or for specific functions such as water closets or control rooms.

Trevin had assured them that the ship was not as insubstantial as it appeared. While it was made out of solid cloud, it had a mithral and adamantite framework that outlined and supported all the rooms and corridors. The cloud walls, floors and ceilings were all maintained by runes fashioned into the mithral and adamantite frame. The Nimbus was a seventh-generation cloudship and as such, was highly tested and reliable, Gnorbert assured them.

That was all quite nice, intellectually, but Jenn's insides were still finding the cloudship to be rather discomforting. It had been clear that Gastropé had shared her misgivings, and she suspected that Elrose and Maelen might as well. None had seemed tremendously enthusiastic. Elrose, however, had spent a considerable amount of time probing Trevin over the wizardly details of the enchantments that kept the ship together.

"Knock, knock," Gastropé said from the hallway outside.

"Come in," Jenn told him. Gastropé split the curtain and came in, looking around. He was frowning at her bed for some reason. "What's the matter?" Jenn asked.

"You've got a normal single-person bed in your cabin, as does Maelen, I noticed," Gastropé told her.

"So?" Jenn was not following him.

"Trevin made a big deal about showing me my room and how comfortable it was, and what a nice roomy feather bed for two I had," Gastropé said worriedly.

Jenn laughed, and he turned his head to give her an annoyed glare. "See what you get for wearing those short silk pants and that skimpy vest? She's obviously interested in what you are showing off," she teased him.

"What? This is standard fine fashion in Turelane. Everybody dresses like this!" Gastropé protested. "At least everyone who can afford to," he admitted a bit more softly, privately realizing that maybe he did try to dress a bit more stylishly than some.

"Uh huh." Jenn just shook her head. "You reap what you sow. That's all I'm saying."

"I don't have any other style of clothing; everything I own is similar to this!"

"See, regular wizards don't have this problem; it's hard to look too attractive in a bulky wool robe," Jenn told him.

"Yes, and have you ever had to stand near one of them in the summer? It is not pleasant, thank you. This is summer and I want to be comfortable, not smell like a barn, and I want my arms free for casting spells," Gastropé protested.

Jenn shrugged and started heading for the hallway. "As Master Hortwell always says, all choices carry risks!" She pulled the curtain aside. "Let's head to the—what did they call it? The bridge?"

"Argh." Gastropé was feeling frustrated by the situation. "Yes, that was what they called it. I have no idea why, though. It doesn't make any sense."

The two headed down the hallway for about 200 feet before they located the spiral staircase on their right that led to the other decks of the cloudship. Gastropé gestured for Jenn to go first; she nodded and started carefully up the winding cloud stairs.

"I think it helps if you don't look at where you are stepping," Gastropé advised.

"Probably," Jenn admitted, "but looking up into the all-white spiral makes me dizzy."

"I'm thinking going by touch would be best; treat it like it was a normal spiral staircase."

"And then how do we know when to exit?" Jenn asked.

"Experience?" Gastropé shrugged. "I'm guessing we are going to be on this thing for some time."

They climbed past three other floors before exiting on the top floor of the staircase. This hall was named the conning hall, and it began from the bridge at the front and ran along the top spine of the cloudship. Periodically there were ladders leading to hatches that let onto the top deck.

Jenn found it interesting that the entire ship was sealed from the outside. According to Trevin, the ship could get extremely high, higher than even aetós could breathe. In fact, it had to, to leave the Grove above its giant mountains. The cloudship, therefore, was what Trevin referred to as "pressurized." Elrose had found this quite interesting and the wizard had made Gnorbert promise to show him how it was done.

It was funny; most of her classes with Elrose had been on sorcery, but he was also a Master Enchanter as well, and she often forgot this. Jenn had to admit, Lenamare's school did have one of the most talented rosters of wizards of any school. Both Lenamare and Jehenna were Master Wizards, meaning they were certified Masters of Sorcery, Enchantment, Thaumaturgy, Pyromancy, Conjury and Rune Magic. Many schools did not have a single Master Wizard; having two was quite unusual. Hortwell was a Master of Conjury and Rune Magic, and Elrose a Master of Sorcery and Enchantment. Trisfelt, on the other hand, was officially a Master of Thaumaturgy yet also of Geomancy; however, geomancy, unlike pyromancy, was not recognized as an official school of magic. Rather, it was considered a sub-discipline of thaumaturgy.

It had always seemed odd that pyromancy would be its own school when aeromancy, geomancy and aquamancy were sub-disciplines of major schools of magic. From what Maelen had implied, animages treated all the elementalists equally: pyromastery, aquamastery, geomastery, aeromastery—and she had no idea what they called the study of the fifth element, spirit, or sometimes just man. She shook her head. Maybe if she ever became a Master Wizard, it might make sense, but she suspected it was more likely a political issue rather than any legitimate classification.

Of course, before she could become a Master Wizard—Jenn laughed a little at her own thoughts—she needed to master at least one school of magic; in her case, thaumaturgy. That was getting increasingly more difficult the way things were proceeding. She had not had a class in weeks, no learning assignments, no real education. Well, no formal education. She was getting an education in combat magic, demons and politics.

She supposed that, to be fair, very few students of wizardry ever had the opportunity to meet and be involved with the entire Council of Wizardry, or go on quests with the legendary Trevin D'Vils —a literal walking legend, the Enchantress of the Grove. And almost no human ever set foot in the Grove, let alone got to participate in a bacchanalia. Okay, almost no one would even know what that word meant, but everyone did know that the fae and in particular the satyrs, centaurs, nymphs and dryads threw incredible parties. She had been to one! That was, Jenn had to admit, a great story to tell people. Assuming, of course, that she lived through this insane quest to hunt down a defunct goddess.

They passed through the red curtains to come on board the bridge. "Permission to come on the bridge?" Gastropé asked the people already there. Gnorbert had told them that protocol dictated that one ask permission before coming up onto the bridge. The idea was that the bridge was the main control center for the ship and that if the situation was difficult, too many people on the deck of the bridge could get in the way. Thus, they stood inside the doorway at the base of stairs that led up to the bridge room.

"Permission granted," replied Aêthêal, the Nimbus's first mate. Aêthêal was a very striking, an amazingly tall woman aetós. They had been introduced to her topside before descending into the ship. She was standing next to Trevin and a tall rialto alfar in a long trench coat with brocaded sleeves. Maelen and Elrose were already on the bridge, as were numerous crewmembers in uniform.

Trevin stepped forward. "Gastropé, Jenn, may I introduce our captain, Xavier Ehéarellis." She swept her arm back slightly to indicate the alfar in the trench coat.

Gastropé and Jenn both nodded their heads to the captain, who nodded politely back.

"A pleasure to welcome you aboard the Nimbus, my new friends." The captain smiled politely at the two young wizards. As he said this, a deep bass bell sounded on the bridge.

"Excellent," the captain said to Jenn and Gastropé. "You have arrived on the bridge just as we've reached sufficient altitude to clear the Rings."

Aêthêal suddenly reached up above her head and pulled a hose out of a previously hidden compartment in the ceiling. The hose had what looked like a funnel on the lower end. The upper end was not visible, as it was somewhere in the compartment. She placed the funnel near her mouth and started speaking. "All hands!" Jenn jumped slightly as the first mate's voice reverberated around them quite loudly. "We have reached Grove departure altitude. All stations are hereby elevated to Defensive Configuration 4. Prepare for departure!"

"Defensive Configuration 4?" Maelen asked Trevin.

The Enchantress smiled. "We have six levels of alert on our ships ranging from Configuration 5, which is routine operations, to 2, which is battle stations. Level 1 is in battle; 0 is abandon ship. We hope to never get to that level." Trevin shuddered lightly. "The ship's armoring and defensive spells are also keyed to these levels. At Configuration 5 we have no defenses raised other than some repulsion spells for birds and insects; Configuration 4 activates our base level of shielding for potentially hostile territory."

"Exiting the Grove is going into potentially hostile territory?" Elrose asked.

Trevin chuckled. "In the days of the Anilords, we left at either Configuration 3 or 2." She shook her head as if remembering great unpleasantness. "Today Astlan is quite safe, but remember we are multi-dimensional here so we are crossing more than just a border to Astlan; it's a single border between the Grove and all Grove-connected realms, some of which are more hostile than Astlan." Trevin shrugged. "And while we don't expect any problems, you never know who might want to take a pot shot at us. Or what happens if we stumble onto... say... I don't know, an orc hunting party on dragonback?"

"Orcs on dragons?" Gastropé croaked out.

"It happens. Obviously, dragons like mountains, and what better mountains are there than those around the Grove? Further, there are multiple tribes of orcs that use trained dragons as mounts to swoop down and ransack and pillage villagers. Nightmarish for the victims, I can assure you." Trevin shook her head.

"Of course, we would come in at too high an altitude for them to immediately attack us, but we don't typically maintain this altitude; we tend to go lower, since higher altitudes use up more of the ship's reserves, and we can't replenish breathing air and so on." Trevin smiled and waved towards the front of the room and to a railing at the edge of the bridge's deck. "Moving up here, you can see where we are going." On the other side of the railing was a very large mirror, or glass lens—Jenn was not sure which, really. It looked like a large window, but given its location in the cloudship, it could not be.

Through this lens, mirror or window was a breathtaking view towards the front of the cloudship and the incredible ranges of mountains they were preparing to pass over. "I think you'll find the view quite breathtaking. I always do."

Jenn shook her head in awe; she had never imagined being this high up, Astlan stretching out at her feet, viewing the tops of the insane mountain ranges around the Grove. She could not even really make out much of the detail of the land below, they were so high. Was it her imagination or could she actually see the curve of the planet? It was one thing to intellectually know that your planet was a sphere despite the fact it seemed flat; it was quite another to actually see it for oneself.

"Oh, my goddess..." Gastropé murmured as he came up beside her.

Maelen made a whooshing noise. "I can See many things, but this is one I have never seen, or Seen, before."

Elrose, standing next to Trevin, asked, "So how high are we?"

Trevin glanced over to a sidewall, where there was what appeared to be a mirror with colored writing on it. "We are currently at 61,350 feet above sea level, or 3.873 leagues; and roughly 55,000 feet above the floor of the Grove, or 3.47 leagues."

"Correct me if I'm wrong, but normal clouds never get that high, do they?" Elrose asked.

Trevin smiled. "You are correct, my fellow Enchanter. The highest natural clouds, which, as a Sorcerer, you know are mainly ice particles rather than actual air, have a maximum altitude of about three leagues. However, this is no natural cloud by any means. You recall my earlier comments about pressurization and how I just mentioned that traveling at high altitudes like this requires significant resources?"

The group nodded.

"We are funneling a fair bit of mana into keeping the cloud stable at this point." She pointed at several crew members gathered around desks with various gems and mirrors on them. "Those crew members are monitoring the mana flows, and are in constant communication with Gnorbert in the engine room."

"Engine room?" Maelen asked. "I'm not sure I understand the term. An engine is an automaton that does work of various sorts, so how can a room be an engine?"

Trevin chuckled. "That's the phrase for it; it is more precisely a very large room filled with a great number of different magical engines which perform the hundreds of tasks necessary for all of this"—she gestured around the cloud expansively—"to work." She smiled and then added, "If you manage to get a look inside one of those flying ships of the Oorstemothians, you will find that they too have 'engine rooms.' " Trevin had a small gleam in her eyes. "However, they have nowhere near as many engines as we have. For one thing, they use mundane materials—wood and non-ferrous metals—in their flying ships, rather than amorphous clouds."

"That would seem a bit easier," Elrose noted.

"True, but they power them primarily by geomancy and then use aeromastery with the sails for propulsion. This limits their altitude; they cannot get that far from the ground, and being open vessels, they cannot adjust atmospheric pressure. They have a maximum altitude of less than two leagues above whatever altitude the ground is."

"But if the mountains rise in altitude, they could repel against that and still climb over the mountains." Elrose pointed to the large mountains they were now passing over. "I thought you said the Oorstemothians could not scale them?"

Trevin smiled. "In theory, you would be correct, but they cannot pressurize their ships, so they would run out of air. However, perhaps they could create special suits. The bigger problem is that of propulsion up and down the mountainside. The steepness presents their method with serious problems. Their ability to climb in altitude decreases with the incline of the ground they are traveling above." Trevin grinned with delight while explaining this. "In other words, geomantic lift works perpendicular to the ground. Steep verticals mean they are pushing away from the mountain horizontally. They can correct for that, but they lose climbing capability as the slope becomes infinite. If a mountain slope were completely vertical, up and down, they would have nothing to push off of that would take them up. Add to that the horribly unpredictable winds around such tall mountains and they need incredibly powerful aeromastery to control those winds, fill the sails and not get the ship ripped to pieces."

Trevin leaned back against the railing. "I wish balling wizardry had always been what it is today; I would love to have shown you their attempts to serve notice on the Grove four hundred or so years ago. It was most amusing—for us, at least." She grinned wickedly.

"So how high could the Nimbus go?" Jenn asked Trevin.

Trevin made a small grimace as she thought. "Well, technically, it's only limited by how much mana we have to burn. It's that resource question again."

"So could you travel to either of the moons?" Jenn asked.

"I'm not at all sure why we would want to do that," Trevin said with a shrug, "but if we could figure out how to get enough mana, then probably. I suppose I have never really thought about it. There is nothing of interest on either of the moons, so I see no point in going there. It would also take a really long time."

Elrose frowned. "The air would be too thin, so how would you move without air?"

"Well the bigger issue is keeping the cloud and what air we have together; however, we can already do that at this high an altitude. Technically, in the absence of air there is vacuos, which can be manipulated by enchantment, as you know. But it would be slow going. However, I am sure Gnorbert could come up with something. It is an interesting thought, I suppose; an excellent theoretical exercise. Hmm." Trevin was lost in thought for a moment. "Yes, it would be tricky. I am probably going to be thinking about it all night, unable to sleep." She made a mock stern face at Elrose. "Thank you for sticking that in my head." She shook her head. "Fortunately, it's one exercise we won't ever have to do for real."

Trevin turned slightly to smile at Gastropé. "Maybe I'll need to figure out something else to keep me occupied tonight?" Gastropé gave her a small, tight grin, presumably being polite.

Jenn shook her head at the ancient wizard's more-than-obvious designs on poor Gastropé. She glanced again at the woman's way-too-revealing clothes. At least she did not have anything to worry about. Gastropé would never fall for Trevin; she was obviously way over a hundred. An image of the woman from last night, dancing on the satyr's lap, suddenly resurfaced in her mind. She had forgotten that. For some reason, at the bacchanalia Trevin had appeared young and stunningly gorgeous!

How could that be? How drunk had Jenn been? Did she have something to worry about? Wait— what was she thinking? She had no interest in Gastropé, so why was she suddenly worried that Trevin might steal him away or something? It was not any of Jenn's business! If the two wanted to... ugh, she did not want to think about that. Jenn closed her eyes for a brief moment to get a grip on herself. It was just her naturally competitive nature getting the better of her. She had seen Trevin's advances and her competitive streak had just kicked in, creating an artificial interest in Gastropé out of a sense of competition. She did this sort of thing all the time. She was sure it was only the fact that Lenamare was so insufferable that Jehenna's interest in him had not made her competitive.

Jenn shuddered. She did not like where this was going; she needed to change gears. She had nothing remotely like any interest *whatsoever* in Jehenna's and Lenamare's personal lives. So why should she care about Gastropé? Yes, he was clearly much more handsome, and much more pleasant—actually quite agreeable. Or at least he was after he stopped trying to kill her. Of course, she had easily beaten him on that front. That was satisfying, from a competitive point of view. Not that he was a slouch in the magic department; he had been really good on the ship fighting the Oorstemothians, and to be honest she had learned some good tricks of combat magic from him.

Oddly, he had turned out to be a decent friend. Really one of her better ones, other than Rex and Alvea. Of course, Rex was dead and Alvea was now being harangued by Jehenna. Maybe that was it: Trevin's advances on Gastropé bothered her because they were friends and she recognized that involvement with Trevin was not in his best interests. Yes, that made a lot of sense, Jenn realized.

"Don't you think, Jenn?" Gastropé asked her.

"What?" Jenn replied, realizing she had zoned out the conversation around her. She had no idea what he had asked her. "Sorry, I got lost in my own thoughts staring out this… what exactly is it?" She turned her head to Trevin.

Trevin grinned. "It's a sympathetic lens. We have lenses stationed at multiple points around the ship and we can tune this big lens to any of those lenses and see what we would see through them. Not completely different from mirrors. Actually simpler, in fact."

"Neat!" Gastropé said.

"Indeed," Maelen seconded. "I have seen an amazing number of new things on this short adventure so far. It's always nice to find new things at my age."

Trevin chuckled. "Wait until you get to be my age. I'm almost hoping we actually find this goddess."

"There are some new things I'm not so sure I need," Elrose replied drily.

Chapter 94

"Neat!" Rupert exclaimed.

"What the hell are they doing?" Reggie asked.

The group had just come over a ridge after a brief walk from the boom tunnel. Boggy and Tizzy had decided that the first stop on their tour of the Abyss would be some place called "Hellsprings Eternal." Tom had noticed the smell of sulfur immediately upon exiting the boom tunnel. Reggie and Talarius both took a few extra moments to notice it because they were reeling from the *boom* of the boom tunnel.

They had trudged up a well-worn path in long-ago-solidified lava rock to gaze into a valley with wide molten lava streams flowing out of a large crater about a thousand feet upstream of them. There were numerous shanties and other odd buildings lining the valley. However, what had gotten Reggie's attention was the fact that the valley was populated with quite a few demons of various shapes and sizes engaged in strange behavior.

There were quite a few that seemed to be wading, albeit slowly, in the molten lava streams. Others were lying on glowing red rocks near the lava flows as if they were sunning on a beach. About four hundred feet away, there was a group of demons apparently submerged to their necks in a pool of glowing hot, molten lava, just chatting away.

"Welcome to Hellsprings Eternal!" Boggy said, waving his hands broadly to announce the place.

"I haven't been here in at least a century," Antefalken said. "I have to admit, after the panic of that stupid spell and our near-permanent death experience at the hands of our new colleague" —he gestured towards Talarius—"a day at the spa sounds wonderful." He patted his pocket. "The day is on me! If anyone wants a massage or other spa treatment, or just some refreshing blood wine or Denubian Choco-Coffee™, just let me know!"

Boggy grinned. "That's mighty demonly of you, Anty!" He gestured to the lava streams. "There's no charge for dunking in the lava flows or just lying on the shores. The services are all at the various huts in the valley and they all list their prices. And all prices include tax."

"Tax?" Reggie asked. "Who is charging tax?"

"Moloch," Antefalken replied. "He's the demon prince that owns this part of the Abyss. He charges the vendors a tax on all sales and services. It's actually not that bad of a tax, as such things go, only fifteen percent."

"That's mighty reasonable," Tizzy said. "I don't remember him being all that reasonable, though."

Boggy shook his head. "That's because you were sleeping with his daughter."

"Oh, right. Forgot about that." Tizzy shrugged. "But technically, neither of us was sleeping…" Tizzy grinned lecherously. "If you know what I mean." He winked very broadly.

"What do you mean?" Rupert asked.

Boggy slapped his head. "Now see what you've done—you've opened Pandora's box with the boy."

"That's right! I had forgotten. Her name was Pandora, and I certainly opened her box… that was why Moloch was so mad at me. The young thing was only a couple centuries old when we 'slept' together."

"I'm confused… I thought you said you *didn't* sleep with her," Rupert said.

Tom coughed. "Technically, Rupert, demons don't need to sleep unless they are hurt. So when Tizzy says they were not sleeping together, he just meant they were spending down time together."

"We got down, all right." Tizzy chuckled.

"You aren't helping!" Boggy punched Tizzy in his upper left arm. "Just let it drop."

"Argh, all right." Tizzy frowned at Boggy. He then quickly rotated to Talarius. "You up for a dip in the lava, Paladin?"

"How many times do I have to tell you? I. Am. Not. A. Paladin," Talarius told Tizzy through obviously clenched teeth.

"Yeah, yeah. You're one of those knights with a rampant body part," Tizzy said.

Talarius clenched his mailed fists in frustration but said nothing.

"We are here to relax and show our guest a good time. So no baiting him, okay?" Tom scolded Tizzy.

Tizzy glanced at Tom in annoyance. "You know, you really can be a party pooper."

"We want to show Talarius that demons are people too. We like to laugh and play and get drunk, just like people, and there are good demons and bad demons," Tom reminded everyone.

"Propaganda will not work; I've been trained by the best," Talarius said.

Antefalken shook his head. "I think I'm going to head up to the gift shop. Maybe I can find us a game to while away the hours back in the cave."

Talarius harrumphed. "You expect to find a deck of cards and a whist marker, perhaps?"

Antefalken looked thoughtful. "Do you play whist?"

"Of course."

"Excellent. Then we shall look towards that as our principal objective. Come along," Antefalken told the knight.

"What? Are you saying that demons play whist?" Talarius asked, sounding shocked.

"Of course. It's a great way to pass the time, and demons often have a lot of time to pass. And it keeps one sharp," the bard replied.

"Yet it requires obeying the rules and detailed analysis, along with the application of logical principles," Talarius said as he followed the demon bard towards one of the shanties.

"Exactly why we like it. Demons have a thing for rules; we are bound by them and very fond of trying to exploit them, which makes us great game players!" Antefalken said.

"I think you are playing a game with me now."

Tom could see Antefalken shaking his head. "Sometimes, Talarius, a cigar is just a cigar."

~

"Trisfelt!" Hilda exclaimed as he wandered through the infirmary, where she was tending to patients.

"Excellent, I'd hoped you'd still be around!" Trisfelt exclaimed. "I was afraid Lenamare and Jehenna might have sent you fleeing the palace in terror, never to return!" He came up to her and gave her a brief, light hug.

Hilda beamed at the familiarity; one did not get a lot of hugs in Tierhallon. "Nonsense. I've served on battlefields and seen horrors nearly as bad!" She laughed lightly.

"Well, you were incredibly graceful and attentive to them, despite their typical patronizing attitudes," the wizard congratulated her.

"Again, nonsense. I've spent some time dealing with nobility and all sorts of high and mighty who really just don't know any other way to interact with people."

Trisfelt smiled. "I suspect that is part of their problem. I have to admit, they did seem to enjoy your company far more than they do most people's." He shook his head and rolled his eyes. "At breakfast this morning, Jehenna actually said they enjoyed your company last night!" He raised his hands in amazement. "I have never heard her say anything like that before. It was practically a miracle!"

Hilda beamed brightly and laughed. "I hardly think it a miracle. They are very talented people and quite fascinating; one just has to have a bit of patience and understanding."

"Patience and understanding? My dear, you have the patience and understanding of a saint!"

Hilda laughed and patted Trisfelt on the shoulder. "You flatter me; I am hardly a saint! I have over-indulged on more than one occasion." She paused and flashed him a grin. "As you may be aware."

They both laughed at that. "Say, you've been so generous with entertaining me, would you allow me to do the honor of returning your hospitality sometime? Perhaps tonight?"

Trisfelt smiled, pleasantly surprised. "Why, I'd love that, most certainly!"

"Excellent." Hilda made a deprecating gesture with her hands. "Now, I have these contractors that are redoing my clinic, which is the main level of my house; they were supposed to be finished while I was at the wedding, but…"

"A siege may have interfered?" Trisfelt suggested with some mirth.

"Apparently, it's hard to get wood and stone into a city when there is an army surrounding it." Hilda shook her head in mock surprise. "Plus, I think they sort of underestimated the time, and are possibly using this as an added reason." She gave a gentle sigh of exasperation.

"Thus, I fear that I am staying in a hotel and treating my patients in my parlor, ugh." Hilda made gestures with her hands as if calming her nerves a bit. "However, it is a decent inn; it's the Havestan Gardens."

Trisfelt raised an eyebrow and smiled. "What a happy coincidence. By sheer chance, I am sure, they happen to have the best wine cellar in the city, outside of a few private cellars in the palace."

"Do they?" Hilda overtly pretended to be ignorant of this fact. Trisfelt chuckled.

"My dear, your palate can no longer surprise me! I am sure you knew this full well when you checked in. Indeed, I am wondering exactly how upset you are by the delays to your reconstruction?"

"Dear Trisfelt, I assure you it is a horrible inconvenience, and I have no choice but to console myself from the inn's cellar each evening!" Hilda gave him look of feigned inconvenience, and they both laughed.

"I would be honored, My Lady." Trisfelt told her.

"Excellent. Shall I see you around the same time as last night's dinner?"

Trisfelt nodded. "That is an excellent time."

"Splendid!" Hilda smiled and then got a slightly surprised look on her face, as if she suddenly remembered something. "You know, Danyel was with the servants last night and they were all talking about the balling of the fight outside. He was told that it was quite spectacular. You don't by any chance have an idea of where a copy might be had? I myself have heard so much, but not actually seen it."

"Yes, yes, you should see it, it's remarkable. I saw it later, after the Council, because I was outside, as you know. Apparently, there are numerous shoddy mirrorings of the event around; but you must see the balling. The Council has made copies for all the councilors; Lenamare and Jehenna each have a copy. I am sure I can borrow one of theirs; particularly when I tell them that it's for you to see."

"Oh you are such a dear, and I'm sure Danyel will be as grateful as I!" Hilda exclaimed.

~

"Well, hello there!" A voice called to Tom as he was walking past one of the shanties. He turned to look towards the open-faced shanty to see Sam lying on a padded table getting a massage from a rather large, homely demoness.

"Hey, Sam!" Tom replied, walking over to the table.

"Yesterday was quite the workout, so I thought I'd come by here and get a massage. My muscles are killing me. The problem with this form is that I have it memorized at a certain point in time, and that somehow never includes having muscles that are used to mountain climbing. You would think I could manage to memorize the form after climbing rather than before." He shook his head. "Of course, if I did that, then I wouldn't feel the need for a message from my favorite masseuse, Helgadavichanova here." He nodded his head back towards the masseuse.

"Nice!" Tom grinned. "Looks relaxing. Do you come here often?"

"Mainly for the massages, although sometimes after a cold day skiing, it's nice to relax in the lava," Sam said.

"Did you bring your company here for some fun?" Sam asked.

"Yeah, we were feeling a bit cooped up, so thought we'd come and stretch a little, relax," Tom said.

"Excellent idea—this place is great for that," Sam said.

"Well, I better let you get back to your massage. It's not very relaxing if you have to twist your neck to talk to me." Tom laughed.

Sam laughed as well. "Very true. As great as it is to see you again, you are correct. Take care!"

"You too!" Tom said as he strolled off. Despite what Tizzy had said, Tom rather liked Sam. He was the most normal person Tom had met in the Abyss. And that included Talarius, whom he had brought to the Abyss with him. He shook his head. Finally, a normal person!

~

Gastropé was enjoying iced tea in the starboard lounge and watching the clouds go by below them at the launch reception. Jenn, Maelen, Elrose, Trevin were there, as was Second Mate Trefalger and several crew members he had been introduced to but frankly could not remember the names of.

They had just passed over the outer rim of the Grove's mountain ranges and the sky above and to some extent below was iridescent with various bands and streaks of color. Trefalger had explained that the streaks were auroras caused by the intersection of various planes with the Grove.

Elrose and Maelen were both standing near the room's viewing lens, practically pressed up against it, watching every sight go by. Gastropé would probably have been there too, but he wanted to try to seem a bit more cosmopolitan. It was difficult, however; this was the closest he had ever been to interdimensional travel.

Well, except for his multiple trips to the Abyss. Okay, he supposed that more than counted. While there were numerous powerful wizards and Sidhe that travelled the Planes of Man to the localverse and beyond, very few ever travelled to the Abyss. At least not travelled and returned. That was something he and Jenn had on everyone else onboard the Nimbus—well, except for Maelen, who had done it once.

Gastropé grinned despite himself. The crew of the Nimbus might travel the localverse and the Planes of Men with barely a thought, but he and Jenn (okay, and Maelen) had been to the Abyss and returned. Multiple times, in fact! Of course, the interesting thing now was that they were actually on several planes at once. He did have to admit that was pretty exciting.

Gastropé tried to remember the names of the different worlds they were currently in: Astlan (obviously), Etterdam, Nysegard, Romdan, Avalon and Targella. Those were what they called the immediate localverse. Apparently, there some other worlds in the localverse, but the Grove was not connected directly to those. They key point of the localverse was that the rules of magic were the same in all of them. A wizard spell that worked in one of the worlds would work in any of the others. Typically, the exact same spells did not exist in each of the worlds, certainly not by the same name; however, there were analogues for many of them. Any spell Gastropé knew and had components for, he could cast on those worlds and get the same results.

Gastropé was trying to think how this must work when suddenly the room—the entire ship, in fact—rocked violently. The ship seemed to tilt aftward and to port briefly before righting itself. A klaxon sounded loudly and the mirror on the back wall suddenly started flashing: "Defensive Configuration 1."

Trefalger ran over to the mirror and shouted at it, "Trefalger here, connect the bridge!" The image in the mirror suddenly shifted from the room to one of the mirrors on the bridge. There, several people were scrambling to clear the bridge through one door and others were running in through a second door.

In the lounge, Trevin rushed to stand next to Trefalger. "Status?" she asked.

A gnome that Gastropé did not recognize responded. "We've taken an aft hit from below off the port side. It appears to be an ice blast that momentarily destabilized that part of the cloud. We've gotten the temperatures back up above freezing now."

On the mirror, another crewmember shouted, "Bringing generators to full. Lightning batteries will be ready in thirty seconds."

Gastropé could hear a large humming sound; it seemed to permeate the ship. He suddenly realized that the walls of the room were getting very dark, like a storm cloud!

"Elemental water portals online!" someone on the bridge shouted.

"Elemental air portals also online, Captain!" a third person shouted.

"What hit us?" Trevin demanded.

Aêthêal appeared in the mirror, standing over the gnome. "Surveillance is detecting three storm liches on ice dragons aft and below port!" she said loudly.

Another voice shouted, "We've spotted two more coming up from starboard!"

"There!" Maelen shouted. Everyone in the lounge except for Trevin and Trefalger turned to look.

"Illiana protect us!" Jenn said loudly enough for everyone to hear.

Gastropé felt the blood draining from his face. Down and aftward on the giant viewing lens, he could see two bluish-white dragons with riders in great black cloaks. They were distant, but approaching rapidly.

"Nysegard?" Trevin demanded of Aêthêal.

"Has to be. But we've never seen five of them ready to hit us, and at this altitude!" Aêthêal said.

"I thought this was too high to breathe?" Maelen asked.

Trefalger replied, "They are storm liches—being undead, they don't breathe. The ice dragons can hold their breath for a very long time. Or so it seems; maybe they don't breathe either. Whatever the case, they can and have attacked us this high. But never with this many." Trefalger was shaking his head.

"Scramble carpets!" the captain shouted. "High altitude com circlets are a must!"

"We have another sighting directly ahead. Four more liches on ice dragons!" someone on the bridge shouted.

"Dungnation!" Trevin shouted. "This has to be a trap! They had to know we were coming out and the general vicinity!" She looked around.

"Gastropé!" She stared right at him, and he jumped. "We need all available hands. You were in Exador's army, yes?"

Gastropé nodded, but he had no idea what he could do.

"Get your combat magic components and follow Zed here"—she tapped a satyr on the shoulder—"to the flight deck."

"Uh…" Gastropé started to say as Zed came towards him. He felt the blood draining from his face. They wanted him, Gastropé, to fight liches mounted on dragons?

"Jenn, you are a thaumaturge. Not a lot of green or ground up here, but you can heal, right?" Jenn nodded. "Good, go with Talinea to the catcher carpet bay!" She gestured at a two-foot-high Sidhe of some sort. Jenn started making similar noises to those Gastropé had made. "Catcher carpets fly below and catch aetós and others that get knocked out of the sky, and heal them —or try," Trevin explained, seeing Jenn's confusion.

"Maelen, we'll need you on the flight deck with a com-link to the bridge for Seeing. Be ready to heal our wounded that can't be dealt with by the catcher carpet teams."

"Elrose…" Trevin turned to the wizard.

Elrose nodded. "I'll grab my stuff from my room and head to the flight deck. We are in my element up here!" Trevin smiled and nodded.

Gastropé could hear no more, as Zed was physically dragging him from the room. The ship lurched as it took another hit. Gastropé was more than a bit concerned; they were presumably at full defense now. That must have been a nasty hit.

~

"This way!" Zed instructed Gastropé. They had retrieved the bag he had prepared for combat magic back in the Grove, and now Zed led him quickly aftward along the cloudship. By this point, the walls of the cloud were darkly mottled black and gray with flashes of lightning coruscating through the walls and the parts of the floor not covered in carpet. The whine of the generators was now loud enough that they had to shout to be heard.

"Storm liches are a real pain! They are the biggest pain we typically face," Zed shouted as he led the way. "Being liches, they are quite resistant to lightning, which is the ship's primary ranged weapon system. The ice dragons do take some damage from lightning, mostly impact related. At least it slows them down."

"What about fire?" Gastropé was trying to remember some of the more esoteric things he had learned. He had never in a million years expected to have to fight liches *or* dragons. That was not something normal people did! That was the stuff of bards' tales and legends!

Zed shook his head. "Ice dragons take some damage from fire—it can melt their armor—but it's gotta be hot! The liches are so cold that they can typically shield the dragons. Really hot fire can in theory damage them, but their intense coldness acts like very good armor. So they might as well be immune to it."

"Crap!" Gastropé yelled as they headed up a spiral staircase to the top floor. His only real attack spells were fire and lightning based. So what was he going to do other than be dragon fodder? As they reached the top floor, he realized it was a different top floor than he had seen before. This was a good-sized room with people scrambling about readying carpets.

Zed led them to a gnome who was handing out various pieces of equipment. Zed gestured to the gnome with two raised fingers and was promptly handed two circlets. "Here, put this around your neck! Pull it apart in the back."

Gastropé took the circlet—really, a solid neckband that was open at the back, but which appeared to have some sort of clasping mechanism. It was made out of gold and silver-colored metal with various rings of different colored stones embedded in the band. It was a tight fit, but he got it around his neck.

Zed had his on already. He came up to Gastropé and snapped the back into place so it was locked. He began twisting the colored gem bands on the circlet. "There, I've tuned it to the same linkage that we will use on our carpet."

"What is this?" Gastropé asked.

"It serves two purposes: first, it's a life support system. It will keep you warm and supplied with air on the carpet. We are way too high up to breathe otherwise, and it's colder than a lich's teat out there. Or almost." Zed shrugged, realizing they would soon have to fight liches and discover how cold that might be. "It also has links to allow us to send and receive communications with others. I just set the default link to the one we'll be using on Peter's carpet." He added, "There is also the general command frequency that we can all hear messages on. We try to not use it except for priority orders and instructions."

Zed was now leading them over towards a carpet where the human boy, Peter, was adjusting straps and talking to others about to board. Peter was the combat pilot they had met on the trip up to the carpet.

"Understand," said Zed, looking Gastropé in the eye, "this is going to be trial by fire for you—or rather, freezing in this case. Normally, we don't fight at this altitude. Storm liches and ice dragons are about the only thing that can attack us this high. It is just below freezing out there, and the air is too thin for even the aetós to fly. Spell casting is going to be very tricky and dangerous. They appear to have sent almost all the storm liches against us; they had to know we were leaving about now and where we were going and therefore exiting." He shook his head. "That's why we are sending everyone, including new people, out to fight."

Gastropé swallowed hard and nodded, knowing his face had to be showing his terror. He had to try to suck it up. Be brave and not look like a complete imbecile. They were counting on him. He only hoped he could count on himself.

"Gastropé!" Peter called with a smile. "In the fight! Hah! No better way to learn than to jump into the nastiest battle we've had in centuries!"

"You are nuts, Peter!" a young woman in an extremely tight-fitting suit of stretchy material said. She glanced at Gastropé. "I am Penelope and yes, I am a nymph and yes, I can do something besides make wild passionate love for hours on end."

"But she's very good at that!" Zed exclaimed with a leer. She glared at the satyr. "She's also a combat geomancer, which is something we are going to really need today!"

"Why? We are so high up that—" Gastropé began.

"Gravity sucks!" Penelope shouted and gave him a quick kiss on the cheek. She then strode to a cushion on the carpet and began strapping herself in.

"She's right. The force of gravity is still quite potent up here, and neither liches nor dragons have any real defense against it." Peter smiled as he pointed to a cushion for Gastropé.

Zed took the very back center cushion; Peter moved towards the front center cushion. He and Penelope were in the two side-by-side cushions. "This is one of the older, smaller carpets. We are using nearly everyone today, so we've put some heavy hitters that don't normally fly combat on the newer six-person carpets," Zed told him. That explained why it had fewer seats.

"On the bright side," Peter said, grinning as he strapped himself in, "this is the carpet I used to set my speed record. It's a lean, mean flying machine!"

Gastropé got himself situated and strapped in; Zed double-checked from behind him. "Strapped in!" the satyr called.

Gastropé quickly began trying to shove his component bag into the pouch before him. He wished he had been able to wizardize his staff; that would have been really useful. As it was, he had a wand of fire bolts he had been barely able to afford in Freehold. It was one that was wizard-powered, meaning it had no mana of its own, but worked as a catalyst so he didn't need the regular material components. Just some key phrases, will power and mana. Unfortunately, he hadn't realized he'd be fighting creatures nearly impervious to fire, or he might have gotten something else. Nevertheless, what did he have that might be useful? He could do lightning bolts, but that would have to be done the traditional way and on a high-speed carpet, he'd likely fumble the spell and kill them all.

The carpet seemed to lurch as it came alive. Peter grinned. "We all good?" Everyone nodded. He smiled and turned around. "Up, up and away!"

The carpet began moving upward rapidly. Gastropé looked up to see the stormy cloud ceiling approaching quickly. He was sure they were going to crash into the roof when the clouds suddenly parted and they were up and out.

"Peter on carpet 69, we are cloud free!" Peter shouted. The link channel to the command center came online as someone, Gastropé could not tell whom, gave Peter some instructions. Gastropé, however, was lost staring up above them. The observation deck and view lenses had mainly been looking down or to the sides. He could now stare straight up into the darkest blue-black that he could imagine.

Nearly overhead and a bit to the east, mighty Fierd was a giant, angry ball of fire. However, off beside Fierd the sky was not the normal blue, but rather the inky blackness of the night sky. Only as one's eyes dove towards the horizon did the sky turn blue. Gastropé gulped at the overwhelming majesty of the sight.

"We have our target!" Peter shouted as the carpet banked heavily to starboard. Gastropé grabbed onto the rope handle beside his seat as the carpet tilted. He had never felt this degree of motion on a carpet before.

They came out of the bank and raced over the roiling, angry cloudship, then suddenly there was open air below them, and they were diving at a terrifying speed. Up ahead he could see the small forms of the dragon-borne liches towards which they raced, below and aft of the ship.

Gastropé furrowed his brow as he watched the rapidly approaching dragons. "Zed, you said that the air was too thin for the aetós to fly?"

"Yep," came the satyr's reply over the linked circlets.

"So how are the ice dragons able to fly up here?" Gastropé asked.

ZZzzsssttt! Gastropé jumped as a giant bolt of lightning arced overhead towards the lich and dragon. It appeared to only briefly hit the dragon's wing, but he could not be sure. The odd part was that the thunder was very mild and subdued compared to the size and proximity of the bolt. Clearly the air was too thin for loud thunder, just a zapping noise.

Peter ignored the lightning and laughed, as did Penelope.

"That is an excellent question!" Zed replied in answer to how ice dragons could fly at this altitude.. "One that we carpet warriors have often debated."

"Fortunately," Peter said, "we have come up with the only possible explanation!"

"Which is?" Gastropé asked.

"It's magic!" The other three all shouted in unison before bursting into laughter. *ZZzzssstttt!* Went another quiet lightning.

~

Elrose hurried towards one of the topside portals. As he had gotten to the upper deck, he had been handed a high-altitude com unit for communication, breathing and warmth. That would save him some effort. A satyr had helped dial him into the same link that Maelen and the others on the top of the ship would be using.

It had taken him longer to get here than one might have hoped. He had not yet properly unpacked his baggage and so had been forced to scramble through his trunks and wardrobe to get everything together. Fortunately, he kept his combat robe stocked and mostly ready to go. He'd swapped out a few of his wands for ones he thought be more appropriate, and had a few seconds of debate on the choice of rings. Several of them did not get along with each other, given elemental affiliations and such. However, he had felt that some additional lightning protection would be worthwhile.

He also had to load up on the most relevant potions. He grabbed several vials of plain water as well. One could not store potions in a combat robe; most potions had to be relatively fresh. He had swapped out his boots and belt and finally grabbed his primary combat staff. He took only one staff, since he would need the other hand for wands.

He noted the pressure spell keeping a barrier between the ship and the ladders leading topside. He stepped through and felt the air pressure drop and temperature decrease quickly. Fortunately, the com circlet was doing its job. He would need to study these units, if he survived.

Elrose awkwardly climbed the ladder; the staff and his long robe made it tricky. He finally made it to the roof of the cloudship. There was Maelen near the front of the ship, looking towards the newest arrivals. As he headed toward the seer, a carpet rose through the roof of the cloud to his left and then quickly spun and headed aft of the ship and down towards the majority of attackers.

"What do we have ahead?" Elrose asked the seer.

"These four liches and dragons are further out, so the carpets have been going aft. We now have two carpets headed to the forward targets, and a third is nearing launch," Maelen responded.

Elrose nodded. "Trevin?"

Trevin came in over the command channel. "Go ahead, Elrose."

"Alright if I take one or more of the forward attackers?" Elrose asked.

"By yourself?" Trevin sounded uncertain.

"It's been a while, but I think I should be able to manage at least one, and do damage to a few of the others," the wizard responded. Maelen raised an eyebrow, impressed.

"Go for it," Trevin came back.

Elrose smiled at Maelen. "Never fought a lich, but I wrote a paper on ice dragons once. Have a pretty good idea how to deal with them."

"Then have fun turning theory to practice," Maelen chuckled.

Elrose grinned and concentrated on his boots, reciting the keyword to activate his link to them. His robe began to billow as the boots brought up air pressure underneath and around them, allowing Elrose to rise above the ground. He nodded to Maelen with a grin and said, "Gotta run!" Maelen nodded as Elrose took off running very quickly towards the forward dragons.

~

Jenn gulped as the very large carpet they were on began surging downward. It felt like her stomach was going to come up through her mouth. She gritted her teeth and hung on tighter.

The catcher carpets were larger and more complex than the combat carpets. The main carpet was good sized and could, in theory, seat eight. However, some space was reserved for those who were caught, so the crew was only five people: the pilot, a backup pilot, Jenn, an aeromaster named Paulinas who could also do some healing, and a large fellow about whom she knew nothing. The most obvious thing for him to do was probably to reel people in.

The carpet was odd in that the "carpet" part of it, while good sized, was not out of line for a large room carpet. However, around the edges of the carpet, including the corners, were large nets extending another fifteen feet from the carpet. Magical buoys at the inner and outer corners of the netting supported the nets in the air. Apparently, these carpets actually caught falling people.

Their pilot, Talinea, had told her they were fortunate today in that there would be no aetós in the air due to insufficient air to provide lift for their wings. Therefore, they would be concentrating on spotting and catching people knocked off carpets. That and coming alongside carpets to try to heal people.

Jenn took a deep breath. If she had thought healing people on the sailing ship was a task, this was insane! As they plummeted to get below the rear attackers, she noted that the large fellow was paying very close attention to the carpets that were approaching the dragons. She suddenly realized that he must have some form of magical vision to spot people.

That gave her an idea. She had not been sure what she as a thaumaturge could bring to the table, but she could enhance her eyesight with a spell she knew. That would allow her to spot people in trouble. She grabbed the necessary components and began the spell.

As the spell took hold, she blinked to adjust her new high-powered vision. She decided she would also turn on wizard sight, as that might help spot potential issues. She blinked again and looked over towards the liches. Crap! She wished she had not done that. The ice dragons appeared about as she would expect, although what she expected she did not know, but the liches were coiling masses of blackness. Not at all pleasant; in fact, quite disquieting.

Jenn spoke to her carpetmates on her circlet. "I've upped my eyesight and wizard sight. Should I keep an eye out across the board, or should I focus on particular carpets?"

The large fellow turned and grinned at her. "Teamwork, good."

~

Crap! That thing is big! Gastropé thought to himself, seeing the ice dragon as they swung in closer to the dragon-mounted lich. He really had to focus on the giant ice dragon, which was about one hundred feet long from nose to tail. The reason for his focus on the ice dragon was due to the fact that he had tried to look at the storm lich and had nearly soiled his pants.

For once, he was glad to have faced down Tom in the valley, because while the lich was completely terrifying, it was still less terrifying than a greater demon. Actually, Tom was terrifying, but was not sickening. That was the difference, Gastropé decided in the few moments he had to think about it. A greater demon radiated awe-inspiring power, making one feel feeble and insignificant; the lich sent deep, ancestral chills down one's spine.

The storm lich was probably about seven feet tall, emaciated and wearing rotting formal clothes with a huge, ragged black cape. But the rotting clothes were nothing compared to the lich's rotting flesh. His first look at the lich's eyeless face had revealed what appeared to be maggots crawling from the lich's eye sockets, as well as holes in its cheeks. Further, the cold near the ice dragon and lich were far worse than the already sub-freezing wind temperature.

"*Idire nox firatus!*" Gastropé shouted, launching a fireball from his wand nearly point-blank at the lich where it was perched on the dragon's back. He did not want to stare directly at it. The carpet quickly banked, even as the ice dragon stumbled in the air just below them. Penelope's gravity spell or whatever it was had rocked the dragon.

Gastropé twisted his head to look back at the dragon and lich to see if his spell had done much. Apparently not. Another carpet was coming in on the same trajectory they had just used. Fireballs, lightning bolts and some more weird light disturbances from the gravity wave rolled over the dragon and lich. Gastropé could not see much more of the latest attack, as they were moving quickly away to get lined up again.

"Incoming!" Zed shouted. Gastropé twisted to the rear to see rapidly approaching icicles coming at them from the lich. "*Idire tres firatus aerus!*" Gastropé shouted and pointed towards the icicle barrage with his wand, releasing a superheated blast of fire to melt the missiles.

Zed cursed and started patting his curly hair. "You nearly fried my locks!"

"You prefer singes or ice daggers to the heart?" Gastropé asked.

ZZzzssstttt! A silent lightning bolt from the ship struck the dragon.

Wow, those things are huge compared to the ones I can create, Gastropé thought to himself as he saw it up close.

Penelope was busy concentrating on her next spell. He wished he could think of something big and nasty that would work, but he really did not have much ready other than fire and lightning. That was usually fine for most combat magic. Clearly, his training had not considered beings immune to such things. Gastropé frowned. Given that besides the Oorstemothians, most of the opposing forces he had gone up against had been either demons, ice dragons or liches, none of whom were that bothered by fire, he really needed to get some new spells.

As they banked for the next round, Peter called back, "Gastropé, aim for the dragon's face this time. See if you can melt its eyebrows, get water in its eyes, blind it, and distract it. Penelope's about to try to hit it hard with a giant gravity suck to try to pull it to the ground. We are so high, I'm not sure how well it will work, but it's worth a shot, and the more disoriented it is, the better."

"Got it!" Gastropé yelled back. Actually, he did not need to yell with the com circlet, but his ears were so plugged from the altitude that it was hard to hear. At least the wind was not that bad, given that there was very little air.

Gastropé chanted quickly to start upping the mana level for his next wand blast. He was going to try to do a sustained cone of fire. The carpet spun and started heading straight for the lich and dragon. "*Idire tres firatus aerus mesapus!*" Gastropé shouted, aiming. The fire from his wand expanded outward in a cone as expected; what was unexpected was the return of the dragon's icy-cold breath! The cone of flame and somewhat conical ice blast met between the two parties, sending blasts of fire, ice and water in all directions, including back to the carpet. Gastropé wanted to curse, but he needed to keep his concentration on the cone of fire. He muttered the incantations to up the power and replenish the flow, but this was going to be hard.

Suddenly Penelope shoved both her arms out towards the dragon and swept them downward. The dragon lurched hard and began plunging towards the ground. The lich screeched, an absolutely terrifying sound, and seemed to rise off its saddle as it scrambled to hang on, its ride suddenly hurtling towards the ground. The two dropped from sight even as the carpet moved over the area where they had been.

"Wow, that must have been one loud screech if we could hear it!" Zed laughed.

The four on the carpet cheered; glancing at the other carpet, they saw several thumbs up. Gastropé was thrilled. That was exciting! He glanced over at the other battles; there had been five dragons and liches aft of the ship. There were ten carpets behind the ship, two per dragon and lich pair.

As he turned his eyes back to their partner carpet, he saw it lurch dramatically as an enormous lightning bolt from the lich struck the pilot. The carpet began quickly spinning, twisting and losing altitude. It somersaulted a couple of times and then the rear pilot managed to regain control; however, on the last roll the wounded front pilot was wrenched from the carpet and began free falling through the air. There was smoke from the front of the carpet; the pilot's straps had probably been burnt off.

Crap! Gastropé was appalled to see how fast the pilot was falling. He peered over the edge to see a catcher carpet moving through the air at an amazing speed, trying to position itself under the falling pilot. Gastropé could not see if the pilot was caught, as Peter banked the carpet, causing the catcher carpet and pilot to go below Gastropé's line of sight.

"Problem, folks!" Peter called. "Our friend is coming back up!" He pointed down, into the bank. Sure enough, the lich and dragon they had sent speeding downward were returning quickly, climbing almost straight up. "Penelope, if we dive bomb them, can you gravity blast them back?"

"I will try!" Penelope yelled and began preparing a spell.

"Hang on, everyone!" Peter called as he spun the carpet in a tight circle and then directed it almost straight down in a collision course with the lich and dragon.

Gastropé shook his head; he had no real idea what to do other than repeat his last attack. As they got into close range, Gastropé pointed his wand and chanted the key phrase for another extended cone of fire. The fire leapt from the wand and Gastropé worked hard to adjust his aim. At such long distances it was tricky, as every movement caused the tower of flame to wave in arcs from side to side or up and down as he adjusted his aim.

Penelope yelled something and their carpet lurched hard as if in recoil. There was a roar as the ice dragon fell back and began plummeting again. Peter righted the carpet; they were now below the catcher carpet. Gastropé hoped they had caught the plunging pilot.

Suddenly the carpet's edge frosted over and Gastropé's butt got extremely cold.

"Crap! The bastard hit us directly from below!" Zed shouted from behind Gastropé.

Peter wrestled for control of the carpet; it had suddenly become hard to maneuver, as the carpet's flexibility was lost due to ice on the bottom of the carpet.

Gastropé frowned. *This is not going well*, he thought.

Elrose was finally within range of the dragon and lich he had selected. On foot, he was slower than the carpets heading for the other dragons and liches, but he was able to use that time and his Sight to study his opponent. Things looked as expected.

The ice dragon was made out of ice, frozen water, and while the lich's cold aura along with the dragon's own made it very hard for fire to get close, there were other ways to induce a phase change. This was one melee in which combat sorcery trounced the showier pyromancy.

With his staff, he could bypass the normal material and somatic components; he need only chant the verbal components and point. Time for the first phase change spell. Actually, time to hurry—the dragon was within range and appeared ready to blast him.

"...*eratos notros morphum!*" Elrose finished his chant and directed his staff directly at the ice dragon. The dragon shook hard and was suddenly quite a bit smaller. *Argh! That was annoying. Once more!* Elrose blasted a second phase change spell at the dragon.

The dragon screeched loudly as it turned completely to water. "Now!" Elrose shouted and followed with a third, yet different phase change spell. Water could easily become ice once again; steam would take more work! Elrose chanted and released the spell.

Even as small crystals of ice began reforming above the now-falling lich, those crystals suddenly turned to steam. Now for his second area of study: enchantment. Using his staff instead of the material components, Elrose cast a spell to create a high-pressure region in the middle of the dragon steam and let it dissipate into the surrounding low-pressure region, sending dragon steam far and wide! The ice dragon would eventually reform, but it would be a while. Quite a while. For now, it was just the lich.

Elrose glanced down at the lich, which had regained its composure and was now flying on its own, heading towards Elrose. Elrose grinned—he loved sorcery.

He chanted a quick spell of true aim, relying on sorcery's seeing powers, and quickly lobbed a vial at the lich. The potion bottle arced perfectly through the air. As it reached the lich, Elrose gestured with his staff, exploding the bottle, which contained only simple water. The staff's spell simply used the water as a material component to open a portal to the Elemental Plane of Water.

The portal would not stay open for long, but it would be long enough for several thousand gallons of water to flow through, surrounding the lich in the freezing atmosphere. A more mundane phase change then occurred as the several thousand gallons of water surrounding the lich froze into a solid, giant block of ice. *Thank you, Mr. Lich,* Elrose murmured.

The lich-cube began plummeting to the ground. Elrose doubted the lich would be able to free himself before it hit the ground. He grinned and turned his attention to the next dragon and lich pair.

~

Jenn worked feverishly on the pilot's burns. She was still on a massive adrenaline rush; the chase to catch the fallen pilot had gotten her blood racing. They had maneuvered under the falling pilot and Paulinas had been able to use aeromancy to slow the pilot's fall.

The pilot had landed in one of the nets and Jorg, the large fellow, had hauled her in. Jenn had then quickly set about working on treating her burns. They were very nasty electrical burns; a bit out of her normal range, but something she was trained to deal with.

No, she could deal with the burns, particularly with some added help from Paulinas; what was really keeping her adrenaline up was seeing Gastropé on another nearby carpet. This could easily have been Gastropé. That bothered her greatly for some reason. She knew it was irrational; they had been in combat together before, and with each other. They both knew the risks, so why was she suddenly so concerned for him?

~

This was definitely not going well, Gastropé thought. Their partner carpet was back online, but was in a dangerous state with a missing pilot, given that it was a larger, six-person carpet. According to Peter, the big carpets were less maneuverable with only one pilot. The smaller carpets like theirs were more maneuverable and could get by with one really good pilot, but the larger ones generally needed both pilots to keep things steady in combat flight and allow the spell casters to work.

That meant that Gastropé's group's carpet was doing much of the work. At least, all of the sweeping attacks. The other carpet worked as a mobile platform, but its lower mobility meant that it was easier for the lich or dragon to hit. Thus, the casters had to work more defensively, and the attacks were easier for the lich to avoid.

ZZzzssstttt! Another quiet lightning bolt shot by to their left. It missed.

They had made several more passes at the lich, but the results were not much better than before. They were keeping the lich and dragon from the Nimbus, but that was about it. They needed to shake things up; they needed another weapon. The tools they had were not sufficient.

A loud explosion came from their port direction. Gastropé glanced to see another carpet working a different lich spiraling down with a large cloud of black smoke trailing it. His vision was not good enough to see, but it looked like many of the carpet riders were bent over or lying down.

This was not good. Gastropé looked at the lich with his wizard sight. It was so disturbing, that oily black cloud of foulness, but he had to find some advantage. There was no obvious answer and he was getting tired, as was Penelope. He hung his head for a moment as they began banking for another turn.

As he looked down, his wizard sight still active, he saw the link to Tizzy. Did he dare? Bringing that crazy demon here could be suicide! However, surely Tom would be upset with Tizzy if Tizzy killed Gastropé. Would that not keep the demon in check? He had to take the risk. They were not going to win at this rate.

They came around for another pass. Gastropé launched his cone of fire against the dragon's wings, hoping to melt them slightly. Penelope targeted the same wing, trying to tilt the dragon and pull it down. They had tried to repeat the gravity suck thing a few times, but the lich had gotten skilled enough to thwart them each time, resulting in only minor downtime for the dragon and lich.

The flames and gravity blast did not do any more than expected. Gastropé shook his head and decided to go for it. He chanted the spell to open the link, a summoning prelude for a bound demon.

"*Tizzy?*" Gastropé asked. Suddenly, faster than he would have imagined, he saw Tizzy's smiling face, or rather the demon's head, in his mind's eye. Gastropé blinked in surprise. Tizzy was buried to his neck in molten lava!

"*Greetings, Accursed Master!*" Tizzy shouted back, apparently very happy to see him.

"*Are you okay?*" Gastropé asked, concerned to see the demon in the hot lava.

"*Sure, just relaxing! Going with the flow, as they say.*" Tizzy flashed him a bright grin. "*So what's up?*"

"*Uhm, I'm sort of in a jam and I need your help?*" Gastropé said.

"*You need my help? Moi?*" Gastropé had not thought it possible, but Tizzy's grin got wider.

"*Yes, and I need it fast. I'm on a flying carpet and we are fighting a bunch of storm liches on ice dragons and things aren't going that well,*" Gastropé explained.

"*Storm liches? Ice dragons?*" Tizzy asked; he suddenly looked upset. "*Why wouldn't you invite me to that party? I thought we were friends! How could you go partying with them and not invite me?*"

Gastropé shook his head at the demon's insane mental processes. "*We are really high in the stratosphere, where the air is thin. Aetós cannot fly here, but for some reason ice dragons can. Can you?*"

Tizzy snorted. "*Adding insult to injury?*" He shook his head. "*I am a demon! I can obviously fly there; I can fly anywhere I damn well please!*" he retorted before tilting his head a bit and frowning. "*As well as several I don't please.*"

"Well, could you maybe come help me out? Eviscerate a few liches, dragons and such?" Gastropé asked. They were taking another pass by this point, but Gastropé sat it out; he needed to talk to Tizzy.

"Hmm, can I bring some friends?" Tizzy asked.

"You mean Tom?" Gastropé asked. That would certainly fix the lich problem, but could create quite a few others.

"Nah. He, Antefalken, Rupert, Reggie and Talarius are over at the shanties shopping." Tizzy shook his head. *"Guys?"* He was apparently talking to some other demons. *"You up to disemboweling some liches and melting some ice dragons?"* Tizzy nodded and grinned.

"Well?" Tizzy asked Gastropé.

"Sure, the more help the better!" Gastropé was getting desperate; the others on the carpet were now watching him, trying to figure out what he was up to, and the lich was going to be attacking them soon. His conversations were all mental, so to them he appeared to be in a trance.

"Excellent; so make some fire, and recite the standard chant for a fiend. I can bring them through with me," Tizzy instructed.

Gastropé looked up and around at the others. "I hope this isn't insane." They looked at him askance; he shook his head and quickly activated his wand, shooting fire out over the edge of the carpet. It was tricky to maintain that and chant the fiend ritual, but he needed to do this.

He heard Penelope behind him. "Am I crazy or is he trying to summon a demon on a flying carpet moving at fifty miles per hour?"

"No… I think that's what he's doing. He's the one that's crazy!" Zed said.

Gastropé ignored them and hoped this would work. He did not know Tizzy's true name, but with the binding, he should not technically need to speak it, or even think it. It should be built into the binding.

As his chant came to an end, three figures began forming in his wand's fire cone. One was Tizzy; the second was a large, craggy humanoid demon with large wings, and the third a shorter, chubbier demon who even so, was still rather ferocious. If he had to guess, the other two were fiends like Tizzy.

He heard Penelope and Zed gulp behind him.

Peter glanced over and his eyes widened as he saw the three demons. "Unholy shit!" he exclaimed.

"Thanks!" The short, chubby one waved at Peter.

"Where's dinner?" Tizzy asked.

"There!" The craggy, humanoid demon pointed to the lich and dragon.

"I love ice carving!" the short one yelled as the three demons took off at high speed towards the lich and its dragon.

Somehow, Gastropé could hear the smaller demon ask the others, "Liches are dead, right? So how do we kill them?"

"No idea!" Tizzy said. "I think that will make it fun. We just shred it into lots of pieces and see if it regenerates."

"Abyss, that geezer looks a might moldy as it is!" The craggy one said. "I bet he's all squishy and mushy!"

"If not now, he will soon be!" Tizzy yelled.

The three demons descended on the lich and ice dragon. Suddenly ice chips were flying everywhere. Dark clouds of smoke and a horrible stench rose from the battle. How did they smell a stench? Gastropé wondered. Or was it just him with his link to Tizzy? He shook his head; it was not quite clear exactly what was going on.

There was a ton of screeching and lightning bolts started raining down on the demons, but they apparently had little trouble shrugging them off. The entire group was suddenly engulfed in a large cloud of ice crystals as waves of cold began reaching the carpet. Thunder rolled from the cloud as the blackness quickly enshrouded everything.

There was a loud *boom* and suddenly everything was silent. Gastropé was concerned—scared, really. Had the lich slain the demons? Suddenly the cloud began breaking apart and the three demons came flying raggedly out of the black cloud, laughing and slapping each other.

"Woo hoo! Now that was fun!" Tizzy said. All three were definitely looking a bit worse for the wear, but seemed to be in pretty good shape.

"Got any more?" Tizzy asked.

Gastropé pointed towards another of the lich dragon pairs.

"Ho! You didn't tell me it was an all-you-can-slaughter smorgasbord!" the craggy demon yelled at Tizzy. "Charge!" The three demons charged off and up in the air towards that next dragon and lich.

~

Elrose finished his second lichcicle and started running over to where three carpets were attacking the next lich. The remaining two liches each had three carpets on them, thanks to his now tried-and-true combat scheme. The rather long walk, and climb, gave him time to observe the situation.

Two of the carpets were keeping the lich and dragon quite busy with swooping attacks of fire, lightning and what appeared to be very intense beams of light. The light beams seemed the most effective, as they were clearly putting dents in the ice dragon, and several more holes had appeared in the lich's clothes after a few beam attacks.

The third carpet was sitting a short distance away and remaining stationary. A wizard was standing straight up on it and was casting something. It took a few minutes for Elrose to realize that the wizard was actually casting a Cloud of Disintegration.

"Time to pause and do long-range attacks," Elrose muttered to himself. He had no desire to get near a COD. Given the results he had witnessed during the siege, the fellow on the carpet could probably go head-to-head with Lenamare for egomania. There was no way that could be a stable conjuring situation!

However, the COD was successfully formed and started moving towards the lich and dragon. The cloud did not get far before the lich noticed it and took direct aim at the wizard controlling the carpet. A giant bolt of lightning raced toward the carpet faster than Elrose could see what was going on.

There was a loud *crack* as the lightning bolt hit a wall—or rather, a shield of ice that had formed in the bolt's path. Clearly, the other wizards on the carpet were prepared to deal with such attacks. This also gave the other two carpets a couple of free shots at the lich and dragon. They managed to score several good hits before being forced to pull back due to the approaching COD.

Elrose's magically enhanced sight could see the concerned expression on the lich's gruesome face. It shook its head and jerked on its dragon's reins, kneeing it. The dragon dove down fast and hard, banking away from the carpets and the COD.

Elrose blinked. The lich was fleeing; the dragon had summoned a large burst of speed and was flying away as quickly as it could. They were also diving quickly. Elrose reflected that was probably a good idea. Given how high up they were, the lich had a lot of vertical distance where gravity would seriously assist its speed.

Clouds of Disintegration were notoriously unmoved by gravity, so it was limited to the same speed in all directions. The carpet with the COD caster started to follow, given that there was a range limit on how far the caster could be from the COD. However, they soon stopped, realizing they could not catch the lich.

The lich and dragon suddenly vanished in one of the auras, apparently plane shifting out of the border region and back into Nysegard. The three carpets cheered.

"We are going to keep the COD active and slowly move towards the fourth lich," said a voice over the circlet. "You guys go ahead and join the other three carpets."

Elrose looked to where the fourth lich and dragon were. Six carpets should be enough. He glanced towards the rear of the ship to see how the others were doing. He had to up the power on his enhanced sight to find the other battles. He blinked as he saw multiple carpets along with three slightly wobbly flying figures heading towards what appeared to be only two remaining lich-dragon pairs. Where had those wobbly red flying figures come from? He upped his sight again and then groaned. It was Gastropé's demon and two other fiends.

It was bad enough that a Master Wizard might summon a COD from a flying carpet in the middle of battle, but a young wizard fresh out of school summoning and controlling three fiends from a fast-moving flying carpet? This day just kept getting more insane!

Elrose shook his head. Time for a line of sight teleport!

"Gotta hand it to you, Gastropé; I thought you were insane, but those demons of yours are kicking some lich butt!" Peter said, shaking his head as the three fiends headed towards their fourth lich and dragon.

"Amazing how joyous they seem even though they are taking a severe beating themselves," Zed noted.

"In my experience, demons don't look at things the same way we do," Gastropé said, shaking his head. "They look at this as sort of a vacation. The Abyss is a really miserable place, trust me."

"Trust you?" Penelope asked, looking at him oddly. "You sound like you have firsthand experience."

Gastropé chuckled. "More than I want."

"You've been there?" Peter had twisted on his cushion to look at him.

Gastropé nodded. "Multiple times. The first time was when I was working for Exador; he took his entire army through the Abyss as a shortcut to get to Lenamare's school."

"He sounds insane!" Zed said.

"Yes, well, it turns out he is most likely an archdemon who has been disguising himself as a human for several millennia," Gastropé said. "So insane is really not the half of it."

Everyone on the carpet stared openmouthed at Gastropé. "Are you saying you worked for an archdemon?" Penelope asked in shock.

"Well, I didn't know he was an archdemon at the time; he was pretending to be a wizard. He fooled the entire Council of Wizardry including Trevin, who I am sure has had dinner with him." Gastropé felt he needed to defend himself a bit. It was rather awkward to have to admit to having worked for the Forces of Evil.

"You are going to have to tell us all about this when we get back to the ship!" Zed exclaimed.

"Wait—you said there were more times?" Penelope asked.

Gastropé sighed; he should have kept his mouth shut. "Yeah, similar idea—Jenn and I, along with a few others, have passed through it a couple times to get to or from various locations in Astlan."

"How?" Peter asked.

"Talk about a detour!" Zed exclaimed.

"Well, this is a bit awkward, but… you know that demon that kidnapped Talarius and stole mana from Tiernon?" Gastropé asked.

"Yes. We haven't seen this crystal ball thing, but we've heard the stories. Actually, I think you told us some of those stories at the Bacchanalia?" Zed reminded him.

"Oh, yeah." Gastropé frowned. "Well, we did it with that demon. He took us to a cave of his in the Abyss that was a bit cooler than most of the Abyss, and we used it as sort of a waiting room until he could make contact with someone else to help him open a gateway to Astlan."

"You are telling us that you were the house guest of the demon that stole mana from a god?" Penelope asked.

"Well, to be fair, he had not yet done so at the time," Gastropé said.

A cheer broke out as the three demons finished killing their fourth lich-and-dragon pair. A second cheer then broke out over the com circlets as the final pair were vanquished by the other carpets. They all looked over to where the final set of carpets were watching something fall to the ground.

Gastropé blinked; was that Elrose standing in the air between two of the carpets?

"Hey, that flying human stole our next entrée!" Tizzy yelled as the three demons flew up to the carpet.

Gastropé looked over at them. Wow, did they look bad. Tizzy's two friends had holes in their wings; the craggy one even had a broken horn. They all had dark spots covering their bodies. It was much clearer on Tizzy, who was lighter skinned and not scaly, but the dark spots appeared to be bad frostbite and/or cold burns. How cold was a lich's teat if they could freeze demons? Gastropé wondered.

"Sorry," Peter said to Tizzy as the demon flew nearby.

Tizzy looked Peter up and down. "You're a human on a Grove carpet?"

"Uhm, yeah. Sort of a long story," Peter said.

Tizzy twisted his mouth back and forth a couple of times before saying, "Unusual."

Zed stared at the demon. "You know about the Grove?"

Tizzy shrugged and pulled his pipe out of nowhere. "I've done some business there; been a long time though."

"You have been to the Grove?" Penelope asked, looking horrified.

Tizzy gave her a wide grin and a completely terrifying leer. "I was indeed, my pretty! Perhaps next time I'm there, I should look you up?"

Penelope shook her head back and forth, not wanting to have anything to do with the octopodal demon.

"How can a demon get into the Grove?" Zed asked.

"Same way as a human!" Tizzy pointed to Peter. "You get invited!" The demon grinned.

~

Antefalken came up to Tom, wading in what he figured must be a molten iron bath. "So, you about ready to head home?"

Tom smiled. "Yeah. It's been a good trip, but probably time to leave."

Antefalken grinned. "Yeah, I haven't been here for at least a decade. It's been great to stretch out and relax."

"Where are the rest?" Tom asked.

"Reggie is teaching Rupert and Talarius to play a card game called blackjack," Antefalken said. "Last time I looked, the others were over in the main lava flow."

Tom nodded. "You grab the card players and I'll get the others. We'll meet up on the ridge we came over from the Boom Tunnel."

"Sounds good!" Antefalken took off.

Tom pulled himself out of the molten metal. He had to shake some metal droplets off his legs. He didn't want any to harden between his scales. He then headed over to the main lava flow.

When he arrived it took him a moment to spot the guys, but he eventually spotted them out floating on their backs in a deep orange hot region. He took to the air and flew over to them. "You guys ready to go?" Tom asked.

Boggy opened one eye. "Already? We just got back not that long ago!"

"Argh!" Estrebrius moaned, keeping both eyes closed. "I ache all over and I've still got some bone-deep chills from where that second dragon bit my leg."

"Whine, whine, whine!" Tizzy groused. "I don't think my rear left toes have grown back yet! At least you two didn't lose any appendages!"

"What are you three talking about?" Tom asked, puzzled. "You've been soaking in lava for hours now."

Tizzy grinned. "We got a bloody call from my accursed master!"

"Bloody good bloody call, if I do say so myself!" Boggy added, keeping both eyes shut.

Tom shook his head. "Your accursed master? He summoned you while you were here? All three of you?" This didn't make any sense.

Tizzy grinned and shook his head, somehow causing small lava ripples. "Well, he called. He was all up in the air over a bunch of liches on dragonback that were kicking his and his friend's butts, so we all decided to go help out."

"Best workout in a century!" Boggy sighed.

"Wait, I'm confused," Tom said. "Your accursed master summoned you and had you bring friends? That makes absolutely no sense!"

"Well, he's also a friend, so we said what the heck!" Tizzy said.

Tom shook his head. "Your accursed master is your friend? You are now back tracking on everything you and Boggy have told me about wizards and demons."

"Yeah, Tizzy does that sort of thing," Boggy said. "However, it's really a case of him leaving out a lot of details, like who this so-called accursed master is."

Tom sighed. "Okay, so who is your accursed master? I don't think you've mentioned him before."

Tizzy looked up and gave Tom a puzzled stare. "What are you talking about? Pretty sure it was your idea!"

Tom stared at the floating octopod and blinked. "What are *you* talking about?"

"When we entered Freehold, wasn't it you that suggested that Gastropé be my accursed master?" Tizzy asked.

"Tom sold you into eternal slavery?" Estrebrius looked up and over at Tizzy. "That's not very nice!"

"I don't think he got paid, so not sure it was a 'sale' exactly," Boggy said. "At least that's what I heard."

"Stop." Tom raised a hand. "You are confusing me. Are you saying you are still pretending to be Gastropé's slave?"

Estrebrius squinted at Tizzy. "I don't know... That binding doesn't look that pretend to me!"

Tom looked back and forth between the two. He then looked at Tizzy with his demon sight. Sure enough, there was some sort of wizard link or binding going up and off plane.

"Where did that come from?" Tom asked.

Tizzy shrugged and closed his eyes again, relaxing. "It just showed up at some point."

"Links don't just show—no. I am not going to do this. I already know I cannot win this discussion. I will just take things at face value." Tom sighed. "So can we go? The others are ready to head home."

Boggy sighed. "I suppose. I'm going to want to take a nap though."

"Me too," Estrebrius said, rotating to an upright position. Tom was not sure how it was possible for them to move in molten lava so easily. The iron had been extremely thick and hard to move in; lava had to be worse.

Tizzy sat up, grunting. "Spoilsports!"

Chapter 95

"They went where?" Lilith asked Rosencrantz for the second time.

"Hellsprings Eternal," the cringing demon messenger replied.

"Why in the Abyss would they go there?" Lilith asked Asmodeus, who was sitting in a large, winged armchair beside her sipping on a glass of blood wine.

"To celebrate, I would assume," Asmodeus replied.

"They have half the Abyss as well as Tierhallon looking for them. This is hardly lying low," Lilith pointed out. "Did no one notice who they were?"

"Not so much as I could tell, mistress." Rosencrantz shrugged. "Most of these people are vacationers and may not have heard the news yet."

"And no one noticed a Knight of Tiernon randomly wandering the Abyss?" Asmodeus asked.

"Well, it wasn't like he was swinging his sword and looking to do battle or anything. A few people raised some questions, but once the greater demon told them the knight was with him, they sort of let it go," the messenger said.

Lilith shook her head. "I really don't see the point of this move. I would have assumed he'd have rendezvoused with his allies and minions to advance their scheme."

"Who was with him again, Rosencrantz?" Asmodeus asked.

"Uhm, the bard Antefalken, the miniature fourth-order that looks like the big one, Tizzy and Bogsworth, plus an incubus and some fiend we had no identification for."

"An incubus?" Lilith asked.

"Yes my queen, he was quite busy with the lady patrons of the springs. As one might imagine."

"Why would he have an incubus working for him?" Lilith asked Asmodeus, who shrugged, having no idea. "Is he creating an army of these mini versions of himself?" Lilith shook her head.

"Under any normal circumstances, the fact that he's got Tisdale with him would make me discount any true threat; however, circumstances have proven to be quite far from normal," Asmodeus said.

"Exactly. Who takes a hostage to a spa?" Lilith took a large gulp of blood wine to punctuate her exasperation.

"So you say they relaxed at the spa for a good part of the day, so to speak, and then simply went back to that hole in the ground they are staying in?" Asmodeus asked.

"Exactly. About six or seven hours by Court Time, Your Lordship." Rosencrantz nodded as he replied.

Asmodeus sighed. "None of this makes much sense to me. Do we really understand what precipitated all this? Yes, I know the city was under siege, overrun by a demon army, but do we know whose? I forget."

"Well, it's not completely clear; however, I do believe Ramses is involved and most likely Exador," Lilith said.

"Exador?" Asmodeus asked.

Lilith shrugged. "An archdemon of shifting alliances. Rather aloof actually. Apparently he's been masquerading as a human in Astlan for the last few thousand years."

"Ugh," Asmodeus said with distaste. "Why? The amenities there are sadly lacking."

"Maybe he likes the cold?" Lilith shrugged, not particularly caring.

"Are either of them aligned with a prince?"

"Not currently that I am aware of. Ramses has been on good terms with Belphegor and occasionally Naamaha. I have seen him conversing at parties with Moloch and Azaziel, but nothing particularly suspicious."

"Hmm, so perhaps nominally in Sammael's camp?" Asmodeus asked.

Lilith made a face indicating uncertainty. "He's not in mine, and as you know, my default assumption is that if you aren't in my camp, you're in his." She set her glass down to pour some more blood wine. "However, that doesn't prove anything."

"Has Sammael mentioned anything to you about this demon?" Asmodeus asked tentatively.

"No, but then he wouldn't." She gave her head a slight shake. "He knows that any such mention of something this interesting would likely rouse my suspicions that he was somehow involved. So either way, he'll remain silent."

Lilith suddenly noticed that Rosencrantz was still in the room. She glared at him. "Return to your partner and remember nothing from this room," Lilithshe commanded her servant.

~

DOF +3
Evening 15-20-440

"My dear lady, this was a most magnificent feast!" Trisfelt said as he leaned back in his chair, trying to surreptitiously adjust his robe's belt.

"Thank you so much, but I fear I can claim no credit, save for hiring Chef Jerod and his team." Hilda beamed to the hearthean as he entered the room to ensure his crew were clearing the table properly.

"Chef Jerod, you are a true genius!" Trisfelt complimented the chef. "Never have I had such a delicious preparation of jahiva fish. The citrus marmalade was an incredible touch that perfectly complemented the fish's spiciness. And the soup, as I said after eating it, was heavenly."

"Did you not enjoy the appetizers?" Chef Jerod asked worriedly.

"My dear man, of course I did. They were marvelous! I simply had to pause to gather air to continue. Before you ask, the salad was the best I've had outside of the Grove and it could give anything there a run for its money," Trisfelt assured him.

"Excellent!" Chef Jerod said, beaming. "But I fear we only have three more courses to go!" He shook his head worriedly. "Perhaps I should get to work on another course? We are about to serve the entrée; I should have time."

Trisfelt's eyes popped open wider, "My dear sir, are you trying to explode me?"

Hilda grinned. She had to give silent thanks to Tiernon for her sainthood so that she could actually enjoy such meals without the fear of gaining weight, or even getting too full. Chef Jerod was the best chef in the city, and certainly the most expensive; however, her managers had greatly increased her budget, thanks to her excellent results.

"Ugh, I fear I shall never eat again," Trisfelt moaned after finishing the final course of roasted and spiced nuts. They had literally gone from soup to nuts this evening. Hilda smiled; she too had enjoyed the meal, perhaps almost as much as Trisfelt appeared to have enjoyed it.

"Shall we adjourn to more comfortable seating?" She gestured towards the sofa and stuffed chairs in the main part of the parlor.

"I'm not sure I can move," Danyel moaned. He looked quite sick, Hilda thought. The lad, being young and inexperienced, as well as mortal, did not have the gastronomical fortitude of a professional like Trisfelt or a saint like herself. He had left food on his plate at every serving, starting with the entrée. It was as if he had gotten full on the amuse, appetizer, soup, and fish alone. He had left a third of the venison and vegetables on his plate, ate half his slice of cake and only picked at the nuts. He had, however, finished the sorbet that had come after the venison and before the cake.

The lad had also stopped taking new wine with each course at about the same time. He had not even had a sip of the dessert wine accompanying the cake. The poor lad could not have known what he was missing. And the cognac with the nuts? He had not even touched it. Youth was clearly wasted on the young, Hilda reflected. However, she could not help but smile, knowing that Danyel had most likely never anticipated being able to enjoy such a meal in his life. Rod members typically did not get to eat such meals unless they were to advance to knighthood, and not many ever managed that.

It really felt good to be able to mentor young people and show them new experiences. Teaching and mentoring had been one of her favorite duties in the Sisterhood. It was not something she was able to do in her current job, or even her previous job. Maybe she could convince the powers that be to reassign her as sort Tierhalloc envoy, or more accurately, a spy, on a permanent basis. She had to chuckle. Would that not be true heaven!

"Ahh…" Trisfelt sighed as he sat down on the sofa. "I must say, tonight you have been an absolutely heavenly hostess!" He shook his head. "I fear I shall never dine or drink so well again in my life!"

"You flatter me, Master Trisfelt." Hilda smiled brightly, not least at the unintended reference.

"So, My Lady, shall we all watch the balling now?" Trisfelt asked.

"Excellent idea!" Hilda exclaimed. "However, before we start, shouldn't we open another bottle of wine?" Danyel made a gulping noise in his chair behind her, apparently not feeling the need for more wine. *Youth.*

Trisfelt chuckled. "I swear, my dear Hilda, it is as if someone dropped you from heaven into my camp that night!"

Hilda laughed. "Oh, my. What a lovely and poetic, if slightly preposterous thought!" Hilda replied, while admitting to herself that technically it was a fairly accurate statement. "What variety shall we have?" She looked over to the wine chest. The chest had two compartments: one for reds, the other with ice in it to nestle the bottles of white wine. "If we don't have it, then I can have Bowker, Chef Jerod's wine steward, retrieve it for us."

"No need for that, my dear. I must admit, I am so full and sufficiently tipsy that I think we should stick with something tasty, yet mundane. I am not prepared to savor something like we had with dinner."

"Hmm, perhaps a drier white? A hint of citrus, perhaps?" Hilda asked while shuffling through the cold half of the chest.

"Excellent. I await your choice."

Hilda selected a bottle and took it to the glass cart that the wait staff had brought in with dinner. She selected three appropriate glasses and then took screw to bottle. "Danyel, it was you who wanted to see this. Get your hind end over to a proper chair or the sofa!" she called to her servant good-naturedly. "On second thought, take a stuffed chair. Should you decide to relinquish your dinner, I don't want you doing so on Master Trisfelt!" She poured the three glasses of wine as Danyel slowly made his way to one of the two stuffed chairs flanking the sofa.

Hilda brought a glass to Trisfelt and set it on the coffee table in front of him where he was setting up the crystal ball on its portable viewing stand. She set Danyel's down on the end table beside him and went back for her own glass, along with the bottle, which she also sat on a coaster on the coffee table. Trisfelt finished his preparations and sat back to take a sip of the wine.

"Now, I'm not terribly familiar with using these in portable display mode," Hilda said. "Should we turn the lights down?"

"I think that's best; even when doing a single viewing in the ball, low lights are better. This will be projecting the image above the ball and coffee table," Trisfelt said.

"Excellent, then." Hilda swept her arm around the room; all of the lamps went out except for a small lamp that she left on to keep the room from being completely dark.

"If you have any questions, feel free to stop me. We can pause, freeze, go back, go slow, whatever is needed," Trisfelt told the other two.

"Excellent!" Hilda said, taking a sip of her wine.

Trisfelt gestured and muttered something, and a three-dimensional scene of Talarius and a human-sized demon appeared in the air above the table.

Danyel sat up straighter. "That's impressive!" He shook his head. "Other than the much-better angle and unobstructed view, it's just like I remember! I can't wait to see the part I missed."

Hilda smiled, but not completely comfortably. She was slightly concerned about what might happen if the lad saw himself assisting the demon; that could be traumatic for him. Trisfelt was looking at Danyel oddly. Hilda suddenly realized Danyel's slip. She hoped it would not mean too much to Trisfelt.

"And here we go," Trisfelt said as he waved his hand, and the scene began to unfold.

The scene played out for a short time and then Hilda interrupted, "Could you pause, please?" In the light of the projected scene, Trisfelt could see that she was quite puzzled. "Did that big demon just say the smaller demon was a child?" she asked.

"Yes, the big one said it was a child, and that it has a human form—which it did. Everyone in the camp was talking about the child that had been found in the nearby forest that had turned into a demon. Apparently, its human form was that of a child. He called himself Rupert," Danyel answered.

Trisfelt choked on his wine and started coughing. He took a second sip of wine to try and quell his throat.

Hilda turned to look at Trisfelt, who was looking extremely pale and seemed rather shaky. "What's the matter? I have to admit to some surprise about this claim of a child demon; that's why I stopped it."

Trisfelt looked intently at Danyel. "You said the boy was named Rupert? How do you know this?"

"Well, many people heard him tell Talarius." Hilda coughed slightly, gave Danyel a quick stare and then took a sip of wine. Danyel got a puzzled expression on his face and then suddenly remembered he was not supposed to be a Rod member. "When I was doing recon for my lady, shortly after the events, the camp was buzzing with talk about it. The story is fairly well known among the Rod members I talked to."

Trisfelt was shaking his head as if in disbelief. "It can't be coincidence. About what age was this boy?"

Danyel frowned, uncertain as to what to say. "Well, a boy—not a young man. Apparently, the story he told was that he had been abducted by a demon that had been flying over camp and was shot down by the Rod. They recovered the boy from the nearby woods and he spent the night, only to be recognized the next day by one of the high priests who said he was from the larger demon's entourage.

When unmasked, he turned into a demon and attacked Talarius and the priest. Talarius slew him."

"Impossible!" Trisfelt muttered, looking positively ill.

"What is?" Hilda asked.

"There is a boy—or was a boy, a rather odd boy, about ten years old. An orphan who came to the school with lots of talent and was accepted on scholarship. He was a very nice boy, very kind, gentle, even shy. He was also something of a loner and introverted. His name was also Rupert."

"And this so-called child demon"—Hilda gestured to the scene before them—"came into the Rod's camp in human form, calling itself Rupert?"

Trisfelt looked to Danyel.

Danyel was on edge now, having come close to slipping up. "Well, that's what I gather from my questioning of people…"

"And Talarius recognized him as this demon, and it also appears the child demon recognized Talarius." Hilda paused to think. "Surely it must be coincidence. Surely, Lenamare would have detected that he was a demon?"

Trisfelt spread his hands palm up on his knees. "One would surely think so. We go through a large battery of tests during the entrance exams. I cannot see how something like that could possibly have been missed. Every master in the school interviewed him!"

Trisfelt shook his head, staring at the small demon's image before him. He blinked suddenly. "On the road to Freehold, before Exador's people attacked…" Trisfelt thought for a few moments. "I asked Rupert to help with the horses as we set up camp. He did not want to; he was quite panicked, in fact. Jenn and I brushed it off as childish fear, but he proved to have good reason. The horses were scared to death of him and went into a panic when he approached. I never thought much about it until now, but…"

"The horses must have sensed he was a demon," Hilda added.

Danyel was shaking his head. "So this smaller demon had infiltrated your school years before?"

Trisfelt shrugged. "So it now appears. But the boy was such a good kid! He was very sweet and shy; I can't possibly see how the boy I knew could be a demon!"

Hilda sighed. "From what I have heard and read, you would not be the first to be so fooled."

"But if the Rupert demon truly is a child, how could it play such a tricky game for several years? Hiding among two of the greatest conjurors alive today?" Trisfelt asked in befuddlement.

"Well, I'd have to assume it is as Talarius said—the big demon is lying. The Rupert demon is not a child; it is simply pretending to be," Danyel stated.

"To what end? Simple infiltration?" Trisfelt asked. "We really are not that interesting of a school. Despite Lenamare's claims."

Hilda thought for a moment. "As I understand it, Exador and Lenamare were at war over a book in Lenamare's possession." Trisfelt shrugged and nodded.

"Is it possible this Rupert demon was searching for the book? On behalf of this larger demon?"

Trisfelt shrugged, shaking his head. "At this point, anything is possible. So then, is this larger demon in league with Exador? Is that how Exador knew he had it?" Trisfelt shook his head in exasperation.

"I'm not sure we can answer anything on this now; let's move on," Hilda said.

They moved on to the part where Verigas started ranting. Hilda motioned for Trisfelt to pause it at the point where Talarius stopped the argument between Tom and Verigas. "Well that certainly confirms what Jenn and Gastropé said," she stated.

"From that perspective, it does seem like the Rod sort of overreacted," Trisfelt said.

"Be that as it may, the ends were justified!" Danyel stated confidently.

Trisfelt shook his head again. "So if the big demon and Rupert were in collusion with Exador, why would they bring the Rod right to the gates of the city and the huge horde of demons? And it seems very sloppy to select a priest of Tiernon as your gateway in such a case."

"To say the least." Hilda was shaking her head. "Let's table this as well and move on."

They continued the balling, getting into the fight. Hilda gestured at Trisfelt to pause shortly after the demon had started shooting those electric ice bolts and blasts at Tiernon. "That circle around the demon, it appeared a bit ago. We have no Sight with this recording, but I'm reasonably certain the priests have encircled the demon with a draining ritual of some form," Hilda said to Trisfelt and Danyel.

"Yes, that's correct. The priests worked in full support of Talarius, using both animus and mana draining rituals; they also used mana-funneling rituals to Talarius. Then, as you'll see shortly, archers began shooting Arrows of Quôlume at him with very nasty payloads," Danyel replied enthusiastically as Hilda made faces at him trying to get him to be quiet.

Trisfelt glanced curiously at Danyel, his suspicions reawakened. "That's very specific knowledge you seem to have."

Danyel blanched suddenly. Hilda intervened, waving her hands as if it were nothing. "I sent Danyel out to make inquiries among the Rod, particularly during the time you and I first met. And then a few more times since we've been back in the city. Over the years, he's proven an able assistant in ferreting out useful information on my behalf."

She needed to distract Trisfelt. "However, what I find odd is that these rituals that Danyel mentioned, are they not dark rituals? It was my understanding that priests of Tiernon were proscribed from using dark rituals."

Trisfelt looked surprised. "Now that you mention it, I seem to recall hearing that as well. Very odd that they should do so." Hilda looked back to Danyel, who was looking even more uncomfortable, if that were possible.

"I am sure it must have been approved by the Arch-Diocate," Danyel said nervously.

Hilda smiled gently. "Well, then, I am sure he'll be more than prepared to answer for and explain his actions, should this Host of Tiernon or what not, ever show up." She chuckled lightly, as did Trisfelt.

"You are right as ever, my dear!" Trisfelt clapped his hands, putting Danyel's apparent in-depth knowledge behind them. "I would not want to be in his shoes!" He laughed and Hilda joined in, flashing Danyel a seemingly good-natured glance which appeared to make him even more nervous.

"Anyway, let us continue." Hilda waved at the scene and then reached for the bottle to refill their glasses.

As the giant demon fell to the ground and the priests rushed in to heal Talarius, Hilda had Trisfelt pause the balling. She was looking quite annoyed. "Am I misremembering? Wasn't the agreement between the demon and the knight that it was to be a one-on-one duel?"

"It was indeed," Trisfelt said. "The Rod was not particularly good about keeping its word."

Hilda was shaking her head, most annoyed. "Demon or no demon, this is not honorable; nor is using dark rituals. While we have no Sight with this, I am sure those clouds are seriously dark magic."

She stood up abruptly. "I need to get more wine. I find it very troubling that I should be feeling any sympathy for a demon!" She marched over and opened a bottle of red wine, paying little attention to which one. She was feeling extremely vexed.

She came back as Trisfelt and Danyel both gulped down the remainders in their glasses. Hilda poured out large glasses of the red wine, emptying the bottle between the three of them. She sat down and placed the empty bottle on the floor beside the sofa. She sighed. "Let us continue."

The battle proceeded with the possession and defeat of Talarius, his surrender followed by his treachery. Hilda was feeling a deep-seated anger at this point. It was then that the god mana started flowing. This was what she had noticed; this was the high-powered miracle that came through the back door and was thus inadvertently allowed. She wished she could See what was going on. It was very impressive to say the least. Then came the turning of Excrathadorus Mortis.

As the hole closed and the balling ending, Hilda could not help herself from feeling that some sort of justice had been done, despite the fact that it was her own team that was on the receiving end. That Talarius had cheated was undeniable; that he had broken nearly every rule of honor in Tiernon's book, undisputable. And did the Arch-Diocate and Vicar General seem okay with this? Apparently. Hilda let out a sigh.

"You know what I can't figure out?" Trisfelt said.

Hilda opened her eyes and shook her head. "There is an immense amount here that I cannot figure out."

"We all know what demons are like," Trisfelt said, the other two nodded. "Yes, they lie. We cannot trust what the demon said at the end about simply wanting to protect his own and live in peace. It is, by every known account of demons, complete nonsense." Everyone nodded his or her head. "So then, why did he stop? Why did he just leave? With the level of power he used to turn that artifact, the dagger—"

"Excrathadorus Mortis?" Hilda asked.

"You know of it?"

Hilda chuckled, suddenly feeling exhausted. She was emotionally drained. "By legend only; obviously, I've never set eyes on it. It's extremely famous."

"Really? I guess I assumed so," Trisfelt nodded.

Hilda shrugged, too tired to prevaricate. "Talarius was awarded with being its keeper nearly a decade ago. This extremely sacred blade was used in Etterdam by Sentir Fallon to slay the demon prince Orcus."

Trisfelt sucked in his breath. "It was used to kill a demon prince?" the wizard asked, agape.

"Permanently, forever and ever, amen," Hilda said, nodding.

Trisfelt slowly shook his head and sat in silence. "So, more to my point," he eventually continued, "with that much power at his command, with the power of multiple high priests, why did he not turn that magic against the Rod? If he could reverse an artifact of that magnitude, then surely he could have used it against the Rod and priests of Tiernon?"

Hilda froze as Trisfelt pointed this out. She had not thought of that. No one had. Clearly, the demon could have done serious damage to the Rod and its priests. He could have decimated them. A ten percent casualty rate would be minimal under the circumstances. He could have conceivably taken out half or more of them. Particularly given the chaos of the possessed soldiers, the people in shock, distracted—he might have wiped out the entire Rod and the priests! It made no damn sense at all.

~

DOF +4
Predawn 16-01-440

The avatars sat in stunned silence, staring at the end of the balling Hilda had just brought them. This was Hilda's fourth time watching it. She had asked Trisfelt if he could leave it so she could review it again once she was completely sober, promising to return it to him on the morrow. They had set an appointment for brunch and planned to discuss the balling in more detail. In the meantime, she had watched it twice more while Danyel slept and had then taken it with her to the predawn meeting with Moradel and the others.

Having seen it and begun to formulate her own thoughts, Hilda simply sat back and waited for the three avatars to discuss. They all sat silently for some time before Sentir Fallon finally spoke up. "This is disturbing on so many levels, I don't know where to begin."

"I have had reports that the Church in Astlan had gotten a bit morally relaxed, and to be fair, I may have even tolerated it," Moradel began.

"You are not the only one. As I recall, we have discussed this before, and it's been discussed at higher levels as well. It's the eternal question of whether the end justifies the means, and it's never an easy question," Beragamos said.

"At the least, we can ignore the child-demon malarkey," Sentir Fallon stated. "At first I found that troubling, but it makes too little sense."

Moradel looked to the elder avatar. "Are there not half demons?"

Sentir Fallon shrugged. "Of course; that is canonically known. However, such children are either lesser demons or mortals with a few demonic traits. If this child demon is able to change form, it must be a greater demon in its own right. For that to be the case, the sire would, at the least, have to be a demon prince."

"At the least? What more is there?" Hilda asked, shocked.

Beragamos chuckled. "I think Sentir's point is that there is no more beyond that, and even then such a thing would be extremely rare; thus, the demon must be lying. The only child demons are half demons, and no half demon can be that powerful."

"Do demons not breed with each other?" Hilda asked; she was not particularly familiar with demons.

Beragamos shook his head. "Not that I am aware of. For demons and in fact, any immortal being to reproduce, both parents have to sacrifice a bit of their own essence beyond sperm and egg. Which most do not, in fact, have." He shook his head. "This requires a level of unselfishness that demons do not possess, and it requires a level of love and commitment they cannot meet."

"Do they not have to do the same with a mortal?" Hilda pursued the question.

"Yes, but not as much is required because a fertile mortal woman needs very little to provide the seeds of life. It is a much smaller sacrifice for the male demon. A female demon would only conceive with a mortal male as part of a grander scheme or reason. Not for love or mere dalliance; it would require a lot of her own resources, particularly for a powerful child," Beragamos said.

Moradel looked at him closely. "So again, highly unlikely to be a greater demon."

"Unless maybe the mother is Lilith," Sentir Fallon chuckled.

Beragamos smiled. "That would be the most likely bet, but seriously doubtful. As would Sammael fathering a child on a mortal woman. As I see it, those are the two most likely possibilities to achieve a greater demon. Remotely, the father could, I suppose, be one of the Triumvirate who literally got lucky. Again, I did say at least a demon prince. Theoretically, it could be any demon prince that somehow managed to get things just right. Perhaps some sort of giant nursery full of mortal broodmares, each one trying to get it right."

"That would be faster than Lilith bearing lots of children to mortal men," Sentir Fallon noted.

"Could a mortal woman even survive such a pregnancy?" Hilda asked suddenly.

Beragamos nodded. "An excellent point; that is another extremely good reason I find the half-demon idea to be extremely unlikely."

"So Occam's razor? The simplest answer—the demon is lying?" Moradel asked.

"I would say so," Beragamos said.

"What about the breaking of Talarius's word and the use of dark rituals?" Hilda asked.

Moradel frowned. "To be honest, Hilda, the questions raised by all of this are not well answered by the senior avatars. Tiernon himself has been pragmatic about it. I personally feel that breaking one's word to a demon is far less of a sin than the use of the dark rituals. But I think we will have to have further inquiry into this."

Beragamos sighed. "And before we can even do that, we shall have to come to some decisions internally about how we shall deal with this sort of moral slippage. If it is happening here, it is happening elsewhere. I can only imagine Etterdam. I would hate to have to take this to Tiernon, but if the hierarchy can't agree, we may need to bother him."

Hilda gulped. Had she uncovered something worthy of Tiernon's own attention? That thought made her stomach twist in knots. Old proverbs made it very clear that one did not one to draw a god's interest; it was never healthy. While that was officially for mortals, she suspected it would not be that much better for a minor saint.

"And so the mana theft? The reversal of Excrathadorus Mortis?" Hilda asked.

"Which brings us to the central question of this demon. I have no idea who it actually is, unless it's one of the princes in disguise, which I think seems to be most likely," Beragamos said.

"Not some demon prince who has been hiding in the deep backwaters of the Abyss? That place is so big, there is no telling who or what is hiding in the backwaters," Moradel said.

Beragamos shrugged. "Certainly a possibility. The only other one, in fact. This being is obviously a demon prince; I cannot imagine an archdemon capable of what we have seen. In fact, I refuse to imagine such a thing due to the sheer terror of all the archdemons learning to do this."

"There is one other possibility," Sentir Fallon said softly.

Beragamos looked at him. "What am I missing?"

"The business with reversing Excrathadorus Mortis—that would require considerable knowledge of the blade, millennia of planning, and the sort of power we've witnessed. What just happened could only be done with Tiernon's own power. A demon seeking specifically to destroy this blade might spend centuries or even millennia researching how to do what we've seen, should they wish to ensure the blade's destruction," Sentir Fallon told the others.

"But who would go to so much trouble to destroy this blade? And then locate it and set this up?" Beragamos asked.

Sentir Fallon sighed. "Someone who had very real reasons to fear it as the one known thing that could stop him."

Moradel started coughing. Hilda turned pale.

Beragamos said softly, "You can't possibly mean…"

Sentir Fallon sat up. "I can't mean a resurrected demon? Or one that we thought was dead, but isn't?"

"Hell," Beragamos said.

Moradel put his head in his arms on the table. "So, should we have Hilda be on the lookout for a sudden uptick in the number of warlocks running around?" he asked.

"Not a bad idea," Beragamos replied.

Chapter 96

"So okay, Vaselle wants another day. He thinks he's close," Tom said to the group in the cave. "I told him to take whatever time he needed to do it right. I am hoping he will come to his senses and back out. I'm still a bit nervous about this business, even though I see the points several of you have made." He and Estrebrius had just returned from Astlan through the gateway. Tom glanced over and saw Reggie paying more attention to his privates than to what Tom was saying.

Tom looked down at his own crotch, now covered by a stretchable loincloth that had come as part of his new belt. With a small loan from Antefalken, Tom had purchased a dragon skin belt that came with an attached loincloth/adjustable kilt yesterday at Hellsprings Eternal.

The belt was pretty cool-looking to Tom's eyes. It had a large skull buckle and a very stretchy curtain of dragon wing skin that could be unfurled to act as either a loin cloth or a wraparound kilt. He had been pleasantly surprised to see that they had one in his size. The best part was that it had several sealable pouches and some loops for hanging or attaching various things, like a utility belt. He had been somewhat nervous leaving the arrowheads in the cave; now he did not have to, he could take them with him.

"So then, where are we going today?" Rupert asked excitedly.

"Well, per our agreement today is Tizzy's choice, since the spa was mine," Boggy said. "He'll have trouble beating it but…"

Tizzy snorted. "You have to admit the best part of yesterday was thanks to my accursed master!"

"Yes, but not everyone got to go kill liches and dragons. And thanks to my idea, we were able to get a nice relaxing soak afterwards," Boggy replied.

"I wish I could have gone with you. It would have been great to see Gastropé again, and lich killing sounds like fun."

"Someone is going to need to explain where those ice dragons came from and how they are related to the dragons here in the Abyss," Tom said.

"That's actually a good question," Boggy said. "They seemed to be all ice—frozen water. They weren't biological or demonic as far as I could tell."

"They were fun to chip away at though," Estrebrius said.

"So where are we going, Tizzy?" Rupert asked, changing the subject.

Tizzy beamed. "Well, I'm not sure there is a formal name for the place, but I call it *crystallus cavernis infra montem fata*. Or sometimes just *fata cavernis* for short. It's beautiful."

Rupert was looking puzzled. "Is that wizard tongue? It sort of sounds like it, but not quite."

Tizzy shook his head. "No, it's a language called *romanus vulgaris*."

Boggy shook his head. "Okay, so what is this place? I've never heard of it. Have you, Antefalken?"

Antefalken shook his head. "Never heard of it, which is rather strange."

Tizzy shrugged. "Well, that's what I call it anyway. It's a large series of underground caverns."

"Caverns?" Talarius asked, sounding annoyed. "You want to get us out of this cave by taking us to see caverns? I'm not sure how that's supposed to be an improvement."

Tizzy grinned at the knight; the octopod's red, burning ember-like eyes seemed to glow even more brightly than usual. "Oh, I think you'll like these caverns. They are truly huge, incredibly beautiful and most of them have crystals dripping from the ceiling and growing from the floors. Rubies, sapphires and diamonds are very abundant." Tizzy chuckled. "Assuming you ever get back to Astlan, you're going to need to make amends, and I'm thinking a sizable donation might go a long way to redemption."

The knight harrumphed. "You cannot buy salvation." He crossed his arms and sighed. "However, the father church is always in need of resources. I suppose it would be rather ungallant of me to spoil our outing today by complaining; I remove my objection."

Tizzy chuckled, as did Antefalken.

"We can certainly use some gems when we get back to Astlan. It wasn't a lot of fun being poor traveling from Gizzor Del to Freehold," Rupert said.

"We should have bought some bags at Hellsprings Eternal," Boggy said.

"Do gems work as money in the Courts?" Tom asked Boggy.

Boggy shrugged. "They're much more valuable in the worlds of men. You can sell them for money in the courts, but they do not have the same sort of value. They are mainly good for jewelry, as decorative items. In Astlan and the other planes, they are a popular way of storing money, but those places don't have large central banks."

Tom frowned, "The Courts have a central bank? You mean like one that prints money?" Tizzy nodded. "That seems rather advanced."

Antefalken shrugged. "Value is a bit different here, and it is tied to power and the ability to do work or get access to physical goods that are useful or wanted. The Abyss is strongly connected to the elemental Plane of Earth and therefore metals and gems are found more easily here than some other planes. The bigger value is in crafting those elements into something useful." He gestured to Tom's table and chair.

"So Lilith and Sammael created the central bank to store value, and they issue coins that work as a unit of value to make trade easier," Boggy continued.

"And that's what makes them so powerful and feared?" Tom asked.

Boggy and Tizzy shrugged.

Antefalken finally said, "I suppose it's some of that, but mainly I think it has more to do with the fact that they capture, mercilessly torture and then obliterate and eat the souls of all those who oppose them."

Tizzy nodded thoughtfully in agreement. "Yeah, that could be it."

~

Hilda hurriedly made her way up the stairs to Trisfelt's quarters. She was running late. It had taken the forensics team more time than expected to copy the balling. It was not a mechanism that was widely used in Tierhallon; however, that might change, given the high quality 3D playback. At any rate, they had eventually got it back to her and she'd popped into the forest around the city at the closest safe distance. She should probably drag Danyel and the horses to the launch point and have him attend the horses. Of course, that would be much more obvious than a single woman on foot in a tweed robe exiting in the predawn hours.

She had gotten back to her hotel room only to find the sword, Ruiden, there. The sword was getting impatient with her lack of progress. Being in a hurry to get to brunch with Trisfelt, she'd tried to brush it off but it was quite insistent, so she'd succumbed and given it a brief rundown of what she knew that wouldn't be too dangerous to let the sword know.

In short, she had ratted out Lenamare as the demon's master. It was true—not that Lenamare was going to be doing anything about such a fact in the near future. He had been quite clear that he had no desire to try summoning the demon any time soon. She was reasonably certain that Lenamare and Jehenna would be more than capable of dealing with the walking sword on equal footing; something she doubted most mortals could claim.

She knocked on Trisfelt's doors. It took but a few seconds for the wizard to respond and open the door with a warm smile.

"So good to see you again this late morning, my dear!" Trisfelt welcomed her cheerily.

Hilda smiled and grasped his arm in warm greeting. "So good to see you. I trust you had sufficient time to recuperate this morning?" she asked.

"Mostly... I'm thinking I may need a bit of medicine, perhaps a Bloody Tatania?" The wizard asked, ushering her into his quarters.

"The perfect cure! Which one of us is the healer here?" Hilda asked with a laugh as she came into the chambers. She had only been here briefly previously. It was a decent suite—nothing to compare with Lenamare's, of course, but still nice. Perhaps the main thing was the lack of personal items. There were numerous professional instruments and quite a few boxes, but overall the suite looked rather unlived in.

Trisfelt must have noticed her looking around. "You'll have to forgive the bare nature of my quarters. They were just procured for me upon my arrival in Freehold, so I haven't moved in." He paused and a look of consternation settled on his face. "And Lenamare managed to vaporize-slash-disintegrate most of my personal possessions back at his school. Some of us didn't get a lot of room for baggage." He gave a small grin of mild exasperation.

Hilda grimaced. "I didn't even think of that. I'm so sorry."

Trisfelt shook his head, implying it was no big deal. "A great inconvenience, but nothing more. We thaumaturgists are known for being rather nomadic and living off the land, so to speak. Unlike many other wizards, most of our components and tools are readily found in nature."

He gestured for her to sit down on the couch. "I also have a small cabin—really more of a sort of tree cabin, out in the woods, not that far from Tris." He sat down himself. "That's where many of my most personal things are kept. It's my hideaway, where I go for a respite now and then."

"A tree cabin?" Hilda asked, puzzled.

Trisfelt had begun mixing Bloody Tatanias from the ingredients and pitchers on the coffee table. He chuckled. "It's basically a hut built inside the hollow of a very large tree."

Hilda got a slightly puzzled look on her face. "It must be a very large tree. And I thought you were a thaumaturgist, not a druid," Hilda joked.

Trisfelt laughed. "No, not a druid. There are a few druids nearby; it is not that far from a satyr encampment. I first encountered the region a decade or so back while researching satyr beer and wine."

Hilda sat up a bit straighter. "Now you have my attention! Did you find satisfactory refreshment?"

Trisfelt chuckled. "Indeed, some of the best beers in all of Astlan, and I suspect the best non-alvaren wine to be found. Much more grounded with very rich, earthy overtones, and far cheaper but every bit as interesting for one looking for new experiences."

Hilda looked quite excited. "Well then, I hate to impose, but once this current"—she gestured around, indicating the entire city and region—"whatever it is, is over, you must invite me for a visit!"

Trisfelt smiled brightly. "I would love to do that. It is quite gorgeous out there. Rustic, I fear, but very relaxing."

"I grew up in a small village in deep woods at the base of the mountains; it was a bit of a backwater." Hilda smiled. "So rustic is something I'm quite familiar with." She got a wistful look in her eye as she remembered Rivenrock. She closed her eyes for a moment and then reopened them and smiled, taking the glass Trisfelt offered her.

"Are you okay? You seem suddenly a bit distressed," Trisfelt asked.

"I'm fine. Simple nostalgia for one's youth. My village is no longer there, it's been reclaimed by the forest, so I sometimes get a bit wistful."

"I'm sorry to hear that. Did it just become too hard to make a living?" Trisfelt asked.

Hilda grimaced. "Unfortunately, a necromancer—well, it's unpleasant and painful."

Trisfelt was startled. "A necromancer! Oh my goddess, I'm so sorry, I should not have pried!"

Hilda waved him off. "No, no, it's a perfectly natural question on your part. I've come to a small level of peace over it with time."

"Well, let me change the topic. I have our brunch being served shortly." He gestured to a dining table set for two. "Waffles with syrup from the region I was just telling you about, as well as ham and a potato-and-egg dish."

"Mmm," Hilda said. "Sounds delicious. We should talk more about the balling. Do you wish to do that before, during or after brunch?"

"My only thought would be to reserve discussion when the servants are here," Trisfelt said.

Hilda nodded. "I agree. I assume they are general palace staff"—Trisfelt nodded—"and no telling who they might share information with."

"Exactly."

"I guess my big question is about this Rupert demon. Are you going to tell Lenamare?" Hilda asked.

Trisfelt shuddered. "I think not; at least, not yet. I still have trouble believing it is the same lad. I just do not see how we could have missed it. Telling Lenamare at this juncture would only serve to make him even more paranoid, and I cannot predict how he would react. Generally unpleasant, most likely with initial disbelief, possibly an insulting interrogation of Danyel and the two of us. So, until I can confirm personally, I think I would like that possibility to stay between the three of us."

Hilda nodded. "I would agree. While I don't know Lenamare that well, what I do know gives me pause before accusing him of allowing a third or lesser fourth-order demon to sleep under his roof undetected."

Trisfelt chuckled darkly. "Then you know him as well as any. That is exactly my concern."

A knock came at the door. "Valet service, My Lord," a voice from the hall called.

"Come in, come in!" Trisfelt called as he stood and moved towards the door. He glanced back to Hilda. "I hope you brought your appetite; I can smell it already!"

~

"Tizzy, dear chap... you might have mentioned that this place is on the other side of the Abyss!" Boggy complained to Tizzy. "My wings are still regenerating from yesterday's revelry!"

"What are you complaining about? I'm the one carrying the giant canned meat!" Tizzy retorted.

"It is a bit out there," Antefalken noted.

"I'm getting more than a little tired, I have to admit. This flying business is still pretty new to me," Reggie agreed.

Tom was fine, surprisingly; the prolonged flight was helping him keep his fidgetiness and even his indigestion in check. Sort of like a good workout. He kept thinking that his symptoms of mana overindulgence would subside at some point, but they had not yet. The massage at the spa had helped, as did today's exercise.

"I'm good. It's very scenic; I don't generally venture this far out on my own," Estrebrius put in happily.

The party had flown to the nearby boom tunnel, and Tizzy had set the coordinates and they had gone through. Tom had assumed a half hour or so of flying, but it ended up being nearly two hours, and then they ended up at another boom tunnel.

"It's been nearly two hours since the last boom tunnel. I don't think I've had to use two boom tunnels in more than two centuries," Antefalken complained. "I know the tunnels all have maximum ranges; were you hitting the max on those two tunnels?"

Tizzy shrugged. "Probably. There's another boom tunnel up ahead, but it's been turned off for quite some time."

"Turned off?" Boggy asked. "Why would anyone turn off a boom tunnel?"

"Save power?" Tizzy asked, shrugging.

"Save power?" Antefalken asked. "Who in the Abyss cares about conservation of anything?"

Tizzy just shrugged.

"So that's the one we would have gone to if it had been on?" Tom asked.

"Nah, that's the one we are going to try and turn on to get where we are going," Tizzy answered. Talarius jostled in Tizzy's hands, obviously perturbed.

"What do you mean *try?*" Boggy asked. "Are you saying that after all this flying and tunneling, we might not get where we want to go because we can't turn it on?"

Tizzy tilted his head for a moment. "No, I'm pretty sure I can turn this one on."

"Well that's a relief," Talarius said sarcastically.

"It's the one that we are going to that's likely to be the problem. Turning on a boom tunnel remotely is kind of tricky. Sometimes they are so drained that they don't get the activation signal to wake up," Tizzy said.

"Ah, fargsbottles!" Boggy cursed.

Antefalken looked over to Tizzy as they flew. "What do you mean, wake-up signal? Boom tunnels are always on."

Tizzy shook his head. "Not if no one uses them. They go to sleep after about a decade or so, to save power."

"So the one we are heading to now has been off for over a decade?" Rupert asked. "Why didn't we just do the remote activation thing for it?"

"Range is too far for the remote activation signal. The one we just came through gets used every few months or years, I think. This next one, not very often."

"At least a decade, I guess," Tom said.

Tizzy shook his head from side to side. "I can tell once we turn it on, but my guess is over a hundred."

"So this place really is in the boonies!" Estrebrius exclaimed.

"So I'm guessing these caves don't get many tourists?" Tom asked.

Tizzy shrugged. "Just me in the last thousand years, I would bet. Not a lot of people would remember them."

Boggy looked at him closely. "You know you always avoid this question, mate, but exactly how old are you? You were here when I got here."

Tizzy shrugged. "No longer counting. Too long."

Estrebrius nodded. "You were the first person I ever met."

Antefalken was looking around at the others strangely. "You know, you were also there when I showed up. Apparently you've been doing the welcome committee thing for some time?"

Rupert was nodding excitedly. "Yeah, Tizzy was the first demon I met after Tom!"

"That seems a bit odd, doesn't it, Tizzy?" Tom asked, looking back at the octopod.

Tizzy shrugged. "What can I say? "I smell buttah!" Tizzy said in a sort of mock version of his yenta voice. He cleared his throat and looked a bit sheepish. "Sorry, can't really do that unless I actually smell buttah."

"So you can smell new arrivals?" Reggie asked.

Tizzy shrugged again.

"Would you stop doing that?" Talarius asked. "It makes me start swaying uncomfortably."

"Eh, not sorry," Tizzy said, looking down at the knight. "Yes, it's a gift or a curse. But it's useful for meeting people." Tizzy went silent and then suddenly turned his head a little and stared. "There we go, the next boom tunnel!" He started moving faster in the direction he had looked. "You would think that after all those welcoming committees, I'd be able to get a date, but nooo!"

It took them another five minutes or so to get to the boom tunnel. Tizzy quickly moved up to the boom tunnel arch and placed his upper right hand on the plate; he then closed his eyes in concentration. This lasted about twenty seconds and then a single, low *woohhhmmm* vibrated the ground and air around them. About fifteen seconds later, a second woohhhmmm came, and then after about ten more seconds, a third, and then within a few more seconds, the regular throbbing of a boom tunnel could be felt all around them.

Woohhhmmm… woohhhmmm… woohhhmmm… woohhhmmm… The tunnel vibrated as various undulating shades of red filled the previously empty archway.

"Tiernon, but these things set my teeth on edge!" Talarius muttered.

Boggy sidled up to the knight. "Well, that's no wonder. It's like your entire suit is vibrating and rattling with the throbs. That's why you shouldn't wear clothes."

"I don't know," Reggie said. "I can feel it throughout my whole body, and I think it's a big turn-on."

Tom glanced down at him without thinking. Yes, Reggie was apparently enjoying the "good vibrations." *Sheesh.* Tom shook his head.

Tizzy was still concentrating at the archway's panel. Suddenly the undulating red light was replaced by undulating black light and the throbbing suddenly became much more intense and audibly quite loud. Within about thirty seconds, all were covering their ears as the throbbing was getting almost painful. Talarius's armor was very clearly rattling now, as were Estrebrius's teeth in his grinning mouth. He did seem to be enjoying this outing.

Suddenly there was a huge throb, the ground shook beneath their feet, and with that, the boom tunnel's blackness turned back to red and the throbbing slowly began to subside to normal.

Tizzy let out a loud sigh, as if quite tired, and then removed his hand from the plate. "Voilà!" he exclaimed, pronouncing it with a hard V sound. "Voilà, what a toila! Yada yada yada... I did it!" He was grinning from ear to ear, quite proud of himself. "You will note that I, a humble fiend, can do something that most greater demons can't do, and a few of the archdemons don't even know how to do!"

"How is that? I would think the archdemons would know something like this," Tom said.

Tizzy shrugged. "Most aren't old enough to have been around when the boom tunnels were built and so never learned. To be honest, it doesn't need to be done that often, so most likely they were never taught and the method was forgot." Tizzy waved his hands around. "You'd be surprised how common Antefalken's assumption is that boom tunnels are always on."

"How long ago were the boom tunnels built?" Rupert asked.

Tizzy rolled his head. "Sheesh, that's a good one. It was a really, really long time ago. The princes hired sleestak wizards to come in and install them all around the Abyss."

"Sleestak wizards?" Tom asked, puzzled. Antefalken and the others were looking equally puzzled.

"Yeah, you know: wizards who are sleestaks." Tizzy shrugged.

"By *sleestak* do you mean a sort of human-shaped insect-lizard race with big black eyes?" Tom asked, thinking about certain really old children's programs and a horrible movie.

"You've met some!" Tizzy said, surprised. "That's impressive. They are really hard to get a hold of, always jumping around time and space and such. You almost need a police box to catch them. DeLoreans aren't fast enough." Tizzy was shaking his head. "I don't think I've seen one in"—he paused and suddenly stared around at the others—"a really long time."

Tom raised an eyebrow. Did Tizzy not want to reveal his age? How old was the octopod? Could it be that maybe Tizzy was not so much crazy as simply senile?

"Anyway, let's head on through!" Tizzy said and immediately turned and marched into the boom tunnel. Estrebrius shrugged, smiled and flew in after him.

"Talarius?" Tom offered. The knight walked through, followed by Boggy, Reggie and Rupert. Tom brought up the rear.

~

Randolf was hunched over his large notebook, working on formula translations between Lenamare's demon banishment wards and his own project. Randolf really hated to admit it, but Lenamare was damn good. Amazingly good. Randolf was no slouch; some of the greatest djinn masters had trained him, but this was absolute mastery. He supposed it should not be a surprise.

When Lenamare was a youth, he and Exador's current incarnations, or whatever they were, had appeared to be about the same age. Lenamare had continually matched Exador toe-to-toe, and Exador was a wizard with thousands of years of experience. Okay, not all as a wizard; sometimes he had been simply a general, possibly a priest even. Then there was time he had spent with the Anilords. But nonetheless, the fact that Lenamare, a mere human like Randolf himself, could have shown such mastery at such a young age was rather humbling.

If only times had been different, and Lenamare had not been such a total cortwad. The two of them might have been allies and sent Exador to his doom years ago. Randolf sighed. The what ifs—they were the seeds of useless ruminations. He shook his head and tried to get back to work.

Donngg went a warning bell. Randolf looked up from his work; someone was in the outer entryway. A chime sounded even as Randolf started to get up. He sat back down; the chimes indicated that Crispin had returned. Their under-palace lab was very tightly guarded and only certain very specific codes tied to specific auras could get in.

As always, he chuckled at the fact that he, the Archimage of Turelane, could not actually have his own sacred inner sanctum and laboratory in Turelane. He had a minor one of course, befitting the buffoon he played. Unfortunately, the Mage of Turelane, Exador, would have immediately spotted any truly guarded sanctum, any place protected from the prying eyes and ears of an archdemon.

Thus he was forced to create his true sanctum in the warrens of the Council Palace. In the warrens, it was just one highly guarded laboratory among many dozens. Every council member, every committee member, every major lackey had a highly secured layer, knowing who owned what without physical exploration and a great deal of effort, thus setting off a great number of wards among a great number of wizards. This made Randolf just one more needle in a haystack.

Crispin entered through the mantrap, shutting the final door behind him. "Hey ho!" The djinn exclaimed in greeting as he walked over to Randolf. Randolf stood and gave Crispin a hug and quick peck on the lips.

"So was the ball as big a hit in Djinnistan as it was here?" Randolf asked.

"Every bit as much!" Crispin said, chuckling. "A couple of elders nearly choked to death when the greater demon got busy with the Armageddon-summoning routine, as I am becoming fond of calling it."

"And have they come to any conclusions?" Randolf asked.

Crispin grabbed an apple out of a nearby bowl and bit into it, slowly savoring its juiciness. "I love the material world…" he murmured. Suddenly he looked back at Randolf, who was waiting for an answer. "What do you think? They're going to be debating this for the next hundred years!" Crispin shook his head. "How long did it take them to come to any consensus about Exador?"

"I wouldn't know—some of us hadn't been born then," Randolf said drily.

"Oh, sorry. I forgot." Crispin grinned. "I was but a boy myself, or more of a boy than I am now."

Randolf rolled his eyes. "Yes, yes. You are but a teenager in djinn terms at the ripe young age of what… 183?"

"I'll be 184 next week; I hope you won't forget my birthday present?" Crispin asked, twisting his head coyly.

"Hmm. Therefore, you were about fifty when Abancia fell. Barely out of diapers," Randolf noted.

"You are missing the point—my present?" Crispin asked with a grin.

"I thought you genies were supposed to be the one handing out presents?" Randolf asked with a smirk.

"Oh, you'll be getting a present alright, if I don't get one!" Crispin laughed.

Randolf laughed as well. "I have something very nice picked out for you. Rest assured." Crispin smiled brightly. "Although I'll have to alert the palace fire marshal before we try to light your cake!"

~

"Holy marathon, batmen! I'm getting a stitch!" Reggie complained while trying to reach around with his right hand and rub his back between his two left arms. They had just landed at the entrance to a large cave at the bottom of a rather deep canyon.

After coming through the sleeping portal, it had been another hour of flying across an unusually flat and arid plain with very few fireballs or columns. They had headed towards a range of extremely tall mountains in the distance. The mountain range was not that extensive in that it did not span the horizon. In fact, it was more of a cluster of extremely tall mountains that simply rose out of the flat plane, and a few large canyons that seemed to radiate out from the mountain cluster.

Rather odd, but then the entire region had a slightly odd feeling to it. This region, after the last boom tunnel, seemed especially desolate. Which was, Tom admitted, a rather tough feeling to pin down, since the Abyss itself was thinly populated to begin with. Actually, other than people coming to visit him, Tom never saw other demons in the Abyss except at the Courts and at Hellsprings Eternal. *Agh,* Tom thought to himself as his own back twinged from exertion. He would need another massage after this trip.

"Here we go…" Tizzy pointed to the cavern entrance, which was probably twenty feet high and perhaps ten to fifteen wide. Plenty big enough for everyone except Tom, for whom it was basically a rather narrow hallway. "We have about a half-hour hike through the corridors until we reach the first of the large caverns. At that point, we enter a long sequence of caverns of different styles. All a wonder to behold!"

"Talarius, you're going to want to turn your armor light on," Rupert said.

"Very well, demon," Talarius agreed, once again not wanting to reveal that his helm let him see in the dark on multiple levels.

Tizzy chuckled. "Once we get to the caverns, both stone and crystal, we will all want light. Black-and-white night sight does not do this place justice. Especially the crystalline and mirrored caverns."

"We need to go single file, or at least I do," Tom said. "Tizzy, since you know where we are going, why don't you go first? Then me, then Talarius and Reggie, Rupert and Estrebrius. Boggy and Antefalken, bring up the rear? Everyone stay together, we don't want to get separated and lost."

The others nodded. Tizzy shrugged and headed in with Tom following. The cavern tunnel was mostly fine, plenty of headroom for Tom. At a few points as they made their way it dipped to about thirteen feet, but Tom had no serious problems as long as he did not stretch to his tallest height.

Actually, the floor was surprisingly smooth and level for a natural cavern. It was not perfect, but it was relatively flat and not V shaped as he might have expected for something so ravine like. Of course, the same was true of his own cave. Tom frowned; actually, he really was not sure how caves and such had come to be in the Abyss. There was neither rain nor any kind of water for erosion, and not much in the way of wind. At least not severe wind, from what he had seen. It was just hot. Okay, some regions were dusty and there were volcanos and lava, but by and large, normal weather would not have shaped things like they had on Earth, or Astlan for that matter.

They walked down the tunnel for some time, perhaps fifteen minutes, before they came to a branch in the tunnel. Tizzy took the left turn. "I always go left," the demon told them, looking over his shoulder. "I find it more sinister; which is something I appreciate as a demon."

Tom shrugged. The demon was making about as much sense as ever. If they did stick to that path, then tracing their way back should be easier. They just needed a better way to tell distance. It was a bit irritating to have no mechanism for telling time. Tom was used to just pulling out his iPhone, or before that his iPod Touch, to check the time. He would settle for one of his watches, which he never wore. Of course, it was not clear what good that would do, since Astlan had a twenty-hour day and the Abyss had no nights or any real time at all. How did demons know when to meet up with each other?

"Antefalken?" Tom asked.

"Yes?" the bard replied from behind him.

"You've dealt with the higher-ups in the Courts, who presumably have meetings and gatherings and such…"

"Yes."

"With no night or day, how do demons know when to show up for a meeting, or party or gathering?" Tom asked.

"Any decent party lasts a couple days and you can come anytime," Boggy said.

Antefalken chuckled. "The princes and archdemons can summon their followers by tugging on their links to them. They just summon them when they feel like it. They can get a feel for their minion's distance from the link and so have an idea how long it will be."

"And there is a clock in the tower of the Notorious Dame," Tizzy interjected.

"What's it based on?" Tom asked.

"Legend has it that the Abyssal day is defined as the maximum time Sammael and Lilith can stay in the same room and not try and kill each other," Tizzy replied.

"Is that true?" Rupert asked, rather surprised.

Tizzy shrugged. "About as true as any of the other legends."

"It is not, however, tied to Astlan time," Antefalken said. "It's mainly used for relative time measurement in the Courts. No one outside the Courts would have any idea what Court Time was."

"There are 666 deminutes in the day," Tizzy said. "That is then divided by six into periods of the day, each 111 deminutes long."

"So deminutes are pretty long units of time." Tom said.

Tizzy shrugged and Antefalken said, "Well, it's completely arbitrary, since there is no Fierd here. That's just the schedule they use for night and day simulation in the courts. You start with two periods of daylight: morning and afternoon. Following that you have one period of evening or dusk where it gets darker, and then two periods of darkness, first night and second night. Finally, or technically firstly, you have one period of dawn where it gets progressively lighter."

Rupert had been fiddling with his fingers. "So basically, 333 deminutes is ten hours in Astlan?"

"Maybe." Tizzy shrugged.

"Okay, thirty-three deminutes is roughly an hour in Astlan, so eleven deminutes is a third of an hour. Nothing rounds nicely," Rupert complained.

Boggy chuckled. "It's not really worth wasting your time on, since no two demons can ever agree on the time of day. It's actually a miracle that Sammael and Lilith were able to agree on that stupid clock."

Tom chuckled. At least he had gotten people talking; they had been pretty silent up until the branch. He supposed it was recovery from the long flight. Unfortunately, as the efforts of the flight wore off, his own fidgety, wired feeling was returning, along with that weird feeling of having overeaten. If it had been food, the feeling would have passed, literally. However, he had no idea how to get rid of mana stuffing, other than to start blasting fireballs all over the place. That did not seem particularly productive.

The group marched on for another five deminutes or so, Tom guessed, and then took another left at a split. From there they travelled about the same distance before the tunnel opened up into a larger cavern. They spread out upon entering and Talarius turned up the lighting to reveal a massive cavern full of stalactites and stalagmites.

"Whoa!" Rupert breathed out.

Tizzy turned around and spread his arms, his brightly glowing red eyes wide with rare joy. "Wander and wonder! See the wonders of the SubAbyss! The UnterAbyss!"

"Everyone stay in the cavern—we don't want to hunt you all down if you wander off!" Tom called. Why did he feel like a schoolteacher on a field trip? Tom smiled as he made his way around the giant cavern. He was pretty sure caves were new to Rupert. He himself had been to a few smaller caverns. Indian Caverns and Indian Echo Caverns in Pennsylvania, and when he was little, one in Arizona on a family vacation. This cavern was huge and incredibly impressive. He scanned the ceiling, wondering if there were any bats. He did not expect to see any—they would have to be bats out of—or rather, still in—hell. He shook his head.

Tom paused, looking at one of the stalactites. How did stalactites and stalagmites form in the Abyss where there was no moisture? He rubbed his fingers together. Yes, the cave was cooler than outside, but it was still quite dry. You needed moisture for this sort of cavern structure to form, pretty much by definition. Tom furrowed his brow and then shook his head. He supposed it was getting a bit too late to start questioning the landscape features of the Abyss. There was no way those crazy pillars could have formed either.

If he started questioning things like these rocks, he would have to start questioning all of his current reality. Tom was pretty sure nothing in his current reality could handle too much scrutiny, so better stop while he was ahead. Or at least, stop before he started drowning.

[Appendix: Time of Day]

Tizzy eventually led them out the leftmost of three exits, relative to the one through which they had entered the cavern. This was a fairly narrow slit passage at an angle. Tom's companions, being sufficiently smaller, had no serious problem, but it was tricky for Tom, as the angle of floor and ceiling were such that he could not stand upright and had to hunch over, his wings scraping on the roof.

The slit passage led to another large cavern, this one strewn with large boulders and sharp protrusions here and there. As they crossed the cavern, Talarius's light lit up a deep chasm about ten feet across that spanned the cavern.

"We'll need to hop over," Tizzy said as he came up behind Talarius to lift him and fly him over. Talarius gave the chasm what Tom could only surmise was a sour look, thanks to the knight's helmet hiding his face. He assumed the knight did not like having to cross a chasm he could not return across on his own power.

Leaving the other side of the cave through the only exit, the group made their way about a hundred feet to the entrance of another large room.

Tizzy stopped and turned to face them. "Okay, magic lamp," he said, pointing to Talarius, "time to turn up the light as we enter the first room of what I call the Corundum Corridor."

Talarius's armor started glowing brighter and brighter until the demons were all blinking as their eyes adapted to the light. The first thing they noted was blue. Lots and lots of blue in the room behind Tizzy. Tizzy turned and entered everyone else followed.

"Holy shite," Boggy muttered.

"Good lord almighty and then some... is this all sapphire?" Antefalken asked softly.

"I don't believe this," Tom said. "I don't think this can be natural." The room was irregularly shaped, about thirty or forty feet per side with an irregular ceiling about twenty to thirty feet high. Embedded in the walls were ribbons of blue crystal. Clear, crystalline sapphire and a milkier stone like sapphire with white streaks. Where the previous caves had stone stalactites and stalagmites, this room had sapphire stalactites and stalagmites.

"This can't be real..." Talarius whispered, rotating in the center of the room as he tried to take it in. His steel boots clinked as they knocked loose sapphire stones around.

"Now I know I'm dreaming for sure," Reggie whispered.

" Do not get too greedy; we have got several more corundum rooms before we even get to the diamond room. The gold and silver caverns are going to be pretty boring after all of these," Tizzy observed.

"We are freaking rich!" Rupert shouted.

"Welcome to the Land of Bling!" Reggie shouted in agreement.

"I guess I get the point about gems and gold not being so valuable in the Abyss," Tom said.

"Fargelsworth... I had no idea they were this common!" Antefalken breathed as they sifted through loose gemstones. "I should have brought a lot more bags..."

~

"Good news!" Damien told the Council once everyone had taken their seats. "The Rod has certified that we are demon-free and Oorstemoth has signed off on it!"

"Excellent news," Alexandros Mien said, nodding to Damien with a tight smile.

"In front of each of you is the current status report of the palace and the city, including reserves and our current active forces," Gandros said. "We are doing remarkably well."

"Do we have estimates on cleanup and repair of the damage?" Sier Barvon asked.

"Not yet; it depends on how soon we can "lift the siege," so to speak. We need craftsmen and materials from surrounding cities, such as your own city of Yorkton," Damien said.

Sier chuckled. "You see through me."

"I know that your sister is married to Burgomaster Falron and that you both come from a long line of woodworkers and masons." Damien grinned back.

"You can't take the merchant out of the Archimage," Sier said, chuckling.

"To that point, Oorstemoth and the Rod are both willing to step down and reduce their forces, and have agreed not to invade the city unless the demon horde comes back." Damien told the Council.

"And that means exactly what?" Zilquar asked.

"It means that Wing Arms Master Heron and a few of his ships will be returning to Keeper's City to work on the pursuit of the demons; but they will be leaving about two thirds of their fleet here in case the demons return." Several councilors frowned at this. "The Rod is also reducing its forces by about half. They claim to be going to a maintenance mode and are simply going to be here to assist in case the archdemons return, and maintain a staging point if they have to ramp up again."

"So, in short, they aren't going anywhere soon," Jehenna said.

"So it would seem, but they are reducing their military footprint and they have said they would like to operate on more cooperative terms," Damien said.

"What exactly are cooperative terms?" Randolf asked whiningly.

"It means they would like to allow small groups of their people into the city for leave and to purchase supplies, and that they would like to work with the two Councils to coordinate a defense in case demons return."

"And how do they determine if demons return?" Davron asked.

Damien made a small grimace. "Sir Sorel, another Knight Rampant of Tiernon, will be using Sir Talarius's Mirror of Demon Detection and flying over the city periodically to inspect the number of demons. I have told him that once the wards are down, we would expect some demons to return, as they are vital to the work of many of our residents. They are okay with a handful of demons in the city. Just no archdemons, greater demons or demon hordes."

"I'm okay with that myself," Tureledor said. "I don't like having any of those in the city. I am still embarrassed that we allowed it to happen."

"I will be asking the Committee on Demonology to come up with some method of regularly monitoring demon activity and overall presence within the city," Gandros said. "It is something we should have thought of long ago."

"So what do they have, a stable of flying horses? Or is this Sorel also going to use Talarius's horse?" Davron asked. "My understanding is that such horses are quite intelligent, and it is probably wanting to charge the gates of the Abyss as it is."

Damien had an amused expression on his face. "Apparently, Sir Sorel's steed is a griffin."

"A griffin?" Sier repeated incredulously. "These knights aren't much for subtlety, are they?"

"Not at all. Sir Gadius is also outside our walls. You don't want to know what he rides."

"Okay, Damien, what does he ride?" Davron asked.

"A unicorn." Damien smiled at the two councilors.

"The man's a virgin?" Jehenna asked.

"Don't most religious types take vows of celibacy? It's part of the same psychopathy that leads them to take up religion in the first place," Tureledor observed, shaking his head.

"Well, I have to say, it does make those otherwise boring goody-two-shoes far more interesting," Davron admitted.

"Are we getting off track here?" Alexandros asked.

"Probably," Damien admitted with a smile. "To get back on it, we need to talk about lowering the wards."

"Yes," Lenamare said, "and to that point, I am working to hand back full control of the wards to the normal team." Lenamare nodded to Gandros. "My recommendation is to take them down to a minimal level, which I will detail to the team, so that they can be brought back up very quickly if needed."

"So then are you pulling yourself out?" Sier asked.

"I am," Lenamare stated. "I am concerned that if Exador actually is an archdemon, he may come looking for me to continue our battle. In such a case, it might be best for me to leave the city quickly. I can't easily do that if I am in the wards."

"So you are leaving?" Tureledor asked.

"Not at this time. I have my students to worry about and my obligation to them. Now that Exador has destroyed my school, I think this is the best place for them, along with what is left of my staff."

"Didn't *you* blow up your school?" Randolf asked.

Lenamare glared at the Archimage. "He invaded my lands, laid siege to my castle, killed a number of my people including students, and was on the verge of ransacking it and slaughtering everyone. We had to escape, and I needed a diversion. He forced my hand; I had no other choice. I therefore consider his actions the reason my students and faculty no longer have a home."

"Ahh, I see…" Randolf said, steepling his hands before him and gazing at them intently. "So you knocked over the blocks and left?"

Lenamare glared at the archimage, who pointedly ignored him.

"Okay, let us let this point go," Gandros said. "I do think we need to get the wards down; they are extremely expensive to operate."

"We may need to bring in additional components from outside," Sier noted, and Damien nodded. "Most of the extremely expensive components are non-consumables, but there are enough moderately expensive consumables that it adds up, and we have limited supplies of such on hand in the city."

"Given current supplies, how long could we continue at the current level?" Tureledor asked.

"At least another quarter month. With some more scavenging of the city, perhaps thirty days," Lenamare said.

"Hmm. Then we really should see about turning them down and restocking," Gandros stated.

Damien was heading back to his rooms after the meeting when a figure stepped suddenly from a doorway along the corridor.

"You are Councilor Damien? The Inquisitor of the Council of Wizardry?" A rather odd-sounding voice asked him.

Damien had to blink to take in the extremely armored man accosting him in the relatively dark corridor. He immediately shifted to a more defensive position. "I am; and who are you?"

"I am Ruiden, Sword of Talarius, and I am investigating his abduction. I wish to consult with you on your investigation into the offending demon."

"Okay…" Damien said, rather befuddled. Did the man just claim to be a sword?

~

"I suppose we could always come back with more sacks," Antefalken sighed as they sat and rested, sorting through their treasure. It was simply too much: the blue sapphire room followed by the pink, orange and yellow sapphire rooms, the emerald room. The ruby room had been, Tom thought, both beautiful and insane. However, that was nothing compared to the diamond cavern. It could have been the crystalline Fortress of Solitude from the Superman movies. Tom's jaw had been wide open the entire time. How could any of this be? The caverns were the sort of place that only King Midas could have imagined.

"I think we will have to," Boggy agreed. "Tizzy, I am so sorry about doubting you during the long, long journey here. It was worth every league and more."

"I have to admit, the discomfort of being demon handled for that distance is drowned out by the sights of this cave system," Talarius said, shaking his head. "The level of temptation here is incredible. It is an excellent opportunity to test myself versus the sin of greed. Truly a worthy challenge."

"I see you are packing gems into those small bags you pulled out of your armor," Boggy commented.

"As the octodemon pointed out, I'm going to need to make some significant donations as part of my penance," Talarius said.

"So you're donating it all to the Church and the Rod?" Rupert asked.

Talarius fidgeted. "Directly and indirectly," he finally said.

"Indirectly?" Estrebrius asked.

"Well, the church has numerous expenses supporting my efforts. If I can relieve those expenses with some small personal wealth in pursuit of my mission, well, that is indirectly."

"What expenses does a Knight Rampant have?" Antefalken asked rather incredulously. "If you are in Eton or anywhere your pantheon is, you get free room and board."

Talarius coughed. "Do you have any idea how many bales of hay it takes to feed a flying horse? They eat twice as much as a normal horse!"

"It's such a long haul back and forth; it's a shame to have to make multiple trips," Rupert complained. He was fastening his one bag to his rope belt.

Before leaving, Antefalken had gone to his home and returned with rope and some sacks. Those without belts had created rope belts to fasten one or two sacks to. Antefalken had only four sacks that could hold about a gallon each, three smaller bags and a few small pouches of his own. Boggy, Reggie, Rupert and Tizzy had each taken a large sack. Estrebrius had taken two small sacks; the large sacks were simply too large and ungainly for his frame. Talarius had a few bags of his own somehow secreted in his armor, and also took the third smaller bag. Antefalken made do with his small bags, and both he and Tom had belt pouches.

"Hmm... you know, one hole in the ground is about as good as any other," Tom mused. "I've got my only possessions from the cave in my belt pouches. I suppose we could set up shop here."

"Interesting." Antefalken frowned, thinking. "From the point of view of back and forth to Astlan, it doesn't make any difference, but I have to imagine, given how far out we are, getting back and forth to the Courts could be a pain. Your current cave is only a single boom tunnel away from the Courts."

"True. But if Lilith is looking for Tom, I'm thinking this might be a better location," Boggy mused.

"I cannot disagree with that," Antefalken admitted.

"Well, you haven't even seen most of your planned new home yet," Tizzy stated. "We really should move on and see more."

"Hmm, well, we could just carry what's easy and leave the other piles here for now," Antefalken said.

"Yeah, I like that idea. It's not going anywhere, and we know where this room is relative to the diamond room," Estrebrius said.

"It was a straight path," Boggy agreed.

"What's down the other paths we didn't take, Tizzy?" Rupert asked.

Tizzy scratched his chin. "Well, that depends on the path. Some will take you to the other rooms on alternate paths. Some are dead ends and some... are just cave rooms not that different from Tom's cave."

"So you've explored this entire cave system?" Antefalken asked.

"A lot of it. There are some deeper regions I haven't ventured to. It's a very big system," Tizzy answered.

"So what's next? You said there were gold and silver rooms?" Rupert asked.

"Yes... they are a ways away though; they are on another side of the mountains. So it will be a long trek," Tizzy answered. "Back in the day, though, streams of silver and gold were quite a sight to behold."

"Streams? You mean molten gold and silver?" Tom asked with a furrowed brow, trying to understand how that could be.

Tizzy shrugged. "Probably not flowing now. A long time ago, there was a very large and active volcano at the heart of the mountain range. It's been cold for several thousand years now, so I suppose the molten metals will have stopped flowing and solidified."

Antefalken shrugged. "Well we have nothing else to do, and if we are thinking about hanging out here anyway, we might as well go take a look."

"Cool! Lead on, Tizzy!" Rupert shouted.

Tizzy made a gesture indicating where he was going. Everyone who had been seated stood and straightened their leftover piles of gems and then lined up behind Tizzy as he started off down a corridor.

Tizzy had not been lying. The journey was pretty long and meandered through a number of twisted tunnels with lots of branches. They were definitely relying on Tizzy to find their way out. It would have been quite easy to get lost in here. Finally they came to a cavern with six exits in addition to the one they had entered.

Tizzy stopped and rubbed his chin. "I think we want that one there." He pointed to one of the tunnels.

"What do you mean you *think?*" Boggy asked rather shrilly.

"Well, it's been several hundred years since I've been to the crystal caves, and probably almost four thousand since I regularly wandered these tunnels," Tizzy replied.

"Nargh! We are relying on four-thousand-year-old memories of Tizzy's?" Antefalken complained.

Tizzy twisted a bit to give Antefalken a grin. "Aaah, not that bad. I've been down most of them at some point." Tizzy paused and closed one eye and tilted his head to the left. "I think." He shook his head. "Let's go this way." He took off.

Tom quickly gouged a mark in the tunnel they had just exited, and another near the entrance of the one they were now going down. He should have been doing this all along. It really was pretty stupid to trust Tizzy on this. The demon had just been behaving so reasonably lately; he had forgotten exactly how unreliable he really was.

The group proceeded for another two hundred feet before they took a right at a three-way intersection. Tom marked the one they had come through and the one they were taking with new symbols to distinguish them. He was done relying too much on Tizzy. After another five hundred feet, they came to a large metal portcullis.

"Why is there a portcullis in the middle of a cave passage?" Estrebrius asked.

"Were these caves once inhabited?" Antefalken asked.

"Are they still inhabited?" Rupert asked nervously.

"I hope not." Reggie said nervously.

Tizzy shook his head. "There used to be some miners and others here, thousands of years ago. However, the entire region has been abandoned for at least thirty-five hundred years, if not more. Like I said, when I used to come here regularly, when I had people to visit, it was over four thousand years ago."

"So why did they abandon it?" Boggy asked curiously.

"War—sort of a rout, you might say," Tizzy said while examining the portcullis, shaking it for weakness.

"War?" Tom asked.

Tizzy shrugged. "War used to be pretty common in the Abyss. The demon princes, occasional dark demigods, Knights of Chaos and such enjoyed battling it out. Much like human princes. This place was abandoned about the time of the last major shakeup among the princes. Since that time, most of the squabbles have stayed at the archdemon level or lower."

Tizzy turned to Tom. "Can you try and lift this? I do not think it is locked down, just very rusty and heavy. Demons would have been fleeing out rather than in, so I doubt they locked the thing behind them."

"Demon wars?" Rupert was looking very curious. "But if demons fight in the Abyss, and they die, they die permanently, right?"

Tizzy grinned and nodded. "If you kill them bad enough! If you chop up a demon or a knight"—he glanced pointedly at Talarius—"beyond what they can regenerate and they die here; there is nowhere else to go."

"So what happens to their animus and mana?" Tom asked as he tested the portcullis to see if he could lift it.

Tizzy shrugged. "Well, if you're lucky, you just sort of dissipate or evaporate and it's like going to sleep, I'm told. Less fortunately, something powerful nearby eats your soul and consumes your mana."

"Eats your soul?" Reggie asked with a tremor in his voice.

"Like Lilith or Sammael," Antefalken stated.

"Or any demon prince, and some archdemons," Boggy added.

"Ick," Rupert said.

"Yeah, from the screams of the consumed souls, I'd have to say it isn't pleasant," Tizzy remarked as Tom grunted and lifted with his legs. There was a huge and painful screech and the portcullis lifted.

"Don't let him freak you out, Rupert," Boggy interjected. "That is a worst case scenario. Remember, we regenerate quickly and efficiently. In order to kill someone permanently, you have to halt the regeneration process somehow."

"How do you do that?" Rupert asked.

"Well, there are several ways," Boggy said.

"The simplest is to make regeneration so difficult and time consuming that they just give up and stop trying," Tizzy said rather somberly all of a sudden.

"Okay, everyone through." They all scurried through and Tom gently lowered the portcullis back down. "I have no idea how to keep it up."

Tizzy pointed to a nearby alcove. "That was, or is, the wheelhouse for it. There would be a hook for the chains, but it's not important." He motioned and they continued down the corridor.

At this point, Tom was able to note that the corridors were a bit more even, as if the tighter spots had been carved out to be wider and more uniform.

"So did a lot of demons die permanently in these wars?" Rupert called up to Tizzy.

"Often. That is why so many demons you meet today are not that old, generally not much more than three thousand years, give or take. While many did die, an equal number of battle-scarred demons tired of the demon princes' games and high-tailed it out to places unknown in the Abyss. Off to the Hinterlands."

"So there are other demon societies? Ones not tied to the Courts?" Tom asked.

Tizzy shrugged. "I suppose. I'm sure some of them set up other demon villages or cities. At the time, it was mainly greater demons and below who left, a few archdemons as well. Obviously almost no princes."

Antefalken shook his head. "I really should be taking notes. Lilith and friends never mention any of this."

"Why?" Reggie asked.

Antefalken shrugged. "I am sure they want everyone to believe that they are the only option. Either submit to them or you are on your own versus everyone else in the Abyss. Standard power consolidation. Start with us versus them, and then make sure everyone believes the 'them' are solitary hermits with no resources, luxuries or hope."

They wandered on for another half period or so, taking seemingly random openings that Tizzy chose, with Tom marking each turn or branch. As they moved along, going through two more portcullises, the evidence of human, or rather demon masonry and construction became more obvious. There were now sections with carved stone bricks, and areas where the floor had been flattened out with stone masonry, presumably for wheeled vehicles.

In short, Tom realized at one point, they were now in a dungeon. The only difference between this and a video game or an RPG was that, technically, as demons *they* were the wandering monsters. Of course, they did have a Paladin with them. *Sorry—Knight Rampant,* Tom corrected himself.

"Did you hear something?" Estrebrius asked suddenly. They had all been quiet, lost in their own thoughts for some time when Estrebrius spoke up.

"Only the sound of us clunking down the corridor," Boggy replied.

Estrebrius shook his head. "No, it sounded like nails scraping on stone."

"Like hooves? All but one of us has hooves." Antefalken was shaking his head.

"No, more like scratching." Estrebrius said.

"Where did you hear it?" Talarius asked; they had all paused. Tizzy was in front, Tom behind him, filling the entire passage. Talarius and Rupert were next. Boggy and Reggie were following them, and Antefalken and Estrebrius were in the rear.

Estrebrius pointed behind him.

"*Grrrrrr...*" A rumbling came from the dark to which Estrebrius was pointing. A second growl almost immediately joined the first. Staring down the corridor, Tom could see four red orbs reflecting the light of Talarius's armor back at them.

"I know this goes without saying, but didn't you say this place was abandoned?" Reggie called back to Tizzy, who was scrambling to see around Tom.

"It should be," Tizzy replied, puzzled.

Rupert was looking nervous. "What is it? Or are they?"

"Apparently something terribly spunky, if they're willing to attack a party of demons," Boggy noted. "Estrebrius, let's switch places." Boggy moved to swap with the smaller demon and took a crouching position.

Antefalken pulled a short sword from his belt. Tom blinked; he did not recall ever noticing the bard carrying a short sword. It was rather more like a full-length sword for his childlike size.

Talarius motioned for Reggie to trade places with him and began dimming his armor. "I am thinking I might want to turn off my light, as that seems to be what is attracting them."

"How are you going to be able to see?" Rupert asked, looking at the knight.

Talarius turned his head to Rupert and the boy could see what looked like a grin through the vertical air slit in the knight's helm. The knight reached up and flipped down the crystalline visor that covered the cross-shaped slits in his helm to protect him from arrows.

"My visor has infrared, ultraviolet and several other night vision options," The knight said.

"So you've been walking around like a giant moth magnet all this time for nothing?" Tizzy complained.

Talarius shrugged in his armor. "I work on a need-to-know basis." The knight crouched in a combat position. His right hand slid down his thigh and suddenly there was a short rod his hand. He gave the bottom end a twist with his other hand, and the head of the rod suddenly popped wide with flanges, creating a mace. The mace began to glow at the same brightness as the knight's dimming armor.

"Is that a Rod of Smiting?" Antefalken asked quickly, taking his eyes off the red orbs to glance back at the knight.

"Yes," Talarius replied tersely.

"Is it even possible to disarm you?" Tom asked in exasperation.

"No," the knight replied, pointedly fixing his gaze on the growling red orbs. Suddenly another set of red orbs appeared with the first two.

As the light level from the armor dropped, Tom's demon sight was able to make out the bodies containing the orbs. "Large, heavily muscled dogs," he noted aloud.

"Of course," Talarius stated.

"What are they?" Rupert asked nervously.

"One of two, maybe three things. I would advise blunt trauma," Talarius said tersely.

Suddenly one of the dogs leaped at Antefalken, choosing the smallest front line target. The dog moved amazingly fast, its giant jaws reaching to try to engulf the bard's entire head. Antefalken's sword lunged forward, squarely hitting the dog's throat. Boggy roared and his right slashed out, his black claws ripping through the dog's neck, jerking a bit as the demon severed the dog's spine. The dog fell to the floor writhing.

"I daresay, that wasn't so bad!" Boggy smiled, pleased with himself and looking back at the others.

Talarius was shaking his head. "Look!" He pointed to the dog's body. Something really odd was happening at the base of the neck. The severed spine had split vertically, like strands of licorice pulling apart, Tom thought. Suddenly red muck was swarming up the split spinal cords from the bloody neck stump. The dog's body scrambled, headless, to its feet and backed up towards its compatriots.

"What is going on?" Rupert asked in shock. The two spine halves were each now accumulating a bloody mass that seemed to wrap around the bone.

It took but seconds before Tom realized what was happening. "Shit! It's growing new heads!" he shouted.

Talarius said, "A hydra hound!" The knight shook his head. "I was afraid of this. For every head we chop off, two more grow back. Quickly." The hound now had two much smaller heads which were quickly growing. "As a side note, they also breathe fire, but I don't think that should be a problem for any of us."

"How do we fight this?" Tom asked the knight.

"Blunt trauma to the head. Pulp, but don't sever or break the spine. You can also gut the body, rip off the legs and incapacitate it. Whatever you do, do not cut or break the spine. If you were to break one's back, I'm betting we'd get two front halves."

"This is not on!" Boggy said. "Making a fist with demon claws is a royal pain."

"I want everyone to duck," Tom ordered those in front him. Everyone crouched down as Tom extended his arm and unleashed a red-hot blast of fire at the hounds. The flames quickly engulfed the hounds; but to Tom's surprise, rather than howling in pain, the dogs just growled louder and started advancing.

"Hydra hounds are usually immune to fire," Talarius observed. "That typically, although not always, comes from the ability to breathe it."

"Now you say," Tom said letting his flames die down.

"Bard, trade places with me," Talarius ordered Antefalken. The bard quickly complied.

The knight gestured at the hounds, making a beckoning motion. "Come, you worthless mongrels. Come taste the wrath of Tiernon!" The red lights blinked for a second, as if surprised by the knight's words, and then the hounds charged. Three large, angry hounds; four ravening jaws of teeth with tongues dripping spittle in fury.

As they charged, Talarius began swinging his rod with brutal efficiency, smashing against the first dog, coming between the two heads to hit the head on his left and then back to hit the head on the right. It was like ringing a bell, twisting the hound one way and then the other.

The second hound bounded onto Boggy, who managed to get his fist up just in time to punch the dog in the throat, keeping its maw from closing on his head. As Boggy tilted back under the dog's momentum, the demon brought his hoof up to kick the dog right between its rear legs. That caused a howl.

After a moment of hesitation, Rupert jabbed his claws into the dog's side, trying to disembowel it as it straddled Boggy. Antefalken, who had scrambled back, swung his sword down on the dog's rear leg, trying to sever it. Reggie tried making some not-very-effective punches at the dog.

The third dog dodged around the fallen Boggy and his hound to lunge at Rupert. Rupert screamed in pain from the dog's bite. Furious at the dog, Tom extended his arm with its six-foot reach and grabbed the hound around the midsection, ripping it off Rupert and smashing it against the ceiling. He then squeezed as hard as he could, feeling the dog's innards squirt out around his fingers. He tossed the remains down the hall.

As he looked down, Boggy and Antefalken had finished very successfully gutting their hound.

Talarius was standing over the first dog, its two heads smashed to pulp. The knight stared at the corpse, making sure no new heads were growing.

"Well, that was a spot of fun," Boggy said, brushing the dog guts off his arms and shaking the blood off his hands.

"Guys," Estrebrius said from between Tom's hooves. He pointed down the hall. "There's some commotion down there; I think there are more."

"Tizzy?" Tom looked to the demon behind him. "Get us out of here, maybe through another portcullis?"

"Sure thing!" Tizzy grinned and nodded. He motioned with his head. "Come on!"

Tom stepped up against the wall. "I will take the rear for now. Talarius and Boggy, why don't you go up with Tizzy?"

Tizzy took off at a much faster pace down the corridor, the others keeping pace. He took them right at the first branching, then left at the one following that. Tom took time to mark the passages, but he was not sure he wanted to backtrack at this point.

As they hurried down a new corridor, Tom suddenly picked up the sound of barking behind him. The dogs, or rather their packmates, were giving chase. "Tizzy? We've got company! We need that portcullis or something!"

"Next room up ahead, something even better!" the octopod shouted back.

Soon they were entering a very large room that was more cavern-like than the first rooms they had encountered today. It had stalactites and stalagmites and, most importantly, a very large chasm that was at least forty feet across, and deeper than Tom could see down. Talarius held his arms out and Tizzy got behind him and grabbed him. The two flew across the chasm, as did the rest.

There were two tunnels on this side of the chasm. The dogs' howls and barks were clearly audible from the corridor down which they had come.

"Can they jump this?" Tom asked Talarius, who was now standing on his own again.

"They should not be able to, but I've only encountered them in Astlan. They're on their home turf here so…"

"Great. Tizzy, which corridor?" Tom asked.

Tizzy was pointing back and forth at the two tunnels. Tom raised his eyebrows. If he did not know better, which he frankly did not, he would have sworn the demon was doing "Eeny, meeny, miny, moe." Tom closed his eyes for a moment, praying to he had no idea whom that this was not the case.

Now Tom heard more barking and clamoring from the right-hand tunnel.

"I think the one on the left!" Tizzy said suddenly, just as a horde of hounds came bursting out of the right-hand tunnel.

"Battle stations!" Talarius cried.

There had to be a dozen hounds coming out of the mouth of the tunnel! Suddenly Talarius was a whirlwind of motion as his mace spun and smashed at dogs. Boggy roared and began punching dogs in the face, with Antefalken slashing at the dogs' legs from behind. Reggie began flailing and pounding with his four fists. Estrebrius launched himself in the air and began looking for an opening to swoop down upon the creatures. A dog leaped on Tizzy and the two began wrestling.

Rupert began kicking at two dogs charging him. Tom grabbed the first one approaching him and picked it up with both hands. It was huge! He spun and threw it as hard as he could down the chasm. It howled and then the noise was squelched as it hit the far side of the cavern.

Tom yelled in pain as a hound pounced on his back and bit the base of his left wing. His tail whipped up and stabbed the hound in the belly, unleashing his tail's signature electrical blast. The dog howled and fell back to the ground, spasming and shaking. Tom lifted his hoof and stomped down on the dog's head as hard as he could, smashing it flat. He tried to release the pressure after crunching the skull; he did not want to break the spine.

"Rupert!" he yelled at the boy demon, who was busy punching and kicking his dog. The boy had numerous bite and scratch marks. "Electrocute him with your tail! That will incapacitate him, and then stomp his skull!" Rupert nodded even as Tom felt the jaws of another dog close on his arm.

"What the hell?" He glanced and saw more dogs pouring through the right tunnel entrance. He twisted and struck the dog on his arm with his tail. The dog spasmed and hung loosely on his right arm, its teeth still latched around his forearm. Tom twisted and shook his arm hard, sending the paralyzed dog over the edge of the chasm.

Reggie had fallen on his butt and was wrestling a dog, using his four arms to pry the dog's four legs apart. Suddenly the dog howled at an incredible level as Reggie managed to ingloriously and bloodily rip the dog's four limbs off. The writhing and biting head and torso fell onto his body. Reggie started shouting obscenities and began batting at the dog's torso to get it off, even as it bit him in the shoulder.

Talarius had left a pile of three dogs behind him, but was now at the chasm's edge with two dogs attacking him. Boggy and Antefalken were battling their third dog with Estrebrius periodically plunging down to skewer the dog's body. Tom moved to grab one of Talarius's dogs when from out of nowhere, two other dogs attached themselves to his legs.

Tizzy had four dog haunches, one in each hand, and was busy smacking two other dogs with them. Their pack mates writhed on the ground with no hind legs, and severely mangled or missing forelegs.

"Fuck!" Tom yelled, whipping his tail around to one dog to zap it into paralysis and then grabbing at the other with his right hand claws. He ripped the non-paralyzed dog off his leg and forcefully threw it into the chasm even as he saw a third dog join the two on Talarius. It was too much; Talarius overbalanced and went over the edge with two dogs on top of him and the third yapping on the ledge!

Tom lunged but the paralyzed dog on his leg tripped him up. He fell to his knees with a thud, attracting the attention of the dog yelping where Talarius had gone over the cliff. Tom used his other leg to kick the spasming dog off his leg; it took a couple of tries. Talarius's third dog was now on him. Tom grabbed the dog by the maw; one hand on the jaw, the other on the snout. He pulled with all his strength.

There was a horrendous noise from the hound as Tom ripped its jaw off. He then tossed the dog and its jaw down the chasm and prepared to dive after Talarius. Even as he moved to do so, Talarius rose from the chasm, whacking at a dog still attached to his leg. The knight could fly! What the hell?

Whap! Talarius's rod succeeded in dislodging the dog, and it fell into the chasm with a loud yelping noise. Talarius flew to the ledge and landed. Rupert had finished his previous dog and was just helping Boggy with the final dog. Reggie was standing in the bloody pulp of his dog. Tizzy was busy gnawing on the haunches of the dogs he had shredded. Apparently, he had worked up an appetite.

Tom stared at Talarius as they regrouped. "So you fly," he said to the knight. Tizzy stopped eating long enough to stare at the knight.

The knight shrugged. "What people don't know can't be used against me."

"Yes, but I've been lugging your fat tin-canned ass all over the place!" Tizzy sputtered, spewing chunks of bloody hydra hound meat. Rupert grimaced as a chunk hit him in the face.

"Watch where you're spitting your food!" The boy complained.

"Thank you. I'll fly on my own from now on," Talarius said. Tizzy just shook his head and took another bite.

Tom shook his head and gestured for them to head down the remaining tunnel. As they started down, hounds entered the cavern from the same tunnel they had. There were at least another dozen, if not more, on that side. Fortunately, they did not seem capable of leaping the cavern.

~

"You lost them?" Lilith asked the prostrate form of Rosecrantz.

"Yes mistress... I am so sorry..." One could hear the fear in the demon's voice.

Lilith inhaled, savoring the smell of fear that the demon before her was radiating. She remained silent, allowing the fear to increase. She had no intention of punishing the demon, but neither did she have any intention of letting him know that.

Antefalken and the greater demon had gone through multiple boom tunnels to their next destination. Overall, given that they could go in any direction after leaving a tunnel, the wide-open spaces and the required distance her minions would need to keep, following them even through two tunnels was actually pretty decent. The question was, why had they gone through multiple tunnels? Did they know they were being followed and were purposefully obscuring their trail? That would be the most logical.

Lilith sat there pondering. After some time she realized that Rosencrantz was still groveling on the floor. "Very well. I am most displeased. Failure like this cannot be tolerated. I will overlook it this once. Return to your compatriot and stake out the greater demon's cave; I am sure they will return."

~

Tom had lost track of where they were. They had gone down the tunnel from the chasm cavern and made a few more turns. At several points, it had sounded like dogs could be heard within some tunnels, so they had chosen others. Tizzy seemed less and less sure the further they got. This was turning into a fiasco. The price of greed, Tom was sure Talarius would say. Fortunately, unlike humans, they had no need of food or water, or even air, so they had all the time they needed to find their way out. The trick was to do it without being eaten by hydra hounds.

Tizzy had stopped at a T intersection and was looking at the far wall of the right-hand passage. "What are you gawping at?" Boggy asked.

Tizzy pointed to what appeared to be a marking, a sign on the wall. It appeared to have been painted there. "Does this paint seem a little too fresh?" Tizzy asked.

Boggy peered closer and then reached out and touched it. "Yes. I'd say it's pretty recent, within a few years."

"Do hydra hounds use paint by any chance?" Rupert asked.

Tizzy and Talarius both shook their heads no. "I've never seen a dog that could paint." Tizzy said. "It's not like playing poker."

"Do either of you recognize the language?" Tom asked the two demons, who shook their heads.

Antefalken and Talarius both looked. "Nothing I am familiar with," said Antefalken with a shrug.

"Agreed," Talarius stated.

"So we go the other way?" Tom asked. Tizzy shrugged. Tom glared at him. "You are our resident expert; *can we go the other way?*"

Tizzy squinted down the corridor to the left and shrugged. "It appears we can."

Antefalken turned to look at Tizzy. "What do you mean, it *appears* we can? Will that passage take us where we want to go?"

Tizzy shrugged again. "Where do we want to go?" Everyone but Tizzy let out sighs of exasperation.

"We were going to the gold and silver rooms, but at the moment, I'd settle for a way out," Boggy said firmly.

"Yeah. Well, I'm not sure," Tizzy said.

Talarius let out another sigh. "Why are you not sure?"

"I don't remember ever being in this part of the cavern system before," Tizzy said honestly.

"You're saying we're lost?" Tom asked in disbelief.

"Well, I know where I am, and I know where you all are. So none of us are technically lost," Tizzy said.

Estrebrius shook his head. "So then, where are we?"

"Here, at a T intersection." Tizzy said overly patiently, as if talking to a child.

Rupert groaned. "So we are lost!"

"Shit!" Reggie cursed. "I am in a lot of pain right now; I've got all sorts of bite holes. I just want to get home and rest!"

"How can we be lost if we know where each of us are? I do not need to find any of you. You are here. If you were lost, we would have to search for you. Like when I misplace my pipe. It's then lost and I have to look for it."

Tom rubbed the bridge of his nose. "Okay. We all need to remember we are talking to Tizzy."

Tizzy gave him a strange look. "I'm standing right here; how would you forget you are talking to me?"

"I mean you operate on a higher plane of consciousness then most of us," Tom said. It was the politest way he could think of to tell the demon he was crazy.

Tizzy gave a nod of thoughtful agreement, put his pipe in his mouth, and lit it with his left thumb.

Tom pointed in the opposite direction from the markings and the group proceeded down that passage. This part of the cavern system was a bit different. There were large swatches of demon-built masonry interspersed with dark rock. It was a very different sort of rock than previously. Before, the rock had been whiter and smoother. This rock was much craggier and far darker.

They came to another T intersection. "Right or left? Tom asked the group.

"Since we have no idea, let's just pick one. Right?" Antefalken proposed.

Tom nodded and they headed right. He made a mark to indicate they had passed this way. They had followed the passage for several deminutes when Tom suddenly said, "Is it just me, or is it getting lighter?"

They all stopped and looked around. Antefalken nodded. "It does seem brighter, but it's not as consistent as Abyss light."

"I'm thinking we should move cautiously and quietly," Talarius proposed softly. Tom nodded, as did the others. They proceeded along and soon they could see that the slowly flickering light was coming from up ahead. They could also now detect what sounded like conversation; however, it was not normal demonese as far as Tom could tell. It was more guttural.

Soon they got to a point where the corridor turned and they could clearly tell that the light and sound were coming from around the corner. Antefalken put a finger to his lips and crept quietly up and peered around the corner. He frowned slightly and then crouched and moved around the corner. Tom heard a small gulping sound, and then Antefalken snuck back around the corner.

He gestured them all to a huddle. "We are at the mouth of a ledge overlooking a large chamber. There is only room for a few of us at a time, and we need to keep low and peer over the edge to the floor about sixty feet below. I suggest we go two by two and take a look."

The rest nodded. Tom motioned Talarius and Boggy to go next. When they came back, Boggy had a puzzled expression, but Tom could not see what the knight was thinking due to the helmet. Estrebrius, Rupert and Reggie went next, and then finally Tom and Tisdale. As the two looked over the edge, Tom noticed Tizzy's eyes get wider and then he made a *tsah* noise with his teeth and tongue.

They scurried back to the group and Tom gestured for them to head back down the tunnel so they could talk with more confidence of not being heard. After a few deminutes, Tom gestured for them to stop. "I think Tizzy recognized what we saw. Anyone else?" Tom asked.

What Tom had seen was basically a large living chamber or barracks, perhaps for a tribe. He was not sure what to call it. In the chamber were a number of very oddly uniform-looking demons. They seemed to be of a specific type or form, not the usual hodgepodge. They were all different, but they shared the same core characteristics. All were eight to ten feet tall, most were red and pretty ugly. However, they had something of what Tom would call a porcine look. They had hooves, but their legs were much shorter than those of most hooved demons, and further apart. More like pigs' legs, if pigs could stand on their hind legs.

The demons were also very large around, and many of them extremely muscular. They had bat-like wings, as did most demons, but they had no horns. At least, most didn't seem to; rather, they had huge mouths with large bottom tusks growing upwards, sometimes to eye height or higher. The other odd thing was that most of them were wearing some form of clothing; at the very least, loin cloths and bands of different colored cloth. They were also all heavily armed.

The demons were basically milling about talking, some resting on beds. Some were standing around a giant firepit in the center of the room. That seemed to be where the light was coming from. It was clearly magical fire, as there were no logs or anything else to burn in the Abyss. The chamber looked like army barracks or something similar, although there were both men and women in the barracks. Tom had no idea what to make of it. He looked to the others.

"They look like really big ugly orcs with hooves and wings," Talarius said.

"D'Orcs." Tizzy nodded in agreement.

"Dorks?" Tom asked.

Tizzy shook his head no. "D'Orcs, like Demon Orcs or Damned Orcs or Dangerous Orcs or Doomed Orcs or Dark Orcs or Death Orcs or—"

"I think we get the idea," Tom cut him off. "So they are orc demons?" He was not sure if he had seen any orcs in Astlan, but if it was a fantasy world, it probably had them. Tizzy nodded. Tom looked to the others, who seemed about as puzzled as he was. Antefalken looked as if he was searching his memory for something.

"So are you saying there are distant planes with orcs on them that get summoned by orc wizards?" Tom asked.

"I've never heard of an orc wizard," Talarius said firmly. "Orc shaman, yes; wizard, no. Doesn't seem in their nature." The knight looked at Tom more intently. "However, I am not sure I follow you."

"We can go over that later; it's part of why I brought you to the Abyss. However, at the moment, it's most likely not useful to our current situation," Tom said. "Tizzy?"

Tizzy shrugged. "Sort of, but not really. There used to be a cult of orcs that worshipped an orc god who would reward the greatest, nastiest, meanest warriors by transforming them into D'Orcs upon death. I suppose it was sort of like sainthood, but rather than being saints, the orcs ended up being demons in the Abyss."

Tom shook his head. "So one deity's idea of punishment is another's idea of reward?"

Boggy snorted and said, "And neither is accurate."

"So what was the point of this? Why would the orcs want to end up in the Abyss?" Tom asked Tizzy.

Tizzy frowned as if it were obvious. "Orcs love battle, and their god promised them the right to fight for him for all of eternity. Why would they not jump at that? That's a promise so-called 'good' gods make all the time." Tizzy glanced over at Talarius, who said nothing.

"Uhm, so where is this god of theirs?" Rupert asked, looking around nervously.

Tizzy shrugged, "He called down the final battle and lost. Bummer when that happens. He died, as did all those with him. These guys must have been left doing rear guard or something. Huge disgrace to not die in battle with your god." Tizzy was shaking his head. "You really have to feel for the poor saps."

Boggy shook his head, staring at Tizzy. "You really are daft, mate."

Talarius sighed. "No, the octopod makes a lot of sense. The sense of failure must be crushing for them."

Tom shook his head. "So what are they doing here?"

Tizzy shrugged. "Where else would they go? They wouldn't have been welcome in the Courts, so it would make sense to get far away and hole up in a defensible location." He gestured to their surroundings. "Seems like this place would do nicely."

Antefalken chuckled. "Well, *we* were thinking about holing up in the Crystal Caverns to avoid Lilith, so yes."

"By the way, I've changed my mind. I want to go back to Tom's cave," Boggy said. The others nodded in agreement.

"Okay, well, we don't want to go that way"—Tom pointed back to the lit area they'd just left—"so let's go back to the last T and take the other direction ."

They returned to the T and continued on straight. This corridor went along for about four hundred feet before it made a turn to the right. Antefalken went ahead and looked around the corner carefully before gesturing them forward. This passage seemed to be going downward at an angle; that was not a particularly good thing, Tom felt. Down was further from the surface and closer to the floor of the barracks room.

The passageway eventually led to a landing with a large iron door that opened onto it.

"Hmm, not so good," Antefalken said softly. "I'll try listening at the door to see if I hear anything, but it appears rather thick and soundproof." The demon put his head up to the door, twisting it awkwardly to get his ears as close as possible despite his protruding horns. Everyone remained silent while the bard listened.

Tom examined the seals around the door. They seemed pretty tight. He had been thinking that if there had been space below the door, he could have turned to flame and gone through; unfortunately, that did not appear to be the case.

Antefalken pulled his head back, shaking it. "I don't hear anything. Whether that's because there is nothing, or because the door is thick, I don't know." The short demon shrugged.

Talarius sighed. "That seems to be the norm. I had hoped perhaps your demon hearing would be better than human or alfar, but the same thing always happens when I find an iron door in a dungeon." He flexed his hands. "We need to be ready for whatever is there, and be prepared to fight or flee as the case warrants."

"You do this often?" Boggy asked, rather surprised.

The knight made an exaggerated nodding motion in his armor so they could see it. "Yes. In the quest to rout out evil, one often has to march through underground warrens, mazes and dungeons." He shook his helmeted head back and forth. "For some odd reason, evil seems to prefer the underground, away from the light of day."

Antefalken rolled his eyes. "Okay, so everyone get ready." They braced themselves as the bard moved to the handle, slowly placing his hand on it and then twisting and pulling. Tom was not sure the demon was strong enough to open the giant door. However, the door moved. Demons were very strong for their size. But then the door stopped moving with a soft clank. Antefalken shook his head. "It's locked."

"I don't suppose you know how to pick a lock?" Boggy asked.

Antefalken gave him a withering look. "I'm a bard! Of course I can pick a stupid lock. You don't need to be rude." He shook his head and reached into his belt pouch to pull out some lock-picking tools. "One nice thing about D'Orc-sized doors: the keyholes are good sized. Hearthean locks are quite the pain. And due to both size and complexity, they are quite complex. They are excellent locksmiths and lock picks!"

The bard fiddled around in the keyhole for a short time before there was a clicking noise. He put his tools back in his belt and nodded to everyone to be on guard. He twisted the handle and pulled. Surprisingly, the door did not make anywhere near the screech Tom had expected. It was not silent but relatively quiet. Antefalken looked through the door, and then stuck his head through the door. He pulled back and opened the door wider, gesturing for the others to go through.

On the other side of the door was a corridor running perpendicular to the corridor they had just come down. This corridor went some distance to the left and right, with various openings and doors every so often.

"So now we enter a more fortress-like environment," Antefalken observed softly.

"Are we sure we want to go this way?" Estrebrius asked. "It seems way too populated."

"Well, the hydra hounds are the other way, and if this area is more populated, there must be an exit somewhere," Boggy noted.

"I believe the barracks we saw are that way." Talarius pointed to their right.

"So let's go the other way," Tom suggested. The knight nodded.

They began moving carefully down the hall away from where they thought the barracks were. They continued down the corridor for several deminutes, ignoring doors and side passages. Eventually the corridor ended in another T intersection.

Tom gestured right and the party turned the corner.

"*Aaagghhhh!*" A rather high-pitched scream erupted in front of them, followed by a clatter of what appeared to be a stone sword falling to the floor. Standing there was a rather short, thin D'Orc, mouth agape and screeching. The D'Orc immediately turned tail and began running madly in the opposite direction, shrieking, "ACHTUNG—INVADERS! WE UNDER ATTACK! PREPARE FOR BATTLE! INVADERS! INVADERS!"

"Okay, not quite what I was expecting," Tizzy observed, pulling out his pipe and puffing away. There was a commotion distantly echoing from the direction they had just come.

Talarius pointed his sword in the third direction. "That way, fast!"

They all charged into that corridor. Suddenly gongs were ringing from multiple directions, although none seemd to be coming from the direction they were going, which was good.

Tizzy was scrambling along on his four legs and came up beside Tom. The hallway was rather wide at this point. "I always hate it when a home invasion goes wrong!"

Tom glanced over at the demon, troubled by his statement. He guessed that technically this was a home invasion. Sort of like when he invaded the dragon's lair. His stomach sank with a bad feeling. "That D'Orc seemed a lot smaller than the ones we saw in the barracks; you suppose they have children here?" Tom asked the group.

"Looks like it!" Rupert said.

"Anything is possible. We saw both men and women and if you're spending thousands of years locked under a mountain, sex is probably a popular pastime," Antefalken called back.

"I wish you hadn't said that! Now that you put the idea of them making babies in my head, something has come up that's making it harder for me to run!" Reggie yelled.

"Demons don't have families," Talarius retorted to Antefalken's claim, ignoring Reggie.

"Tell my dad that!" Rupert pointed to Tom.

"If your god is dead set on not making any more of your kind, babies are the only way to maintain or grow your population," Tizzy noted.

"Why would they be doing that?" Boggy asked Tizzy.

"More soldiers for a war of vengeance?" Tizzy noted.

"Damn it, octopod, you're starting to make too much sense," Talarius harrumphed.

"Do you hear barking?" Estrebrius asked while flying down the corridor.

"Crap." Now that he tried, Tom could hear barks and howls that sounded like hydra hounds, as well as the clamoring of what sounded like shields and spears, mixed with shouts and commands.

"It sounds like hounds and a small war party," Talarius commented.

"That could be a problem. Adult D'Orcs are the best of the best when it comes to orc combat. Most of them are major demons and their leaders are greater demons," Tizzy said.

"Are you saying that our current plan of retreat is better than standing and fighting?" Talarius asked.

"Pretty much," Tizzy said.

"Very well then," the knight said matter-of-factly.

They rounded another corner.

"Should we branch off at some point to try and elude them?" Tom asked.

"There are various theories of castle design and dungeon design, but long hallways often lead to exits. Unless the builders are particularly crafty, dwarves and drow being very good examples of such. Orcs are not crafty. Sneaky, untrustworthy and ruthless, but not crafty. I am thinking the best bet is to try and get to an exit. They know these halls far better than we," Talarius said.

The point might be moot, Tom realized, as they had not seen any side corridors or even doors since they had turned that last corner.

"Crap!" Antefalken exclaimed as they emerged into a larger room. The group stopped, as there did not appear to be any place else to go.

The corridors for some time had been mostly masonry. The front half of this room was the same; however, the back wall was rough brown stone leading all the way to the top of a forty-foot-high ceiling. There were no doors or other exits.

"This is not good; we will have to backtrack," Talarius said as he moved around the room, apparently searching for secret doors or who knew what. He shook his head and walked back to the center of the room near the back wall, staring down the corridor through which they'd entered.

Tom blinked at the wall behind the knight. He thought he could see what looked like a drawing on the wall. The knight's armor light was off, so the room was completely dark, but the drawing on the wall seemed to be softly glowing. It had not been doing that when they'd entered.

"Does anyone else see that?" Tom pointed to the wall behind the knight.

"Yes," Antefalken said.

The others looked and nodded. Talarius turned and clearly saw it as well.

"What the...?" The knight walked up to the wall. As he did so, the writing grew brighter. There was what looked like a door drawn on the rock wall, covered with all sorts of runes and designs both on the door and on the door's drawn frame.

"Do you recognize the writing?" Tom asked.

"It seems to recognize you," Reggie said.

The knight's helmet moved back and forth. "Some of it looks familiar. It may be very old Etonian, or even Ætòênyân. However, I've only seen it in some very old books and engravings."

"I don't suppose you can read it?" Tom asked Tizzy.

"Sorry. Not big on reading religious propaganda, so never learned," the demon said.

"Talarius, step back. Let's see if it goes dark and if it will light up for anyone else," Tom instructed.

Talarius stepped back, and the light dimmed and then went out as he moved further away. Each of the others moved close to the back wall; however, the wall remained dark.

"So for some reason either Talarius, or maybe something on him is causing the runes to show," Tom said.

"So these are Etonian runes? How would they get here in the middle of nowhere in the Abyss?" Antefalken asked, clearly troubled and puzzled. More noise came from the corridor.

"They are getting closer," Tom said. "Any of you know much about rune magic?" They all shook their heads except for Antefalken, who made a so-so motion. Tom looked at the bard. "What do we need to do? Read them out loud?"

Antefalken shrugged. "Not necessarily; they could be instructions or maybe a riddle, or maybe you read them aloud to a particular response. It's hard to say without actually reading them. You really have to get into the runes and understand them somehow."

Get into the runes? That might be an idea. Maybe Tom could trace them like a link or something. "Talarius, move up to the runes so I can see them." The knight did as Tom asked. As he did, Tom opened one of his belt pouches and carefully removed an arrowhead and hid it in the palm of his hand. He stared intently at the writing, looking for a starting point. The lower right-hand corner looked as good as any. He got down on his knees up close to the runes and carefully, so that the knight could not see what he was doing, tried scratching at the first rune with the arrowhead. It did not seem to do anything.

He concentrated his essence into a strand, as he had on the battlefield, and channeled it through the arrowhead. Thinking more, he tried to reach into himself to the wad of god mana that had been giving him indigestion. Trying to separate it out was not easy, but it was the only thing he could think of. As he scratched, he tried to force his stream into the arrowhead and insert it into the rune. He imagined himself, his essence stream becoming part of the rune, even as he had done with the mana streams, treating the rune, which was clearly magic, as if were a stream or a priest that he wanted to possess.

There! It caught; he was coursing through the rune. In his mind he heard a noise that somehow he knew was the verbalization of the rune. All the runes were lightly connected. He allowed himself to flow from one rune to the next, and as he did, he could mentally hear the runes speaking their sounds.

"They are getting closer! Any luck?" Antefalken asked.

Tom could not spare his attention to answer; he was too busy flowing through the runes. He did try to speed up the process though; he poured more of the god mana into the runes.

"Whoa!" came a voice behind him—Boggy's, he thought.

"He's doing something; they are getting brighter, rune by rune," Estrebrius said.

"I've never seen runes do that, but then I don't usually deal with hidden glowing runes," Antefalken said.

"They are definitely powering up," Talarius said. "For something."

"All the rune words are lit; the door and frame are still dim," Reggie observed.

The sounds of the runes were echoing in Tom's head. He did not need to touch the runes to keep the link. He stood back up, palming the arrowhead. *Find the starting one—there.* Tom proceeded to intone the sounds he heard in his head aloud one by one; with each completed rune word, he injected more mana.

"I don't know that language at all," Antefalken said.

Talarius shook his head. "Nor do I."

Tom completed the intonation and felt a cracking sensation. Suddenly the dimmer outlines of the door and frame flashed brilliant blue. As the light faded, they could clearly see the door and frame as real objects. The barking was very loud now from down the corridor, accompanied by what sounded like shouts of victory. Tom reached out and twisted the door handle and pushed the door open. Behind it was a landing with stairs leading upward. "Hah! A stairway to heaven!" They all cheered.

"You better hope it's not going to Tierhallon!" Tizzy shouted.

Tom went through the door and made room for the others to come through. They all quickly did, even as a large arrow slammed into the rock frame of the door before bouncing off. Tom looked through the door to see a large horde of very big and angry D'Orcs charging into the room. He quickly slammed the door and began pulling himself out of the runes, with luck depowering them. "Everyone go, up the stairs! I'm trying to lock the door behind us." The handle he was holding suddenly vanished, leaving a solid stone wall with no markings.

Tom leaned against the wall to rest. He could hear angry shouts and yells from the other side. The stone wall and door had been rather thick, but not insurmountable. They might be able to break down the wall, given time. They needed to hurry. He charged up the steps after the rest of the group.

The stairs went quite some distance and ended on a landing that had more steps going upward on the other side of the landing. The more interesting thing, however, was on the wall to their left. In the center of the wall was an ornate marble entranceway, or rather door frame, with a very white marble door with a heavy vault handle, a wheel sort of thing, and giant stone hinges on the right. It looked to Tom a little Greek or colonial in style, but the door and the frame were heavily inscribed with more of the same runes.

This time as Talarius approached the door, it was his armor that started to light up. "This is most unusual," he said.

"Why would Etonians be wandering around in the Abyss making runic doorways?" Antefalken asked.

"How would they even get down here? That would be an act of war that would trigger all sorts of repercussions," Boggy said.

"Do you know anything, Tizzy?" Tom asked.

Tizzy shrugged. "Never been through that invisible door. Certainly never been in this room. Back in my day, no Etonian in their right mind would have set foot in the Abyss."

"So none of this was here when you were last here?" Boggy asked.

"No idea, but I think that if it had been installed at that time, there would have been a lot of dead bodies lying around. The demons that lived here would not have let an Etonian in, I can guarantee you that."

"So what's behind the fancy door?" Rupert asked.

"Up for another try?" Antefalken asked.

"Uhm…" Estrebrius made a hesitant motion. "Perhaps it's locked up for a reason? Maybe it's dangerous?"

"Dangerous for whom?" Tizzy asked. "I cannot think an Etonian would try to protect demons from something."

"I find this very disturbing," Talarius said. "I must confess, I am very curious. I am also very hesitant, but this should not be. It's very wrong."

"Okay, so I think we open it," Tom said. Antefalken and Rupert shot him big grins.

Tom stared at the runes. They looked exactly like the runes downstairs, so while he knew how they were pronounced, he had no idea what they meant. He decided to start by just reading the runes aloud.

"*Darwaltho omnibois pertuum, fetenagathan larthow mewem. Dest naturume sanct vastros deum. Narth faltosth agck demolscrius bitem. Saveros tootos freeyum nathos, eternolom cretenexos verum. Argwolo beat sact fetenagathan. Barthfarlon omnibus bitem,*" Tom intoned.

Nothing much happened. "That didn't help." He walked up to marble vault wheel and examined it. Clearly it could turn, and probably released giant bars inside the door. At the center of the wheel was a small insert, almost like a screw hole; probably the axis the wheel turned on. Tom passed his palm over it and pushed the arrowhead into the hole. He was still attached to arrowhead and so it took no time for him to start sending himself into the stone axis.

At first, he didn't detect magic per se, but then suddenly he hit against what he guessed was the door itself. It flashed against him painfully. The door was definitely alive with magic; much more magic than the runes below. This was heavy magic; it vibrated with power. He closed his eyes to try and feel the power. Yes, the vibrations resonated with the magic in the arrowhead. This was Tiernon's magic. He needed more of it. Tom reached back to what he imagined in his mind was the wad of divine mana within himself; that which he had taken from the umbilical cord but still had not digested, so to speak. He pulled on it and let it suffuse the threads of his own being, much like infiltrating the priests. This he sent up against the magic wall.

In his mind, his mana stream flattened against the wall of magic, the two sets of mana not quite in sync. Very close to being in sync; just not quite. He tried spreading his flattened-out stream, imagining it as a coat of paint upon the mana wall. He imagined his coat of paint absorbing the vibrations of the mana wall, synchronizing with them, relaxing and oozing into the pores of the mana wall until they were one. *Relax, let go, sink into the wall of mana. We are one.*

There—he was the mana wall, at least the part near the handle. He carefully let more mana, both his own natural and the undigested god mana flow into the wall, a trickle of animus riding along to guide it. Flowing, engulfing, becoming one with the mana wall, one with the door and the runes. At the edge of the door the mana vibration changed. The magic in the doorframe was different; it was locked firmly to the door's magic, but different.

Tom tried to do the same thing again. It was exceedingly tricky, much harder this time, as he had to maintain the same frequency, or whatever it was, as the door, but also try to match the doorframe to infiltrate it and keep it all as one piece. It was hard, very hard. He could see what he needed to do, but trying to balance three different frequencies was extremely taxing.

He had no idea how long it took, but suddenly he was in. He could feel himself and his mana inside the doorway. He let more mana in. It was slow going because he had to shift and match frequencies, but soon he had engulfed the doorframe's magic.

Now, he could see clearly what he needed to move the giant rods within the door; he needed the frame to let go. There—those were the rods he needed to release in the frame, pinning the doors in place. He suddenly realized that the archway was connected to the room. He could feel the room. The magic wall of the doorway was part of the overall magic wall shielding the twenty-by-twenty-foot room on the other side of the door. He could not tell what was in the room, but he could tell its size.

Tom willed the room to relax, to rest. He realized he needed to synchronize the magic of the room/doorway with the door. If he did that, he could make the pins slide and the door open. *Relax, calm, and synchronize,* Tom thought, willing the three parts of his mana self. Over and over, like calming a puppy.

There! They were all synched. He willed the doorway pins to move. *Slurk, slurk, slurk...* a fury of noises came from the wall as he did so. Tom began turning the wheel, now suddenly aware of the room and of his friends standing up after having been seated on the floor during this long ordeal.

The pins rolled back into the door. Now he needed to pull the door open. It was heavy and he had to push against the floor hard with his legs, but it swung open very smoothly. A cloud of very stale air escaped the vault as new, fresher air entered.

"Wow, how long was that?" Tom asked, slumping against the door. He had to slowly withdraw himself from the room and door. He palmed the middle of the wheel and willed the arrowhead back into his hand.

"About an Astlanian hour, I think," Rupert said. "We watched you with demon sight. It was pretty wicked."

"It felt like I was doing a bank job," Tom said with a laugh. The others looked at him strangely. "Never mind. What's inside?"

They all peered into the room. It was, as Tom had seen, a twenty-by-twenty-foot room with nothing in it except at the very center. There were two marble blocks covered in runes about six feet apart, linked by a black metal bar that seemed fatter on one end than the other. It looked as if the blocks had been formed around the two ends. Almost as if the bar had been set in concrete that was allowed to harden. Except that the blocks were marble, not concrete.

"All that, for this?" Boggy asked, clearly disappointed. Tom had to agree. A dull metal bar encased on its ends in rune-covered marble. What could make a metal bar that important? Or was it the blocks? Tom reached out with his mental fingers. No, the blocks were Tiernon magic, like everything else. The bar was something else; something very different. It did not like the Tiernon magic, but whatever it was, it was very weak at this point. It did not actually seem to have much, if any, magic in it. It was more residue at this point, a faint trace of past power.

"I think whatever it was, it's harmless now," Tom said. "The runes on the blocks are Etonian, like the locks and all. The bar is different, but there is not much of any magic left in it. I would say a small residue, but no real, active mana in it," Tom said.

Antefalken was peering at it more closely. "See these two lines that entwine the bar?" He pointed to two parallel lines that striped the bar, sort of like a barber pole if the red line were composed of two different colors. Although at the moment, both were pretty dark. "They are crystalline, and each appears to be an unbroken single piece. That is very unusual. The only place I've seen anything like it was in the Crystal Caverns, but those were straight lines. How you would get crystal to grow like this is beyond me."

Antefalken stood up. "Of course, that might explain the residue of mana you sense," Antefalken said. Tom looked at him curiously. "Crystals are often used for mana pools."

"I've heard the term, but am not that familiar with them," Tom said.

"Mana pools are constructs that wizards and others use to store mana in. You can put mana in them and link them to a magical artifact to provide mana, or you can link to one yourself to draw on it for extra capacity in battle or as needed," Antefalken said.

"So that's why wizards like gemstone rings!" Tom exclaimed.

"Yes—to a point. You can really only safely attach to one mana pool at a time. Trying to keep two of them in synch with yourself and each other is extremely difficult and can result in feedback loops, which can be unpleasant or even deadly," Antefalken said.

"Good to keep in mind," Tom said.

"Which makes this device odd," Antefalken added.

"Why?" Estrebrius asked, and Tom nodded.

"Because there are two different crystalline strands here: one ruby, the other sapphire, I believe. That would imply two mana pools in the same artifact, which would be highly unstable."

"Unless one is for the device, and one for the user as a personal pool?" Talarius suggested.

Antefalken's eyes widened. "Yes, that would make sense. Your knowledge surprises me."

Talarius shrugged under his armor. "I am a mana wielder myself, and as you may have noticed, I have a couple of arcane objects on me. I'm not a stranger to the mechanics of mana manipulation."

Antefalken smiled. "I see that."

There was some noise outside the door, in the distance.

"Did they get through the wall?" Rupert asked.

Estrebrius flew out to the landing and listened. "No, I think the noise is coming from up the stairs!"

"Curse it!" Talarius said angrily.

"We took too much time with this stupid thing," Antefalken complained.

"Sorry," Tom said.

"Not your fault; we were all curious," Boggy said.

"Well if we are going to fight our way out, I want something for it. I'm taking the bar!" Tom proclaimed.

"Seems reasonable. If nothing else, you can use it as a club to pound D'Orcs," Tizzy said.

Tom grabbed the bar, intending to pick it and the marble blocks both up, but it would not budge. "Shit!" He could hear the noises from outside, still distant but getting closer. He moved to the block at the thinner edge of the bar. He scraped the runes with the arrowhead, forcing himself into the runes. They fought back; he was going too fast. *To hell with it.*

Tom reached deep inside and gathered up as much pure mana as he could and shoved it hard into the runes. He would overwhelm the damn thing. In he went, racing through the runes, filling them with power. To his surprise, he found himself mentally jumping over the rod to the second block; the two blocks were linked. He filled those runes , flooding them with power, willing them to release, unlock, dissolve.

They did not want to budge; the space between the blocks was glowing now, as if the bar of metal was inside a force field or something. "I think you guys might want to get out and onto the landing; I think this is going to blow!" Tom yelled.

He shoved mana into the blocks as hard as he had shoveled it into the dagger. *KABLOOM!* The blocks shattered into dust. Tom was thrown back by the force of the explosion, stunned. The metal bar fell to the floor with a loud thud.

"Shit." Tom shook his head and got back up and moved to the bar. Now that the ends were free, he could see it was more like a staff, or would be a staff for a human. For Tom, it was more like a bat or club. The narrow end had a silver-rimmed end cap with a very sharp nine-inch long metal spike on the bottom. The wider end came up to a hexagonally shaped top cap about six inches across from side to side, and from that rose a two-inch round cylinder or neck with a large metal ball, or sort of amorphous blob of unshaped metal, about the same diameter as the hexagon cap.

"Okay, it will work as a mace then," Tom said to himself. He grabbed it. "Ouch!" The damn thing had shocked him! He was pissed. He had just freed it and now it was going to shock him! Yes, he knew it was an inanimate object, but he was in a hurry, and getting angry.

Tom reached down and grabbed it again, ignoring the shock, and willed himself into it. He did not need to use the arrow this time, which would have been bad. The thing did not like the arrow's magic, he could tell that. This thing was a mana pool, huh? Well, he would see what would happen if he filled it.

He willed himself into the rod even as it shocked him. He was determined to win. He would treat it like an unwilling priest, or an unwilling rune. He flooded it primarily with his own mana, but also god mana. In and in, envisioning himself becoming one with the mace, intertwining his essence with its molecules and atoms. He mixed and merged until he could feel the crystalline pools. There were only the two crystals, as Antefalken had said: unbroken ruby and sapphire strands. He flooded them with mana; the sapphire with god mana, the ruby with his own.

He *was* the crystals, he was the adamantite bar, and he was the mithral end caps, the mithral ball. He, Thomas—Tommus! He was the rod, the mace, the staff. This was the Rod of Tommus and *he* was Tommus! They were one; they were the same. Tom suddenly realized that the rod was not fighting him; it was embracing him, joining him. Welcoming him. He did not know how he knew this, but he did. He was the rod, the rod was him!

"Yes! We are Tommus!" Tom shouted at the top of his lungs. The rod flashed, its ruby and sapphire strips glowing brightly and radiating the room in red and blue, melding into purple.

The room suddenly lurched. Was that him? No, the room lurched again. Earthquake!

"What the hell are you doing in there?" Boggy called to him. The others filed back into the room, blinking in the purple light from the rod.

"So... you recharged the mana pools?" Antefalken said.

Tizzy was grinning from ear to ear and doing a little dance for some reason.

"Cool!" Rupert said.

"Wicked!" Reggie slapped his thigh with his lower left hand.

"Did you feel those tremors?" Tom asked.

"Yes. Did you do that?" Boggy asked.

"No, not that I know of. I just took control of the mace," Tom said.

"I have to say, that is one nice mace," Talarius said. "I am hoping we don't regret this."

"Why?" Tom shrugged. "I fully control it, and it's like a part of me. I have no idea what I can do with it other than smacking people, but for now that's about all we need." The ground rumbled again beneath their feet.

"I think we need to get out of here," Boggy said as the ground shook some more. "We just need to face the D'Orcs up above and be done with it."

"I agree," Talarius said as yet another tremor rocked the room.

"I will go first," Tom said, leading them out onto the landing and heading up the stairs. The stairs went up and up for a long way.

"It's amazing we can hear any noise from the top, given it's so far," Boggy said.

"Perhaps there is a very large echo chamber at the top," Antefalken suggested.

"You know, it seems a lot quieter since the tremors," Estrebrius noted.

"Maybe it scared the crap out of them!" Rupert said excitedly.

"I doubt that," Tizzy said. "Not yet, at least," he added softly.

They finally reached a landing at the top of the stairs. At the opposite end of the landing was a marble portcullis engraved with Etonian runes. On the other side of the portcullis was a large room with wall carvings and several Tom-sized benches as well as more human-sized benches. There were also marble tables of various heights between the two. At the opposite end of the room was a large double door that had apparently been opened recently, given the tracks in dust on the floor. However, no one was in the room. Light was streaming from beyond the door.

Tom examined the runes, found their starting point and quickly intoned the runes. The portcullis began rising on its own. Very slowly—it took about a deminute—but eventually it was raised.

"That's convenient," Reggie said. "I guess."

They went across the room to the open door. Tom peered through and then opened the door wider and stepped through. He found himself standing on an open bridge with a deep cavern beneath his feet. The bridge started at the door and went about fifteen feet before opening up onto a huge platform.

Tom looked up, and up. There was sky above them! The others filed out onto the bridge with him. They were in a large… something. It was a huge oval room open to the sky above. Its walls were somewhere on the order of two thousand feet high. Along the walls, starting at about two hundred feet up, there were openings like balconies, spanning both sides of the oval room. There were probably a dozen rows of balconies on each side.

The platform spanned the center of the room, with various bridges to other doorways or landings around the room. The platform appeared to be suspended over a large chasm. On the platform at the end of the bridge was a raised dais about forty feet across with steps leading up from the bridge to a dais. The dais appeared to be square or rectangular with large black-and-gold marble pillars at each corner. What appeared to be large gold braziers were set on the top of each pillar. In the center of the dais was a massive malachite throne, its back facing them, trimmed in mithral and adamantite with very large gems on the back posts and possibly on the arm end posts, although it was hard to tell from this angle.

As Tom's gaze went to the top of the throne and pillars, he suddenly realized there was a huge metal emblem over the door they had entered through. He had to turn and look up—the angle was very bad—but it appeared to be an absolutely huge, upside-down pentagram.

That seemed a very odd thing for an amphitheater in the Abyss. Pentagrams were a symbol of demon slavery. Of course this one was upside down; did that make it a symbol of power? As he was thinking this, the ground lurched again and what sounded liked an enormous burp came from underneath them. Their attention was whipped to the right side where, between three and four bridges down, a bunch of rock came spitting up and then a glob of hot lava jumped up and fell back down.

"Okay, this goes without saying, but didn't you say the volcano was inactive?" Reggie asked Tizzy. Tizzy was grinning widely. "Only for the last four thousand years. Apparently only napping."

"Well, that explains where the D'Orcs would have gone. They've fled the volcano," Antefalken said.

"Maybe." Tizzy shrugged, his grin fading. "Maybe not."

"Why would they stay?" Reggie asked Tizzy. "That would be insane, to stick around an active volcano?"

Boggy's eyes suddenly widened. "Maybe not," he said. Rupert and Reggie turned to Boggy. "What were we doing yesterday?"

"Playing in the lava flows of a small volcano?" Tom said. Tizzy grinned.

"So you think the D'Orcs have decided to open a health spa at the exact moment we arrived?" Talarius asked sarcastically.

"No, only that an active volcano is not that big a deal for them." Tizzy shrugged. "After all, they were here when it was active before. For them, it's probably like the furnace kicking in after a long summer."

"They were here when the volcano was active?" Reggie asked incredulously.

"So that's why they are here? Are you saying this is where their dark god stationed them?" Antefalken asked.

Tizzy shrugged. "That would make sense."

"None of this makes any sense," Reggie complained.

Due to his height, Estrebrius had mainly been flying since they had encountered the hydra hounds; he could fly faster than his stubby legs could walk.

After the first eruption, while the others were talking he had floated up to see over the dais. Now he floated down. "Uhm, sorry to interrupt, but the D'Orcs haven't actually gone anywhere," he said.

"What do you mean?" Talarius asked.

"They're on the other side of the dais. A few thousand, I would say. More are filing in as we speak."

"So why can't we hear them shouting?" Reggie asked.

"They seem to be on their knees in front of the dais," the little demon said.

"Kneeling?" Tom asked incredulously.

Estrebrius shrugged and made a puzzled expression with his mouth.

"Well, if we hadn't already established that lava isn't a problem, I'd have said 'crazy volcano death cult waiting for the end.' But that no longer seems so likely," Reggie said.

"Maybe we should just go up and take a look from the dais?" Tizzy asked. He turned and started walking towards the dais.

Tom looked to Talarius and Antefalken.

"Well, we either go and look, and if need be head straight up, or we shoot straight up and out of this place right now," Talarius said.

"I suspect they know we are here, as we aren't that quiet, so if they're going to shoot us out of the sky as we leave, or pursue us, going up to the dais probably won't make a huge difference." Antefalken shrugged.

Tom looked back to Talarius.

The knight sighed. " This is your world, demon. I am a stranger here and don't know the protocols of war on this plane."

"I guess we follow Tizzy. However, when we get up there, I should probably take the first look. If they charge or start shooting stuff, I can probably fend them off long enough to give you guys time to flee." Tom pointed straight upward.

He started down the bridge to the dais. He caught up with Tizzy at the foot of the stairs; the demon had not been walking that fast. Tizzy grinned at him. "Good, I was hoping you'd come. I'd much prefer you to go out there first in case they start shooting."

"Thanks," Tom said. That was what he had offered, but Tizzy made it sound worse.

"No problem!" Tizzy took a puff of his pipe.

Tom headed up the stairs, the others following. The stairs were sized a bit large for most of the other demons, but a bit small for him. Maybe they were D'Orc sized. Tom came to the top of the stairs behind the throne. It was a very large throne; it would be good sized even for Tom. He adjusted his grip on his mace, the Rod of Tommus, and confidently stepped out around the edge of the dais, ready for pandemonium.

The throne was raised a few feet above the dais, which appeared to be actually part of the throne. As Tom came around the right side of the throne, there appeared to be a holder for a rod about the height of Tom's rod. Apparently, the previous owner of the rod had owned the throne as well. That would make sense.

As he came around the dais, he could see a large crowd of D'Orcs, perhaps two thousand as Estrebrius had said. They were all well ordered in sections of about 100 each, and all were on their knees, staring at the dais. There were a few still coming in from rear bridges and quietly kneeling in formation. He noticed they had been whispering, but they fell silent as Tom came around and stood before the throne.

Silence ruled. Tom had no idea what to do. For the moment he stood reviewing the mass of D'Orcs. They were rather ragtag and worn. There were men, women, and now more obviously children. All kneeling before the throne silently; a very unexpected turn of events. There was a loud rumbling from below them and another large burp. He watched for a reaction from the D'Orcs to see if they were frightened or concerned. Surprisingly, while most acted as if nothing had happened, some of the younger D'Orcs seemed excited or happy about the lava burp, as if it was hard to contain their glee.

He supposed he should say something. *But what?* Maybe he should start with something simple. He had no clue what to say that would not get him attacked. He had no idea what was going on. Maybe it was the rod they respected; raising that for them to see might be a good idea.

"Greetings. I am Tommus!" He raised the Rod of Tommus above his head for all to see. He had no real idea where this Tommus vs. Thomas pronunciation came from; it had just popped up and sounded a lot cooler. More demon-like.

A loud cheer rose from the D'Orc horde and they all suddenly started shouting. "Tommus! Tommus! Tommus!" Tom felt his stomach drop a bit. *Okay, not expecting that. Really.* This was getting stranger and stranger. They were chanting his name loudly and enthusiastically. He needed to initiate some real dialog, figure out what was going on. He gestured them to be quiet so he could speak.

"Who speaks for you?" Tom asked when they had quieted down.

There was a second or so of a pause and then a relatively well dressed, extremely large female D'Orc in the front row center stood up and bowed deeply before marching forward to the foot of the dais. She then knelt and bowed, her head touching the floor.

"Oh Great Master, Lord of Lords, Demon of Demons, I am Zelda, daughter of Trogthor, son of Mythgar, son of your faithful steward Grognar, who gave his last breath to defend this fortress from the clutches of Lilith the Eternally Damned. I am the last adult of my line and the leader of the Faithful. We have longed for this day when you would return to us reborn, oh mighty one! Long have we waited, bearing our shame and the shame of our forebears, and today we are overjoyed at your prophesied return!"

Still bowing and not looking at him, Zelda rose and gestured to the crowd behind her. "We beg your forgiveness for our sorry state, but rest assured we are ready for your commands, ready to strike your vengeance against those who have so gravely wronged you!"

Oh, shit, was the only thing Tom could think.

Chapter 97

Jehenna took a sip of wine and gazed out over the city. She sat on Lenamare's terrace with him as they wound down their long day. The glow of the wards cast a rather eerie light over the city.

"I was questioned by a sword today," Lenamare said suddenly, apropos of nothing.

Jehenna blinked and glanced at him. "Someone questioned you at sword point? Why would you permit that?"

"Not at sword point. *By* a sword," Lenamare replied, taking a sip of wine.

"A sellsword? I am not following," Jehenna asked, puzzled.

"Yes, it was most odd. A walking, talking, intelligent sword," Lenamare said matter-of-factly.

"Obviously, I am familiar with intelligent swords, but not ones that walk and talk. I am having trouble even conceiving of what that would mean," Jehenna said.

"Think of an extremely finely crafted adamantite golem with a lot of razor-sharp edges. Clearly beyond what any normal wizard could create," Lenamare said.

"So it just walked up to you and began interviewing you?" Jehenna asked, frowning.

"Well, it invited me back to my quarters to speak in private, but yes."

"What on Astlan did it want?" Jehenna asked.

"Well, it calls itself Ruiden. Apparently it was, or is, the sword of Talarius and it is investigating his abduction."

"Well, that's unusual." Jehenna was still frowning, trying to take this in. "What did it want with you?"

"It was aware that I was the first person to summon the greater demon," Lenamare said.

"So what did it want?" Jehenna asked. "Did it want you to conjure it?"

"Indeed, it did. I demurred, saying the wards prevented it, and that even then, I would be hesitant to summon it to a place where people might be harmed."

"Altruistic of you." Jehenna said.

Lenamare chuckled. "The sword works for the Rod. That is the sort of logic they would consider, or at least one expects that they would. It seemed to understand."

"So the interrogation was cordial?" Jehenna asked.

"Quite." Lenamare shrugged. "I have to say the sword seemed quite reasonable, for a tool of death at least."

"That's nice, I guess." Jehenna shook her head. "What else did you tell it?"

"I claimed that I had not realized how powerful the demon was and that subsequent information that the Council obtains makes me suspect that this greater demon was tied to the archdemons in the palace. In particular, I thought it, Ruiden, should consider speaking with Exador, should he ever come back; and that the Council believed Exador was an archdemon, likely in charge of the greater demon."

Jehenna did a double take. "And did it buy this argument?" She seemed doubtful.

"The sword was noncommittal, but it did say that it had seen the crystal balling and had spotted Exador on the carpet with Ramses the Damned and the woman. It said it would be speaking to Exador upon his return."

"Well, that's something. I suspect that Exador will not like being quizzed by a sword. Particularly if the sword accuses him of being an archdemon."

Lenamare grinned. "Exactly my thought."

Jehenna chuckled and the two went back to silently looking out over the city, relaxing over their wine. After a few minutes of pleasant silence, Jehenna spoke up again.

"You know, I'm not sure about this proposal of yours today," Jehenna said.

Lenamare glanced over at her. "My proposal? To the sword?"

Jehenna gently shook her head. "No, not that one. I am talking about the one that has us leaving the city should an archdemon Exador return to try and retrieve the book."

Lenamare tilted his head in thought. "I'm not so sure it was so much a proposal as laying the groundwork for future options."

"Hmm." Jehenna took another sip and then continued with her point. "While I might agree there is some value in heading off someplace where Exador can't find us to work on the book, should he actually find us, I think we are in a much more defensible position here."

Lenamare chuckled softly. "Long term, or I suppose in general, I agree with that assessment. Weighing the extra safety in being somewhere Exador is unlikely to find us versus the increased risk when he does find us is a difficult proposition." He took a sip of his own wine. "I'm not sure I want to have to make that calculation. On the other hand, the argument that the city and the Council would be much safer if we were gone when an archdemon Exador comes looking for us is a very easy argument to make."

Jehenna grimaced. "I'm not sure I like your newfound altruism."

Lenamare chuckled. "Far from altruism my dear; it is the foundation for doing what I suspect we may have to do anyway."

Jehenna looked at him directly. "I'm not following."

"I am coming to suspect that we are missing a key to opening this book. At this juncture, with the stakes this high, we can't afford to outsource finding the key to another group of ne'er-do-well adventurers. We may have to seek it ourselves." Jehenna nodded at this. "It is also unquestionably true that dragging our students along with us would be a huge hindrance."

"Ahh." Jehenna nodded, finally seeing his point. "So if we have to leave, and the reason we leave is the safety of the city and the Council, and that of our students, then we can get people here to take them off our hands for a while."

"Exactly." Lenamare smiled. "I'm looking for some babysitters." They both laughed.

~

Arch-Diocate Iskerus looked up from the maps on the table to stare at Arch-Vicar General Barabus on the other side. "Once again, are we sure this is the best option?"

"And once again, I say I have no idea. I'm at a complete loss. The Knights are determined to rescue Talarius and seek vengeance and I—we—have a responsibility not to lose any more knights. So we must explore this option."

"You will keep me informed of what you find in Keeper's City? I find it very hard to trust the Oorstemothians," Iskerus said.

"Church lawyers are confident of the Rod's safety in Keeper's City and our right to leave Keeper's City, regardless of whether an agreement can be reached. We just need to verify that they can do what they claim they can do. Once that is done, it is an entirely different document for the joint resolution of whatever the hell flimflam they call it. Which again Church lawyers will relentlessly scour. Further, if we did do a joint mission, we would have our own lawyers with us to negotiate any disputes of interpretation that may arise."

"Fine then. Your men will take the gateway to Hoggensforth in the morning, and then make sail for Keeper's City in the evening."

"Yes. We will station the remainder of the men we are withdrawing from here outside Hoggensforth, in preparation for whatever comes of the next round of negotiation, or whatever happens when the wards are lowered here," Barabus said.

"I guess we are set then." Iskerus shook his head, standing up.

"And Ruiden?" Barabus asked.

Iskerus shrugged. "I have not seen him today. I believe he has taken his investigation into the city."

"And the city and palace guards are fine with a walking sword wandering around?" Barabus asked.

"It appears he took a ring of invisibility from Talarius's arcane armory," Iskerus said. "I had a brother keeping an eye on him and at one point, after exiting the burnt remains of Talarius's tent, the sword vanished into thin air."

Barabus raised his hands slightly as if pleading to Tiernon. "A magical sword wearing a magical ring?" He sighed. "I think I have now heard everything."

Iskerus chuckled. "We are certainly living in interesting times."

"I'm ready to go back to some boring times," Barabus groused, shaking his head.

"I will second you on that," Iskerus said, raising his hand in a farewell gesture as he moved towards the tent flap. "I will leave you to make your final rounds, so you can get some sleep for tomorrow." He walked to the doorway. Looking back before exiting, he said, "And if you do reach an agreement for the next phase? Please do not feel obligated to invite me along." Iskerus turned and left as Barabus chuckled.

~

"Excellent," Tom said, realizing he had to say something. He needed to think fast. "We have much work to do." He was making this up as he went along; he needed time to regroup. Looking down the dais at the demoness, he noted that there were stairs leading up from the platform to the dais. "You, all of you, have permission to be at ease. You may look at me. You are warriors, yes? Stand tall, stand proud."

A ripple of something—relief, perhaps—seemed to circulate among the crowd. Zelda stood and looked at him proudly, and Tom thought, quite happily. Tom looked back at the throne; he needed to sit down, to think. It was a rather odd chair with what appeared to be two backs: the normal back he had seen from behind and then an inner back made of posts. He suddenly realized that the inner posts were actually cutouts for his wings. There was also a tail slot and a rather conveniently shaped seat. Tom turned and stepped up onto the throne and sat down, carefully fitting his wings between the posts. It really was surprisingly comfortable.

He placed his rod into the stand, its pointed end neatly fitting into the base. The world spun. Tom's head was suddenly reeling as the staff to which he was intimately connected immediately merged into the throne, into the dais, into the platform, into the volcano! He could actually feel, sense the entire mountain region. The volcano, the caverns. His mind was able to trace every corridor, every room, every trap, every watch point. He had to close his eyes, it was so overwhelming. For the moment, he *was* the entire mountain range.

He released his grip on the rod and the feelings eased. He was still linked to the rod and thus to everything else, but the immediacy receded. He shook his head to clear it. Several of the D'Orcs laughed and others clapped. Clearly, they had known or suspected what would happen. "Well, that is something," Tom said. Many other D'Orcs laughed at that.

"Our lord has now completely reestablished his dominion?" Zelda asked.

"I'm connected to it. I may have a few things to work out and understand," Tom said, shaking his head.

"Great One, may our people approach and directly swear our fealty to you now?" Zelda asked. Tom had another "*oh, shit*" moment.

If he did this, he would be locking himself into being their leader under false pretenses. There would be no going back. It was a huge step. However, if he did not, who knew what would happen, how they would react. He was busily racking his brain trying to think how this sort of scenario played out in books and movies he had read and watched. At last, he gestured to Zelda. "Come to my throne; I would consult with you directly."

Zelda nodded in acceptance and carefully climbed the dais, then approached the throne and knelt briefly before standing again. He gestured for her to come up close on his right-hand side, which she did.

Tom leaned down to speak with her privately. "I know this must come as a complete surprise, and very sudden for the people. We must, of course, have the swearing; however, are you sure that all of your people are ready and prepared for this after so long? I seek complete, unwavering loyalty and if we do this too quickly after so long, some may end up with reservations. I want no reservations." He was pulling this out of his butt; he just needed to buy time to talk with the others.

Zelda blinked at this, uncertain, perhaps puzzled. He hoped he had not insulted her or her people. "I, uhm, had not thought of that. I just know that we have been waiting. Many were… on the verge… of losing hope. Many did lose hope, and so perished. You are right, My Lord, this is sudden. We should have a feast prepared to celebrate the oaths; we do not. We were not expecting you."

"I think a celebratory feast is clearly necessary," Tom said, grasping at anything. "How long will that take to prepare?"

Zelda shook her head. "I do not know; perhaps a few days. We need to get supplies from somewhere…"

"We need to plan. This must be done right!" Tom said decisively. "We will set the date once we have the feast planned."

Zelda looked at him and nodded. "Perhaps I might simply introduce my commanders today?"

Tom nodded and stood up. "My people," he began. Okay, that was presumptuous; he needed to play the part, though. "The Oath Taking is a momentous event and will deserve a celebratory feast. We will need time to prepare the feast; we must therefore plan for that and plan a time for the Oath Taking. Thus, for now, I would have Zelda present her commanders to me."

Tom sat down and motioned to Zelda, who moved forward to address the crowd. "Commanders, attend!" At this order, about twenty D'Orcs came forward and knelt before the dais. Tom gestured for Zelda to bring them forward. She looked at him and made a gesture of one or all.

"Bring them all up together, as we will be for war councils," Tom said, getting smiles and cheers from those who heard. The twenty D'Orc commanders came up the dais and knelt before Tom. It was getting a bit crowded; these D'Orcs were big.

"While we are at this, I should also introduce… uh, my entourage." Tom could not think of what word to use. He seriously doubted that dark overlords had "friends." He gestured behind the throne, hoping the others would see and come up, cautiously filing two by two around the throne and into view of the D'Orc commanders.

"One of the commanders suddenly choked and grabbed for his battle-axe. "Treachery! A knight of Tiernon!" The others all stepped back, suddenly very concerned and nervous.

"Relax!" Tom ordered, realizing this was all about to blow up. "He is my hostage." *Something true!* "He will not harm you, nor will you harm him. He is part of my strategy." He glanced at Talarius, who of course was glaring at him through his visor, or at least Tom assumed he was by his stance.

"Ack!" another, older-looking D'Orc said as the previous D'Orc's motion had freed this one's line of sight. "This is a validation of the prophecy I did not need!" He was pointing at Tizzy.

"Hey, Darg-Krallnom! Long time no see!" Tizzy smiled and waved.

"You know this demon, Darg?" the first upset D'Orc asked.

"Yes. The master used to allow him the run of the mount, and on occasion sought his advice," Darg-Krallnom said.

"Yes," a third older D'Orc warrior with a broken right tusk said. "Probably the only prince in the Abyss to listen to that trickster!"

Boggy looked over to Tizzy. "Well, apparently you haven't changed much in four thousand years or so."

Tizzy shrugged. "What can I say? You stick with what works!" Tizzy turned to the third D'Orc. "Good to see you too, Arg-nargoloth! Still haven't seen a dentist?"

A D'Orc beside Arg-nargoloth had to restrain the D'Orc commander from rushing forward to throttle Tizzy.

Tom shook his head, looking at Tizzy. He was starting to suspect a setup. He was not sure how that could be; things seemed too random, and yet... Tizzy knew these D'Orcs? *Then why had they been running from D'Orcs?* Tom glanced back at the D'Orcs who knew Tizzy and realized that the expressions on their faces most likely explained why they had been fleeing. Apparently, a significant number of demons who knew Tizzy wished him ill.

"Yes, well... seems like some of us know each other already," Tom said. "Tizzy many of you know. The demon Boggy," he said, gesturing to Boggy. "Talarius, Knight Rampant of Tiernon, we have established is in my custody and not to be harmed. Beside him is Reggie, an incubus in my service." One of the commanders got what Tom thought might be a reflective look on his face thinking about an incubus. He was not sure though; maybe it was simply indigestion.

Next Tom pointed to Estrebrius. "Estrebrius is another associate and confidant of mine." He then pointed to Antefalken. "My bard, Antefalken." Antefalken nodded. "And finally, Rupert—"

"Of course," Zelda interrupted with a big smile. "Clearly, we recognize your son; he is identical to you, even as the prophecy said he would be."

Tom froze in his tracks. He wondered if his eyes were as wide as Rupert's were. Tom coughed. "Aah... yes. Yes, indeed. We should talk more about this prophecy later."

Zelda nodded. "Allow me to present my commanders by seniority."

Darg-Krallnom stepped forward. "I am Darg-Krallnom of the Krall Tribe of Astlan. It is an honor to see your return, Master." He stepped back and Arg-nargoloth stepped forward.

"Arg-nargoloth, the Narg Tribe of Etterdam." He gave a bow and stepped back to allow the D'Orc who had been upset with Talarius's presence to approach.

"Roth Tar Gorefest, of the Hun Horde of Romdan. I apologize for my reaction to your prisoner. Old habits..." He gestured, not knowing what to say.

Tom nodded. "Very understandable." Roth Tar Gorefest stepped back.

Another D'Orc, this one short and rather squat, stepped forward. "Vargg Agnoth of the Ag Clan of Nysegard. Welcome back, My Lord." He nodded as best his short neck allowed and then stepped back.

"Delg Narmoloth of the Delg Tribe of Earth," a rather old-looking, tall, thin, bald D'Orc stated, stepping forward and bowing.

"Earth?" Tom sat up straighter. "I wasn't aware there were orcs on Earth." He suddenly hoped Tizzy's history had been correct.

Delg Narmoloth chuckled. "Not for millennia. Our tribes began migrating at the same time as the other jötunnkind. I myself was reborn by your previous self after personally slaying a hundred Valkyries at Ragnarök."

"You were at Ragnarök?" Tom asked incredulously.

"Yes. We were able to force the Æsir back across Asbrú, the rainbow bridge, which, with Loki's assistance we were able to destroy and thus block the Æsir's access to Earth, and all of Midgard for that matter, once and for all. Unfortunately, however, they had to do it from Jötunheimr and that sealed the last of the jötunnkind from Midgard as well. Or so I understand; I was busy dying at that exact time."

"So how long ago was this?" Tom asked.

Delg Narmoloth grimaced. "Millennia, as I said. It's hard to tell time here. It was a few lifetimes before"—the D'Orc suddenly seemed uncomfortable —"the incident."

"The incident?" Tom asked, puzzled.

"Your death," Tizzy suggested helpfully.

Delg Narmoloth looked relieved that Tizzy had said it rather than him. Tom sighed internally; a dark overlord probably would not want minions mentioning his defeat.

Tom nodded. "Understood." He nodded at Delg Narmoloth, who quickly stepped back after having almost stepped in it. So to speak.

The next D'Orc to step forward was extremely burly with pointed tusks and very shiny, pointy teeth. Clearly he brushed, which seemed a bit odd. His pectorals were huge under his armor.

"I am Helga Dourtooth of the Dourtooth Clan of Nysegard," the D'Orc said in a slightly higher-pitched voice than the others. *This was a woman!* Tom nodded and smiled grimly. That was a surprise.

Another female D'Orc stepped forward. "I am Ayega DeathTusk. I am daughter of Fenwith DeathTusk of the DeathTusk Horde of Romdan." She bowed and then stepped back. Given that she gave her father's name, was she born here? Tom wondered.

A third female warrior stepped forward, this one much more obviously female than Helga. "I am Frigda Normaghast, daughter of Blargh Normaghast of the Houofa Horde of Ithgar."

As she stepped back a rather wiry, but still very muscular D'Orc stepped forward and bowed. "Zog Darthelm, son of Neth Darthelm of the Elm Clan of Gormegaest, Antilles star cluster."

"Antilles star cluster?" Tom asked curiously.

"My Lord, as my father related to me, the Plane of Orcnaes is called Gormegaest, and on that plane the Elm Clan roamed between the stars and planets of the Antilles star cluster in great metal ships," the commander told him.

"Ah," Tom said. Had 40K got it right? He had always preferred the original, but if it turned out to be based on a real place—wait, he was already stuck in one crazy fantasy world. No need to think about gaming in another. He shook his head. "Such metal ships might prove interesting."

Zog nodded and stepped back.

The next commander stepped forward stiffly and bowed. "Fester Dourtooth, son of Helga Dourtooth of the Dourtooth Clan of Nysegard."

"Helga"—Tom gestured to the burly female—"is your mother?"

"Yes, My Lord."

"And you have risen to commander, as well. Your prowess honors her," Tom said. He really had no idea what to say to show appreciation, but he figured that anything you might say to praise a Klingon should work for D'Orcs.

Fester made a very slight grin—hard to detect, but noticeable. Helga seemed pleased as well as she stared at her son. *Mother and son fighting side by side in battle.* Tom mentally shook his head. He had not even been here an hour and already he was starting to think like a D'Orc—or a Klingon, at least.

Another female D'Orc stepped forward. She was, as they all were, quite muscular, but this one was noticeably a bit smaller, perhaps younger, than the last few commanders. "My Lord, am Velma Snargspitter, daughter of Heathgol Snargspitter, son of Hera Snargspitter of the Snargspitter Clan of Verasai."

Tom was right; she was from a newer generation. He nodded in solemn greeting at the younger D'Orc.

"I am Morok Deathstealer, son of Arshog, son of Arog, son of Pharog and Vesog, daughter of Ysog, daughter of Ithog Deathstealer of the Deathstealer Clan of Attanoobe Five on the Plane of Orcneas, Visteroth," said the next D'Orc, who was very unusual. He was very tall, quite thin and pale as a ghost, but he did have the other orc-like attributes.

Tom blinked. That was a very different genealogy than the others; was it incestuous? No time for that. He needed to get through this, but he was curious. "From the name of the plane and the planet name, can I take it that the Deathstealer Clan are space travelers?"

"Yes, My Lord. We plied our star system as traders and explorers," Morok said.

"Fascinating," Tom said. Morok stepped back and a very craggy-looking D'Orc stepped forward. He was very bulky, but still seemed rather young.

"M'Lord. I be Ferrus RockSmasher, son of Aeris RockSmasher, daughter of Plumbum RockSmasher. "We are from the RockSmasher Clan of Nysegard."

Another male commander of about the same age as Ferrus stepped forward. "M'Lord, I am Hewith Bilespitter, son of Hegron, son of Haeron Bilespitter of the Bilespitter Clan of Verasai."

The next commander was a bit smaller and younger yet. She seemed a bit more hesitant. "My Lord, I am Ruthus Tarpit, daughter of Rufus Tarpit, son of Teeg Tarpit, daughter of Reeg Tarpit of the Labraen Horde of Romdan." Tom nodded at her. Yes, same generation as Zelda.

The last of the male commanders stepped forward; he appeared to be fourth generation, if Tom was getting the hang of this. "I am Kraukus Skullspitter, son of Kraig, son of Kaela, daughter of Raig of the Skullspitter Clan of Verasai."

The last three commanders were women and of what Tom took to be the fourth generation. The first of the final three stepped forward. "I am Flora Lifender, daughter of Lucreza, daughter of Amethyst, daughter of Fauna Lifender of the Lifender Matrimony of Targella."

The next one stepped up holding a rather odd-looking battle axe. It was very long along the hilt and narrow compared to what the others typically had. "I am Serah Sidesplitter." She stressed the L in Sidesplitter, apparently to differentiate it from the various "spitter" clans. "My father was Trog Sidesplitter, whose father was Seroh Sidesplitter, whose father was Dagog Sidesplitter of the Splitter Horde of Excelsion." She nodded and stepped back as the last of the commanders came forward.

"I am Vespa Crooked Stick, daughter of Selma Crooked Stick, daughter of Hazel, daughter of Vera of the Crooked Stick Tribe of Astlan."

Tom nodded at her with a tight grin, as he had tried to do for all the others. "Well met. I shall rely on your strength and courage even as Zelda does. I am confident I shall be well served," Tom said, once again making it all up as he went along. He had really never planned on being a general or a leader, and certainly not a dark overlord of a demon army. His nerves were really starting to fray. He just wanted to curl up into a fetal ball and make the world go away. Intellectually he knew he should be enjoying this—it was straight out of every teenager's power trip fantasy—but all he could think of was how this was all going to blow up horribly once the D'Orcs figured out he was faking it.

~

Hilda made her way back towards the inn. She had sent Danyel ahead about an hour ago to prepare her a bubble bath and collect some strawberries, chocolate and sparkling wine from the inn's tavern before the kitchen closed. It had been a rather lengthy and trying day. What with the ball viewing in Tierhallon, brunch with Trisfelt and strategizing, a round with her various patients in the palace and then a long dinner with Trisfelt, Gandros, Damien, Lenamare and Jehenna, she was feeling a tad worn. Dinner with the two schoolmasters was not a trivial task; however, the presence of the head of the Council and the Chief Inquisitor had them on slightly better behavior.

She was pleased to be making connections with other members of the Council. Such inroads were critical for maintaining her vantage point and access to critical information. Hilda smiled to herself. If she really were an animage healer, these would be invaluable business connections. She grinned more widely, suddenly realizing that technically, they could be considered invaluable business connections for a spy—her current profession.

Amusement or not, it was taxing and she just wanted to get home and relax as soon as possible. Which was why, when she spotted an upturned cart and all sorts of commotion on the city street between her and the inn, she chose to take a series of side streets, more like alleys. She had explored them briefly in the daytime; rather dank and dark even in broad daylight. Certainly not a great route for a woman alone in the middle of the night. However, being previously deceased, she really did not have much to fear. It was rather hard to kill someone who had been dead for centuries and who could heal any wounds within moments. She chuckled to herself at that.

Naturally, because she had bothered to entertain such thoughts, it was not at all unexpected when a dark shadow rose in front of her within no more than a minute. She supposed it was almost de rigueur. By the sounds, another three people had also materialized behind her. Not in the way she could materialize when coming down from Tierhallon; these individuals had simply stepped out of the deep shadows of a large doorway on her left and another doorway on her right. The man in front of her had simply stepped out from behind a large canister of refuse.

Fortunately, she could see perfectly well in the dark and so realized instantly that it was beggars that were accosting her; although not, she suspected, in the manner typical of beggars. Hilda stopped before the man in front of her, noting a fifth man coming up behind him with one eye covered in a patch, pockmarked skin, poorly dressed and limping. The beggar in front of her had a hook for one hand and a crutch under his arm on the opposing side. One of the men behind her had a peg leg, by the sound it made on the stone cobbles. Another man behind her had some sort of condition that caused his breathing to sound mucus-filled and quite unpleasant. The third she could not tell.

Sternly yet politely, she asked the man in front of her, "Can I help you gentlemen?"

"You can stop screwing with people's livelihoods, bitch," the man growled at her.

Hilda blinked in the dark. "My, that seems to be poor manners for someone whom I suspect is about to make a request of me," she said, shaking her head even as she began drawing in mana from both her illuminaries and from upstream in Tierhallon. She had a good idea where this was heading, so she needed to be prepared. "However, I am but a simple healer, so I have no idea what you are talking about. Now if you'd please excuse me, I'm tired and would like to get home."

"You know damn well what we are talking about!" the main beggar snarled.

"You destroyed Rathbart's career!" The man—no, woman—behind Hilda who was not rasping, nor peg-legged, said.

"I'm not sure about this Master Rathbart of whom you speak," Hilda said pleasantly, stalling for time and preparing herself for what was about to come.

"One of our guildmates. You healed him! You took away his livelihood. No one is going to give money to a healthy, able-bodied beggar!" the peg-legged man behind her stated.

"So the beggar meister wanted us to talk to you," the lead beggar stated.

"Hmm, I think I know this Master Rathbart of whom you speak. However, he came to me begging for aid, so I gave it to him in the manner I'm best suited to give. I am a professional healer, so I gave him his health," Hilda said innocently. "Typically, I charge a fair amount for the services I provided him for free."

"You ain't stupid, lady; we can tell that by your speech. You know'd damn well you'd be hosing his ability to beg!" the main beggar told her angrily.

"I'm deeply sorry that you feel that my well-meaning help was inappropriate, but it is my job," Hilda said as her hands inside her wide-sleeved robes began the necessary semantic gestures to raise defensive wards about herself. As the beggar continued, she subvocalized the verbal parts of the warding ritual. Not strictly necessary, but it would strengthen the wards.

"The beggar meister has instructed us to bring you to Rathbert so you can undo your damage," the main beggar told her.

Hilda shook her head. "I'm sorry; I'm under oath to do no harm," she lied to them. All followers of Tiernon were allowed to do harm if it served the purpose of justice. Saints in particular were quite capable of doing vast amounts of damage, if necessary. However, she was pretending to be a healer, and most healers had strong vows against using their knowledge and power to harm others.

"The beggar meister thought that might be the case, so we've been instructed to teach you a lesson," the principal beggar said menacingly.

Hilda sighed, rather theatrically, she felt. "And by *lesson*, do you mean grievous bodily harm?" she asked.

The main beggar smiled over Hilda's shoulder to the woman behind her. "See, I told you she was smart."

Hilda shook her head sadly. "And how do you propose to grievously harm someone who can easily heal themselves?"

Both men in front of her grinned evilly. "We're betting you can't heal without hands," the second one said, brandishing a large dagger.

It was Hilda's turn to grin and chuckle evilly. "I personally would not place a bet on that." Her face turned very serious suddenly. "Since you have been honest with me about your intentions towards me, let me now be honest about my intentions towards you."

The peg-legged beggar behind her snorted, and the raspy guy gurgled a laugh. The men in front of her smiled condescendingly. "Sure, you do that. It won't matter much." The first one chuckled.

Hilda shrugged. "Nonetheless, I feel I must give you this opportunity to flee, for I intend to make a very serious lesson of you five for the rest of the guild. Leave this alley now and you will avoid your fate."

The beggars all chuckled.

"She thinks she can kill all five of us?" The woman laughed and the others quickly joined in.

Hilda let them cackle a moment as she locked her defensive wards into place. "Kill you? Oh my dears, I think you misunderstand!" She shook her head as if in disbelief. "Remember, I have a code against doing harm to others."

"So then your lesson's going to be pretty lame, isn't it?" the second man in front of her said.

"Not at all, I'm just going to heal all of you, as I did for Rathbart." Hilda said, and then her eyes and voice hardened. "After that you will go back to the beggar meister and tell him that if he doesn't back off and leave me and mine alone, I will hunt down every single beggar in this city, heal them and then place a Geis upon all of the beggars in this city, to never willingly allow themselves to be harmed or maimed. I will then place a second Geis upon them that forces them to compulsively bathe and clean themselves daily, and a third Geis that will make them feel anxious and restless if they aren't doing back-breaking manual labor every day while Fierd is up." Hilda grinned. "Is that clear?"

The beggars had stopped laughing. "I think we may need to do more than hurt you," the main beggar said.

Hilda shrugged. "You have been warned."

The man in front of her whipped his crutch towards her legs, trying to knock them out from under her as he simultaneously lunged at her with his hook. Hilda adroitly leaped over the cane, easily seeing it coming in the dark and aided by her defensive wards, which redirected the crutches away from her. She grabbed the beggar's forearm where the hook's cup was strapped on. Hilda mouthed a quick prayer and healing mana surged into the man's arm. The beggar leaped back as if struck by lightning, which in some ways he had been.

"Fraggin rat's tails!" The man began screaming and cursing and shaking his hook. He dropped his crutch and began trying to get the hook's cup off his forearm. "Midas's nuts, it itches! It stings like a thousand scorpions!"

The gurgling, raspy man, formerly behind Hilda but now to her right, lunged towards her with a knife. Hilda batted the man's knife arm away and palm-punched him in the chest, chanting loudly in Etonian at the same time, sending another shockwave of healing power into him. The man collapsed to his knees and began violently hacking his lungs out. All the pus, mucus and disease in his lungs were being violently expelled by his coughing and retching.

The peg-legged man glanced at his compatriot and came lunging at Hilda with a sickle. Hilda shook her head, dove under his poorly wielded sickle and grabbed his peg, pulling it and his leg up and to the side while infusing the leg with healing power. The man tumbled to the ground as she let go and started thrashing and screaming in pain, trying to get the peg unstrapped from his rapidly healing leg.

"Sorry about the pain, guys," Hilda shouted. "This is healing combat, which is basically the opposite of combat healing." She moved towards the woman who had unfurled a whip and had only been waiting for the peg-legged man to get out of her way so she could use it on Hilda.

This woman had a terrible case of—*leprosy!* What the...? Hilda shook her head. How in Tiernon's worst nightmare were they allowing a leper to run around the city? It was a figurative miracle that there had not been a huge outbreak. But clearly it was leprosy; she could see the craggy skin nodules, the missing fingers from the woman's left hand. She was blind in one eye, her right foot twisted and club-like. This one was going to need a huge rush of antibiotic mana to eliminate the bacteria and then some widespread regeneration.

This was going to hurt the beggar woman like crazy! Hilda dove and tackled the woman before she could bring her whip around. Hilda wrapped herself like a blanket around the leprous woman, essentially irradiating her whole being in healing mana while chanting multiple rituals of healing.

The woman screamed like bloody murder. "Sorry!" Hilda said, standing up to face the man with the big dagger and one eye. He was picking up his dagger from the ground; Hilda suspected he had thrown it at her and it had been deflected by her wards.

"Healing Combat," Hilda told the man as they began to circle each other, "is like Combat Healing in that it has to be done in the middle of battle, but with Combat Healing I am rapidly healing one of my own, so while I have to work very fast and use a lot of excess mana, I can also suppress the patient's nerve endings to numb the pain of healing too quickly.

"In the case of Healing Combat, I am in combat and don't have the necessary links to my patient, so all I can do is shove out an excessive amount of healing mana very quickly. This leads to extremely abrupt healing and regeneration, which typically itches, tingles and overwhelms the nerves. It also taxes the body's systems to a huge level, weakening them as their natural regenerative systems are forced into a very unnatural overdrive," Hilda explained as she warily faced down the man with the dagger. She was not completely sure why she felt the need to explain why their healing hurt so much. Perhaps it was guilt about inflicting pain.

"In any event, you are going to be healed," Hilda told the one-eyed man with the dagger. "You don't have to like it, but it's going to happen. We can do this the easy way or the painful way. Your choice."

"Screw you, bitch!" The man lunged at her with his giant dagger, clearly mistaking a large target for an easy target. Hilda shook her head and stepped to her right, twisting sideways as he lunged forward and then away from where she'd stepped, deflected by her protection ritual. As he skittered by, trying to reorient after what must have seemed like a mystifying miss, Hilda brought her left palm around and slapped him hard on the eye patch, at the same time channeling a rapid ocular regeneration ritual into his head. He was about to have one nasty migraine.

The beggar dropped his dagger and grabbed his head and started screaming. Hilda quickly started chanting and extended a silence spell over the section of the alley they were in. There had already been a lot of screaming; with luck, the city guards in Freehold were as lax as they were in most cities.

The man started to stagger away; Hilda could not allow that. She quickly ran after him and grasped him by the waist while chanting a ritual to rapidly clear and clean his skin. Of course, that meant getting rid of some nasty bacterial infections and a few viruses. This was really going to hurt.

The beggar dropped to his knees, frantically scratching at his itching skin. This was not going to help skin regeneration. Hilda quickly performed a mild paralysis ritual to slow him down. It would not completely paralyze him, but he would not be able to scratch at himself effectively and disturb the healing.

Thinking better of her previous actions, she did the same for the other beggars, who were also writhing, the exception being mister hacking lung, who needed to continue to clear out his lungs. After they were stabilized, she cast a Ritual of Unnoticement on their area to keep prying eyes from seeing too much. It was time to roll up her sleeves and get to work properly healing her new patients.

When she was done, they would all have fresh, youthful complexions, perfect health, no deformities and no disease. Now it would be too cruel to do the Geis of manual labor, but she was not above a Geis of not allowing themselves to be willingly harmed. She had done no such thing to Rathbart, but he had not tried to harm her. These thugs needed more punishment. Thus, she would Geis them to stay clean and well-presented and to avoid allowing themselves to be willingly maimed or hurt. They would still be able to get hurt defending themselves or someone else; they just wouldn't be able to sit still and allow themselves or someone else to wound or maim them for the sake of employment as a beggar.

It would be exhausting—she would really need that bubble bath at home, and then maybe even a short nap before her planned morning rooftop adventure—but it was fun. It was a great opportunity to do Tiernon's work and unofficially take a bit of revenge on those who had sought to harm her. She felt she was allowed some small sin of satisfaction in this. She grinned and got down to the work at hand.

~

DOF +4/DOF +5
Late Period 6/Early Period 1 16-02-440

Tom closed the giant double doors behind them and waited to hear the two D'Orcs who had escorted them to the Master's Suite, as they had called it, leave. Unfortunately, from the sound of their giant axes thumping to the right and left of the door, he assumed they had taken up guard.

He looked around the giant entryway to the suite. It was huge and quite opulent, if a bit heavy on the gold and silver for his taste. He spotted the double doors leading to the bedroom and gestured everyone to follow him through. He then shut the door behind them.

The place was rather dusty. Zelda had apologized profusely, but they had not known he was coming. He had assured her it would be fine. He just needed somewhere to rest and contemplate, even as he was sure they did. That *contemplate* line did not seem to sit well with her though.

"Okay, how the hell did that just happen?" Tom asked raising his hands above his head as he paced nervously in the room. "This has got to be the most insane thing yet! I am in so far over my head!"

"Demon, your ruses are getting tiresome. Why do you insist on this charade? Clearly this was all part of your plan to regain your powers!" Talarius stated.

Tom spun and stared at the knight. "Are you serious? You have been with me this entire time, heard everything I have said, seen everything I have done, and participated in the process. You chose many of the passages we followed!"

"You are cunning, I give you that," Talarius said.

"Seriously? Seriously! You think I got enslaved by Lenamare, trapped in Freehold and was then forced out only to have you shoot down Rupert and need to come rescue him and then end up battling you?" Tom waved his hand.

"Next, I would have had to know that you would cheat! You recall my shock at your methods? So I *knew* that the virtuous Knight Rampant of Tiernon would be outside the city ready to trap Rupert as bait for me, we would end up dueling and you would cheat to almost defeat me, and then I would have to pull a rabbit out of a hat! I had to do something no one even conceived of as possible—intercept a god's mana stream and possess a bunch of priests—then defeat you and reverse the dagger and store up a ton of extra god mana for later use?"

Tom was pacing in circles around the knight, clearly frustrated. He tossed his mace on the very large bed and watched a cloud of dust rise up and then settle before resuming his pacing. "I then wait for you to rest up and get healed, and somehow get Boggy to take us all to a spa for massages and heated lava, as well as some lich-slaying on the side for some of us. Then I somehow get us to ALL agree to a long hike through the Abyss to the Crystal Caverns, without saying much of anything. I then convince *you* to stock up on gems and arrange it so we all start on an underground trip to get more gold."

If Tom had hair, he would have been pulling it out. "I then manage to get us lost and have us all nearly eaten by hydra hounds as we randomly run around corridors. I knew that by random chance we would wander into a lair of D'Orcs who would think we were invaders and chase us along the passageway *you* chose that led to a dead end."

Tom pointed a claw at the knight. "As I recall, it was you and your armor that allowed us to see the runes. Runes put there by Etonians. Runes that no demon should have been able to open. So I just reused some tricks I'd learned fighting you, along with mana I stole from your god, to activate the runes and open a magical doorway that let us escape.

"When we then found the vault, we *all* agreed to see what was inside, even though we were under time pressure." Tom started pulling on his horns. "We got into a room no one in the Abyss could have gotten into, using mana that no demon should have been able to steal, but that I had been able to, thanks to your cheating! I then use it to free a rod or staff thing, which when I charge it up, starts a volcano. We then march out into an auditorium, through a portcullis that again, no one in the Abyss can open. Where all the D'Orcs are kneeling with the belief that the guy who stole the rod and relit the volcano is their messiah returned!"

Tom let out a loud breath and collapsed into a very nice renaissance-era French chair of his size. "And you seriously think I planned all this?" He stared at the knight.

Talarius was silent for some time; they were all silent. The others were probably surprised by Tom's outburst, but also reflecting on the improbabilities of the current insanity. Finally, Talarius sighed.

"Well… when you put it like that, it does seem to be outside the range of what a greater demon could do. It's a bit too devious for a fourth-order, I admit."

"Thank you!" Tom raised his arms in the air as a sign of victory.

"However, clearly the D'Orcs' god must be a demon prince, and certainly such a series of events is not outside the range of the devious machinations of a demon prince. And since you've now revealed yourself to be their long-lost master, you have therefore admitted to being a demon prince!" Talarius said with a note of triumph in his own voice.

Tizzy started laughing uproariously. Tom let out a soft wail of despair. Boggy also started laughing and Antefalken was shaking his head with a broad grin on his face.

"Have you ever thought of going into politics, Talarius?" Tom asked wearily.

The knight seemed puzzled. "No, why?"

"Because you would make an excellent politician. You can twist any absurd set of facts around until they fit your idea of how the universe should be, without so much as batting an eyelash," Tom said. "Look, you know that Rupert and I were in the city; you saw us come out over the wall. You scanned the city; did you see any demon princes in your mirror?"

Talarius was quiet for a moment. "No, but you could have been in disguise, hiding your power."

Tom looked at him. "So you are saying that your mirror, powered by your god, was not infallible? That it could or can make mistakes?"

Talarius was silent and finally cursed. "You demon princes are truly masters of confusion."

"For the last time, I am not a demon prince. I am a greater demon who really hasn't been around that long compared to say, Tizzy, Antefalken or Boggy." If Rupert were not in the room, he would have gladly told Talarius the truth—not that he would have believed it.

"So, the rest of you? What do we do?" Tom asked.

Boggy was the first to pipe up. "Well, we need to work with Zelda's lot to arrange the party. Out here in the middle of nowhere, that could get challenging. However, Tizzy and I should be able to figure something out." Tizzy nodded in agreement. "Bard? You know how to throw a good party; you need to be on the committee as well." Boggy started rubbing his chin in thought. "Got any idea how to get hold of some Denubian traders?"

"Out here?" Antefalken slowly shook his head, thinking. "It's going to be rough."

Tom was staring at the three of them in shock. "Are you three serious?"

Boggy looked at him in surprise. "Of course. This is the hinterlands; you expect them to have good food and drink clear the way out here? No, they are going to need professional assistance."

"You do know that planning the feast was just a way to buy time before they all try and swear eternal allegiance to me?"

Boggy looked puzzled. "Buy time? Why would you want to buy time? I mean the celebration, and having some prep time for such a big event makes sense. But otherwise, why try and put it off?"

"Because that makes me their leader? I end up taking over a giant demonic horde?" Tom asked rhetorically.

"And the problem with that is...?" Estrebrius asked.

"Yeah, I agree. Sounds like a great gig," Reggie added. "Why would you pass such a sweet gig up?" Reggie's hands started to drift towards his crotch. "Think of all the big D'Orc booty you could get! Dark lords always get the hottest groupies!"

Tom twisted his head back and forth, trying to stare incredulously at all of them. He finally turned back to Talarius. "You do understand what I'm saying? I can't go through with this, right?"

Talarius shrugged. "Why do you ask me? This was your plan, right? You led us here, why would you back out now? Are you still trying to convince me that you did not intend this? Obviously, as a spokesman for the Forces of Good, I cannot recommend you form a new evil horde, or for that matter, re-form an evil horde."

Tom put his head in his claws. "I am surrounded by crazy people!" He lifted his head and looked around at everyone. "You do all realize that I am not a demon prince, Talarius's paranoia aside. If I pretend to be their reborn dark lord, and take their allegiance, then everyone in the Abyss and beyond is going to think I'm a demon prince and will therefore come after me and my horde!"

They were silent for a moment. "Well, technically they already are," Rupert said. Tom looked at him askance.

"The boy's right," Antefalken said. "We are hiding down here in the Abyss, worrying about a Heavenly Host descending on Freehold in pursuit of us out of vengeance for your actions. In addition, we were just talking about hiding in the Crystal Caverns because Lilith is on the lookout for us. She really wants to know your secret so she can do it herself. You can bet all the other demon princes will be thinking the same thing."

"Really not seeing a downside, my lad," Boggy said, shaking his head. "You were already in over your head; a horde of D'Orcs might be able to keep you afloat. It will certainly give people pause before they attack you."

"Not to mention there's a crapload of money downstairs in the caverns," Rupert said.

Tom looked around, feeling completely beaten down by this crazed reality. "I need some rest; I am going to lie down. There are other rooms in the suite; if you want to rest and heal from the hounds, that would probably be a good idea." He looked at Boggy. "If you want to go help plan the party, go ahead. Just don't make any major commitments for me beyond the party."

Antefalken nodded. "Good point. As Tom's closest advisors, people will come to us trying to get an 'in' with Tom. Be very careful."

"Hmm, there were quite a few hot warrior babes out there in the crowd. Might go see if any of them want to party now, so to speak," Reggie said, making a lascivious face. Tom just shook his head.

"I'm going to explore the suite and then take a nap. I'm beat, and still have dog bites I need to heal," Rupert said.

"I'll go with you guys," Estrebrius said to Boggy.

Talarius simply marched out of the room, presumably to find a place to rest.

Tom stood and went over to the giant bed, grabbed his mace and lay down on his side, curling up as tightly as he could. He had used a lot of mana on the various runes and charging the mace, but it was not just that; it was this whole sudden crush of responsibility coming down on him.

He had somehow blundered into agreeing to take on responsibility for a few thousand down-on-their-luck D'Orcs looking for a savior. He was teenager, for God's sake. Suddenly becoming Rupert's fake dad had seemed like too much responsibility; now he was going to take on responsibility for a giant horde of demonic orc warriors out for vengeance? *Agghh.* He just wanted the world to go away for a while!

Chapter 98

DOF +5
Period 1 16-02-440

Bess surveyed the gardens as Usiris climbed the steps to the villa's terrace. She smiled and gestured to the pitcher of fruit juice and glasses on the table beside her.

"Greetings. It's been some time," Usiris said, sitting down in the other chair.

"Too long, my dearest." Bess smiled back at him as he poured himself some juice.

"May we live in interesting times." Usiris raised his glass in their traditional toast, to which Bess joined with her glass.

"Indeed, we are." Bess laughed lightly. "I can feel the electric tension in the air. The Wheel of Life has the entirety of New Nyjyr practically jumping out of its skin."

Usiris gave her a quick grin. "Well, we have a lot of souls needing bodies to incarnate into, so every fertile adult needs to get busy! We shall have a bumper crop of babies in a few months!"

"Unless you are planning on a lot of multiple births, I'm not sure we have enough people," Bess replied, looking worriedly across the valley below.

Usiris smiled again, more broadly. "True. However, our faithful agent Merit-Ptah in Natoor"—he pointed vaguely upward in the direction of the continent of Natoor on the giant planet that provided the light over the valley this evening—"has been hard at work."

"Really? Do tell," Bess said.

"She has summoned, or rather created, a brand-new incubus," Usiris said.

"An incubus? If she wanted to get laid, she should have just come here." Bess shook her head and gestured at the recently extra-fertile valley around them.

"No." Usiris laughed. "Although I am sure she is enjoying this young incubus's services. No, we shall load the incubus with a serum I am deriving from the Wheel of Life's energies."

"You are planning on using an incubus to seed followers in Natoor?" Bess asked curiously. "How will we shepherd them in the faith? We have not been able to keep a priest alive down there for a very long time. And we don't have that many followers left there for secretly home schooling that many."

"I have some ideas that I'm working on," Usiris said.

"Go on..." Bess purred.

"The key is that we need someone to run interference with the Etonians to keep our priests alive while we get them established in communities. Our problem has been that just having an experienced priest, pretending to be of any profession, suddenly move into these communities gets suspicious. Etonian church officials notice and arrest our priests," Usiris said, pausing to take a drink. "So we need to keep the Etonian hierarchy occupied and allow our priests to slip in more gradually during a period of confusion."

"I assume you have a plan for distracting them?" Bess asked.

Usiris chuckled. "I am counting on a cloud to obscure the Etonians' view of what's happening."

"A cloud?" Bess was completely puzzled.

"From the Grove." Usiris grinned wickedly.

"Ahh," Bess said. "But they turned down our priests' request for help last time."

"This time, we are not asking . Their own nosiness, this insanity in Freehold with the Rod being spanked by that demon, sprinkled with some visions I have been seeding to various parties for the last half a year or so, shall position them where we need them to be."

Bess smiled, feeling good for the first time since the debacle at Freehold. The idea of using that to their advantage brought her a warm, satisfied feeling. She leaned back in her chair, gazing up to the beautiful planet of Astlan dominating the sky above her. New Nyjyr, now on Uropia, had a much better view than those stuffy old outer planes they had had to maintain at such cost. Yes, it was much smaller, and thus a bit crowded, but as they grew, they could expand to Anuropia easily enough. With control of the two moons, their oversight of Astlan would be solidified. Add in the power of the book, and the Etonian pestilence could be eliminated from at least one plane of the multiverse. From this secure base, they would eventually take back other worlds and return themselves to their rightful place in the scheme of things.

~

DOF +5
Dawn 16-02-440

Tom woke suddenly, realizing he had dozed off. Boggy and the others were in the main room, talking rather animatedly; perhaps that was what had woken him. In any event, he was feeling better. That was the one indispensable thing about sleep; it gave one a break from consciousness. It made the world go away for a while and when you woke up, things often seemed better.

At least they did for a few minutes, until he heard the name *Vaselle*. He closed his eyes again. Today was supposed to be the day the wizard turned himself over to Tom. He had somehow forgotten about that in all the insanity of yesterday. Why was he doing this again? Why couldn't he have just said no? It would be nice to blame Vaselle; the wizard seemed so needy, so desperate, as if he needed love and acceptance. Tom suspected that the wizard had what his stepdad called a codependent personality. It probably was not a good idea to be mixed up in a relationship with such a person.

Except that he could hear the guys talking; they were planning a shopping list of items for Vaselle to buy for the party. Seriously? The wizard was in a city under siege! Where was he going to find supplies for a party for two thousand plus D'Orcs!

Enough! Tom decided. He could not worry about everything; he needed to delegate. Maybe a warlock was not such a bad idea; Vaselle could be sort of like a personal delegate, or a personal assistant. He did not know. At the moment, he did not want to think about it.

Tom stood up and grabbed the mace by the ball. It poked him. That was weird; he looked at the amorphous metal ball head of the mace. Odd. It was not quite so amorphous anymore. It was still rather putty shaped, but it now had two sharp little points about twenty degrees down from the top of the sphere and about halfway from the center to the front on two sides. They were curvy points coming out from the side of the sphere and then pointing up. On each side of the sphere with a point, another point more towards the center and a bit down was also forming.

The sphere was also not that spherical anymore. If he rotated the sphere so that the big points were on opposite sides, the space between them had gotten bumpy and had some dimples and almost a little mesa or something. He rotated the sphere to look at it from different directions. It was starting to look like a head. In fact, if he did not know better, he'd think it was a very blurry version of a demon head! Horns, ears, muzzle, brow… was it supposed to be *his* head? It was too hard to tell yet, but it was changing.

Given that he was rather intimately connected with the rod, it would not be completely unreasonable that the top would shape itself to look like him. Just a bit weird. A little narcissistic perhaps, but not completely out of the realm of possibility. Tom shook his head and walked over to the doors to the parlor. Opening the doors, he found Boggy, Antefalken, Tizzy and Estrebrius sitting around a table scratching away at various papers with pencils or something.

The sitting room was opulently furnished, if dusty. There were a few formal chairs and a sofa for his size, and another set that was perhaps small D'Orc or large humanoid size. The three demons were sitting on high stools around a table suitable for Tom's height. It was near a large set of French doors with actual glass panes.

The French doors opened onto a balcony overlooking the volcano platform. If he were to guess, it was just inside the upside-down pentagram. The light from outside was rather unusual for the Abyss. Tom moved to the doors to look out and up at the sky.

Black and purple storm clouds were starting to swirl around the top of the volcano. That was very strange; he had never seen clouds in the Abyss before. Actually, how would you even get clouds in the Abyss? It was too hot and dry. There was no real moisture.

"You guys notice the clouds?" Tom asked.

"Yep," Boggy said, still scribbling away.

Antefalken looked up briefly. "Tizzy says they were extremely common back in the day."

"Really?" Tom asked the octopod.

Tizzy nodded. "Sure. Only place in the Abyss I've ever seen it rain."

"It rains here?" Antefalken looked up in surprise. He finally stopped scribbling.

"Yeah, and when it does it's like a giant steam sauna. Water sizzling on lava. Gets downright chilly here, in fact. Sometimes drops to a third of the boiling point of water."

"You mean like 33 Celsius?" Tom asked incredulously.

"Not often, but on occasion as I recall," Tizzy agreed.

"So humans could actually survive here," Tom said.

"Not sure about the acidity of the rain, but presumably," Tizzy said.

"Actually, that would be a very comfortable temperature for orcs," Antefalken mused.

"Do you know, that would be helpful with the refreshments," Boggy suddenly added, looking up from his paper. "We're not likely to be able to get our hands on any Denubian Choco-Coffee™, nor any blood wine, so we'll probably need to whip up some x-glargh, which boils somewhere near the same point as water. It's best served cold, around a quarter of the boiling point of water."

"X-glargh?" Tom asked.

"It's an extra-potent form of glargh, a favored intoxicant of orcs according to Hezbarg, the quartermaster." He gestured to Tizzy. "X-glargh has some extra ingredients that increase the potency so that it affects demons." Boggy frowned. "It's nowhere near as potent as blood wine or Denubian Choco-Coffee™, though, so we are going to need a lot of it."

"Anyone know what the X is?" Antefalken asked the room. "I know how to make glargh, but I'm not sure about the X part. We are going to need to let it sit and ferment for a while."

"I do," Tizzy said. "It is mainly nightshade and arsenic. The amount is sort of to taste. Oh, and a good bit of nitro-glycerin—that's what gives it a kick—plus a few other slightly more esoteric things, like a splash or two of mercury."

"The fermentation is going to be a problem," Antefalken said.

"Not if you can find a thaumaturgist to speed it up," Estrebrius said.

"I don't suppose Vaselle is a thaumaturge?" Boggy asked the smaller demon.

"No, don't think so. But he could probably hire one for a gem or two," Estrebrius said.

"Jenn's a thaumaturge," Rupert said, entering the room from a side chamber.

"Something tells me she might not want to play cocktail waitress at a D'Orc party," Tizzy said.

"Okay, here's my count, assuming x-glargh," Boggy said. "If we assume two quarts per demon times 2,000 demons, that's 4,000 quarts or 1,000 gallons or about seventeen barrels. I think we should really assume at least twenty barrels in case the count is off. So I think a nice two dozen barrels should be perfect."

"I don't know that we can make that many barrels," Antefalken said worriedly. "If I could get a hold of some of my Denubian contacts, that would help. No one could possibly drink two quarts of Denubian Choco-Coffee™. A quart and you'd be well beyond passed out."

"Plus, the Denubians are equipped for mass production and distribution of the stuff. You can get it by the barrel, and you do not have to keep it cold. Just heat it up when needed," Boggy said.

"Unfortunately, Hezbarg has said that it's not safe for D'Orcs to go to the Courts, where we could, with enough cash, buy what we needed," Antefalken said. "And I don't know how the rest of us could lug everything we need."

"Speaking of which," Boggy said, turning to look at Tom, "we are going to need you to pop open some gateways for some cattle, goat and pig raids for the food."

"Huh?" Tom asked, puzzled.

"Well, it will not be a problem for a D'Orc hunting party to round up the groceries, so to speak, if you can open a portal to a plane that has the aforementioned grocery items," Boggy said.

"And how am I to do that? I need someone summoning me, or some other summons I can intercept," Tom said.

"Well, your predecessor used to contact orc shamans all the time to do that sort of thing, according to Hezbarg," Boggy said.

"Okay, first, I don't know any orc shamans, I've never even met an orc, and I don't speak orcish," Tom told the demon.

"Shouldn't be a problem, given that we are all speaking Universal," Tizzy said.

"What?"

"What, you never noticed that demons can talk to people who summon them, no matter the person's language?" Tizzy began shaking his head. "And you didn't think that odd? How else would they command us? If they can contact demons, they can communicate with us. Seriously, who would want to learn Denubian the mundane way? You need at least two mouths to speak it natively; Universal takes care of it for us."

"Is that why the D'Orcs don't sound like orcs?" Rupert asked suddenly, as if he had just realized something.

"What do you mean?" Antefalken asked.

"Well everyone knows that orcs always talk funny with really stilted, mangled vocabulary. Very brutish like, but the D'Orcs sound like normal people."

Antefalken laughed. "Orcs only talk like that when speaking foreign tongues. Their jaw structure and tusks make speaking most of the human or alvaren tongues rather tricky. If you talk to them in orcish, they sound very normal."

Boggy nodded. "So if you were to speak to an orc in Universal, he or she would hear orcish and reply in orcish, but you would hear Universal. They would sound just as normal as the D'Orcs do here."

"Cool!" Rupert said.

Antefalken shook his head as if in dismay. "Elitist cultures often mock foreign tongues and the way foreigners speak the tongue of the elitists. In fact, the word barbarian comes from the *baa-ing* noises that sheep make. The elitists who invented the word joked that the foreigners' home tongue sounded like the bleating of sheep. Hence baa-baa-rian." He grinned. "And of course, when the barbarians tried to speak the tongues of the elitists, they did so poorly, so the elitist generally assumed the speakers were primitive, ignorant and of lower culture."

"But if the elitists tried to learn the tongue of the barbarians, wouldn't they sound equally stupid?" Rupert asked.

"Precisely." Antefalken said. "However, it is the side with the better historians that ends up dictating who the elitists were and who the barbarians were."

Tom closed his eyes. Was it possible, he wondered, to change his mind at this moment and decide this was all a dream? He shook his head. "So anyway, I'll see what I can do about contacting an orc shaman."

"You know, if we do that, they might be able to help us get glargh already in barrels," Antefalken said.

"Then we just add the X and mix it up!" Tizzy clapped his lower hands. "Excellent idea! As soon as Tom purchases his warlock, it can get us the X ingredients in that wizard city of his, no problem."

Tom wandered over to Rupert, who had gone over to the very large fireplace. There was very large spit in it. Had his predecessor cooked his own dinner here? Or his victims? Tom wondered. "Where's Talarius?" he asked Rupert.

Rupert pointed to the third door leading off the room; there were a total of five, including the one to the hall. "He's in there; it's another smaller bedroom."

"How are you doing with this craziness?" Tom asked.

"Great! Isn't it amazing how the prophecy knew that you would come here with me, just like we did?" Rupert asked with a big grin.

"Yeah, except I don't think I'm the reincarnation of some orc god. As I was saying, I have never even met an orc before. Have you?"

Rupert thought for a moment. "No, not met. I saw some in Exador's army though, from the walls."

"I don't know how accurate this prophecy is, or how we could be fulfilling it."

"But the fact that you were prophesied to come, restart the volcano and have an identical-looking son?" Rupert tilted his head while looking up at Tom and smiled. "How do you explain that?"

Tom sighed. "I don't. I don't know anything about prophecies. Or how one could have prophesies or fate when you've got gods and demons princes messing around with stuff." He shook his head. "I'm definitely going to ask about this prophecy. Find out exactly what it is they think I am going to do. I hope I don't have to conquer a world or something." Tom thought back over the discussions with the commanders. He turned towards Tizzy back at the table.

"Tizzy?" Tom called. The demon looked over to Tom.

"Darg-Krallnom and Arg-nargoloth both recognized you, and said you used to hang out here with their old master. Yes?"

Tizzy got a slightly awkward look. "Yes…" he said out of one side of his mouth.

"The same dark master that was the dark god who turned orcs into D'Orcs?"

"Yes," Tizzy said.

"And these guys seem to think I'm the reincarnated version of this dark god?"

"Apparently." Tizzy shrugged.

"Did this dark god have a name by any chance?" Tom asked as Antefalken started paying attention to the conversation as well.

"Yes," Tizzy said.

"And that was…?"

Tizzy grimaced. "Uhm, Orcus?"

Boggy and Estrebrius went silent at that. All eyes were suddenly on Tizzy.

"Orcus? Like the demon prince Antefalken was telling us about? The one who was killed by Sentir Fallon in Etterdam?" Tom looked down at his mace, if this Orcus was the same as the fantasy Orcus from his world. "And they think I am him reborn because…?"

Tizzy grimaced and shrugged. "Because you reclaimed that." He pointed to the Rod of Tommus.

"And that means my Rod of Tommus is really…"

"The Wand of Orcus?" Tizzy said hesitantly, apparently knowing full well that he had been hiding information.

~

Lilith was relaxing in her spa; a small imp was giving her a pedicure. The imp had just placed her feet in the pleasantly hot blood bath below her spa chair when a knock came at the door. That should not have happened. Lilith carefully raised her hands to remove the Denubian Space Cucumbers from her eyes, being careful not to disturb the moisturizing mask on her face. "Come in," she commanded warningly.

"Sorry, mistress, but this demon was carrying a high-priority token and said it was imperative to see you," the extremely nervous guard explained.

"Come around where I can see the two of you better." Lilith was not going to rotate her chair and disturb the blood bath, nor twist her head and disturb the mask. She recognized the guard. The smaller demon, a fiend, stood nervously beside the guard, wringing its hands.

She stared at the fiend, trying to remember who he was. She saw the token he was clutching nervously in his claws, noted the gulp of fear at her stare. She just could not remember who he was. "Your name?" Lilith demanded.

"Lesteroth Garflog, Your Dark Majesty," the fiend yammered hesitantly.

Lesteroth Garflog. Lilith pondered the name. She had heard it before, a very long time ago. She raised an eyebrow. "Your commander is?"

"Darflow Skragnarth, Dark Majesty."

Lilith shot straight up in her chair, spilling the bubbling pot of coagulating blood at her feet. "Everyone out and away from the doorway, now! Not you, Lesteroth Garflog," she added as the small fiend started to retreat. The imp and the guard quickly fled through the door, shutting it behind them. "If you can still hear me, you will be worse than dead if you don't get out of my voice's range, now!" Lilith called.

She waited a few moments, Liliththen looked back to Lesteroth. "What word do you bring? It had better be important."

Lesteroth gulped and nodded. "My commander bade me tell you 'Mount Doom awakes.' "

Lilith, who had been leaning forward in her chair, now sat straight up. "That is not possible," she said with an icy coldness.

"There have been multiple tremors, lava has been spotted flowing and storm clouds gather." Lesteroth gulped again. "I swear, Dark Majesty; I have seen it with my own eyes, as have all the demons of Doom's Redoubt."

"This cannot be possible! There is only one way to wake that volcano, and HE assured me it could not be done!" Lilith stood, spilling the remaining blood from the foot bath, and began to pace, tracking coagulated blood over the white fur rug. Her face was taut and frowning with concentration. "I must see this. Prepare to return with me," she ordered Lesteroth. "But first call all my attendants and get this mess cleaned up and me ready to travel!"

~

The Wand of Orcus? He had stolen and activated the Wand of Orcus? Tom sat down on the nearby sofa. This was turning into one very bad campaign! First the Monty Haul dungeon of gems, now the Wand of Orcus? Any serious dungeon master putting this in an adventure would be run out of a convention! The only way you could have a Wand of Orcus sitting around was if it was at the culmination of, say, a five- or six-year-long campaign in which everyone played religiously. But even then, the Wand of Orcus? It was such an incredibly overused trope that... that... seriously? The Wand of Orcus?

He had only been a demon for a bit over a month at most! Now he had the Wand of Orcus and a horde of D'Orcs who thought he was Orcus reincarnated! Could this day get any worse?

Estrebrius suddenly leaped off his stool. "Tom! It's Vaselle—he's summoning me. We need to go collect your warlock!"

Tom just stared in shock at the little demon. His mind was starting to numb over again.

~

"Well, there some of them go," Lenamare said to the others. He was standing atop a tower on the city wall in the early morning light, peering through the semi-translucent wards as a good number of Oorstemothian ships rose into the air and began their turning arcs to return home. Some distance away, one could see the light of the runic gateway where a long string of Rod members, two by two, were leaving for Hoggensforth and their ships.

"It would be nice if they were all going," Hortwell said.

"I suppose," Trisfelt replied. "However, I am not that opposed to their presence if it provides a deterrent to another demonic invasion."

"Is the sword going with them?" Lenamare asked.

"That's a good question," Damien replied. "I am sort of doubting it."

"What are you two talking about?" Gandros asked.

"Talarius's sword," Damien answered.

"It's running around interrogating everyone involved with the greater demon." Lenamare shook his head from side to side. "It's a most unsettling magic item."

Gandros blinked. "How is a 'sword' running around asking questions? You do realize that sounds nonsensical, yes?"

Damien nodded and then shrugged. "On the surface, yes. However, the sword transformed itself into one very impressive metal golem that can speak."

"I have never heard of such a thing." Gandros frowned in consternation. "I'm also wondering why no guards have tried to stop it from running around the palace, or even so much as reported it to me."

Lenamare gave a somewhat dismissive expression and replied, "It seems to appear and disappear in random locations. It can either become invisible or it teleports. I wasn't looking with wizard sight when it accosted me."

"An invisible or teleporting, shapeshifting sword? Where would such a thing ever come from?" Gandros asked.

"One would think such a powerful sword would be well known, along with other famous magical weapons," Jehenna said.

"Talarius is from Eton, maybe it was well known over there," Damien said.

"Is it aggressive? Did it seem to be threatening?" Gandros asked.

Damien shrugged and looked at Lenamare, who also shrugged. "Other than its natural appearance, which is rather intimidating, it seemed quite professional to me," Damien said. Lenamare nodded.

Trisfelt shook his head. "I am starting to think Elrose's scryings were only scraping the surface of whatever is going on. It's like every oddity one can imagine is popping out of the woodwork."

"It is starting to seem that way," Hilda said, sipping on her hot chocolate. Jehenna took a sip of hers. It was a bit chilly in the early morning air. Hilda had brought a picnic basket with several insulated bottles of hot chocolate for their morning launch party.

"Back to the original topic, though. I find it is interesting that they have both the Oorstemothians and the Rod have timed their leave takings so closely. It's almost like they are going to the same place, yet by different routes."

Damien raised an eyebrow. "An interesting thought. Both said they were going to pursue the demons elsewhere. I wonder if they have information we do not?"

"I am not sure what that would be, nor am I sure where else they would pursue these demons," Gandros said. "The only lead we have is Trevin's, and I am sure they don't have that."

"I received no indication from them that they had even noticed the flying carpet," Damien said.

"Although the sword did know of the carpet and the individuals on it. It did not, however, mention the woman being a goddess."

"Thus, they probably did not make the connection Trevin did," Gandros said.

Lenamare nodded in agreement. "I think it is but a face-saving statement. What are they going to do? Pursue the demons into the Abyss?" The seven of them all laughed at that ridiculous thought.

Chapter 99

DOF +5
Morning 16-02-440

Vaselle had not slept all night; he was nearly a nervous wreck. He had put the finishing touches on his spell, done some dry runs, packed up his supplies and tried to get some sleep. It did not work; sleep would not come. He was so excited and scared. Really scared. Selling your soul to a demon was clearly a risky, crazy, insane thing —but he could not let himself think of that. Or what hellish tortures might await him. However, if he was faithful and obedient, maybe his master wouldn't torture him too much.

Yes, he had not seriously thought through that torture bit. Gods—at least, Etonian gods—did not torture their priests, at least not in life. They could, of course, be consigned to a horrible fate upon death if they were evil, but that was to be expected.

All through the night, his mind had played through every possible horror he had heard of about demon masters. Which, admittedly, was none. However, he knew the sort of things demons did to victims of misworded commands and such. In theory, though, if Vaselle was a good and valued servant, surely he wouldn't get dismembered or slowly eaten alive. Vaselle was not that good with pain. He really should have considered that before extending his offer to his future dark master.

Vaselle made his way to the clearing. It took a bit longer than usual; some sort of big hubbub with the Oorstemothians and the Rod. Who cared, as long they did not get in his way. Once at the clearing, he had made the preparations for summoning Estrebrius; really not that complicated. He had then set up a small portable table and mirror and begun the preparations. He had a special paste made from his own blood that he used to draw runes on his forehead and chest. Around his neck, wrists and arms were bands with a single linking rune each.

Once done with this part, he summoned Estrebrius. Estrebrius appeared within the flame. "Greetings, master! You still want to go through with this?"

Vaselle was so nervous he could only nod.

Estrebrius could apparently see Vaselle's nervousness because he said, "Don't worry, master. Tom, or I guess Tommus, is a really good guy. You could not ask for a better demon to own your soul. Once you are all signed up, I'll be working for him too... but then, I pretty much already am and it's the best job I've ever had!" Estrebrius paused. "After working for you that is..." He grinned.

Oddly, that incredibly bizarre speech did make Vaselle feel a lot better. Estrebrius made a gesturing motion behind him and suddenly the flames leaped higher and higher, and then a hole opened up in the clearing. It was actually a hole in the middle of the fire, but instead of the other side of the clearing, he was peering into some rather fancy, if dusty, room bathed in odd red light. The room had several other demons in it, including a smaller version of the dark master, and a demon dressed like some sort of Sidhe—maybe a brownie? Then there was that weird demon with all the arms and legs, puffing on a pipe and sort of leering at him. That was disturbing.

Vaselle stopped looking at the room as the dark master came into view and stepped through the opening, crouching a bit in order to do so. Again he was struck by the magnificence of his soon-to-be master. So muscled, so powerful, and his... was he wearing a loincloth? That was new, and oddly disappointing; he was not sure why though. Also new was the giant rod he held in one hand, and a good-sized sack in the other. Vaselle scurried back as the demon stepped into the clearing.

"So, Vaselle," the demon lord thundered. "You are still committed to this?"

"Ughk..." Vaselle coughed and cleared his throat. "I am, oh mighty one!"

"Uh, huh. Okay, then. First things first. When you discuss me with others, you will refer to me as Tommus; that is what I've decided to go by. You can choose the titles, as I have not settled on one. However, when addressing me directly, you will address me as Tom." He stared at Vaselle.

"Tom?" Vaselle said worriedly. "That seems a bit personal."

The dark master—er, Tom—chuckled. "I'm going to possess you at times, Vaselle, inhabit your body, like I did the priests and the Rod members. That's what you wanted, right?" Vaselle nodded. "Well, it does not get much more personal than that."

"Yes, master... I mean, Tom," Vaselle said.

His master—Tom grinned, or at least Vaselle hoped that was a grin; it was really very frightening. "I will have some errands for you to run; you will need money for them." He held up the sack in his hand. "Here are some rough stones; hopefully you can sell them or trade them for what we need." He set the sack down a short distance away. Vaselle just nodded.

"Very well, let us begin," Tom ordered.

"Assuredly." Vaselle quickly went to his table and grabbed a scroll lying on it. It was a good-sized scroll with somewhat large letters; he had tried to make something proportional for his master—er, Tom.

"This is... basically a script," Vaselle explained. "I have words I say, you have words you say. I start by doing a basic incantation to empower these runes." He gestured to the ones on his body. He was wearing only his pants, which were rolled up to expose his ankles with the circles. "Then I create a link which I hand to you. As I do, I will start the words of the script and then we alternate... and then it should be done, at least as far as you commanded me."

"Very well. If you are still willing, proceed," Tom said.

Vaselle nodded and began the incantation as he had practiced without the runes or the few other material components. He established the linking of the runes on his body, empowering them, and then took the magical leash link, as it were, and began reciting from the script. He finished his part and handed the link both mentally and with his real hands to his master.

His master began reciting the words and suddenly Vaselle could feel his master pouring over the link like a tidal wave! It was far beyond what he had expected or been prepared for. It was overwhelming… it was….

~

Vaselle woke lying on the ground. All around him, leaves were charred to a crisp. His pants were also severely charred and quite damaged, but at least wearable. He had one heck of a headache, he suddenly realized as he sat up. He looked around the clearing. Other than a lot of charred leaves and the remains of the summoning spell, now completely dispersed, nothing much had changed. Well, there was that large sack and a note pinned to it.

He grabbed the note.

Excellent! You are now mine. Congratulations!

Well, that was a bit anticlimactic, Vaselle thought.

Please acquire the following goods in the following quantities. When you have done so, exit the city wards and then think of me and call my name.

Tom

Vaselle looked at the list and blinked. It was in his own handwriting! How totally bizarre! "But not as bizarre as this list," he muttered. And the quantities? He shook his head. Freehold was one of the few places all of these things were available, but in these quantities, this would be expensive! He tugged on the sack string to open it and see what the rough stones were; hopefully some marble or malachite something worthwhile. The sack opened and rough-cut rubies, emeralds, sapphires, diamonds and other gemstones spilled out. "Holy saints in their graves!" Vaselle exclaimed at the wealth spilling out of the sack. Who said selling one's soul did not pay!

~

Tom headed immediately back to bed. He needed to curl up again. It was too much —way too much! He shut the door behind him, to the surprise of the others, saying only, "I need to rest some more." He really did not need to rest; he just needed to curl up and freak out!

How had he kept himself together while possessing Vaselle? He was amazed he had been able to do some simple tests of flame in the man's body and then write out the list in Vaselle's hand. He had then released the wizard, sent everyone back to the parlor and closed the link while making a beeline to bed.

When he had possessed the soldiers, he had been in a hurry, with a burning anger and a crapload of mana. He had basically flattened the minds of the people he'd possessed. Here, he had come in and Vaselle had opened himself up to Tom completely and utterly. The wizard had exposed everything about himself—his fears, his frustrations, his loneliness, his despair, his longing, his love, his self-loathing, his pettiness, all his foibles and just said "take me."

Tom tried his best to tolerate it, but it was too much. To see someone else exposed that way was painful in a way he could not explain. It made him ache; ache in his heart, his mind, his soul. It brought forth a very complex wellspring of emotions that he could not even begin to process. When someone did something like that, it was very hard not to reciprocate or resonate or something. Tom did not have the words for it.

He did not want to reject the wizard, but he did not want to meld with him at that level of intimacy. He was torn on so many levels that he could not even process them at the time. He had done his best somehow, mentally, spiritually or something, to "pat" the wizard and welcome him, give him some affirmation. But it was a bit too much. A lot too much. He had not been prepared for it. Therefore, he merely gave him a mental hug and tried to push him gently down and take control of his body to establish a solid link within the wizard. He certainly did not want to go as far as he had with the Rod of Tommus. Nope. Not going to happen; but that was what Vaselle had seemed to want.

Christ, that wizard was lucky he had done this with Tom. He had to imagine most demons on seeing that much vulnerability would be tempted to exploit it. To think of the damage one could do to someone so open and vulnerable. It made Tom shudder. It made him ache. He did not know if he felt embarrassment for Vaselle, pity, love, despair or what? All of the above?

Tom opened his eyes. Was this the sort of thing God saw when people prayed to Him/Her? In this case, he meant the god he had been raised with on Earth, but he supposed it was the same for the local gods. How could they take this, worshippers opening themselves up like this? It would be a living hell, it would take a level of… of he had no idea what to handle this day in and day out.

Fuck! He just wanted to cry, or maybe scream. Or both.

~

Lilith stood beside Darflow Skragnarth looking Abyssal Southwest (ASW) from Doom's Redoubt, her secret fortress built to keep an eye on Mount Doom and its occupants. She had originally had it built about ten or twelve thousand years ago as a base station for her spies to keep an eye on Orcus and his machinations. After his demise, she had repurposed it to be more of a garrison to ensure the D'Orcs did not get too out of control.

"How long has it been since you've performed a D'Orc culling?" Lilith asked her commander. A culling was what they called the periodic raids they performed on the D'Orcs to whittle down their numbers, test their defenses. It was expensive, in that she generally lost about as many soldiers as the D'Orcs; however, it would have been more expensive if not for her troop's greater magical resources. Their arcane devices and mana-wielding demons were more than enough to neutralize the D'Orcs home field advantage.

The D'Orcs had no magical defenses left. In the old days, no demon prince in his right mind would have even thought of attacking Mount Doom, the most powerful fortress in the multiverse. Like any truly great fortress, it had only fallen through treachery. Of course, since its fall she could have wiped them all out permanently, but that would have required drawing on her regular resources enough to cause people to wonder where those resources were going.

Darflow's mission was quite secret. No one at the Courts even knew of the D'Orcs' continued existence or any of her history with Mount Doom, and she was determined to keep things that way.

"It's been just over a decade since the last culling. We're due for another one in about half a year; we've already begun the planning and training. As per your orders, we try to be irregular in the schedule so the troops cannot become complacent."

Lilith nodded, thinking. "Continue your training, but I'm not so sure we will want to go ahead with that, given this." She gestured to the now-smoking giant volcano ringed by both mountains and storm clouds. She shook her head. The return of the storm clouds meant the portal to Water had reopened. The Abyss obviously had Earth, Fire and Air. Add Water, combine with the raw Spirit of demons, and you had a recipe for a giant mana factory. Which is exactly what Mount Doom was. How Orcus had ever constructed such a place was beyond her ken. He had done so without her or Sammael's knowledge, before the advent of the boom tunnels.

Altrusian technicians—highly evolved sleestaks that normally existed outside the primary time stream—installing the boom tunnels some twenty-five thousand years ago had discovered the mountain range. Of course, it was not until about fifteen thousand years ago that the Council of Princes had realized the full significance of the storm clouds; they had previously just assumed Mount Doom was Orcus's overly theatrical secret fortress. Lilith chuckled, fondly remembering the bitter and heated arguments when the other princes had first confronted Orcus. Those had been the days! She had to admit, completely obliterating one's enemy was not as satisfying as one might think. It rather left a void in one's daily life. Her current enemies were so much less interesting.

Yes, there was Sammael, but she knew him too well, and he her. They had known each other for such an incredibly long time that all real mystery and uncertainty about each other had long since vanished. Not for the first time, she wondered if Adam had made the right choice after all. Her slight smile hardened. Right choice or not, that bitch Eve had no business offering it to him. Lilith shook her head. There was no point going down that path. That was so far long gone into the mists of time, it was inarguable at this point. It was but a bitter pill, lodged deep within her metaphorical heart.

~

Gastropé and Jenn wandered into the map room behind the bridge, where Trevin and the Captain were going over maps with Elrose and Maelen. "If we can follow the northwest side of the mountains, along the Murgandy border, we can descend straight south into Western Noajar," Trevin said.

The Captain grimaced slightly. "It will be slow going, given the winds coming up from the coast and blowing against the mountains, but I agree that it is preferable to Eastern Noajar."

"What's in Eastern Noajar?" Maelen asked.

The Captain pointed to a series of villages at the base of a mountain near some standing stones. "Treojar."

"Yes, we want to avoid them," Trevin agreed, looking at the two wizards.

"Why?" Maelen asked.

"They're rather unsavory, or more precisely, their gods are, and they don't like interlopers," Trevin said.

"But Aêthêal said that our height and the fact we are a cloud allowed us to slip through political borders without people on the ground having a clue we were even there," Jenn said, puzzled.

"In most cases, but not all. For example, we would not cross over Oorstemoth or Freehold without first obtaining permission. Both would likely spot us. In Freehold there are too many wizards that might see us, and in Oorstemoth—well, they are very much aware of our cloudships," the Captain explained.

"You now have firsthand experience that the Nysegard Storm Lords, as they call themselves, do not like us and in Nysegard have no problem fighting us at any altitude," Trevin said with a rueful smile.

"In the case of Trojar, it's their rather hands-on deities." The captain shook his head in dismay.

Trevin was nodding. "Not very powerful deities in the grand scheme of things, pretty local actually, but quite deadly and fueled by sentient blood sacrifice."

"Sentient blood sacrifice?" Gastropé asked, concerned.

"Interlopers, prisoners and people they just don't like," the captain said. "They aren't powerful enough to bring a ship like the Nimbus down, but they could damage us, or at the very least distract us unnecessarily."

"It's not safe to send carpets against these deities either, as they can easily take them down," Trevin said.

"Well. Then we should definitely avoid them," Jenn said, shaking her head. "Although the fact that we are even mentioning fighting 'lesser' gods has me more than a bit bothered." She frowned.

"But to be fair," Gastropé pointed out, "before this trip, the thought of battling liches on dragonback at the very top of the atmosphere would have bothered both of us."

Jenn glared at him for some reason.

"What? I am just saying that one becomes acclimated after a while. Wandering the Abyss with a greater demon, blasting liches off the backs of their dragons in the stratosphere, you sort of get used to what was once insane."

"You do know that is what they call a slippery slope , yes?" Jenn asked him.

Trevin chuckled and the two glanced at her. "My dear, you are so correct. At times it seems like my entire life has been one long slippery slope. Trust me, at some point you cannot even imagine how to get off the slope. You just try to optimize your speed going down and hope to avoid crashing."

Gastropé sighed and returned to staring at the map. "On a lighter note, I thought we were heading to Natoor. Why are we going to Noajar? It seems rather out of the way."

Maelen nodded. "It is, but it's also the closest place where there were Nyjyr Ennead temples. You see these pyramids on the map? Those are, or rather were, sites of both tombs of rulers and temples to the gods."

"So we are hoping to get lucky with a shorter trip," Trevin said, grinning. "Admittedly, Noajar was something of an outpost for them, and we don't think there were any really large temples there."

"However," Elrose added, "there were also fewer Etonians hunting down Nyjyr Ennead followers in Noajar. With lesser temples, there was less need for desecration and we are hoping for better a chance of finding intact artifacts and altars."

"How long until we reach Noajar?" Jenn asked.

"Optimizing wind currents for optimal cruise speed, which means not taking a straight line, we have nearly 900 leagues to traverse," the captain said. Gastropé raised his eyebrows at the huge distance. The captain continued, "That's not as bad as it sounds. Following the air currents and adjusting altitude to get the best paths, we can cruise at about eleven leagues per hour, every hour of the day." He smiled. "So about four days."

Gastropé frowned, trying to do the math. "So the Nimbus is over five times faster than a sailing ship?"

"Indeed; under favorable conditions, our cruising speed is," the captain replied. "Under unfavorable conditions, we are still generally better by a factor of two or more, given that we can adjust altitude to get more favorable winds, whereas a sailing ship cannot. And beyond that, unlike a non-magical sailing ship, if need be, we can nearly double our cruising speed for short periods."

"Wow!" Gastropé said in surprise.

The first mate, Aêthêal, had entered the room during this discussion and smiled at Gastropé. "If you think that's fast, you should ask your combat carpet buddy Peter to take you out for a fast run. He holds the current speed record of forty leagues per hour."

"Forty leagues per hour? A hundred and twenty miles in a single hour? Doing that at any lower altitudes would blow you off the carpet!" Jenn exclaimed.

Aêthêal grinned and nodded. "He did it at about thirty-five hundred feet, not that much lower than the other day, but even so, I would probably not recommend launching any forward fireballs at that speed."

She, the captain and Trevin all laughed.

~

"Thank you for inviting me to lunch," Randolf said to Lenamare as the two sat down at the dining table in Lenamare's suite.

"Not at all. I appreciated the notes you sent me on the wards. You had some good insights and ideas and I would love to discuss them with you," Lenamare said, smiling.

"I am quite excited to talk about them as well. As I said, truly masterful work. I had always thought the original wards quite interesting, but these new modifications for expelling things inside the wards are truly revolutionary," Randolf said. He had been sure to include lots of detailed praise in his note. Flattery would be necessary to get Lenamare on his side, but it would have to be sincere flattery. The man was quite brilliant.

"Your reworking of Hierophan's postulate to increase the energy channels was particularly remarkable. Especially given that the wards were active at the time of the reworking. Historically, one would have had to recreate the wards from scratch," Randolf said.

Lenamare nodded. "Yes, it was a bit of work, but something I'd realized could be necessary in many circumstances. After the incident at my school, I took a long look at options for in-place upgrades of the wards. Of course, I'd had no idea that I'd need to do such a thing so soon; but I had been thinking on it for some time."

"Well, the power to actually expel archdemons along with all the others would have been otherwise unimaginable," Randolf said.

Lenamare nodded. "Again, not something you would ever expect to need to do."

Randolf nodded in agreement, although he had been thinking about the need to do so most of his life. It was one of the first unmet needs he had experienced in life; in particular, the need to get rid of Exador once and for all. "And conveniently, it exposed the duplicitous and malevolent nature of your rival," he said.

"Yes." Lenamare frowned. "Sorry to deprive you of your mage."

Clearly, Lenamare was still a bit sore about not being selected as Mage of Turelane, thought Randolf. However, Randolf had needed Exador closely tied to him in order to contain him, more than he needed an actual mage. He gave a short laugh. "Nonsense. I am better off not having a secret archdemon working for me. You have done me a great favor!" Randolf shook his head. "No one in their right mind would trust a bound archdemon, let alone an unbound one." He tilted his head and frowned. "Although I'm not sure if there are any bound archdemons."

"That remains to be seen," Lenamare said sourly.

"Ahh, yes… that extra-greater demon of yours." Randolf shook his head. "Rather troubling."

"It is," Lenamare agreed.

"Well, with all of this, you must at least be glad to have an explanation for Exador," Randolf said casually.

"An explanation?" Lenamare asked, puzzled.

"Certainly. Now everything makes sense!" Randolf exclaimed, raising his hands as Lenamare looked at him in puzzlement.

"One thing I have always wondered is how nature managed to produce two such brilliant minds, such powerful intellects with so much innate talent as you and Exador at the same time! Normally, such individuals only come along every few hundred years. However, both of you were 'born' near the same time and in close proximity."

"Yes." Lenamare nodded, intrigued by where Randolf was going.

"I mean, think of it; every time you made a breakthrough, there was Exador releasing some sort of 'me too' breakthrough! What is the probability of that happening? How could there be another person so close to you in insight and power?"

Lenamare nodded, taking in the archimage's logic.

"The fact that Exador has been shown to be an immortal archdemon puts all the pieces in place. He was not inventing new things at the same rate as you! No, he was simply unveiling things he had done centuries or maybe thousands of years ago, but had kept secret. Your innovations made him jealous; he felt upstaged, so he began releasing his centuries of work to the public so that it would appear that he was as gifted as you."

Lenamare tilted his head, considering this idea.

"Who knows how much of it was actually his," Randolf continued. "If an archdemon has free reign over multiple planes over thousands of years; his discoveries might simply be stolen wizardry from other planes that he passed off as his own work!"

Lenamare stared at Randolf for a moment and finally shook his head. "You are so right. I had not thought of this, but it makes so much sense as to be almost obvious!" Lenamare smiled ruefully. "Nothing has irritated me more than how

Exador seemed to match every breakthrough I had. It now makes so much sense! He cheated!"

Lenamare was so excited, he got up and began to pace, ignoring the food and wine on the table. "How could I have not seen this? You are so right!" He shook his head. "We had Alexandros Mien and then myself, and Jehenna is no slouch... if you add in Exador as a match for me, you have to ask how so many great minds could be alive at the same time! It defies probability!"

"Exactly!" Randolf said enthusiastically.

Lenamare paused to stare at Randolf in frank admiration. "Your insight on this is brilliant!"

Randolf made a deprecating gesture. "I only wish I could have come to this realization sooner. I had always been puzzled, but who could seriously expect an archdemon to be posing as a wizard? A conjuror, for that matter?"

"No one. It defies what everyone knows about demons and archdemons in particular." Lenamare tapped his forehead. "I mean, think about it. We have always assumed that the amount of power necessary to get an archdemon to manifest in the Planes of Men would be inconceivable. Yet here he is, and has been for a long time."

"It would argue that archdemons have a means of traveling to and from the Abyss aside from being summoned," Randolf said.

Lenamare shuddered. "So how is it we are not overrun by demon armies?"

Randolf shook his head. "That is a very good question."

~

DOF +5
Mid Afternoon 16-02-440

Sentir Fallon sighed as he opened the door to his suite. He had been in a meeting for the last two hours discussing the questionable tactics of the Rod in Astlan as well as on a few other planes. It appeared that numerous branches had started to show signs of overzealousness in the pursuit of justice and righteousness.

He had to admit, he had been suspecting as much for some time now. What had not been clear was the level to which these overzealous attitudes had apparently crept into standard dogma. To be honest, however, he was not convinced that it was quite as bad as some others believed. He willed the light on in his resting chamber and entered, heading directly to his master wardrobe to get out of his vestments in order to take a relaxing shower.

"Good evening, Sentir." A deep, throaty, and oh-so-very-female voice came from the shadows behind him.

Sentir felt his stomach drop at the sound. He slowly closed his eyes to gather his composure and turned to look his guest sternly in the eyes. "You know it is not safe for either of us for you to be here," Sentir stated.

"Yes," Lilith said slowly and with great import from the low-backed chair in which she reclined, her long, midnight-black feathered wings wrapping around the back of the chair. As she stood, she briefly stretched her giant wings, blocking light from the parlor door. Her low-cut, red-trimmed black gown seemed to thrust her cleavage at the archon. He remembered the feel of them quite well. He brought his eyes back to hers.

"I am aware of the risk," Lilith said. "However, I am also aware of the threat we now face." LilithShe brought her wings in and glided across the carpet towards him.

"And what threat is that?" Sentir asked sternly.

"Ahh, you are not then aware?" Lilith asked.

Sentir looked at her curiously. "Do you mean the events in Astlan?" The theft of Tiernon's mana was clearly the greatest threat to Tierhallon, but not necessarily to her. For all he knew, she could be in league with the demon thief.

Lilith smiled mischievously. "I suppose they are the same. But I am actually referring to something more specific." She turned to look around the room, providing her voluptuous profile for his review.

"And that is what?" Sentir asked, starting to lose patience for her games. Tempting as it may be, her presence here was too dangerous.

"Ahh, I forget—those of you in the Outer Realms are cut off from information in the Abyss." Lilith turned back towards him.

"It does seem to have some natural barriers to our eyes and ears. As you know," Sentir stated.

"Well, then, it is good that I came to tell you the news." Sentir looked at her, eyebrows raised, and she said simply, as if discussing the weather, "Mount Doom is once again active."

Sentir blinked, staring at her. His stomach knotted and rolled a few times. "What are you talking about? That is not possible; it cannot be."

Lilith smirked, clearly enjoying herself. "Perhaps, but nonetheless I have seen it with my own eyes. The volcano is active and storm clouds gather."

"The only way that could happen is if the Wand had been freed and then somehow miraculously tuned to the person retrieving it, and that particular person also happened to have a vast reserve of mana to restart the mountain." Sentir stared deeply into her eyes, trying to read her lies.

"Further, I sealed that Wand within the Holiest Wards of Tiernon, within an impenetrable and ciphered chamber behind shielded and warded gates. Only a major Archon of Tiernon equal to or greater than myself could have released the Wand. Even then, they would have needed to overpower and retune the wand and then flood it with enough mana to restart the mountain. It is not possible."

"Well..." Lilith said, putting her index finger to her pursed lips. "I should note that a certain party of demons, along with a hostage of your religion, were last seen making a beeline to Mount Doom, less than a full day before the mountain restarted."

Sentir Fallon's eyes widened and he backed up, feeling for the chair he knew had to be behind him. He sat down hard, even as he felt his innards try to sink below the chair. What had he and the Astlan team just been discussing in regards to Excrathadorus Mortis? He had not seriously believed that. It had seemed like such a worst-case scenario that it needed to be put on the table, but not too seriously considered. But this? "You know this demon destroyed the blade the three of us forged to kill Orcus?" Sentir asked, not able to look at the demoness.

"I did not know that that was the blade. However, once Mount Doom reignited, I began to wonder if the so-called "Holy Dagger of Tiernon" might not be our blade.

Sentir nodded. "It was. I saw a crystal balling of the event."

Lilith chuckled. "I find it rather funny the Paladin called it the Holy Dagger of Tiernon, for it most assuredly is not holy. It is pretty much by definition unholy. A perversion of Tiernon's power designed to permanently destroy animus. The dagger was suffused with antimus."

"Which is why this cannot be Orcus reborn!" Sentir stated vehemently. "I saw him die—I saw his entire being engulfed by that negative energy, watched it follow his links to the D'Orcs in Etterdam, watched it devour them as well. As, for that matter, did you!"

"I know," Lilith said. "I was watching, even as I shut down Mount Doom to destroy his ability to get more mana to try and save himself."

"So how could this be?" Sentir asked. His stomach was churning horribly at this point.

"Well, clearly this demon, whatever or whoever he is, has somehow figured out how to break your so-called Holy Ciphers. If he can steal mana from your clerics' streams, surely he could infiltrate and corrupt your wards by the same mechanism. Further, he had a lot of stolen mana to play with. It's not inconceivable."

"So you don't think this is Orcus?" Sentir Fallon asked.

Lilith shrugged, her wings dipping slightly. "I don't see how it could be. Which is why I had completely forgotten the forlorn prophecy of the D'Orcs and the orcs."

"Prophecy?" Sentir asked.

"Yes," Lilith said sourly. "I had completely dismissed it and banished it from my memories until one of my commanders, who has been keeping the D'Orcs in check, reminded me of it."

"And this prophecy says?" Sentir asked.

"About a hundred years after we killed Orcus, an orc shaman in Etterdam supposedly had an oracular vision, and it somehow managed to spread through the entire localverse and to the D'Orcs remaining at Mount Doom."

"Yes?" Sentir prodded.

"It said that their lord and master would be reborn and return one day, and would bring mana from the heavens to claim his wand, relight the fires of Mount Doom and bring vengeance on those who had wronged him. Along with some other signs and details that frankly, I don't recall right now."

"Mana from the heavens?" Sentir asked worriedly.

"Yes. Thought you might not like that part," Lilith said rather snidely.

"Have you told our other conspirator?" Sentir asked.

Lilith laughed. "No, and I will not for now. You know his boss. I have no doubt they are aware and likely concerned about this prophecy. If they knew of these events, well, I think that might cause more problems than we need right now."

"In hindsight, maybe we should have paid more attention to it ourselves," Sentir said.

"Perhaps." Lilith smirked. "But, naturally, I dismissed the prophecy because, as you know—"

"A prophecy requires a deity or similar higher power to see the prophecy through," Sentir finished. "But what god is there for demons? Not to be rude, but you are a rather godless lot."

"Thank you! That is actually one of the nicer things I've ever heard you say about us." Lilith smirked. "However, your point is valid. What deity *is* seeing this prophecy through? I don't suppose you are aware of any angry deities out to get us?"

Sentir looked up at Lilith, and his face got just a little paler.

Chapter 100

The great demon lord Tommus sat broodingly upon his magnificent double-backed throne, contemplating his newfound dominion and its many inhabitants, while idly rotating the Rod of Tommus in its holder on the right arm of the throne. Steam and smoke mixed in the air above the suspended platform of the Great Hall at the base of the active volcano that was his fortress.

Yes, Tom decided, "broodingly" worked particularly well. It seemed to him that if a demon lord was going to sit upon his throne in a large empty room, he should do so broodingly. Clearly that was all a dark lord could do—brood—and were not all demon lords dark lords by definition?

He shook his head. He had ended up taking another nap after binding Vaselle. At the time, he had thought he was unusually worn out. However, after flying down from his balcony to the throne and spending an hour or so following the throne's links to the rest of the complex, Tom now understood why he had been so tired. It turned out he had been unconsciously feeding mana through the Rod of Tommus to the entire complex. Basically turning it back on.

It had taken quite a bit of mana to relight a dormant volcano. There were all sorts of wards that had been hibernating but were now waking up. Plus, there was some sort of elemental portal thing to… well… "Water" was the only term he could think of for it. It was that portal which was pulling moisture into the air above the volcano and creating the storm clouds that were now raining down on the mountain and creating huge amounts of steam as the rain struck the lava below the platform.

What was weirder, though, was that the steam seemed to be permeating everything, every room, every tunnel and wrapping himself, the D'Orcs and his friends in its embrace. The steam was oddly pervasive in and of itself, permeating everything—the people, the rocks and even the flames. And with all this, the hidden runes in the complex were somehow collecting mana. It was as if the complex, or more precisely, the elaborate hidden runes within the complex were able to extract mana from combining fire, air, water, earth and animus.

According to the books in Freehold, mana was created by the friction between the five elements. Was it possible that this complex was some sort of engine to capture this friction? What was clear was that since the rain had started, the drain on his own mana had decreased as the complex had started to collect mana from this network of runes. He could follow his own mana flow through the system and see the interconnections. He just was not sure what all those connections were doing.

The other thing that he had discovered was that the complex had a number of interesting chambers and many different sets of runes and spells. Many of these runes were still dormant. It would be very interesting to know what these systems of runes would do. Clearly some of them were for protection, as well as energy generation, but he had no idea what the rest did.

Darg-Krallnom entered the platform inhaling the steaming vapor along with the gentle, pleasing scent of sulfur from below the platform. He stuck out his arms to feel the gentle rain upon his bare skin. He was still some distance away, but Tom was pretty sure the D'Orc was smiling, or at least pleased. D'Orc expressions were even harder to discern than regular demon emotions.

"Permission to approach?" Darg-Krallnom asked as he reached the base of the dais. Tom motioned for him to come up. "My Lord," he said, bowing as he approached. "Your return is truly welcome! I despaired of never seeing the mountain fully functional again."

"This mountain is truly a wonder." Tom smiled. "There is so much that is still dormant, but that will change as the mana levels build."

"Indeed." Darg-Krallnom nodded. "It has been nearly a decade since the Eternally Damned One's forces have raided us. We have been expecting them for some time now. It will be good to have the fortress's full defenses available for the first time since…" he trailed off awkwardly.

"Lilith's forces raid the mountain periodically?" Tom asked, concerned.

"Every decade or so, generally between seven to fifteen years. They like to keep us off guard."

"Why? What do they seek to gain?"

Darg-Krallnom shrugged. "We have debated this; we have not given them any particular provocation. We have no interest in them and ignore them in their fortress. We trade with demon clans further out than ourselves. No one ventures to the Courts. We suspect they are trying to keep our numbers in check."

Tom shook his head. "Then she must fear you —fear the D'Orcs becoming a threat to her reign." He smiled, as did Darg-Krallnom, and Tom nodded appreciatively.

"We shall repay her treachery against you, My Lord. Now that you have returned, her vile betrayal shall be repaid," Darg-Krallnom told Tom with a truly heated passion.

"At some point I will need your reports on her actions so that a full accounting can be made against her," Tom said, going along. At this point, he was playing a role he barely understood. He was under no illusion that any of this treachery had happened to him, but clearly, the D'Orcs had suffered and felt a need for vengeance. Although if his world's idea of orcs was anywhere close to being accurate, it probably did not take a whole lot of treachery to demand vengeance.

"Indeed, those of us who failed you must atone," Darg-Krallnom replied somberly.

Tom shook his head. "I am not interested in the atonement of any of the D'Orcs. You were betrayed as well, correct?" Tom was swinging into left field here.

Darg-Krallnom nodded. "We should have been better prepared for her treachery, her sabotage. We did not keep our guard sufficiently raised in her presence and she was able to disrupt the mountain's mana generation even as the Unholy Terror of Tiernon struck you with the vile dark blade. We failed you at your hour of greatest need!" Darg-Krallnom was clearly anguished, bending over as if in pain.

Tom reached out and grabbed him by the biceps. "You did not fail. You were betrayed! Do not forget that." He squeezed his arm to get the D'Orcs attention. Darg-Krallnom inhaled and stood up, nodding his understanding of Tom's implicit command.

"If it will make you feel better, I have essentially destroyed Excrathadorus Mortis; I reversed it completely. It is now a blade of healing. It can no longer serve its former purpose." Darg-Krallnom's eyes widened in surprise. "In fact, I am pretty sure the priests of Tiernon are scared to even touch it at this point."

Darg-Krallnom chuckled. "I am very relieved that threat is gone. How did you manage to find it?"

Tom smiled. "The knight—my hostage? After I defeated him and his soldiers and chose to show him mercy and spare his life, he shoved it into my stomach."

Darg-Krallnom's eyes widened again. Tom smiled. "The knight had cheated in battle, so I too went outside the rules. I intercepted his god's mana streams to his priests and used Tiernon's own mana to cleanse the wound and reverse the blade."

Darg-Krallnom inhaled, closing his eyes for a moment, and then reopened them. "Of course, as the prophecy said—you come with mana from heaven!" He chuckled. "We have often wondered what that meant, but it is now clear. It literally meant mana from heaven." The D'Orc commander shook his head in amazement.

"I am not aware of this prophecy; where did it come from?" Tom asked.

Darg-Krallnom blinked. "Well, we assumed that you revealed it to the shaman who spoke the prophecy." He seemed surprised. Tom might have stepped into it.

"When was this?"

"About 100 years Abyss time after your death, My Lord."

"And the shaman?"

"He was a shaman of the Nart tribe of Etterdam, the same tribe as Arg-nargoloth. A very respected shaman named Tiss-Arog-Dal. His prophecy revitalized the very disillusioned tribes of Etterdam and quickly spread throughout the localverse and the Abyss," Darg-Krallnom explained.

"Tiss-Arog-Dal?" Tom asked, somewhat suspicious of the name. It sounded a little too much like someone else's name.

"Yes. As I said, a very respected shaman."

"Is there any record of anything unusual about this shaman?" Tom asked.

"Unusual? You mean more unusual than normal for a shaman? They are all a bit off-balance."

Off-balance; well, that fit. "I mean physically? Anything odd physically? Any deformities?" Tom asked.

Darg-Krallnom seemed puzzled by the question. "Not that I'm aware of, but I never saw him. By the time I heard the prophecy, the shaman had passed away. Why?"

Tom shook his head. "No reason; just trying to put some pieces together." Tizzy was adamant that he could not shapeshift, so he could not have been this shaman. Had Tizzy perhaps had a son with an orc woman? Alternatively, was Tizzy feeding the shaman information, or was the name Tiss-Arog-Dal completely coincidental and Tom was just getting paranoid? To be honest, Tizzy really did not seem to have the sort of attention span necessary for even formulating a prophecy, let alone guiding one over thousands of years. However, Tom could not help remembering how pleased Tizzy had been when he had mastered the Rod of Tommus.

"Not to change the topic, My Lord ..." said Darg-Krallnom respectfully. Tom gestured for him to continue. "Would it displease you greatly if the younger folk were to come out onto the platform and take in the rain and steam?"

Tom gave him an odd look. "They want to come out in the pouring rain?"

Darg-Krallnom nodded. "None of the D'Orcs born in the Abyss have ever seen rain before, or water, for that matter."

Tom shook his head and looked around. Sure enough, there were D'Orcs peering anxiously out of various tunnels, entry points and balconies. How stupid of him. They were apparently scared to come out and disturb him while he was brooding.

"Everyone! Come out and enjoy the rain! Whether you have ever seen it or not, come on out and enjoy the rebirth of Mount Doom!" Tom bellowed and gestured for the D'Orcs to come out.

The waiting D'Orcs cheered and began spilling out onto the volcano's platform.

~

"M'lord, you have a *visitor* requesting an audience," Bartholomew announced from the French doors to Randolf's terrace. He stressed the word "visitor" rather oddly.

Randolf glanced to Crispin across the table. They were enjoying their afternoon tea and cucumber sandwiches. Crispin shrugged.

"Does this visitor have a name?" Randolf was puzzled, as typically the lord chamberlain would announce the visitor's name and title.

"I am afraid I did not ask," the lord chamberlain replied abashedly.

Randolf raised an eyebrow; this was a highly unusual lapse on the chamberlain's part. "You forgot to ask?"

"I'm sorry, Your Lordship, but I did not think of it as having a name," Bartholomew answered.

"*It?*" Crispin asked. "You are referring to the archimage's visitor as an *it?* My, that seems a bit contemptuous, even for you, Bartholomew." The djinn grinned; he loved tormenting the chamberlain.

"I have no better word, Your Lordship."

Randolf shook his head. "Very well; show him in."

The chamberlain turned and left the doorway.

"This should be amusing. He seemed rather in a flap," Crispin noted.

In a few moments, Bartholomew returned and announced, "The sword Ruiden, Your Lordship."

Randolf frowned at the very odd title, then his eyebrows shot up when he actually saw the guest. It was a metal golem.

"What in the seven realms?" Crispin muttered from the other side of the table as Ruiden entered the terrace.

Bartholomew turned and left.

"Thank you for seeing me, Archimage," Ruiden said, nodding to Randolf. He then turned his head and nodded to Crispin. "Djinn."

Crispin blinked in surprise at his disguise being blown. "You know I am a djinn?"

"Yes; it is clear looking at your aura," Ruiden said.

"You are good," Randolf stated softly, leaning back, confident that the golem, or whatever it was, was not going to attack. Although it looked quite deadly.

"You are a sword, I believe Bartholomew said?" Randolf asked.

"I am. I am Ruiden, Sword of Talarius, Knight Rampant of Tiernon," Ruiden stated.

"And what brings you here this day?" Randolf asked. He gestured to the pot of tea and plate of sandwiches. "Would you care to join us?"

"Thank you, but I do not digest," the sword said. "I am investigating the abduction of Talarius."

"Ahh," Randolf said, but then gave the sword a questioning look. "It makes sense you would undertake such an investigation, but I am not sure why you would need to speak with me. I was inside the city during the fight and abduction."

"Correct," Ruiden said. "That corroborates what I have already learned. However, you are the employer of Exador, who *was* outside the city, on a flying carpet with Ramses the Damned and an unknown woman."

"Yes, he does work for me, loosely. However, I have no idea why he was out on the carpet," Randolf said. "You would probably need to inquire with him."

"I intend to; however, he is not here now," Ruiden said. Randolf nodded. "Moreover, from information I have gathered, it appears that there is a high probability that Exador may be responsible for the demons within the city, and therefore that the demon that abducted Talarius may be an associate of his."

"Ahh, so you think Exador might have summoned the demon?" Crispin said.

The sword looked at the djinn. "It has already been established and admitted to that Lenamare summoned this demon most recently and had a binding to him. However, the demon that abducted Talarius was well beyond what Lenamare believes he summoned. I suspect that the demon may have been working with Exador against Lenamare."

"Interesting," Randolf said, nodding. "So you think there was a previous binding between Exador and the demon."

Ruiden looked at the archimage. Randolf would have guessed that the sword was puzzled, but its expressions were too hard to decipher. "Why are you prevaricating? My analysis shows a 98.4 percent chance that the three individuals on the carpet were the three archdemons identified by Talarius's mirror. The Council suspects this, and you yourself are working on spells to bind an archdemon. I would presume that it is Exador you intend to trap and bind."

Crispin suddenly choked on a sip of tea.

~

DOF +5
Mid Afternoon 16-02-440

Rupert rounded another corner; this hallway was also empty except for some doors to the right and left. It ended in a large spiral staircase going upward. He was exploring the vast underground complex. Svartbart, Hezbarg's apprentice, had told him that it should be perfectly safe to wander the main corridors. Any private rooms would be locked, and all the D'Orcs knew who he was, so none would bother him. Svartbart had also given him a loop to go around his neck with a small pouch on it. The pouch contained multiple scented salts that the hounds could detect and recognize him as a friend, and thus not eat him.

Hezbarg's other assistant, Shebolla, had led a party out to the chasm room to go down and bring up the hounds they had tossed down the chasm. The problem was the hydra hounds did not fly, and so the dogs, or parts of them, that were thrown down the chasm would regenerate, but then not be able get back out. If that happened, once regenerated they were likely to howl nonstop until someone came to retrieve them. Better to do that upfront rather than have to put up with incessant howling.

There were a number of large barracks chambers similar to the one they had seen earlier. These were where the single D'Orcs lived; at least the more junior ones. There were a number of private rooms where families lived. Svartbart had also indicated that each commander had his or her own room regardless of marital status. What was interesting was that from what he had seen, the D'Orcs actually slept. Tizzy and everyone had been chiding him for sleeping, but many of the D'Orcs slept as well.

There were also numerous training halls and workout halls with balls of various weights as well as ropes and metal bars. He had stopped to watch D'Orcs training a couple of times. Everyone had been very respectful of him. Rupert thought back to the fight with the hounds. It would probably be useful to get some real combat training. His dad was too preoccupied with all the insanity around them, so maybe he could find some D'Orcs to train him.

He climbed the stairs to the next floor and stepped off quickly, nearly colliding with a short D'Orc. "Ack!" The D'Orc made a surprised noise, but then recognized Rupert. Rupert blinked and recognized the short D'Orc as well. It was the one they had surprised in the hallway that had set off the alarm.

"Hey!" Rupert said. "We meet again."

"Yeah." The D'Orc suddenly looked very nervous and uncomfortable. "I'm sorry for running like that. I have shamed myself and my lineage."

"Don't worry about that!" Rupert said, making a waving motion. "Given how things worked out, your running and alerting everyone was the best option. If you'd stood and fought, well..."

"I'd be dead," the D'Orc said morosely.

"Well, I'd hope not. You're a kid like me, right?" Rupert asked.

The D'Orc nodded somberly. "I'm Fer-Rog, son of Zelda, and I have ten Abyssal years."

"Cool!" Rupert said, sticking out his hand. "I'm Rupert, you know my dad too, and I'm, well... I don't know, about twelve Astlanian years, roughly. I don't know what that is in Abyssal years."

Fer-Rog stared suspiciously at the hand for a moment and then awkwardly shook it.

"Your mom is the Steward of the Mount?" Rupert asked; Fer-Rog nodded his head. "Then we should definitely hang out, as I'm sure your mom and my dad will be working together a lot." Rupert paused for a moment. "Who is your dad?"

Fer-Rog frowned. "My sire was Ser-Rog of the Bear Clan of Verasai."

"Was?" Rupert asked, concerned.

Fer-Rog nodded. "He fell in combat during the last raid of the Lilith Spawn, a few days before my birth. He died trying save the life of my grandfather, Trogthor, the Steward of the Mountain. Neither regenerated, and my mother became steward that day."

"I'm sorry," Rupert said, and then frowned. "Wait, you said they didn't regenerate? Why not?" Even the hydra hounds regenerated.

Fer-Rog sighed. "There are multiple reasons. In some cases, the individual's body requires so much repair that the individual cannot summon the mana to bring everything back together, or at least do so in a reasonable number of years; they then give up and let themselves go. In other cases, the demons do have a few weapons capable of ending a demon or D'Orc permanently."

"That's horrible." Rupert shook his head in horror at the thought.

Fer-Rog nodded. "I am told that the frequency of such happenings has increased in the last thousand years or so." He shrugged. "That should end now with your father's return."

"I hope so," Rupert said. "But unfortunately, that won't bring your father back. Again, I am sorry. I lost my mother a few years ago, so I know what it feels like." Fer-Rog looked at him again and sort of nodded in acknowledgement of the pain. "So, where were you going?"

"I have combat training with the others in my age cohort," Fer-Rog said.

"That's a coincidence! I was just thinking how much I needed some combat training. May I come and watch?" Rupert asked.

Fer-Rog shrugged. "I do not believe Xaroth can say no. However, even if he could I would seriously doubt he would. He is a firm believer in everyone being at his or her best. So, I am sure if you ask, he will evaluate you and place you in an appropriate class."

~

"Greetings, master and fellow servant of Tommus!" Estrebrius shouted excitedly as he appeared in his summoning pentagram in Vaselle's lab.

"Greetings, Estrebrius. They've taken down the city's wards against demons and pretty much everything else," Vaselle said. "I've summoned you because I'm going to need help hauling all of these supplies back here so we can send them to Lord Tommus."

"I think he said you could call him Tom. He really seems to prefer that for some reason," Estrebrius said.

"It just seems a bit too familiar," Vaselle said, frowning.

"Well, you did cast a 'familiar' spell on yourself." Estrebrius grinned. "Besides, as demon princes go, he's really extremely nice."

Vaselle's eyes widened. "So he is a demon prince? Official rumor was greater demon, but everyone figured he was one of the archdemons. No one suspected a demon prince in the city!"

Estrebrius rocked his head from side to side. "Well, Tom denies he's a demon prince. In fact, he says he's only a greater demon." Vaselle looked at him, not understanding what Estrebrius meant. The little demon continued, "But, while you were working on your spell, we all went treasure hunting in these caverns that turned out to be under Mount Doom. After a few battles with hydra hounds and fleeing a bunch of D'Orcs, Tom managed to destroy a bunch of Etonian runes and then seized control of the Wand of Orcus and renamed it the Rod of Tommus. He then restarted Mount Doom and is now considered to be the reincarnation of Orcus by something like 2,000 plus D'Orcs!"

Estrebrius stopped for a moment to catch his breath. "And that would make him a demon prince and according to the D'Orcs, the archrival of Lilith, the Empress of the Abyss!"

Vaselle collapsed into a nearby chair. He only understood about half of what Estrebrius was saying, but what he did understand was overwhelming enough. After a moment, he asked Estrebrius, "What is a dork?"

Estrebrius shook his head, "No, a D'Orc. Like 'demon orc.' They are the demon equivalent of an orc. Tom has an army of about 2,000 demon orcs at his command, or at least he will shortly. That's what the supplies are for."

"Huh?" Vaselle asked, not understanding.

"Well, technically not for that. There is going to be an allegiance-swearing ceremony and then a party afterward. We are trying to get booze for the party, but demons need something stronger than mortals to get drunk. So we are hoping to get a lot of barrels of glargh. We then take these supplies you are getting and mix them into the glargh to make x-glargh, which is a favorite of D'Orcs."

"So my first task is getting party supplies?" Vaselle was feeling a bit of a letdown. Here he had been certain all the nasty things he was buying were for some horribly evil scheme.

"Welcome to indentured service," said Estrebrius with a grin.

Vaselle shook his head. He had just summoned Estrebrius to lug supplies around. *Fair is fair*, he supposed.

"I wish I could see the master's new fortress," Vaselle said sadly.

Estrebrius shrugged. "I'm sure Tom will be okay with you coming to the party. There is just the problem of your staying alive there. The Abyss is very hot. Mount Doom is actually quite a bit cooler, especially since it started raining, but it's still going to be like one of those saunas they have in the northern regions."

"Dang," Vaselle said.

"You know," Estrebrius said after a moment. "Rupert once mentioned that Tom had brought several wizard friends through the Abyss and that the wizards had a way of staying cool. Maybe I can find out what that is. It sounded like it was a spell or something."

"That would be great!" Vaselle clapped his hands, jumping up. "Okay, so we should get started. We have some of the supplies ready to be picked up. The rest will be ready tomorrow. Let's go get what we can."

~

DOF +5
Late Afternoon/Early Evening 16-02-440

"The wards are down!" Antefalken exclaimed as he materialized in Damien's chamber.

"Yes, finally!" Damien said, grinning. "I can't tell you how much I've missed your company. Things are insane here, wards or no wards." He shook his head and sat down, gesturing for Antefalken to hop on his favorite chair perch.

Antefalken laughed. "You only think things are insane here. It's much crazier in the Abyss."

"I don't know, the Oorstemothians recorded the battle between Talarius and Edwyrd and there are tons of crappy mirrorings from the wall as well. So everyone is pretty freaked out."

"Well, there were hundreds of demons watching, and they all ran back to the Courts to tell everyone. But it gets wilder."

"Really? Wilder than the fact that Alexandros Mien noticed something odd and drew the Council's attention to a flying carpet upon which Exador, Ramses the Damned and an unknown woman were all having breakfast while watching the battle?"

That caused Antefalken to pause as he digested the sentence. "Well, I think I can beat that, but a) who is the woman, and b) why are the three of them outside the wards when everyone else is inside?"

Damien twisted his head in something like a shrug. "We aren't certain, but as you recall, we suspected that the Ramses the Damned character might have been an archdemon; the woman is clearly something equally unusual; and then add Exador on the rug, outside? We think he may be the third archdemon."

Antefalken blinked a few times. "So you are saying that Lenamare, a mortal, has been going toe-to-toe with an archdemon for the last few decades and that the two kept ending up in a draw?"

Damien pursed his lips. "Well, when you put it like that, I like the theory a bit less. It gives Lenamare way too much of an ego boost, which he certainly doesn't need."

"Well, he did apparently kick three archdemons out on their asses; he deserves some credit for that," Antefalken noted.

"Trust me; he's been soaking it up like a sponge. He's actually been both pleasant and helpful lately."

"Now you are scaring me." Antefalken gave a mock shudder. "So how's your buddy Randolf taking the news that his faithful servant-slash-boss is an archdemon?"

"Surprisingly well," Damien said. Antefalken gave him a skeptical expression. "No, really—I am shocked myself. I almost, and I say *almost*, think he had suspected so already."

"Really? I thought he was clueless," Antefalken said.

"That is the appearance he gave, but I had an interesting breakfast with him. He is far smarter than we give him credit for being. I get the impression that he may feel he has little choice but to play the fool," Damien said.

"That does not add up with anything we know about him," Antefalken noted as he shook his head. "And the third, the woman? Another archdemon?"

Damien gave that same half shrug again. "That would be the most logical explanation; however, Trevin recognized her as being Bastet, a goddess of the Nyjyr Ennead pantheon."

Antefalken nodded, thinking back. "Guardian of House and Home, or some such title; hardly seems like the sort to be consorting with archdemons." He shrugged. "However, they disappeared several hundred years before I arrived on the scene. I have seen their old temples. Very impressive, but again, long gone from the Astlanian localverse, at least. I don't get much outside that, so can't say where they might have gone."

"Well, she mentioned that apparently, both Elrose, who works for Lenamare, and Gastropé's friend, Maelen, got hit by some visions that were tied to all of this; it was the whole reason they'd been traveling to meet each other."

"Seriously?" Antefalken asked.

"Serious enough that Trevin has set off on a mission to investigate the possibility and has taken Maelen, Elrose, Jenn and Gastropé along with her."

"Why Jenn and Gastropé?" Antefalken asked.

Damien chuckled. "You may recall the reason we were surrounded by two armies?"

"Oh, yes… they were persona non grata," the bard remembered aloud.

"Exactly, and fortunately, I had sent the animage Edwyrd and his apprentice Rupert off to hunt down the remaining demons. So no real cause to surround us."

"Hence the wards are down."

"Mostly," Damien admitted. "They are, more accurately, suspended. We can raise them quickly if need be. Say, if Exador comes marching back for revenge with his horde of demons."

"Good idea," Antefalken agreed.

"Yes. Unfortunately, the Rod and Oorstemoth both had similar thoughts and so have not completely withdrawn." Antefalken grimaced. "Although we do have a truce agreement with them. They are technically here to assist us if the horde comes back."

Damien smiled, having given his friend a nice, quick rundown of the insanity in Freehold. "So, what insanity have *you* been up to that's so crazy?"

Antefalken grinned at Damien in a manner the wizard thought seemed almost evil, as if the bard were going to enjoy telling his story a little too much.

~

Hilda and Trisfelt sat on the small balcony of Trisfelt's suite. There was barely room for two chairs and a small table filled with meats, cheeses and of course, wine.

"Ah, one forgets how nice it is to see the night sky again!" Hilda remarked.

Trisfelt chuckled. "Even though it's only been a few days since we were both camping outside the city in the woods."

Hilda laughed too. "So maybe that was a bit melodramatic, but you have to admit those wards rather wore on one after a bit. Plus at night they cast that weird red sheen over everything."

"I completely agree. I am very much an outdoorsman… at least as long as I have the basic necessities." He gestured to the table, indicating the food and wine. Hilda raised her glass to toast his observation, and Trisfelt clinked it with his.

"So life gets back to normal." She turned her head slightly to look at him better. "Or sort of; you are quite out of your routine here in the city. What will your new routine be?"

Trisfelt rolled his head his shoulders. "Well, we must resume classes for the students, which I think shall be challenging with Elrose gone and Lenamare and Jehenna likely to double down on their precious book. It will mainly fall to Hortwell and myself to teach most of the classes."

"What is so important about this book? One would think in such times as this, when they are shorthanded with one master gone, one senior student dead and another off chasing down a goddess, that they would put aside their hobbies and focus on their charges," Hilda said.

"I fear you might be starting to actually believe those charming things you say about them to their faces. You forget they are two of the most narcissistic wizards on the planet." Trisfelt grinned and popped a cube of ham in his mouth. Hilda chuckled and took another sip of wine.

Trisfelt swallowed and continued, "Remember, this is the book that Exador and Lenamare went to war over."

"I thought Exador wanted Lenamare's school and property or some such?" Hilda asked, puzzled.

Trisfelt shook his head. "That was only the pretext told to the Council. The book was the real reason. Lenamare acquired it, screwing Exador over with Oorstemoth in the process. Once Exador had dealt with the Oorstemothian courts, he immediately marshalled his forces and came for the book."

"How did Lenamare get Exador in trouble with the Oorstemothians?" Hilda asked, puzzled.

Trisfelt took a long drink of wine and inhaled. "He hired this group of inter-dimensional brigands…"

"What are inter-dimensional brigands?" Hilda interrupted.

"Well, I don't know if that is the precise term, only that they've somehow made themselves unwanted on multiple planes both within and without the localverse. Wherever they go, carnage and cataclysm ensue."

"You mean like what is happening now?" Hilda asked.

"Hmm." Trisfelt stopped to think. "You may be right, but I think in this case, it was bound to happen anyway." He shook his head. "These brigands are actually quite skilled and very experienced. Lenamare promised them any riches they found other than the book he wanted, plus a large sum of money, and he provided them in advance with quite valuable arcane devices that they could keep as payment."

"A very good deal, then. I take it that it was a difficult mission?" Hilda asked.

"Apparently. I don't know all the details, but I do know that while others had known of the book's location, none had ever retrieved it. These fellows managed to do so."

"Well, that is good, but how—"

Trisfelt raised a finger so he might continue. "What I have not mentioned was that the book was located deep underground in a designated historical preserve of Oorstemoth."

"Oh, and they removed the book from the site." Hilda nodded.

"And, one presumes, a fair amount of other antiquities." Trisfelt poured more wine for both of them. After setting the empty bottle on the floor beside the other empties, he continued. "Now comes the duplicity. The brigands escaped the historical site, but were apprehended by a small army of wizards and soldiers of Oorstemoth."

"Awkward, I'd imagine," Hilda said.

"Indeed, and apparently Oorstemoth suffered severe casualties. However, here comes the answer to your question. You see, Lenamare had given them a special bag to hold the book once they found it. It turns out that this bag was actually a Bag of Safekeeping—you know, the extra-dimensional storage space bags?" Hilda nodded, she had heard of them. "However, this bag was *twinned*, in that there were actually two bags that opened onto the same extra-dimensional space. The brigands put the book in the bag; Lenamare then opened his bag and removed the book. He then destroyed his bag so it could not be traced back. The Oorstemothians were left with an empty Bag of Safekeeping."

"Ingenious, one has to admit," Hilda said.

"Don't tell Lenamare that." Trisfelt shook his head, feeling this fifth bottle of wine. "In addition, those arcane devices he had given the brigands as payment?" Hilda nodded that she remembered. "They had very powerful hidden enchantments on them such that when questioned about who hired them, the brigands always replied 'Exador.' "

"So devious." Hilda shook her head. "Ethically challenged, but devious."

Trisfelt nodded. "So long story short, the brigands went to Oorstemothian prison, where they were held so they could testify against Exador before being executed, and Exador was served notice by Oorstemoth and had to go prove his innocence. This gave Lenamare and Jehenna quite a bit of time to read the book."

"I thought they couldn't open it?" Hilda asked the wizard.

"I said it gave them time; unfortunately, they were forced to use that time to try to figure out how to unlock and open the book. To date, they have had no luck." Trisfelt chuckled.

Hilda shook her head and grinned. "All that for nothing?"

"Exactly."

"So what is in this book? What secrets does it contain?" Hilda asked.

"I have no idea; they are not willing to share that information with anyone."

"So they blew up their own school and disrupted the lives of all their people over a book they cannot read and which none of those affected by this upheaval knows the import of." Hilda shook her head as Trisfelt nodded. She frowned and continued, "But the Council believes that the demon horde was here before Lenamare blew up his school?"

"Yes, that is the theory; they would have had to have been sneaked in over time," Trisfelt said.

"And we believe they were brought here by the archdemons, Exador, Ramses and this woman who may or may not be a former goddess?" Hilda asked.

"It does not make a lot of sense," Trisfelt admitted.

"Unless Exador expected the book to end up here in the end in any event?" Hilda asked.

Trisfelt shrugged. "That sounds consistently paranoid for Exador, or Lenamare for that matter."

"So then, it was the arrival of Jenn and friends, pursued by Oorstemoth and the Rod, that threw the game wide open again?" Hilda suggested.

Trisfelt frowned for a moment, thinking. "So it would seem."

"And their arrival and that of their pursuers were all precipitated by the intervention of Lenamare's greater demon?"

Trisfelt stared at her for a moment. "My dear, I see the rabbit hole you are following. You think that Lenamare suspected that Exador may have set a trap for him in Freehold and so Lenamare summoned the demon as part of a twisted plan to thwart Exador's army of hidden demons?"

"It worked, did it not?" Hilda replied. "He has the book again and Exador, his allies and army have become unwelcome and untrusted within Freehold.

"I do hate to say this, my dear, but I am following your logic and think you may have hit upon something! It appears we are now both thinking like Lenamare or Exador; thus, I can only conclude we have drunk too much wine!"

~

DOF +6
First Period 16-03-440

"Does it seem oddly dark out there?" Boggy pointed out the balcony window. He, Rupert, Talarius and Tizzy were playing whist, while Tom sat on the sofa lost in his own thoughts, simply relaxing and listening to the rain splash against the large metal pentagram outside his open balcony door. Their respective masters had summoned Antefalken, Reggie and Estrebrius.

Tom looked out the door. It was quite dark outside, as if it were night. He mentally dove into the Rod, moving through it to the throne and then to the complex. It did not take him long to notice a new set of runes had come online; he spent a few moments exploring them, or more precisely, inhabiting them.

"It's nighttime," Tom said, startling the others, who had gone back to their game.

"Nighttime?" Rupert asked.

"Yes, the complex has artificial days, just like the courts. The runes controlling the days came back online sometime within the last period or two," Tom said.

"How do you know this?" Talarius asked.

"You remember how I sort of inhabited the Etonian runes where we found the mace?" Tom asked and Talarius nodded his upper body. "My link to the mace and the throne allows me to inhabit the entire complex. There are a huge number of various runes and spells surrounding this place. All of them have been dormant for thousands of years with no mana to power them. I can sense them, and flow into them as I did the Etonian runes. Sometimes I can get a feel for what they are doing; not always though."

"So why are they all coming alive now? Where is this mana coming from?" Talarius asked.

"Me, at first."

Boggy blinked and both he and Rupert turned to look at Tom. Tizzy continued to stare at his hand of cards and puff on his pipe.

"When I established my link with the mace," continued Tom, "I blasted it super-full of mana. That mana then fed from the mace to the complex, which is what restarted the volcano." Boggy nodded. "What I didn't realize until this afternoon was that I never actually shut off the flow of mana once I inadvertently lit the volcano, and my mana continued to flow throughout the mountain, turning things back on. That is the big reason why I was napping this afternoon. I was feeding the entire complex with mana."

"So are you going to go dry and pass out or something?" Rupert asked.

Tom chuckled. "No. I don't understand it completely yet, but this place is actually a giant mana engine. Various runes control access to the elemental planes. Fire, Earth and Air are already here, and thus fairly straightforward to tap. There is also a more complicated portal to Water; once that opened, the storm clouds started forming, and eventually it rained. You combine that with the heat of lava and fire, you get steam. Steam is the demi-element of Water and Fire. As you saw, things are rather smoky out there also. Smoke is Earth, Air and the heat of Fire. Both Steam and Smoke fill the complex and permeate the living residents—the D'Orcs and us. We provide the animus, which is the material form of the fifth element, Spirit. All of these elements rubbing up against each other—"

"Creates the elemental friction that generates mana!" Rupert said, nodding. "It's exactly what I was taught in school!" He shook his head. "Normally it just sort of floats around until absorbed or collected by animus—a person."

Tom nodded. "And it does here, too, but there are invisible runes all over the place that are also collecting the excess mana and using it to feed the engine. As this great big mana engine wakes up, it generates more mana to fuel itself. Thus, I have to provide less and less. In theory, at some point it should become self-sustaining and even be able to generate excess mana." Tom shrugged.

"At least that's what I think Orcus was doing. Apparently, when he was battling Sentir Fallon, Lilith somehow made her way here and gummed things up so Orcus couldn't pull enough mana to overcome Excrathadorus Mortis."

"The bitch!" Boggy shook his head.

Tom nodded. "And that's why the D'Orcs hate her. Her treachery breached their security, a great number of D'Orcs here in the mountain died that day, and yet they feel they failed their master and were in part responsible for his death."

"Are you saying that this demon queen, Lilith, sabotaged Orcus's mana engine to help Sentir Fallon?" Talarius asked.

"That's exactly what the D'Orcs say. They believe the two were allied to bring down Orcus," Tom said.

"I don't believe it! No archon of Tiernon would so subvert himself." Talarius seemed quite angry.

Tom shrugged. "I don't know that belief is required. We do know that she managed to gum up the mana flow here in the mountain while Sentir Fallon and Orcus were fighting. It could have been coincidence."

"It must have been," Talarius stated.

"And yet," Tizzy finally spoke up, "someone returned that mace." He pointed to the Rod of Tommus. "They brought it back here and sealed it in the room where we discovered it; sealed it in a buttload of Etonian runes, wards, seals and what have you. I can guarantee you no demon could have created those blessed wards."

Talarius made a growling noise, clearly frustrated. "I admit to that point; no demon could have made those wards. They were clearly Etonian and I could easily feel Tiernon's presence in them. They were the work of someone very powerful within Tierhallon."

"So how would an archon of Tiernon get down into the Abyss, into these mountains, past all the D'Orcs, and seal the mace inside?" Boggy asked.

"I think someone would have noticed a Heavenly Host marching into the Abyss, and certainly there would have been tales of it in your own church history," Rupert remarked.

Talarius growled again and was silent for a moment. "Demon," he finally said, turning more fully toward Tom. "The longer I am with you, the more uncomfortable I get. The complexity of your machinations in putting me in my current state of mind is clearly on par with what I'd expect from a reborn demon prince."

"Is that a compliment or a curse?" Tizzy asked.

"Both," Talarius replied.

Chapter 101

DOF +6
Morning 16-03-440

Damien poured himself another cup of coffee and bit into his toasted muffin. He had not slept much last night. He had no idea how to digest Antefalken's tale. It all seemed like a perfect series of coincidences, yet an unusually beneficial one for Edwyrd or Tom or whatever the demon's name was. Antefalken seemed to think it was all completely innocent, but Damien had a hard time believing that anything involving demons was innocent.

As he sat back to take another sip of coffee, Antefalken came wandering into the dining room, stretching his arms and shoulders.

"Rough night?" Damien asked the demon.

"It doesn't take too many nights of absence to get out of practice with the maidens. I may have sprained my tongue," the bard said with a smile as he hopped up to the back of his chair at the table. "You look like you didn't get much sleep."

Damien shook his head. "I have decided to admit that your adventurers were crazier than mine."

"Thank you." Antefalken grinned and bowed his head in acknowledgement.

"I am still concerned that this is all too convenient."

Antefalken shrugged his right shoulder and nodded. "I understand; if I had not been there every step of the way, essentially every moment, I would have been suspicious myself." The demon shook his head. "But it is legitimate; there are just too many independent actors all aligning to support what I observed. I have known Boggy for a long time, and Tizzy for even longer; they would not be in on any sort of strange plot to make this seem like a coincidence when it isn't. For one thing, Tizzy can't keep his head together long enough to not slip up."

"I don't know." Damien shook his head and popped a strawberry in his mouth.

"You could come visit, I suppose." Antefalken shrugged. "See for yourself."

"What?" Damien sat up and looked at the bard as if he were insane.

"Well, as you know, Gastropé and Jenn both traveled through Tom's cave with no problem using that cooling spell that Exador showed Gastropé. The mountain complex is actually far more agreeable than Tom's cave, so you would probably be quite comfortable."

"Perhaps, but I'm not sure I want to risk getting trapped there. I'd eventually run out of mana and expire," Damien said.

Antefalken shook his head. "Tom has taken humans to and through the Abyss on multiple occasions and never abandoned them. Talarius is there now, and Tom has been more than hospitable to him. I point out that Talarius tried to kill Tom and his friends permanently, and yet Tom treats him as honorably as any king would treat a formally held noble hostage. You would be there as a friend and ally."

"I will have to think about that," Damien said, shaking his head once more.

"Oh come on; think what a learning opportunity this would be! A human conjuror wandering the halls of the great demon lord Orcus's fortress?" Antefalken gave a short shake of his head and a grin. "Do you have any idea how many wizards, and demons for that matter, would sell their souls for such an opportunity?"

"Uhm hmm," was all Damien would say.

Antefalken frowned. "Speaking of selling their souls, I wonder if Vaselle is going to want to attend the party?"

"Vaselle? Party?" Damien asked.

"Ah, I think I forgot to mention that side event." Antefalken gave him a quick grin. "The party is going to be a celebration after the allegiance ceremony. Tom originally suggested it to buy time to get out of the D'Orcs swearing him allegiance, but we convinced him to go through with it. Vaselle, on the other hand—"

A bell chimed, indicating someone at the main door. Damien's eyebrows rose in surprise, and he got up to answer the door himself. He had sent his assistants off on errands, as he often did when he and Antefalken had their breakfast meetings. He left the dining room and went through the main sitting room to the small entryway and opened the door. A palace valet was there with a wizard a bit younger than himself whom he did not recognize.

The page said, "Greetings, Master Damien. This gentleman says he has important information for you regarding a friend of yours named Tom? He insisted on visiting you rather than making an appointment."

Damien looked at the wizard, most likely a conjuror, and said, "You are?"

"Ah yes, My Lord Councilor, my name is Vaselle. I work for an acquaintance of yours, Tom?" the wizard said.

Damien blinked. "Vaselle? As in Vaselle and the party?" he asked. He nodded and waved to the escort to go, and ushered Vaselle in.

Vaselle was looking quite shocked. "How do you already know about the party?" he asked. "That's why I came; I have some items that I need to acquire for Tom and I need Council approval to get them in the quantity I need."

"Vaselle?" Antefalken came into the living room.

Vaselle looked over to Antefalken. "The bard Antefalken, yes? I recognize your voice from the other side of the portal. Estrebrius has also mentioned you in recounting his recent adventures."

The bard walked up and offered his hand to Vaselle, who shook it. "Nice to finally meet face to face," Antefalken said, smiling. "How are you doing? Getting acclimated to the new job?"

"Yes, indeed. Just trying to get supplies for the party. I told Tom about the restrictions on the nitroglycerin quantities and he told me to come visit Councilor Damien. I'd wondered how I would convince him of the request's authenticity, but clearly the mas... uh, Tom knew you were here."

"I assume this is the Vaselle you were just about to tell me about?" Damien asked.

Antefalken turned slightly to give Damien that same slightly malevolent smile he had used the night before. "Yes, Vaselle is Tom's new warlock!"

~

"So this theory, which you admit is rather out there, supposes that this Lenamare is secretly a warlock belonging to the bit-more-than-greater demon?" Moradel asked Hilda. Their early morning meeting had been delayed, as Sentir Fallon had been tied up.

"I don't know that he has to be a warlock, so much as working in collusion with the demon," Hilda replied. "As I mentioned, I am just throwing out ideas to explain what is going on. Superficially, it seems that all these rather random events just happened. The book issue with Exador and Lenamare is clear enough, if slightly melodramatic, but why had Exador and his allies filled the halls of the palace with a demon horde, if not to trap Lenamare?"

"That does seem logical. And given what I understand of how this Council works, taking the dispute to them would be a logical step. And Exador, being an archdemon with similar allies, would have access to a demon army to assist him in capturing the book once it came to Freehold," Beragamos said.

"So then," Hilda continued, "we either have to believe in complete random chance that this demon would show up and completely disrupt Exador's plans—"

"Or believe that Lenamare is sufficiently skilled to give incredibly detailed instructions to the greater demon and his student to do all the things necessary to draw both the Rod and Oorstemoth to Freehold and then expose the demon horde, and thus give the Council a reason to activate the wards Lenamare had built, and then eventually expel all the demons to be killed by Oorstemoth and the Rod," Moradel said.

"When you put it like that, coincidence seems more likely," Beragamos said.

"Except," Sentir Fallon countered, "you have to add in the events with Talarius and the mana theft." He shook his head. "Clearly this was not a greater demon. An archdemon should not have been able to break the Holy Ciphers, steal our lord's mana, possess our priests and Rod members and then destroy Excrathadorus Mortis!"

Sentir Fallon sighed and finally sat down; he had been standing. "As you know, not even Orcus could overcome Excrathadorus Mortis. I have to come back to our earlier discussion about this demon possibly being Orcus returned."

"In which case, Lenamare must be a warlock. Yes?" Hilda stated.

"Formally or informally," Sentir sighed.

"Informally?" Hilda asked.

Sentir shrugged. "Basically your own argument a few moments ago. A warlock is formally bound to a demon via strong linking spells, as great as those of a priest."

Moradel nodded. "I see your point. If he were so bound, then those wards of his would have complicated such a binding. So perhaps a more informal arrangement; not a true warlock, but a demon's agent nonetheless."

"Assuming the binding could expel a demon prince," Beragamos said.

"The demon did flee the city," Hilda noted.

"Possibly a ruse," Beragamos said. "Clearly he must have wanted to confront Talarius so he could take our forces unaware and unencrypt our ciphers while supposedly battling Talarius."

Sentir twisted his head to Beragamos. "So you are thinking that Talarius's initial victories were because the demon was busy cracking our ciphers?"

Beragamos bobbed his head slightly in a nod, acknowledging his own reasoning. "That would explain much of what we witnessed. At first, I thought it might have been simply a fake-out. However, if he was, in fact, occupied in infiltrating our streams, then Talarius might truly have gotten the upper hand for a bit."

"Devious." Moradel shook his head. "I will need to think about this."

"As will we all," Sentir Fallon agreed.

"What is clear," Beragamos said, "is that we need you, Hilda, to keep a close eye on Lenamare. He now appears to be our best link to this demon. At some point they will be in contact again."

"That is also the sword's reckoning," Hilda said.

"You've had more contact with Talarius's sword?" Moradel asked.

Hilda frowned. "Yes; it seems he has decided to appropriate my living room as his base of operations. He spends his downtime standing in a corner."

"That seems a bit intrusive —standing in a corner watching you and your servant," Sentir Fallon noted.

"It is, but it is much better than if it were to sit on the couch or a chair. The furniture would be slashed to pieces and we'd have to reimburse the inn." Hilda grimaced, thinking about this.

Moradel chuckled. "I admit that I do enjoy your positive attitude, Hilda!"

"So, back to the current issue. Our next step?" Beragamos asked.

"Assuming this is, as we suspect, a plot by a demon prince, whether actually Orcus or not, we need to start marshalling our forces. We can't let this escalate like the last time," Moradel said while turning to Sentir Fallon.

"I agree; we need to be prepared for the worst-case scenario," Sentir said firmly.

"We might also want to acquire more information on this book," Beragamos said.

~

DOF +6
Early 3rd Period 16-03-04

"I need a shower!" Reggie said after materializing in the parlor.

"I've often said you stink!" Tizzy snarked.

"There you go…" Boggy pointed outside to where the rain continued to fall in the morning light of the volcano. Reggie nodded.

"Why do you need a shower?" Tom asked. He had been over in the corner working on some fighting moves with the mace. He probably should join Rupert in training, but he was afraid it might look awkward if the D'Orcs' supreme general was training as a raw recruit. Although that was probably better than getting his butt handed to him in battle. He shook his head and holstered the mace in his belt.

"Last night was rather skeevy," Reggie said.

"What have you been doing with that mistress of yours that *wasn't* skeevy?" Tizzy asked.

"Last night was 'training' as she called it. She had been a bit disappointed in my lack of experience on some matters, so she decided to teach me about dream sex."

"Dream sex?" Tom was glad Rupert was in combat training.

"Yeah, making love to someone in their dreams while they sleep." Reggie shuddered.

"Astral penetration," Tizzy said, nodding to himself. "Remember me telling you about this?"

Reggie grimaced. "It doesn't seem to me a person can truly give consent in a dream. Sure, they dream that they do, but I don't know. Seems a bit rapey to me. I don't like it."

Tizzy shook his head. "Bad attitude; raping, ravishing, pillaging, torture, mayhem, all are standard tools in the demon toolkit. No point in getting mushy about it."

"You are creepy, you old perv!" Reggie said angrily to Tizzy.

"Thank you," the octopod replied. Reggie just shook his head.

"So, what, your accursed master wants to have sex in her sleep?" Tom asked.

Reggie shrugged. "Apparently. Her and a bunch of friends of hers, I guess."

"A bunch of friends?" Boggy got interested. "You mean like an orgy?"

Reggie shook his head. "No, more like one-on-one romance. Sort of wine and dine and bed them in their dreams. She keeps stressing that I am supposed to romance and love them, pleasure them beyond their wildest dreams, and not force the issue. However, they're still asleep, so…"

"So more like a dream gigolo," Tom said.

"She's pimping you out!" Tizzy giggled.

"Maybe, but either way I'm not that comfortable doing it. She says that many of them are married! They just want some extra romance," Reggie said.

"Well, if they've come to her for assistance, that seems okay," Boggy said.

"Far more ethical than a love potion," Talarius noted. He had remained silent up to this point. "But still, not particularly savory. Sex should only occur within the bounds of matrimony." Talarius shrugged. "Ideally."

"Does your religion allow premarital sex?" Tom asked, suddenly curious.

"Well, it's frowned upon, but not forbidden. As a rule, it is very disadvantageous for younger women, particularly if they are virgins and using that fact to woo a husband. However, that is more an issue of familial duty than religious duty. Tiernon only demands that the partners respect each other and don't take advantage of or harm each other, emotionally or physically."

"Hmm, seems oddly rational for a god," Boggy noted. "So are knights, priests and such chaste?"

Talarius shrugged. "That depends on the knight and his or her vows. As far as priests, monks and Sisters, that is a function of their order. If one joins an order that has a vow of chastity, one has to keep one's vows, the same as joining an order with a vow of silence."

"Hmm, seems rather reasonable to me," Tom said. Talarius gave him an odd look. Or maybe he did, it was very hard to tell through the helmet, even with the visor up.

"You know, I can lower the temperature in this room if you want to get out of your armor for a bit," Tom said suddenly.

"What trick is this?" Talarius demanded, suddenly on his guard.

"There are all sorts of crazy runes hidden in the walls," Tom said, "including runes for heat, cold, air purification. As it is, it is actually cool enough now that you would not die, you would just be uncomfortably hot. I can cool it even more."

"And then, once I'm out of my armor, you turn on the heat and bake me!" Talarius said.

Tom glared at him. "At what point will you start taking me for my word? When have I ever violated my word to you?" He bent his head and stared straight at the knight. "Can you say the same?" Talarius did not respond.

Tom shook his head. "I tell you what. Follow me." He headed into the room that Talarius had been sleeping in. "I'm going to show you the runes for heat and cold. I will be glad to power them, but if you prefer, you can power them yourself, assuming you know how. Which to be honest, I am not sure how to tell you, given that I am an animage and you are a Knight Rampant. In any event, once I show you, you can come in here and cool it when I'm gone, and I won't know that you are not in your armor and ready for roasting."

"I think you meant to say he is a Paladin!" Tizzy shouted behind them as they entered the knight's room. Talarius stuck his fist out behind him, making a rude gesture at the demon.

Tizzy smiled and turned to Boggy. "He's growing on me. I'm starting to like him." Boggy just shook his head as Tizzy asked, "Do you think maybe he's starting to like me?"

~

Tom stood looking over the maps in the command center. Zelda, Arg-nargoloth, Darg-Krallnom, Roth Tar Gorefest and Vargg Agnoth were also around the large table. It was rather an impressive mapping system. Like most things in the complex, it was rune powered and could display a vast array of three-dimensional maps of the Abyss and other worlds.

"How many worlds does it contain maps for?" Tom asked.

Zelda was shaking her head in amazement; the map table had never been powered in her lifetime. Tom himself was amazed; the table was of carved stone, reminiscent of a very large pool table when dormant. Active, it was essentially the 3D map table used in science fiction movies where unscrupulous mining companies schemed to steal Unobtanium from theoretically helpless blue aliens.

"As many as there are tribes with shamans who worshipped you, lord," Vargg said. "The shamans used special crystals you provided to dream travel to the Ethereal Realm of their world and map it. Not all are complete, and obviously after this many years, towns and roads may have changed."

"In the very old days, when we had enough shamans on a world, we could have live views of events on the grounds," Arg-nargoloth said. "That was impressive."

"And frustrating," Darg-Krallnom said.

"Frustrating?" Tom asked.

"We were able to observe your battles with the FOG." Darg-Krallnom shook his head.

"Fog?" Tom asked, not understanding why he, or rather Orcus, would have been fighting *fog*.

"Forces of Good," Vargg said.

"Or so they call themselves," Roth said bitterly.

"Hypocrisy of the highest caliber," Arg-nargoloth said.

"Leave it to both the alfar and the humans and their gods," Roth said. "They have the best media. They always end up spreading their side of the story to the other races, and we always end up looking bad."

"Not always; the Drow and most of the Dok Sidhe have been good allies of the orcs," Vargg noted.

"Not all of our allies have been completely reliable. Many of the so-called 'dark races' are a bit unhinged," Darg-Krallnom noted to Tom on the side.

"I will never work with necromancers again," Roth stated firmly. "Bad news."

Vargg was shaking his head. "I think the real problem is that these groups try to force some sort of huge narrative on everything. Every conflict must be a battle between the so-called 'good' and the so-called 'evil.' It's not just a territorial or trade dispute. No, it's an ultimate battle for the survival of their way of life!"

Arg-nargoloth sighed. "Seriously? A trade route? That's the one thing that allows you to keep your way of life intact. Your entire civilization will collapse without that trade route through our territory, and you can't afford to pay us a toll for traveling on our land?"

"What about grazing lands? Or a mine that they absolutely must have, that we happen to possess?" Darg-Krallnom said. "Really, unless we hand over our mine at sword point, your way of life is over, and the FOG is defeated?"

"In any event," Vargg said, "that was why you, or rather your previous self, so proudly chose to take on the mantle of the FOE, the Forces Of Evil. Someone had to stand up for the oppressed and downtrodden. And you, Great One—you saved us!"

"Your leadership allowed our people to build unified armies to defend ourselves against the depredations of the FOG," Roth said proudly. Once again, Tom was feeling a heck of a lot of weight on his shoulders. What had he signed up for?

"So…" Tom said, attempting to move the topic along and pull this group out of the funk it had suddenly descended into. Who had ever heard of depressed orcs? Tom wondered, but maybe that was just FOG propaganda. "We need game for the feast; that means we need to send out hunting parties, which means we need to open gateways to the Planes of Orcs and the localverse, and that means reestablishing links with any remaining shamans."

Vargg sighed and scratched his chin. "After this long, it may be tricky. On none of the planes do our people live longer than about one hundred Abyssal years, maximum."

"Generally, a lot less," Darg-Krallnom snorted.

"Shamans live longer than most warriors," Roth said.

"In any event…" Vargg cut them off. "The temple will have link stones to the various tribes. On the off chance anyone out there is listening, you may be able to contact them."

"The temple?" Tom asked.

Vargg grinned. "We call it 'the temple' because it's where we store the talismans that are the other side of the shamanic links, and thus it is where the dream walkers are drawn to."

"That makes sense," Tom said.

"Back in the day, we had someone monitoring it in case a dream walker showed up," Arg-nargoloth said. "If we are activating the links, we may want to do that again." Tom nodded in agreement.

"I will set up a rotation schedule so someone is always on duty. In fact, I believe my great grandfather said his father had two on duty at all times," Zelda told Tom.

"Indeed he did," Vargg agreed. "Kept them from falling asleep, and if a dream walker did appear, there was always another to attend the dream walker while the first called on the master or steward."

"Excellent; let's head over to the temple to see who we can contact," Tom said.

"As you wish, My Lord." Zelda nodded with a truly horrifying smile. "The Temple of Doom awaits!"

Tom blinked at her in surprise and then grinned himself. Naturally, one would expect the temple in Mount Doom to be the Temple of Doom!

~

Exador materialized in the arrival alcove in his suite in Freehold. Time to deal with the Council and get the details of what had been going on since his forced departure. He did not expect it to be pleasant, but it should still be better than listening to his Nysegard allies whine about their defeat at the hands of the Nimbus.

If they were going to whine like this after their own failure to marshal sufficient forces to take advantage of the intelligence he had provided, it would probably have been better to not have told them. Talk about ungrateful.

That is odd, Exador thought to himself, suddenly realizing that the wards to his suite had been triggered. Someone had been in his suite, at least once.

He had not received an alert due to Lenamare's giant barrier, or so he assumed. This was quite unusual; Exador went around his suite, through the multiple rooms but did not see anything obviously missing. Nothing sensitive was kept here. His laboratory was a different matter, but he could sense that the wards were on and fine. Perhaps Randolf would know something.

Exador headed out, down the hall in the direction of Randolf's suite. As he walked along, he surveyed the damage done by his escaping demons. He had to admit this whole fiasco had been a learning experience; he shook his head thinking about it. It took him a good ten minutes, but he finally decided that people he was encountering were acting a bit odd.

Not everyone, but several people he passed gave him odd looks. Once he noticed the first person or two, he noted what he thought were people whispering behind him as he proceeded. Something was definitely amiss; very few people were willing to look him in the eye.

This was not normal. True, given his normal temperament and reputation, not that many people enjoyed making eye contact with him, but rarely was it this obvious. As he came closer to Randolf's quarters, he encountered more of Randolf's lackeys; all of them seemed to give him a wide berth.

Exador spotted Bartholomew, Randolf's lord chamberlain. "Lord Chamberlain!" Exador hailed the man. Bartholomew turned at the hailing; was it his imagination or did the man seem to wince and then swallow, suddenly seeming very uncomfortable? "Is the archimage in his rooms?"

"Ah… as far as I know, Magi," Bartholomew said nervously.

"Good. Run ahead and tell him that I am coming for a visit. I would hate to arrive unannounced and interrupt his consultations with Crispin." Exador gave the chamberlain a malicious grin. He knew the man hated to be reminded of the archimage's activities. Personally, Exador found simple pederasty to be a bit "vanilla" for his own tastes, but to each his own.

The lord chamberlain scurried off to find Randolf while Exador headed to Randolf's formal parlor. He entered the parlor and took his accustomed seat to await Randolf's arrival. While he waited, he contemplated the best ways to make Randolf uncomfortable. Certainly, simply explaining the odd behavior of the people in the palace should make the man uncomfortable. Actually, everything made Randolf uncomfortable; that was one pleasant thing about the man.

The other door opened and Randolf came in, looking hurried and harried as ever. "My dear Exador! So good to see you again!" Exador stood and shook the archimage's hand; they did not go into the formal title thing. Technically, Randolf was his liege, but the archimage did not push the issue.

"I had to leave suddenly the other day; I am sure you made appropriate excuses to the Council for me?" Exador asked as they both sat down.

Randolf gave him a rather odd, sickly grin. "Yes, well… I tried…" Exador raised an eyebrow, questioning Randolf's statement. Randolf grimaced. "It seems there was well, some awkwardness."

"Awkwardness?" Exador asked.

"Yes, well, as you know, there was this interesting battle outside the walls between Lenamare's greater demon and the Knight Rampant Talarius."

Randolf looked at him, clearly indicating that Randolf knew that Exador knew, despite the fact that Exador had planned to say he had left before the wards went up and forced the demons out.

Exador adjusted and said, "Yes, I have been made aware."

Randolf grimaced a bit more. "Well, my dear Exador, that's sort of where the complication comes in."

Exador shook his head slightly, not following.

Randolf made a sort of disturbed hand motion and said, "Well, I suppose I just need to get this out there."

Exador simply stared at the archimage.

"The Oorstemothians balled the entire thing and a special meeting of the Council was called that afternoon to watch the balling," Randolf told Exador.

The mage shrugged. "So the Council had a close-up view of this battle and the rather remarkable events. I am sure they were quite shocked."

"Oh, indeed, indeed they were. However, the battle was only one of two things the Council found interesting."

"Oh, yes?" Exador was getting impatient; the whining imbecile would not get to the point.

"Well, by pure happenstance, Alexandros Mien noticed something in the background at one point and drew the Council's attention to it," Randolf said hesitantly.

"Yes, already. Spit it out."

"We zoomed in to discover a flying carpet watching the battle," Randolf said.

Exador felt his eyes hardening in their sockets. He twitched his mouth into a small, tight smile. "A flying carpet?"

"Yes." Randolf grimaced again. "There seemed to be something of tea party going on between the three occupants as they watched the battle."

"Do go on," Exador said through clenched teeth.

"Yes, it appeared, at least, to everyone other than myself, of course"— Randolf gave Exador one of his sickly grins —"that you were one of the occupants, along with a woman of Natooran descent and a gentleman who looked remarkably like the portraits of the Anilord Time Warrior, Ramses the Damned."

"Indeed, I did have a nice viewpoint for the battle," Exador said, forcing himself to be calm. "I take it that the Council found it unusual that I might have chosen to watch the battle from outside the city walls?"

Randolf gulped and looked around, clearly hoping for a cup of tea or some other object to allow a mild distraction. "Well, as you may recall, the Knight Rampant, Talarius, had claimed that there were three archdemons in the palace."

"I do seem to recall that," Exador said tightly.

"I know it's ridiculous and I assured everyone on the Council that it was completely impossible…"

"But?" Exador prompted.

"But they seem to have this silly notion that the three individuals on the flying carpet were the three archdemons who had been expelled by Lenamare's pentacles," Randolf finished rather timidly.

Exador sat there staring at Randolf for several long moments. Several very long, very uncomfortable moments as Exador watched Randolf sweat. Finally, when it looked like Randolf could take it no more, Exador suddenly burst out laughing, slapping his thighs and bending over in his chair in a completely uncharacteristic display of mirth.

"Gods above and below!" Exador wheezed when he had finally stopped laughing hard enough to breathe in some air. "Me? An archdemon? That is incredibly rich! Oh, I cannot believe it! I have never been so flattered in my entire life!"

Randolf stared at his magi. Clearly, this was not the response the archimage had been expecting. Exador got up, still bent over from laughter, and moved closer to the archimage, clasping him on the shoulder. Randolf could see the tears of laughter running down Exador's cheeks.

"Truly, my friend, you have made my day!" Exador hugged him. "You have no idea how funny this is! I think this has to be one of the best moments of my life." Exador stood up, wincing as he placed his hand on his side, obviously tending a stitch from laughter. "To think the entire Council of Wizardry, including that fool Lenamare, thinks that I, Exador of Turelane, am an archdemon!" He shook his head. "This is just too rich! No wonder everyone was looking at me so oddly."

The mage started pacing to work off his laughter, his smile wider than Randolf had ever seen it. "I think I shall enjoy their tiptoeing and fearful gazes a bit longer before disabusing them of this ludicrous notion!" Exador turned and grinned quite broadly at the stunned Randolf.

Chapter 102

DOF +6
Late Afternoon (Murgatroy Time) 16-03-440

Tal Gor El Crooked Stick trudged down to the stream to fill his leather water bag. His scrying exercises were using up a lot of water, and this meant he had to spend an inordinate amount of time trudging back and forth from his small tent to the stream. This in turn meant he was spending quite a bit of time in pain. The weight of the water basket on the end of his carrying staff put quite a bit of strain on his bad leg. Once again he cursed the fates for allowing him to live after he had failed to kill the wyvern that had mangled his left leg. If he had died like Dar Oth Non, Sep Tar On and Fer Bar Seth, at least he would not have to live with being a crippled apprentice shaman to a dying shaman of a less than sober bearing.

He had dreamed his whole life of being a great hunter and warrior like his father, Sal Gor El Crooked Stick; his mother, Mar An Crooked Stick; his sister, Soo An Crooked Stick; and his two older brothers, Bor Tal El Crooked Stick and Fel Nor El Crooked Stick. Okay, to be fair, he had dreamed of being a greater warrior than his older siblings. Instead, on his second hunting expedition they had encountered a wyvern that had managed to kill the rest of the hunting party before his father, who had been trailing half a league behind the young hunters for just such emergencies, had arrived to finish off the wyvern.

Horrgus Trifeather, the shaman, had been off at a trading post in Murgatroy and only the healing woman, Fesha No Al, had been around to tend him for the first two days. By the time the shaman had returned, his wounds had set in and while between the two of them, his life had been spared, he would never be truly fit for battle again.

That had been four years ago, shortly after he turned thirteen. If not for the shaman detecting a spark of spirit magic within him, he would have been reduced to being a cook's assistant or some similarly ignoble fate. As it was, he had become apprentice to Horrgus.

He should not complain; shaman was an honored position. Even if the tribe's own shaman was a bit—well, *drunk* was the only word he could come up with. He might have said "shabby," but to be fair, the entire Crooked Stick tribe was a bit shabby and poor these days. The tribe was down to only three bands, totaling no more than 150 warriors and another forty or so children and others, including one shaman and his apprentice.

Tal Gor trudged along, waving to Feth Bar, the lad currently tasked with bringing dinner to the warg camp. The boy was pulling the meat cart, which was currently filled with several large, squirming and roiling sacks. Tal Gor smiled; the wargs were getting live meat tonight. They would be happy. They really only had the resources to capture live game for the wargs a few times a week. Most of the time they fed wargs from the scraps and entrails from the band's primary kills. It just took too much time and effort to catch and preserve live game for them every day.

Not that there were that many wargs. They did not even have enough for every warrior in the tribe. Certainly not one for Tal Gor to ride regularly. Only on migrations did he get to ride. On those long journeys, his leg had proven to slow him and thus the tribe down. In the old days, he would probably have been left to die or given the coup; but in this day and age, the tribe needed every semi-able hand they could get.

Tal Gor eventually made it back to his tent with his water bucket. He hung it on its small tripod and sat down on his pillow to massage his aching leg. He peered into the empty copper bowl he had been using for scrying. He had not been getting much in the way of results. Today he had worked with chemical components to effect a Viewing; five attempts and nothing. He really was not much of a shaman. He sighed as he rubbed his leg to ease the pain. He would never even be as good sober as Horrgus was drunk.

Tal Gor liked to think all this was not just him. His entire tribe was not what it used to be. He snorted, remembering two years ago on the western plains when the tribe had passed by one of the abandoned fortresses raised by Ferundy thousands of year ago to defend the land from the Orc Hordes. Horrgus had told them that the Ferunds had built multiple lines of defense, fortresses behind fortresses to hold back the tribes. Today the Ferunds only garrisoned the inner fortresses, and barely those. The tribes had not been able to mount a credible force in hundreds of years, and even that last one had been nothing compared to the great days thousands of years ago.

He shook his head and bent over to rummage through the loose pile of mementos that he held on to for no good reason. He grabbed the one that had captured his imagination the most when he first found it buried deep in one of Horrgus's trunks. It was a roundish stone with two protrusions on the sides near the top, like horns, or so Tal Gor imagined. The worn and barely recognizable face of some orc-like creature was carved on the front of the stone. Horrgus had laughed and said that it was the scrying stone of a long-dead god. The thought of such a god had resonated with him. It seemed to perfectly symbolize the fortunes of his tribe, and his own dreams. He had pestered Horrgus for details of the god, but the shaman had put him off time and again. Only slowly over the years had he learned the tales that Horrgus knew regarding the dead god. Only slowly had he been able to connect the long-dead god to myths told by storytellers.

The tales had been fantastic; at every feast or gathering of the tribes he would ply other shamans and history tellers, as well as storytellers, with questions about the long-dead god. Eventually, he became a sort of resident expert. No one particularly cared about the long-dead god anymore. Even though all remembered his name, and the warriors and history tellers told stories of him now and then, they all considered the god and any related tales fictitious. This was why it took Tal Gor nearly a year to put together the myth of the storytellers with the talisman of the long-dead god. Once he had started to know more, he had enjoyed pretending that he was the last shaman dedicated to the long-dead god.

DOF +6
Evening (Murgatroy Time) 16-03-440

Tal Gor returned to his tent, ready for bed. Tonight had been his night to help with cleanup and he had spent the pot-scrubbing ordeal listening to his brothers and their friends discussing their last hunting trip and their bravery. He wished so much that he could go hunting again, but he was too much of a burden on the others. It was an old complaint of his; he should get over it. Most nights when he did not have to be out by the main fires, he would return to his tent to study or practice.

He really should work more on his scrying, but he was tired and really did not feel like making another useless attempt. His agitation was enough, though, that he would probably have trouble sleeping if he went to bed immediately. He frowned and then smiled on seeing his dead god's talisman.

He quickly filled his copper bowl from the water bag. He lit two candles on small wooden stands on each side of the bowl. He then sprinkled scrying herbs in the water. He was the priest of the Lord of the Underworld, the mighty demon lord Orcus! He needed to summon his deity to advise him on a matter of great import.

He grabbed his dagger and pulled it from its sheath. He cut the palm of his left hand and, laying the dagger aside as blood lightly filled his palm from the cut, he picked up the talisman and placed it facedown in his palm to feed the god's mouth his blood.

"*Orgnath falgon, zartoth Orcus!*" Tal Gor chanted softly. He did not want others hearing his games. He was basically ad libbing, putting together normal chants to the spirits with what he imagined he would need to contact a deity. "*Anoboth, trigoshlog, nargh fal doth toman. Graghl foth zartoth!*"

He thrust his fist with the talisman into the water… and screeched as the cut in his hand burned with pain. The herbs were apparently painful against the open wound, or so Tal Gor thought until he started getting woozy and the room started to swirl around him. He glanced worriedly down at the bowl. Had he cut too deep? Was his life's blood overfilling the basin?

Red blood swirled in the water, casting a red tint to the reflected candle light. The bowl was oddly bright and shimmering. What was that in the bowl? Tal Gor wondered woozily. It was not his reflection. The young shaman suddenly passed out.

"Well, that was faster than I would have expected," a craggy baritone voice crackled. It sounded like that of an elder warrior.

"What are you talking about?" another deep but female voice asked.

An extremely bass and darkly disturbing voice said, "Use your demon sight. We have an insubstantial visitor that has just joined us." *Demon sight?* Tal Gor wondered groggily, trying to open his suddenly sleep-heavy eyelids.

"Over by the calling stone with Astlan's symbol on it," a third craggy voice stated. "A dream walker has come to us."

"Ahh, I see. He looks rather young," the woman's voice said.

"Interesting in that we had not actually tried calling to him; yet he shows up on his own shortly after the temple's runes were reactivated," the disturbing deep voice said.

Tal Gor finally managed to get his eyes open and stared in awe at the room around him. He was sitting on the floor hugging a large silver talisman that looked very much like his stone talisman, yet unworn. He was in a large, carved-stone chamber with a number of large pillars around the edges. He himself was seated between two of the pillars. The voices were coming from the other side of the room, about twenty feet away. There were five very large, very odd-looking orcs and an even larger something else.

The odd-looking orcs were impressively massive, yet had cloven hooves and wings. The orcs were of widely varying colors. The giant creature was truly frightening; it had a lower body like that of a satyr, but instead of being hairy, this being was scaly and had a long tail with a spade on the end. The being's upper torso was very orc-like, but hugely massive, with far better defined musculature than any orc he had ever seen. The being had huge bat-like wings, not unlike the weird orcs, just a lot bigger. His arms were huge with massive claws. His muzzle was more snout-like than that of an orc, more bestial with huge fangs rather than tusks, and very sharp teeth. The demon, for clearly it could be nothing else, also had huge horns, much like on the talisman.

Tal Gor gulped as he stared at the creatures, who were staring back at him as well. Finally, Tal Gor stammered, "M- My Lord God Orcus?" It was probably hard to hear, but he was feeling rather stunned.

"Well, at least the boy knows where he is," the woman, who was standing next to the large demon, said.

The large demon, or so Orcus Tal Gor supposed it was, grinned. At least, Tal Gor hoped that that horrifying visage was a grin. "I am Tommus," it said, "the new Master of Mount Doom. What is your name?"

"Tal Gor El Crooked Stick, son of Sal Gor El and Mar An Crooked Stick. I am apprentice shaman for the Crooked Stick tribe."

"Vespa will be pleased that one of her tribe was the first to actually contact us," the woman said.

A man who had not spoken before said, "I must admit, the Crooked Stick bloodline must be strong if an apprentice shaman can seek out and find this temple on his own after all this time. I had expected that locating any shaman still capable of hearing us would have been a task, and here an apprentice comes to us before we call."

The giant demon stood; it had been seated on a low-backed throne behind an altar. It was huge, twice the height of Tal Gor. It pulled a huge mace with a metal version of the talisman as the ball of the mace. It walked over and stood before Tal Gor. "Rise, shaman," it commanded.

Tal Gor gulped and stood up. Surprisingly, he felt no pain as he stood. He glanced down at his leg to see it as it always was, yet it did not hurt.

The demon lord noticed his glance. "So you've been wounded?"

"Yes, My Lord. I am sorry for my weakness," Tal Gor said, looking to the ground ashamed.

The demon lord chuckled. "Strength comes in many forms. Do not belittle yourself. You have come here today, uncalled when we were about to look for you. Your strength as a shaman has impressed the commanders of the D'Orcs, and it has impressed me. You have chosen to come to me, and I could use your assistance. Will you swear to be my shaman?"

Still in shock, Tal Gor nodded.

"Grasp the head of my mace and swear by your name and tribe that you shall serve me faithfully as my shaman," Dark Lord Tommus commanded.

Tal Gor reached out and grasped the head of the mace with his cut hand. "I, Tal Gor El Crooked Stick, son of Sal Gor El Crooked Stick and Mar An Crooked Stick, Apprentice of Horrgus Trifeather, do hereby solemnly swear to be shaman of Lord Tommus, Master of Mount Doom, with all the duties and responsibilities that ensue." Tal Gor was improvising based on other oath-taking ceremonies he knew of; specifically, the shamanic oaths of service.

"I, Tommus, Master of Mount Doom, do hereby take thee, Tal Gor El Crooked Stick, to be my shaman with all the duties and responsibilities that ensue."

Suddenly, Tal Gor felt himself overwhelmed by the presence of Tommus. Strange visions and things he did not understand swept through him and he felt weak and dizzy and lost, and then suddenly he felt a warmth and an embracing that was unlike anything he'd felt before.

Tal Gor, return to your sleep now. My commanders and I shall have work for you. We will need to hunt, a great deal, and will need your assistance to come into your realm. I shall contact you when the time is right, Lord Tommus boomed inside Tal Gor's mind.

~

Tom waited for his new shaman to disappear before turning to his commanders. "Well, that went strangely well."

"Indeed. Would that shamans from other planes came so easily," Darg-Krallnom said.

"I have, obviously, never witnessed a shamanic binding before," Zelda said.

Tom shrugged. "To be honest, I have never done one before. I based it on what I've done before for binding warlocks and similar tasks."

"It seemed pretty much identical to what your previous self did," Arg-nargoloth said. "The words were different, but then, the ritual always varied according to the individual."

Tom hoped so; he did not know for sure he was doing any of it right, warlock or shaman. He had spent considerable time analyzing what he had done with Vaselle, comparing it to his possession experiences, and had tried to refine it, make it less intrusive. He was not sure a warlock binding and a shaman binding would be the same, but he presumed they would be similar. Did not shamans channel spirits, sometimes being possessed? And presumably the shaman would want to call on his aid or power. Tom was not sure how such power sharing might work, although the *aid* part at least made some sense. He had a link to both Vaselle and Tal Gor and could roughly sense where they were. Presumably, he could send mana down that link the same way whoever had been upstream of the priests sent mana down to them.

"So that's one down in Astlan. We should see about contacting some more shamans," Tom said.

"I was thinking on the glargh," Roth said, and Tom looked to the commander. "Neth Darthelm, Zog's father, used to brag of how they 'mass produced' glargh in giant barrels on moving platforms in large breweries on planets that their tribe inhabited."

Tom nodded. "A spacefaring tribe would probably have access to advanced manufacturing and mass production." Except for Roth, the commanders looked at him as if he was speaking a foreign tongue. "Meaning I agree, that might be the best option," he quickly added.

"For the hunting though, we want to do that the normal way. We have many warriors that would love to hunt the Planes of Orcs again," Vargg said.

Zelda laughed. "Do you have any idea how many people have requested to be in a hunting party?"

Tom shrugged. "If we get enough shamans, perhaps we should do this more often. I think it would do a lot to sharpen skills and work off frustration."

Darg nodded. "I like that idea, and I am sure the D'Wargs would like it as well."

D'Wargs? Tom wondered. Like demon wargs, giant demon wolves ridden by orcs in Tolkien's and other fantasy books. "You have both D'Wargs and hydra hounds?" he asked.

Vargg nodded. "The hounds are a bit small for riding."

"And they tend to roast the prey before we get a chance to kill it," Darg-Krallnom added.

"The hydra hounds go sort of flame crazy when they get out of the Abyss. Everyone here is immune to fire so they never get to toast anyone," Roth said, shaking his head in sorrow for the poor hydra hounds.

"I like my bison and ox on the bloody side; I'm not a fan of eating cinders and ash," Vargg said.

"I'm hoping we can catch some wyvern," Darg-Krallnom said. "You have any idea how long since I've had a wyvern steak?"

"About as long as it's been since I've eaten anything," Roth said.

"Or any*one*," Arg-nargoloth finally chimed in, and the D'Orcs all laughed. Arg-nargoloth had been over examining various talismans and had finally wandered back to the group. "I've got a likely-looking one from Etterdam here," he said, holding up a silver talisman. They had all noted that some of the talismans were shinier than others. He was not sure if that meant anything, but the Astlanian one that Tal Gor had appeared around had been shinier, and was even brighter now.

Tom shrugged. "Well, let's give it a try and see if anyone is home."

~

DOF +6
Sixth Period 16-03-440

Talarius sighed with pleasure. It was the first such sigh he had uttered in a very long time. The pleasure was coming from the gloriously wet washcloth he had dunked in the washbasin full of rainwater in his room. He had finally decided to let his guard down, a small amount. The demon Tom was out with the D'Orcs, probably planning a war to take over the multiverse, so Talarius had filled the large washbasin in his D'Orc-proportioned room off of Tom's suite with rain water from the balcony and brought it back to his room.

He had then shut the door and barred it with the wardrobe. He knew it would not stop the demon entering, but perhaps he would have enough warning to get some of his armor back on. He had then cooled the room using the rune that the demon had shown him. Finally, for the first time in what felt like an eternity, he had peeled his armor off, along with the padding.

Tiernon almighty, did that feel good! There was no soap, but he did not care; he scrubbed himself clean with the washcloth. It felt so sinfully pleasant. The water was quite warm, but still cooler than any place outside this bedroom. He savored the opportunity to wipe the dried blood, sweat and caked dirt from his skin and his healed wounds. To be outside his reeking armor! Yes, it was a sustainable environment under adverse conditions, but sustainable was not the same as comfortable. Not when the outside temperature was nearly the boiling point of water.

It felt so good to be clean. Talarius stared at his underclothes and padding. How he wished he had the time to wash them out and let them dry. However, he clearly did not. He had no idea how long the demon would be distracted with his machinations. The best he could hope for was to let the clothes dry out from his own sweat and stench.

Talarius glanced at the bed. It was quite large, yet not unnaturally so, and oddly comfortable, even in his armor. Why a demon—or more precisely, a D'Orc would need a bed was a bit strange. Demons notably did not sleep. True, the demon Tom did, but then he had been busy charging the fortress. Rupert and Reggie slept, but they had been doing so in the cave. As far as he could tell, Boggy, Antefalken and Estrebrius never slept, and Tiernon knew that damn multi-limbed menace never shut up. If it was not talking to someone, it was talking to itself. Talarius shook his head. The only time it was silent was when it was billowing foul-smelling smoke from its pipe.

Talarius glanced again at the bed. It was night, he was quite tired, and he was powering the cool rune, so he might want to conserve his energy. Maybe if he arranged his armor for quick dressing, he might be able to lie down for a few minutes. Of course, "quick" dressing took about a third to half an hour but he would at least get his breast plate on before he was overwhelmed by demons. He would keep the Rod of Smiting in his hand, just in case.

~

"So how did your beloved servant, Exador, take the news that he is an archdemon?" Crispin asked Randolf as the wizard entered his bedroom.

Randolf frowned and then sighed. "Far better than I'd have hoped, or for that matter, feared." He shook his head. "I was fully prepared for him to take it very badly; in fact, I expected a rather destructive reaction," he said as removed his dressing gown and hung it up.

"He wasn't his normal destructive self?" Crispin asked, puzzled.

Randolf shook his head. "Quite the contrary; he laughed his head off. Never in my life have I seen him more amused. He acted like he'd just pulled off the greatest joke imaginable upon the Council."

Crispin frowned. "That seems very odd."

"Indeed," Randolf said, sliding into bed. "He was so convincingly moved by the preposterousness of the very idea that he almost had me believing it was all some sort of hoax. If I didn't know the man better than anyone else on the plane, I'd have been tempted to believe him."

"So what, then?" Crispin asked. "Is he just going to brazenly go around and laugh his ass off at whomever is so ridiculous as to accuse him of being an archdemon?"

"Perhaps." Randolf shrugged. "There are not a lot of good ways for him to salvage something like this. He'll need to come up with some good excuses as to who his compatriots are and why they were out there on a carpet, as well as provide counter suggestions as to who the archdemons were, if not he and his compatriots."

"That seems like a very tall order," Crispin observed. "However, probably not as hard as convincing Ruiden that he is not responsible for the demon that kidnapped Talarius."

Randolf chuckled. "Either way, I should hope so; I don't want Exador wiggling out of this. He needs to be exposed once and for all," he said. "I'm going to need the Council's help to banish him from this plane for eternity."

Crispin chuckled. "I am reasonably certain that, no matter what else, Lenamare will volunteer to help you!"

Randolf grinned back at the djinn as he moved in for a kiss.

~

Hilda sighed as she relaxed in her bubble bath. It had been a somewhat vexing day. She had spent a good deal of it doing what she called "deep snooping." She had tried, unsuccessfully, to detect any signs of Lenamare being a warlock. Quite difficult, it turned out. They had all eaten lunch today and Hilda had noted that while Lenamare was famous for so many things, it was clear that his true forte was conjury. She had gently pleaded with him to recount how he had decided and then succeeded in becoming the preeminent expert on demonology in the world; unsurprisingly, it had not taken much effort.

The "interview" had taken another three hours. Poor Trisfelt had had it far worse, and the poor man was nodding off every few minutes after the first hour. However, it was amusing to watch Jehenna's reactions to some of Lenamare's accounts. Between Jehenna's reactions and Hilda's own truth readings, she felt like she was getting a fairly accurate accounting. That was what was so frustrating. There was not much there.

After that first hour, she decided to get a bit more technical; something she could do given her own knowledge of multiversal topology. Those classes in Tierhallon had finally been useful for something! She kept the admiration going, but peppered the dialog with observations and technical questions that she knew the answer to so as to get him to dig deeper and reveal information that a normal mortal would not, particularly when it came to bindings, links and similar magic. The large basket of wines she had brought as a lunch gift also helped Lenamare relax; but again, to no avail.

She eventually had to dial it back as Jehenna started to show signs of puzzlement at Hilda's rather advanced knowledge. Lenamare was too wrapped up in his own story to notice, but Jehenna, having heard it all before, could pay more attention to Hilda. That was dangerous, so Hilda worked to assuage her concerns by emphasizing her general animage training. Jehenna would have no knowledge of that. Hilda also purposefully mentioned a few common misperceptions and mistakes people made, so as not to seem too much the expert.

During all of this she had also had her saint sight on; yet again, to no avail. For one thing, the man had a lot of links and bindings on him. Jehenna quite a few herself. All of them, however, seemed to be traditional one-way bindings or very simple link spells. She traced them all and saw nothing remotely similar to a clerical upstream link, which is what she supposed a warlock would have.

The long conversation had given her plenty of opportunity to examine him, and it was truly frustrating! The man seemed to be exactly what he said he was.

Further, his ego was so clear in all of this, she was not sure he was even capable of collaborating with another wizard who was not subservient to him, let alone a greater demon or higher.

She took a sip of sparkling wine. She had needed to stay sober this afternoon while the others had gone through that exquisite collection of fine wines. So frustrating to not fully enjoy those luscious wines. Tonight, though, she would make amends. She plucked a chocolate-covered strawberry from the table beside her and bit into it, relishing the sweetness.

~

Ragala-nargoloth was roused from her slumber by a very odd sound. The shaman sat up on her cot and looked around her tent. It was a rattling noise and it seemed to be coming from a chest on the other side of the tent. The chest she actually used as a table because she had not needed anything in the chest for a decade or more.

"What in the dried-up tusk of Risk Athanon's mug could that be?" Ragala-nargoloth climbed out of bed, made her way to the chest, and quickly began taking items off the lid so she could open it. After clearing the tabletop, she opened the lid.

Nothing was rattling on the top shelf, so she removed that. The lower layer was just a big open box filled with trinkets, totems, amulets, jewelry and talismans. She dug through them, moving in the direction of the vibration that was rattling all of the items. Her hand grasped something on the bottom; a lumpy round stone by the feel of it.

As she fully grasped it, what felt like electricity lanced through her body. It hurt, and this naturally ticked her off. She grunted in frustration and pulled the stupid rock out of the trunk, wanting to smash the thing. "*Ffargdar Quetusqare Fardus*," Ragala-nargoloth muttered, causing the candles in her tent to light so she could more clearly see the offending object.

She squinted at it and snorted. It was the Talisman of Orcus! "What in the name of the Bloody Bilestone?" she asked herself aloud. "You've been dead for four thousand years! Not since the days of Tiss-Arog-Dal has anyone even talked about you!"

Ragala-nargoloth grabbed a fistful of Tikaraok powder as she moved to a meditation position. She quickly snorted the powder and centered herself, looking with her Sight into the talisman. "Bloody fragging Bilestone's bones!" she shouted as she felt herself almost forcibly pulled into dream space.

Ragala-nargoloth blinked as the world shifted around her. Suddenly she found herself not in her tent but in some sort of stone temple between two columns. Instead of the small stone talisman, there was a bright silver talisman in her lap that she, or rather her dream self was clutching. Her head was reeling and she felt incredibly disoriented.

She looked around the room to see several very odd-looking orcs with wings and hooves. D'Orcs? They could not be; D'Orcs were long gone from the localverse. As she eyed the apparent impossibilities, she suddenly recognized one from a stone painting in one of the tribe's holy sites.

"Arg-nargoloth?" Ragala-nargoloth breathed in disbelief. The greatest warrior in her family's bloodline—the most revered of all her ancestors?

"Hah!" the vision of Arg-nargoloth roared in triumph. "My name lives on, my blood survives! Name yourself, shaman!"

"I—I am Ragala-nargoloth, First Shaman of the Nart Tribe," she said in shock.

Arg-nargoloth nodded in obvious satisfaction. "When we have more time, you must recite your lineage to me so that I may know of my heirs and of their triumphs!" He was chuckling with nearly unbridled joy, it seemed.

Ragala-nargoloth noticed someone rising behind Arg-nargoloth. This someone was very large, and not a D'Orc. As the being moved into view, she saw a giant mace, a rod, a wand swinging at his belt. She felt her blood go cold, or was it hot? She had no idea. No one remembered what Orcus looked like, other than that he was different, not a D'Orc, and that he had possessed a giant mace, the Wand of Orcus. This mace, with its metal head that looked identical to the demon lord's own head, could only be the Wand of Orcus.

Ragala-nargoloth quickly abased herself before the demon lord. "My Lord and master, as the prophecy of Tiss-Arog-Dal has foretold, you have returned!"

"Greetings, Ragala-nargoloth, heir to the blood of Arg-nargoloth. You are welcome in the Temple of Doom." The demon lord pulled his mighty mace from his belt. "I am Tommus, the new Lord of Mount Doom, and I am preparing to accept the oaths of the D'Orcs. We have work to do, now and going forward. Are you willing to assist me?"

Ragala-nargoloth was in shock, which was not something she had ever experienced before. She actually thought "shock" was a weakness of non-orcs, but what she was feeling now could be nothing else. She nodded her head and whispered, "Yes, master." She could not even look the mighty demon lord in the eye at this point.

"Are you ready to be bound to my service?" The mighty demon lord, heir to Orcus asked.

Ragala-nargoloth gulped. "I am, My Lord."

The head of the mace moved towards her head. "Grasp the mace and prepare to repeat after me."

Ragala-nargoloth tentatively raised her left hand and reached out towards the head of the mace and to her new future.

~

DOF +7
Second Period 16-04-440

Tom checked the runes controlling night and day within the mountains. He had discovered they worked pretty well as a clock. It would be dawn before long. They had managed to contact three more shamans beyond Tal Gor and Ragalanargoloth: Beya Fei Geist of the Olafa Horde of Ithgar, Farsooth GoreTusk of the Rockgut Horde on Romdan, and Leftenant Trig Bioblast of the Oak Clan and Second Shaman of the OCSS Skull Crusher in Gormegast.

Leftenant Trig Bioblast caused the most confusion among his commanders, Tom had noted. The shaman had made several technology references that went right over the heads of the D'Orcs present. Tom was at least familiar with science fiction versions of the things Trig had mentioned. He was definitely going to want to visit Gormegast as well as Visteroth, if they made contact with it. He wanted to see a world where technology and magic worked side by side. It seemed extremely implausible, but then at this point he was not in a position to define possible and impossible.

"Zelda, you mentioned wanting to get the first party out with dawn?" Tom asked the steward.

She nodded. "I think it's going to take us a few days to gather enough game and butcher it. Hezbarg and his team have been cleaning up the kitchens. They told me that power has reached the freezers, so we should be able to store our game."

Tom nodded. Yesterday morning Boggy had asked him to make sure the freezers' runes got activated. He had been surprised that the mountains had several large kitchens with cold storage. Apparently, Orcus had been known for throwing parties. In fact, the party they were planning used to be normal for major events. He had suggested that they might make these hunting expeditions routine. To his surprise, Vargg had later mentioned that in the old days, the D'Orcs used to stage hunting expeditions with the various tribes, clans and hordes that had paid homage to Orcus.

Tom found himself a bit disturbed to find that several of his suggestions had been routine operations under Orcus. It was more than just a bit disconcerting. He knew for an undeniable fact that he was not Orcus reincarnated. For one thing, he knew firsthand what that dagger did. If everyone said it had killed Orcus, then it had utterly killed Orcus and destroyed his soul. While not an expert on reincarnation, it seemed logical to believe that one needed some sort of soul to actually reincarnate into a new body.

Tom shuddered, thinking about Orcus's fate. Of course, to be fair, that was what true death was. Therefore, the ritual the Rod had been preparing for all of them would have done the same. That seemed an unbelievably evil thing to do to someone. Of course, back in Jersey, he had not really believed in any sort of afterlife, so why did a true death seem so much more horrible now?

The answer, Tom reflected, was that now he knew that there was, at least for believers, the chance for life after death. Antefalken had stated unequivocally, and the others had all agreed that if Talarius died in the Planes of Orcs/Planes of Men, that he would go to Tierhallon to be with his god. Others had said similar things. That was the thing: heaven and hell were real. Maybe not what his grandparents believed, but there was something. There was also the possibility of nothing. That was what made the difference. Gods were real, and of course; so were demons.

"As I recall, Astlan time in Jötunngard and Doom Time were pretty close," Arg-nargoloth said. "Etterdam and the lands of the Nart were about a period or so behind. I am not sure of the others."

Roth Tar Gorefest nodded. "While obviously I am anxious to return to the hunting grounds of Romdan, I do think we should go in order of shaman. Thus, we first send a band to Astlan, followed by one to Etterdam with its dawn. We move on to the others tomorrow."

Vargg nodded. "We will need the time to process the kills in the kitchens. Everyone is out of practice."

"Some of us have never gotten to practice," Zelda noted somewhat bitterly.

"The price of being fourth generation." Darg-Krallnom laughed, slapping her on the back.

The thought of Zelda being fourth generation D'Orc, born in the Abyss as many of the younger D'Orcs were, made Tom suddenly realize that something was fishy. Demons were immortal, so how did they age? He had just assumed that Rupert had aged because he was half-human, yet clearly he was every bit as powerful, every bit as much a real demon as any first, second or third-order demon. Except, Tom suddenly realized, Rupert stopped aging when he started to show signs of being a demon. He had shape-changed into his younger self and stayed that way. Everyone thought he was younger than he actually was.

Tom shook his head; this did not make a lot of sense. He needed to sort this out, probably with Antefalken or someone else who understood demon physiology. *Clearly not Tizzy, though.* However, this was not the time; they had a hunting trip to plan.

~

Bess took a sip of Denubian Choco-Coffee™ and sighed. "Complications, complications."

Astet chuckled. "Who was it that liked to warn everyone about how lies and deceptions end up entangling one more than chains and ropes?" Astet was drinking iced tea, which she had to work to keep cool in her hand as they were sitting in a rooftop "garden" in the outpost. The plants that would grow in the Abyss were extremely odd plants.

As a goddess associated with Air, she had no problem summoning a nice breeze, but all the air in this quite literally god-forsaken hellhole was insufferably hot. One reason she did not come down here that much. Upon reflection, she supposed the very existence of the outpost meant the place was not completely god-forsaken, but it was still a hellhole.

Bess chuckled. "Yes, it was me." She shook her head. "Those stupid Oorstemothians! Who would expect them to record the whole thing? And capture us on the carpet?"

"Times, they are a changing." Astet shook her head. "When we were in Astlan officially, such wizardry did not exist yet."

"I know; it's one of the things so many of us prefer about the magic-based worlds over the tech worlds. If there is no visual or audio recording of an event, it's a lot easier to tell one group one thing, and another group something else," Bess said with a smile. She had always been big on being up front wherever possible with people. Which is what made her current situation so ironic.

"Takes some of the fun out of godhood, doesn't it? You lose plausible deniability for mysterious actions and such," Astet remarked before taking another sip of her super-chilled iced tea.

"It does sort of put a damper on 'working in mysterious ways,' " Bess agreed.

"So," Astet said, "now you have to pretend to be a mortal wizard in Freehold?"

"It's looking that way." Bess shook her head. "Exador wants us all to show up and demonstrate our humanity."

"And how do you do that?" Astet asked.

Bess shrugged. "I have no idea what Exador plans. Perhaps have them put the wards back up?"

"But didn't that cause you all flee the city?"

Bess chuckled. "It caused *them* to flee the city, and it did rattle my sinuses, making me feel quite twitchy, along with a nasty headache. However, I was able to locate the source very quickly and surmised what was happening. Being the consummate actress, I simply played along with my cover story."

Astet laughed. "That, I will grant you, is one of your skills. I would lose patience, break character and smite those two buffoons."

"Well, I guess it's good that I took on this task." Bess grinned.

"So you are to be a goddess pretending to be an archdemon pretending to be a human?" Astet shook her head from side to side. "Those tangled chains of lies again."

~

Tal Gor tossed restlessly on his sleeping mat. He was still a bit freaked out by his nocturnal experience. Once he had woken from dream walking last night, he had put the talisman on a small tray beside his bed and prepared to bandage his hand. However, he had quickly discovered that the cut was healed and that the palm of his hand was now scarred with what appeared to the same image as the talisman. The ridges of the scar appeared well healed, as if he had had it for years. He shook his head and looked at the talisman. The formerly worn imprint on the stone appeared new and fresh in the candlelight of his tent, rather than worn and old, as it had before his dream walking.

Tal Gor had hurriedly left his tent to tell Horrgus about his experience, but the old shaman had been passed out drunk on his cot. He had then gone to the main fire, where several warriors were still talking and drinking, and tried to tell them about his dream trip, but they had all laughed at him. They insisted he had fallen asleep and had a normal dream, and that he should go back to bed.

It was late and he had been tired, so he had gone back to bed. He needed to think about the events anyway. He supposed it made sense that none of the younger warriors would believe him; he could not really believe it himself. Tal Gor finally sat up. The light of predawn was seeping in through the loose closure of his tent flaps. He crawled over to the water bucket; the tent was so small there was no real point in standing up to get to the leather bucket's tripod.

He grabbed his washrag and dunked it in the water to wash the sleep from his eyes and the dried sweat from his body. As he was doing this, his left hand began tingling.

"Greetings, Tal Gor El Crooked Stick!"

This was weird; Tal Gor could hear Lord Tommus in his head!

"Are you ready to hunt? You may select a total of twenty of your best hunters to join Commander Vespa Crooked Stick and her hunting party. Since the party flies, we will bring D'Wargs for your selected hunters to ride on the hunt."

"Hunt? Ah, I had no idea it would be so soon—I need to gather hunters!" Tal Gor exclaimed in his head.

Lord Tommus grinned in Tal Gor's mind. *"Our hunters are gathering now. They have not been hunting in a very long time and so are anxious to enter Astlan. Make sure you have a good-sized fire going and make room around it for us to come through. I will be reaching out to you shortly to open the gateway!"*

Tal Gor raised his eyebrows in surprise, scrambled from his tent, and hurried quickly to the main campfire, where the band was gathering to break their fast. "Everyone! Listen!"

"Still talking to your dream gods, Tal Gor?" his brother Fel Nor teased him with a broad grin.

"It's no dream! Lord Tommus and his D'Orcs want to hunt! They are coming soon and twenty of our best hunters are invited to hunt with them!" Tal Gor exclaimed.

Horrgus turned and gave him a bleary eye. "What are you babbling about, boy?"

Tal Gor quickly recounted his experience last night for the tribe members who had been in their tents when he had told people last night. He could see people rolling their eyes at his story. Clearly, no one believed him any more today than the group late last night had.

Sal Gor, his father, shook his head. "Tal Gor, did you hit your head or something? You are making no sense."

"It is real, father, I swear! You will see shortly when Lord Tommus brings his hunting party here! They are also going to bring D'Wargs for our hunters to ride today."

"D'Wargs?" His older sister Soo An asked.

Tal Gor shrugged. "I assume they are demon wargs. All I know is that the hunting party will be flying and so they need to bring flying mounts for our hunters!"

Bor Tal, his oldest brother walked up to him and put a hand on his shoulder. "We need to check you brother, perhaps you were bitten by a viperclaw? Its poison causes false visions." He gestured to Tris An, his aunt the band's healer, to come over.

"I was not bitten! I am telling you, Lord Tommus is the ruler of Mount Doom and the heir to the mighty Orcus!" Tal Gor tried to explain. At this point, even Horrgus was rolling his eyes in disbelief. Tal Gor shrugged off his brother's hand and marched up to the main fire.

"You need to listen! Lord Tommus will be coming soon, and his hunters shall hunt. We have an invitation for twenty hunters to join them. This is something that hasn't been seen on the plains of Norelon in thousands of years!" Tal Gor told them, turning around to face the gathering band. At this point most of the band had come out of their tents to see what all the commotion was.

Horrgus shook his head and then winced. He came over to Tal Gor. "Come, boy, let's go back to my tent with Tris An so we can take a look at you for bite marks."

"Why don't you believe me?" Tal Gor asked, annoyed.

"You do understand this is a bit farfetched, yes?" his father asked him.

"No. I am a shaman and I am sworn to Lord Tommus, see?" Tal Gor stuck out his palm for people to see the scar. Horrgus stared at it, as did Soo An. His father also came closer to look.

"That's a fully healed scar!" Horrgus said, rubbing it.

"It looks like it's been there for years," Soo An added. "But I'm sure I would have noticed you getting that scar. It's also an odd scar."

"It mirrors the image on the Talisman of Tommus!" Tal Gor said.

"The Talisman of Tommus?" Horrgus asked.

"Well, it used to be the Talisman of Orcus, but since Tommus replaced him..." Tal Gor trailed off.

Horrgus shook his head. "You know those stories are myths? I know you've always been fascinated with the dead god and tales of glory, but at this point they are just tales."

Tal Gor shook his head. "No, they are real, and there is going to be a hunting party, today!" Tal Gor could see several heads shaking in disbelief. They thought he was crazy. Suddenly his hand ached.

"Ready to open the gate?" Lord Tommus asked in his head.

"I am not having a lot of luck getting others to believe me, My Lord," Tal Gor replied.

He felt the demon lord grin. *"Their belief is not necessary; reality should be sufficient. Go to the fire and thrust your hand with the scar into the flames. You won't get burnt."*

"Boy?" Horrgus asked the zoned-out Tal Gor.

"He's coming. They are coming, now you will see!" Tal Gor shook off their concerned hands, ducked around them and walked as quickly as his leg would let him to the central fire. He thrust his left hand into the flames.

"Tal Gor!" His mother yelled, thinking he had lost his mind.

"Lord Tommus, Master of Mount Doom, come now, enter our world of Astlan! Bring forth your hunting party!" Tal Gor shouted. His brother Bor Tal moved towards him to pull his hand from the fire; yet even as he did, the large campfire burst into twice its height, completely engulfing and obscuring the grate with the porridge pot on it.

"My porridge!" Toth Bagg the cook screamed in concern.

The flames continued up and up, overflowing the rocks of the fire pit. The fire was now roaring far louder than should have been possible for the amount of wood present. It was bigger than the largest bonfire Tal Gor had ever seen. Suddenly, the middle of the flames seemed to tear, ripping open into another reality. There was a giant, one-sided hole in the flames! Nearby orcs scrambled to peer into the tear in reality.

Through the hole, one could see what looked to be a large staging area, crowded with a very odd assortment of large, winged orcs with supersized tusks and hooves. There were also what looked like a bunch of huge wargs, also with wings and tusk-like fangs.

Suddenly the large head of Lord Tommus popped through the hole from one side, and then his entire huge body stepped through into the camp. He grinned down at Tal Gor, or at least Tal Gor hoped it was a grin. "Thank you, shaman." He surveyed the band and the camp, his eyes narrowing slightly, most likely at the rather sorry sight the band presented.

"I am Tommus, Master of Mount Doom," Tommus announced in his booming voice. Tal Gor had to clench himself; the demon lord was far more terrifying in person than he had been in his dreams. "Mount Doom is preparing for a feast and our hunters need to hunt in the Planes of Orcs once more." He looked around to the various warriors of the band. "In exchange for the assistance of your shaman"—he gestured to Tal Gor—"we invite twenty of your tribe to hunt with us."

He looked around, obviously noting that none of the tribe were geared for hunting yet. Tal Gor hung his head at his failure.

Suddenly there was movement at the hole as a woman stepped through into the camp. Tal Gor had to blink. *Wow!* he thought to himself. She had to be the most beautiful woman he had ever seen. Okay, so she had wings and hooves, but was she ever gorgeous! Tal Gor looked around and noted that he was not the only man in the camp staring at her. He had heard humans call certain women breathtaking, all orcs had, but this had to be the first time he had ever seen a woman who could literally be said to take one's breath away.

"Allow me to introduce my commander, Vespa Crooked Stick," Lord Tommus said.

Crooked Stick? Tal Gor felt his heart thud. This incredible D'Orc woman was blood? How had Crooked Stick blood ever created something like this? He could see several other men shaking their heads with the same thought.

"Shut your gaping holes, morons!" Vespa yelled to the men of the camp whose mouths were open. "You look like you've never seen a woman before!" She scowled in disapproval. "I could have gutted each and every one of you vermin by this point." Tal Gor noted several warriors uncomfortably adjusting their loincloths or pants, depending on what they were wearing.

"Now, I see none of you so-called warriors is ready to hunt." She shook her head. "Understand this: you are of my tribe. If you ever ignore the instructions of Lord Tommus's shaman again, you will answer to me. Is that clear?" Several of the warriors nodded; others mumbled acknowledgements.

"I can't hear you, worms! I asked you a question; I expect an answer. Fail me again, and I will beat you into a coma that will last a quarter month!" Vespa snarled.

The band members answered affirmatively this time with "yes, ma'am," "yes, Commander," and other similar verbal responses, many of them quite enthusiastically. Tal Gor had to admit, this woman was an old-style leader, and her charisma and leadership style clearly matched her beauty.

Vespa nodded and glanced to Lord Tommus, who nodded approvingly. Commander Vespa gestured towards the hole for others to come through, and suddenly people had to scramble to make room for the large D'Orc warriors decked out in their hunting gear to come through the inter-dimensional gateway in the middle of their cooking fire.

Tal Gor counted twenty D'Orcs of various ages and bloodlines, some of which he had never seen before. The two tall, thinner, pale white orcs with red eyes were particularly unusual.

"This is Virok Soul Wrecker of Erdnalia III on the Visteroth plane. He is our huntmaster today." Vespa gestured to the older of the two tall, pale orcs. "In matters of the hunt, his word is my word and law. Do you understand?" She glared at the Crooked Stick orcs.

"Yes, ma'am," or some variant was heard from each member of the tribe.

"As I'm sure you are aware, Tal Gor shall be selecting twenty of you to join us on this hunt." Vespa grinned. "I'm sure many of you will be regretting your failure to trust his word earlier. Try not to sob too hard at losing out on what will certainly be the most glorious event in all of your lives to date. If you aren't chosen, that means you'll just need to prove your worth to our shaman before we return to hunt here again!"

Tal Gor tried to suppress a joyous grin and look properly annoyed. This was clearly the best day of his life; he certainly did not want to show it!

Chapter 103

Talarius woke with a start. *What time is it?* he wondered. It was dark in the room, of course; there was no window and he had been lighting the room with his armor, which had gone out once he fell asleep. He willed the armor to light and began to get dressed. It was somewhat disturbing to note that his padding was completely dry. The air in the room was a bit dry, at least compared to the rest of the mountain complex since the rain had started. It was not, however, dry enough that his under-padding should have dried out within a few minutes.

Talarius walked over and dragged the giant wardrobe away from the door as soon as he was girded with his various vestments, armor, weapons and accouterments. Even with the strength boost he got from his gauntlets, the dresser was heavy; the very reason he'd used it to block the door. He opened the door and walked out into the main room to see daylight streaming through the balcony doors. The octopod and Boggy were playing some card game, Antefalken was perched on a chair back, oiling his harp, and the other demons were off somewhere.

"Well, if it isn't sleeping beauty?" Tizzy asked or perhaps stated, grinning maliciously at Talarius.

Talarius glared at the demon through his helmet. Apparently, the demon somehow knew he had fallen asleep without his armor and was intent on irritating him.

"Where is everyone?" Talarius asked, ignoring the demon's jibe.

Boggy looked up. "Rupert is off with Fer-Rog somewhere; Tom is with his commanders arranging hunts for the feast; and Reggie and Estrebrius are still in Astlan as far as I know." By coincidence, even as Boggy spoke, Reggie materialized in the room, sighing and quickly sitting down.

"Rough night?" Tizzy's eyebrows were making those obscene leering motions again. Talarius found this exceedingly discomforting. Not that there was anything particularly comforting about the vile multi-pod; however, this was even more disquieting than his usual behavior.

Reggie closed his eyes. "Yes, more dream sex training. I am not enjoying it."

Tizzy shook his head as if not understanding. "Kids today! In my day, it was all sex, drugs and rock and roll! What has become of this new generation?"

Reggie glared at him. "You are a twenty-plus-thousand-year-old demon. How do you even know about rock and roll?"

"I used to party with Keith Richards every time he came to the astral plane, which was quite often," Tizzy said.

Reggie shook his head, clearly not sure who that was; Talarius certainly had no idea.

"What I want to know," Boggy interrupted, "is how do these wizards know how to train an incubus? Doesn't that seem a bit odd?"

Antefalken looked up. "A bit; however, it's not impossible. Wizards and animages have employed both incubi and succubi for centuries. While I am sure it is not taught in any normal schools, the knowledge is probably out there."

Boggy shrugged. "Where is your accursed master? Do you know?"

Reggie shrugged. "I've really only seen her tower, but she and one of her associates mentioned Memphis. I assume it's not the one I am familiar with."

"Never heard of it," Boggy said. Antefalken also shook his head.

Talarius supposed it was a good thing these demons did not know Astlanian geography. "It's in Natoor," he said.

"What is Natoor?" Boggy asked.

"It's a continent south of Eton, immediately west of Najaar," Talarius replied.

Antefalken was nodding his head. "I've been to both of those continents. I don't recall a town called Memphis, though."

"It is an archaic name for New Krinna. The name Memphis has not been widely used in a thousand years," Talarius said.

"Ohh, okay, New Krinna I am familiar with. Never been there," Antefalken said.

"How old is your master that he uses a thousand-year-old name?" Boggy asked Reggie.

Reggie shook his head, "Mistress. And she's not that old, maybe thirty."

Talarius shrugged. "Perhaps she is a heretic."

Boggy looked at him. "A heretic?"

Talarius nodded. "There have been heretics on both continents ever since we arrived to free the people living on them. Throwbacks to their old dead gods."

"You mean like Orcus?" Tizzy grinned.

"Orcus was a demon, not a god." Talarius glared at Tizzy. "Since you were apparently buddies with the foul one, I should think you would know that."

"The orcs thought he was a god," Tizzy said, still grinning. Clearly, the annoying creature was needling him.

"Orcs? Orcs are unethical, malignant barbarians and thugs. I'm not surprised they would have such low standards for a deity."

"I dare you to go out in the corridors and start shouting that," Tizzy said slyly.

"I am not stupid, demon," Talarius replied. Why did he even engage this annoying thing? It had been gratifying to note that several of the old D'Orcs had not appeared too fond of Tizzy. Apparently the demon had been remarkably consistent over the last several thousand years.

~

Tal Gor finally finished selecting the twenty band members to join the hunt. It had actually been quite difficult, they were all essentially family. Or at least extended family. That, in fact, had been a big problem; he had his mother and father, two brothers and his sister. He finally decided to pick his siblings and told his parents that next time they could go. After that, well, he frankly went with those who had been the nicest to him over the last few years. A few had been more than difficult, or made nasty remarks about wishing him dead. They did not get selected.

His selected hunters sped off to their tents as Tal Gor turned to watch what was happening at the gate. Lord Tommus came over to him.

"I have another hunting party to send out in Etterdam in a few hours, so I will leave to take care of that and some other issues. What Vespa and I have discussed is that, when you have one or more large kills, contact me through our binding. We will then create a gateway to haul the kills to Mount Doom. We will store the kills for your warriors there in a cold room, and when the party returns, we will open a gate here and deliver the kills directly to camp. This will be much more efficient than trying to lug them around all day."

"Yes, My Lord." Tal Gor nodded. "How many kills are you expecting?"

"As many as we can reasonably and honorably get. I've got a lot of D'Orcs expecting a feast and they can eat a lot of meat." Tommus smiled and patted Tal Gor on the shoulder. The demon lord's giant claws caused Tal Gor to tense a bit in apprehension, but the demon lord was careful not to skewer him. Tal Gor felt a tingling of excitement; Lord Tommus had said he would be creating a gateway from the kill sites so apparently he would get to go along. This was truly the best day of his life.

He glanced over to see a couple of the D'Orcs at the edge of camp swatting at the tall plains grasses. He could not figure out what they were doing. It was extremely odd behavior, so he started wandering closer.

"Who ever heard of hairy ground?" one of the D'Orcs asked the other as he started pulling on some strands of four-foot high grass.

"It makes no sense. Why would the ground need hair? It does not sweat. It does not feel cold," the other D'Orc said.

One of the more battle-scarred D'Orcs sneered at them. "It's grass, you morons!"

"Grass?" the first D'Orc asked, looking up with a scowl.

"You mean the stuff that you old timers used to smoke after battle?" the second orc asked.

The older D'Orc shook his head in frustration. "No. That's just a word we used for it. What we smoked was a distant relative, more like a weed that grew in hillocks and groves. This is regular grass. It is a plant that is eaten by a wide variety of animals, including those we hunt today."

The older D'Orc turned to head back to the portal and spotted Tal Gor. He grinned. "These idiots were born in the Abyss, and have never been to the Planes of Orcs. Teaching and talking only goes so far; at some point you have to *do*." He paraphrased the old orc saying. "You and your tribe mates won't be the only ones on their first winged hunting party! We are going to be lucky if some of these bone-brains don't get the heads and tails confused and slit the tail rather than the neck!" He shook his head and grinned.

Tal Gor chuckled as he turned his attention back to the portal.

The D'Orcs had just finished carrying tack and other gear through the gateway when a loud ruckus started on the other side. It sounded like a few hundred wargs! There were not actually that many, but they were loud and eager to hunt. D'Wargs were larger than the largest wargs Tal Gor had ever seen, and they had massive wings and claws nearly as fierce as Lord Tommus's. The unusual tack that the D'Orcs had brought through now made sense.

About four D'Wargs had come through; others were preparing to follow when there arose some truly hideous snarls and growls. The D'Wargs that had been lined up to come through were forced back as what had to be the ugliest, scariest-looking D'Warg of them all barged through the gateway; spitting and snarling.

Tal Gor had no real idea how to judge age on a D'Warg; he supposed it was similar to a warg. If so, this was a rather old and very heavily scarred D'Warg. Its snout and jaw had apparently been broken and reset at some point, and its eyes were slightly off kilter, as if its skull had been somehow skewed. The head was huge with teeth so large and twisted, the D'Wargs' lips could not close over them.

Further, as the D'Warg walked, it limped slightly. Not so much as in pain, as Tal Gor did, but more as if its leg lengths were different; or perhaps, Tal Gor thought, its hips and shoulders were at different angles. In any event, the ugly beast was glaring at everyone and everything as it came through the gate; the other D'Wargs fell back to give the hissing and spitting creature room.

Vespa groaned. "Tar Roth Non!" she yelled to a younger D'Orc on the other side of the gateway, who was working to get the D'Wargs through. "What is Schwarzenfürze doing here? You know no one can ride her! She won't tolerate anyone and hasn't since my great grandfather, Helmut, passed!"

"I'm sorry Commander, but when she saw the hunters gathering the saddles and harnesses, she started making all sorts of noises. Then when I began selecting the D'Wargs for this hunt, she butted through them and insisted on coming. I tried to grab her and stop her, but you know what she's like!" Tar Roth Non shook his head forlornly. "When she's in a mood like this, she doesn't respond to commands!"

Vespa closed her eyes and shook her head as the beast glared around the camp and began snorting and sniffing at various orcs, all of whom tried to give her a wide birth. "Argh, did you get another then? We need enough for our companions."

"Uh, yes, ma'am. I did," Tar Roth Non said, stammering.

Tommus was grinning. "You seem to have things under control, Vespa, except perhaps for this D'Warg." He chuckled; it sounded quite evil. "I need to get back. Tar Roth Non, can you clear some space?"

The young D'Orc nodded and shepherded a couple of D'Wargs out of the way, and Lord Tommus went back through the gateway.

Tal Gor jumped as something wet banged up against his bad leg. He glanced back and around. He had been so distracted by Lord Tommus's departure that he had not seen the ugly D'Warg make its way around to him. It was poking its nose at his bad leg, and then in his butt crack, sniffing. Tal Gor stood perfectly still; this was clearly not a friendly D'Warg.

The D'Warg, Schwarzenfürze they had called her, stepped back and eyed him up and down as if trying to decide if he was a worthy meal. It then snorted as if in contempt and looked around the camp. After a moment, she moved again towards Tal Gor, pushing him with her muzzle, shoving him in the direction she had been staring.

Tal Gor nearly lost his footing; he twisted to stare at Vespa, not sure what he should do. Vespa was staring back at him, or more precisely, at Schwarzenfürze, and she seemed to be completely shocked.

"What does she want, Commander?" Tal Gor asked rather helplessly as the D'Warg shoved him again.

"I am not sure. It certainly can't be what it looks like. I've known her my entire life; this is not like her."

"What should I do?" Tal Gor asked.

"Unless you want to fall and be trampled by her claws, I'd suggest you move where she's pushing you," Vespa said. The other D'Orcs were also staring at the D'Warg.

She pushed him again, so Tal Gor moved forward, and the D'Warg pushed him again. He just kept moving where she pushed him. After a few pushes they were next to the saddles and harnesses the D'Orcs had brought through the gateway.

"By Lilith's bloody teat!" one of the D'Orcs cursed. "I think the bitch wants him to ride her!"

"Ridiculous!" another exclaimed. "She won't let anyone ride her. Even when she was mortal, she was a mean one; only Helmut could ride her. Even Vera, his wife, couldn't get close."

Tal Gor suddenly found himself sprawled on a saddle after the D'Warg pushed him into the pile. He looked at Vespa.

The commander was shaking her head. "Well, lad, I cannot in a million years believe this, but I think I'm going to have to show you how to saddle Schwarzenfürze. A D'Warg is different than a warg; the wings and the fact that you fly a thousand feet or more above ground makes the harness quite different." She shook her head. "The rest of you Crooked Sticks, pay attention now. All the other D'Wargs will be simple to saddle in comparison."

~

"You know, I find Trisfelt's lady friend, Hilda, quite charming. She seems extremely perceptive and bright for a layman," Lenamare observed apropos of nothing while applying butter to his toasted muffin.

Across the small breakfast table, Jehenna arched an eyebrow and glanced up from the letter she was reading. "You would think that," she snorted.

Lenamare paused in mid-motion, tilting his head to ask, puzzled, "What exactly do you mean by that?"

"Oh, come on." Jehenna shook her head. "You must have noticed." She reached for her cup of tea.

"Noticed what?" Lenamare asked, clearly confused and not understanding what she meant.

"Yesterday?" Jehenna gently shook her head from side to side. "She was buttering you up better than you're doing to that muffin!"

Lenamare looked taken aback. "Seriously? You must be joking!"

Jehenna sighed. Putting the letter down on her lap, she stared directly at Lenamare. "You cannot tell me that you, Lenamare the Great, do not know when someone is flattering you?"

Lenamare's mouth opened in a stunned O. He finally shook his head. "What possible reason could that woman have for flattering me? What end would that serve?"

Jehenna sighed heavily. "Men! You are all so dense. I don't know why we women put up with you." Lenamare was completely baffled at this point. Jehenna just stared at him. Finally she said, "She obviously has a crush on you!" She raised her hands in hopelessness. "She's like any senior student infatuated with a famous professor!"

"No…" Lenamare denied. "That cannot be." Now he was shaking his head. He paused and looked thoughtful.

"Men are always the last to realize when a woman is flirting with them," Jehenna noted archly.

"But I thought she and Trisfelt were courting?" Lenamare said.

Jehenna gave her head a small shake. "Clearly, she's simply using him to get access to you."

Lenamare grimaced. "Ah, poor Trisfelt. Here I had been hoping he might have finally found himself a companion."

"It is a shame, particularly since the woman is clearly working a lost cause," Jehenna stated firmly.

"What do you mean, 'lost cause'?" Lenamare asked, looking slightly insulted.

Jehenna closed her eyes briefly, and then reopened them. "It is a lost cause because you are with me, and that is not going to be changing. Is it?" Jehenna asked sternly. There could clearly be only one correct answer.

"Oh. Of course not." Lenamare replied, startled and slightly embarrassed at having missed her meaning.

~

"I just want to stop by my suite to check on everyone before we launch the next hunting party," Tom said. "I assume, since we are calling on Ragala-nargoloth, that you will be commanding the hunting party, Arg-nargoloth?"

"It would be my honor, Great One," Arg-nargoloth said, clearly trying not to sound too pleased.

"I too would check on Fer-Rog, who I believe is with Rupert," Zelda said.

"We shall meet the rest of you back here in the assembly area before long." Tom nodded to the commanders. He and Zelda headed off towards Tom's suite.

As they made their way through the corridors Tom asked Zelda, "Do you wish you were going?"

Zelda snorted slightly. "It would be a great experience. However, as steward, my duty is here in the mountain."

Tom nodded. "But at some point, perhaps it would be good for you to go on a hunting party. After all, as the Steward of the Mount, you must intimately understand all details of the Mount and its provisioning." He glanced at her.

Zelda nodded, "You are quite wise, My Lord, and when appropriate, I shall be honored to add to my skillset in order to serve the Mount." Tom was not sure, but he thought he detected a bit of extra brightness in her eyes and the subtlest whisper of a miniscule grin of pleasure on her face.

"Excellent!" Tom smiled.

They entered his suite to find Reggie, Antefalken, Boggy, Tizzy and Talarius all there. Estrebrius was presumably still with Vaselle; Rupert and Fer-Rog were off someplace.

"You two are back!" Tom smiled at Reggie and Antefalken. He looked over to Talarius, who seemed a bit different. It took Tom a minute to register the difference in the knight's posture. "Got a good night's sleep, I take it?" Tom smiled at the knight, who immediately seemed to get agitated.

"I did rest for a bit," Talarius admitted.

Tom grinned. "I see no one roasted you in the night."

"No. They did not." Talarius said tersely.

"Talarius, for the last time, I will not roast you or kill you down here. At some point, I will see to your safe return to Astlan. You have my word on it. Provided, of course, that you don't try to or succeed in killing any of the others under my protection while you are here."

Talarius made a harrumphing noise.

Zelda shook her head. "Knight, why do you doubt the word of Lord Tommus? Surely you know that in his previous existence, Lord Orcus was known as the God of Oaths and the Punisher of Perjurers. There was no greater crime that one could commit before Lord Orcus than to break one's oath or to be foresworn."

Hmm, do not remember that from the Monster Manual, Tom thought to nn ¼himself. Not a bad thing; he really did get sort of bent out of shape when people broke their word. He shook his head. He needed to keep his own head pulled back into reality, or whatever passed for reality around here. He was not Orcus reincarnated.

"Speaking of oaths," Antefalken said, breaking into the conversation, "as you might imagine, I managed to freak Damien out a little with our adventures. It might not be a bad idea for you to pay him a visit and reassure him that nothing has changed."

Antefalken chuckled. "I think Vaselle and I, between the two of us, may have been a bit much."

"So the two of you double teamed him? Great!" Tom shook his head.

"Yeah, and by the way…" Antefalken paused; Tom nodded. "…one thing I suggested to reassure him was that perhaps he could come for a visit. Gastropé and Jenn have both been to the Abyss and lived. Talarius is here now, and seeing the knight safe might reassure him."

Tom shrugged. "I have no real problem with that. He would need to know how to do the Cool spell that Gastropé and Jenn use. I am sure they could teach him." Tom paused. "Or Jenn could—Gastropé is flying around killing liches."

Antefalken grimaced. "Jenn is with Gastropé."

Tom looked at the bard, puzzled. "Really? That seems odd. I didn't think she cared that much for him."

Antefalken shrugged. "The short answer is that the Council needed everyone who was being hunted by the Rod or Oorstemoth to be gone from the city, so they sent them on a quest. I am guessing that's how they ended up flying around in the clouds fighting liches on dragonback."

"A quest? A quest to rid the world of liches?" Tom asked.

"Well, the Council and many others have now seen a crystal ball recording of your battle, and apparently the Council noticed the flying carpet that we spotted before the battle. And they pretty much reached the same conclusion we did."

Tom nodded, remembering the flying carpet with Bess, Exador and Ramses on it. Tom, Antefalken and Tizzy had assumed they were the three archdemons.

"By the way, I was thinking about Exador being an archdemon. It just seems bizarre. He's a wizard known for enslaving demons," Tom said.

"Slave, minimum wage employee—hard to tell the difference." Tizzy shrugged.

"So you are saying he wasn't conjuring and enslaving demons, but paying them money?" Tom asked incredulously.

Tizzy and Boggy both shrugged. "Yeah, most of the soldier demons are employed by higher-level demons," Boggy said. "Not a life I would want, but to each his own. It pays for the Denubian Choco-Coffee™."

Tom twisted his mouth and tilted his head with a small shrug. "I guess that makes sense; seems a lot easier than pure compulsion." He shook his head. "But back to what you were saying: how is this related to a quest?" he asked Antefalken.

"Well, it seems that Trevin D'Vils…" Antefalken began.

"Pagan whore!" Talarius interrupted. Tom rub cf ed the bridge of his nose, trying not to poke his eyes out with his claws. As much as he wanted to ask about this Trevin D'Vils and why she was a pagan whore, he needed to keep this conversation on track.

"Continue," Tom told Antefalken, raising his hand to hold Talarius off.

"Anyway, Trevin recognized her as possibly being Bastet or Bestat, Defender of House and Home," Antefalken continued.

"That's a rather odd title for an archdemon," Boggy noted.

Antefalken shook his head. "No, Trevin says that Bastet was a goddess of the Nyjyr Ennead, a pantheon of deities previously worshiped in Natoor and Najaar."

"Heretics, false deities, thankfully long gone!" Talarius stated proudly.

"Wiped out by the Etonians," Antefalken said, nodding to Talarius.

"Heretics?" Reggie asked. "You mean like my accursed mistress?"

Antefalken turned to stare at Reggie, as did Talarius. Tom looked back and forth between the three, not having any idea of what they are talking about.

"Same heretics. Memphis was one of their holiest cities. Fortunately, your heretic mistress worships gods that are long dead," Talarius said, nodding emphatically.

"Or maybe not." Antefalken countered.

The knight swiveled to look at the bard. Again, it was really hard to read the knight's expressions inside his giant helmet. Tom thought about lowering the temperature of the entire mountain, except it might interfere with mana generation. There was too much he still did not understand about this fortress.

"The Council, and in particular Trevin, think that the third archdemon might not have been an archdemon at all, but the goddess Bastet. They are on a quest to discover the truth," Antefalken said.

Tom shook his head. "I'm rather new to Astlan, but isn't goddess hunting a bit dangerous?"

"Sounds like it to me," Boggy said.

Antefalken raised his hands. "Don't ask me, I'm just relaying what I was told. I am not sure they seriously expect to find a goddess."

"But why would a goddess be slumming as an archdemon?" Reggie asked.

Tizzy released a large cloud of smoke. "I've been asking myself that same question ever since she and her avatars popped up in the Abyss about a hundred and fifty years ago. Built themselves a scary fortress and all started pretending to be demons." Tizzy shook his head. "Always seemed a bit déclassé to me."

"Well, I should think the real estate down here would be cheaper," Boggy noted.

"Tizzy, are you saying that this Bess, the archdemon ally of Exador and Ramses, really *is* a goddess?" Tom asked.

Tizzy shrugged. "Well, that has been my assumption. I smelled them when they first showed up here, all at the same time, which is very odd." He took a quick puff on his pipe. "The odder thing, though, was the smell; they didn't smell so much like buttah as marzipan." He pronounced *buttah* in his yenta voice but otherwise spoke normally.

"Marzipan?" Talarius asked, puzzled.

"Yeah, it's an almond paste, smells a lot like cherries," Tizzy told the knight.

"I know what it is; I'm asking why they smelled like marzipan," Talarius said, annoyed.

Tizzy shrugged. "Why do others smell like buttah?" Again, the demon used his yenta voice for *buttah*.

"You are the only person I know who can smell new arrivals," Boggy said. "I don't smell anything."

"What did Talarius smell like?" Reggie asked.

"Like blood, sweat and piss," Tizzy said. Talarius glared at him.

Tizzy grinned. "I should know, I carried him all the way back to the cave, got quite a whiff." He shuddered slightly. "But the smell only comes when someone manifests a new body. Talarius came through a hole, a portal; he didn't incarnate a new body as is what happens with new arrivals."

"So the goddess and her avatars created new demon bodies for themselves?" Antefalken asked.

Tizzy shrugged again. "So it would seem, but like I said, it didn't smell right and they all showed up at the same time. Fortress popped up very shortly thereafter, too soon to have been built normally. That smelled weird too, like iron and sulfur. I got there with some cookies just after the fortress was completed. They'd just shut the door behind them, so I had to knock."

"Hey, you didn't bring me cookies!" Boggy said, annoyed. "A hundred and fifty years ago? You also didn't bring me along to check out the fortress."

"You were probably working." Tizzy gave Boggy a glare. "Remember, you hadn't eaten your accursed master then."

"Well, technically, that would have been the grandfather of the accursed master that I ate," Boggy pointed out.

"You ate your master?" Talarius said incredulously.

"Best way to get rid of him once and for all," Boggy said.

"Seems pretty gross," Reggie said. "But then, where I come from there's this religion where every time they have a worship service, they eat bread and wine and pretend they are eating the body of their god. The oldest version of this religion actually believes the bread they eat and the wine they drink transubstantiate to become the actual physical flesh and blood of their god."

"Ritualized cannibalism?" Talarius asked with distaste. "Clearly these people are heathens of the worst sort."

Tom interrupted, "Guys, we are getting off track here."

"Sorry. Back to the topic," Reggie said. "Why didn't I get cookies either?"

Tizzy held up his upper hands as if trying to placate them. "I'm sorry, but the cookies were a house-warming gift. Did you just move into a new Dark Fortress?"

"No, but Lord Tommus just did," Zelda pointed out.

Tizzy closed his eyes and grabbed his horns with his upper hands, rocking his head from side to side. "Okay already, I'll bring cookies to the feast! But it's going to take me some time. Do you have any idea how long it is going to take me to bake three or four hundred dozen cookies in my oven? I can barely fit a whole dwarf in it!"

Boggy gave him an odd look. "You have an oven? I've never seen it."

"Guys… please?" Tom felt like he was going to lose it. He was under enough stress as it was; trying to work with Larry, Moe, Curly and Shemp all at once was too much. "I have to get back to open a gate for the next hunting party. So let's get to what needs to be done."

Antefalken frowned. "What were we trying to do? I've forgotten at this point."

"We were talking about teaching Vaselle and Damien the Cool spell," Tom said. "Or maybe they could make amulets or something like Talarius's armor. Actually, that would be the best thing."

Antefalken scratched his chin. "Well Vaselle told Damien and me that he runs a shop and creates arcane devices. I am not sure what type, and I am sure Damien could make one too. Let me discuss it with them this afternoon when Damien summons me."

"Fine. I will contact Vaselle and have him get some clothes for Edwyrd, and we'll come by."

"Who's Edwyrd?" Reggie asked.

"He's me—it's my human form," Tom said, noting the knight turn to face him.

"So *you* are the Lord Edwyrd who sank the Oorstemothian ship?" the knight asked.

Tom sighed. "Yes, I was disguised as a human so as not to cause a panic. We were told the Oorstemothians were pirates attacking our ship, and having been hired to defend the ship from pirates, we tried to defend it. But then they nearly killed Rupert—in fact, I thought he was dead—so I sort of took the battle to them and sank their ship."

Talarius was silent for a moment, thinking. "That makes some sense, but—"

"But being a demon, I can't be trusted with the truth! Do you want to really know what was going on?" Tom asked. "Let's get it out there before I go sending more D'Orcs into Astlan."

"Go ahead," Talarius said.

"Exador's men ambushed a caravan with Rupert, Jenn and a bunch of others from Lenamare's school who were fleeing Exador's siege of the school. Gastropé was one of the soldiers, but Jenn fought him to a standstill. Jehenna summoned me; but she used a broken ring, so I came through of my own free will. Everyone else fled or perished, so I agreed to escort Rupert and Jenn to Freehold for their safety."

Zelda, Reggie and Talarius had never heard this story and so were watching Tom closely.

"In any event, along the way, Exador sent several major demons to locate us and they distracted me and managed to capture Jenn." Tom sighed. How many times had he told this story now? "Rupert came up with a scheme to infiltrate their camp as a lost boy, not unlike what he did in your camp." Talarius nodded. "They put him in the tent with Jenn and Gastropé. Rupert, being a demon, was able to free himself from his ropes and then freed Jenn and summoned me. I opened a portal and pulled Jenn, Rupert and Gastropé into my cave."

"These two people were either very brave or stupid," Talarius said.

"Well, if you know Exador, he's not a pleasant person. Staying was not an option," Tom said. "Actually, given that we now know he is an archdemon, I can say he is pretty much everything you, Talarius, expect an archdemon to be. Not all demons are, but in Exador's case—he seems to fit the stereotype." Tom shook his head.

"Anyway, Gastropé and Jenn used this Cool spell to survive the heat in my cave, but it wouldn't last long, so I had to find a way back to Astlan. I went searching and found your high priest, Verigas, summoning a demon of his own. I intercepted that call and opened a portal to let Rupert, Jenn and Gastropé back into Astlan. We tried to assure your priest we meant no harm, but he apparently overreacted and called out the Rod once we left. I was just trying to get Jenn and Rupert to safety in Freehold."

Tom shook both hands in Talarius's direction. "So, to be clear: there was no planned invasion, no nothing! All of that Lord Edwyrd's invading demon horde crap was made up by Verigas to make himself look good after admitting to summoning demons. And the Oorstemothians? Well, they shot first; I considered it self-defense."

Talarius just shook his head. "What a complicated story you have created."

"Look, you can believe it or not, I don't care. I have now told you the truth; I have put it out there. I have yet to lie to you about anything. So you can judge for yourself based on what you see me do."

Talarius seemed to shrug. "I will take your story under advisement, as I do everything else."

"That's all I ask." Tom sighed. "Antefalken, are we set? I am going to visit Vaselle later this afternoon; you tell me when. He and Edwyrd will then come visit you and Damien. We can put Damien's mind at ease and discuss constructing some sort of Abyssal life support system for Astlanians."

Antefalken nodded. "I expect him to summon me about a period after noon local time. Anytime after that."

Tom nodded. "So early fourth period; that works."

~

After a small eternity, the D'Wargs had been saddled, and the D'Orcs verified they had fastened securely. Tal Gor had run to his tent to retrieve his crossbow and quiver of arrows. He had not used them for much other than practice in years. Since the wyvern, he had only hunted small game and his crossbow was a bit over-powered for that, so he had been using bow and arrows. For large game, though, the crossbow was ideal.

All the D'Orcs had been amazed to see Schwarzenfürze harnessed. It was obvious that she was not much enjoying the gear, but she was permitting it. It took a few tries and a fair amount of patience from the D'Warg, but eventually he was mounted. Schwarzenfürze squirmed and seemed to be trying to force Tal Gor to a more balanced location while the other orcs mounted their D'Wargs.

Vespa lined them up two by two so that each orc could launch one at a time. Three D'Orcs hovered in the air around the takeoff area, prepared to help if any of the orcs had issues. Naturally, the orcs grumbled about being babysat, but the huntmaster was adamant; he wanted them to get some practice in first and be prepared for the eventual chases of the hunt.

As the shaman, Tal Gor was one of the first two in line, along with Soo An, his sister. As they were ready to begin flying, Schwarzenfürze seemed to finally settle down a bit, almost sighing. Suddenly, from directly behind Tal Gor, a very loud series of moist, splattering explosions erupted. The D'Warg behind him jumped out of line with loud snorting noises, causing its rider, Fel Nor, to reel to the left, where he began coughing and hacking before jamming his fingers in his nostrils.

Looking over his shoulder, Tal Gor was surprised as the other second-line D'Warg began moving away as well. It was at that point that the putrescent stench struck his own nostrils. Apparently, the aim of the noxious gas cloud had been straight back, and it had taken a few moments for the cloud to drift back to Tal Gor's nose. He gasped for breath through his mouth even as Soo An did the same.

The third line of orcs began waving their hands in front of their faces even as their D'Wargs began giving them trouble. D'Orcs standing nearby began plugging their own noses and a few were almost retching, even as they laughed uproariously.

"Lilith's dusty udders!" Virok cursed even as he plugged his own nostrils. "I thought I'd never have to smell this again!"

"It's been over four thousand years since she's eaten! How is this possible?" Vespa yelled between guffaws.

"Knowing Schwarzenfürze, she's probably been saving it, letting it ferment for four millennia!" Virok said, laughing. His two brothers behind him finally had their D'Wargs back in formation, but the D'Wargs were snarling and snorting in displeasure. The poor beasts had no way to block their nostrils. By this point, everyone was laughing at the ornery D'Wargs.

"Tal Gor," his brother Fel Nor exclaimed, "never in my life have I smelled something so disgusting. You could leave entrails out on a rock for days and not have such a smell! I shall never ride behind that D'Warg again."

"Relax, Fel Nor," said Vespa, still laughing. "I am sure it will take Schwarzenfürze at least a few moments to recharge!"

Tal Gor rubbed Schwarzenfürze's neck, truly enjoying her attack, of sorts, on his brother. This day just kept getting better!

~

"So what exactly is Exador proposing?" Lord Gandros asked the councilors in his room.

"That is not completely clear," Randolf said.

"Not clear?" Damien asked. "He says he can prove he's not an archdemon, yet he's not clear how?" The wizard shook his head in disbelief.

Randolf shrugged. "He said he and the guests he had staying here would be more than willing to pass any test the Council decided was reasonable."

"He sounds rather confident," Jehenna noted.

"Too confident." Zilquar squinted at his fingers, concentrating as he spoke.

"So we come up with a plan to test him and his colleagues, and if they pass, we know they are not the archdemons?" Davron said.

"Or they have managed to trick us," Damien noted.

"All well and good, but what if they don't pass? What if we expose them?" Lenamare asked drily.

"Then I am guessing we have three very embarrassed archdemons in the middle of the Council Chamber," Gandros snorted.

Davron and Zilquar both grimaced. "I'm relatively sure that won't be pleasant," Davron observed. Zilquar nodded in agreement.

"In such a case, we would need to be prepared to bind them," Randolf stated.

Damien arched an eyebrow and looked askance at the archimage, who had apparently just lost his senses. "Bind them? Bind three archdemons?"

Randolf shrugged. "Well, I admit, three is more than I bargained for, but I have been researching traps for a single archdemon."

Lenamare looked at Randolf, giving a slight inhale of sudden understanding. "Interesting; I now see what you were getting at during our discussion the other day."

Gandros did a double take between the two councilors. "The two of you were having a discussion? Have heaven and hell united?" Jehenna was also looking at Lenamare oddly.

"Strange situations make strange bedfellows." Randolf grinned. Several other wizards grimaced, slightly uncomfortable with the allusion to the archimage's catamite.

"How much more work do you have to do?" Gandros asked.

Randolf shrugged. "Thanks to Lenamare's assistance I was getting close, but I'll need to recalibrate to hold three archdemons."

"Perhaps we should do them one at a time?" Davron asked.

"That would be best, but how do we schedule that? If the first one is an archdemon and doesn't return to the Abyss, won't the other two get suspicious?" Damien asked.

Zilquar frowned. "We could put the wards back up really fast."

"That would get rid of all three," Gandros noted.

"Unless they are prepared for it, under the assumption that that is the test we would devise," Jehenna said.

"And we do need to come up with a test, still," Lenamare noted.

"This is going to be tricky," Gandros stated.

"Assuming we do discover that they are archdemons, and we put the wards up, how long can we keep them up and keep out three angry archdemons?" Damien asked.

"Long enough for the Rod and Oorstemoth to recall their forces, I should hope," Lenamare said reluctantly.

"And then what? Previously, they did not use their full strength because they were in hiding for some reason. There would be no such constraint at that point," Davron noted.

Gandros shook his head and sighed. "I would like to convene a meeting with Alexandros on this; he was not available this morning." The Archimage rubbed his temples. "We need to buy some time, time to think this through. Time to look into bindings, time to look into banishings." He looked back and forth between Lenamare and Randolf. "Is there a way to ban them from Astlan for a few centuries?"

Lenamare blinked and Randolf shrugged. Finally Lenamare spoke. "Well, we don't quite know how they got here. All previous research indicated that manifesting on the material planes was very complicated and power intensive. That's why we never expected to have to do such a thing."

"In hindsight, a contingency plan for one of those times an archdemon did manage to manifest might have been a good idea," Randolf noted.

Damien sighed. "I am wondering if we might need to consult with some religious authorities."

Lenamare snorted. "I doubt such narrow-minded and opinionated mana channelers would have any useful advice to offer."

Damien shook his head in annoyance. "They deal with extra-planar beings all the time: ghosts, vampires, undead, saints, angels. As I recall, they also like to do exorcisms; isn't that demon-banning?"

Lenamare just snorted again and shook his head at the ridiculousness of consulting with clerics.

Jehenna interjected. "It may come to that, but perhaps we can do more research on the subject before needing to take extreme measures." She glanced at Lenamare to make sure he was mollified.

"So what do we do in the meantime?" Zilquar asked.

"Business as usual?" Randolf shrugged.

"Business as usual?" Davron asked non-rhetorically.

Damien nodded in agreement. "We tell Exador that we are investigating testing mechanisms because we must be sure; but for now we take his word as a trusted member of the Council of Wizardry."

Gandros nodded. "I agree. If he or his friends are archdemons, they have been that way for longer than any of us have been alive, and could have killed us all long ago. So for now, status quo."

Davron sighed. "I guess. It seems better than any alternative."

"I am not really seeing any alternatives at the moment," Damien said.

~

Tom closed the gate behind the last of the Etterdam hunting party. He figured he had a few hours before he would need to create more gateways. Actually, that would be a problem with his visit to Damien and Antefalken. He would not be able to create a gateway to the kitchens if he was in Freehold. He would need to change that with Antefalken before the bard left.

He headed back towards his quarters, Zelda following. As they walked down the corridors to his suite, he was reminded of the other doors along the corridors. "Zelda, are these other suites in use?"

"No, My Lord. The suites on this level have been closed off since the treachery," Zelda said.

"Who used them?" Tom asked.

Zelda shrugged. "Various high ministers, some guests." She pointed to one they were just passing. "It is said that this suite was reserved for Loki when he visited."

"Loki?" Tom asked. "The same one Delg mentioned?"

"Indeed, the jötunn lord," Zelda replied. "Although this was a very long time ago, before Ragnarök. He perished battling Heimdallr to destroy Asbrú and thus all access to the realms of Midgard." Zelda smiled. "Or so I am told; I am much too young to remember this. I know for a fact, however, that Delg would be more than happy to tell you far more than you could ever wish. In fact, my understanding is that if he gets drunk, he might not stop telling his stories, over and over again."

Tom chuckled and nodded. It would be interesting to know how young she actually was, but he had to assume that asking a D'Orc woman her age was in as poor taste as asking a human woman.

"Can we assign a suite to some of my other friends?" Tom asked. "Talarius and Rupert each have their own rooms, but I think it would be good to have another suite for the rest. I don't know the layouts, but ideally each should have a bedroom of their own."

"Of course, My Lord. They can each have their own suite if they want. We have a lot of extra space in the Mount. At its height, we had over twenty thousand D'Orcs stationed here," Zelda said.

Tom shuddered and closed his eyes; the D'Orcs had lost over ninety percent of their forces. "That's a lot of casualties."

Zelda nodded sadly. "We were just under four thousand after the defeat. We have encouraged children, but D'Orc babies are difficult to make and general attrition to Lilith's forces and despair have taken their toll."

Tom sighed, feeling depressed. He hoped he was not building up false hope. He suddenly realized he wanted to help the D'Orcs, a lot. They had welcomed him unlike any other group in the Abyss or Astlan, and they needed help. He could almost feel their suffering and pain. Of course, they were D'Orcs and they had been part of an Army of Evil for Orcus, which was probably not that pleasant of a thing. He should not be under any illusions as to who they were. He was familiar with the tales of orcs and Orcus.

Of course, he was also familiar with tales of demons. Before becoming a demon himself, he had believed many of the same things as the Astlanians. Now, with the orcs and D'Orcs, he was seeing them as real people, not the monsters of fairy tales and fantasy novels. Could the stories of orcs and D'Orcs be every bit as much bullshit as the stories of demons? Why not? The victors, not the losers, wrote history.

Could all those fantasy tales be some sort of elvish or alvaren propaganda? Was there a dark side to pipe-smoking wizards with big hats and large-footed, short friends? He needed to keep an open mind. He realized he had been quiet for some time as they walked; he should get back on topic.

"So how many bedrooms per suite?" Tom asked.

"Most have two, and some have three."

"Actually, that is something I am curious about. I note that these suites have bedrooms, and the barracks have beds, even though demons don't generally need to sleep," Tom noted.

Zelda smiled. "Well, beds are useful to make babies."

Tom grinned. "In that case, I guess you guys are working pretty hard."

Zelda chuckled. "But you are correct; D'Orcs need sleep no more than any demon. However, my understanding—and we should be verifying this shortly now that you've returned—is that the Mount's mana generation and accumulation competes with a demon's or D'Orc's ability to collect mana."

Tom nodded, thinking. "So by sleeping, D'Orcs can conserve mana and replenish easier."

"Exactly! While operating, the Mount creates a lot of mana, but it sucks a lot of it right back up to power itself and charge its mana pools. That means the ambient levels for demons and D'Orcs to replenish from is lower."

"So you sleep more." Tom nodded.

"Yes. Of course, the Mount has been dormant for thousands of years, so we didn't need to sleep as much," Zelda added.

Tom chuckled. "But you did need babies."

Zelda grinned. "Indeed we did. But also because… well, to be honest, many of the elders were filled with despair and sorrow. This caused them to sleep more, and sometimes worse."

Tom shuddered, thinking about the depressed D'Orcs. "And I suppose x-glargh hasn't been particularly available?"

Zelda nodded. "We have the wealth of the Mount, but that's most valuable on the Planes of Orcs, which we've had no way to access."

"Are there not any shaman D'Orcs?" Tom asked as they approached his suite.

"I am told there were, but the majority was with your prior self and perished. The shamans here were the front line in repelling Lilith and her forces after the treachery. We lost all but a handful at that time. About two thousand years ago, we lost the last of our shamans to attrition and despair." Zelda sighed. "We are so sorry, lord, for failing you. For not trusting your prophecy and believing." She sounded truly heartbroken.

"Do not be sorry. You have been hardened by these trials. You are the survivors, the strongest of the strong, and you have bravely carried on. There is nothing to be sorry for." Tom rested his hand on her shoulder for a moment before turning to open the door to his suite.

"Thank you, lord," Zelda said as he turned.

In the room were Rupert and Fer-Rog. It looked and sounded like Rupert was teaching Fer-Rog a card game. The room was otherwise empty, and the other doors off the suite were open.

"Where is everyone?" Tom asked.

Fer-Rog looked up and grinned at his mother.

Rupert moved a card and then grinned at Tom. "Reggie, Tizzy, Boggy and Talarius all found large sacks and headed back to the gem caverns to gather our gem piles."

"Antefalken is wandering the halls, exploring I guess," Fer-Rog said.

"Do they know how to make their way back through the tunnels?" Tom asked Rupert.

Rupert shook his head. "No, they flew up and out of the volcano. They plan to go back in from the entrance."

"Good enough," Tom said. "If you see Antefalken, tell him that I need to push back my visit to Damien until the evening. I'm going to be busy with hauling game back to the kitchens today."

"Mother, when can I go hunting?" Fer-Rog asked excitedly.

"We'll see. There is a long line of hunters with seniority who want to go first," Zelda told her son.

"I want to go too!" Rupert said.

"Okay, at some point you can. As the steward says, we have a long queue," Tom said. He really was not sure that big game hunting was the greatest idea for a kid. Although it could not be any more dangerous than being caught in a tent with Talarius and his sword. In addition, if they were in Astlan, Rupert could not be permanently killed. Okay, maybe not a bad idea, Tom decided.

Tom turned to Zelda. "Speaking of beds, I want to rest a bit before the first gate is needed. Powering this place up is still quite draining."

Zelda nodded. "I will have rooms made up for the others. What assignments do you want?"

Tom thought for a moment. "Maybe a two-bedroom suite for Boggy and Tizzy, and then a three-bedroom suite for Antefalken, Estrebrius and Reggie? Or whatever combination they want, I don't care."

"The rooms will be ready later this afternoon. I will be down near kitchen one, awaiting the first kills," Zelda said.

"Thanks!" Tom said.

"Fer-Rog, you will need to be in the kitchen when the kills arrive; you need to learn how to prepare them," Zelda said. She looked at Tom. "As do I, for that matter. I've been taught but never done it, since I'm not that old."

~

DOF +7
Midday (Murgatroy Time) 16-04-440

"I am starting to think this place is a very comfortable prison," Gastropé said to Maelen as he entered the port observation lounge, where Maelen was relaxing on a sofa and sipping tea as he gazed out the large port viewing lens. He sat down next to the seer.

"A very nice prison with good food, wine and a very nice library of work done by non-humans," Maelen said, smiling and gesturing to the wall of books to their left. "I have to tell you, getting access to alvaren texts is quite a treat for me. Add in Modgriensofarthgonosefren works, as well as several others, and I could spend years floating on this cloud."

Gastropé chuckled. "I should probably be a better scholar. Although I am learning a lot about aerial combat magic with Peter, Zed and the other carpet warriors. This ship truly is incredible. That, in fact, may be the problem."

Maelen gave him a questioning look.

"On a ship, you feel the sea's rocking motion continuously. You can walk on deck and get the wind in your hair, smell the salt of the sea. You feel the movement, the progress of the ship's journey. This cloud moves incredibly smoothly when not under attack. I cannot even discern that we are moving other than by staring at the ground so far below us. And that is through a lens, not even a real window!" Gastropé complained.

It was Maelen's turn to chuckle. "You will, however, at least admit it's a far better view than you get in the middle of a sea, yes?"

Gastropé grinned. "I will give you that. It's a view I could not even have imagined from a flying carpet until this trip!" He shook his head. "It just doesn't feel quite real."

"And during your combat practice? I heard you were drilling with the carpet warriors," Maelen asked.

"That is more surreal than real. I try very hard not to look at or even think of the view there; otherwise, my muscles would freeze over faster than a storm lich's butt."

Maelen grinned. "I will take your word concerning flying on a combat carpet. As for the Nimbus, I understand. I have been a traveler nearly my entire life. I have never traveled in such luxury or with such ease. I doubt the gods themselves could arrange better transport than this cloudship." He shrugged again. "So, I shall enjoy it. It's a rare luxury in this world—or any, I should imagine."

"I just like this piped-in water they have!" Jenn said, joining the conversation as she entered the lounge. "Imagine, just turn a knob and a pipe delivers water into a basin or a tub. Then imagine two pipes, one with cold water, the other with hot! This is wizardry at its finest! It would be an unbelievable luxury on the ground, but in the air, leagues above the ground? It's like living in some sort of fairy tale!" She grabbed a biscuit off the tray next to the teapot.

"If your fairy tale has dragon-riding liches that like to attack you every so often." Gastropé grinned at her.

"True, I could do without them in my fairy tale." She shook her head. "Everything has its price."

So where are we now?" Jenn changed the subject, leaning over the sofa back to look out the lens.

"The forest below us is The United Federation," Maelen said, pointing to the large forest that they were passing over. "A very large and dense forest, with significant logging operations and paper production."

"Yeah, at my old school we ordered all our paper and books from the UF," Gastropé said. "I didn't exactly know where it was, just a long way southeast of the school. Over-Grove One, Master called it."

"It and Murgandy have somehow managed to survive millennia of wars with the jötnar races without using extensive defenses," Maelen said.

"I'm not sure I would completely agree," Elrose said, walking into the lounge. "The UF has walled cities and clusters of keeps to protect their eastern farmlands."

"True, for their eastern farmlands. However, there are large sections of exposed forests where their rangers have done a very good job of keeping out undesirables," Maelen replied. "On the other hand, Murgandy has no fortresses and even trades with the various orc tribes."

"Yes, but have you ever been to their forests? A place only Trisfelt could find even remotely tolerable, and then only for the beer." Elrose shook his head and continued, "A very rough and tumble, primitive region filled with more than a few unsavory rogues and brigands."

"But they seem to have a relatively good relationship with the orcs. And given that a lot of the citizens are alfar, that's saying quite a bit." Maelen noted.

"Sounds like a fun place." Gastropé said.

Elrose grinned. "Well, you'll get a taste soon enough. We'll be heading right by Murgatroy and then down to Murgandor, where we will be making our first stop."

"Why are we stopping in Murgandor?" Jenn asked, apparently not liking the description of the region.

Elrose nodded understandingly. "Seamach has contacts there who can give us recent information on Murgandy, Ferundy and Noajar. None of us have been to this part of the world in a long time, so we need to get up to speed on current events in the region."

"Yes—for example, if the rat and mouse problems have suddenly improved considerably," Maelen said, grinning.

Gastropé shook his head, not understanding at first, and then suddenly remembered who they were looking for. He chuckled at the seer's joke.

~

Tal Gor gripped Schwarzenfürze's neck harness with his left hand, his right hand tightly gripping the long-handled and very sharp scythe, hooking his right thumb under the harness. His legs squeezed the D'Warg's shoulders tightly as they dove out of the sky with insane speed, swooping down on the gazelle that had been separated from the herd.

"Stick Vengeance!" Tal Gor screamed as the D'Warg rocked hard underneath him. With a mighty roar, the D'Warg's long front claws grabbed the gazelle at the base of the neck, and her rear claws grabbed at the flanks. He felt the D'Warg pushing up against him as her mighty wings beat at three times their previous rate as she pulled up sharply, lifting the three of them off the ground.

Tal Gor raised his right arm and brought it down and around as he had been shown, slicing the gazelle's neck with a dark splatter of blood. The animal's struggles slowly ceased as it perished and Schwarzenfürze banked hard to the right while still lifting them higher into the air to return to the agreed-upon collection spot.

"Best hunt ever!" Tal Gor shouted, even though no one other than Schwarzenfürze could hear him. The others were all pursuing other herd members. They had broken up into ten teams of four, two D'Orcs and two orcs with D'Wargs, and gone in different directions to find game. Tal Gor was amazed at the speed of the D'Orcs and D'Wargs. Their ability to fly faster than an orc could run allowed them to cover an unprecedented amount of ground. When one combined the speed with the aerial vantage point of several hundred feet, locating and tracking game herds became almost too easy.

How would his tribe members ever want to go back to normal hunting again? He chuckled. The D'Orcs had been unbelievably true to their word! This was the greatest honor an orc hunter could wish for, to be able to hunt like this, to be the ultimate predator. The adrenaline rush was amazing! Tal Gor had never felt so alive in his life.

He glanced back to ensure the other group members were also returning with their kills. They were doing well; Vespa and Bor Tal both had kills. Kirak Doth Nar, the other D'Orc in their group, was going in for his kill even as he watched, swooping down and landing on the gazelle's back as if mounting it. However, instead of grabbing the neck to hold onto, he reached his huge claws around and slit the animal's neck with his left hand before wrapping both arms around it and clamping his legs around the flanks. He then pulled up, lifting the still-twitching gazelle into the air.

Tal Gor grinned and waved his scythe to the others in triumph. "What a glorious day!" he yelled joyfully at the top of his lungs.

They reached the designated collection point. It took quite a bit longer to get back to it than it had coming outbound. Lugging the gazelle carcasses significantly reduced speed, although not proportionately different than lugging an animal on one's back slowed one's march, Tal Gor suddenly realized.

They came in low and slow. Schwarzenfürze released the body and continued on, finally coming to rest about two hundred feet away. They wanted to collect all the carcasses in one spot. Vespa dropped her gazelle and flew over to where Schwarzenfürze had landed. Both Vespa and Tal Gor were grinning in pleasure.

Bor Tal dropped his kill and flew to join them; he was laughing and shaking his scythe in the air. "This is the best way to hunt!" He shook his head and looked straight at Tal Gor. "I am so sorry for doubting your sanity, brother. If these are the visions caused by a viperclaw bite, then I want to be bitten every day!"

Kirak Doth Far had deposited his kill and was heading over to them. "Vespa, this is a great day indeed! I have longed to do this, to hunt the Planes of Orcs as my parents did. If only my father had survived to do this again. My mother shall revel when her turn comes!"

Tal Gor was puzzled. "So you have not done this before either?"

Vespa grinned at him. "Neither of us has. Virok and several of the others have. Kirak is second generation, I am fourth; only first generation D'Orcs have hunted, or for that matter warred upon the Planes of Orcs."

"I am not sure I understand *generation* as you use it," Bor Tal said.

"First generation D'Orcs were mighty orc warriors who were raised upon death to become D'Orcs, a warrior companion of Orcus. The later generations of D'Orcs were born in the Abyss to D'Orc parents. We have always been D'Orcs."

Bor Tal was shaking his head. "You mean the first D'Orcs, the oldest ones, were once orcs like me, my tribe?"

Kirak Doth Far nodded. "My mother and father were both mighty warriors, my father of the Crooked Stick tribe nearly five thousand years ago. He grinned, remembering. "He would tell me of the great raids upon the wall of keeps guarding Ferundy, before the desolation. He was in the D'Orc raid that caused the desolation!"

Bor Tal was staring at Kirak Doth Far in awe. "Your father was at the Desolating?" Kirak nodded. "Ah, the tales he must have told." Bor Tal sighed. "To hear firsthand of that battle. If I were not here, hunting with you on this D'Warg, I would not believe such a thing. It is simply too glorious!"

There was a whooping noise and a loud thump over by the carcasses. Soo An and Dider An Sep had just dropped a very large ox carcass. It had taken both of the D'Orc and Soo An's D'Warg to carry the large carcass. The two started over towards the group.

"Dider An Sep, she is first generation," Vespa told them. "She is of the Fen Horde on Romdan." As the new arrivals came up, she asked them, "Good hunting?"

Soo An shook her head. "Damn oxen are too slow. It is very hard to slow down enough in a dive to get a clean kill! And once they start moving, they are nearly impossible to stop! The momentum is incredible!"

"It takes patience," Dider An Sep said with a chuckle.

"D'Warg and D'Orc claws do work a lot better than crossbow bolts taking these wild oxen down."

Tal Gor was enjoying the hunt talk. He had missed this so much. Of course, with Vespa standing right beside him, it was bit difficult to keep one's eyes focused on who was speaking, unless it was Vespa herself. She was so enticing. *The blood splatter on her cheek was so...* He shook his head. He needed to focus on the hunt around him, enjoy being part of that and not be a mooncalf for a sexy woman.

"So why are you now needing to hunt on the Planes of Orcs after so long?" Bor Tal asked Vespa. Tal Gor had missed some of the conversation, but this brought his attention back.

Vespa nodded. "For many years, over four thousand in fact, after the fall of Orcus in Etterdam" —here the D'Orcs all made an odd gesture of respect —"we have not been able to get to the Planes of Orcs. All the D'Orc shamans who could do so perished with Lord Orcus or not long after." She shook her head.

"What did you eat?" Soo An asked.

Vespa smiled. "D'Orcs are similar to demons, jötunn, djinn and similar beings in that we don't need to eat or drink. Although we do enjoy it."

"Now that Lord Tommus has returned as promised, we can once again hunt," Dider said as Vespa nodded.

"Lord Tommus has returned? Was he there before?" Bor Tal asked.

Dider shook her head. "No, not exactly."

Vespa continued, "A century after the debacle in Etterdam, a great shaman named Tiss-Arog-Dal foretold that Lord Orcus would return, reborn as a new demon prince, and that we would know him when he returned to us with his identical son and an entourage. It was foretold that he would locate and release the Wand of Orcus, thus restarting Mount Doom. He would finally end the dark status quo that had been established with his death in Etterdam."

"And a few other assorted odd details," Dider added, "not relevant at the moment."

"So this Lord Tommus is Lord Orcus reborn?" Soo An asked.

"Well, that's what the prophecy said, or something similar. It was in a rather convoluted and ambiguous language, as prophecies always are. But that is how we interpreted what was foretold. Every other interpretation we could come up with made no sense. There was some other nonsense about a book, but how many orcs have books?" Vespa looked at Tal Gor. "No offense shaman."

"Uhm, I actually have only two books—quite a number of scrolls though," Tal Gor said.

"Scrolls, I understand; they often have maps. Books are too long-winded, take up too much time," Dider said. "Just tell me what I need to know, spare me the useless details."

Bor Tal nodded. "Who do we fight, when do we fight, and where do we fight!"

Kirak nodded and smiled. "Exactly!"

"And who's bringing the glargh for afterwards!" Dider added.

"We are not going to have enough glargh to wash down our meat after this giant hunt!" Soo Ann suddenly worried.

Vespa laughed. "You think you have a problem? We are hunting here and on other planes to feed two thousand D'Orcs. Getting enough glargh—or as we drink, x-glargh—is going to be a true challenge. We are going to need at least three dozen barrels!"

"The steward thinks she has some ideas on getting glargh to make x-glargh, but it is a lot to pull together on such short notice," Dider said.

Bor Tal shrugged. "Well, I don't know about three dozen, but you should be able to get a dozen barrels in Murgatroy."

"That's where we get barrels for the tribe gatherings." Soo An nodded.

The D'Orcs looked at each other. "Is this Murgatroy far away?" Vespa asked.

"Quite a ways, but if we are flying at hunt speed? A bit over a day's flight, perhaps."

"That's a lot of hunting time." Vespa shook her head. "It would take us until after fierdset to get there. Let us discuss this with the steward and Lord Tommus. We might be able to return tomorrow to get glargh."

"Or," Dider said, "Astlan is mana rich. D'Orcs and D'Wargs need no sleep. After we hunt, we could travel through the night to this Murgatroy. Our hosts, who know where we are going, would need to sleep on D'Wargback, which I suspect would not be pleasant."

"We can ride all night for glargh!" Bor Tal said with a bit of indignation. "We are Crooked Sticks, after all!" He grinned.

"I would be game for that!" Tal Gor said. He did not want this day to end, so if he could extend it through tomorrow, that would be ideal. Bor Tal and Soo An nodded in agreement.

Vespa grinned and nodded her head.

Chapter 104

"You are looking a bit… sickly, master," Vaselle told Edwyrd hesitantly as the animage finished dressing in the clothes he had asked the wizard to purchase for him.

"You are starting to sound like Tizzy," Edwyrd said, chuckling. "You do know that if I walked about the city in my true form, there would be mass panic and the wards would be immediately snapped back on?"

Vaselle shrugged. "Yes, but it seems a small price for not sacrificing your comfort. Surely squeezing your true magnificence into such a small and weak form must be uncomfortable?"

Edwyrd looked at Vaselle and grinned. "You are amazingly perceptive, Vaselle. It is quite uncomfortable, particularly when I haven't been in this form for several days. It takes adjustment. However, we need to go see Damien and I can't enter the palace as Tom."

"Have you have finished with your hunting parties?" Vaselle asked.

"I brought the last game back from Etterdam right before I came here; however, I will be retrieving the D'Orcs in the morning. They are feasting with their hosts tonight and wanted some more time outside the Abyss. The guys here in Astlan are feasting now and will be heading to someplace called Murgatroy overnight to try and get barrels of glargh."

"Murgatroy?" Vaselle said, trying to recall if he knew where that was. "I assume that must be somewhere near Jotungard?"

Edwyrd shook his head. "I barely know where Freehold is relative to Gizzor Del and Lenamare's castle." He frowned. "I've got maps, or at least old maps. I should study them. If I had more shamans I'd have them update the maps, but that's a big undertaking."

"You could just buy some maps here in Freehold," Vaselle observed.

Edwyrd grinned. "Mount Doom's maps are pretty cool; you will want to see them." He chuckled. "I probably should get some normal maps for an interim update, but I am not sure how long paper maps will last in the Abyss." He shook his head. "So much work to do!"

Edwyrd reflected on his conversation about maps with Vaselle as they made their way to the palace and Damien's suite. He had mentioned all the work he had to do to bring Mount Doom up to date, and that was very true, but the real insight was that it was *something to do.* Up until he had freed the Rod of Tommus, he had not really had anything to do. He had had no goal other than getting by day-to-day. Now he had something worth doing, something constructive to actually do with his time. That was exciting. It was surprising how much better he felt having something to do, something to plan for and look forward to. He had been feeling pretty depressed in his old day-to-day rut, bouncing from disaster to disaster and contemplating doing that for thousands of years. However, rebuilding Mount Doom and the D'Orcs and their networks—that was something to keep him occupied for centuries, if not longer. There were infinite worlds to explore. Things to do, places to go. Really, this could be a lot of fun!

Of course, there was the small detail of the Church and Rod of Tiernon, and presumably this Lilith woman who hated D'Orcs for some reason. However, he should be able to reach an accommodation with them. He had no desire for conquest, just for ensuring good lives for his people. It would take some effort, but he was sure he could work out deals. He hoped so, at least. He had seen how difficult Talarius could be; Tiernon and the rest were probably worse.

They were just starting up the stairs to Damien's suite's floor when he realized that he was thinking about negotiating a treaty with a god. Okay, somebody's ego was getting out of check! Edwyrd grinned to himself. The two walked down the hallway to Damien's suite and Vaselle knocked on the door.

One of Damien's valets opened the door and let them in. Damien came into the sitting room from the dining room.

"Welcome back, Edwyrd, Vaselle," Damien said, reaching his hand out in greeting to Edwyrd and then Vaselle. "I think the later time worked out better because we can have dinner."

"Definitely. I've been looking forward to catching up and getting your advice on various issues," Edwyrd said. "Plus it's a great opportunity to talk to both of you about making an arcane device that I think would be quite useful."

~

"So you have no idea what was behind those Etonian wards?" Damien asked after Edwyrd had finished relating his story. He had gone back to the major turning point in the story. Obviously a rather hard-to-believe incident.

Edwyrd shook his head. "Not a clue." He gestured to Antefalken and said, "We were just out for sightseeing and picking up some treasure. We then got lost and in over our heads. It was purely random chance; a case of being in the right place at the right time."

Antefalken nodded. "I admit, if I had not been there every single step of the way, I would never have believed this story."

Damien closed his eyes and shook his head. "But how does one accidentally stumble upon the Wand of Orcus?" He opened his eyes. "Lost, hidden and shielded by Etonian runes for thousands of years, right in the old seat of this demon prince's lair?"

Edwyrd chuckled. "And not only that. These were not just Etonian runes; this stuff was pure Tiernon magic. I could easily see that, and the trick I learned in battle, how to decode their mana streams—I used the same trick on these runes and then used the excess mana I'd stolen to meld with and subvert the wards. I was basically masquerading as an avatar of Tiernon." Edwyrd blinked as he said this, having not really thought of that angle before.

"How do you plan something like that?" Antefalken asked.

Damien shook his head and shrugged. "I have no idea; I could not have foreseen the results of your battle with Talarius, let alone the way in which the battle came about thanks to Lenamare."

"Exactly, it was completely random that we went treasure hunting at Mount Doom," Antefalken said.

Edwyrd frowned. "Well—I'm not so sure on that point."

The others looked at Edwyrd. "It may simply be his insanity, but when I freed the Rod of Tommus from the stones, Tizzy was looking happier, more ecstatic than I've ever seen him. He was literally dancing, or at least I think that was what he was doing. It could have been a seizure."

Antefalken squinted. "Well, it *was* his idea to go there."

"And he knew a lot of the D'Orcs," Edwyrd pointed out. "And they didn't seem to like him."

"Which proves they probably did know him," Antefalken pointed out.

"But the idea that Tizzy planned all this doesn't make much sense, given that it *is* Tizzy we are talking about. You've known him much longer than I have; have you ever known him to be able to carry out anything that required planning?"

Antefalken shook his head. "I've known him since I first arrived in the Abyss. The only thing he ever seems to reliably remember to do is to restock his pipe stash. Otherwise, he is very unreliable. Actually, the fact that he's stuck around so long with us is pretty remarkable."

Edwyrd nodded. "That's what I've noticed. Although I still don't know where he's keeping his pipe and stash."

Antefalken grinned. "I can guess about the pipe." His grin was suddenly replaced by a frown. "Although now that I say that, as a fiend he should not be able to do that." He shook his head. "Whatever. I don't think it is relevant, other than I have no idea where he gets the stuff he smokes."

"If this is where this conversation is going"—Damien shook his head and reached for the wine decanter—"I'm going to need another drink."

"Me too," Vaselle said, lifting his glass towards the decanter so Damien could refill it.

"You would need a drink if you'd been stuck in a cave with Tizzy going on and on the whole time. If not talking to us or irritating Talarius, he would just start up conversations with himself," Edwyrd said, smiling.

"You mean like the heated debate he had with himself over ruined buildings in the Courts of Chaos? And why someone might choose to live in a ruin?" Antefalken asked, laughing.

Edwyrd laughed and looked at Damien. "Tizzy is nuts. It's just that this prophecy stuff from the D'Orcs has me getting a bit paranoid." He turned back to

Antefalken. "Before one goes too far off the deep end, it's always critical to step back and take a rational look at reality and who one is dealing with."

Damien chuckled and lifted his wine glass in a toast.

~

Tal Gor groaned as Schwarzenfürze was buffeted by a particularly strong wind current. He was strapped in pretty tight and resting his head on the D'Warg's neck and the back of her head. He was trying to sleep off a bad case of glarghvost as they flew to Murgatroy, but it was a bumpy flight. He could only imagine how his family and tribemates were doing on their D'Wargs. Evil D'Orcs had been having great fun at their expense. Glargh could not make D'Orcs drunk, but they had failed to tell anyone that, so that had led to drinking challenges that his tribe had all promptly failed. It was very hard to outdrink someone who could not get drunk.

The D'Orcs had eventually explained to everyone that they drank x-glargh, which was a more potent (as in *fatal* to orcs), version of glargh. They wanted to get glargh in Murgatroy so they could doctor it into x-glargh for their party. At this point, Tal Gor could not even imagine a party with glargh, let alone x-glargh.

They had had an incredible feast and party after they had returned from the hunt. No one in the tribe could remember a bigger haul for a hunting party. Nor could anyone recall stories of one. The D'Orcs had let the tribe keep as much as they could readily eat or preserve, and the rest had been hauled through a portal to Mount Doom for the feast of Lord Tommus.

The tribe had eaten better this evening than they had in at least a generation! It had been a feast to remember for a lifetime and everyone was exceedingly pleased. The hunters had regaled the rest of the tribe with the events of the day, their great kills. He smiled to think how jealous those who had been left behind were. None of them had ever hunted from the air before. So much glory! So much honor!

Even through his lingering drunken haze and severe headache, Tal Gor felt deliriously happy. Now they were on their mission for more glargh. The plan was to go and buy as many barrels of glargh as they could; he would then summon Lord Tommus. They would then all go into Mount Doom, bringing the glargh with them. Lord Tommus said they would do the swap in the freezer so as not to be roasted. Very odd comment, but apparently it was quite hot in the Abyss.

Lord Tommus had left his son Rupert and Rupert's friend Fer-Rog with the tribe. Apparently, Lord Tommus could communicate with Rupert. He would summon Lord Tommus to open a portal, and then the orcs could return to camp without having to make the long return journey, bringing a couple of barrels of glargh back with them.

It would have been a lot of effort to carry a dozen or more barrels of glargh on the long flight back to the camp. Tal Gor shook his head, thinking about how much easier life was when you could fly and open shortcuts to other planes to travel through. It was literally the stuff of legends.

As he eyed the dark, distant ground below him, he wondered what it would feel like to be puked on from above. Certainly worse than bird droppings. Something or someone down there might have to find out soon. His stomach was no happier than his head. He gently petted Schwarzenfürze's fur as they flew; doing so was rather soothing to his glargh-addled body.

~

"This place is awesome!" Fer-Rog exclaimed to Rupert as they came up to a wide stream. He jumped in the water and splashed around. "Water that stays on the ground? That you can walk into and through?" Fer-Rog shook his head. "It is almost as weird as the hairy ground!"

"Tall grass," Rupert corrected for the third time. "Most of the ground in Astlan has stuff growing on it. Except for deserts, or so I am told. I have never seen a desert other than, I guess, the Abyss.

"Yeah, and those wooden sticks growing out of the ground are pretty cool too. Who knew wood was all fluffy on the end? We have so little wood at Mount Doom, and all of it really old and heavily preserved." Fer-Rog hunkered down to sit in the stream.

"It is so cool, cold even. I have never felt anything like it." He ran his claws through the water, watching it whirl and part around his fingers. He looked towards the east as Fierd came above the horizon, and his eyes widened. "Don't look now, but there is a giant ball of fire that just came over the horizon!"

Rupert chuckled. "That's Fierd. It is coming up and will follow an arc through the sky, bringing light to the world!" He traced Fierd's path through the sky with his arm. "Wow, I just realized this is your first fierdrise!"

"What's a fierdrise?" Fer-Rog asked.

"It's what we are watching: Fierd rising above the horizon, starting its journey while providing light, energy and life to plants," Rupert explained.

"So it's orbiting Astlan? I remember being taught that Astlan, and most worlds, are spheres." Fer-Rog asked.

"No, Astlan orbits Fierd; Uropia and Anuropia orbit Astlan. That greenish crescent we saw in the sky last night was Uropia, the closest moon. Anuropia should be in the southern hemisphere now and visible during the day. Not sure where we are, but given where Uropia was in the sky, we might see Anuropia near the southern horizon today."

"Okay…" Fer-Rog said, trying to figure it out.

"Fierd and Uropia traverse the sky from east to west; Anuropia moves from either north to south or south to north, depending on the time of year."

"Seems complicated." Fer-Rog shook his head.

"Yeah, it is, but you gotta know all about this stuff if you're a wizard because where the moons are affects the astrological signs and can have a major influence on spell casting. Most spells are associated with the five elements, and the moons determine the season and thus the current elemental affiliations," Rupert said.

"And that makes a difference?" Fer-Rog asked.

"Spells of the opposite sign are harder to cast and are less effective; spells that are of the same sign are easier to cast and are more powerful. So yes, it can. Unless you are someone like Lenamare, who can toss enough mana into a spell to counteract the astrological effects on the elements. Most normal wizards can't," Rupert said.

"Lenamare is that crazy wizard you studied under?" Fer-Rog asked, trying to remember what Rupert had told him about life in Astlan.

"Yep, that's him. He's one of the most powerful wizards in the world," Rupert said.

"He would have to be in order to summon a demon prince." Fer-Rog said.

"Yeah, well, I think and have always figured that my dad wanted Lenamare to summon him so he could be reunited with me. So as I figure it, father just used Lenamare and his summons as a focal point. Sort of like the calling stones he is using to locate the shamans."

"So why did he take so long to come find you?" Fer-Rog asked.

Rupert frowned. "I'm not really clear on that. He does not want to talk about it for some reason. Maybe he didn't know my mom had died? Or maybe he was busy on other planes doing things and that was as soon as he could get to Astlan. Or, who knows—maybe it is part of the prophecy, and I was meant to experience life as a human for several years."

Fer-Rog frowned. "I've never met a human, unless that knight of your dad's is a human; can't tell inside his armor. I've heard stories about them, though; while physically weak, they are shifty and untrustworthy, only slightly better than the evil alvar, who no one can trust."

Rupert shrugged. "Many of them are nice enough, but it is true that a number of them are petty and mean and lacking in honor. Talarius is a human; he killed me once here in Astlan and tried to kill all of us permanently about a week ago. That's when my dad kicked his butt and took him prisoner."

"Why did he try to kill you? I mean, I know that is what followers of Tiernon do, just like the demons that follow Lilith, but I'm not sure why," Fer-Rog asked.

Rupert shook his head. "He's convinced that all demons are evil and out to overthrow humanity and all goodness in the world. He has therefore made it his job to kill all demons he encounters."

"Seems rather racist if you ask me," Fer-Rog observed.

"Tell me about it, but it's a pretty common belief among humans," Rupert said.

"So why didn't anyone try to kill you previously?" Fer-Rog gestured up and down at Rupert. "You're pretty obviously a demon."

Rupert chuckled. "I don't always look like a demon, see?" He suddenly shifted into his human form.

Fer-Rog splashed backward in the stream in shock and surprise. "What did you do?" His eyes were wide.

"I changed my form!" Rupert grinned. "This is how I managed not to get killed among the humans. I was disguised as one." Rupert was not ready to admit he was only half demon.

"You can do that?" Fer-Rog was staring at him intensely. "That's a pretty sickly-looking form, very puny and weak, even compared to an orc!" He shook his head. "I can't imagine wanting to look like that."

Rupert grinned. "I know, it's not that pleasant, and now it feels very cramped and confining, but that's how I survived for my entire life up until my father showed up."

"Wow! I'm so sorry, I thought we had it bad at Mount Doom, but I can't imagine being trapped like that and knowing that if you turned into yourself you'd be killed." He looked up and down at human Rupert and grimaced in distaste.

"Yeah, but I'm good now. Actually, I have had a lot of fun pretending to be human since my dad arrived. It's a great way to infiltrate humans and sneak among them and get information," Rupert said. "At least, up until a knight kills you."

"Yeah, you mentioned that before. If Talarius killed you, why aren't you dead?" Fer-Rog asked quite reasonably.

Rupert laughed. "That's the best part of Astlan. Short of really spectacular efforts, demons can't die here. If you get killed, you just rematerialize in the Abyss. It hurts, and you have to regenerate, get your energy back, but you aren't dead."

Fer-Rog pondered this. "So you could go into battle, kill your foes, and if they somehow killed you, you'd just end up in the Abyss and could return to fight some more?"

"Once you've rested." Rupert nodded.

"Great Orcus's balls!" Fer-Rog cursed in amazement. "That's like being in heaven!"

Rupert chuckled. "I think that was the point. As I understand it from Tizzy, Orcus turned the greatest of the great orc warriors into D'Orcs upon death so they could serve in his army. They could travel the multiverse fighting battles and if they died, they were simply penalized by having to stay in the Abyss for a while."

"Yeah, that makes sense now. That is sort of what I've been told, but differently. It never really sank in before. But I get it now," Fer-Rog said.

"Wow, that would be so cool!" he added after a moment. "I wish I could change form; I'd change into an orc and just travel around Astlan looking for fun and adventure, and if I got in over my head, I'd still be safe and could regenerate at Mount Doom."

Rupert nodded. "Exactly, because if you are in disguise as a non-demon, anyone trying to kill you wouldn't know to take the extra precautions to kill you permanently."

"Oh, they can do that?" Fer-Rog asked nervously.

"Some people can, but it is very hard to do. Only a few wizards, and of course the priests of Tiernon, know how to do it. And even the priests, they need a big ritual to do it, so if you've got time to escape if you need to," Rupert explained. "Of course, when I learned that, we were all trapped in a magical net, so we couldn't fade to the Abyss, which was scary."

Fer-Rog shook his head. "I wish I could change my form. That would be so cool!"

Rupert shrugged. "How do you know you can't? D'Orcs are demons, and all the more powerful demons can do it."

Fer-Rog frowned. "Well, I've never heard of a D'Orc doing that."

Rupert frowned and thought for a minute. "But then, why would they need to? None of the D'Orcs have been able to get out of the Abyss since Orcus was killed; and before that they were all busy making war! Plus, given what I've seen at Mount Doom, how many D'Orcs would want to shrink down into a little orc without good reason?"

Fer-Rog nodded. "That would be cool! If only someone could teach me!"

Rupert grinned and gave what he hoped was an evil chuckle. "Well, I have taught someone before... and I've been practicing link spells, so now it should be even easier to show you how to do it!"

"Excellent!" Fer-Rog clapped his hands in the water, splashing Rupert.

~

Ragala-nargoloth flopped down in her four-poled hammock bed and lit one of the cigars from her hidden stash. She was sparing in her use of tobacco since it was expensive, but this was certainly an occasion. Normally, she would have shared it with her partner, but they had only barely finished their ninth session of the night when Lord Tommus had called on her to open a portal to collect the D'Orcs and D'Wargs.

As she exhaled a large plume of smoke, she idly reflected on her rather spectacular evening. As shaman, she was naturally aware of all the taboos and customs of her people in regards to marriage and fooling around. And while sex between direct descendants was against custom, did it count if the other party was an ancestor from over four thousand years ago, and now technically a different species?

Hmm. Clearly something to ponder —but not too hard. She chuckled and then coughed on the smoke in her throat. Arg-nargoloth was clearly the hero of legends. His stamina was unorcish. Well, she supposed it was D'Orcish. He could take his time and please her, and then immediately reset and continue.

"Once you get a D'Orc in the sack, you'll never go back!" Ragal-nargoloth chortled to herself. From the sounds she had heard last night from around the camp, she was pretty sure she would find lots of agreement in the tribe.

~

DOF +8
Start of Third Period 16-05-440

"Good morning!" Antefalken called to Tom as the bard walked into Tom's quarters. "I like my new bedroom. There are some decent-looking D'Orcettes here; I think the bed should be most useful!"

Tom chuckled. "You could also sleep in it. The competition for mana with the complex tends to make demons sleepy. We are all going to be taking up Rupert's bad habits soon enough, I fear."

"Well, if I'm going to need to sleep, I'll want a companion or two, that's for sure." The bard grinned. "Is Rupert in there sleeping now?" He pointed to Rupert's bedroom.

Tom shook his head. "He and Fer-Rog stayed the night in Astlan with the Crooked Sticks. Later today they are going to help me create a gateway to the Crooked Stick camp, so we can return the orcs who went to Murgatroy for glargh."

Antefalken nodded. "Very nice shortcut. Might be handy if you could teach Rupert how to make those gateways. It's going to be a pain if you have to play gatekeeper all the time."

"True. We really need to find some others who can do this stuff. Maybe some training sessions."

"That's a very undemonic way of doing things. At least in the Courts, it is. There, it is everyone for themselves," Antefalken observed.

"Yes, but like orcs, D'Orcs are very tribal and band together for the common good. I'm pretty sure it's one reason they have been able to resist Lilith's periodic purges." Tom shrugged. "I want to do some rebuilding and help the D'Orcs get back their standing."

"Admirable," Antefalken commented.

"Not so much admirable as something to occupy my time," Tom admitted. "Something to give me a purpose. Sitting bored in a cave, waiting for others to make a move that I would then need to react to is not a lot of fun. This makes me feel more in control of something." Tom tilted his head. "I know that Tiernon's folks are going to come looking for me; you said it yourself. I know my helping the D'Orcs is going to make Lilith mad. So, might as well do what I can to deal with these threats in advance."

"I did," Antefalken said, smiling, "and I agree." The bard hopped up on the back of a chair. "The only thing that gives me pause is how others will react to your actions."

Tom shrugged. "We are out here in the middle of nowhere. It will be some time before people notice that Mount Doom is active."

"I bet Lilith knows. She has that fortress watching the place. Or she will know before long," Antefalken reminded him.

"I am sure, and therefore, we need to be ready. But she still doesn't know much about me, and I would think that might slow her down, although I could be wrong," Tom said.

"One would hope it would give her pause. She's very hard to read on such things," Antefalken answered. "However, that will happen one way or the other. I might be more concerned about D'Orcs showing up in Murgatroy."

"It's an orc trading city; you think the D'Orcs will freak out the orcs?" Tom asked.

"Well, it's not so much an orc trading city, as a city to which orcs and a lot of others come to trade. It is the others that concern me."

"Meaning the humans in Murgatroy?" Tom asked.

"A little, but really, the alvar are a bigger concern. There are quite a few alvar there, living tenuously with the orcs, but there. Alvar live for thousands of years; they are bound to know what D'Orcs are. Pretty sure it will freak them out."

"Great! This would probably have been good to consider before I agreed with their plan." Tom shook his head and chuckled wryly. "You never stop by with happy news or thoughts!"

"Oh, I don't know. That actually reminds me, I was working on the music for the feast. We have several musical bands that want to play."

"Excellent!" Tom said.

"And to that point, they wanted me to ask you if you could make sure the sound system is active and that the lightning cables are working."

"Sound system and lightning cables?" Tom asked, puzzled.

"Yes; they have arcane devices to amplify and even modify the sound. Then they have some instruments they haven't been able to play in over four thousand years that use these special cables that provide the instruments with lightning."

"You mean electricity?" Tom asked.

Antefalken thought for a moment. "Exactly!"

"So they have electrical instruments?" Tom asked.

"That is my understanding; they've had to make do with more traditional instruments in the interim. Unfortunately those instruments don't produce the same effect for the type of music most D'Orcs like."

"What type of music is that?" Tom had a feeling about where this was going.

"Well, given this is Mount Doom and most of their instruments have metal strings, their favorite type of music is called Doom Metal, but they also like all sorts of D'Orc rock. Anything that lets them really go to town on these metal stringed instruments. We get some of it at the Courts. I am not personally a huge fan, but I know a lot of demons who are. Of course, we do not call it D'Orc rock in the Courts, but I expect that it is similar. "

Tom laughed. "Well, this should be more exciting that I'd expected! Sounds like we'll be doing some serious head banging!"

"We may all want to, after two thousand orcs all line up to personally swear to you. I'm figuring that's going to take a day or two," Antefalken said.

"Yeah, that's something I need to discuss with Zelda," Tom said. "I am thinking we do it by commander. That way they all see their immediate comrades swear, but they don't all have to be in the throne room the entire time if they don't want to be. I am thinking some would get restless standing for a day or more at a time."

Antefalken nodded. "I haven't had any real experience with D'Orcs until now, but assuming they are like orcs, huge amounts of patience and just standing around is not their thing."

"My thinking exactly," Tom agreed as he stood. "I need to head down to open the gate to Ithgar. Beya Fei is awaiting us with the Olafa Horde."

"Ithgar? Isn't that a ways out there? It's not in the Astlan localverse, is it?" Antefalken asked.

"It is not. Apparently the rules of magic are a bit different, but nothing too significant to cause problems. Frigda is one of our most experienced commanders and she is from there. We're going to Romdan a bit later this morning once we clear the staging area, and that is in the localverse." Tom told him.

"I spent a few years there with a master early in my career. I liked the place just fine."

"The more interesting one that I want to see is Gormegast," Tom said. "I am thinking about a visit this afternoon."

"It's a high-tech plane, as I recall," Antefalken noted.

"Exactly."

"I had a friend who was stuck chained to a mech for about a century there." Antefalken shook his head. "Is this the Antilles Cluster where Zog Darthelm is from?"

"It is, interestingly. Given the vastness of space, I find that odd. Of course, I find it odd that on the magic planes we always seem to end up on the same planet. Why don't some gateways open up to other planets in a particular universe?" Tom mused.

"How do we know that they don't?" Antefalken asked.

Tom looked at him, puzzled.

"Well, what if the planes that we call 'the localverse' all observe the same rules of magic because they are other planets in the same universe? If they are on opposite sides of the galaxy, or different galaxies, we couldn't even tell by the position of the stars," Antefalken said.

Tom shook his head. "My head is spinning. The multiverse is huge—an infinite number of infinitely large universes with galaxies and stars!"

"Yeah, I try not to think about it. The nice thing is that with no night in the Abyss, we don't have to stare up at the night sky and think about such things," Antefalken replied.

~

Shortly before midday, Tal Gor and his compatriots landed about a thousand feet from the southwest outskirts of Murgatroy's wargtown. With luck, the D'Wargs would get along with the wargs. Wargs from different tribes were often prickly around each other. D'Wargs and wargs would probably be even worse. With wargs, the promise of food and water, along with finishing a long journey, was usually enough to take the edge off. However, D'Wargs did not need to eat, drink or sleep, and really did not seem to get worn out.

In any event, Tal Gor would be glad to get off Schwarzenfürze. They had stopped at dawn to relieve their cramped legs, cramped bladders and cramped intestines. The orcs also ate trail bread and refreshed their water pouches from a nearby stream. The bread, water and walking around had helped clear their heads of glarghvost. Not completely, but it made the morning journey much more pleasant.

As to be expected, the D'Orcs spent most of the journey ribbing the orcs about their pathetic constitutions and being unable to hold their glargh. They liked to come up behind you and slap you hard on the back while screaming a loud greeting in your ear. Further, they also took great joy in discussing the most disgusting foods they had ever eaten, trying to make the glarghvost-suffering orcs toss their stomachs.

In all, a swell group of guys, Tal Gor thought. It was probably natural, in that the first generation D'Orcs had been chosen by Orcus as the best-of-the-best orc warriors. Therefore, you had these walking orc archetypes, and the best bloodlines the multiverse had to offer for the younger generations of D'Orcs. In particular, that explained Vespa, who was just so amazing! Yesterday, she had congratulated him on one particularly superior kill by punching him so hard in the shoulder that both Bor Tal and Fel Nor had had to help him relocate his shoulder in the socket afterwards! Tal Gor grinned and shook his head in appreciation of her magnificent strength. His shoulder still ached today.

As they were coming in for a landing, he could see orcs of various tribes, along with a good number of wargs coming to the edges of the wargtown to see them land. Several had their hands to their brows, trying to get a clearer view in the glare of fierdlight from above. Others were readying their weapons, naturally expecting an invasion. That is why they had landed a thousand feet away, to give those in the town time to realize they meant no harm.

Soo An had unfurled the tribe's banner while they were in air. The flying tack had pole cups and straps for two banner staves. Vespa explained that, as their guests in this world, the D'Orcs were marching under the Crooked Stick banner on this mission. Soo An would also be carrying the colors with them into town.

They landed and the orcs dismounted.

"Keep your weapons sheathed and D'Wargs heeled," Vespa ordered. "We'll march with Tal Gor and myself in the lead, Soo An to my left flank, Virok to Tal Gor's right flank. We keep our arms to our sides and in plain display." It was a standard neutral formation for potentially rival tribes when approaching. The very presence of D'Orcs and D'Wargs guaranteed that those in the wargtown would be suspicious.

They approached the main corridor of the town. It was not walled, obviously, being a place for wargs to relax and wait for their orcs to return from the city. The wargs wanted to be free to come and go. From the main corridor, where a crowd had gathered, a large, heavily scarred, old orc shoved his way to the front, along with an orc in a vet coat and a one-eyed orc who looked to be nearly ninety years old, yet still quite burly.

Vespa chuckled and whispered to Tal Gor, "I am enjoying our visit as much as I can see you are. In the Abyss, we only have trading missions with various demon groups, and they are either notoriously hard to impress or the kind of spineless weasels you would just as soon step on as talk to."

They came within twenty feet of the wargtown's advance party. The leader was looking Vespa directly in the eyes; the other two were leering at her in a mixture of lust and barely concealed terror. Tal Gor chuckled. This woman's mere presence could defeat an entire orc troop. The crowd in the town was staring and pointing at the D'Orcs and the D'Wargs. The wings were clearly confusing them.

The wargtown leader nodded to Vespa. "I am Meat Maker of the Broken Tusk Clan, Master of Wargtown here in Murgatroy," he stated loudly. "This is WargDoc Toothsetter of the Nan Tribe, Vet of Wargtown." He gestured to the orc in the vet coat. "To my left is Tiberious Smashfinger of Murgatroy, Watch Commander of Wargtown."

Vespa nodded to them. "I am Vespa, daughter of Selma, daughter of Hazel, daughter of Vera Death Sister of the Crooked Stick tribe. I am Commander of the Nineteenth Regiment of the Dark Lord Tommus. My D'Orcs and I ride today under the banner of the Crooked Stick tribe at the invitation of Tal Gor El Crooked Stick, Shaman to the Dark Lord Tommus and the Crooked Stick tribe." She gestured deferentially at Tal Gor.

Her right arm then gestured to Virok. "And this is Huntmaster Virok Soulwrecker of Erdnalia III in Visteroth." That caused a number of mumblings.

"Apologies," said Meat Maker, nodding to Virok, "I am not familiar with your clan?"

"I am from the plane of Visteroth; it is far outside this world's localverse." Toothsetter and Tiberious Smashfinger's eyes both got a bit wider. The volume of noise in the crowd also spiked with this statement.

Tal Gor smiled. While there were certainly plenty of legends of offworlders, none had been seen in millennia.

"And you, commander?" Meat Maker made a gesture up and down, taking her in. "You and some of your compatriots are a bit unusual in appearance. Who is this Lord Tommus that you serve?"

From behind them, Kirak snorted. "You would think they had forgotten about D'Orcs!" Several other D'Orcs made snorting noises.

"You are the D'Orcs of legend and myth?" Meat Maker was now clearly looking troubled.

"We are," Vespa stated. Tal Gor could sense her pride in the statement. "We serve the Dark Lord Tommus; the prophesied heir to the throne of Orcus and the new Master of Mount Doom!" She gave the crowd a very pleased, yet still rather frightening grin. The three leaders shifted quite uncomfortably as the crowd in the wargtown started babbling excitedly behind them.

"Uhm, so what brings you to Murgatroy?" Meat Maker asked nervously.

Vespa smiled. "What else? We come to trade. We have business in town and need a place for our D'Wargs to rest while we are here." She held her arms out wide. "On this, we are no different than anyone else here." She gestured to the town.

The three leaders stared warily at the D'Wargs, who stood off to the side snorting, spitting and periodically expelling snot, as was their wont when idling. Much like wargs, actually, just a lot more so.

Tal Gor glanced at the D'Wargs, controlling a smile. He could not blame Meat Maker for his trepidation; the D'Wargs were a surly lot. If he had not spent the day hunting with them, he would have been nervous himself. Of course, the way the D'Wargs were eying the wargs in the town... well, it was quite unsettling, suggesting a sort of hunger, but given his knowledge of wargs, he was sure it was more of a mating hunger than physical hunger.

"So you want a pavilion for them to rest in?" Meat Maker asked uncertainly.

Virok shrugged. "That is a convenient way to arrange it. My guess is that the D'Wargs may want to take the measure of some of the wargs here." He grinned, his eyes glowing deep red in his otherwise gray face. "Perhaps in a few months some of your other guests may end up with some mighty nasty pups."

"We will leave the customary two handlers here to ensure that none of the wargs are accidentally killed or eaten by the D'Wargs," Vespa said, producing two large silver coins. "Will this be sufficient to rent a pavilion until midafternoon?"

Meat Maker eyed the two large, very old coins. Suddenly he seemed to relax and get much friendlier. He nodded. "It will do; however, it does not cover glargh for your handlers. That is extra, paid at the bar."

Vespa nodded.

~

Sir Gadius and Peace Bringer solidified on the shore of the small island along the coast of Norelon, en route to Keeper's City. Gadius pulled his helmet off, placing it under one arm as he moved to a large rock to rest. His iridescent chain mail rattled under his surcoat as he sat. Peace Bringer wandered over to a patch of tasty-looking grass and began munching.

Gadius chuckled. "I might join you," he said. "I'm not hungry, nor I suppose are you; but at this point, after the last five hours traversing the aether, any semblance of normality would be welcome." To outside observers, the unicorn would seem to be ignoring him; however, Gadius could feel his companion's amusement at his desire for normalcy. Gadius had never like traveling through the aether. True, one never tired or got hungry; nor did one have to worry about landscape features, if one did not care to. He did not like running through mountains and hills, though. It was too unsettling. He preferred to go over such obstacles.

Sea travel was much better, unless the waves were really high; aethereally "splashing" through the waves, and sand dunes for that matter, was much less unpleasant than moving through solid stone.

He sighed. Officially, they were taking a break in the material world to relieve the *otherness* of the aether, but the two of them had spent days and nights traversing the aether when time was critical. One needed neither rest nor sleep in the aether. Time was important, but the arch-vicar general's ships set the length of time for the journey, not the two of them. He had no desire to arrive in Keeper's City before the fleet.

No, he had no fear of Keeper's City; it was simply his distrust and distaste for the Oorstemothians. This proposed alliance did not sit well with him. However, their planned undertaking required resources that neither the Rod nor the church possessed. This Chancellor Alighieri claimed to have built the ideal tool to achieve their goal of rescuing Talarius.

It would be a long and difficult journey, if it even truly worked, but it was their solemn duty to try and rescue their brother knight. He could only imagine the horrors the good fellow must be enduring. With a cruel thought, Gadius suddenly wondered if Talarius had been reconnected with his doomed, damned ladylove, Melissance.

Sir Gadius shook his head at his own pettiness. Such a horrible thought was unworthy of him. Still, if they at least met up for a short while, maybe the knight would stop obsessing over the woman. It had been long enough ago at this point that Talarius's continued dwelling on her had become more of a pathology than an emotional sentiment.

Gadius suddenly had a horrible thought. What if Talarius refused to leave the Abyss without rescuing Melissance? It would be his one-time opportunity to do the unimaginable. Gadius shook his head at that thought. Where would one even begin to look for her, who had been but a poor lost soul consigned to the Abyss upon death, deprived of the grace of Tiernon? An unholy beast like that which had kidnapped Talarius would surely stand out in the Abyss; even if not, they would be able to track Talarius, given that the knight would be the only other thing in the Abyss to radiate the power signature of Tiernon. A lost soul, however, would be nearly impossible to find.

~

"Mistress?" One of her pages requested Lilith's attention.

"Yes?" The demoness asked, gazing at her servant over the top of the old scroll of infantem vellum she had been reading.

"Lord Asmodeus is here to see you," the page replied nervously.

"Show him in." Lilith

The page closed the door and a few moments later the door opened again with the page ushering the demon prince in. Asmodeus came in with a firm jaw, but a distinct twinkle in his eye. The page left the room closing the door behind itself.

Lilith gestured at the chair opposite her in front of the ice-place for him to join her.

He glanced at the icy flames in the ice-place. "Cozying up with a good book?"

Lilith simply smiled and handed him the scroll.

As he took it, he noticed the feel. "Infantem vellum? It must be a good read." He glanced briefly at it. "Indeed, I had thought this lost for a few millennia."

Lilith smiled and shrugged. "I was cleaning up one of my remote palaces and found it."

"Hmm, perhaps I should do similar to see what I might find." Asmodeus chuckled.

"Knowing you, it's more likely an issue of 'who' you might find. You tend to be in the middle of torturing someone, get distracted and then forget about them for a few centuries or more."

Asmodeus shook his head from side to side in a short arc. "Are you prescient?"

Lilith raised an eyebrow.

"I did happen to find someone I had misplaced," he said.

"Really?"

"Yes, although this had only been for a few decades."

"Go on… I assume this must be something relevant to one of our current endeavors or you would not rush right over to tell me." Lilith chuckled.

"Indeed." Asmodeus nodded. "You recall this knight of Tiernon that the greater demon captured? Talarius?"

Lilith nodded. "My understanding is that he's one of Tiernon's greatest knights in Astlan."

"Indeed, but that is not all. Like most heroes, he had an exploitable weakness."

"Had?" Lilith asked.

"That's just it. One of my archdemons had been working on this corruption deal with his vampire agents in Astlan, and they had encountered this Talarius and were working to corrupt him."

"And?" Lilith was getting intrigued.

"Well, it seems they put a challenge out to him, and he rose above it and sacrificed his one true love to maintain his holy vows." Asmodeus smiled.

"So the corruption exercise failed." Lilith shrugged.

At this point Asmodeus's grin became wicked. Lilith always enjoyed this grin. "Yes, but he has apparently been tormenting himself ever since." Lilith nodded for him to continue. "And of course, we still have the bait—he sacrificed her and my agent has her soul!"

Lilith clapped her hands. "Excellent! Once he finds out, he will be compelled to mount a rescue mission. We then get him, and with him will come the greater demon!"

Asmodeus smiled. "This should drag this so-called greater demon out of that stupid cave he's holed up in!"

Lilith's grin faded and turned to a frown and then a grimace. "Yes, well, about that…"

Asmodeus looked at her curiously.

"There has been a bit of a complication. He and his entourage have relocated," Lilith told him.

Asmodeus shrugged. "So where did he go? We will just track him down there. He didn't leave the Abyss, did he?"

"No," Lilith admitted, "but that might have been better. You aren't going to like this."

Asmodeus looked at her askance, puzzled by her meaning.

Chapter 105

The guards at the gates to Murgatroy had observed the interaction in the wargtown and apparently decided this rather odd lot was safe to enter. From what Tal Gor's parents and others had told him, including Soo An, Murgatroy was known to welcome more than its fair share of suspicious travelers. Which was all well and good, since he doubted the town had ever seen characters more unusual than the D'Orcs. Demons were always frowned upon, of course, but unbound, winged demons that looked like orcs and went about of their own accord? He was sure that was unheard of. He was thus pleasantly surprised that they were not stopped.

On second thought, Tal Gor realized they were a hunting party of nineteen orcs and nineteen D'Orcs, Zerg Fel Far and Fed Tal having stayed behind in the wargtown to watch the gear and the D'Wargs. He had to admit, one would have to be rather crazy to try to stop such a group, especially when they were coming in peace to buy lots of stuff.

They were traveling down a rather wide boulevard towards the town center. He noted a number of taverns and brothels nearby. Given the proximity of the town to this gate, this was probably the main entrance for orc warriors. Tal Gor had not been here since he was a child. Soo An and his brothers came more frequently.

Naturally, everyone in the city stopped what they were doing to watch them walk down the street. The D'Orcs were giving the townspeople mean glares; clearly enjoying themselves. Bor Tal and Soo An nodded or waved occasionally to merchants or townspeople they recognized. He let his eyes smile, noting the way his tribemates were working so hard to pretend they did this sort of thing every day. He chuckled softly in his throat.

They were part of a legend come to life! For once, he felt the sort of glory the mighty heroes of old must have felt as they marched through conquered cities. True, they had not conquered Murgatroy, but they were looked upon with awe, trepidation and even fear. He was very pleased to note a number of small children crying with fright. As they passed one opening, a bunch of human youths who had been trying to get a look at what was coming down the street saw them, screamed in fear and ran the other way.

"Heaven," Tal Gor said to himself.

Vespa laughed beside him and turned to give him a big grin.

Dider spoke up behind them. "Commander, there is a market up ahead, I am thinking we should pick up ingredients to make bread to go along with the meat."

"Excellent idea; why don't you take two D'Orcs and two orcs and buy several bags of grain and, if you can, eggs and yeast, yeast first. Kirak, see if you can get some sacks of root vegetables. Turnips, potatoes—whatever, and as much as you can find," Vespa ordered.

"How about a wagon or two? That way we don't have to make too many trips," Tal Gor suggested. "Fel Nor and maybe one of your warriors could see about renting a wagon?"

Vespa nodded. "Excellent idea, but what is renting?"

~

"Why are you dragging me out here, Bastien?" Neelon demanded of his great grandson.

"I think you need to see this. I believe it is something that hasn't been seen in Astlan since before my father's birth," Bastien told the elder. "But I need your confirmation."

"So you need me for my geriatricity?" The old alfar complained.

"I would use the word *wisdom*, sir," Bastien corrected as he dragged his great grandfather out onto the roof deck overlooking the marketplace.

"It had better to be important to rouse me from my meditation," the old alfar harrumphed.

Bastien tugged him by the hand to the wall and pointed to the large square. "There, in the market!"

"What am I looking for?" Neelon groused, squinting out into the market.

"You cannot miss them," Bastien replied.

Neelon stared out across the market for a moment before his raspy breathing stopped. His back stiffened as his full attention became riveted on the market. He began scouring every inch of the market, counting under his breath.

"They came in with a similar-sized group of orcs. Prior to entering the city, they stopped to stable their mounts in the wargtown," Bastien said.

"You mean their wargs?" The elder asked in an odd voice, hopeful yet resigned.

"Wargs only in the way those fellows with wings are orcs. They were bigger, nastier, winged wargs!" Bastien said with clear worry in his voice.

Neelon shook his head. "What do they want? Why are they here?"

"Apparently they are buying supplies—food, glargh, beer. I have no idea why; it must be some sort of subterfuge."

"Or perhaps a great gathering," Neelon sighed.

"Are they what I think?" Bastien said breathlessly, turning to stare again into the marketplace.

"Assuming you think they are D'Orcs, the infernal and eternally damned minions of the Dark Lord Orcus, then yes. Yes, they are." Neelon said, sighing again. "This is truly an ill wind and a dark day for both the alvar and the mortal races we shepherd."

"What should we do?" Bastien asked worriedly.

"You and your fellow rangers need to get word to Murgandor as fast as possible. Send one messenger now, and another after these foul creatures depart, so that we can give a full accounting of their activity. They will be able to get word out to the rest of the alvar and to Prince Ariel and the Grove. Make all haste; do not rest on the journey." Neelon sighed once more and turned to peer out into the marketplace in despair.

~

Tal Gor expected the presence of the D'Orcs to cause the merchants to haggle less. Apparently, however, the orc merchants, at least, did not seem that impressed. Once a merchant determined they wanted to buy his or her wares rather than kill him and take whatever they pleased, the merchant's tone changed considerably.

Tal Gor was standing by the wagon that Fel Nor had rented and was directing the packing of foodstuffs. The glargh merchants were going to deliver the glargh barrels to the wargtown. While this was going on, a large orc dressed as a chieftain of some tribe Tal Gor didn't recognize, approached him.

"Who are you and what are you doing here?" the chieftain demanded loudly.

"I am Tal Gor El Crooked Stick, Chief Shaman of the Dark Lord Tommus in Astlan." So, maybe he was giving himself a new title, but since he was the only shaman of Lord Tommus on the planet, he figured it would be okay.

The chieftain snorted and sneered. "And who are your ugly compatriots?"

The chieftain was definitely intimidating, but Tal Gor knew he could show no fear. "They are my hunting partners, the immortal D'Orcs of Mount Doom, servants of my master, Lord Tommus. And who are you to question me?"

The chieftain gave him a huff and another nasty sneer. Tal Gor could smell glargh on the man's breath. Clearly he was in his cups. "I am Gal Trog, Chief of the Arrow Clan."

Tal Gor had not heard of the Arrow Clan; maybe it was one of the newer clans? "I am not familiar with your clan; however, if your tribe and your shaman wish to swear allegiance to Lord Tommus, I am sure others will soon know of your tribe," he said with more confidence than he felt.

"Swear allegiance? To some unknown lord? I think I'd rather pound you into the ground a couple times," Gal Trog threatened, raising his fist.

"I am not sure you want to move your arm further. Unless you wish me to rip it off and shove it up your soon to be greatly enlarged anus," Virok hissed as he suddenly appeared behind Gal Trog. His claws locked on the chieftain's upraised elbow.

Gal Trog turned his neck as much as his collar plate armor would allow and then twisted his eyes up and to the side to look into the blood-red eyes peering from Virok's thin, pale gray face. The chieftain swallowed audibly. Virok was nearly a foot taller than the large chieftain.

Vespa came up behind Tal Gor. "Tell your tribe to prepare. Lord Tommus, Master of Mount Doom, has claimed his rightful place as the heir to Orcus and shall tolerate nothing less than complete obedience to his will." Gal Trog's eyes darted back and forth between Vespa and Virok.

"Understood," he finally said. Virok released his grip on Gal Trog's arm.

The chieftain lowered his arm and glanced briefly towards Tal Gor and nodded before sidling off and out of the crowd of D'Orcs and Crooked Sticks that had converged on the wagon. Within moments, he had vanished into the rather noisy crowd, all of whom were now talking about Lord Tommus and Mount Doom.

Tal Gor chuckled. "Well, hopefully that will stick with him."

"If it does not, I will stick him with his arm, as promised," Virok replied somberly.

~

Tom was walking down one of the many hallways in Mount Doom, contemplating a nap. Between turning on the electrical system, retrieving the Etterdam party, launching two more hunting parties and providing the baseline power for the complex, he was getting a bit worn out. He wondered if he would need to go back to his old cave just to nap and rest up without having to compete with Mount Doom for mana.

He was going to need to get more D'Orcs, or demons or any sort of living creatures into Mount Doom if he was going to get it to a self-sustaining state. The problem was, he had no idea how to make D'Orcs, and even if he did, it did not seem particularly ethical. If an orc died in the course of war or other circumstances and he brought them over, that would be one thing; but killing orcs just to make D'Orcs was no more ethical than what Lenamare had done to him.

Perhaps he could get some demons to move in? Maybe they could provide support services for the D'Orcs so they could focus on training and getting ready for battle. Battle? He was thinking about getting ready for battle? Tom shook his head; he had to be honest, that was exactly what he was thinking. Between Lilith and Tiernon, one of them would eventually come a-calling and he wasn't sure he could talk either of them out of their plans for war.

Or did he want a war? That was probably what was disturbing him. If he admitted it to himself, he sort of wanted to wage war against his enemies. He suspected it was that whole demonization of his thought process that he had been worrying about a few weeks ago when he had popped that soldier and been so uncontrollably violent. He hated to admit it, but the violence and the battle felt energizing at times. Being around a bunch of battle-lusting D'Orcs probably was not helping either.

Speaking of which, down the hall he noted a second D'Orc hauling a bunch of large pieces of metal equipment down a cross corridor. When he reached the corridor, he turned right and followed the D'Orc.

The corridor went about another thousand feet before ending in what could only be called a blast door, right down to a large metal wheel and locks, not unlike the vault in which he had found the Rod of Tommus. In this case, however, the door was heavy metal and wide open.

Behind the door was a large room lit with overhead electrical lights. The room had metal grating on the floor and several long rows of metal booths or cabinets. Down the first corridor of booths, the last D'Orc he had seen coming this way was putting his gear in one of the open cabinets and connecting cables to the equipment. He could hear some other D'Orcs banging around in other aisles. Tom walked down to this one to see what was going on.

As he approached, the D'Orc glanced over and saw Tom. He suddenly stopped what he was doing, setting a large metal contraption down on the cabinet bench and turning to bow low to Tom. "My Lord. Varn Starsplitter at your service."

Tom gestured for him to rise from his bowed position. "Greetings, Varn Starsplitter. I noted you and some others carrying a lot of gear this way and came to observe."

Varn grinned and nodded. "A glorious day, thanks to Your Lordship! For the first time in four thousand years, we can charge our equipment!"

Tom nodded, suddenly realizing what he was seeing. "Ah, yes. The electrical system has been down for a long time, and now it's back on."

"Exactly. At long last I can charge my battle suit and my blaster, as well as the batteries for the range finding and ignition systems for my other weapons. Clearly, requiring a battery for the rocket launcher's ignitions system was a tactical flaw. However, traditional fire starters don't work so well in a vacuum." Varn shrugged.

"How much tech equipment do we have here at Mount Doom?" Tom asked.

"A fair amount. We used to plunder base stations and conquered ships and haul stuff here and then our engineers would rig it to work in the Abyss on the lightning grid," Varn said. "Commanders Zog and Morok have put a team together to bring the Tech Command Center, or TCC, back online. It is the second door to the right when you enter the main command center. It will be a great advantage should Lilith's forces try another attack. She has not devoted much in the way of tech resources to her local fortress; she has not needed to since we lost power. I expect she will have trouble reallocating those resources. High-tech stuff requires good climate control, which we have at Mount Doom, but is very rare outside of here and the Courts."

"Excellent. I would love nothing more than to give her a surprise." Tom grinned.

Varn grinned widely. "We will once more have radar for monitoring incoming threats, as well as radio communication between commanders in the field and the TCC." He chuckled evilly. "And I think they will find our anti-air and spacecraft artillery to be quite good at knocking demons out of the sky, as well as existence."

"The complex has that sort of heavy artillery?" Tom asked, surprised.

"Yes, sir. We had been working on adapting force field generators we had liberated, but the war in Etterdam put that on hold and then we no longer had the power or resources." Varn shook his head sadly. "We were probably within less than a decade of having force fields on top of the runic wards."

"Science and magic working together!" Tom marveled. He grinned and clapped Varn on the shoulder. "We shall carry on and rebuild everything!"

Varn smiled, thrilled to finally begin the return to glory.

~

"Reattach the saddles to the D'Wargs' harnesses," Virok ordered once they had returned to the wargtown and the large tent they had rented for the D'Wargs to rest in. Because the pavilions were designed for wargs, they were outfitted with water troughs and food troughs. D'Wargs did not need to eat, but since the food and water were included in the price, the D'Wargs had spent the last several hours eating, drinking and investigating the wargs.

"It was just socializing," Fed Tal told Tal Gor as they grabbed the saddles for their D'Wargs. They had left most of the harness on the D'Wargs and just detached the saddles and extra pieces of tack, such as weapon holders and saddlebags. Those extra pieces could be hooked and strapped into place quickly in the event a quick departure was needed.

"What do you mean?" Tal Gor asked his tribemate.

"A number of them mated," Fed Tal said.

"With wargs?" Tal Gor looked curiously at the other orc. "I wonder if they can interbreed?"

"I don't know, but if so, I pity whoever has to deal with the pups!" Fed Tal chuckled.

"So did you watch, you pervert?" Tal Gor grinned.

"Tal, trust me; everyone observed. It was so noisy and violent that it would have been impossible to miss," Fed Tal said. "Pretty hot, actually."

Tal Gor shook his head at Fed Tal's weirdness. He had to admit, warg mating rituals were interesting if one had never seen one, but they were not erotic to any rational person. Or at least, not to him.

"Were any of the wargs brave enough to approach a female D'Warg?" Tal Gor asked.

"No, they were too frightened of the D'Wargs. But a couple of the D'Warg bitches did manage to force themselves on male wargs."

Tal Gor laughed. "It figures! They've been stuck with the same partners for thousands of years!"

Tal Gor and Fed Tal finished saddling their D'Wargs and walked with them out to the staging area.

The staging area was about a thousand feet outside of the town. Zerg and Fed had marked off an area after the first wagonload of supplies had come back from the city. Nagh Felwraith, one of the D'Orcs, had stayed behind to help guard the supplies. D'Orcs were so new to the people of Murgatroy, they did not feel they would need too many guards to defend the supplies. Especially with a pack of twenty snarling and slobbering D'Wargs a thousand feet away.

While saddling the D'Wargs, Fed Tal told Tal Gor that the orcs in the town had been more wary of the D'Wargs than Zerg. Or they had been up until he began winning too many drinking games. Naturally, neither Fed nor Zerg had mentioned that D'Orcs could not get drunk on glargh, ale, wine or anything else. After about a dozen orcs passed out, and a good number of the onlookers had lost more money betting than they'd spent on drinks, the wargtown orcs finally realized that Zerg and his infinite glargh-gut were a bigger threat to their wallets than the D'Wargs were to their hides. Fed Tal showed Tal Gor his now-rather-stuffed money pouch.

Tal Gor had laughed and clapped his friend on his back. "So while we were in town spending Lord Tommus's treasure, you were out here making money?"

Fed Tal was quite tipsy by this point and simply gave him a wide grin, as if he had been caught eating warg droppings.

As they approached the staging area, they shifted their direction to come up beside Vespa, who was manipulating a large abacus.

"So what's the total haul?" Tal Gor asked.

"Very impressive!" Vespa said. "We may want to come back here for more supplies at some point."

"Given that you are paying in gems and chunks of precious metal, I am pretty sure you will be welcome!" Tal Gor said with a grin.

"I am sure we were taken advantage of, but we are in a hurry," Virok commented drily as he walked by while arranging items for transport through the gateway.

"Did you get all of what you needed?" Fed Tal asked.

"A great deal. We managed to get a dozen and a half barrels of glargh, six barrels of ale and two barrels of wine. We also picked up two large sacks of ground salt, three sacks of cornmeal, four sacks of ground wheat and five sacks of oats." She paused and looked up from her abacus, grinning. "The D'Wargs are going to be excited for us to make wargmeal for them."

"I thought the Abyss was a desert? Where do you get water?" Fed Tal asked.

Vespa grinned. "It is. You were paying attention to our stories last night!" Then she mock frowned. "And apparently sober enough to remember them! As for the water, now that Lord Tommus has returned, the storm clouds and rain have returned to Mount Doom."

"Lord Tommus made it rain in the Abyss?" Tal Gor asked, awed.

"Indeed he did. His power is as described in the legends. Glorious days lie ahead!" Vespa said before looking back to her abacus. "However, for this celebration, we will be using x-glargh, oats and meat to make the wargmeal."

"Lucky D'Wargs!" Fed Tal pounded his fist into the palm of his hand.

"They are." Vespa chuckled. "As far as inventory, we also got a case of large snake eggs and two cases of chicken eggs. A cask of sodium bicarbonate, that was a nice find! Or so I am told. I have no idea what it is," Vespa said.

"It can be used for several things, but for bread, it makes it bubbly," Fed Tal said.

"So you will not want to use it in Schwarzenfürze's wargmeal!" Tal Gor joked, and they all laughed.

"In any event, there are a dozen other sacks of things: potatoes, turnips, ginger, beets. I won't bore you with the entire list," Vespa said.

Virok came back and nodded to Vespa. "We are set, commander. Whenever you and Tal Gor are ready, we are ready for Lord Tommus." Vespa looked to Tal Gor.

"I am ready. My brother Bor Tal has a fire started over there." He pointed to the far side of the staging area, away from the wargtown. Quite a number of orcs were watching them from the town, obviously curious as to what they were up to. Given that the wagons that had brought the barrels had left and the orc they had rented the other wagon from was returning with it to Murgatroy, there was no obvious way for them to transport their goods.

Tal Gor went over by the fire and stared into it while reaching for the summoning stone. As he had done yesterday, he cleared his head and began a ritual chant that calmed his mind and let him reach out to Lord Tommus over the link, using the fire as a bridge. It was surprisingly easy.

Lord Tommus, we are ready, Tal Gor thought through the link.

One moment, came the reply. A few silent moments passed and then suddenly the small campfire blazed up higher and higher. When the flames became larger than the amount of wood present would permit naturally—taller than Tal Gor—reality split itself down the middle of the flames.

Tal Gor was certain that no matter how many times he saw this, it would still disconcert him. It simply was not natural; one's mind instinctively recoiled from the sight of the overlaid realities. Lord Tommus stepped through, and Tal Gor and the nearby orcs all stepped back, overcome by the awesome sight of their lord.

Tal Gor could hear a scream or two coming from the wargtown as people started fleeing in terror. He had thought the town to be far enough away, but he must have been wrong. The D'Orcs started chuckling as they looked back to the town to see the wide range of reactions.

Lord Tommus looked at their haul and smiled broadly. "Excellent! Much more than I had hoped for! Hezbarg is going to love you!"

~

"Aggghhhh!" Fer-Rog bellowed as he exhaled the breath he had been holding.

Rupert grinned. The funny part, aside from the fact that Fer-Rog did not actually need to breathe, was that when the D'Orc let the air out of his lungs, he expanded rather than contracted.

"That is really hard!" Fer-Rog exclaimed.

"You managed to stay orc sized for over a minute!" Rupert exclaimed, clapping. "That's great progress, given that you did your first shape-change this morning!"

"Whooo, it is so hard to hold that smaller form. I have no idea how I am going to make my wings disappear or change my appearance and keep it all together." He shook his head in frustration.

"Yeah, but the fact that you could make yourself shrink means you can do it. It will just take time and lots of practice," Rupert told him.

"Well, watching you do it through that link thing was what did the trick. Once I could sort of 'feel' you do your own change, it gave me a place to start," Fer-Rog said.

"It just feels weird though, like I'm going to explode at any moment when I'm in that smaller form," Fer-Rog observed.

"Well, just think about my dad. He squeezes down from his normal size to a skinny human for days at a time!" Rupert said. "I myself only have to squeeze down about a foot or so. Can you imagine being in a body about one-third your normal size?"

"Not at all. But then your dad is Lord Tommus; I bet there is very little he can't do," Fer-Rog replied.

"Well, I…" Rupert trailed off as he felt the link from Tom. He mentally let Tom know they were out a little ways and needed to return to camp and that he would summon him as soon as they got back. It was rather weird how one communicated over the link like that. It was not so much thought as… he had no idea. "We need to head back to camp," he said to Fer-Rog. "The orcs are ready to return."

"That sucks! I'd like to stay here longer!" Fer-Rog complained.

"Yeah, I know. This has been fun!" Rupert said, motioning for them to head back towards the camp.

"I think we've got everything we need," Tal Gor said to Vespa as the last of the supplies they had requested from Murgatroy were brought through the portal: specifically a barrel of glargh, one of beer and a sack of potatoes. "We haven't unsaddled the D'Wargs yet; we should do that now, I am thinking," he added.

He and almost half the orcs were on the Astlan side of the gate along with Fer-Rog, Rupert, Virok and Vespa. The rest were in the cooled staging area where the D'Wargs were.

Vespa smiled and shook her head. "That's okay, we are going to take them back to their cave and unsaddle them there so we don't have to lug all the tack back to the cave as well."

"Okay, then." Tal Gor gestured to the rest of his tribe, who were still in the Abyss. "Say the last of your goodbyes and come back through!"

"Vespa, Virok, it has been our honor to hunt with you!" Tal Gor told the D'Orcs.

"Tal Gor, it has been our honor to hunt with you. May we hunt again soon!" Virok said as Vespa grinned and nodded.

"Ouch!"

"What the…?"

"Move it or I'm going to get trampled!"

"Argh!!!"

There was a lot of yelling coming through the portal as orcs who had been trying to come through were suddenly shoved aside and started falling over. Vespa frowned. "What the Abyss is going on over there?" she yelled.

"It's that—" someone yelled before being cut off.

There was a large, splattery, moist, sickening explosion on the other side of the gate. Suddenly the cursing doubled, along with the shouts and yells of orcs and D'Orcs. The immediate area of the gateway completely cleared and out came Schwarzenfürze! She burst through the gateway, still saddled, wings batting away anyone trying to stop her.

She plunged through the orcs on this side of the gate, even as they had begun to scatter as the hideous stench released by the D'Warg's bowels floated through the gateway. Bor Tal had been next to the gate; he bent over retching, as did several others.

"Damn!" Vespa cursed as the smell finally reached her nose. "I knew we shouldn't have fed the D'Wargs!"

Schwarzenfürze charged across the staging area and then circled around to the other side of the camp.

"Tar Roth Non!" Vespa yelled through the gateway. "Get your damn D'Warg!"

Tar Roth Non stumbled through the gateway, his eyes still watering from the deadly miasma released by the cranky old D'Warg. He launched into the air and flew over to where Schwarzenfürze was parked on the other side of camp. Tal Gor and several others, including Vespa, ran over there too.

When they arrived, they found a showdown in progress. Schwarzenfürze was standing stiff legged, claws dug into the ground and baring her truly ferocious teeth at Tar Roth Non, who was trying to convince her to come with him.

"What is wrong with that D'Warg?" Vespa demanded.

"She doesn't want to go back to Mount Doom," Tar Roth Non said.

"No warg dung!" Virok cursed.

"She was in Mount Doom and when we started coming back, she charged through with us!" Fel Nor noted.

"Apparently she wants to stay in Astlan?" Vespa said, shaking her head.

"Why?" Tal Gor asked.

Virok snorted. "She's Schwarzenfürze—you do not ask why with her. Remember, we did not ask why she wanted to come to Astlan in the first place and then wanted you to ride her. You are the first person in well over four thousand years to ride her. In fact, I would argue only the second, maybe third person ever."

Vespa sighed. "Fine. Be that way, you crazy bitch!" she snarled at Schwarzenfürze. "She's been a huge pain for everyone at Mount Doom. If she wants to stay here, I will ask Lord Tommus to let her stay." She glared at the D'Warg.

"You do understand, Schwarzenfürze, that if Lord Tommus orders you back, you will be going back?" Vespa asked the D'Warg, who simply narrowed her eyelids.

Vespa flew over the camp to the portal to seek out Lord Tommus. Tal Gor turned his attention back to Schwarzenfürze. Why would she want to stay here? This D'Warg was mighty strange. Although, of course, since this was all completely new, all the D'Orcs and D'Wargs were strange.

Vespa flew back over and hovered in the air nearby. "Okay, Lord Tommus has agreed to let Schwarzenfürze stay, but she will need to report to Tal Gor. Is that clear?" She stared at the D'Warg, who stared back silently.

It was not as if the D'Warg could actually say yes, Tal Gor reflected. Wait a minute—that meant he, Tal Gor, was being entrusted with one of the nastiest death-dealing monsters from the depths of the Abyss that had ever walked the Planes of Orcs! Tal Gor reeled a bit at that thought. He almost felt giddy.

Vespa shrugged. "Back to the gate!"

They all headed back to the gate, the D'Orcs flying, the orcs walking.

The orcs had all come back through and Vespa was just following Virok through the gate by the time Tal Gor finally got back. He cursed his bum leg.

Lord Tommus was standing on this side of the gate. He grinned at Tal Gor. Of course, only the shaman link between them told Tal Gor that his lord's hideously frightful expression was grin. Anyone else would think the demon was about to eat them.

Lord Tommus chuckled. "Good luck with your D'Warg, shaman. I expect you are going to need it." He nodded to the orcs. "We appreciate your assistance and hope you have another good feast. We will hunt again!"

I shall contact you again in a day or so, Lord Tommus told Tal Gor in his head. With that, the demon lord stepped through the gateway, waving a final greeting to all, and the strange rip in reality suddenly vanished.

His tribe mates and hunting partners all started whooping and clapping their hands together to celebrate their adventure. Bor Tal came over and gave Tal Gor a very uncharacteristic hug. Tal Gor looked at him, shocked.

"I have never been more proud of you or any other family member in my life, brother!" Bor Tal told him. The other orcs all came and surrounded him, shouting "Tal Gor, Tal Gor" over and over again. Tal Gor's chest was thudding so hard he was having trouble breathing. He had never felt so much a part of his tribe in all his life.

After several more minutes of shouting his name and joyfully punching him hard on the back, the side, the front and the head, they all started moving off to talk to the rest of the tribe.

"I better go check on Schwarzenfürze," Tal Gor told his brother Bor Tal.

Bor Tal chuckled. "To repeat the words of our great Lord Tommus: good luck!"

Tal Gor chuckled and made his way back to where Schwarzenfürze was. She was still standing in the same place, looking wary. "It's okay," Tal Gor told the D'Warg. "The gateway is closed; no one is going to drag you back to Mount Doom against your will."

The D'Warg looked at him for a few minutes, did some sniffing and then relaxed her legs and started walking over towards him. Tal Gor watched her, not sure what she wanted at this point. She got right up next to him and then began rubbing against him.

No, actually she was rubbing the harness and buckles against him. She wanted him to take them off. Tal Gor shrugged and began unsaddling the D'Warg. She stood relatively still and let him take of the saddle, the bags and holders and then the harness. He was sorting the pieces together, wondering where to store them—he guessed with the warg gear—when Schwarzenfürze just started wandering off toward the camp.

"Where are you going?" Tal Gor asked in vain, since there was no way she could answer him. He shook his head and gathered up the gear, or as much as he could easily carry, and lugged it off to where they stored the warg gear. He hoped the D'Warg would not eat any of his tribe while he was stowing the gear.

It took him two trips to lug all the gear and stow it with the warg tack. He had not heard any screaming, so he assumed she had not eaten anyone, or worse, farted. He looked around the camp but could not see her. He walked up to Soo An. "You didn't see where Schwarzenfürze went, did you?"

His sister said nothing, but gave him a big smirk and then pointed behind him. He turned to see that she was pointing at his tent. He headed over there and raised the flap. It was especially dark inside for some reason; and then he saw why.

Schwarzenfürze had entered his small tent, knocking everything over. She was currently sprawled over his bedroll along with most of the rest of the interior, apparently sleeping! Tal Gor raised his hands helplessly. What was he going to do? There was barely room for him in the tent! Now that Schwarzenfürze had taken it, where was he going to sleep?

~

"My Lord?" Zelda asked, approaching Tom as he prepared to leave the staging area.

"Yes, Zelda?" Tom asked his steward with a smile.

"If you have a moment, this is Völund, the Smith of Doom," Zelda said, introducing a short individual, meaning about six feet tall, who was somewhat hunched over, walked with a substantial limp, and did not have wings. Therefore, he was not a D'Orc, nor even an orc, although, he was almost ugly enough to be an orc.

"Völund, a pleasure to meet you." Tom nodded at the smith.

"Likewise." Völund shrugged and stood there.

Zelda stood for a moment waiting for the smith to say more, but apparently he had nothing more to say. Interestingly, he did not seem particularly awed or impressed by Lord Tommus. Tom was getting used to people being slack-jawed at the sight of him. In this case, however, Völund just stood there chewing tobacco or something similar. He appeared to be on the verge of spitting it out on the floor.

"Uhm," said Zelda, shaking her head. "Völund here is in charge of making all our weapons and armor, but at the moment, more importantly, he is also in charge of the mint."

"The mint?" Tom asked, puzzled.

"Yes, the mint," Völund stated, and then said nothing more.

"You mean like a coin mint?" Tom asked.

"Yep," the smith replied.

Zelda sighed and continued, "Naturally, once Mount Doom shut down, the metal founts solidified, and in fact without access to Midgard, the Planes of Orcs, we had no huge need of coins—"

"Now we do, so we do," Völund interrupted, "and the founts are starting to run again."

"Yes," Zelda finished. "So Völund is seeking your permission to start minting new coins. He proposes to use the same denominations as before, but to replace the coin's head with your portrait instead."

"Uhm, okay." Tom was not sure what to say.

"It will be much more efficient for trading with orcs and such," Zelda said. "Right now, lumps of metal and gems are very imprecise payments, and we can't be sure we are getting an accurate value for our treasure."

Tom nodded. "That actually makes a lot of sense. They will take our coins in Midgard?" He was starting to like saying "Midgard" instead of "Planes of Orcs" or "Planes of Men." It was much more efficient and he would not accidentally sound racist when talking to different groups.

He had never thought about it until he had heard the D'Orcs calling Astlan and the other planes "the Planes of Orcs," but it did make sense that the term "Planes of Men," as the wizards used, was hugely condescending and racist to all the other races and species living there. Not to mention the women. He wondered suddenly if there were tribes of Amazon women who referred to Midgard as the "Planes of Women."

"Definitely. Foreign coins are never a problem. Every large merchant has an assayer, or has basic skills as one and can measure volume and weight to verify the density of a coin, and thus the value," Zelda noted. "Actually, it's a skill most orcs learn early on. Since you can only carry so much loot from a city, you want to take the most valuable coins."

"Back in the day, at the height of the Doompire," Völund said, "our coins were more valuable than those stupid tokens the Courts issued."

"The Doompire?" Tom asked.

Zelda shook her head, indicating it was not that important. "That was a slang term for the Empire of Mount Doom, as it was known for several thousand years. It was not an official title."

"When was this?" Tom was curious.

"Shortly after the Courts realized we were here, so I'd guess between twenty thousand to five thousand years ago." Zelda shrugged.

Tom gave a small shake of his head. The historical timeframes he was dealing with just kept getting longer and longer. It really took some getting used to.

"So," Völund said, interrupting his thoughts. "Good?" The fellow was not a man of many words.

"Yes, I think it's a great idea," Tom said.

"Well enough." Völund pulled some sort of contraption out of a bag that hung from his belt. He quickly brought it up to his eyes and pointed the other end at Tom. It appeared to be some sort of steampunk binoculars, with various odd protrusions and some extra crystals on little arms jutting out from the sides, top and bottom.

"Smile," Völund said.

Puzzled, Tom smiled. Suddenly there was a huge flash of light and a crack of thunder. Tom blinked in surprise. As his eyesight cleared, Völund was lowering the device.

"Should have a proof of the casting by tomorrow. If approved, we can mint the inaugural coins right after we finish the ceremony, before I get too drunk," Völund stated rather matter-of-factly. He then turned and walked away, muttering, "Looking forward to that drunk, so I am. Four millennia is too long to be sober."

Tom gave a puzzled glance to Zelda as the smith walked away. "He's not exactly social, but he is good at what he does. The only smith who can even compare is Hephaestus, and he's a god," Zelda told him.

"So what is Völund?" Tom asked after the smith had hobbled off down a tunnel. "He's not a D'Orc."

Zelda grimaced slightly. "I don't exactly know. He is jötunnkind, and according to the stories he's told while drunk, or so I am told, he used to bed Valkyries fairly routinely, so he must not have been a stranger to Valhalla or Ásgarðr'. He has been here since Ragnarök. I'm told that in the old days, he and Loki often went on long benders together."

~

Dider, Zerg, Nagh and Vespa began positioning the last round of D'Warg saddles on the saddle frames in the tack room. Dider chuckled.

"What is so funny?" Zerg asked.

"Just thinking about the great time we had. It's been so long since I have hunted on the Planes of Orcs," she replied.

"It has been a long time. It was good to hunt with my tribe again," Zerg said. He was a first-generation Crooked Stick, and unlike Vespa, had been born as an orc in Astlan.

"So," Tegh Nornfell asked as he brought in the last saddlebag, "were the Crooked Sticks so relaxed in your day?"

"Relaxed?" Zerg asked, puzzled.

"They did seem a little at ease. I noticed that myself," Dider An Sep added. She was of the Fen Horde on Romdan, like Teg Nornfell.

"I am not following what you mean," Zerg said suspiciously.

"Well, I'm just saying that I saw none of the typical signs of their being on a war footing. It seemed a bit unusual," Dider said.

"I didn't really notice, but then I've never met an orc before," said Nagh, who was third generation in the Abyss.

"Exactly, Dider. The band seemed a little pacifistic to—" *CRUNCH! THUD!* Tegh never finished his sentence, as he was interrupted by Vespa's fist smashing into his face with a loud sound of bone crunching, followed by a large thud when he hit the back wall of the tack room twenty feet away. The D'Orc slid down the wall.

Tegh reached his hand up to his nose to pinch off the bleeding. "Sorry, Vespa," he mumbled.

"Apology accepted." Vespa said sternly as she strode over to the downed D'Orc. "It's just that we are talking about my tribe, and well, you know us women. We can only put up with so much damn vulgarity before we get pissed and have to act. And, you gotta know, if you're going to be tossing the P-word around when talking about my tribe, I'm gonna have to put my fist in your face."

Tegh nodded, holding his nose with one hand and reaching up to take Vespa's outstretched arm to assist him in getting back up. "I do. It was thoughtless and stupid of me. It has been so long; I think I've forgotten most of my manners." He shook his head slowly, trying to determine if his neck was broken. "Sorry."

"I understand. And to be fair, they did not seem completely battle-ready to me either," Vespa admitted.

Dider snorted. "Well, on the bright side, as far as I could determine they had no lawyers or diplomats!"

The D'Orcs all burst out laughing at such a preposterous idea.

"Aye," Nagh said. "Things could always be worse!"

"If I found one of those in an orc tribe, I—well, I don't know what I'd do. Pretty sure it would demand war," Tegh said awkwardly through his broken nose.

"Remember the first rule of conquest: kill the diplomats first and the lawyers second, before you do anything else!" Dider declared.

Arg-nargoloth walked into the room at this point and snorted with amusement. "Truer words were never spoken of conquest!" The others all laughed at this. "But let me advise you from experience: do not be too hasty on the sequence of events. One lawyer's skull between your claws is worth two diplomats in a carriage any day!"

They all grinned at that.

Nagh, being the youngest, asked, "Really? I was taught that diplomats were worse."

Arg-nargoloth shrugged. "They are. Diplomats are full of lies and deceit and they seek peace"—he spat on the ground—"above rightful conquest! But, when given the opportunity for a guaranteed lawyer skull crushing over a theoretical gutting of diplomats, take the guaranteed option. If you pass up the lawyer for the diplomats, all three may get away."

Tegh spoke up at this point. "How do you gut something that has no guts?" he asked with a grin on his face as they all began laughing.

"An excellent question," Vespa observed as the laughter died down. "However, to Arg-nargoloth's point: do not let the ideal become the enemy of the good!"

"Exactly!" Arg-nargoloth nodded in agreement.

Chapter 106

DOF +8
Start of Fifth Period 16-05-440

"Fer-Rog and Rupert are in danger of having too much fun," Zelda observed as they gateway closed behind the two boys.

Tom chuckled. The Olafa orcs of Ithgar were going to repeat the Murgatroy exercise, as were the Rockguts of Romdan. In the case of Ithgar, the band they had joined up with was only an hour's flight from a trading city, so they wouldn't necessarily need to do the two-gateway trick. Once they had acquired whatever they could trade for, they would bring everything through to the Abyss, and then the orcs would fly back to camp and open a new gateway to get their share of the goods and return the D'Wargs.

In the case of the Olafa Horde, they had about a day's flight as well, so Fer-Rog and Rupert had gone to join the after-hunt festivities on Ithgar, where they would spend the night again and help open the gate in the afternoon. The interesting thing was that Rupert wanted to try open a gate himself from Ithgar back to Mount Doom. If he could do that, it would be incredibly helpful. They needed more people capable of opening gates.

Tom had thought about trying to figure out a way to create more permanent gateways, but then realized that since all of the orc tribes he had met so far were nomadic, that would not be practical. For now, at least, they would need to be used ad hoc at different locations.

"So," Tom said, "we want to see about contacting some more shamans, as we discussed. Can you round up some appropriate clan representation for the different worlds we think we might be able to contact? I think it's useful to have someone of the same bloodline available."

Zelda nodded. "Agreed. The temple, about thirty to forty deminutes?"

"Sounds good." Tom nodded and smiled. Zelda took off to gather people and Tom headed back to his quarters.

Tom entered his quarters just as Antefalken and Estrebrius materialized in his living room. "I'm starting to think this is the main entrance to Mount Doom!" Tom joked.

Antefalken laughed. "It's because we all spend so much time here, we just return to wherever we were last summoned from when we do it the old-school way. Not all of us can run around ripping holes in reality wherever we please." Everyone laughed at that.

"We will want to work on that. We need better egress in and out of here. Rupert's going to try opening a gateway from Ithgar to Mount Doom tomorrow."

"That would be useful." Estrebrius nodded in agreement.

"How is progress coming on the environmental devices?" Tom asked.

"I think well. Vaselle is quite good at arcane device construction, and while Damien is no slouch on that front, his access to Council resources and the library are quite valuable," Antefalken said.

"And the gems from Mount Doom are also very useful!" Estrebrius added, grinning.

"Good. Any idea on how soon they can be ready?" Tom asked as Boggy walked into the room from the hallway.

"Well, how many do you need?" Antefalken asked. "You indicated that you might have some people coming in addition to Vaselle and Damien. Are you planning to invite Lenamare?"

Tom stared at Antefalken in shock until he realized the bard was joking; he then broke out laughing. "Okay, I'm going to have the thought of him here in Mount Doom at a banquet with D'Orcs for a very long time."

Antefalken grinned.

"Actually, I think it is a great idea. He can be the main course!" Boggy was nodding his head up and down. "That's what I advocate!"

Tom gave Boggy a snarky grimace. "I hardly think that Damien is going to feel at ease watching one of his fellow Councilors of Wizardry being eaten."

"He can be dessert!" Boggy said.

"No," Tom said firmly. "To be clear, no one is going to eat, or even talk about eating my guests, particularly in front of them."

"Egh. You're not a bit of fun!" Boggy sulked.

Tom stuck his tongue out at Boggy. "Now, back to the question. Yes, Damien, Vaselle, Tal Gor, Beya Fei Geist, Farsooth GoreTusk and Ragala-nargoloth."

Boggy nodded. "I'm sure Arg-nargoloth will be thrilled to see her here."

Tom looked at him, puzzled. "Why, did they not get along?"

Boggy grinned wickedly. "According to Arg-nargoloth, they got along very well; many times, in fact." He chuckled and said, "I'm willing to bet that if she is at the celebration, they'll get along several more times."

~

Hilda sighed as she waited for the others to arrive in their usual conference room. It was quite odd to have a late-night meeting. She had spent the day—well, technically a good part of the last two days—working with Trisfelt on his new rapid brew process for beer. It turned out that her ability to see and work at the cellular level was of great benefit to Trisfelt in understanding the exact details of the fermentation process. Not only could she help him more accurately measure the effects of different ingredients, she could detect when his magical efforts were causing more problems with the fermentation than they were helping.

She had found it quite exhilarating, a completely new type of research. The best part was that it was centered on improving something important to her: alcohol production. Trisfelt had a very detailed system that, while taking some time to understand, was clearly useful in testing and experimentation. He called it the scientific method, a most wonderful method. Trisfelt had told her that it was the basis of modern wizardry and was why wizardry had progressed so much in the last few hundred years. It was all in the methodology. The method of magic! How glorious!

Of course, based on her experience, such a method might work well in the Planes of Men, but all bets would be off in the Outer Planes. Everything here was pretty much there due to the direct desires of the pantheons and their assistants. Even the refleca-wood chair she was sitting on at the moment. Sure, it looked like wood, as did the table before her, but it was not actually wood. It was but a reflection of wood from the material planes.

That was the secret of the Outer Planes; they were but reflections of the material planes as seen through a god's eyes. Or the eyes of multiple gods and goddesses, some of whom didn't always agree with each other as to what the current state of reality should be. That did make things interesting. Thankfully, the disagreements only affected the common regions of the pantheon's outer planes. Tierhallon itself was pretty stable; or at least, the regions where the avatars lived was stable.

The regions where the "deceased" lived were quite malleable by the gods, avatars and in many ways, the deceased themselves. In the Etonian religions, a good part of one's afterlife was of one's own subconscious choosing; subject, of course, to the constraint of one's particular deity's overall framework and rules.

The door to the room opened and Beragamos walked in. He smiled to see Hilda, much like a kindly old grandfather, and shut the door behind him. "Good to see you, Hilda!"

"A pleasure as always, Your Lordship," Hilda replied with a bright smile.

Beragamos chuckled. "Feel free to call me Beragamos in private, my dear."

"Thank you sir, Beragamos," Hilda replied with a bright smile. What a great honor this was.

Beragamos sat down with a loud sigh. "If you'll pardon the expression"— the supreme archon tilted his head to give her a wry expression under his brows— "it's an ungodly time of night to call a meeting! If you ask me." He chuckled.

Hilda chuckled as well. "It is a highly unusual time."

"Is there wine?" Beragamos looked around the room, frowning as he saw none.

"Allow me, your… Beragamos," Hilda said. "I will retrieve some from my wine locker." She held her hand out above the table as if holding a bottle of wine by the neck and summoned a bottle of Romden Heart Valley Portsooth, 1470 RV.

The bottle appeared in her hand and she set it down on the table. She had dug deep into her wine locker for this one. It was not every day one got to have wine with a supreme archon of Tiernon. Beragamos clapped as he peered at the label.

"My dear! What impeccable taste you have! Here I had hoped for some simple table wine, and you bring a masterpiece." He waved his hand and two refleca-crystal wine glasses appeared on the table. After a moment of hesitation, he motioned and two more appeared.

"I will not rush such a fine bottle of wine, so I fear we must be prepared to share it with Moradel and Sentir." He shook his head. Hilda just grinned and pulled her travel corkscrew from her pocket. One always needed to be prepared.

Hilda had just begun to pour the wine into Beragamos's glass when the door opened and in came Moradel and a young saint whom Hilda did not recognize.

"Oh drat, a fifth!" Beragamos muttered under his breath.

"Good evening my friends," Moradel said rather grimly. "Unfortunately, Sentir is occupied and won't be able to join us."

"How unfortunate!" Beragamos said with what sounded like great emotion, even as he withdrew his hand from creating a fifth wine glass.

Moradel glanced at the bottle of wine, his eyes widening as he recognized the label. He snorted. "Yes, I am sure you are truly disappointed, Beragamos." He shook his head with a slight smile.

He turned to gesture to the young saint. Hilda thought of him as a young saint because he appeared to be in his early twenties so he must have died young, but he was also young given his aura. She would be surprised if he had been a saint for more than sixty or seventy years.

"This is Saint Stevos Delastros, Patron Saint of Travelers of the Border Forests," Moradel said, gesturing to Stevos, who nodded politely to each of them. Clearly the youth was feeling a bit overwhelmed to be in the meeting, even as she had been but a few days back. It was funny how quickly one became accustomed to the previously unbelievable.

Moradel shut the door and Hilda poured wine for the four of them. Stevos nervously took a seat that Hilda gestured for him to take and Moradel sat down at the final seat. He raised his hand to give them pause before trying the wine.

"I think you will want to wait to drink until after you've heard what Stevos has to say," Moradel said solemnly.

Beragamos raised an eyebrow at this as he pulled his hand back from his glass. "Very well," he replied. "But first, where exactly are the Border Forests?" Hilda was glad he asked; she had no idea.

"Uhm, they are on Norelon, Your Lordship," Stevos replied hesitantly. "They are the forests between the Abancian wasteland and Jotungard. Where the Kingdom of Murgandy and The United Federation are."

"I am not sure I like where this is going," Beragamos said firmly yet hesitantly at the same time. " If there is trouble in that region, historically it meant orcs."

Stevos nodded. "But it's worse, Your Lordship."

"Worse?" Hilda asked, puzzled.

"Yes, ma'am," Stevos said.

Hilda smiled tightly. While technically a term of respect, the word always put her on edge; it made her feel old. She had only just celebrated her two hundred and forty-sixth birthday one month—okay, a month and a half ago. She was by no means old; at least not amongst present company. She glanced at the two archons.

"Go on, Stevos," Moradel said.

"Well, as you know, our presence in that part of Norelon is minimal and has been so for some time," Stevos began.

"Since the Desolation," Beragamos added.

Stevos nodded. "While we do have resources in the Cythanian Federation, and of course Noajar, Ferundy and further north have not been particularly welcoming."

"Alfar, orcs, and assorted brigands are not our ideal worshipers." Beragamos smiled.

"Aye, My Lord, but I do what I can in the region. I support a number of itinerant priests who do try to support the faithful that we find there," Stevos said.

"Admirable work, lad." Beragamos smiled.

"Thank you, sir," Stevos said somewhat breathlessly, clearly nervous. "So as it is, not having a huge number of illuminaries to deal with, I tend to pay special attention to those I have."

Beragamos smiled and nodded, trying to ease the young saint's nerves. "Excellent."

"So, one of my priests, Teragdor—" Stevos began.

"Teragdor? That is an odd name," Beragamos interrupted.

"Yes, Your Lordship. He's half-orc, half-human," Stevos acknowledged awkwardly.

"Half-orc?" Beragamos blinked. "We have half-orc priests?" Hilda was shocked herself.

"Yes, Your Lordship. He was a child of rape, naturally, and his human mother abandoned him with one of our priests," Stevos said. "It's a long story, but eventually the boy entered the priesthood and has done quite well. Given the difficult circumstances of the region, I would say quite well indeed."

"And you are sure of his devotion?" Beragamos asked.

"Yes," Moradel interrupted. "I am aware of this particular priest and he has been thoroughly vetted, as you can imagine. He is sincere, and to be honest I would probably trust him more than some of our people surrounding Freehold."

Beragamos chuckled. "Verigas?"

"Of course," Moradel said. Stevos looked back and forth, not understanding.

"Go on then, Saint Stevos." Beragamos nodded with a smile.

"Well, Your Lordship, this evening he began a very urgent and relatively sophisticated set of ritualized prayers to ensure he contacted me," Stevos said.

"Something more than a bedtime prayer, I take it?" Beragamos joked.

Stevos nodded. "The Prayer of Dire Deliverance."

"The PDD?" Beragamos blinked as Moradel nodded.

Hilda shook her head in amazement; none of her illuminaries had ever tried that. Very few did; in fact, it was usually only done by a high priest.

"So what information did he want to relay?" Beragamos said.

Stevos exhaled and then took a deep breath. "Today, in broad daylight, a band of twenty orcs entered the city with another twenty large, winged, orc-like beings. In the wargtown, they stabled twenty large and very mean winged wargs which the orcs had flown in on.

"Winged orcs?" Beragamos was looking quite pale.

"And winged wargs..." Moradel sighed.

Stevos nodded. "Teragdor reached out to some of his alvaren contacts—"

"A half-orc with alvaren contacts?" Beragamos shook his head at the nearly incomprehensible thought. Hilda found it odd herself, but certainly no odder than a half-orc priest of Tiernon.

"Indeed. As I've said, he's been quite useful." Beragamos nodded and gestured for him to continue. "They told him that these winged beings are D'Orcs."

"Dorks?" Hilda asked, not sure she'd heard correctly.

"No—D'Orcs. You need to stress the D, a slight pause and then the O, trailing with the rest: D(uh) O(rcs)," Beragamos said softly.

"What are D'Orcs?" Hilda asked, puzzled.

"They are the unholy warriors of the demon lord Orcus," Beragamos said softly. Moradel nodded confirmation.

"Orcus? As in the supposedly dead demon lord whose warlocks I am supposed to be on the lookout for?" Hilda said with a feeling of incredible despair.

Beragamos shook his head in disbelief. "To be honest, I thought Sentir was being ridiculous, exhibiting paranoia from one of the most difficult battles any avatar of any religion has ever faced. I never seriously thought that Orcus had returned."

"How else do we explain the D'Orcs returning to Astlan?" Moradel asked. "We sort of assumed there were scattered remnants left somewhere in the Abyss. However, they had never had the ability to enter the material planes without powerful shamans attached to Orcus."

"So could the orcs have summoned these D'Orcs directly?" Beragamos asked.

"Ahem," Stevos interrupted. The two avatars and Hilda looked at him.

"Sorry, sirs, but I got a few more things from my illuminary. There was a young shaman with them; he seemed, however, to be crippled."

"A crippled young orc?" Moradel looked surprised. "Old, crippled orc warriors might go on if they can continue to fight, but young ones born deformed or maimed early are almost always left to die." Beragamos nodded in agreement.

"Be that as it may," continued Stevos, "he seemed to be one of the leaders, along with a large female D'Orc and a tall, but very skinny grayish-white orc with blood-red eyes. According to my priest."

"A skinny gray orc?" Moradel looked puzzled.

Beragamos nodded. "Most likely a Soulwrecker, Soulstealer, Soulsmasher, Soulslayer or similarly named clan of space-faring orcs from Visteroth." He shook his head. "They are particularly unpleasant, even for orcs."

"Space faring?" Hilda asked puzzled. Beragamos shook his head and gave her a small gesture, meaning that discussion was for another time.

Stevos continued, "Also, the orcs said they were from the Crooked Stick tribe."

The avatars shook their heads, not getting the significance.

Stevos explained, "According to Teragdor, the Crooked Sticks were once one of the largest and most feared tribes of orcs, but today are but a very sorry remnant of their former glory. They are often used as an example of the failing of a weak tribe. They've been reduced to only two small bands of nomadic orcs."

Beragamos nodded. "So unlikely to have a shaman powerful enough to summon individual D'Orcs. Assuming they knew any true names."

Moradel nodded. "That is what I am thinking."

Beragamos sighed and closed his eyes. "Hilda, you cannot know how grateful I am for your wine locker." He reached out and took a sip of wine. The others all did the same. Hilda tasted it. Ahh… perfection. It would have been the end of her if it had soured after all this drama.

Stevos's eyes went wide in surprise upon taking a sip; likely he had never experienced such a fine wine. She was pleased that both senior avatars seemed to appreciate it.

"This came from your stock, Hilda?" Moradel asked. Hilda nodded. "I am going to need to start inviting you to more meetings." The avatar grinned, and Hilda chuckled.

"Ahh, I have to admit this helps immensely," Beragamos said. "I am going to alert the attendant archons of the Astlanian localverse and other nearby realms that were historically plagued by Orcus. We need to know how far-flung his machinations are."

"Indeed." Moradel raised his glass in agreement and took another drink.

~

DOF +9
Midnight ?? (Olafa Camp, Ithgar) Ithgar Date Unknown; 16-06-440 Astlan

"This passing-out-drunk thing seems to have some advantages," Fer-Rog said to Rupert. "If we stared at a D'Orc like we are staring at these passed-out orcs, we would be pounded into meat coins."

"Yeah, it's really helpful to have a model to stare at to practice a new form," Rupert said.

"There are a few mirrors in Mount Doom, but if I stared at myself, I'd see my wings and I think that would be distracting as I try to make them disappear," Fer-Rog said.

"Probably. I find it easiest to change to a form I know well, but I think if the two forms are too similar it would be hard to keep them apart," Rupert replied.

"Yeah, that's about it. What do you think?" Fer-Rog asked Rupert.

Rupert stopped working on his own form and looked at the large, older-looking orc sitting naked next to him. Fer-Rog had been wearing clothes, but had taken them off to practice shifting. Many of their models were a lot bigger than they were. "That's pretty good. You need to work on the wrinkles, though. It's the details that get you. That would be one benefit of shifting to a young orc; you wouldn't have so many wrinkles, scars and other details to remember."

"I have to think clothes could hide a lot too," Fer-Rog said as he relaxed and shifted back to himself.

"And being closer to our own age, we would not have to worry about acting old," Rupert added.

The two boys were out by one of several groups of passed-out orcs. The D'Orcs were in other parts of the camp. Sober or not, the shapeshifting would have had them freaking out. This band of orcs was a lot larger than the Crooked Sticks.

Several D'Orcs were busy mating with orcs; others had gone around from campfire to campfire to tell their stories to new groups. Fer-Rog had said he bet that the D'Orcs were having as much fun telling their old stories to people, who had not heard them every other day for the last four thousand years, as they'd had on the hunt.

Given that D'Orc children did not come along that often, every one of them were immediately inundated by old warriors who needed someone new to marvel at their stories. At this point in his life, Fer-Rog had heard most of them, and a couple of them twice.

Rupert concentrated and shifted into another orc passed out nearby. It was different in that the orc was technically a bit larger than his true form, so he did not feel as compressed, but it was still uncomfortable. He just needed to concentrate on the form. He had no plans to use this particular form, but just practicing any new form, particularly an orc form, would be useful.

"So, what are you two little demons up to?" a stern woman's voice asked behind them. Both boys lost their assumed forms as they spun in surprise.

It was Beya Fei Geist, the shaman Tom had contacted. She chuckled at their surprise. "Skin-walking lessons is it?" She walked over to the dying campfire and tossed another log onto it, stirring the embers to cause it to blaze up. "Very impressive for two such youngsters, demons or not, to be teaching themselves skin walking." She gestured to a nearby log. "Sit." She sat herself.

"So, you are both impressive and fierce-looking young warriors. Why would you want to look like far less fierce orcs?" Beya asked.

The two boys looked at each other sheepishly and shrugged. Finally, Fer-Rog spoke up. "I have lived my entire life at Mount Doom. I want to go to other places, have adventures, maybe get to fight someone who has not been training for thousands of years and have a chance at winning."

Beya burst out laughing. "Okay, that last bit, the wanting to fight someone who has not been training for thousands of years. That is a new one for me!" She laughed once more. "An admirable response. I can see where such combat could be frustrating for you."

Beya turned her attention to Rupert. "And for you, son of Tommus?"

"I too have had a sheltered life. Now that I am starting to come into my own strength and power, my father is always there, casting a large shadow. I'd like to get out and make something of myself on my own, prove my worthiness to be his son," Rupert said.

Beya nodded thoughtfully. "Another good answer. One I've heard many times, but still a good answer." She was silent for a moment, thinking. "So you would pretend to be normal orcs, so as not to frighten everyone you encounter?"

The boys nodded in unison.

Beya chuckled again. "You see, that is the difference between demon youth and orc youth. The orc boys and girls dream of going places and have people quake in fear. You two seek the opposite." She smiled warmly and looked Rupert directly in the eyes. "Clearly you understand the fear you can cause."

Rupert nodded and the three sat silently by the fire for a few moments.

"Very well then," Beya finally said. "I know something of skin walking. My precise methods may not be your methods, but perhaps I can teach you a few things that would be helpful. At least during your short visit tonight and tomorrow."

~

"Are you ready, My Lord?" Zelda asked as Tom opened the door to let her into his suite.

"All set. Where are we doing this?" Tom asked.

"I have the commanders and other team leaders meeting in the command center. We also have maps of the Doomplex to discuss the arrangements."

"Excellent; let's go." Tom joined her in the hallway. "Maybe we'll pick up the guys who are here." He gestured to the other suites in the hall.

Zelda squinted in thought. "Boggy and Tizzy are in a lower kitchen, cleaning it up and organizing."

"What for?" Tom asked, puzzled.

"The cookies!" Zelda grinned.

"He's going to make them? And here?" Tom shook his head. "Where is he getting the ingredients?"

Zelda shrugged. "He's got a stream of type I and II demons hauling in supplies from the closest boom tunnel. Including Estrebrius."

Tom shook his head in wonder. "Well, he does seem to know almost everyone in the Abyss; I wonder how he got them to haul all this stuff for him?"

Zelda chuckled. "I have a sneaking suspicion he's offering them room and board in your house."

Tom chuckled too. "Would you be okay with that?"

Zelda shrugged. "We have the room. We used to have demon servants and even some warriors back in the old days. As long as they swear allegiance to you, it would not be unprecedented. I am sure several of my senior staff would appreciate having more hands to do work. As you can imagine, D'Orcs aren't much for doing routine chores."

"And we will need to maximize our combat readiness. If the D'Orcs are free to train and prepare, that could be useful," Tom said.

Zelda nodded with a smile. "Exactly my thinking, My Lord."

"Okay, so Reggie is with his accursed mistress; Rupert and Fer-Rog are in Ithgar."

"Talarius is with Antefalken, working on the x-glargh," Zelda noted.

"Really?" Tom looked at her as they walked down the corridor. "Talarius is actively involved?"

"I heard Antefalken tell him the Astlan hunting party had brought in some barrels of wine for the mortal guests, so I suspect he wanted to try that out," Zelda commented.

Tom chuckled. "So do you have the basics for the ceremony worked out?" That was what they were going to the command center to work on with the various leaders.

"Yes, we are thinking to do the swearing in, in pairs, if that will work for you. Each will swear an oath, but they will come up in pairs. I think that will save some time," Zelda said.

Tom nodded. "Do you have a good time estimate?"

"At least a full day. If we put in some breaks and adjust for the rotation of people working on preparing the party, I am thinking about a day and a quarter," Zelda said.

"And we start…?" Tom asked.

"The last of the parties will be back by noon tomorrow, or shortly thereafter. So we are thinking to start early fifth period." She paused, then added, "Oh, and before I forget, can you have the Ithgar crowd purchase some tanning supplies? I have a list somewhere."

"Tanning supplies?" Tom looked her askance. Why would D'Orcs want to tan? There was not even a sun, or rather Fierd, in the Abyss. Normal demons could not tan; a good number were red already.

"Yes." Zelda looked at him, surprised by his surprise. "We have all these kills, and we have a lot of D'Orcs who could use some new clothes. The hides, bones and ligaments of the kills are going to be more useful in the long run than the meat!" She seemed surprised he had not considered this.

"Oh yes, of course. I was thinking of a different type of tanning." Tom shook his head. Tanning like tanning a hide, making leather. Clearly, he was a city demon.

"Another type of tanning?" Zelda asked.

"It's not important. Humans like to lie out in the sun, I mean Fierd, to darken their skin; they call that tanning."

Zelda blinked. "That doesn't make much sense. Why would you want to dry out and age your skin like that? From what I've read, nobles and rich people like pale, soft, supple skin, not the leathery skin of a field worker!" She shook her head. "I do know that Morok and his tribe, who have very pale skin, have to use special ointments when on planets to avoid starburn."

"Same idea, but on some worlds people of light complexion sometimes try to do a little bit of starburning—more like starbaking, I guess. In that sense the 'tanning supplies' I was thinking of were ointments to control the amount of darkening of the skin," Tom said, realizing as he said it how stupid and pointless such an act would seem to a D'Orc, or an orc.

"Wow, you've had to deal with some really strange cultures and people on your journey home!" Zelda shook her head, marveling at the strange lands he had seen.

Tom smiled. He liked the idea of this place being home.

~

"Excellent! I think that covers everything for now. Are there any other issues?" Tom asked the leadership team in the command center. They had just finished a long discussion of the ceremony and the party afterwards, as well as discussions on guard duty rotation during the party. They needed to ensure there were some at least some semi-sober sentinels on duty. That meant that they had to rotate people in and ensure that no one scheduled to go on duty drank too much. On-duty soldiers would have food and traditional glargh or ale, which would not get them drunk.

This included sentinels in the Command Center, which was currently seventy or so percent functional, as well as guards at the entrances. After one of their first meetings, Tom had ordered increased security and monitoring of all entrances, such as the one he and his friends had used. His hope was to eventually have wards on all gates to alert the control center and then just use patrols; but for now, guards and locked portcullises would be the order of the day.

All of his commanders had just signaled they had no other details to discuss when a loud cheer came from the adjoining Tech Command Center. Tom and a few other commanders, particularly the tech-based ones, headed into the Tech Command Center.

"What you DIB's yammerin about?" Arg-nargoloth growled as he entered beside Tom. Tom had learned that DIB stood for D'Orc in Back. It had been adopted from GIB, or Grunt in Back, because on medium-sized starships the scanning and radar operators often sat behind the pilots. Years ago, they had continued it here since the Tech Command Center was sort of a back room off the main Command Center.

"We've got the phased array radar antennas online and working again!" said Horken, one of the senior DIBs.

"Or we will have; I've got one more array I'm tweaking the SNR on," said Varn Starsplitter, the D'Orc Tom had met in the armory.

"SNR?" Tom asked.

"Signal to Noise Ratio. It's an adjustment we do to distinguish background topology from active targets," Varn explained.

"The other twelve arrays are tuned correctly and we are able to discern standard known landmarks." Horken pointed to what Tom realized was a translucent computer screen. "We have a database of what the base topology should look like; the computer then filters it to show us only what shouldn't be there. See all this?" He pointed to numerous orange objects on the screen, along with numerous white items.

"Yes?" Tom asked hesitantly.

"The white stuff is missing landmarks that used to be there; the orange stuff is new stuff that's there now. We have to go through and confirm that previously fixed objects have moved."

"What is moving?" Tom asked.

Horken chuckled. "In the normal course of things, it would be targets. However, after four thousand years, the landscape is bound to shift a little bit. Particularly after Doom shut down and then restarted. The first would have caused settling of geological features; the second would have meant some minor quakes which could dislodge stuff."

"Got the SNR on thirteen!" Varn shouted excitedly.

"Excellent; next up is twofold," Horken explained to the commanders who had entered with Tom, Zelda included. "We have to update the geographic database as I just mentioned, and then we need to start fine tuning the aperture synthesis algorithms."

"The aperture what?" Zelda asked.

"Aperture synthesis. It's a post-processing algorithm that we used to track moving objects with a phased array. We then supplement it from our secondary Doppler radar antennas. The phased array units that use PDP—sorry, pulse Doppler processing—also need to be calibrated; however, full calibration of that requires the sweep antennas to be active, and those will take more time since they have a lot of moving parts."

"So, in short, a lot of sophisticated electronic equipment is coming back online without a lot of issues after four thousand years?" Tom sounded a bit incredulous.

Horken chuckled. "Oh, there are issues, but we had quite a bit of redundancy. And most of the systems are heavy duty, built for deep space military craft and bases. The Abyss around here is not that much worse. At least, it isn't when Doom is dormant."

Tom looked at him, puzzled.

"Metal equipment does not like water," Horken explained. "That is one of the biggest issues. In space, the problem is ice crystals that can melt. In the Abyss, when there are no storm clouds, it is very dry, so rust is not a problem. Dust can be a problem, but again, almost no wind if Doom is sleeping. You may have noticed the only place in the Abyss that actually has weather is Mount Doom."

"And we have not had any of that in a very long time!" Varn added.

Several other DIBs laughed at this. One whom Tom did not recognize added, "We started cleaning the arrays and equipment shortly after Your Lordship's return. We had been hoping to get these babies back up."

"This is excellent!" Tom was very pleased.

Horken and the others nodded in acknowledgement of the praise. "There are some more advanced detection systems we will eventually bring up. But we cannot calibrate those until we have the simpler systems fully calibrated and functional," Horken said.

"How long before you will be able to detect invaders or trespassers?" Darg-Krallnom asked from behind Tom.

"That depends on the size," Horken replied. "Something large, or a large swarm, we would see now." He shrugged. "One or two demons, though, we won't be able to detect for at least a day, maybe longer. We have always had problems with smaller demons. Imps, shadows, smaller fiends by themselves are too small to detect. It varies a bit from region to region, depending on the equipment we have in a given region."

Horken gestured to the main Command Center. "The real calibration will begin once we've got full control of both rooms. Then we can start to correlate information from the runes and wards system to the tech systems. That will take a few weeks, or likely months."

Tom thought for a second, feeling the outer regions of the rune network. "How far out can we go with the tech systems?"

"Sweep times get longer the further out we reach, so it gets tricky, but with this system we can go about thirty to forty leagues out in all directions. Some of the more advanced stuff can go further, much further, but a lot of that is tricky to bring up. Always was, being on the ground and not in a starship."

A very old DIB snorted. "We got one system we managed to acquire that has a very extreme range. Unfortunately, we have never had enough power to use it, but if we could, it could irradiate a three-dimensional radius of several thousand leagues with huge tachyon flux. We could monitor the damned she-beast, Lilith, herself!"

Horken rolled his eyes. "Even if we had the power to turn it on, none of us are qualified to calibrate it. We have no engineers left that understand FTL engineering."

"FTL engineering?" Zelda asked.

"Faster than light," Tom quickly replied.

Horken and the old DIB grinned brightly at him, having not expected him to know the reference. "My Lordship knows his technology." Varn clapped his hands.

Tom chuckled. "You DIBs know more than I will ever know. Keep up the good work." He looked over at Zelda. "I need to head to the temple to send invitations to my shamans for the ceremony and party. I also need to check in with Vaselle to see how the cooling devices they are making are coming along."

"Excellent, My Lord. I am going to head to the kitchens to check on the staff preparing things. Tegdolar is in the temple right now, monitoring for any dream walkers that might show up." Tegdolar and his sister Tegleesa were the two younger orcs assigned to monitoring the temple along with their mother, Teg-Gala, who was one of Zelda's best confidants.

"Good lad, Tegdolar," Tom said with a nod. He had said "lad," but Tegdolar was probably twice his own age. It was amazing how one fell into certain roles. He nodded goodbye to his commanders and left the command centers. He was feeling pressured and warn out again. He was still fueling at least a third of Mount Doom, and it was getting exhausting. It was a continuous drain on his ever-lowering reserves. They really needed to get some more bodies into this place to generate more mana.

~

"So do you have a plan yet as to how we prove ourselves human?" Bess asked Exador as they sipped on Denubian Choco-Coffee™ at the Outpost.

"I and my team have been working feverishly on amulets that will nullify the effects of the wards," Exador said.

"This assumes they turn the wards back on," Rameses said. He was normal-sized and wearing an elegant silk robe rather than his war garb. "What if they invite the Rod in with that stupid mirror?"

Exador sighed in frustration. "Unfortunately, I am but a single archdemon…"

"With a staff of over a thousand demons," Bess noted.

"Most of whom are incapacitated and regenerating after the Freehold incident." He shook his head. "Further, most of them weren't any good at wizardry or magic."

"What about that sycophant of yours?" Ramses asked.

Exador shot him a look indicating the demon was insane. "Randolf? Ignoring the fact that he's one of the councilors I must convince, he is also singularly unqualified to do much of anything arcane."

"He's an archimage, which must mean something," Ramses said.

"Do I have to keep pointing this out? Archimage is a political title; it means he owns a country! It has nothing to do with skill, of which Randolf has very little," Exador said wearily.

"So who is this team?" Bess asked.

"I do have a couple of decent demon wizards in my employ, as well as one warlock in Etterdam and two in Romdan," Exador said.

"You conduct business in Etterdam and Romdan?" Ramses asked, puzzled.

Exador gave him a puzzled look. "Yes, why?"

Ramses shook his head. "Nothing—it's just that your insistence on living in Astlan for so long had convinced me you had a singular unnatural attachment to that plane."

Exador shook his head. "It comes and goes. I have estates on other material planes, but the time I spend in Astlan depends on my current interests. Since the Abancian incident, I have spent quite a bit of time in Astlan. Once that arrogant prick Lenamare showed up, I admit that I did end up spending the majority of my time there."

"You have to admit, Ramses," Bess said in defense of Lenamare, "the book was, or is, in Astlan, which is something that in my opinion justifies Exador's attention."

"True," Ramses conceded. "Has Lenamare made any progress?"

Exador shrugged. "I rather doubt it. Apparently, two of his wizards have disappeared with Trevin D'Vils on some crazy quest. Therefore, I have to imagine he is quite shorthanded with his school. Further, I suspect he would be the one in charge of proving that I am an archdemon."

Bess shrugged and took a sip of her delicious beverage. "That is whom I'd hire. Those wards were quite remarkable." Exador glared at her.

She chuckled. "What is this crazy quest?"

Exador shrugged. "I have no idea. It is tied to some visions by Lenamare's sorcerer and this seer from the Society of Learned Fellows. Trevin is leading it for the Council."

"The Society of Learned Fellows?" Ramses asked, sounding surprised. "They still exist?" Lenamare waved his hand, indicating that they apparently did.

"This Trevin—remind me who she is again? I am not as familiar with Astlan as the two of you," Bess said.

"She's the Enchantress of the Grove," Exador said.

"The Grove? Is that a health food store or something?" Bess asked, causing Ramses to snort Denubian Choco-Coffee™ through his nose.

Exador grinned as well. "No, it's some sort of extradimensional refugee camp for misfits, losers and tree-huggers."

"A homeless shelter then," Ramses snarked.

"As I recall, a rather difficult homeless shelter that caused you more than a little grief," Exador said to Ramses.

The archdemon grimaced. "They are tenacious and have some very powerful defenses. We eventually gave up on them."

"Well then, let us simply assume that these quest people are out of the picture, and hindering Lenamare's progress with the book," Bess said.

"I should think it would," Exador agreed.

"We really need to get that thing into our hands and safely back in the Abyss," Ramses said.

"Safely in the Abyss?" Exador asked. "I might question how safe this place is for that book."

"Can you think of any place Lenamare is less likely to follow it?" Ramses asked. "After all, he sent his agents into Oorstemoth. There are very few places he won't go."

"I guess that leaves Tierhallon, or one of the Sibling realms," Bess joked.

"Yes, there's an idea. Hand the book over to Tiernon and see the end of the Abyss," Ramses said. "He would use it to slay every single demon permanently."

"Terribly unsociable fellow, it seems." Bess grinned.

~

Sam stared out over the valley from the ledge of Tom's cave. The cave was decidedly empty. He had been monitoring it for some time. Tom and his entourage had left on some expedition the day after he had met them at Hellsprings Eternal. They had not returned as he had expected. They had been gone for a good five days now.

The more troubling thing was that during the night, Rosencrantz and Guildenstern had left their clandestine post as well. That meant Lilith was not expecting Tom to return either. Had she captured them? Surely his spies in her camp would have alerted him. *Wouldn't they?*

Sam turned and reentered the cave. He had scoured it several times, both physically and magically, and there really was no clue as to where they might have gone. He felt thwarted. He did not like being thwarted.

Had he been spotted spying on them? Lilith's toadies had no idea he had been monitoring them and the cave. He had spotted Rosencrantz and Guildenstern immediately, and shielded himself from them on several levels. They were incredibly inept, but it was possible, and in fact quite likely, that Tom was far more capable of spotting him than those two.

Of course, one reason for introducing himself as he had was to try to win the demon's friendship. Tom had seemed receptive, so if he had been spotted, would Tom not have confronted him? Unless, of course, someone had recognized him.

Tom had not seemed to recognize him. Certainly, Sam did not have a clue who Tom was. He was sure the two of them had never met. Antefalken the bard, he knew; however, the bard should not have been able to see through his disguise. He was very tightly disguised on all levels in this almost never-used form.

The incubus and the two friends, Boggy and Estrebrius, were known entities and of no consequence. The mini-Tom demon was an unknown, as much as was Tom. Then there was Tisdale.

That walking, talking clown was always around when something big was about to happen. He had a way of always being at the fringes of everything important. He never got involved, never took sides; in retrospect, that was probably why he was still alive. Could Tizzy have recognized him?

While Tizzy was only a fiend, he was a very old fiend. Sam had known of Tizzy for longer than just about any demon other than Lilith. While they rarely traveled in the same circles, a meeting every few decades over countless millennia did breed a certain level of familiarity.

Even if Tizzy had somehow recognized him, it would be unusual for Tizzy to have said anything unless directly questioned. Even upon direct questioning, there was no guessing what the demon might say. Sam shook his head. He would need to go talk to his agents in Lilith's camp as well as in others. Perhaps there was some other key event that had happened recently that might give him a clue where Tom and his entourage had gone.

Chapter 107

DOF +9
Early Morning 16-06-440

Sirs Gadius and Gaius walked down the tightly manicured boulevard running from the west gate of Keeper's City towards the government buildings. As expected, entering Keeper's City had been complicated. Having been warned by the Church lawyers and diplomats, who specialized in Oorstemothian protocol, they had known that as members of a recognized military organization, their entry would be more complicated. Members of known militias were required to sign in and out of the city and present their papers at the gate and have them on them at all times.

It had been for this reason that they had chosen to enter the city on foot rather than their more traditional mounted style. If they had done that, it would have drawn too much attention and once inside, only one of them would be registered.

"However do they keep these smoothly paved streets so clean?" Gaius asked Gadius, gesturing at the boulevard of clean white stone pavement, curbs and planters. His obsidian chain mail and black leather gauntlets made a sharp contrast to the white stone as his arm swept out.

"By arresting the dust and debris religiously?" Gadius responded jokingly.

"One would think they must." Gaius shook his head. "Did you by any chance nod off when that one visa official started rattling off the rules of work within the city? I thought I saw your eyes close and heard a small snore."

Gadius laughed. "I may have; these people are incredibly long winded. Where is this recommended tavern?" he asked, referring to the tavern that the Church diplomats had recommended as a rendezvous point within the city. The Rod had no presence within Keeper's City; nor, for that matter, within Oorstemoth. This was completely due to Oorstemothian Defense Regulations regarding foreign military forces. The Church, on the other hand, had a relatively robust, purely non-military presence within the country.

It was only under the very odd circumstances being negotiated by the leadership teams of the Church and Rod with Oorstemoth that allowed the Rod's presence within the nation. They had had to show the papers provided them by Heron's people to get into the city at all. Of course, as Knights Rampant, they could come and go unofficially as their Holy Mission demanded, and if discovered, the Church and Rod would back them and deal with any repercussions. After the first few hundred years of this, however, and more than a few "repercussions," the Church had decided to do two things: first, increase stealth capability via both training and Holy Relics of the Knights, and second, increasingly counsel patience regarding Holy Missions within Oorstemoth.

"The tavern is down three more streets, then to the left and about another block," Gaius said.

"I swear you seem to hear more outside the tent and a hundred feet away than I do inside the tent." Gadius shook his head.

Gaius smiled. "And isn't it the same for you?"

Gadius shrugged; when he was outside, he was not as enthusiastic about listening in on distant conversations that Gaius might be having. Gaius was the one with all the curiosity. He shook his head. "It should be the same either way!"

Gaius grinned even more broadly. "I think it's because inside the tent, one is too distracted by the stench of sweat and oiled armor. Not to mention the claustrophobia of being inside a tent with half a dozen Rod members."

"It would be better if other Rod members bathed more," Gadius admitted, making a distasteful expression. The two continued in silence for a while, gathering stares from the other pedestrians.

Gadius was not sure if this was due to the fact that they were non-Oorstemothian military, or to their admittedly unique appearance. Two knights of near identical height and weight, one with alabaster skin and fair hair dressed in shimmering white mail and a white tabard trimmed in silver, the other with a deep midnight complexion and tightly cut, military style black curly hair, dressed in obsidian black chain mail with a black tabard trimmed in gold. Both tabards were emblazoned with the Rod's symbol, as were their great cloaks. Both knights were armed to the teeth with weapons strapped to their bodies and giant swords crossed with pikes with either pearlescent or obsidian heads.

Gadius shrugged; in most places, it was their striking appearance as individuals or as a pair that garnered the attention. Although if either of them was mounted, the attention was always on the mount. He grinned; this was the one place where he was not sure of the source of the stares. All Oorstemothian soldiers were immaculately uniformed in expensive outfits. Given that all civilians seemed remarkably unarmed, the presence of well-armed knights not of Oorstemothian origin should be unique as well.

They turned the corner on the designated street and continued on silently for a block before coming to the door of the recommended tavern.

"The Unicorn's Tale," Gadius observed sourly, reading the sign.

Gaius laughed. "Well, at least it's a story and not a tail."

"Such jokes are not funny; nor are such plays on words," Gadius stated firmly.

Gaius laughed again and slapped Gadius on the back. "You really should not take everything so seriously or personally. Do you think anyone in Oorstemoth has even seen a unicorn? Unicorns are merely myths here."

Gadius gave him a dark grin and a stare. "So you are saying it is good we entered the way we did, so as to continue the myth? That would seem to do nothing but perpetuate stereotypes. Better to let people understand the reality, to accept it."

"How many times must we argue this? Yes, the truth is best served by openness and honesty, but sometimes more good can be served if there is some mystery left in the world," Gaius said.

Gadius smiled. "Neither of us will win this argument. I am too pragmatic to force any such issue in the real world prematurely, so we are where we always are."

"Where almost everyone has been for centuries. Fortunately, scarcity makes the choice effectively moot," Gaius said as they walked up to the bar. He made a small motion with his hand to end the discussion now that others were present. They had noted the posted time of day during which alcohol was sold at the door's entrance. It was still a bit early, but the tavern was open for alcohol now, and they had been travelling the aether for several days.

"Ah, my good barman, might we purchase one of your fine libations? An ale perhaps?" Gaius asked.

The barman nodded in greeting at the two. "Certainly; two ales it is then?" Gaius nodded.

Smiling, the barman reached down below the bar and pulled up two sets of documents bound by a small string loop in the upper left corner. The documents appeared to be some form of contract. "I just need you to sign the waiver of liability, the acknowledgement of the health dangers of alcohol, tobacco and other substances within our foods, along with the absolution of responsibility for any actions taken by you after partaking in food and beverage within these premises." He waved his hand dismissively. "Just the standard stuff you have to sign everywhere these days. Nothing unusual, all on the same old eight pages." He shrugged. "Oh, and of course, an ID to verify the name and signature."

Gadius shook his head and grinned. He had heard stories, but no one seriously believed them. He now believed. These Oorstemothians were something else. He found it amazing that Oorstemoth could maintain such an efficient and flexible army and navy with so much paperwork. Normal soldiers everywhere else could barely read, let alone understand and sign contracts. He frowned. Oorstemoth must have a very highly educated population if they were all expected to sign and understand legal contracts for everyday activities. After they had signed the documents, the barman handed them each a small bracelet with an odd charm on it to wear on their wrists.

"These indicate that we have your paperwork on file. You can add charms from other taverns and bars if you need to," The bartender said.

"Interesting… quite useful, it would seem," Gaius noted to the man.

"That's the advantage of the strong guild system here. The Tavern Keeper's Guild ensures that all inns, bars, taverns and other similarly licensed establishments all cooperate to ease the overhead cost in ensuring that all patrons are properly informed and up to date on their agreements with the establishments."

"Curious," Gaius said, looking at the charm and ensuring it was not too magical. Simply a small, inscribed runic symbol with an object link back to a centering piece in this tavern.

While the two knights were fastening on their bracelets, the barman poured each of them a house ale from a cask. Gadius raised his eyebrows in surprise as the barman set down two frosty glass mugs of ale. He was not sure if he was more surprised by the glass mugs, or the fact that they served their beer cold. He and Gadius generally preferred cold beer, but as Knights Rampant they were often adventuring in backwaters without the resources to chill beverages.

Sitting at a table near the bar, the two knights had finished about half of their ale when the tavern door opened and a loud, deep tenor voice called, "Like night and day—if it isn't Salt and Pepper!" The two knights grinned to each other and turned to salute the new arrival with their ales.

"Sir Lady Serah!" Gaius greeted the arriving knight.

"That's Sir Serah to you, Knight!" Serah laughed. "You know what I think of that 'Lady' crap. I ain't no lady, I'm a Knight Rampant of Tiernon."

"You really can't blame the Church hierarchy for maintaining archaic and patronizing forms of address," Gadius said. "It's just part of their nature, ingrained for millennia."

Serah snorted as she pulled up a chair to their table. "Jaedall, a pint of Neurien mead!" she called to the barman, flashing a bracelet with multiple charms on it.

It was Gaius's turn to raise an eyebrow. "I take it you are familiar with the city?"

She flashed him a grin as she pulled her large helm off and shook her insanely long hair, nearly two inches long, free of the helm. "Not officially." She grinned.

"You really need a haircut, soldier," Gadius said with a grin. He knew how much she disliked having long hair. She must have been on a rather intense mission.

"Tell me. Fortunately, I have paperwork with a couple of good barbers here," Serah replied.

"You need to sign papers with a barber?" Gaius asked.

"What if they cut your neck by mistake while trimming your beard?" Serah asked.

"Is that actually a problem you have to worry about?" Gadius asked her. She punched him in the shoulder.

"You get my point; a barber brings a sharp blade close to people's throats. They are all bonded and insured. Also, my understanding is that for certain high officials, it's best to have a clear design plan agreed upon before starting to style said person's hair. It avoids a lot of court time if they are unhappy with the new look."

Gadius and Gaius shook their heads in wonder at the complexity of this city.

"So other than that, what all can you tell me?" Serah asked. "I'm sure I got the same initial message, which sounds appalling, but then I got a second message to come here when I couldn't get to Freehold before you left."

"Are you up to date on Freehold?" Gaius asked.

"All I know is that Talarius was cruelly defeated and kidnapped by a demon." She shook her head. "It sounds impossible. He's bested more demons than I can count."

"Not just any demon, an archdemon. And there were at least two more, along with a few greater demons," Gadius said.

"Archaedemons? Multiple archaedemons?" Sera asked.

"Well, yes, and well over a thousand other lesser demons that had been infesting Freehold." Gaius shrugged.

Serah gave them a double take. "You are going to have to tell me more!" she commanded.

~

"This place makes Gizzor Del seem civilized!" Jenn complained as she, Gastropé, Danfaêr and Treyfoêr made their way down the cramped stone street towards the apothecary. As cramped as the small street was for her, she could only imagine what it felt like to the aetós.

They had arrived shortly after dawn. Trefalger, the second mate, and Seamach began putting together landing parties. All five people from the Council party were going down: Trevin, Maelen, Elrose, Jenn, Gastropé, along with Seamach the scout, Bealach the navigator, Trefalger, four of the aetós guardians and four of the dwarf guardians.

"I have not been to Gizzor Del, but I have heard of it," Danfaêr said. "But given these horribly confining streets, I can't see how it could have been conceivably worse!"

"I do not like all the little tunnels where people's homes have extended so far over the street that they are bumping into the apartments on the other side and cutting off the sky above!" Treyfoêr said.

"Why even groundlings would want to live like this is beyond me! It's like a cage, complete with a dung-strewn floor!" Danfaêr said, trying to scrape some excrement off his right boot.

"Who would have thought being cooped up for days inside a cloud would feel less confining?" Gastropé added with the others nodding in agreement.

They had made a quick descent on the carpets, diving out of the sky at a far faster pace than they had when going up to the Nimbus at the first town, albeit more restrained than during combat. The pilots had landed them outside of town and they had split up into different groups to gather various supplies. The plan was to all rendezvous at a large tavern named "The Alfar's Arse," oddly enough run by an alvaren couple for the last seven hundred years. It had a good-sized banquet room that Seamach had rented out for the day. Seamach had told them that there would be snacks, beer and wine available and paid for throughout the day and that they would be having dinner in the evening with some of his friends.

It seemed like a pretty good deal to Gastropé, albeit a bit odd. Seamach had talked about his contacts in the alvaren intelligence community, but they were not being particularly circumspect. True, there were plenty of alvar in town, so that was not unusual, as well as a fair number of dwarves, heartheans and other races compared to Freehold or most of Turelane, for that matter. However, the only aetós in town were the ones with them, and that did attract quite a bit of attention. Tall, extremely attractive humans with large, colorful feathered wings and wild hairdos were not common anywhere that Gastropé had ever heard of. Most thought the aetós to be creatures of myth and legend. He felt rather sorry for their discomfort. In the more crowded areas people, especially children, would just randomly reach out to touch their wings. Gastropé had to imagine it felt rather awkward to be continually groped and touched like that. However, Danfaêr and Treyfoêr seemed to maintain a pleasant demeanor.

Eventually they were able to see the sign for the apothecary. They had a list of chemical and alchemical ingredients they needed to pick up for the ship; ingredients that helped keep the air fresh when it had to be recycled at high altitude, along with items to keep the stored water pure. Apparently, there was what Gnorbert called a *sophisticated life support system* onboard the cloud, and it was rather high-maintenance. While all the organic components were generally available in the grove, there were some elements that were easier and cheaper to obtain in Murgandy and a few other areas.

After awkwardly crossing the crowded square, Treyfoêr opened the entrance to the store. He ducked at the waist and tightened his wings close together to squeeze through the door. Gastropé noted the door was a bit larger than a normal human door, but still a bit tight for the winged warrior.

Jenn followed Treyfoêr and then Gastropé entered, with Danfaêr bringing up the rear. As she entered, Jenn drew a soft but sharp breath. He glanced ahead to see what had caused her reaction and blinked at the sight of an extremely ugly fellow behind the counter. His skin was green and pockmarked all over. He was balding with greenish black hair streaked with white. His nose was rather snout-like and his mouth sported a set of huge bottom teeth and two rather large tusks.

An orc, Gastropé realized in surprise. His first thought was that the orc had broken in and killed the apothecary; but then he realized the orc was wearing a white lab coat. This was quite unusual. He, and he was sure Jenn, had never encountered an orc actually engaged in legal behavior.

To be fair, he had only encountered orcs infrequently in Exador's army, so technically he had only experienced them as part of an Army of Evil, of which he himself had been a member. As of the time they had left Freehold, the Council still had not ruled on Exador vs Lenamare, so in theory that might have been a legal activity, except for Exador being an archdemon. Which, he was pretty sure, was illegal in most regions.

"Yeah?" the orc behind the counter grumped at them. He seemed none too pleased to have customers.

"Uhm, yeah… we need to purchase some items?" Jenn asked rather hesitantly as she unfolded the list.

The orc gestured for her to hand him her list. "It's in Noralese, do you read Noralese?"

The orc looked at her as if she was insane. "I speaking it now! What you think, I stupid?"

"No, not at all," Jenn said. "I'm sorry."

"Would be shitty business orc if I not speak and read Noralese and Etonese. I also good in Gnomish Prime and can talk Mogradin if have to. No read stupid runes. Who put words as pictures? Dumbies, that who! No alvaren, any kind. Crappy language, too complicated to bother. Don't speak wingdings either." He pointed to the aetós.

Danfaêr and Treyfoêr looked at each other in puzzlement; they had no idea what "wingdings" was. Treyfoêr had told Gastropé that the aetós generally spoke either Noralese or Etonese, depending on where they lived. The actual aetóên language was only spoken in High Council, ceremonies and when privacy among other races was essential.

"I apologize; can we please get what's on the list?" Jenn said.

The orc gave her a stare, nodded and looked at the list. "Lot of weird dung here." He glanced up at the two aetós. "Must be Grove business, those crazy always do weird dung." He shook his head. "Need half candle to put together." He gestured to a candle that was lit on his counter, even though most of the room was lit by lanterns. Some merchants used candles as an indicator of time, Gastropé remembered his father saying.

~

"I am getting spoiled in Tierhallon," Hilda told Stevos as they entered Murgatroy. Beragamos had asked her to introduce Stevos to their new tactic of using "on-the-ground intel." He had mentioned that everyone had been so pleased with her quick success, they were going to be doing a lot more on-the-ground work and that if she was interested after this was over, she would be a huge asset to the new team.

Hilda has smiled graciously and replied that it was a huge honor. She had left it at that. She really had not been sure how much she wanted to have a job that required a lot of travel. Although, if her expense account continued at the current level, that would more than compensate. At least, that's how she felt until she and Stevos arrived in Murgatroy. *Ugh!*

Muddy, dung-filled streets with no sidewalks other than a few wooden planks here and there. Rough wooden buildings right up alongside poorly constructed stone buildings. The smell? Horrible. The town was overrun with animals and some odd beasts of burden. And there were orcs. Lots of orcs. Quite a number of alvar as well.

Truly amazing that the city was still standing with both alvar and orcs in it. It had been her understanding that the two races frequently clashed, even in non-wartime situations. If alcohol was involved, it was considered guaranteed. Yet there was no question that there was alcohol in this town. Bad alcohol, vinegary and nasty, mixed with the smell of vomit and urine. Every alleyway they passed was an assault on her nostrils. Seriously, the damn wards around Freehold had been less of an assault on her person than the stench from some of these alleys.

Fortunately, she was not in her saintly attire. Since they were undercover, she was dressed in leather breeches and sturdy leather boots. Hidden beneath her rather large leather coat, she had a knit shirt and silk undergarments, fortunately. Otherwise, there would be no question of chafing in the stifling heat of this city. The humidity was quite atrocious. Her hair was apparently on strike and curling in random directions.

Stevos was dressed similarly and appeared quite happy to be out of saintly attire. Even as she was thinking this, he spoke up. "It's really nice to be back in normal clothes."

Hilda grinned at him. "*You* think it's nice? Try walking through the mud in slippers and a white gown with gossamer lacing along the bottom trim."

He shuddered and grinned back. "Yeah, women saints have it far worse, I agree with that."

"At least those of us from the Sisterhood. The women Rod members have a better getup," Hilda noted.

"Yeah, but think of the knightly saints; they have to wander around in full armor all the time."

"How is that different than how most of them lived their entire lives? How often have you seen a Knight Rampant or a Paladin not in armor?"

Stevos grinned at her. "Point taken. Although, in my defense, we did not get a whole lot of knight anythings down here. Mainly Brothers and Sisters, along with priests and an occasional Rod detachment."

"Given what I've seen so far, it is probably a good idea to keep the knights away," commented Hilda. "There are too many suspicious characters here, most almost certainly up to no good. Plus all the orcs, goblins and other unsavory types would probably distract them and cause all sorts of unwanted political issues."

Stevos nodded. "The Church keeps a much lower profile down here. We also interact more with the churches of the Holy Siblings than in other parts of Norelon."

"And probably in Eton," Hilda said. "I lived in Eton and while we saw Sibling church members, we had very little interaction with them. Rather odd, I always thought, but who was I to say?"

"Do you ever encounter any avatars from the Sibling Hosts?" Stevos asked.

"Only at official dinners. They will show up to those, but they generally only interact with the highest ranking avatars on our side." She paused. "Where does this illuminary of yours, Teragdor, live?" she asked, adjusting the subject to their current business.

" 'Around' is about the best I can say, unfortunately." Stevos said with a grimace.

"Around?"

"He's itinerant and travels the area around Murgatroy and many of the deeper villages of Murgandy," Stevos said. "He just happened to be in Murgatroy when the D'Orcs came to town."

"He is still here?" Hilda asked.

Stevos shrugged. "I would think so; it was just last night that he contacted me. If he's not still in the city, he is going to be close by."

"Very well, then. Can you follow your illumination line to him?" Hilda asked.

"I should be able to. I have never really had to do it from the Planes of Men before. Normally I'm doing it from Tierhallon and so—"

"I know." Hilda beamed at him and gave him a small pat on the shoulder. "It is trickier here because everything is close and the lines tangle. From up there, the lines spread out over all of Astlan so they become easier to track. Down here, it is like being in a bowl full of noodles trying to follow a single noodle!"

"Exactly. Let me try." Stevos stepped up against a nearby wall and closed his eyes.

Hilda waited patiently while he worked to trace the illumination line. She looked around at the Stone Age village they were in. The best buildings were crudely carved stone; many were of fieldstone and a fair number were timber of various sorts. As she was looking around, she noted a beggar surreptitiously heading their way. Hilda softly chanted a ritual to distract his attention elsewhere, quickly making the semantic gestures inside her sleeves.

The beggar suddenly looked to his right and started scuttling to his left. Hilda smiled; she was not up for starting any more beggar battles. Freehold had been enough for her; she would leave well enough alone down here. For one thing, she thought with a grimace, there appeared to be a lot more people, all of various races, missing limbs or with scars, so the beggar pool was potentially far larger here.

"Got him!" Stevos said, opening his eyes. "He's that way, near the city wall." He pointed around the corner to their right.

"Lead on, my dear. Lead on!" Hilda encouraged him.

Stevos followed the illumination line through the crowded streets, around several corners and between a couple of buildings. Finally, they came upon a smithy, where an individual in priestly robes with the symbol of Tiernon emblazoned on the back was bent over, healing someone.

As they came up, they could see he was tending a young girl in a smith's apron who had apparently burned herself. The smith, presumably her father, was hovering over her. Stevos and Hilda waited quietly for the priest to finish his healing. After another minute, the priest stopped praying and stood up.

"How does that feel?" he asked the girl.

"Much better, Teragdor! Thank you." She gave the hooded priest a hug. The smith nodded and reached out to shake the priest's hand. Hilda noted a small silver coin donation in his hand. Very good, she thought, nodding in appreciation.

"Good day, Master Sorensen!" The priest nodded, turned to leave and saw the two of them standing there watching him. Hilda got a good look at him. Mmm. Ugly young man. He appeared to be in his twenties, with a large jaw and mouth. Oversize teeth, but no tusks. Large eyes with a vertical irises, like a cat. His skull was rather large and square, somewhat out of proportion to his large-boned, yet very thin frame and his large, bony hands.

He nodded at the two humans staring at him. "Good day. May the peace of Tiernon be upon you," he said in the traditional greeting, preparing to move past them. As he did so, Stevos put out a hand.

"The peace of Tiernon be with you as well, Teragdor. Might we speak with you somewhere private?" Stevos asked gently as Hilda gave the man one of her bright smiles.

Teragdor looked at them suspiciously. "Have we met?"

An oddly suspicious reaction for a priest, but Hilda assumed that being a half-orc priest of Tiernon was not always easy. Nor would being a priest of Tiernon of any sort in this region.

"Not directly." Stevos smiled.

"Not directly? How do you know my name?" Teragdor asked.

"Your patient spoke your name." Hilda grinned at him, trying to relax the young priest.

"What is this about?" Teragdor asked.

"Events that occurred here yesterday that you reported last night," Stevos said with a grin and a flash of his eyebrows.

The priest got a shocked look on his face. "The missives I sent to the Father Abbot could not possibly have reached anyone yet. It would take a solid day for my crow to get there."

Stevos chuckled. "Not that missive; the other one that you sent to me."

"We really should go somewhere a bit more private," Hilda said, taking one of the priest's elbows. "Do you by any chance have a room at a local inn?"

Teragdor was so busy being puzzled by Stevos's comments that he was slow to answer Hilda. "Uhm, no. I usually camp a ways outside in the woods."

"Can you name a good, safe, quiet inn?" Hilda asked. "We are paying."

"Uhm, the Blind Orc's Gut is about as reputable as any place in town, and they usually have a spare room or two. They are a bit pricier than some, which is why," Teragdor stated, his attention now on Hilda.

"Excellent, dear. You may help guide us on the way." She had him by the left arm and Stevos by the right. Clearly, the priest was nervous and confused.

"Are you with the Church? I am a reliable and honest priest. The Father Abbot can vouch for me!" Teragdor said nervously.

Stevos chuckled softly in a friendly manner. "Teragdor, you have nothing to worry about. We just need to work with you to understand and fully appreciate the report you sent me last night."

"I only sent a report to the Father Abbot. I didn't send a report to you."

"Well, technically I guess it's not exactly a report, but a Prayer of Dire Deliverance tends to work in a similar, if expedited manner," Hilda chided him gently.

Teragdor inhaled suddenly and tried to halt in place. "What? You mean…"

Both Hilda and Stevos worked to keep him moving. "Yes. That's why we think it best to discuss these matters in private," Stevos said. "I am Stevos Delastros; last night you sent me a Prayer of Dire Deliverance, and now it's being answered."

Teragdor was staring at Stevos in shock. "Seriously? You are Saint Stevos Delastros? You are real?"

Hilda snorted. "An all-too-common reaction. Oh, ye of little faith. I swear, some of the priests are worse than the lay people. Tell me, why would you bother praying to a saint for intercession if you didn't expect to get it?"

Teragdor turned to stare at Hilda. "Are you a saint also?"

Stevos grinned. "Teragdor, may I have the pleasure of introducing the Holy Saint Hilda of Rivenrock!"

Teragdor grimaced slightly. "Sorry, Your Holiness. I'm not familiar with you or your work."

Hilda grinned. "I'd be highly surprised if you were! I'm from Eton and we are deep in the heart of Norelon, so it would be very unusual for anyone here to have heard of me." She patted him on the back. "Don't you worry, though. Who we are is nowhere near as important as what you saw!"

~

DOF +9
Late Third Period 16-06-440

Lilith entered her bedchamber planning to disrobe the old-fashioned way and take a nice cooling whirlpool bath. With a flick of her hand, she lit the lamps in her room, bringing light to the darkly curtained boudoir.

"Good day!" Lilith was so startled by the man's voice that she nearly destroyed her bedroom with lightning bolts before realizing it was Sentir Fallon.

"What the Abyss are you doing here?" Lilith shouted at the avatar.

"Not pleasant having strangers just mysteriously popping up in your bedroom, is it?" the avatar asked in amusement. "Tit for tat."

Lilith closed her eyes for a moment and shook her head. "You've made your point."

Sentir Fallon shrugged. "You must admit, given that no one can ever be allowed to know of even the existence of these meetings, there are few better places for privacy and security."

"Security?" Lilith asked incredulously. "You know you've just doomed a large number of my guards to certain horrible torture and death?"

Sentir Fallon shook his head. "It's not their fault and you know it. You did not detect me in here, waiting in the dark. If you could not detect me, then how can you blame them for not detecting me?"

Lilith frowned and then said tartly, "Because I'm a psychotic, mean-ass, vengeful bitch?"

Sentir Fallon grinned and shook his head. "Now who is starting to believe their own press?" He wagged a finger at her. "I do recall having more than one conversation with you about the dangers of starting to believe your own lies... Do you?"

Lilith sighed and shrugged. "Fine. They'll live."

"Good. And besides, if you did kill them or torture them, then they and others would know that they failed to stop someone, and they would start to wonder whom they failed to stop. It might give others reason to try. In short, pretending this meeting did not happen is probably best all around," Sentir observed.

Lilith sighed again, relaxing more this time. "You are right. But that still doesn't explain why you are here."

"He's moving fast," Sentir stated.

"Fast?"

"It has only been nine days since he defeated Talarius, and in that time, he has found the wand, started the volcano and has begun reconnecting with the orc tribes on the material planes."

That caused her to pause. "He is reestablishing his old connections on the material planes?"

"Indeed. They were spotted in Astlan yesterday. A combined D'Orc and orc hunting party came through a village called Murgatroy, where they were purchasing supplies. We have our people looking for similar situations on other nearby planes. We expect to find more examples."

"He's building armies in the material planes." Lilith shook her head.

"Or laying the groundwork to recruit more D'Orcs."

"That should take years, if not decades or centuries," Lilith said.

"One would think; but on the other hand, before four weeks ago, no one had even heard of this demon." Sentir spread his hands. "Now he is rocking everyone's boat."

"So what do we do?" Lilith asked.

"We need to have some understanding of what is going on inside Mount Doom. I'd suggest a scouting party, or maybe rattle their cage with a raid," Sentir said.

"And if that pisses him off?" Lilith asked.

"Better to piss him off now, before he is at full power. Don't you think? At this point we may still be able to bargain with him," Sentir said.

Lilith looked at the avatar sideways. "If he's someone new, maybe. If he is Orcus reborn, there will be no bargaining. He will be pissed. Very pissed."

"In which case we are screwed already. We might as well find out how screwed we currently are." The avatar grinned at her.

~

"Tiernon's pauldrons!" Sir Lady Serah exclaimed when Gaius had finished relating the story of Freehold and Sir Talarius's defeat. She shook her head. "I heard all sorts of crazy rumors, and of course that he had been abducted!" Her eyes were wide at this point. "But stealing mana and possessing priests and Rod members? This creature is fell indeed!"

"An unholy terror unlike any the Knighthood has experienced in our lifetimes," Gaius stated.

Serah suddenly got an odd look on her face. "Yet you made no mention of an intercession?"

Gadius lifted his hands palm up, signifying it was a mystery. "We expected some word from upstairs after this heinous event, and yet we hear nothing. No instructions, nothing. So we are left to our own."

Serah shook her head. "I could understand such a lack of attention for simply kidnapping Talarius. But stealing mana from the illumination streams? Possessing high priests, priests and Rod members? A demon of this caliber? I can't imagine why there has been no inquisition or concern from above."

Gaius shrugged. "One supposes. However, while we hear of such intercessions, has anyone we know actually seen a saint or avatar in Astlan?"

"Well, there are reports of saints all the time," Gadius noted.

Gaius shook his head. "By a reliable source—priests, monks, Sisters, Rod members? An actual documented case?"

Serah shrugged. "Not in my lifetime that I am aware of. There is documentation of it from the last century, of course."

"Apparently times are changing, and so are the attentions of the gods." Gaius sighed.

"So what are we doing?" Serah asked. "We can't abandon Talarius to this horrible fate!"

"That's why we are here, in Keeper's City," Gadius told her.

"I've been wondering about that. There are rumors of an alliance?" Serah asked incredulously.

"Yes. Apparently this demon's activities have deeply offended the Oorstemothian government," Gadius said.

"Lawyers have been negotiating all week on the terms. We are here to see if they can back up their claims," Gaius said.

"And they claim…?" Serah asked.

"They claim to have the capability to serve warrants, and thus justice, in the Abyss, as well as do judicial extraction, recovery, remedy and executions," Gadius said.

"And how is that possible? Everything I have ever read or heard about the Abyss makes me question the feasibility of such a thing," Serah replied.

"You are not alone on that one," Gaius said.

"Which is why we are here. The fleet that came with us arrives tonight," Gadius said.

"So will we see the proof of their power tonight then?" Serah asked.

"One might hope, but first there is a formal dinner and I am sure there will be all sorts of speeches," Gadius said in a very dry voice.

"Speeches? By Oorstemothian bureaucrats?" Serah asked nervously.

Gaius and Gadius just smiled evilly at her.

"Why couldn't I have waited until tomorrow?" Serah complained. "There is no way for all of them to finish their speeches tonight!"

~

DOF +9
Early Fourth Period 16-06-440

"That's the last of the supplies. Including the late ordered tanning supplies," Zelda said as they brought the last of goods from Ithgar through.

"Did you two have a good time?" Tom asked Rupert and Fer-Rog.

"The best!" Fer-Rog exclaimed happily.

"Beya was a great host!" Rupert said.

"Excellent," Tom said. "Let me say goodbye to her." Tom stepped back through the gate to bid farewell to the Olafa orcs.

"Wow. We need to figure out how to get back to her for more training," Fer-Rog said.

"After we got back from the Crooked Sticks, I spent time looking at the stones in the temple. I think I should be able to contact her or Tal Gor through them and then use them as an end point to open a gate," Rupert said.

"So how would we get back?"

"That's the trick. But they have people manning the temple now for dream walkers," Rupert replied.

"Tegdolar and Tegleesa!" Fer-Rog said excitedly.

"Exactly. I think we can make a deal with them to be on this side of the stones."

"We just don't want their mother to find out. She's a good friend of my mom's," Fer-Rog said, and Rupert nodded in agreement.

Tom stepped back through the portal, waving to the other side. "I will contact you in about half a period for the ceremony, Beya!"

The shaman said something the boys could not hear, and then Tom shut the gateway.

"So Beya is coming?" Rupert asked.

"As is Tal Gor, Farsooth and Ragala-nargoloth," Tom said.

"Vaselle and Damien too?" Rupert asked. Tom nodded and smiled.

"Excellent. I haven't seen Damien in a week!" Rupert chimed in.

Tom grinned. "Let's head back upstairs. There is a lot of work to do to clean up from the return and get the supplies put away before the ceremony starts and we don't want to be in the way."

"Okay, we can go see how preparations are going!" Fer-Rog said happily.

"Well, first though… your mother"—Tom nodded to Fer-Rog—"has had special clothes made for both of you."

"Clothes? I hate clothes! Demons don't wear clothes!" Rupert complained angrily.

"Yes, but D'Orcs do, and I do, sort of." Tom gestured to his belt and kilt combination. "I probably should get some new clothes at some point as well."

"I think my mom had some of your old clothes adjusted to fit you!" Fer-Rog said.

"What old clothes?" Tom asked, puzzled.

"Are you saying you never looked in the closets and wardrobes in your suite?" Fer-Rog asked mischievously.

"Clearly, I did not." Tom admitted shaking his head with a smile.

~

Hilda set down her glass of barely palatable wine and smiled at Teragdor on the other side of the small table in their room. It was not much of a room. Two narrow beds, a small table, a chest and a single chair in a room about eight feet per side. Trisfelt's camp in the woods had been far more comfortable, and the wine and food had been several magnitudes better.

However, she did have to admit she found Teragdor to be interesting company. They had finally convinced him of who they were and had him recite everything he had seen and learned from yesterday. Hilda had also been quite curious on his own background and dug a little bit there. Only enough to be polite, though; she would have loved to know more about someone with such a different background, but that would be rude and ungracious on a first conversation.

"So, I am thinking we might want to go out to this 'wargtown' place you mentioned. They seemed to have the best view and some of the longest interactions," Hilda said.

"Uhm, I suppose. I did talk to them a bit, but did not want to appear too nosy. They are a rough lot," Teragdor replied.

"As I would suspect, however, we have all been very impressed with your ministries to the various 'rough lots' in this part of the world and are confident that if you can guide us on the basics, we can take it from there," Stevos told the priest.

"I can be very persuasive," Hilda said.

Teragdor looked at her rather neutrally. "Okay."

That caused Hilda to blink. Normally when she said that, beamed at someone and turned on the charm, they comfortably agreed. This could be interesting.

The three agents of Tiernon trudged down the dusty road to the Murgatroy wargtown. Hilda was once again grateful for her leather garb over her saint clothes. Everything about this place was dirt and dust. She had lived in a relatively small village; had it been this bad? She certainly did not remember it as such.

They were approaching the tents of the wargtown and already, before they had even arrived, were getting some very hostile stares from the occupants. Hilda glanced at the very large, very heavily armed orcs inside the tents and pavilions. Her attention was quickly drawn to the huge, slavering wolf-like beasts—wargs, she realized they were—which seemed eager to eat anything or anyone. Their multi-colored, bright eyes glared malevolently at the three of them.

"So you said the winged wargs were bigger and meaner than these?" Hilda asked Teragdor.

"At least half again larger. Scarred with bigger teeth, huge claws. Completely monstrous," the priest replied, causing Hilda to grimace.

"Last time I saw wargs, they were chasing me," Stevos said quietly.

"Was that the cause of your canonization?" Hilda asked.

"No, not that time. I got away. It did add to my legend, though." Stevos chuckled.

"Is Meat Maker present?" Teragdor asked loudly at what appeared to be the main avenue of the town.

Looking at the unsavory occupants, Hilda crossed her arms inside her large sleeves, where she could make some semantic gestures while whispering some rituals for speed, dexterity and strength. Given what she knew of orcs, all from tales, she suspected physical confrontation and a show of strength might be necessary.

After a few minutes of rustling and loud whispers inside the suddenly quiet town, a very large, very old and scarred orc shoved his way forward. Beside him was an even older, more scarred, one-eyed orc. Both were more than a bit intimidating.

"Who seeks Meat Maker?" Meat Maker asked ominously.

"Master of Wargtown, I am Teragdor, priest of Tiernon," Teragdor stated firmly.

"I am aware of you, failed orc," Meat Maker said.

"I am not a failed orc. I am a priest of Tiernon," Teragdor said firmly.

The one-eyed orc rolled his single eye in exasperation.

"You are but half an orc, and chose not to follow in your father's path. How is that not a failure?" Meat Maker asked.

"Success is judged on many levels. We will simply have to disagree. I want no argument." Teragdor bowed his head slightly in respect.

Meat Maker shook his head and started to leave.

"Master of Wargtown, I have matters I would discuss with you," Teragdor said.

Hilda was continuing to prepare. This was not going that well, just as she had feared.

"I have nothing to say to you, failed orc," Meat Maker said.

These orcs were far more articulate than Hilda had expected. Suddenly she remembered that she was speaking universal and that Teragdor and Meat Maker were speaking orcish. That was a real problem with universal; it was always hard to know what language you were speaking.

"Yesterday, I spoke with some who had been in the wargtown when the D'Orcs arrived with the Crooked Sticks," Teragdor said.

Meat Maker turned back to stare impassively at Teragdor and then shrugged.

Teragdor said, "My compatriots here would like to know more about the great warriors that came to Murgatroy yesterday. They have learned that you were the one who spoke with them the most, and would have words with you."

Hilda noted that the half-orc's orcish seemed a bit awkward. Apparently, it wasn't his first language.

"What do I care? They may talk with themselves." Meat Maker shrugged and started to turn again.

Hilda figured it was her turn. "Meat Maker, Master of Wargtown, attend me. I am Hilda of Rivenrock, and the priest Teragdor has brought me to you at my request. I would share glargh and words with you to learn of the great event that happened here yesterday." She beamed at him in what she felt was a very respectful and yet truthful manner. She was tossing in more than a little Saintly Charisma to boot.

Meat Maker stared at her for a few moments then spit on the ground and started to turn again and walk away. Hilda had never met that sort of indifference to her charms. Apparently, her powers of persuasion did not work as well on orcs.

"What? Did the sight of the mighty D'Orcs yesterday so frighten you that you are afraid to speak of it?" Hilda shouted suddenly. Meat Maker stopped, and the crowd quickly moved away from him with some chuckles and grunts. Clearly, she had hit home.

Meat Maker came back and stood within arm's reach of her, staring down at her. "I am not frightened of anything —orc, D'Orc or human." He glared at her. "You are simply not worthy of my time."

"I am not worthy to buy you a drink to hear your wisdom and insight?" Hilda asked belligerently. This was a bit odd for her, but she needed to simply let the spirit of Tiernon flow through her. Teragdor was looking at her as if she were insane. She could not see Stevos where he stood behind her, but she expected from his small coughs that he was thinking the same.

"Yes," Meat Maker said, staring her in the eyes. She stared back, unblinking.

"If that is the case, then you are not man enough to be allowed to tell me your tales, and you clearly have no wisdom or insight to impart. If you will not speak to me, then you are not worthy of the title Master of Wargtown." The crowd went completely silent.

To Hilda it seemed as if all of time had slowed to a crawl. She smiled grimly, knowing that this was her rituals kicking in. She saw Meat Maker twist and pull back his giant fist, preparing to punch her in the face and send her flying, most likely killing any normal human. She stepped back slightly, widening her stance, digging her feet into the ground and flexing her knees to absorb the impact. As Meat Maker's fist came forward, Hilda held up her right arm, palm first, to block the fist. She braced her right arm and hand with her left and leaned forward to brace for the impact that was so clearly coming. She chanted one more prayer for strength; a very high-speed one, given her elevated state.

The fist came forward, crashing into her palm. The fist was actually larger than her palm, so only his two middle fingers actually collided with her. But that was enough to send pain racing through every bone in her body and for feet to dig two small trenches in the dirt as she slid back about two inches. However, other than that, she held. She did not collapse, did not fall, did not go sprawling. Her hand and arm ached like crazy, but as time started to go back to normal, she could hear a scream of pain coming from Meat Maker that was nearly ear shattering.

Hilda made sure everyone could see that she was still standing and then took a few steps back, sweeping her coat out of her way, and launched into a flying dropkick to Meat Maker's jaw. Her legs ached with the impact as the two of them went sprawling backwards into the orcs behind, bowling them over.

As Meat Maker rolled on the ground, Hilda leaped free and stood over him, staring him down. "Apparently, they don't breed orcs like they used to!" she shouted and then laughed. Meat Maker was on the ground, still in pain, reaching his aching hand up in the air. Hilda adjusted her position and reached down to grasp his hand and pulled the huge orc to his feet —a task that would require considerable strength for an orc, let alone a human.

Thanks to her rituals, that was not a problem. She got Meat Maker to his feet and he rubbed his aching jaw.

"So, can I buy you some glargh now?" She grinned at him, gesturing over to a nearby plank bar, behind which the bartender was staring at her in awe. "Or do you feel like another go?" She put her best charm into her smile.

"Glargh, woman, glargh." He chuckled. "You are big boned and brawny for a human. If not for your ugly face, I might think you were of orc blood."

Hilda grinned and nodded in acknowledgement of his praise. "Glargh on the house, my treat! I want to hear the stories of the mighty D'Orcs!" She yelled as cheers went up around the tent.

~

Rosencrantz relaxed in the soothing lava pit at Hellsprings Eternal. It was one of his favorite pits, secluded and off the beaten path. He had not been to the springs in several years; however, tailing the demon Tom to the springs had reminded him of how much he enjoyed them. Lilith had given them a few days off for their good work and so he had returned to the springs and his favorite pit.

Quite frankly, he was relieved to get this break. He had less than no desire to stake out the new Master of Mount Doom in claustrophobic underground tunnels. Thankfully, Lilith had an entire army of nearly forgotten demons stationed nearby to deal with that sort of thing.

Rosencrantz started to raise his right arm out of the lava to scratch his head when he suddenly realized the lava was putting up a lot more resistance than usual. In fact, an unprecedented amount of resistance. Was it going cold? He stared at the orange-red lava with chunks of black rock; it appeared the same as ever. It certainly felt as hot as ever, if not a bit more. However, he could no longer move.

Rosencrantz's eyes widened as the lava before him in the center of the pit began oozing upward. A ball shape was rising from the lava on a black lava stalk. He blinked as the ball began to shape itself; within moments the ball was clearly a human-like head on a neck, albeit made out of lava.

Rosencrantz felt his non-existent bowels churn as fiery red threads of lava formed what appeared to be hair on the head , along with a red beard and mustache. Two very pointed horns rose from the temples. Black eyelids opened to reveal deep, burning-red ember eyes.

The face was clearly recognizable. The red-lava hair also rather clearly gave the individual away.

Rosencrantz stuttered. "Uh, uhm—oh, Great One! What an honor!" He gulped. This was a horror between horrors. The springs were in Moloch's territory and thus neutral ground. This should not have been a problem; he should have been off limits.

"You may cease with the small lies, Rosencrantz. I can sense your fear. You positively reek of it," the Co-Factor told him.

"I beg your forgiveness, your greatness. However, my mistress would do most horrible things to me if I were to so much as speak with you," Rosencrantz said, nearing a state of panic.

"Well in that case, what is done is done. We've obviously been speaking," Sammael stated with a small, tight smile.

Rosencrantz made a sad, squeaking sound.

"Relax. I would rather she not know we are speaking. We are in neutral territory, a remote area and I have shielded my presence beyond what anyone nearby can detect. If you say nothing, I will say nothing; thus you have no reason to fear your mistress." Sammael grinned at the smaller demon. He knew how difficult it could be, and how dangerous it was, to keep secrets from Lilith. "I simply note that the demon you were following has apparently relocated. Where did he and his entourage go?"

"I am not sure what you are talking about, Great One!" Rosencrantz protested. The demon felt the lava around him start to compress.

"I am not in the mood for games. I have no problem ending you right here and now. I have been feeling a bit puckish lately," the Lord of the Abyss stated.

Rosencrantz gulped. "How did you know this?"

Sammael scowled in frustrated annoyance. "I was also spying on him and then he left, and you and Guildenstern also left. So he has obviously gone somewhere else. Where?" Sammael demanded.

"Doom," Rosencrantz admitted. He really wished he could sweat. It would be very useful at the moment.

"Doom?" Sammael asked, puzzled.

"*Mount* Doom."

Sammael's eyes widened in surprise. "Mount Doom? Why would he go to that abandoned dump?" He twisted his head in thought.

"Uhm, to restart it," Rosencrantz volunteered, trying to perhaps buy a few more moments of life.

Sammael shook his head in surprise. "Start it?" He blinked a couple of times. "He would need the wand to do that."

"Uhm, I don't know, your greatness, but it is active once more," Rosencrantz said.

"Doom is active?" Sammael was shocked. He then chuckled. "The woman must be shitting in her dress!"

Rosencrantz nodded, staring at the Lord of the Abyss in terror.

"You have done me good, Rosencrantz. I will not forget." Suddenly the head glopped back down into the lava and Rosencrantz's arms could move, free once more. The demon sighed and tilted his head back. He needed to get out of here. This place was no longer that relaxing.

~

"So, this is the Abyss?" Damien asked Antefalken rather nervously as he and Vaselle walked down one of the rather poorly lit corridors of Mount Doom. They had just left the Temple of Doom, as Tom called it for some reason: the chamber that the D'Orcs used for much of their interdimensional communication.

"Well, it is Mount Doom, which is in the Abyss," Antefalken said. "It's actually a very pleasant place compared to most of the Abyss."

"Really?" Vaselle asked rather nervously, looking around.

"It's a lot cooler and significantly more humid," Antefalken noted. "Tom has cooled the majority of the Doomplex, as we've started calling it, down to the equivalent of a very hot summer day, so that your amulets won't be taxed as much."

Antefalken gestured around them. "And, as you can tell by the fact that there are furnishings that somehow survived four thousand years of very dry and excessive heat, the acidity level is not toxic." Antefalken grinned. "That is considered a major selling point."

"So how hot is it normally?" Vaselle asked. "I hear that water boils here."

"That is true on the plains. We are at a higher altitude here and so when the volcano was dormant, the temperature was probably only about three-fourths the temperature of boiling water."

"So the volcano starting made it hotter?" Damien asked.

"I guess. For a while, we didn't really notice, since it did not get any hotter than the rest of the Abyss. However, once the storm clouds formed and it started raining, the temperature quickly cooled. And then Tom started the cooling runes."

"Cooling runes—you've mentioned those before," Damien said.

"Yes, there are runes throughout this complex that do a wide variety of things; some of them are cooling runes that basically produce a cooling spell upon the air. They are actually very popular in the Courts of Chaos," Antefalken said.

"Why do they want cooling at the Courts if they are all demons?" Vaselle asked.

"Because they have furniture, paper, clothing and food and drink that doesn't fare well at the ambient temperature. Therefore, the higher-ups tend to use various forms of arcane cooling in their homes and palaces."

"Is that why most demons are naked? Because clothes wouldn't hold up well in the Abyss?" Vaselle asked.

Antefalken shrugged. "Well, it's more like most don't care about nudity, and don't bother acquiring clothes. Particularly since tailoring them to fit an odd shape gets expensive for most demons, and then, as you say, the temperature would not be good for many materials over time. If they have the money, most prefer to spend it on something else."

"But you wear clothes," Vaselle pointed out.

"Yes, but I'm a professional entertainer; I need to wear clothes or all the women in my audience would swoon!" Antefalken grinned.

"I thought you said demons don't care about nudity?" Damien asked his bard snidely.

"Well, generally speaking, but when one has a particularly outstanding physique…" Antefalken said.

"So you have to spend quite a bit of money on clothing?" Vaselle asked.

Antefalken looked at the wizard, slightly perplexed by the question. "Well, something like that. I didn't always wear clothes."

"You know it's very odd, now that I think of it. You wear the exact same clothes probably ninety percent of the time and yet they are always impeccably clean and pressed," Damien said, furrowing his brow.

Antefalken coughed. "As I said, I'm a professional; I need to look my best at all times. It is also about branding; people need to be able to recognize you. Ask any celebrity!"

"So are you taking us on a tour?" Vaselle asked.

"We will be doing a tour, but I'm showing you to what I'm calling the mortal suite." Antefalken said.

"The mortal suite?" Damien repeated dubiously.

Antefalken grinned at the wizard. "It's a suite of rooms overlooking the volcano and stadium, with a balcony. There are quite a few suites like that, but this one was apparently designed with mortal guests in mind as opposed to immortal guests."

"And what are the differences?" Vaselle asked.

"Well, the number one difference is a room for number one and number two." Antefalken smiled brightly at the humans, who did not seem to get the reference. He sighed. "A toilet. Bathrooms with toilets and running water. Running water *now*, I should say. The water did not work after the reservoirs went dry, but they work now." He waved his hands reassuringly. "Also, the beds and furniture are more human sized, although this varies, as demons come in extremely different sizes. And the rooms have much finer temperature controls. You won't need your amulets in them."

Antefalken opened the double doors to a large suite with very nice furniture and some rather odd paintings of demons and other creatures. There were six doors to other rooms, plus French doors leading out to a balcony. The lighting in this room was considerably better, with multiple lamps lit throughout the room.

"Seems like a lot of rooms for two people," Damien observed.

"Well, on that matter," Antefalken began, "we have some other mortal guests coming. Tal Gor, Ragala-nargoloth, Beya Fei Geist and Farsooth Gore Tusk. Unfortunately, Trig Bioblast had watch and so was unable to come."

"Those are very odd names," Vaselle stated suspiciously.

"Well, they are orcs," Antefalken admitted.

"Orcs?" Damien asked, surprised.

"Tom is being sworn in as king of the D'Orcs, which are based on orcs. These four, or rather five with Trig, are his shamans. Tal Gor is from Astlan, down near Jotungard and Murgandy."

"So I take it they had longstanding ties to Mount Doom?" Damien asked.

Antefalken shook his head. "Not at all. Tom had to seek them out to get supplies for this party. Not a lot of stores or merchants nearby."

~

"Welcome, Beya!" Tom greeted the final shaman as she came through the portal.

"Lord Tommus, it is my honor to be at this glorious occasion!" She bowed her head.

"We have a suite of rooms for our mortal guests; each of you will have your own room off a common living area. We think we've got everything covered, including water and reliable cooling," Tom said as he closed the portal. "There is a balcony that will provide a great view of the ceremony; however, you are also welcome to attend on the main floor of the arena. It will be a very long ceremony, as I have mentioned, so come and go as you please. I, of course, will be busy most of the time, but I will have someone available to assist all of you."

"You are most gracious, My Lord." Beya nodded again.

"I shall take you to the suites. My demon bard, Antefalken, will be giving a tour prior to the ceremony," Tom told her as they walked along. "The others are already there."

"Antefalken?" Beya said.

"Yes, have you heard of him?" Tom asked.

"There is a famous orc bard from about three hundred years ago by the same very unusual name," Beya said thoughtfully.

"Well, given all the demons I've been uncovering pretending to be mortals lately, I suppose it could be the same. However, my Antefalken doesn't look anything like an orc. He's way too small, and as far as I know, he can't shape-change."

"Ahh, speaking of that. It would be good if we could speak at some point regarding your son and his friend, Fer-Rog," Beya said.

"Did they cause problems for you?" Tom asked, suddenly concerned.

Beya smiled and bowed slightly. "Not in the manner you fear. But they might cause you some issues," she said with a chuckle.

"Rupert does have a tendency to get in over his head," Tom admitted.

"I think both boys have great shamanistic potential, and that is what I would like to discuss," Beya told Tom.

"Really? That is great news! We need more shamans here in Mount Doom if we are to resume interactions with Midgard. I can't open every portal myself, and we need end points in both locations."

"Exactly." Beya smiled as they approached the suite. "Which brings me to the question I am most interested in."

"Which is?" Tom asked, smiling back.

"Well, you've brought your shamans and wizards through to Mount Doom and closed the gateways behind us. How exactly are we going to get back with no one on the other side?" Beya asked curiously.

Tom stopped in his tracks. "Shit. How did I not think of that?" He felt his stomach sink to his knees.

Chapter 108

Randolf, Exador, Gandros, Lenamare, Jehenna, Tureledor and Davron had just finished a conclave to discuss the conditions for the tests to confirm the humanity of Exador and his colleagues. They had filed down from the small Atrium of Archos, where the meeting had been held, and had just entered the grand foyer of the palace, which was the closest crossway to each councilor's respective regions of the palace, when Randolf noted Ruiden approaching them.

Randolf blinked. While there was a fair amount of fierdlight coming through the large windows of the grand foyer, Ruiden seemed to be reflecting an ever-increasing amount of light as he approached. It had to be some sort of magical effect, which swords were, in fact, known to have under various conditions. Ruiden had not been glowing when Randolf had spoken with the sword, and none of his colleagues had reported this either. He was not sure what to make of this, but it did not bode well.

"Councilors!" Ruiden came up in front of the small group before they could split off to go their own directions.

"Ruiden." Gandros, Lenamare and Tureledor all nodded and greeted the sword. All the councilors with the exception of Exador and Trevin had been interviewed by the sword at this point. Randolf had to suppress a small chuckle at remembering how Gandros had expressed the wish that the rest of the Rod were as pleasant to deal with as the sword.

"Councilor Exador," Ruiden addressed the mage.

Exador, of course, had no idea who Ruiden was; he had not been present at any of the council meetings where the sword and its investigation had been discussed.

"What are you?" Exador said rather tersely. He was looking at the now very obviously glowing sword.

"I am Ruiden, Sword of Talarius."

"You are a sword?" Exador asked, frowning at the odd statement.

"Yes. I am the sword Ruiden, currently in the service of the Knight Rampant of Tiernon, Talarius." Ruiden nodded politely. "I am investigating the abduction of Sir Talarius and have been interviewing all relevant parties."

"Nice to meet you. I will leave you to interview whichever colleague of mine you wish." Exador gave the sword a small smile and nod and attempted to pass.

"I am sorry, Councilor; I was imprecise," Ruiden said.

Exador had moved towards the sword's left, but turned his head to respond. "Not a problem. It was interesting to meet you."

"Councilor," Ruiden said, turning to face Exador. "I have already interviewed your colleagues here and would now like to interview you. I realize you have been quite busy, but I have been trying to reach you for an interview and this is the first moment I have been able to make contact with you."

Exador stopped again and stared for a moment. "As you say, I am very busy, and am under a number of time constraints. I fear I don't have time to be interviewed at the moment."

"Quite understandable," Ruiden said politely. "May we please set a time and place that we may talk?"

Exador sighed, annoyed. "Why do you need to interview me? I was not a participant in the battle and have no knowledge of anything useful to you."

"I am sorry, but I respectfully disagree," Ruiden said. "Other than Councilor Lenamare, you are perhaps the most relevant person for me to interview in this case."

Exador shook his head, not understanding. "Why do you say that?" His temper was starting to rise'.

Randolf was more than familiar with the mage's tone. He quickly got a sick feeling in his stomach as his adrenaline levels started to rise. *"Crispin,"* he called to the djinn over their master-djinn link. *"I think the situation with Exador may be about to go critical. Start breaking out the gear. Get down to the lab and start prepping it to move to the Grand Foyer if I should need it."*

"Seriously?" Crispin responded over the link.

"Afraid so. Hurry!" Randolf ordered.

"Well, first and foremost, you were the closest wizard to the battle between Talarius and Lenamare's demon," Ruiden stated.

Exador interrupted, "How do you determine that?"

"Councilor, we have all seen the balling with you, Ramses the Damned and another demoness watching the battle."

"What are you talking about? I did observe the battle from a carpet, but I was not on any carpet with Ramses the Damned and a demoness," Exador said. "Those were my human associates."

Ruiden tilted his head to the left slightly. "Unfortunately, the balling does not allow me to verify that the woman was a demoness; however, the garb of your male colleague was unmistakably that of a Time Warrior. I am personally familiar with the outfit. He also looked the same as I remember Ramses the Damned looking from a similar distance."

Exador shook his head in disbelief. "Are you saying you've seen any one of the Anilords named Ramses? And that you have personally seen Time Warriors?"

"Councilor, I have slain Time Warriors, and I have seen several of the Ramses on the field of battle, although I have not engaged them," Ruiden stated without emotion.

"You've slain Time Warriors?" Jehenna asked incredulously.

Ruiden looked at her and nodded. "I have, several; albeit with different wielders. They are, or were, very difficult to kill."

"Well, that's all interesting, but have you stopped to think that my compatriot might just be a history buff?" Exador asked, clearly not amused by this line of questioning.

"If Ramses the Damned were a demon lord, it would explain his multiple incarnations and his ability to be here now," Ruiden stated.

"Yes, but you have no proof that he was or is a demon. We have, in fact, just come from a meeting to discuss how to prove his humanity," Exador said.

Ruiden nodded in acknowledgement. "True, but given that your colleague was on the carpet with you, it seems highly likely that he is also a very powerful demon."

Exador squinted slightly and said very coldly to Ruiden, "What exactly do you mean by that? I have just stated that I am working with the Council to establish categorically that my colleagues and I are not archdemons!"

Ruiden seemed to shrug, which was a very odd motion for a metal golem, Randolf thought to himself.

"I do not know if you are an archdemon." Ruiden stated in his dry voice. Exador smiled grimly in triumph. "But you are very clearly a demon of considerable power."

Several nearby people, perhaps some of the other councilors, gasped at this very provocative statement. Randolf had to suppress a grin. He was nervous as the Abyss, but the sword was going to force the issue once and for all.

"Ruiden," Gandros interjected, trying to calm the situation, Randolf suspected. "That is a very serious allegation that the council is working to verify. It seems to me that additional accusations are not needed at this stage."

"Thank you, Chairman," Exador said coldly.

Ruiden glanced at the chairman of the Council. "It is not an accusation. It is a statement of proven fact."

Gandros gave his head a small shake. "What do you mean, 'proven fact'?"

"You note," Ruiden said, "that I am glowing brightly at this moment?"

"Yes." Several councilors nodded in agreement.

"You all note that I did not glow in any of your presences?" Ruiden asked. The councilors all nodded.

"This is because none of you are demons. I am glowing like this because I am in the presence of a demon—a very powerful demon," Ruiden said.

"Enough! This is ridiculous!" Exador shouted. "Talarius could turn you on and off at will!"

"I am not sure how you would know that, Councilor," the sword stated. "However, Talarius is not here. That is why I am conducting this investigation."

"Why should we believe you? How do we know you are not glowing in order to accuse Exador?" Randolf asked, playing devil's advocate —about as literally as possible, Randolf thought, chuckling to himself.

Exador nodded in appreciation at him. "Because I was forged as a demon-slaying sword. Identifying and slaying demons is my principal purpose," Ruiden stated. Several people gasped and more than a few councilors stepped back.

"In short, I know a demon when it is in my presence. Even as I recognize the other extra-planar beings running around the city."

Exador snorted. "Other extra-planar beings?" He turned to the other councilors. "This is nonsense. I will not stand here and listen to these lies." He was very angry at this point. "We have agreed on a system; we will stick to it."

"At this point, I have not verified that you are responsible for the demon that kidnapped Talarius; therefore, I have no need to prove you are a demon. I simply need to ask you some questions as to your involvement with that demon and the incidents leading up to Talarius's abduction," Ruiden said. "However, if it would help to clarify things, I can have Arch-Diocate Iskerus bring the Holy Mirror of Erastimus to us." Ruiden looked to the other councilors. "It is the mirror that Talarius used to detect the demon infestation; I trust that its credibility and accuracy have been satisfactorily proven?"

Exador threw up his hands. "This is complete nonsense. We cannot trust Tiernon's priest's magical artifacts!"

"The mirror did prove to be remarkably accurate," Jehenna said.

"Perhaps we should have Iskerus just bring it and be done with this issue here and now," Tureledor said.

"I agree," Davron seconded.

"I am a Councilor of Wizardry; I do not need to stand for this treatment!" Exador said, spinning to march away.

Ruiden was suddenly in front of the mage; he had moved there faster than Randolf's eyes could follow. "Councilor, given your recalcitrance in answering my questions, I fear I must insist on obtaining your word for scheduling an interview, or engage in one now. We can go somewhere more private."

"I refuse to be intimidated by a stupid artifact!" Exador waved his left arm and suddenly Ruiden was flying through the air, crashing hard into one of the columns lining the foyer.

"Exador, there is no need for violence!" Gandros shouted, even as the sound of some sort of air vortex started to drown the archimage out.

As if in slow motion, Randolf saw what appeared to be an insanely large, four-pronged glaive, spinning clockwise through the air, fly across the room from the column into which Ruiden had been thrown. The glaive, moving at whirlwind speed, cleaved Exador in two at the waist and continued on to crash into the top of an archway on the opposite side of the room.

Randolf had not even been able to process it in real time; it was only after the loud crashing that he had been able to understand what had happened. People began screaming and running for cover even as the roar of a loud fire rising from where Exador's two halves had fallen drowned out the screams.

There was a huge blaze where Exador had fallen; out from that blaze stepped a re-formed Exador. The wizard was now fully clad in his infamous war regalia: his highly ornate and archaic blackish-purple armor, horned great helm and large black sword.

"You have chosen the wrong battle, sword!" Exador shouted in rage.

"Crispin, get your ass and the gear up here now!" Randolf shouted through his link to the djinn.

"Lenamare! Get the wards up!" Tureledor shouted.

Gandros spun to the guards, who were scrambling to figure out what to do. "Sound the alert, evacuate the palace immediately! Get everyone out and away from the palace! Clear the surrounding areas of the city!"

Randolf cast the djinn-taught spell to summon his staff; whirling dust from all over the room rose and moved towards him, coalescing into the form of his staff. As he did this, he noted Jehenna leading Lenamare to the edge of the foyer, Lenamare obviously distracted trying to reach out to the members of the warding team.

Tureledor was quickly surrounded by a shimmering globe; most likely a kinetic bubble to protect him from flying objects. Davron was shouting into a mirror, clearly shouting orders to his people.

Ruiden crashed to the floor below the archway and quickly stood to face the oncoming Exador. "Well, I hope that surviving a cleaving should be sufficient proof for everyone of your demonic nature?" Ruiden said.

"I am going to take great pleasure in disenchanting you, artifact!" Exador hissed, bringing his giant black sword around to strike at the sword golem. Ruiden raised his right arm and countered the giant blade.

Randolf shook his head. Exador was going into combat against four swords: two arm and two leg swords. This would be interesting, but he had work to do. His staff was now present and he began using its magical end tip to begin inscribing runes around himself in the stone floor. If he was about to go toe-to-toe with an archdemon, a good pentagram would be very useful.

~

An extremely loud klaxon caused Trisfelt to jump up in shock from the chair in which he was seated at a table, reading over a large scroll. "What the hell is that?" he asked no one in particular, being alone in his suite. He quickly ran to the door.

The klaxon seemed even louder in the hallway. A page came rushing down the hall.

"What is that noise?" Trisfelt yelled at the page.

"It's the palace evacuation klaxon!" the page replied, running up to Trisfelt.

"Evacuation?" Trisfelt asked.

The page nodded. "Lord Gandros has sounded the alarm to evacuate; apparently there is a major arcane battle going on in the grand foyer that is liable to cause death and generalized mayhem!"

"Worse than when the demons all exploded from the basement?" Trisfelt asked.

The page shrugged. "Apparently. Everyone needs to evacuate. You should see lit runes near stairwells with directions on where to exit. Gotta run!"

"Crap!" Trisfelt cursed. He needed to make sure the students got out. He prayed to… he had no idea whom that they were all close together. *Where was Hilda?* He hoped she was at home.

~

Randolf finished his carved pentagram and was finally able to glance back to the battle. Things were not really going well for Exador; at least, he was not making any progress. Ruiden was a sword, a very sharp, very hard metal sword. In a sword fight, you fought to wound and kill the wielder of a sword, not the sword itself. Thus, Exador had nothing to actually attack; he was fighting a self-wielding weapon.

There was really nothing Exador could do with another sword to wound Ruiden. While Exador was also heavily armored, his armor had joints so he could move his limbs. This presented a weakness that the greater demon had used consistently against Talarius. Ruiden seemed to be using this weakness fairly successfully against Exador. Every so often one of the sword's blades would bypass Exador's guard and strike at a joint. Shortly thereafter, a flash of light would occur; presumably a healing spell. Actually, considering that Exador was going up against four blades, and the sword's gymnastic skills were quite formidable, it was quite impressive how few such hits Ruiden managed to get in.

"How far away are you?" Randolf asked Crispin over the link.

"I have to get all the stuff outside our wards. Once I've got it all out, I can teleport it all to the foyer. I need about two more trips," Crispin replied.

Randolf glanced over to Lenamare and Jehenna. Jehenna was busy casting a protective circle around herself and Lenamare. That was a good idea, Randolf thought. Lenamare was the keystone to the city wards; he needed to be protected. Assuming he got the wards up, that was.

At that very moment, Lenamare looked up towards Gandros. "Where in the Abyss is Damien?" Lenamare shouted. "I can't reach him and he is a key part of the wards!"

Gandros shook his head. "No idea! What about the rest?"

"They are scrambling into place!" Lenamare shouted.

This was not a good way to communicate! Randolf quickly began casting communication links to the other councilors, with the exception of Exador, naturally. Tureledor was the first to connect.

"*Should I launch an attack, or allow Ruiden to keep Exador distracted while everyone else gets into position?*" Tureledor asked.

"*Let's get everyone into position and get protections up. If we go full arcane, the damage area is bound to get worse!*" Randolf replied.

Davron and Gandros came online at that moment. "*We are working to ward the foyer; we will need to be able to contain the damage as much as possible!*" Gandros said.

Randolf looked; sure enough, the two were making their way around the edges of the foyer, working on trying to create containment wards. They should consider installing permanent runes to make such containment systems easier to bring up. They were really starting to have too many deadly events around here, Randolf thought to himself.

Lenamare came online with the link; Jehenna was still busy casting various protection spells around the two of them. "*Damien is not responding; I have everyone else. You've studied the wards; do you think you can take his place?*" Lenamare asked Randolf.

"*I can try, with the wards in their current state, the destabilization should be minimal,*" Randolf replied.

"*Let us go for that, then. Even once you are in, it's going to take me a bit to get everything back up. Particularly with both of us up here rather than down there,*" Lenamare said.

~

Master Hortwell and Zilquar banged on the door of Sier Barvon. "Open up!" The two wizards shouted over the klaxon. Finally, after a few minutes the door opened.

"What the Abyss? What is that damn racket?" Sier Barvron complained. "Loud enough to wake the dead!"

"But not you!" Zilquar yelled.

Sier shrugged. "I'm a deep sleeper." He stuck his head into the hallway. "It's louder out here! What the hell is it?"

"Do you not attend any of the emergency preparedness meetings?" Zilquar asked in disbelief.

"I'm always prepared, so there is no point in going," Sier stated.

Zargoffelstan snickered behind Hortwell, who shook his head. "Well if you did, you'd know it's an evacuation klaxon!"

"Evacuation? Why?" Sier shouted over the klaxon

"Gandros ordered it after Ruiden cleaved Exador in twain!" Zilquar shouted back.

"Well, that seems a bit rude," Sier said with a shocked expression on his face.

"Exador thought so too, and now the two are dueling it out in the Grand Foyer," Hortwell yelled.

"How do you out duel a self-wielding sword?" Sier asked loudly. "What do you aim for?"

"That's exactly the problem! Exador is going to realize that at some point, give up and start blasting the demon dung out of everything!" Zilquar yelled.

"So, we are sure he's an archdemon then?" Sier yelled.

"Well, how many wizards get cleaved in two at the waist and re-form in a blaze of fire, fully armored with a large sword?" Zilquar replied at the top of his lungs.

"Seems like a fair point!" Sier conceded. "What now?"

"Gandros is putting up a containment field around the foyer; we need to put one up around the entire palace in case it expands beyond the foyer!" Hortwell shouted.

"Abyssal arthritis, that's going to be a pain!" Sier stated, shaking his head. He gestured for them to lead the way.

~

"Lilith fornicator!" Exador screamed at Ruiden as the archdemon fell over after losing his balance when Ruiden sliced his right leg off at the hip.

Randolf looked up in surprise upon hearing the loud clatter of the archdemon falling over. He had just gotten into the wards and was working with Lenamare to stabilize them after the handover.

"Enough with this farce!" Exador screamed as he engulfed himself in flames that seemed to grow higher and higher.

"*I think we are about to experience full archdemon!*" Randolf yelled over their communication link.

"*Really getting tired of demonic invasions,*" Jehenna said; she had come online a few moments earlier.

"*We are almost there on the foyer containment spell!*" Gandros said. "*Zilquar, Sier and Hortwell have rounded up some other senior wizards and they are working on a palace containment spell!*"

"*Where is Alexandros?*" Tureledor asked.

"*I got a reply that he is coming, but not sure how fast he can get here,*" Gandros said. "*He said he had to get some components together.*"

"*I hope they're worth the wait, because this could get ugly fast!*" Jehenna said.

Exador's flames were now nearing the high ceiling of the foyer and a form—a very large form—was appearing. It appeared to be about twenty-five feet tall and probably eight feet across the shoulders. Large pinioned wings, very unlike typical demon wings, appeared on the demon's back. Other than that, Randolf realized quickly, it looked just like Exador.

"Sword!" Exador roared at Ruiden. "You have pissed me off more than anyone has in a long time. Not even Lenamare could annoy me as much as you have!"

Randolf noted that Lenamare, still working on ward stabilization, frowned, possibly insulted by the comment.

"Since you were forged in metal, I will assume fire will not be useful against you, nor lightning. So how about cold?" Exador suddenly inhaled and then pursed his lips and blew—in fact, he whistled—directly towards Ruiden.

Randolf blinked his eyes, realizing that he could actually see Exador's breath, as if on a very cold day. No, he corrected himself, the breath was frost. No, now it was ice and it slammed into the sword golem as a solid blast of what appeared to be liquid ice? Or ice water? Randolf was not sure, but what was clear was that Ruiden was now completely buried, hidden in a very solid mound of ice.

There was a loud clanking noise as Crispin and a large pile of gear suddenly appeared behind Randolf. Crispin went to work quickly to distribute objects in their correct positions.

"What is this?" Exador asked. Apparently, he had heard the noise of the arrival, even over the klaxon. That was very good hearing, Randolf decided. He glanced up at Exador.

"Randolf, my employer. What does your catamite have there? It looks like demon-binding equipment," Exador thundered.

Randolf turned to face him. "Well, my no longer trusted employee, you are astute, I will give you that. Much brighter than most of the demons I've bound."

Exador looked at him as if he had just lost his mind. "Most demons that you have bound? Have you ever bound a single demon?" He chuckled. "And now you think you are going to start with me. You have clearly become unhinged."

"Perhaps," Randolf said. "However, I have begun to question your loyalty. You have been absent way too much recently. I am beginning to suspect you may have other allegiances than Turelane." He was trying to buy time for Crispin to get things set up; he could not leave the pentagram he was in without breaking it.

Exador tilted his head and stared at him. "You are definitely acting oddly; you have not been possessed by the demon the sword was looking for, have you?"

"No, I am afraid not. I am just rather tired of your scary wizard routine. I think it's time for you to move on," Randolf said.

Exador laughed. "So what, are you firing me?"

"Got it!" Crispin shouted. Randolf shook his head; the djinn should have said that over their link.

Crispin's shout got Exador's attention. "Ah, Randolf, sending a boy to do a man's work?" He shook his head. "That sounds like you." Exador waved towards Crispin and a giant bolt of lightning flew from his hand and struck Crispin with a loud crash of thunder. As the flash cleared from their eyes, it was clear that all that was left of the boy was a smoking, extremely charred corpse. More like a pile of charcoal.

Randolf heard gasps of shock over his link with the others. His fellow councilors knew how he felt about Crispin, even if they did find the apparent age difference in their relationship to be morally questionable. Randolf stared at the corpse and then turned back and looked up at Exador.

"You probably did not want to do that," Randolf said calmly.

Exador laughed. "What? Are you upset I broke your toy? What are you going to do about it?"

Randolf shook his head slightly. "No, I, personally, am not that upset. Thus, for the moment, I am not going to be doing anything about it. And for the record, you did not break "my toy" so much as piss it off."

Exador stared at Randolf in puzzlement for a moment, not understanding what he meant. Randolf gestured with both hands to the four fireplaces along the two side walls of the foyer. Exador turned his attention to see large plumes of smoke and ash pouring from the four fireplaces, streaming through the large room towards Crispin's crispy corpse.

"What is this?" Exador asked, puzzled.

Randolf chuckled; the other wizards in the room not busy casting spells also stared in surprise as the four large streams of smoke, soot and ash converged on the corpse into a single black cloud; a cloud that swirled upwards higher and higher. A cloud fed by four fireplaces containing hundreds of years of soot and ash, as well as a deep elemental affinity to fire, air and smoke.

The cloud began to crackle with small lightning bolts as Randolf resumed speaking. "And you did not simply piss *him* off; you will have pissed off his entire race. You know an attack against one is an attack against all, do you not?"

A booming laughter filled the room, emanating from the black cloud of soot over the now-hidden catamite's corpse. The smoke and soot from the fireplaces continued to stream unendingly towards it, the streams then bending and rising directly up above the site of Crispin's charred corpse. The upward streaming cloud was now as tall as Exador, and began to form a cross-like shape. At about waist height, the cloud suddenly lightened and changed.

Within moments, the upper half of the cloud had formed the upper torso of Crispin, or an older, more mature and hugely muscular version of Crispin. His gleaming muscles shone through the sleeveless, open front vest, and rock-hard abdominal muscles showed above a red sash that separated the human-appearing torso from the black cloud.

"Master," the new Crispin said, nodding to Randolf, showing those below the top of his very elegant, formal red turban. "This infidel has tried to damage your property."

"What the...?" Exador's eyes were wide in shock.

"Here's the thing, Exador," said Randolf. "You have been a pain in my family's side for a very long time. However, our closest allies could not move against you until you attacked one of them directly. You have now done so, unprovoked by myself or Crispin." He chuckled. "You see, in order for the djinn to move against you, you would need to attack Crispin in a manner unprovoked by either of us. You have now done so, for which you have my greatest appreciation." Randolf flashed Exador a very wide grin.

"My master is correct, demon. You have now given all of Djinnistan a reason to hunt you down and exterminate you like the vermin you are," Crispin said, grinning at Exador.

"Crispin?" Randolf said.

"Yes, master?"

"I *wish* you to punish Exador for damaging my property," Randolf said.

Crispin grinned widely, steepled his hands before him and bowed at his smoky waist towards Randolf. "Master, your *wish* is my command!" With that, Crispin and his smoke cloud quickly enveloped Exador. The sound of thunder and lightning resounded around the room even as the whistling roar of the air being sucked down the four chimneys rose to a level that drowned out the claxon.

"*Quickly, everyone; we need to move fast while Crispin buys us time!*" Randolf shouted across his link to his stunned fellow councilors. He had to twist his jaw to pop his eardrums; the air pressure in the room was getting quite extreme.

Crack! Crash! Crackle! Crash! Crunch! CRASH! The large upper windows in the foyer were being blown out by the very high air pressure in the room. Randolf had to brace himself as the wind levels within the room began to approach cyclone level. Fortunately, the air pressure had pushed the window glass outwards. Glass shards raining down on them was the last thing they needed while trying to cast spells.

Randolf shook his head and began casting a very local shielding spell around himself and his accessories before they all blew away. Gold braziers and similar instruments were heavy, but there were limits. He just needed to deflect the winds around his small area so he could actually cast some spells.

Once his local air shield was in place, Randolf flicked his wrist at the nearby brazier that Crispin had set up before his metamorphosis, lighting the components within. "*Astuos trineptos, eskelon nor tufos!*" Randolf began his incantation.

"*Is that Herodite's Horrendous Hellion Scourge?*" Jehenna asked over the link, apparently to Lenamare, yet everyone heard.

"*Sounds like it. I've never done it myself,*" Lenamare said, having temporarily forgotten about the city's wards. Randolf smiled grimly as he worked to cast the spell. Unfortunately, the most truly devastating spells against demons relied on a binding link between the master and demon. Thus, against foreign demons, most wizards were forced to use traditional non-demon spells which had varying effects.

Fortunately, there were a few demon-specific spells that could piggyback on a normal wizard link, such as the ones they all had as councilors. Herodite's Horrendous Hellion Scourge was one of those. It was also seldom used due to its complexity.

He had to really concentrate on this agonizing spell, making sure he added the pre-prepared components to the brazier in order. He thus could pay little attention to what others were doing. He did note that Tureledor was sending force bolts into Crispin's maelstrom. That was a great idea; they would have little effect on Crispin's gaseous form, but would be able to do quite a bit of kinetic impact damage to Exador.

Out of the corner of his eye he saw that Davron was creating a pentagram around himself, preparing to use conjury against Exador. *Excellent.*

"*Aargh!*" Exador screamed as a rapid barrage of razor-sharp ice bolts pummeled him. The bolts appeared to come from Gandros's direction. At least, Randolf assumed they were pummeling him, as no one could actually see Exador inside Crispin's smoky cloud. Suddenly Exador was coughing loudly. He must have inhaled after his scream; that would have drawn Crispin into his lungs.

Randolf shook his head; that was not going to be pleasant. Suddenly there was a new whistling sound as all of the smoke and soot began streaming into Exador's nostrils. Once inside the demon's lungs, after being initially inhaled, Crispin was able to pull the rest of his smoke and ash cloud to himself inside Exador. This was a standard djinn attack; Crispin would not only be attacking with lightning from inside, but also increasing the air pressure inside Exador. Mortal creatures generally exploded; that probably would not happen here. Exador would probably shift to fire or some other insubstantial form.

Yep, there he goes, Randolf noted to himself as a huge blaze started inside the smoke cloud. He shook his head while reciting his spell. The wind, combined with Exador's giant flames, were reaching out to the whipping tapestries and drapes. In moments, the upper walls of the foyer were a conflagration to match the pillar of flame in the center of the foyer.

"*Fiat Completum!*" Randolf screamed at the top of his lungs while thrusting his staff towards the flames of Exador, releasing his spell. Greenish-black tendrils each about six inches in diameter extended quickly from his staff and began wrapping around the flames.

Randolf really had to concentrate now, chanting under his breath to direct and manipulate the spell. He had to force the tendrils to wrap around all sides of Exador's flames, as well as above and below. He was going to need to get this in place quickly. The two insubstantial beings were now at a stalemate.

Tureledor's force bolts were now useless with nothing to impact upon; however, the stream of ice bolts was likely still hurting Exador, as the flames were sizzling as the bolts struck. While the bolts did melt, they were also poking holes in Exador's flames. *There!* Randolf mentally yelled to himself. *And now to squeeze.* Holding his staff in his right hand, Randolf began making a fist with his left.

There was a horrendous scream from the flames as Exador began to feel the pressure. Randolf waved his staff in a scourging motion as if he were whipping Exador, which in essence, he was. The flames shifted back to the solid, winged Exador, who was red with fury and glaring with a hideous malevolence at Randolf.

"You sycophantic sociopath! How dare you!" Exador raged. The archdemon pointed at Randolf and giant bolts of lightning flew from his large index finger, crashing against the shielding of Randolf's pentagram, even as Exador's body was pummeled from behind by more force bolts from Tureledor.

Randolf laughed. "Wizards use pentagrams to protect themselves from demons, in case you were not aware of this."

"To the Abyss with your pentagram!" Exador screamed at ear-splitting levels before he started choking again as Crispin again tried to fill his lungs when he inhaled. Perhaps at some point Exador would learn better, Randolf thought, grinning. Around a smoke-formed djinn, breathing was a seriously bad habit.

Exador dove to the floor with both fists forward, slamming hard into the floor while screaming a very loud, very deadly curse word. The ground rocked with the impact, far more than Exador's actual weight would have caused. He had done some sort of geomantic spell; that was obvious now as cracks began radiating out from the impact point of his fists.

The foyer shook with the force of the quake and the smaller tremors that followed. It had to have been some sort of ground-quake spell. Randolf began whipping harder, which naturally caused Exador to scream in pain again.

"He's got two columns!" one of his fellow councilors shouted over the communications link. Randolf could not tell which one it was, but he turned his attention enough to see that a crevice had reached and opened up the ground under at least one of the nearby columns. *Crap!* The columns were definitely load bearing, and were starting to collapse.

"I will work to prop the columns up!" Gandros shouted over the link.

"I'd help, but I'm trying to redirect the crevices from Lenamare while he works on the wards!" Jehenna shouted.

Randolf glanced at her; she was gesturing and chanting rapidly to redirect or ameliorate a very large crevice coming at her and Lenamare.

He turned his attention back to the ground at his feet. His pentagram had successfully stopped a crevice at its borders. Small cracks began appearing all around the pentagram, but not inside. It could block these because the pentagram had been tuned to Exador specifically and it was his magic causing the crevice. He had not been sure whether that level of indirectness would work without a true name, but it was.

Randolf glanced at Davron even as he kept on scourging Exador. Davron's pentagram would not be tuned; fortunately, no large crevices were splitting off near his position. Red tendrils were now twisting out of Davron's staff and were heading towards Exador.

CRACK!

A cracking noise far worse than the windows breaking, came from above. Randolf glanced up to see the ceiling cracking open. He mentally cursed; between wooden beams that were rapidly charring, the tie rods now most likely burnt from the flaming wall curtains, and the shifting of the columns, the stone roof was about to give way.

Exador cursed loudly as Davron's red tendrils began raking him with a new level of pain, added to what Randolf was inflicting. Randolf looked at the demon to see his right fist swing out towards the columns on the other side of the room. As if in slow motion, his giant fist struck through first one column, and then another. There was a large groaning and creaking noise as the archways above the two struck columns began to give way under the weight above them. The archways lurched and suddenly there was a terrific cracking sound from above as the ceiling stones gave way.

"Gandros! If you can keep the side wall from collapsing, I'll take care of the roof tiles!" Jehenna shouted over the links.

"Will do!" Gandros replied, even as the ceiling stones began falling down into the foyer. Jehenna gestured and flung the largest stone away from the area of the fight into an empty part of the room. The ceiling was rapidly fragmenting in a chain reaction. She was going to be busy.

Randolf whipped at Exador with renewed emphasis.

Exador screamed and stared directly at him again. "Okay, you lying deviant! I have had it with you and playing in your world! Time to come play in mine!" he screamed in pain and rage. He twisted his left hand in what almost looked like a rude gesture, and suddenly a circle of flame appeared on the floor halfway between the two of them.

Randolf blinked to see a portal exactly like the one the greater demon had used to kidnap Talarius. He glanced over to see that Ruiden was still stuck under a great mound of ice.

"Let us see how your pentagram works when there is no floor under it!" Exador shouted.

Randolf suddenly realized that the circle of flame was expanding to move under his pentagram. It was an extra-dimensional space. Dung droppings! It was highly unlikely that the pentagram would notice it. It was not an attack targeting him or the pentagram; it was just a void that would happen to come between him and the floor onto which the pentacles were inscribed. However, Randolf's body would still fall right through it, as would all of his gear.

Before he could even begin to try a spell to reverse the hole, the circle passed through his pentagram and he was falling! He was in free fall in a very, very hot place. He looked up to see a twenty-foot-diameter hole in the red sky, with Exador peering over the edge in glee.

"Crispin! I *wish* to be transported to a safe location in the foyer!" Randolf screamed vocally and over their master-djinn link.

Randolf slammed into the floor at the back of the foyer as his djinn did a line-of-sight teleport through the hole between worlds. *Dung beetles, that hurt!* Randolf thought to himself as shooting pain raced up his legs from the impact. He heard Exador scream once more in rage and fury. Randolf's spell had been broken when his components had fallen into the Abyss, but Davron's was still affecting the archdemon. However, Randolf suspected it was not pain but the fury of being thwarted that had spawned Exador's outburst.

"Enough of this!" boomed an incredibly loud voice from above, startling everyone. Randolf looked up to see Alexandros Mien floating through the very open skeletal remains of the ceiling. The still-violent winds were only moderately ruffling his robes, although his thin hair was standing on end and fluttering rapidly.

"Exador, you are no longer welcome in Freehold!" The ancient mage raised his staff as if pointing to something in the sky and swept it quickly down at Exador. As he did, there was an ear-splitting whistling or roaring noise, completely unlike that of the chimneys.

Almost without warning, a large black-and-red object about fifteen feet in diameter came racing out of the sky and smashed into Exador's head with brutal impact, sending both the object and Exador spinning through the hole into the Abyss. Alexandros waved his staff again in the same sweeping motion and another black, fiery object came hurtling out of the sky and through the hole into the Abyss at an even faster rate, smashing into the falling archdemon.

Randolf, Gandros, Tureledor and Davron all moved closer to the hole to observe. Jehenna could see into the hole from her current position. A third fiery rock followed. Randolf drew his breath, realizing that the fiery rocks were meteors. Alexandros was actually pulling celestial bodies out of deep space and smashing them into Exador!

"I think this was worth the wait!" Randolf told Jehenna over the communication link.

Exador and the meteors struck the ground in the Abyss, producing a very large mushroom cloud, into which a fourth and then a fifth meteor crashed. A sixth, very large one followed, and then they heard Jehenna scream into the air and over their link, "Stop the showers, the wards are coming up now!"

Randolf looked up to see Alexandros staring upward, working hard to redirect the course of the next few meteors off to a more harmless location. Suddenly the light level in the foyer changed dramatically as the portal closed when the wards kicked in. At the same time, the sky above the open roof once more turned the familiar red of the demon wards.

Randolf crossed his fingers that all the meteors had been redirected; it was not clear if Alexandros would be able to control them through the magic-blocking wards. Before he could finish crossing his fingers, the wind in the room shifted direction. Suddenly the air, smoke and ash in the room were streaming upwards at a very high velocity.

"The wards were my clue to exit!" Crispin shouted in his head. *"Based on last time, I should be back in half a day or so!"*

Within seconds, the air was completely still, the ash and soot slowly sinking to the ground. The upwards rush of air had snuffed out the flames in the upper foyer. Alexandros Mien landed in the middle of the foyer and looked around at the mess. Gandros had finally managed to bring the collapsing upper walls to a gentle rest as a huge pile of rubble.

"First the demon escape, now this. I think they are going to cancel our building insurance," Alexandros Mien said drily.

Chapter 109

Calyph Ser Sayat Tel Bastios unlocked the wards using his signature code and entered the shielded space of the Calyphadrome. He was the first to arrive. The space was soothing and quite relaxing; being shielded, it was cut off from the cacophony of Djinnistan. Only here and at his home space was there mental peace these days.

How he had envied the Grand Calyphos when he had been a scattered youth. He had foolishly believed that the Grand Calyphos were above the daily rituals, tasks and servitude of the lesser djinn. A common misconception of those not in power about those in power. Yet no matter how many tutors would try to explain to the young that power was but a burden, best shared, a grave responsibility that made one the servant, not the master, the students never believed.

They dreamed and dreamed, and for only a poor few—those who worked and strove relentlessly for centuries to perfect their studies and rise to the height of their profession—only those poor few realized, too late, that their tutors had been correct. Power was a burden, a responsibility that somehow, in a weightless world, weighed heavily upon the spirit of those who held it.

The room flashed with the signatory colors of Calyph Her Tanaya Tel Barthos, quickly followed by the colors of Calyph Te Narthos al Biyam. As the two calyphs entered the chamber, Ser Sayat flashed them pleasant, warm colors of greeting, which they generously returned.

"*We are awaiting Calyph Le Senara al Vistra and Calyph Cryan Ser Viat Tel Malthos?*" Her Tanaya expressed to Ser Sayat.

Ser Sayat flashed a scent of amused agreement. It was no surprise that the other two were late, albeit for very different reasons.

"*It shall be amusing to receive Le Senara's explanatory dialogue this time,*" Te Narthos expressed to them.

"*Hir explanatory dialogues are always a source of great amusement!*" Ser Sayat agreed.

Le Senara was a djinn of the greatest wit. Hir delays were always due to poor time management and organizational skills, yet the witty diatribe of reasons were always fascinating and engaging.

The space flashed with the signatory colors of Calyph Cryan Ser Viat Tel Malthos, who quickly expressed colors and scents of embarrassed apologies. Ser Sayat had to wonder which of hir partners had delayed hir.

Her Tanaya flashed Cryan Ser Viat a scent and color of amused approval, which only served to make Cryan Ser Viat flash more signs of embarrassment. Ser Sayat laughed internally—to be young! Cryan Ser Viat was the youngest of the Grand Calyphos at only 302 multiversal standard years.

The four of them waited quietly for a few more moments before the area flashed with the colors of Le Senara entering, flustered and disheveled as usual. The awaiting members all flashed greetings of amused warmth to Le Senara.

"My apologies, profuse, profuse apologies..." Le Senara expressed.

"And what amazing thing so distracted you this time?" Te Narthos inquired politely.

"Something truly amazing! Unprecedented even. Well, not unprecedented, as it used to be routine, but has not been for centuries upon centuries!" Le Senara gushed emotionally.

Ser Sayat was interested; this was a very different response than Le Senara's normal witty explanation. Ser Sayat and Her Tanaya flashed for Le Senara to continue; the rest flashed agreement.

"One of my students, Xavios De Mien Tel Tarthos"—the others flashed acknowledgement of the student; they knew hir —*"was working on baseline para-elemental measurements and detected malleable levels of para-elements in the Abyss!"*

The other calyphs flashed shock and surprise, as well as a request for confirmation from Le Senara. Le Senara flashed acknowledgement of their surprise. *"Naturally, I rechecked the measurements myself. They were correct!"*

This ignited extensive flashing and expressions of shocked bewilderment between the calyphs, disbelief even. It was safe to say the other calyphs all had appreciably similar reactions and quickly reached a consensus of emotion.

"Were the malleables scattered in any pattern? Were there sufficient coagulations—you did say malleable? That should imply coagulation of para-elements, yes?" Cryan Ser Viat asked impatiently.

"Indeed, they were where we last saw them in the Abyss: Mount Doom! It appears to have awakened and is once again is producing malleables!" Le Senara gushed hir thoughts and emotions.

"Could this be more than simply coincident with the balling we viewed from Crispin in service to Randolf of Turelane?" Te Narthos pondered.

The others flashed their thoughts and emotions for a few moments before Ser Sayat summarized what they were feeling. *"It would seem extremely improbable that two such monumental and, may I express, epic, events should occur in what must be considered a simultaneous period on the timescale of the multiverse."*

"So it would appear this demon that stole the false god's mana used that mana to awaken the volcano?" Te Narthos stated.

"That is likely, but we need to investigate to be sure," Her Tanaya expressed.

"I think, and would like to believe, that we all agree? That re-establishing relations with Mount Doom, and thus the Abyss, is critical to our long-term goals?" Te Narthos expressed. The others all rapidly flashed agreement and emotional support for the suggestion.

"*Then we must begin coagulation of a new golem at Mount Doom so that we may make contact with the new master.*" Again, the others flashed agreement with Te Narthos's suggestion.

"*Le Senara?*" Ser Sayat inquired of the other calyph. "*Since you are most familiar with the situation, might you take it upon yourself, at our request, to begin forming the golem?*" The other three calyphs flashed unanimity.

Le Senara flashed colors and scents of appreciation at Ser Sayat and the rest. "*I would be so honored, and give thanks to the Grand Calyphos for such an opportunity!*"

"*Next, we must consider who our ambassador should be,*" Cryan Ser Viat expressed.

"*Ahh, Cryan Ser Viat!*" Her Tanaya cautioned the youngest member quickly. "*At Mount Doom we are most likely dealing with D'Orcs, which are, at heart, orcs. We must never mention such terms as ambassador, diplomat or similar titles or job functions.*"

"*Agreed!*" flashed Ser Sayat. "*Such words can get our—agent—evicted, or worse, dissipated.*" All five expressed horror and dismay at the thought of dissipation.

"*My apologies. I now recall this.*" Hir contrition shone and smelled quite brightly within the space, causing Her Tanaya to express regret at expressing such a rapid and shrill reaction. She had not meant to shame Cryan Ser Viat; hir only concern had been the proposed mission and ensuring they were all careful.

Cryan Ser Viat expressed colors, scent and soft audibility to acknowledge and thank hir for hir concern.

"*Trying to resolve my memory, I believe the term 'military adjutant' might serve?*" Ser Sayat proposed.

Te Narthos expressed agreement with a hint of hesitation. "*We should verify this, but I believe that's correct. How long until you have a golem ready?*" Te Narthos directed this at Le Senara.

"*Assuming it is undisturbed—base levels are still thin—between five and six Abyssal periods,*" Le Senara replied.

"*Then it would be best for you to get started while we deliberate on a list of candidates. When we have a list, we shall join you to select one,*" Ser Sayat expressed.

Le Senara and the others flashed agreement.

~

DOF +9
Late Fourth Period 16-06-440

"I don't like the way that—creature—back there, is looking at me," Vaselle whispered nervously to Damien as they walked down the corridor towards the main dining hall. "I think it's trying to decide when to eat me." He quickly glanced back to the rear of the party, where Tal Gor and Schwarzenfürze were bringing up the rear.

Antefalken's head quickly ducked between the two wizards. "I am not sure if Schwarzenfürze wanted to eat you before, but now that you've called her a 'creature' and an 'it,' I am pretty sure it's just a matter of time before she does." The bard grinned at Vaselle.

"She can hear me? She can understand me?" Vaselle asked.

"Wargs are well known for their superb senses. Given that a D'Warg is a super-powered warg, I am sure she can hear you." Antefalken shrugged. "As far as understanding you, wargs can't speak particularly well or at all, but they certainly understand orcish and often several other languages, including human ones."

Vaselle gulped as Antefalken continued. "And given that she's a very old D'Warg that's been in the Abyss for a long time—I have no doubt she understands universal and so understands what we are saying."

"Should I apologize?" Vaselle asked, concerned.

Antefalken shrugged. "It might help. But I would do it from a distance."

Vaselle looked at him, eyes wide. "So I would have a chance to run away if she comes for me?"

Antefalken laughed. "Not at all. To give her some sport! Wargs, and thus surely D'Wargs, like to play with their dinners first. There is no way you could escape her! According to Vespa, Schwarzenfürze is the oldest and meanest D'Warg in the Abyss. Which would mean in the entire multiverse. She once took on two greater demons at once and slew them permanently! That's why she looks rather beat up."

"I'm doomed," Vaselle wailed quietly.

"Well, I suppose I could try and put a good word in with Tal Gor for you; maybe he can convince her not to eat you?" Antefalken said.

"Anything, please?" Vaselle begged.

Damien was giving Antefalken a dirty look. Antefalken gave the councilor a wink that Vaselle could not see.

They came into a large kitchen, where a number of D'Orcs were busy preparing extremely large portions of meats, carving and trimming them for roasting. A few other D'Orcs were preparing bundles of wood to go into the ovens.

"This is one of three kitchens where we are slow roasting meat for dinner tomorrow night. We plan to slow roast everything to a nice rare, or medium rare. The wood is to add flavor. Naturally, being in the Abyss, we don't need wood for fire!" Vespa told them.

"We have three other kitchens preparing meat, two preparing bread, and another one preparing vegetables," Vespa said.

"Don't forget Tizzy's kitchen!" Fer-Rog spoke up; he and Rupert were with the group as well. Rupert had been really happy to see Damien again.

"Tizzy?" Damien asked, puzzled. "What is he doing in a kitchen?"

"Baking cookies!" Rupert said.

"That will be nice for dessert!" Vaselle beamed, feeling a little better being in a large room where there were lots of people to see if Schwarzenfürze tried to eat him.

"I would probably advise going easy on the cookies," Antefalken said.

"Are they rich?" Vaselle asked.

"Not exactly, but having smelled his pipe, I am betting he is using a special form of butter," the bard said.

"An extra-sweet and rich form, I bet!" Vaselle rubbed his hands together.

"Yeah, something like that," Antefalken nodded.

Vaselle let out a loud yelp as he felt something wet rubbing against his arm.

Vaselle, Antefalken and Damien looked over to see Schwarzenfürze pull her tongue back into her mouth from licking Vaselle's hand and arm. The D'Warg looked at Vaselle and then opened her mouth wide and ran her tongue almost lovingly over her lips and teeth before snapping them shut. She gave the wizard a creepy look , then turned and walked away.

Antefalken looked at Damien. "See? You doubted me?"

Tal Gor smiled. "See! Schwarzenfürze is not as unsocial as everyone thinks!"

Ragala-nargoloth chuckled, as did Beya Fei Geist. Farsooth GoreTusk just grinned at the D'Warg's game. The orcs were all very familiar with wargs' sense of humor, and a D'Warg's was no different.

~

Rupert pulled at his collar as he stood on the platform behind his father. He had gotten out of the habit of wearing any clothes here in the Abyss; in fact, had never worn clothes in his true form. So it felt really strange. He was wearing a sleeveless gold embroidered black tunic that was open at the back, except at the collar, and then a button below his wings. He then had similar knee-length black pants on.

He, along with Zelda, Fer-Rog, the commanders and most senior D'Orcs, were all on the platform for the initial ceremony. There was a D'Orc orchestra, or a D'Orchestra, he guessed. Okay, it was like twelve D'Orcs, but that was more musicians than he had ever seen in one place before.

Each commander had given a speech about what a great opportunity this was, and how they had never expected to see this day. It was all quite inspirational and rather emotional, but after the first two or three? Rupert rolled his eyes at the latest one. Zelda would also give a speech, as would Tom.

After that, Rupert was to swear fealty, which seemed like an odd thing to do to one's father. But that did sort of sound like the story books, he guessed. Then Zelda and Fer-Rog would swear, followed by all the commanders. After that, Vaselle and the shamans were going to repeat their oaths. Talarius had agreed to swear to abide by the Rules of Hostage or something like that, and the rest of the entourage were encouraged to declare loyalty or friendship, but not required to swear fealty.

Tizzy, though, had a group of demons that he had hauled in for his baking that were going to swear. Apparently, they were all planning on taking up residence here. Rupert grinned at the thought of Tizzy's drinking buddies living here. That should be fun if they were all like Boggy. He wondered if Tizzy would swear? The octopod had been telling his demon friends that he was Tom's Lord High Muckety Muck, so Rupert would think someone with that prestigious of a title would have to swear allegiance. He was not really sure what a Lord High Muckety Muck did, but presumably Tizzy knew.

In any event, after that there would be the first short break as the staff that needed to be rotated for duty, or whose detachment wasn't going to be swearing in for a while, would be excused. At that point, Rupert, Fer-Rog, Talarius and the guests would be free to go. He figured most would go up to the mortal suite, where snacks would be set out for them. True, none of them would need to eat in the Abyss, but most were in the habit, so Tom felt it only polite to have food and wine.

For some reason, Tom referred to it as the "skybox treatment." Rupert looked up, trying to spot the balcony they would be using. There were an awful lot of these skyboxes. It was actually nice to see them clearly again. Tom had been able to part the rain around the mouth of the volcano so that the arena was dry. Or mostly dry; there were water troughs from up high that funneled excess water down to the lava below. Since it was still raining just outside the volcano mouth, there was quite a bit of steam and soot coming up from the volcano.

That soot was kind of a pain. It coated everything near the arena. At least the dining halls were soot free; he really did not want his food covered in soot tomorrow. Actually, outside the immediate area of the volcano, the soot disappeared. That seemed odd. He wondered if there was something in the system that was absorbing it. Actually, the dust level had been going down steadily lately. When they had first arrived, all the furniture had been very dusty in his room. It was less dusty now, yet not like someone had dusted. There was just less of it. Very odd.

~

Fierd was low on the horizon as Hilda and Stevos managed to get Teragdor back to the inn and into one of the small beds. The priest, barely awake as it was, began snoring as soon as they had him on the bed.

Hilda chuckled; Stevos looked at her. "I can see that he has been observing his priestly vows of moderation." She laughed. "Orcs are all known, or so I'm told, to be able to hold prodigious amounts of alcohol. Our young priest here could barely hold as much as a Rod member."

Stevos shook his head. "I don't understand how you so easily drank the wargtowners under the table. Every time I went to the trenches to relieve myself, I had to surreptitiously do a cleansing ritual to stay even close to sober!"

"Ah, youth!" Hilda said with a laugh. "First, aside from being much older and more experienced, I also have a lot more mass! I cannot stress how much that helps. Plus, over the years, and particularly lately, I've gotten very adept at doing cleansing rituals under the table, so to speak. My principal mission right now unfortunately involves my drinking prodigious amounts of very expensive wine." Hilda feigned dismay.

"And here I'm getting second-rate glargh!" Stevos said, laughing.

"Well, one nice thing is that even though buying enough glargh to drink everyone in town under the table while they revealed their secrets was quite expensive, it actually doesn't come very close to my worst tabs in Freehold."

"And no one objects?" Stevos asked.

Hilda shrugged. "It's a bureaucracy, and it takes quite some time for the forms to make it through the system. Fortunately, we've been getting exceptional results, so… no complaints so far."

"Nice work if you can get it." Stevos shook his head.

Hilda shrugged again. "It is a nice change. However, it is a lot more fieldwork and pretending to be someone you are not. Here we were able to tell Teragdor the truth. In Freehold, I am almost in enemy territory. I cannot reveal myself to the Church or Rod outside the city, or to the wizards inside. If I did, they'd all go silent and cagey."

Hilda looked down at Taragdor. "He really did seem to enjoy himself; I imagine he doesn't get a lot of opportunities to socialize with his father's people."

Stevos nodded. "That is my understanding."

"I have to return to Freehold for a few hours, and then we have another late-night meeting," Hilda said. "Can you watch over him, work to ease his glarghvost, I think they called it?"

Stevos grinned and nodded. "That is what it is called. I like that name."

Hilda gave an amused frown. "I like the name better than the beverage." She shook her head. "Don't fully cleanse him, just take the edge off. Part of an experience like this is the next morning. It makes the event more memorable."

Stevos laughed. "I think you really must be an alcohol professional!"

"If only…" Hilda laughed.

~

"Well, it's been nice to be back on solid ground for the day," Jenn noted to Gastropé in the banquet room of the inn that Seamach had arranged for. She plucked a strawberry from the buffet table with her little wooden stick. Much to her surprise, she had found she really enjoyed strawberries with the funny bubbly wine they had at the inn.

"It is, but I am not in a hurry to settle down here," Gastropé told her.

Jenn chuckled. "Fortunately for you, I suppose, I don't think either of us will be having an opportunity to 'settle down' for quite some time."

"Did you have a good day?" Maelen asked, coming up to them.

"It was a bit of an eye opener," Gastropé said. Maelen raised an eyebrow in inquiry.

"There are actually orc shopkeepers here?" Jenn said.

Maelen moved his eyes around a bit in puzzlement. "And?"

"Did you know that orcs could be merchants?" Gastropé asked.

Again, Maelen looked puzzled. "Why couldn't they? I am not aware of any place with laws against it. Although given so many prejudices out there, there might be somewhere."

Jenn shook her head in amazement. "But everyone knows that orcs always side with the forces of darkness and armies of evil, and when not doing that, they are brigands, thieves and unsavory mercenaries."

Maelen nodded slightly in consideration. "There are many that do tend to fall into those occupations and allegiances, but certainly not all of them. Not all humans are wizards, for example."

Gastropé looked puzzled. "Most humans are not wizards."

"And most orcs aren't brigands or thieves. Orcs are generally a tribal people, often nomadic in nature. And yes, they do have a rather martial nature and don't often get along with humans, or elves, but they are just people."

Jenn was giving him a skeptical look. "Yes, but history books said that in most conflicts, they've sided with the forces of darkness."

"Says the wizard who has spent the last month working hand in hand in close proximity with multiple non-bound demons?" Maelen asked.

Jenn clamped her mouth shut for a moment, then took another sip of sparkling wine. Gastropé coughed and took a sip himself.

~

"You smell like a cheap, beer-soaked barn!" Danyel fanned his nostrils as he helped Hilda get out of her over-clothes.

"If it only it had been that pleasant a venue." Hilda grimaced, smelling the armpit of her jacket. "I will clearly need you to run me a quick bath before I go check on Trisfelt."

She had been shocked to find the wards back up and once again unable to materialize inside Freehold. Fortunately, the guards were letting in anyone who was able to enter. She had asked the gate guards what was up and had been told that there had been more demon issues at the palace. Fortunately, while there had been a lot of property damage, no one had died or been seriously hurt.

Her first instinct had been to go directly to the palace, but then she realized she would never be able to explain her stench. Of course, she could have used a cleansing ritual, but she had already planned on a bath, and they'd said no one had been hurt. Thus, the best course of action was a hot bath. She shook her head in dismay at the lack of time. Fortunately, Murgatroy was sufficiently far east of Freehold that she had picked up an extra hour or two of fierdlight.

"So where were you all day?" Danyel asked. "Trisfelt stopped by to check on you after the dust-up. I had to tell him that you had been called to the countryside to assist a client with numerous ill servants."

"Well, that works out extremely well then. It will more than explain my ignorance of the day's events and give me a good excuse for questions." Hilda chuckled. "You are turning out to have a calling for subterfuge!"

"What should I do with these?" He held up her jacket and gestured to the rest of the clothes she was wearing.

"Put them somewhere where they won't offend our noses. I need to wear them again tomorrow." Hilda said.

"Are you going to do a cleaning ritual on them?" Danyel asked.

That gave Hilda pause. "Hmm, for authenticity, I had not planned to, but my principal target there knows who I am." She shook her head. "I think I will wait on a decision until after tonight's meeting. I may have gotten enough information today that Stevos can wrap things up."

"Stevos?" Danyel asked.

Hilda shook her head. "I'm sorry—you asked where I was. I was in Murgatroy." Danyel gave her a blank look and shrug, indicating he had no idea where that was. "It is south and east of here eight or nine hundred leagues."

Danyel raised his eyebrows. "Quite a jaunt," he said dubiously.

Hilda smiled. "Not if you take a shortcut through Tierhallon. Anyway, I was with Saint Stevos Delastro of Murgandy."

Danyel slowly shook his head. "Never heard of him."

Hilda grinned. "I just met him last night. He is young as saints go. I am thinking about seventy or so. It is rather impertinent to ask a saint you have just met about their untimely and always tragic demise. "

"Sensitive subject then?" Danyel asked.

"Yes, but not just for the saint." Hilda shook her head; Danyel looked puzzled.

"Let's just say that if I told you the story that led to the canonization of Saint Tatiana, you would never drink another Bloody Tatiana again!" Hilda chuckled grimly.

Danyel grimaced. "I'll get your bath ready." He laid the jacket on the back of a wooden chair and moved into the bathing room.

Hilda followed. "So anyway, we were in Murgatroy, which is a backwater down in the Kingdom of Murgandy. Not sure it's technically kingdom, or what it is." She shook her head. "Anyway, we were interviewing a half-orc priest about incidents he had reported yesterday."

Danyel paused in preparing the bath. "A half-orc priest? Is that even possible?"

Hilda smiled and made a shrugging gesture, raising her hands. "I know; who knew? However, he is very sweet, quite nice and does an admirable job. The powers that be have been quite impressed with his service."

"Those are not words I have ever heard associated with an orc, or a half-orc." Danyel shook his head.

Hilda nodded in agreement. "It gets even odder. To get direct information, the three of us headed out to Murgatroy's wargtown."

"Its what?" Danyel asked, puzzled.

Hilda nodded her head. "Wargtown. Apparently it is—or rather actually is, since I spent the day there and can attest to it—a place to stable one's wargs." Danyel was looking at her oddly.

"Wargs: those giant, scary wolves that orcs like to ride," Hilda said, thinking he did not understand.

Danyel nodded quickly. "Oh, I know what they are; I think all of us were raised on horror stories of orcs on wargback and their raids. It must have been terrifying!"

Hilda waggled her head from side to side. "Not as much as one might think. The orcs watching over them took more of my attention, and after I got a few glasses of glargh in them, and me, I really didn't notice them that much." Danyel was shaking his head in disbelief. "And, to be fair, being dead and currently an immortal saint does sort of lessen the tension in such situations," Hilda admitted.

Danyel chuckled. "So you were getting the warg tenders drunk to tell you about something that happened?"

Hilda nodded. "Yes. A group of twenty orcs had flown in on D'Wargback the prior day with twenty D'Orcs."

Danyel shook his head and looked completely puzzled. "Flew in? On dwargback with dorks? Huh?"

Hilda sighed. These creatures really had such an awkward name. One would think that after who-knew-how-many thousands of years, they might have realized what it sounded like and gotten a new name? She grinned, preparing to fill Danyel in on more details.

~

Sir Talarius skewered a piece of undercooked roast... *something* and took a bite. Not bad; the spices used were a bit unusual, or was that the meat? He shook his head. At this point, he would not complain. He had not eaten the entire time he had been in the Abyss. He had not gotten hungry, but it still felt pleasurable to resume the habit. He had drunk water of course, from his Flask of Holy Refreshment. It was always cold and fresh, and that had done wonders for his morale.

He wandered away from the buffet table, enjoying being in the presence of two other humans and not needing to wear his helmet. He kept it tucked under his arm, just in case, but it was nice to not have it on all the time. Admittedly, he had repeated his exercise of barring his door and sleeping without armor. It really did help him regain his strength to get a good night's sleep.

He could have done without the orc conspirators of the demon, but while surly, disreputable, disagreeable, smelly, unpleasant to look at, and of low character, they were still better company than demons. He was not that familiar with orc shamans, but they were generally the best educated, or rather the only educated orcs. Presumably, they were capable of civilized conversation.

He walked over to the youngest one, the one with the seriously ugly pet that was sleeping in the room behind him. This young orc seemed to have been wounded at some point; he walked with a limp and one of his legs was twisted very awkwardly and appeared somewhat shriveled under his trousers. Talarius was not a good judge of orc ages, but he guessed by his small frame and relatively good looks—good looks in the sense that Talarius could eat food while looking at him—that this one was a youth of less than twenty years.

"So, how were you injured?" Talarius asked. He was a warrior, not a conversationalist. Yes, as a Knight Rampant, diplomacy, politeness and a courtly nature were intrinsic to his training, but he was a damn hostage to a demon lord in the Abyss. Screw courtliness. He no longer had the patience after the insanity of the last week.

The orc looked at him suspiciously. "Wyvern," he finally said.

Talarius blinked at this information and looked down at the lad's leg and foot. "It appears long set, so not recently?"

Tal Gor looked at him for a bit and then stared straight ahead. "It was my second hunt. I was thirteen. My three hunting companions and I encountered the wyvern. They died; I fought it off long enough for my father, who had been trailing us, to catch up and slay it."

"At thirteen, you held off a wyvern by yourself after it killed three others?" Talarius asked.

"Yes," Tal Gor said. He appeared embarrassed.

"Hmm," Talarius said. "Apparently the legends of orcs being nearly impossible to kill are true. If a youth on his second hunting trip can hold off a wyvern for any length of time—that is impressive."

Tal Gor looked at Talarius angrily. "You mock my weakness?"

Talarius did a double take and looked back at the youth. "Not at all. I compliment your strength and courage. At that age, I doubt I could have done the same. I was twenty when I encountered my first wyvern and it took two others to help me slay it. We were newly knighted and had had the best training available to warriors of the Rod." Talarius shook his head. "No, most human youth of that age would have frozen in place, given up and allowed themselves to be cooked in the beast's breath and then eaten. None could have done better; I doubt any would have lived."

Tal Gor nodded, seeming appeased. He looked back out over the balcony.

"So you are a shaman to the demon Tom?" Talarius asked, probing a bit further.

"Yes," Tal Gor replied tersely. "You are his hostage?"

"So it seems. I have no way of returning to Astlan, and am to all intents and purposes unarmed," Talarius said. Tal Gor looked him over, his eyes briefly touching on Talarius's hidden Rod of Smiting, his Rod of Lightning, and then scanning over the locations of his smaller blades.

"Clearly," Tal Gor said drily.

Talarius chuckled. "You are the first person I have met here that I understand."

"So how did you become hostage?"

Talarius shrugged. He did not want to go into it, yet this orc lad was the only one here who did not know of his shame. "Your demon lord challenged me to a duel for the freedom of his son, there." He pointed to Rupert. "As well as his other friends. I accepted. We fought the fight of my life." Tal Gor was looking at him incredulously. "I thought I had defeated him, and my hubris got the better of me. I let my guard down. He came back from what appeared to be death and possessed the priests surrounding me and quite a few archers. He used them against me. Admittedly, much the same way I had used them against him." That was hard to admit, but what did it matter at this point?

"In any event, I could fight no more, even with healing, and I surrendered." Talarius sighed. "He granted me mercy, and being rather upset, I tried one last time to skewer him with Excrathadorus Mortis."

Tal Gor's eyes widened and his breath was sucked into his lungs. "The blade that Sentir Fallon used to kill Orcus?"

Talarius blinked in surprise, he was shocked that the lad would know such ancient history. "The same. As the foremost Knight Rampant of Tiernon, it was my honor to wield it."

Tal Gor shook his head. "So you missed?"

Now it was time for Talarius to sigh aloud. "No, I did not. I thought I had finished him off."

"Did not seem to work then," Tal Gor said, gesturing to the ceremony.

Talarius shook his head and gave a small, sad laugh. "Indeed, it did not. When he possessed the Church and Rod members, he broke into Tiernon's holy illumination stream. He used the purified mana of Tiernon to heal himself and reverse Excrathadorus Mortis permanently."

Tal Gor shook his head in amazement. "I take it Lord Tommus was not very happy with you?"

Talarius chuckled. "He opened up a hole to the Abyss under my feet and dropped me through it. He and his friends followed. And here we are!" Talarius shook his head. Talking about it, telling the story aloud to someone who did not know it, he came off badly. The demon had accused him of cheating. He had, and he had been dishonorable at multiple points. He shook his head. Why had he behaved that way? Was it hubris, as he had thought? Ignoring the great evil that Tommus obviously was, he, Talarius, had done things that he had always sworn not to do.

Several minutes passed in silence as Talarius was lost in his thoughts and Tal Gor digested the story.

Eventually Tal Gor broke the silence. "So this blade, Excrathadorus Mortis, it killed the demon prince Orcus permanently?"

"Yes, that is what the church teaches, and that's what the demon bard says. If both agree, it must be true," Talarius replied.

"Yet when you used it on Lord Tommus, he easily defeated its power and reversed it completely?" Tal Gor asked.

Talarius chuckled grimly. "Yes. It shocks the mind."

"Yet was not Orcus one of the most powerful demon princes to walk the Abyss?" Tal Gor asked.

Talarius nodded. "That is what legends say. Behind only Sammael and Lilith."

"So if Lord Tommus can easily overcome that which Orcus could not, does that not make him more powerful than the demon prince Orcus?" the young shaman asked.

Talarius closed his eyes. That was a thought he had been studiously avoiding. However, as much as he had wrestled with it, there was really only one answer. "It would seem that way," he admitted.

Chapter 110

"...and know, my fellow colleagues, friends, associates, subordinates, assistants, admirers, articulate adversaries and all those others so assembled here in this gloriously, yet in no way garishly decorated reception hall at this hallowed, historic and honorable happening, that we seek not only to enable and enervate this experimental endeavor that seeks to engender an edifying and equitably egalitarian enterprise to extend the existence of law into the ersatz empire of evil; an expedition that emboldens so many earnest, and certainly not erstwhile exhibitions of emotions of trust and facilitation and goodwill between our organizations..." continued this most recent chancellor or councilor, or something with a title.

Arch-Vicar General Barabus surreptitiously pulled out his pocket watch and glanced at it. He rubbed his eyes. They were only two and a half hours into the dinner. It was scheduled for eight hours. Fortunately, servants kept the food and wine coming. There were also nearby facilities to relieve oneself. It was apparent from both the setup and the behavior of the Oorstemothians at the party that such long dinners were not uncommon occurrences.

He reached for his water glass, glancing next to him as he did so and noting that his dining companion to his left, Wing Master Heron, had his eyes closed. That was actually reassuring to the arch-vicar general; Heron's reaction showed that at least the Oorstemothian armed forces were human.

He glanced down the table to see Gadius and Gaius staring in rapt attention at the speaker. How could those two manage that? The knights did have to go through insane levels of courtly training, but he found it hard to imagine that even the best Church instructors could have prepared them for this particular ordeal.

He had been relieved when he had arrived in Keeper's City to see that Gaius had joined Gadius here. Back in Freehold, Gadius had told him that Gaius was occupied on another Holy Mission. Apparently, that had ended. The knights were generally quite autonomous once they got to the Rampant level. Fortunately, when the chips were down, they always came through. Rescuing Talarius would obviously be something the knights would give a high priority.

As his gaze traveled idly down the table, noting Sir Lady Serah, he wondered where the knights were stabling their unique steeds. Very few stables would take a hippogriff, since that would obviously cause a panic among the horses. The two unicorns, one midnight black—War Bringer—and the other opalescent white—Peace Bringer—would probably not bother the horses much. However, their odd, all-knowing gazes would surely discomfort the grooms.

Actually, as Barabus thought about it, he wondered if mythological creatures were even legal in Keeper's City. As far as he could tell, one needed the proper permit to vacate one's bowels! He was not sure how long he could deal with the Oorstemothians.

Tomorrow they would see this project of Chancellor Alighieri's, the one the chancellor had assured them had been specifically designed for just such a mission as the one they faced now. How that could be, he had no idea, but he saw very few options other than just giving up for now.

Sir Lady Serah's head nodded downward before jerking back up. Barabus grinned in triumph, very pleased to see that even his own knights had some limits of endurance! Yes, an odd thing to be relieved about, but dinners like this were not what warriors like himself, or Heron apparently, were trained for.

~

Dinner had been extraordinary, Gastropé thought, suppressing a loud belch. He shook his head slightly at the pain of choking back a belch. He was sure, however, that their alvaren hosts would have thought him crude.

He had never had pure alvaren cooking before. There had been some alvaren dishes at that crazy feast in the Grove, although his memory was not completely clear on that point. This, however, had been an entire meal of alvaren dishes. The flavors were sublime.

The conversation had been quite interesting as well. He and Jenn had confined themselves to smaller questions. The level of historical knowledge and world geography required to add anything relevant to the discussion was a bit beyond him. He grinned to himself; it was very difficult to sound knowledgeable when discussing history with a table full of people well over a thousand years old.

Oddly, Maelen managed to keep up his part of the conversation, even though he was an admitted babe by comparison. Trevin was also incredibly knowledgeable. While she obviously looked to be well over a hundred, that too would be but a toddler to the elves. However, she talked about events from a thousand years ago as if she had witnessed them herself.

The wine was getting to him; he found himself chuckling again. Yes, the enchantress was incredibly old-looking, but she would have been dust if she had actually seen the things discussed. Jenn glanced at him and his chuckling. She was smiling, having a good time even as he was. Probably the wine affecting her as well.

It was odd, in the soft candlelight of the room, to look at Jenn there smiling and think of her as the weed-wrangling wizard who had changed his career trajectory so much. She had been a most pleasant traveling companion for someone who had tried to strangle him when they had first met. She was also quite attractive in this light. Strange that he had never really noticed that before. Again the wine. He smiled brightly at her.

He was about to say something, probably stupid, when an urgent knock came at the door. It was late in the evening, the servants came and went silently; who would be knocking?

Dresdech, their local host and Seamach's principal contact, rose to answer the door. He opened the door a small distance; Gastropé could not see who was on the other side.

"Bastien? You are a mess! You seem to be a complete wreck. What is the matter?" The concern in the elf's voice was clearly discernable.

Gastropé saw Trevin sit up in surprise and look to the door from her wine glass. The enchantress seemed to find the breech of alvaren composure as shocking, if not more so, than Gastropé.

Gastropé could just barely hear the exhausted Bastien on the other side of the door. "I come straight, without stopping, from Murgatroy at my great-grandfather Neelon's request."

Dresdech shook his head. "What is the matter? He is not ill, is he?"

Bastien still seemed out of breath, or quite tired. "He is fine; however, he bade me to bring this urgent message to the Principality and the Grove."

Dresdech blinked, clearly taken by surprise. "Come in. Come in. It is an ominous coincidence that we are here speaking Grove business this very evening. Trevin D'Vils is here." He gestured for Bastien to come in.

A younger-looking elf entered, clearly disheveled and dirty with wild, windblown hair from a hard ride. His eyes glanced to Seamach, Bealach and Captain Ehéarellis, seeming relieved to see them and giving each a nod. His eyes traveled briefly over each of the aetós with a nod, and he managed to not wince at the sight of the dwarves.

When Bastien's eyes finally lit on Trevin D'Vils, the alvaren ranger bowed deeply and gave her a bright smile. "Mistress D'Vils! Seeing you is a pleasure I have not had in over eight hundred years!"

"At your half-millennial! I recall, Bastien. It was a grand event. Your grandfather and great-grandfather were both so pleased!"

Gastropé blinked and turned to Jenn to see her already staring at him. Trevin was over eight hundred years old? Jenn mouthed something to him. "I take it back, she looks quite good for her age!" was what he thought she said. He could barely suppress a drunken giggle. He had to though, because this was clearly serious.

"What dire news brings you in such haste, good ranger?" Trevin asked Bastien.

"Yesterday, in Murgatroy, a party of twenty orcs flew in." Bastien began.

Danfaêr, also tipsy, exclaimed, "I can assure you, Bastien, orcs do not fly!"

Bastien shook his head and retorted, "They do, Danfaêr, if they are on D'Wargback!" There were gasps from around the room. "Twenty orcs on D'Wargback, along with twenty D'Orcs!" Bastien added. The alvar all gasped; they seemed truly taken aback and upset.

"Dorks?" Jenn asked.

"What are dorks?" Gastropé followed up.

Trevin closed her eyes for a moment. "Not dorks; D'Orcs, pronounced D(uh) O(rcs). Depending on who you ask, they are either Demon Orcs, Dark Orcs or sometimes Death Orcs."

Gastropé glanced at Maelen, who was looking extremely pale and sickly and looking in turn at Elrose. Elrose really could not actually look pale, but he did seem a bit ashen. Gastropé looked around the table; all the alvar were looking particularly nauseous. He did not think elves were supposed to have such reactions. The dwarves seemed more muted, with mixed reactions. The aetós also looked more neutral.

"What are they, though?" Jenn asked again.

Trevin shook her head, lost in thought at her own words and their implication. She sighed. "They are, or were, the agents of the Lord of the Underworld, the Damned Prince, Orcus."

"Orcus? What or who is Orcus?" Gastropé asked.

"A vile being we thought dead four thousand years ago," Captain Ehéarellis said. He looked to Bastien. "Neelon confirmed that these were indeed D'Orcs and D'Wargs?"

Bastien nodded. "I dragged him out onto the roof deck so he could see them wandering about the city."

"Neelon is an expert on D'Orcs?" Darowin, one of the dwarves, asked.

Captain Ehéarellis gave a wry smile. "He spent the first half of his life, four thousand years, dealing with D'Orcs and D'Wargs up until Orcus was thought slain in Etterdam."

Trevin looked sharply at Bastien. "You said they wandered about the town, so it was not an invasion? No massacre?"

Bastien shook his head. "While I was there, things were peaceful. Another messenger is hopefully a few hours behind me with more news. The rangers will be sending messengers every few hours with updates until there is a resolution. Hopefully, they leave."

Trevin nodded. "So while they were there, they were not causing problems."

Dresdech spoke up. "Murgatroy has an even larger orc population than Murgandor. It would be uncharacteristic for D'Orcs to make an unprovoked attack against a town with significant numbers of orcs."

"So what were they doing?" Treyfoêr asked.

"Well, they stabled their D'Wargs in the wargtown and then they came into town and appeared to be shopping."

"Shopping?" Jenn asked incredulously.

Bastien shrugged. "Again, others will have more information, but they seemed to be purchasing supplies."

Dresdech was pacing. "I was young at the time, not even a millennia old, but as I recall, it was not unknown for the D'Orcs to mount hunting parties with local orc tribes."

"You think they were out hunting and wanted to get some salt and glargh for their roast?" Darowin asked rather sarcastically.

"It does seem farfetched. But then there are many extremely odd things happening right now," Trevin said.

~

Hilda and Stevos arrived at the conference room at about the same time. Hilda had come directly from her not-exactly-relaxing dinner with Trisfelt. Leaving Murgatroy, she had been looking forward to it as small point of sanity, a means of touching base with reality that would quite welcome. Something one needed after spending the day hearing stories of D'Orcs and half-dead deities trying to rise from the grave. However, to come home and find the wards up and that the main entry hall that one had become accustomed to passing through each day had been thoroughly demolished by an archdemon? That was not relaxing. Especially when it then turned out that your houseguest had accidentally provoked the archdemon into attempting to obliterate most the Council of Wizardry. She shook her head; she would love to have gotten Ruiden's take on the battle, but he had not returned to the hotel until after she left. She had touched base with Danyel via their link to make sure Ruiden had come home.

"How is your priest doing?" Hilda asked, trying to get her thoughts back to more neutral ground. Neutral ground that before returning to Freehold had been the insanity she had thought to escape.

"Sleeping comfortably now. I cleansed him enough to sleep well. I've also placed a ward on his room in the event our actions may have caused unforeseen repercussions," Stevos told her.

"A wise precaution. There seem to be a lot of unforeseen repercussions happening lately." You never knew when a few questions might set off an archdemon, for instance. Hilda smiled at Stevos.

The door opened and in walked Moradel and Sentir Fallon. "Stevos, may I introduce Sentir Fallon, the other member of our small task force who was not able to join us at our last meeting," Moradel said. "Sentir, this is Stevos, whom I have told you about."

Stevos rose and bowed deeply. "It is an honor to meet you, Your Holiness!"

The young saint was obviously more familiar with Sentir's work than Hilda had been. To be fair, she thought, he did work more with orcs than she did, so there was a good excuse.

Sentir Fallon smiled beatifically at him and made a relaxing gesture with his hand. "At ease, my friend; we are all comrades in the service of Tiernon here. No need for titles or honorifics." He grinned more normally. "Not when the fate of the multiverse may be at stake!"

"Oh, my Tiernon!" Beragamos exclaimed, walking in behind them and hearing Sentir Fallon. "Are we not being just a tad dramatic?" He grinned at the assembled avatars. Hilda twisted her mouth to avoid commenting.

"Down to business!" Beragamos said, shutting the door with a wave of his hand.

Hilda reached down into the bag she had brought with her and retrieved two very nice bottles of wine. "Since we are dealing with Astlan, I brought some better Astlanian wines this time."

Moradel laughed. "Who else is for abandoning our predawn meetings for these new late-night meetings so we can drink more wine?"

Beragamos chuckled and waved five refleca wine glasses into being.

Sentir Fallon shook his head. "Is this what I missed last time? I miss one meeting and everyone starts drinking!" He laughed and sat down. "Here, I have a corkscrew!" A refleca corkscrew appeared in his hand.

"So can a refleca corkscrew open a material bottle?" Stevos asked.

Moradel shrugged as he opened one of the bottles with Sentir's corkscrew. "It can if we believe it can. It's all about faith, my lad." He grinned. "Remember, faith is our core business!"

"So that we may all try both, I will pour slightly smaller glasses for each of us," Moradel said.

After the four glasses were poured, Beragamos reached out and raised one up. "My friends, let us toast to faith! Toast to our faith in Tiernon and that his will be done!"

"His presence be known!" Sentir added.

"His foes be vanquished!" Moradel said.

"His will be done!" Stevos continued.

Beaming brightly, Hilda finished, "His glory and light to shine throughout the multiverse forever and ever!"

"Amen!" They all finished in union before drinking simultaneously.

~

Tal Gor had wandered off from the room to explore a bit more, get his bearings. He somehow found himself back in the Temple of Doom. It was weird to physically be here, so different yet similar to being here in his dreams. To see one's dream made physically manifest! It was amazing. The proof it demonstrated—all of this demonstrated—in his and his people's faith.

Gods were real! Orcus, the lost god of the orcs had returned as Lord Tommus, stronger and more powerful than before. Lord Tommus would set things right for the orcs and the D'Orcs and vanquish those who had sought to thwart his will and harm his people.

The temple was empty now, the normal watchers out at the ceremony. It was highly unlikely that anyone would try to contact the temple at this time. Other than the shaman from Gormegast, everyone who would try to contact Lord

Tommus was already here. He, Tal Gor, apparently was the only one to come uninvited, so to speak. Uninvited, but not unwelcomed. Tal Gor grinned to himself. It felt good to be a part of something so much larger than himself, larger than his tribe or the orcs on his own world. This was a venture that would span the multiverse, bringing redemption and renewal to orcs everywhere. No more would humans and elves be able to treat his people as refuse, as garbage. With Lord Tommus to lead them, those who had shunned and spurned them would have to respect their strength once more.

Lost in thought, he almost did not realize that someone else had entered the temple behind him. The scraping sound of a boot against stone alerted him. A sound he knew well, the sound of someone with a limp. Tal Gor turned to see a very unusual figure in the room behind him, staring at him.

The individual was about the same height as Tal Gor; however, he was quite hunched over. He appeared to be quite old, although at one time quite handsome, Tal Gor supposed. He was also quite muscular. He had no wings, so was not a D'Orc, and certainly not an orc, but he was clearly jötunnkind.

"Hello," Tal Gor said cautiously. The man did not appear threatening, but he was looking Tal Gor up and down quite seriously.

"You are Tal Gor of the Crooked Sticks?" the man asked abruptly.

"I am," Tal Gor replied.

The man nodded. "You came to this temple on your own? Not called?"

"I did." This was a rather odd conversation, or inquisition.

"That miserable fartbag from the depths decided you were a worthy rider and finally left the rest of us in peace?"

"Schwarzenfürze came to live with me. She took over my entire tent, in fact." Tal Gor shook his head.

The man shrugged. "Sounds like her. Going to miss the bitch. Might have to visit." He looked down at Tal Gor's bad leg. "You a cripple?"

Tal Gor frowned. "I am not crippled. My leg was damaged fighting a wyvern, but I hold my own and provide value to my tribe."

The man chuckled. "Me, I'm a cripple and proud of it!" He started turning around. "Come with me, boy, I have something for you!"

He started limping out of the temple.

Tal Gor frowned and followed. "Who are you?"

"Völund," was all the odd man said.

Tal Gor frowned and thought for a bit as they went out into the corridor. He had heard that name. He blinked as memories of the stories came back to him.

"The smith?" Tal Gor asked.

Völund snorted. "Of course."

"The smith who forged Caliburn? Arthur of Avalon's sword?" Tal Gor asked.

"Called by humans Excalibur. Yes. You know human history as well as orcish?" Völund asked.

"When it comes to great weapons. And Durandal?"

Völund sighed. "And that."

"And Gram? Destroyed by Odin and later reforged by Regin for Sigurd to slay Fafnir?" Tal Gor continued.

"Do you simply wish to recite my back catalog, or will you follow me quietly so I can remember the path?" Völund asked.

"I am sorry. But I am honored to meet you," Tal Gor said. Völund shrugged, apparently not caring.

The two wandered down multiple tunnels, going deeper and deeper. Tal Gor began to be concerned about finding his way out. Eventually they came into a very large and complex chamber. The chamber was easily one hundred feet tall and thousands of feet in each direction, with large ducts crisscrossing the room to and from various holes in the walls and into giant buckets with what appeared to be large furnaces or lava pits below them.

It was quite warm in here and he could feel his amulet growing colder as it kicked in to compensate. The smith motioned Tal Gor to follow him towards one wall. Tal Gor had to work to keep his eyes on the smith. This workshop was absolutely incredible! There were tools whose function he could only barely guess at. Many of the furnaces appeared cool. He assumed that prior to the volcano's restarting, this place had been largely inactive.

"No. Not completely," Völund said suddenly. The old man had turned and was smirking at him.

"What are you saying?"

"I am saying," the smith said, "that I know what you are thinking. You are thinking that this place was dead while Doom slept. I am saying it was not completely dead. This is the Abyss. Fire is not in short supply here, nor are noxious combustible gases for forging and welding. My forges have not all been quiescent for millennia. Most, yes. But not all."

The smith continued on towards the wall. "It was more work, not having already molten metal. I had to dig up solid metal and melt it. But mining here is still easier and better than mining anywhere in Midgard." He chuckled as they came up to a set of shelves and the old man began scanning them.

Tal Gor waited patiently for the smith to finish scanning the shelves until he found what he wanted. Rather spryly, the smith grabbed a ladder, and propping it against the shelving, he swiftly climbed up about fifteen feet. He quickly reached in and began pulling out a very long, narrow wooden box.

Tal Gor blinked. Given how hot it was here, how could that wooden box survive? He would have thought it would have dried out quite quickly. The smith managed to wrangle the box down and then carried it over to a large table nearby.

"It's Denubian wyrmwood. Compared to where it grew, this place is quite chilly." The smith seemed to be able to anticipate Tal Gor's questions. The smith grabbed a cloth from under the table and quickly wiped the dust off the box, which had three latches along one side.

"In the old days, Orcus issued staves of power to each of his shamans, each one with a mechanism for mounting the shaman's contact stone. I expect Lord Tommus will want me to create new ones for his new shamans. We shall see." The smith turned to look at him. "Call me an old softy. But when I see someone who shares my impediment, and yet still outperforms all the traditionally abled, I get sentimental." Tal Gor did not know how to respond to this. Völund simply smiled and turned back to the box and began unfastening.

"Now, I have one shaman staff left. I was constructing a rather different staff for one of Orcus's most trusted shamans. Unfortunately, he bought the farm before I finished it. As did Orcus, for that matter." Völund shrugged again. "So I finished it and put it on the shelf. I think you should have it, as the first new shaman and one who has overcome much to be the first, and perhaps one day, the best." Völund opened the box, and Tal Gor moved forward to look at it.

The box was velvet, or some similar material that was heat resistant, and lying in the box was a… staff? It was not like anything Tal Gor thought of as a staff. Yes, it was a long, rod-like device, longer than he was tall. At the base was a large ball, similar to the head of a ball mace. The shaft was intricately carved wood— wyrmwood perhaps?—with metal strands wound about it. At several points there were smooth areas. One was at what would be hand height, so Tal Gor assumed they were grips. At what he surmised was head height, the rod split into two paths, bending into a circular frame before rejoining.

Inside the frame were what appeared to be metal claws or teeth, presumably for mounting the summoning stone. The outer edge of the loop had sharp-looking metal teeth, aligned for slicing an enemy. Above the circle was a large blue sapphire set through another loop in the shaft, and then the shaft continued perhaps four more inches before melding into a large, double-edged metal blade of about two feet in length.

Tal Gor blinked. The "staff" was actually a pole arm with a double-edged glaive at one end and a mace at the other. "Is it a staff or a very unusual pole arm?"

"Both. Use it both ways. The gem there is a mana pool that you should link to; it is designed so that you can bind it as a true shaman's staff in the traditional ritual sense. The large loop holds your summoning stone. With the blades, teeth and ball, you can stab, slash, eviscerate and crush your enemies," Völund explained.

"It's unbelievable! For me, really?" Tal Gor asked breathlessly.

"Yes. Just do not tell the other shamans. I will be making them staves, I am sure, but it will take time. I will put this with your bitch's gear. I got a harness for the box, and a holding cup for the base, and saddle ties for the staff itself. I will tell the D'Warg handlers to keep it safe."

"Thank you so much." Tal Gor bowed deeply to the smith.

"Use it to protect my girl and her rider."

~

Lilith entered her private sitting room off of her bedroom, planning on curling up with a good book for the remainder of the evening. She waved the table lantern on near her favorite reading chair. The sudden light revealed Sentir Fallon. She was mildly startled but refused to show it. His shielding skills were truly amazing. She had not detected him in the dark with her demon sight or any of her other senses.

"So you're back with more news, I guess?" Lilith asked.

"I am. I came indirectly, of course, from a meeting with our Astlan 'Incident Response Team' and have more news," Sentir Fallon said.

"And that is?" Lilith pulled up another chair from a corner into the light of the lamp.

"First, Beragamos has ascertained from the Ithgar archons that D'Orcs have appeared in a trading city there, doing much the same thing as in Astlan."

Lilith nodded. "As we rather feared."

"And according to our on-the-ground agent who interviewed a large number of orc witnesses—"

Lilith interrupted Sentir. "You have an agent on the ground who actually speaks with orcs? Is actually willing to even be in close proximity with them? That doesn't sound particularly Etonian of you." She shook her head suddenly. "Wait—how do you get orcs to talk to one of your agents?"

Sentir smirked. "Yes, our principal field agent for Astlan is quite industrious and is very good at gathering information discreetly. They didn't even know they were talking to an avatar." He chuckled. "But beyond that, we actually have a half-orc priest who reported this."

Lilith slowly shook her head and grinned rather mirthlessly at the avatar. "Things are changing, even within the never-changing world of the Etonians."

"Not that much. We have simply realized that coming down to the material world in all of our celestial glory can sometimes be detrimental to information gathering. So our intelligence services are branching out."

"You have 'intelligence services'?" Lilith asked skeptically.

"Well, yes. Now. We are starting it with this incident," Sentir said. "However, we need to do something about this. We need to stop this demon in his tracks. During her interviews, our agent discovered that the D'Orcs have openly said they will be paying a lot more visits to all the material planes, that their master, Lord Tommus, was planning on reestablishing all the old connections and raising the orcs and D'Orcs back to their former glory."

"So were you two ever planning on sharing this with me?" a very calm tenor voice asked from the still-darkened corner on the other side of the room.

Lilith jumped at the sound of the voice behind her and angrily hopped her chair around to stare into the darkness. "What the Abyss? Aodh? Why are you lurking in the shadows of my private study? Did someone relocate the entrance to the Abyss into my private chambers?"

Aodh, the Hand of Nét, stepped out of the shadows. His silver wings were, as always, a striking match to his long, silver hair. He was dressed in his typical reddish-silver chainmail and crimson tabard emblazoned with the symbol of Nét, the El'adasir god of war. "I believe I have the outstanding question, which should take priority."

"Yes, we just wanted to make sure of the facts on the ground before worrying you. We realized that if the rumors we had heard were true, you and your liege would be quite interested. But we didn't want to cause alarm if none is justified," Sentir replied calmingly.

Aodh stared impassively at the other avatar.

"It's the truth, relax," Lilith told the El'adasir avatar. The high elves were notably moved by little; their gods and avatars even less so.

"A personal illuminary of mine just this evening alerted to me to the events in Murgatroy, having received this information from very high up in the principality." He crossed his arms. "Who is this Lord Tommus that threatens the alvar?"

"Well, that's a long story," Sentir Fallon said.

"All of us in this room are immortal. We have time," Aodh said with no trace of humor.

~

Beragamos sighed. He had been summoned to the Palaestra. It was not the summoning that bothered him—there was nothing unusual about that—it was the location. The Palaestra was the training studio for the Holy Knights of Tierhallon, and to be fair, Tiernon was often there in the mornings, watching his knights train.

The problem was that Tiernon's form in the Palaestra was very similar to his judgement form. It was not Beragamos's favorite way of talking with his deity. Which, of course, was the point of the form when passing judgement. If he were simply acting as an observer, that would be one thing, but in this case he would have to explain a rather complicated situation and as such, would be the brunt of this form's eyes.

Beragamos in his outdoor, winged form flew over the rolling meadows surrounding the five-hundred-foot-tall, refleca-marbled building. The scent of flowers was strong on the air. From a long distance, the Palaestra resembled a fairly standard rectangular building girded in Corinthian columns. Only as one got closer, which took some time, did one begin to realize exactly how huge the building was.

Once more, as he had so often done, Beragamos smiled as he thought about how lucky they were that the outer planes only obeyed those laws of physics that pleased their owners. Otherwise, this building would be completely unstable from an engineering standpoint. The weight of a real marble ceiling of the size of the Palaestra's would need much more support than it had. Fortunately, refleca objects only weighed what they needed to weigh.

Beragamos landed on the top stairs of the main entrance of the Palaestra. He straightened his robes and proceeded forward. The two-hundred-foot-tall marble double doors swung open silently at his approach. He entered, and smiled slightly at the convenient nature of refleca when it came to minimizing energy requirements to open such seemingly immobile doors.

Beragamos passed through the antechamber and into the main arena of the Palaestra. This floor was a large training field, lined inside as well with more columns. Along each of the sidewalls were doors of various heights, all at least fifty feet high, leading to training studios, baths and ancillary chambers.

The avatar walked around the outside edge of the arena, behind the inner columns to avoid the sparring Holy Knights, all of whom were twenty feet tall and armed to the teeth. He purposefully avoided looking toward the far end of the hall, his destination, where Tiernon sat upon his throne.

Even at a fast walk, it took Beragamos's human-sized legs some time to traverse the field. He finally stopped at the right approach to the throne. This was the waiting area to the right of the throne, where those wishing an audience could wait until they were acknowledged and motioned forward.

It was only upon reaching the approach that Beragamos dared look at his god, trying to judge his mood. This was one reason why he did not like this form; it was very hard to judge demeanor and reactions. The scale probably had something to do with it.

Tiernon's form in the Palaestra was one hundred feet tall when standing; sitting on the throne, he was still over sixty-five feet tall. Tiernon was seated in the very ornately carved Palaestra throne; he was clad in sandals with golden leg wrappings that crisscrossed his truly enormous and muscular calves to tie just below the knee.

He wore only a single shoulder toga with three layers of refleca silk. Each sheet was probably a hundred and fifty feet or more long. A wide belt with very a large, golden buckle carved with Tiernon's own face kept the toga tight. Tiernon's form was that of a human man of great but not excessive muscle. The perfection of the human form, without the bulk of a barbarian.

His curly hair, made of strands of real gold, was held in place by a mithral coronet. His right biceps was also encircled with a silvery white mithral band. That was the extent of the jewelry. The god did not need much more than that; the chiseled, square face and the deep black eyes ensured that those viewing the god saw little else. Beragamos had to be careful not to look into the eyes. That was the trap of this form. One could easily get lost in their depths.

Beragamos waited silently for some time as the duels between the various knights played themselves out with Tiernon's all-seeing gaze. Beragamos glanced at the knights. How they could practice under the gaze of Tiernon was beyond Beragamos. The pressure seemed unimaginable to him.

Eventually the knights finished and all bowed deeply before their god. Tiernon clapped in approval, sending shockwaves through the air that visibly moved the looser clothing on the knights, as well as Beragamos's gown.

"EXCELLENT WORK, MY KNIGHTS!" he boomed. "WE ARE MOST PLEASED WITH YOUR EXERCISES. WE SHALL SEE YOU ALL TOMORROW."

As the knights trotted off the field to the showers, the god slowly turned his gaze towards Beragamos. Crap! There it was. He had accidentally met Tiernon's gaze and had to fight to keep from being drawn into those two enormous black spheres. A blackness deeper and darker than the darkest corner of starless space, a blackness so deep it seemed never-ending. However, as one peered more, one could sense that there was something in that blackness—a fire, orbs of fire, brightly burning stars? It was more a sense than an actual sight.

Beragamos blinked; Tiernon had released his gaze. Beragamos shook his head and then bowed deeply at the waist. "My Lord Tiernon! You have summoned me, your loyal servant."

The god had a slight grin on his face. While he never admitted it, Beragamos had a suspicion that the god worked to purposefully trap him in his eyes. Simply because he knew how much it bothered the archon.

"INDEED, BERAGAMOS. APPROACH!" the god intoned.

Beragamos moved forward to stand at the foot of his god and peered upward, working to avoid the deity's terrible gaze.

"WHAT IS THE NEWS ON THIS ASTLANIAN EVENT?"

"Thanks to Saint Hilda of Rivenrock's excellent intelligence-gathering, we have determined that the demon who broke into and intercepted our illumination streams is known as Lord Tommus. In addition to stealing your mana and kidnapping your Knight Rampant, Talarius, he has apparently managed to restart Mount Doom in the Abyss and is now making connections to orc tribes on the material planes."

"HE RESTARTED MOUNT DOOM?"

"Yes, my god." Beragamos nodded.

"WOULD THAT NOT REQUIRE THE WAND?"

"From the accounts of witnesses interviewed by Saint Hilda, when Lord Tommus came through the portal to retrieve his minions from Murgatroy, he had a rod. The witnesses' descriptions of this rod match that of the wand," Beragamos said.

"HOW DID WE GET THESE WITNESS ACCOUNTS?"

"Saint Hilda traveled to Murgatroy with Saint Stevos Delastros and the priest that alerted us, Teragdor. There, they went to the wargtown, where the D'Orcs and orcs had stabled their D'Wargs."

"ORCS WERE WILLING TO TALK TO AN AVATAR OF OURS?"

"Well, they did not know she was an avatar. She has been working undercover, pretending to be human. The priest led them to the wargtown, where the wargmaster was dismissive, but she bested him in short combat and then bought several rounds of drinks for the orcs in town to get their stories."

Tiernon chuckled like thunder in a cloudless sky. "I LIKE THE SOUND OF THIS SAINT. I WILL NEED TO MEET HER."

"Of course, Your Godship." Beragamos was sure Hilda would not be quite so thrilled with the invitation; she was very low-key, and very smart. While some younger saints were foolish enough to long for their god's attention, Hilda struck Beragamos as someone wise enough to know better.

"SO WHERE WAS THE WAND?"

"This was not clear, Your Godship. Sentir Fallon reported that it had disappeared at the time that Orcus's body was dissolved by Excrathadorus Mortis. We have always assumed that it was so tightly linked to the demon prince that the magic of the blade destroyed it as well," Beragamos said.

Tiernon sat silently for a few moments, thinking. "YES, I RECALL SENTIR FALLON'S ACCOUNT. APPARENTLY IT DID NOT DISSOLVE."

"Clearly. It must have faded back to the Abyss, similar to how demons do," Beragamos suggested.

"AND NO ONE NOTICED IT UNTIL NOW?"

"I would guess, and this is only a guess, that the D'Orcs retrieved it and guarded it until the prophesied return of Orcus."

"PROPHESIED?"

Crap! The eyes! Beragamos blinked as he came back from being lost in the god's stare once again. He shook his head and tried to continue. "Yes, My Lord. According to the orcs in the wargtown, there is, or was, an old prophecy made one hundred years after Orcus's death. It was made in Etterdam by an orc shaman named Tiss-Arog-Dal," Beragamos replied.

"A PROPHECY MADE BY A SHAMAN REGARDING A DEAD DEMON?"

Beragamos nodded.

"A TRUE PROPHECY REQUIRES DEIFIC GUIDANCE, PARTICULARLY FOR SOMETHING OVER SUCH A LONG TIME PERIOD. WHAT DEITY WOULD SUPERVISE A DEMON PROPHECY?"

"We have debated this issue, and found no answer."

"DID WE KNOW OF THIS PROPHECY?"

"Not that I have been able to determine, my god. To be fair, if any churchman in Etterdam had heard of it, he would have likely dismissed it due to the lack of any discernable deific presence."

Tiernon nodded, being careful not to make eye contact with Beragamos. He closed his eyes for a few minutes, thinking. "TIS-AROG-DAL." The god reached up and rubbed his jaw. "BEFORE SUMMONING YOU, I REVIEWED YOUR

REPORT ON THE EVENTS NEAR FREEHOLD." Beragamos nodded. "YOU ARE SURE IT IS THE SAME DEMON?"

"The probabilities are such that anything else is very unlikely. First, the demon in Freehold went by the name Tom; the demon described by the orcs in Murgatroy is Tommus. Assuming one had the Wand of Orcus, it would still take tremendous energy to reignite the volcano. It would take, literally, a miracle. And that is essentially what he stole from you," Beragamos explained.

Tiernon closed his eyes in thought, or perhaps Seeing. After a few moments, he opened his eyes again. "IN THE REPORT, YOU SAID THE DEMON HAD SERVANT DEMONS WITH HIM?"

"Yes, Your Godship."

"DESCRIBE THEM TO ME IF YOU CAN."

Beragamos nodded, thankful to Hilda for retrieving that balling. "There was a smaller version of the Tommus demon, identical but smaller. There was another small demon that wore clothes and had a musical instrument, like a bard." Tiernon nodded. "The last one was another fiend, probably second order. Rather weird: splotchy green, four human arms, four human legs. Non-standard wings, more like a fairy's or something."

Tiernon was silent for some time, looking at Beragamos. He then closed his eyes in deep thought. Finally, the god spoke. "THE LAST DEMON YOU MENTIONED —DID IT SMOKE A PIPE?"

Beragamos blinked in shock and surprise. Apparently, gods really could be all knowing! "Yes, actually. Now that you mention it, he sat under a Net of Demon Entrapment, smoking a pipe very calmly. As I think on it, the behavior was a bit odd for the circumstances."

Tiernon sighed. "NOT FOR THIS DEMON. HE IS INSANE."

Beragamos blinked again. "Your Godship knows this demon?"

Tiernon paused and tilted his head slightly. " 'KNOW' IS A STRONG WORD. WE HAVE ENCOUNTERED EACH OTHER ON A FEW OCCASIONS. HOWEVER, I HAVE NOT SEEN HIM FOR OVER FIFTY THOUSAND YEARS. I ASSUMED HE WAS DEAD. AS INSANE AS HE WAS, IT WOULD STAND TO REASON THAT SOMEONE WOULD HAVE ERADICATED THE ANNOYING PEST IN THE INTERIM."

Tiernon was silent for a moment and then continued. "AT THE TIME, I TOOK HIM FOR A FOOL."

"Understandable, my god."

"BUT NOW I SUSPECT HE MAY NOT BE SO MUCH THE FOOL, AS THE ONE PLAYING THE FOOL CARD." Tiernon's face seemed to take on a rueful expression as he shook his head from side to side. "WE SHALL HAVE TO SEE."

Beragamos frowned, not quite understanding his god's meaning. Further, the god finished with a different, odd expression on his face, and as always with this form, Beragamos had trouble interpreting it.

Chapter 111

Jenn gripped the carpet handles tightly as the crazed pilot dive-bombed the ground at record speed. Her stomach was going to come up soon. This was not the sort of ride someone with a hangover enjoyed. She glanced over to see that Gastropé was not pale for a change; his face appeared quite green in the early morning fierdlight.

It really was not a good thing to get world-shaking bad news about the Forces Of Evil (FOE), as the alvar called their enemies, when one was drunk. It was even worse to be plunging into an exploratory mission while hungover.

After receiving Bastien's news, the senior alvar and Trevin went into a private consultation and came back shortly to announce that they were returning to the Nimbus and leaving for Murgatroy at once. It was only about eighty leagues, so the Nimbus could be there shortly after dawn. Jenn had shaken her head last night, trying drunkenly to comprehend such insane speed.

A second messenger arrived shortly before they boarded the Nimbus, but there was not much news beyond what they had already learned. Thus, they left with no clue as to whether there still even was a Murgatroy. Based on the information she had heard, Jenn suspected there would be, but the alvar seemed very paranoid.

Their carpets came in for a landing outside of town, near a large encampment that Seamach identified as the wargtown. It took them very little time to disembark, as the aetós and dwarves came armed and ready for combat, and were quite skilled at carpet landings under hostile conditions.

Jenn was not seeing much in the way of hostile conditions. There seemed to be no real activity coming from the town. There seemed to be a few wargs moving about, but no sign of any orcs moving about.

"Where are all the orcs in the wargtown?" Maelen asked Seamach.

Seamach was staring at the town carefully. "I see some bodies littered in the streets, but no movement."

"Surely the D'Orcs wouldn't have slain orcs in a wargtown?" Trevin asked.

"You would think survivors from the city would have come out to bury them," Elrose noted.

"Not if they slaughtered everyone in the city," Captain Ehéarellis said. "It would not be unheard of."

They all looked towards the gates. The walls of the town were wooden tree trunks knit together. The gates were shut tight and there appeared to be no sign of activity. "Well, it is shortly after dawn," Jenn noted hopefully.

"What sort of town doesn't open its gates at dawn?" Gastropé asked.

"One full of corpses," Darowin said.

"I really hate to admit it, but the dwarf has a point," Seamach noted grimly.

"Guardians: by land and air, standard approach to the wargtown," Trevin commanded.

The dwarves quickly fell into formation, bringing up their shields and moving towards the town. The aetós took to the air in formation and headed toward the town as well.

Once the dwarves got within about two hundred feet, Darowin called back to them. "There seems to be a horrible ruckus going on."

"Ruckus?" Maelen asked.

"It's snoring!" Darowin shouted back a few minutes later.

Jenn could almost feel the tension ease palpably in the air as people's shoulders relaxed. The aetós flew in and began inspecting more closely; the dwarves eased up and moved in as well. After a few minutes, Treyfoêr flew back with a report.

"It appears everyone in the wargtown is completely passed out. In place, not even in their beds or sleeping blankets. A few are, but most seem to have fallen off benches and stools and gone to sleep." He shook his head. "The smell of stale glargh and piss is really bad. It almost masks the stench of the wargs."

"Is it standard orc procedure to allow everyone to just pass out with no guards or fortifications?" Gastropé asked, indicating the openness of the town. Anyone could just walk up and come in, as the dwarves had just done. His brow furrowed. "We have soldiers marching through their tents, and still no one has woken up."

"It is not standard, as far as I know," Seamach said, also frowning. "Although they've been known to let their guard down at some very serious celebrations."

"Hoy there!" came a voice from the direction of the town gates. They all looked in that direction to see the gates being pulled into their day positions. A man, apparently human, was walking towards them. "Don't be pilfering the wargtown or there will be hell to pay!"

"We won't be taking anything. We were simply investigating why there was no movement," Trevin called back.

The man arrived shortly. He was wearing a rather tacky and stained town guard uniform and had not shaved in some time. "Aye, they all went on a bender yesterday afternoon and really never stopped until they all passed out. 'Twas a real pain for the folks who wanted to reclaim their wargs and such. They made do, but I suspect there will be some reckoning of payments at some point."

"Is this normal?" Trevin asked.

"Nah, most of them ain't got the kind of money you need to get this drunk," the guard said, shaking his head before spitting.

"So what was different this time?" Maelen asked.

The guard squinted. "Well, from what I gather from those who returned to town before the others passed out, there was this large blonde woman and her associates who came to hear the tales of the D'Orcs from the day before. 'Course, they didn't want to talk to a human, not until she whupped Meat Maker, but then she bought them glargh all afternoon and listened to their tales."

"And then they passed out?" Elrose asked.

"Nah, that's when a few did return and I learned what was up. But the rest, they kept drinking on their own coins, presumably. Once an orc is drunk, it's hard for them to stop until either their glargh or money is gone. It's either that or pass out."

Seamach snorted and gave Captain Ehéarellis a knowing look.

"So the D'Orcs and orcs who came to town the other day —were they any trouble?" Trevin asked.

The guard shook his head. "Actually not. They were much better behaved and better organized than the majority of hunting parties coming through town. No drinkin', no fights, no rowdiness or noise. They just bought what they needed and then left."

"Left? Which direction did they go?" Maelen asked.

"As I heard it, they didn't go any direction." The guard pointed off east-southeast. "They came from there. They left through a big fire."

"A big fire?" Seamach asked, puzzled.

"A hole in a giant bonfire they started," the guard said.

"A portal to the Abyss," Gastropé said. Jenn nodded in agreement. The two of them had been through more than enough of those things for a lifetime.

The guard shrugged, only knowing what he reported.

Elrose shook his head. "Well, the good news is that they didn't cause any problems."

"But what foul scheme have they cooked up?" Captain Ehéarellis said.

Trevin nodded. "I want my people to run some forensics on the town, the markets they visited. See if we can get any signs, perhaps residual signals that we can read."

Elrose nodded. "That does seem prudent."

"Maybe if we get lucky, they'll come back," Seamach said. Jenn and Gastropé gave the elf looks of disbelief.

~

"Great," Darflow Skragnarth said hollowly.

"What?" Lesteroth Garflog asked his commander.

"That fellow there"—Darflow pointed down the hall to a fiend who seemed to be hightailing it out of the fortress—"has brought us new orders from our glorious Queen of Darkness."

"Didn't she just send orders last night for a recon job?" Lesteroth asked.

"She did."

"And the new orders?"

"Full-on assault, eliminate all the D'Orcs and their new ruler," Darflow said with a sigh.

"Seriously?" Lesteroth said in shock. He grabbed the missive from his commander's grasp and scanned it. "Abyss! She is really serious this time," Lesteroth said with a very surprised look on his face.

Darflow shrugged. "She is sending in reinforcements. Given that we only have about a thousand demons left, I am both shocked at her generosity and pleasantly surprised."

"Agreed. Doom has twice our numbers, and now somebody is driving the pyrotechnics." Lesteroth pointed out to the stormy, rumbling volcano. "If she is sending reinforcements, she must be serious this time."

"So," Darflow said, shrugging, "we are to wait for the reinforcements to arrive. I wonder what sort of reinforcements she is sending?"

"It had better be something serious if she wants to actually pull this off," Lesteroth replied.

~

Hilda was enjoying a breakfast of fresh strawberries, muffins and a glass of orange juice and sparkling wine when a knock came at the door. Danyel rose to answer it. It had been a long night; first there was the meeting in Tierhallon, and then she had returned and spent until dawn listening to Ruiden's firsthand account of the battle. Unfortunately, he had been buried in ice for some of the exciting parts. Fortunately, as a sword he relied on his extrasensory perceptions, which had given him a better vantage point than being stuck inside a giant ball of ice would normally allow.

"It seems oddly early for someone to be calling," Hilda observed.

Danyel opened the door. From the angle, Hilda could not see who it was, but she did recognize the voice. This was most unusual!

"Ah, you must be the young Danyel I have heard so much about," an old man's voice said. It sounded different in mortal form, but was still recognizable.

"I am; and you are, sir?" Danyel was clearly puzzled.

"Ah, yes, iconography and statuary are not what they used to be." Hilda detected gentle humor in the voice. "I am Beragamos Antidellas, and I am here to see the lady Hilda of Rivenrock."

Danyel's face went white; Hilda was afraid the poor lad might faint. Of course, it was not every day that the right hand of Tiernon appeared at one's door. Danyel just stood there in shock, saying nothing.

"Might I come in?" Beragamos asked politely.

Danyel shook his head, trying to recover, and then bowed deeply. "My apologies, your archonship. No disrespect, I was simply overwhelmed!" He scrambled back, gesturing the archon to enter.

Hilda stood and went to retrieve a glass and plate for the archon. Beragamos smiled at her as he entered.

"Your Holiness, what a pleasant surprise. I hope," Hilda said with a bright smile and a bit of concern in her voice. "We had not been expecting you!" She gestured for him to take a seat. "Ever," she added more softly.

Ruiden came alert from where he had been resting and recovering mana in the corner. "Archon Beragamos!" the sword said, coming forward and bowing to the archon.

"Ah, you must be Ruiden, sword of Talarius," Beragamos said nodding. "Forgive me for not shaking your hand, but I just grew these fingers and I'd like to keep them a bit longer!" The archon chuckled.

Ruiden's sense of humor was not particularly great. "I can sheath my finger blades; however, etiquette demands that I bow rather than shake hands."

"Ah, yes." Beragamos's eyes twinkled. "I hear you had a very exciting day yesterday?"

If a sword could frown, Ruiden would have been doing so. "A rather frustrating and unsuccessful day. I was not able to question Exador." Ruiden shook his head. "I was encased in ice when the portal to the Abyss opened. This was very unfortunate."

Beragamos looked slightly puzzled. "Because you were unable to prevent Exador from escaping?"

Ruiden tilted his head in surprise at Beragamos. "No. If I had been able to move, I could have dived through the portal."

"Why would you want to dive into the Abyss?" Hilda asked shocked.

"Talarius is in the Abyss," Ruiden explained as if it was obvious. "Once in the Abyss, I should be able to follow my links to him and free him."

"Ahh," Beragamos said, slightly surprised. "That is admirable loyalty." He glanced at Hilda, who simply shrugged. The sword was driven.

"Can I get you some orange juice and sparkling wine? Or I have evenberry," Hilda offered, changing the subject.

"Why, thank you, my dear! I'll drink what you are having," the archon said, sitting down. "I think I need to be more careful when incarnating. I really only wanted the look, not the associated infirmities of a body as old as I wanted to appear. I think it must be a function of how old one feels inside." He shook his head, his brilliant white bangs shaking slightly. "By the way, your assessment of the ward's effect on archons was fairly accurate. That is why I had to incarnate a new, mortal body so I could get through the wards." He sighed. "The mana expenditure is quite high for physically incarnating like this. Doing this on a large scale for multiple archons would be expensive and require considerable effort."

Hilda poured him sparkling wine and then some orange juice and gestured to the fruit and muffins. "To what do we owe this honor?"

Beragamos simply smiled and held up one finger. He closed his eyes for a second and brilliant golden light suddenly limned the edges of the room before fading to a level only saintly sight could see. "Just to be on the safe side, I have shielded these quarters for our privacy."

Hilda nodded, noticing that Danyel had moved to a nearby sofa and was simply staring in awe at the archon. She had to smile; it was not every day that you met someone right out of the most sacred texts of your religion. Ruiden took a guarding position near the door.

"I am not sure why you simply did not call a meeting; would that not have been easier?" Hilda asked, puzzled.

"Well, based on your experience on the ground, I thought I might try it myself. The situation has escalated and I now need to be very much on top of the game." Beragamos shook his head ruefully.

"Escalated?" Hilda chuckled. "That is one way of putting it."

Beragamos grimaced. "No, no—I am not speaking of events in Murgatroy or even here. Although I am thinking we may want to reopen a temple in Norelon and establish a permanent base for the Rod. However, that too is not my current concern. The escalation occurred in Tierhallon."

Hilda got a concerned and uncertain look on her face, suddenly afraid of what he meant.

Beragamos nodded at her expression; it was as he had thought. "Yes, I was summoned to the Palaestra this morning." Hilda gulped. She knew what that meant.

"Our god read the reports I filed, and called me in to discuss it personally," Beragamos said.

Hilda felt her stomach going through the seat of her chair. This kind of scrutiny could not be good.

Beragamos nodded, but then smiled. "However, on the bright side, after reading about you and hearing of your interviewing the orcs in the wargtown, our god is most pleased with your work," Beragamos said.

Hilda sighed, that was a huge relief. "Well, that's good," she said with a smile.

Beragamos nodded. "It is good indeed. The downside"—Hilda looked concerned again—"is that he wants to meet you in person to get your firsthand impressions on the situation and what your experience has been with this new method of inquiry you have pioneered."

There was a moan from the couch and then a thunk. The two avatars looked over to where Danyel had been sitting to find him on the floor passed out, having slid off the couch. Beragamos looked at Hilda and raised an eyebrow.

Hilda smiled and shook her head. "That is where I would be right now, if I had not already had a bit of sparkly to ease my nerves. Poor Danyel has not had any alcohol in several days."

Beragamos chuckled. "Well then, the lad will not ever want to meet Tiernon in his Palaestral form." He took a sip of his sparkling cocktail.

~

Reggie took time to enjoy the sensation of his room fading in around him. He was back from "work," if you could call having dream sex with women work. It was practice sex, but it was still sex. But he figured it was more like working on a porno film. He kept getting technical instructions from Merrit-Ptah, his accursed mistress. It was not as fun as one might think.

But the good news was, he was getting a night off! Woo hoo! And it just happened to be on the night of the party. Merit-Ptah and her peeps were relocating to a different city, and so she would not be summoning him this coming night. That meant he could be at the party!

He had not been to a good party in a long time. The last one he had been at, Tom had gone and died on them. That had really busted up the party. The weeks after had also been stressful, which is why he had been smoking, trying to take a break, only to die en flagrante, so to speak, and end up here.

"I need a joint," Reggie said to himself. A good blunt would take the stress off. Of course, that is what had gotten him into this screwed-up situation in the first place. Shaking his head, he headed off to the mortal suite.

When he got there, things were fairly quiet. Apparently, the orcs were still asleep. Estrebrius and Antefalken were playing cards. Two individuals he did not recognize were out on the balcony, watching the never-ending ceremony.

"How goes?" he asked the two demons.

"Good up here," Antefalken said.

Reggie gestured with his head to the volcano. "There?"

"Good. Going pretty smooth, might end up a little ahead of schedule even," Antefalken said.

"Only issue was Tizzy running around his kitchen late last night, screeching about needing more butter," Estrebrius said.

"What is with this guy and buttah?" Reggie tried to say it like Tizzy, sort of yenta-like.

Estrebrius squinted. "Don't know, but I think he meant regular butter this time, for his 'magic cookies.' He sent some of his demon buddies out to get more."

Reggie shrugged. "Well, that's easy enough, I guess." He was not sure actually sure where you would get butter in the Abyss, or how one kept it from melting.

"Yeah, but he was freaking because he has to do something with it, melt it down and infuse it with some secret ingredient, I guess, and then strain it out."

Reggie raised an eyebrow at that. "I think I am going to want some of these cookies."

He wandered out onto the balcony and peered over the edge to see the line waiting to go up and swear to Tom. Boy, was this freaky or what? He glanced over to his two companions. They were not D'Orcs, demons, or orcs. There were sort of like really old, ugly humans.

One was about six feet tall but rather hunched; the other looked fairly human, but was under five feet tall and really burly. They both had very calloused hands resting on the balcony.

Reggie nodded to them. "I'm Reggie, a friend of Lord Tommus," he said.

The taller individual seemed to ignore him until the short guy poked him. "I am Völund, Smith of Doom."

"Oh yeah, I've heard of you. You make all the weapons and armor here. Cool!" Reggie held out his upper right hand to shake. Völund ignored it.

The shorter fellow harrumphed. "You'll have to ignore my friend; he's not much of a conversationalist." The two glared at each other.

Reggie reached out to shake the shorter man's hand. "And you are?"

The man laughed. "Oh, sorry. I don't get out much. I am a homebody. People usually come to visit me, and when they do, they obviously know who they came to see. Völund is one of my best friends and about my only equal—"

"Superior," Völund interrupted.

"—in smithery." The man shook his head at Völund. "I am named Hephaestus currently, but my friends call me Phaestus."

"Nice to meet you, Phaestus. Glad we are getting some visitors, it livens things up!" Reggie said.

"Indeed." Phaestus nodded. "And smithing is a tiring, thankless job. I need a break right now, so the party will be good. Help me get rid of some stress." He moved his shoulders around. "I carry it all in my shoulders and upper body."

"Well, Tizzy is making what he calls 'magic cookies.' If they are what I think they are, they will definitely help with the stress!" Reggie said.

Phaestus blinked. "Tisdale is here?" He looked at Völund. "Why in the name of Tartarus did you not mention this?"

"Didn't think it mattered," Völund said, shrugging.

"I've got to go see him. I have not seen him in well over four thousand years. Do you know where he is?" Phaestus asked Reggie.

"Sure, I'm betting he's in his kitchen. I'll take you there."

~

Reggie and Phaestus were wandering lost down one of the corridors from Tizzy's secret kitchen. Well, technically not that secret. The two of them had found the magic treasure. They were moving a bit slowly. Phaestus had quite a limp, but more importantly, they were both pretty cookied. Limps seemed to be pretty common what with Völund, Phaestus and Tal Gor. Reggie idly wandered if there was a connection.

"I wonder where Tizzy gets his weed. The Abyss is a barren wasteland; where does he dig this stuff up?" Reggie asked Phaestus.

"I don't know about up, but I know about high." Phaestus grinned back at him. "My me! It has been a long time! Tizzy's cookies are the only thing that can really relax me. Drinking can sometimes relax me, but often it just depresses me and I get grumpy."

"Grumpy! Like Snow White!" Reggie suddenly said, looking at Phaestus in realization.

"Who?" Phaestus asked.

"Not important; chick that fell asleep. Thing is, though, she had these seven buddies that were dwarfs. Are you a dwarf?" Reggie asked.

"Nah. Get that a lot. They do like me a lot, the dwarves, they do. They've been good to me; I try to be good to them."

"So you are just naturally short?" Reggie asked.

"Yep. Rest of my family are normal sized, most of the time."

"You have a family?"

"Of course I have a family!" Phaestus laughed.

"Does Völund?"

"Not that he'll speak to. Not sure, really. He had a couple brothers. They may have gotten left on the other side of the birefrigerated bridge or whatever it's called."

"Oh yeah, jotuns..." Reggie remembered.

"Something like that. Pronunciation's a bit off."

"Wow, I'm feeling really good!" Reggie said. "I think this has got to be the best time I've had in the Abyss!"

Phaestus snorted. "Not surprised. This place sort of sucks! They used to toss Titans down here to get rid of them. Not into the volcano, but into the Abyss."

"Yeah, not a great place to live. Weather is really terrible," Reggie said.

"Yeah, I think my friend Bess was a bit wacko for building a fortress down here," Phaestus said.

"I bet the real estate is cheap!"

"Yeah. If real estate is all about 'location, location, location,' then she probably got her Abyssal Palace really cheap!" Phaestus giggled. " 'Course, her other place has a view that is literally out of this world! Well, not *this* world, except that it is out of this world, but I mean that the view she has there is out of the world she has it on. Do you know what I mean?"

"Not at all." Reggie shook his head and smiled.

"Neither do I."

"Wah woa woo vad waah!" a voice said off to their left.

"What was that?" Reggie asked.

"I don't know. Sounds like someone who's really drunk!" Phaestus said. The two turned to look into an alcove, from which the voice had seemed to emanate. Some of the stone wall had collapsed and water was trickling out. Perhaps it gave way during the rain, Reggie thought to himself.

"Wah orgus dorg," the voice said again.

It was dark in the alcove, so Reggie turned up his demon sight to max. He blinked. There was a chunky fellow in the alcove, about five feet tall. He seemed rather misshapen, with two arms and two legs that were thick and ungainly-looking. His head and neck seemed to merge into one sort of stumpy head, and if Reggie did not know better, he would swear the guy's skin was mud.

"Hey, a mud man!" Reggie exclaimed.

"Hi, mud man!" Phaestus said.

"Waaan eee orgaass. Shtablish reel ashions!" the mud man said.

"Why would someone put a mud man down here?" Reggie asked, puzzled.

"No, no. He grew here!" Phaestus shook his head.

"Mud men can grow?" Reggie found the idea rather funny.

"He's not a mud man; or rather, *it* is not a mud man. It's a mud golem!" Phaestus told Reggie.

"Is it speaking universal?" Reggie asked. "Because I don't understand it."

Phaestus nodded. "It is, but its vocal cords aren't. Well, technically it doesn't have any. Talking has to be very difficult."

"So why is it here?"

Phaestus shrugged. "Not sure, but I am guessing it wants to establish relations with Mount Doom."

"Yashs!" The mud man said.

"Hmm, I think we are going to need someone who can talk to spirits," Phaestus said.

"Where are we going to find a psychic in the Abyss?" Reggie asked.

"Typically one would use a shaman or seer."

"So we just need to find a shaman. I think I might have seen a few upstairs," Reggie said, giggling.

"I think you are correct, my dear friend," Phaestus said, slapping him on the back, or trying to. Given the height difference, the slap hit Reggie in the butt.

"Do you want to go get one or should I?" Reggie asked.

"Do you know how to get back to the room with the shamans?"

"No," Reggie admitted, shaking his head.

"Then I better go get one," Phaestus said.

~

Tom smiled to himself as Ivan Throat Cruncher swore his oath alongside his wife, Imelda Throat Cruncher. They were a great third-generation team, Zelda had whispered to him. This ceremony was certainly making him feel pumped. Each oath was creating a link between himself and the D'Orcs and Doom.

These links were very similar to the links with the shamans and Vaselle. Perhaps a bit more low-key, since few if any of the D'Orcs were mana wielders, but nonetheless, from the small tests he'd tried during the downtime, he should be able to channel mana to and from them as well as communicate with them.

On some level, Tom recognized that this was sort of creepy; a gross violation of privacy. Very much like the feelings he'd had after linking with Vaselle. But on the other hand, it also felt like family. He could actually feel the emotions of the D'Orcs. Right now, everyone was excited, joyful and full of pride and hope. That joint swelling of emotion from the D'Orcs was overwhelming. He was feeling an intense emotional high from their high. At the back of his mind, a small warning was flashing about what might happen if they got seriously depressed, but for now, he couldn't think about that.

As they switched oath takers, Tom followed the previously sworn links to the command center to get a vibe from up there. He could sense vigilance, but also calm. It was completely non-verbal, but he could sense the military efficiency of the D'Orcs on duty and their calm scrutiny of the grid and the radar screens in the TCC. So far, so good.

He had been super-paranoid about something going wrong during the ceremony. Well, not the ceremony itself; they could be interrupted at any point during it and scramble. What still worried him was the party. Having so many of his troops drunk and incapacitated. It just seemed like a perfect opportunity for Lilith to attack.

Yes, they had made plans to have sober people on duty at all times, but he still felt a bit paranoid. It was silly, really; how could she possibly know when they were at their weakest? As far as he knew, and as far as Zelda and his commanders knew, there was no way anyone here could, or more importantly, *would* be in contact with Lilith's agents.

Tom had to shake his head at his own paranoia. While hiding in his cave, he had had no strong fear of Lilith and friends attacking. Of course, at that time he had not yet seized control of a giant military fortress that she had spent considerable effort decommissioning. He had to believe that restarting Mount Doom would almost force her to act.

He was certain it would, in fact. He had no idea how he could be so certain; was it some sort of joint paranoia of the D'Orcs? The other edge of the two-edged emotional sword he was riding high on right now? He could not know. All he could do was to pay attention to the next oath takers and ride the spirit of the moment.

~

DOF +10
Mid Fourth Period 16-07-440

The shamans stood around the mud golem, contemplating it. Farsooth had summoned a couple of were-lights to light the region better. The D'Orcs were obviously more than able to see easily in low light or no light. Not so much the orcs.

Damien and Vaselle stood watching the shamans analyze the mud golem. "So do you know much about golems?" Damien asked Vaselle.

"I've studied them. I think everyone who wants to create arcane devices does, but they always seemed like too much effort to me. It is a very complicated art, requiring numerous engineering skills, at least for stone or iron golems. I have no idea how you keep a mud golem together; it seems completely different than an articulated and animated statue," Vaselle replied.

"I would have to agree. I've never actually seen one before," Damien said. "Quite fascinating."

"It appears to be made out of the mud in that chamber; they are of the same type," Tal Gor said. The young shaman was standing back, letting the more experienced shamans have the best access.

"That would mean someone built it here," Vaselle said. "That seems rather odd. We are not that far off the beaten path. You would think that someone would have noticed a wizard creating a golem down here for a few weeks.

"The golem has been here no more than a day," Farsooth said, looking back towards them.

"So if it came here, then it was not made from the same mud," Damien stated.

"No, it was created from this mud, but it was done within the last day," Farsooth said. Beya and Ragala-nargoloth both nodded in agreement.

"I don't see how that's possible. That would be pushing the bounds of wizardry. Can shamans do something so quickly?" Damien asked.

Farsooth shrugged. "I have not met one who could, but it is conceivable with enough power."

"No, I think this is djinn-based," Beya said. "I can think of no one else with the skills to do this."

"You are saying that it was created by a djinn?" Damien blinked. He had heard of djinn, but they were beings of legend. They had few interactions with the mortal realms. They were beings of the demi-elemental planes and according to legend, were highly constrained in their ability to enter the material planes.

"Or multiple djinns. I believe the spirit in this golem is a djinn. I cannot say that it is the same djinn or djinns that created this golem," Beya said.

"So djinns can access the Abyss?" Damien asked.

"Why here and now?" Vaselle asked.

"The rain," Völund said suddenly, startling everyone. He had come down with them, but as was his fashion, had remained completely silent.

"The rain." Phaestus nodded. "That makes sense."

"Not to me," Damien said.

"How much do you know of how Mount Doom works?" Phaestus asked.

"I know it's covered in runes and it combines the elements with spirit to generate mana," Damien said.

"Close enough," Phaestus said.

"Not really," Völund said.

"Enough for the purposes of explaining this." Phaestus shook his head.

"I take it the two of you are very familiar with Mount Doom's operations?" Vaselle asked.

Völund shrugged. Phaestus rolled his eyebrows. "Yes, the two of us provided the core engineering skills and created many of the mechanisms in the complex."

Vaselle's eyes got bigger. "That was a long time ago, yes?"

Phaestus nodded and looked at Völund. "What year is this?"

"Fifty four seven sixty." Völund said matter-of-factly.

Damien blinked. "You mean 54,760 years ago? That's when this place was built?" He sounded rather incredulous.

"Foundation," Völund stated tersely.

"What you see today took thousands and thousands of years to build, but Orcus laid the foundation stone 54,760 years ago," Phaestus said.

"Wow," Tal Gor breathed. Vaselle nodded in agreement.

"In any event," Phaestus continued, "the interaction of the five planes creates what djinn call para-elements. In sufficient quantities these para-elements, or demi-elements, become malleable to the djinn. Once Mount Doom restarted, the para-elements began to pile up and malleables became available."

Damien was nodding, putting things together. "Water and Earth become mud. Fire, Air and a bit of Earth are smoke; Water and Fire are steam; Water, Fire and Earth are soot, and so on."

"A mud golem is a para-elemental golem of Water and Earth," Beya added, voicing her agreement.

"Okay, that is the what and how, I guess. But that leaves the why," Vaselle said.

"To re-establish relations with Mount Doom," Phaestus said as if it were obvious.

"Re-establish?" Damien asked. Phaestus nodded, as did Völund. "Orcus had a long history of working with the djinn."

"Really? Why?" Reggie asked.

"Many reasons mutually advantageous to each. The djinn have no other reliable way to access the Abyss, and Mount Doom contains numerous minerals of interest to the djinn. In return, the djinn have knowledge of other realms and can relay information to Mount Doom," Phaestus said.

"So how do we talk to it?" Vaselle asked.

"Someone has to link with the spirit and let it talk through them," Tal Gor answered. The three older shamans looked back and forth between themselves.

Finally, Beya spoke up. "I have done something similar once before."

Ragala-nargoloth nodded her head in respect to Beya. "I have not. Ancestors, Kachinas and similar spirits, but nothing elemental."

"Nor I," Farsooth admitted.

"Very well, then." Beya began rummaging in her pouch and pulled out some stones, which she began placing around the mud golem. "For stability," she said.

The mud golem watched impassively, saying nothing.

Beya began sketching symbols or runes around the mud golem. Finally, she scooped up some mud near the golem's left foot and rubbed it on her eyelids, ears, nose and around her mouth.

With that complete, she began chanting softly and closed her eyes. Damien could neither understand nor even clearly hear what she was chanting. The mud golem closed its eyes, or eye sockets he guessed.

A moment later, Beya began shaking and her chanting stopped. She drew in a large breath and opened her eyes. Damien noticed the other shamans blinking at Beya in surprise. Damien shifted to get a better look at the shaman's face and had to blink too. Her eyes were like crystalline pools of liquid. That description made absolutely no sense and was, in fact, contradictory; however, that was the only thing Damien could think of to describe her eyes.

Clearly, Beya was now possessed by the djinn of the mud golem. The Beya-golem began turning around, slowly looking at each of the people in the corridor. She smiled as her gaze came upon Reggie.

"A sex demon? You might make a very enjoyable anchor." The Beya-golem chuckled. Her voice sounded quite different from Beya's. Much smoother, softer.

Actually rather disconcerting, if truth be told, thought Damien.

As she continued to turn, her eyes came upon Völund. "You are Völund the smith. I have shared visions and experiences of you with our previous military adjutants. It is good to know you are still here."

As her eyes moved to Phaestus, they widened. "Vulcan. You have returned to your creation. Not in Memphis, nor Olympus... but here. It is an honor to encounter you."

It was odd that she clearly recognized Hephaestus, but odd she should call him by a different name, Damien thought.

She continued on, noting but not saying anything to the other shamans. Her eyes crossed Damien's and she stopped and stared at him disconcertingly.

"Inquisitor Damien. You are, perhaps, one of the last people I would have expected to see here." Her head tilted. "With the possible exception of Lenamare or Jehenna." She smiled. Everyone else was now staring at Damien.

"I'm sorry, how do you know me? Or them? I don't believe I have ever met a djinn," Damien said nervously.

The djinn made an amused half-chuckle. "No, we have not met. However, as with Völund, I have shared visons and experiences of you with another of my kind."

"Are you saying that the djinn are monitoring the Council of Wizardry?" Damien asked worriedly. Would they need to put up Lenamare's wards permanently?

She smiled again. "Not directly. We are observing someone else who is of concern to us, and who frequently interacts with the Council."

"Who might that be?" Damien asked. This was making him very uncomfortable. The world was quickly becoming far more complicated than he expected.

She gave him a slight frown. "I'm sorry, but I am afraid I am not at liberty to reveal that information." She looked truly contrite. Or at least as contrite as an orc face could look.

"Can you at least tell me if this person puts the Council in danger with his or her interactions?" Damien asked.

The djinn shook her head slowly. "I think you are discovering the answer to that through your inquisition."

She then started turning again to complete her circle. She nodded, having observed everyone. She paused thoughtfully, and then spoke again. "I have been asked to inquire if Tisdale is here?"

Damien shook his head. "Is there anyone that demon does not know?"

The djinn looked at him. "Yes, you know him. He was in Freehold before the wards went up. He was with the demon that captured the knight. Am I correct in assuming that the new Master of Mount Doom is the same demon that stole mana from Tiernon?"

"Stole mana from Tiernon?" Phaestus stared at Völund. "I think there may be a few things you neglected to mention…"

"He is!" Vaselle spoke up.

The djinn looked to Vaselle. "You are a warlock, yes?"

"I am," Vaselle said proudly.

"To the Master of Mount Doom?"

"Yes."

"I would like to speak with the new Master of Mount Doom when it is convenient," the djinn said.

Vaselle sighed. "Well, he's a bit tied up at the moment. He's trying to finish taking oaths from all the D'Orcs, and then we will have a feast."

"Hmm," the djinn said and then nodded. "I can wait until he is finished with the oath-taking ceremony. I will be in this corridor. Have Beya repeat this exercise to reengage dialogue."

Suddenly Beya's eyes closed and she started slumping to the ground. Farsooth moved quickly to catch her.

"Okay, then," Phaestus said.

~

Barabus thanked Tiernon that the final meeting of the day was over as he and the others marched down the long corridor. Finally, they would get to the point of this long-winded expedition. There had been so many non-informative speeches that he no longer had any idea of what they were going to see.

Following this morning's meetings and speeches, all of the Rod and Church members had to personally sign various legal documents to acknowledge various dangers, liabilities and other nonsense. They also had to sign something called a "non-disclosure agreement," saying that they would never reveal what they saw here today with anyone not designated as being so authorized themselves.

He and Heron were marching side by side behind Chancellors Alighieri, Ain and Sagramn; the three chancellors who, as Barabus understood it, were the principal backers of the project they were about to see. Behind him were his three knights and his top generals. They were walking side by side with Heron's top generals.

"So, Wing Arms Master," Barabus asked Heron. "Have you seen this 'Extender of the Law' thing Chancellor Alighieri has built?"

Heron shook his head. "No, Arch-Vicar General, I have not. I have railed and ranted about its cost in countless councils, chanceries and more than a couple of committees, but I have not seen it. This shall be as new for me as it is for you."

"Yet you know what it does? How it works?" Barabus asked. "I know we have heard many speeches on it, and I understand that it will allow Oorstemoth and its allies to extend the long arm of the law beyond anything currently imaginable. But I'm not sure how exactly it does this."

Heron nodded. "I can understand how, after only the few brief"—he raised his eyebrow on Barabus's side—"meetings and lectures we enjoyed last night and today, that might be. Clearly, the speeches only had time to brush upon the most salient and significant signature statistics, supplying only a circumspectly slight survey."

Heron paused for a moment as Barabus nodded in feigned agreement. Heron then continued, "But rest assured, I have been diligent in deliberating on every detail of its design, development and deployment, not to mention cost, for the last twenty years. Poring over thousands of pages of punctually delivered, pointless papers, each with the predictable pontification. Having done so, I can most certainly assure you that I have no better idea than you as to what this damnable thing of Alighieri's is. All I know is how much I could not spend on more useful military machinery these last twenty years."

At long last they came to the end of the very long, wide corridor that they had been marching down. The chancellors stopped in front of large metal doors, guarded by three soldiers. While Chancellors Ain and Sagramn worked with the guards to show the approved paperwork for the people following them, Chancellor Alighieri turned to the others, smiled and prepared to speak.

"Friends, allies, colleagues, Chancellor Alighieri said, practically glowing. "As you know, I am a man of few words." There was more than one person behind Barabus who suddenly had an urge to cough, both from his side and from the Oorstemothian side. "But on this, what I am sure will be the eve of an auspicious alliance of altruistic activist agnates and advocates seeking solely the cooperative consanguinity of a conciliatory conjoined course committed to coordination in countless endeavors to exceed the extent of justice, jurisprudence and the law beyond its current boundaries, I would like to say a few words."

"Chancellor," Heron interrupted.

"Yes, Wing Arms Master?"

"In the far distant lands into which we expect to extend and elevate our ability to carry out the requirements of the law, there is a saying." Heron paused; the chancellor simply looked at him, waiting for him to continue. "Facts on the ground speak louder than words."

The chancellor shook his head in puzzlement.

"Can you just open the door and show us what you have built? What you have spent so incredibly much money on these last few decades?" Heron asked.

The chancellor grimaced, obviously unhappy about having to skip his prepared remarks. He ran through a small gamut of facial expressions, ending with resignation and finally pride.

"As you will, Wing Arms Master. After countless committee comments questioning the commitment of cash to this carefully crafted construct, I think you will be more than sufficiently satisfied with the result." He gave the wing arms master a tight grin. "Gentlemen," he addressed his fellow chancellors. "Open the doors!"

The large metal double doors opened inward, spreading to reveal a very well lit, cavernous room. The first thing Barabus noted was a metal railing of about ten feet on the other side of the doors. The doors were opening onto a balcony over the cavernous room beyond.

The party stepped into the brightly lit metal and stone room. The room was enormous, well over fifteen hundred feet long and two hundred feet wide with something on the order of a two-hundred-foot-high ceiling. The huge space was filled with cranes, scaffolds and more equipment of different sorts than Barabus could even begin to imagine.

However, all of this was rendered insignificant by the room's primary content: the thing that all the scaffolding and cranes were designed to work with. Barabus's own mouth fell open even as he heard gasps from those behind him, including the knights. For once in Oorstemoth, no one spoke. The entire entourage was silent, staring at the vast... device? ship? vessel? that took up the majority of space in the room.

Vessel. It had to be some sort of monstrously huge vessel, Barabus thought, shaking his head. It was a thousand-plus-foot-long tube with rounded end caps. It was about seventy or eighty feet in diameter and made of solid black metal. Every inch of the metal hull was covered in runes, most currently only dully visible against the metal, but a fair number were glowing ominously against even the bright light of the room.

At each end were small towers protruding a few stories from the top of the thing. In the center, an even taller metal tower rose upwards. Along each side of the tube were large metal fins that stuck out at least another thirty feet. Like the body of the device, the metal fins were also engraved with runes.

Murmurs of surprise and shock finally began to rise from the assembled guests. Barabus looked up from the device and glanced at Heron, who was staring at the chancellor in complete shock.

Finally, Heron addressed the chancellor. "My gods, Dante! What have you wrought?"

Chancellor Dante Alighieri smiled even wider and raised his arms to gesture at his creation. "Ladies and gentlemen! Behold the future of law enforcement! Behold the vessel that shall allow us to extend the law to all parts of the multiverse! In air, water, fire, vacuum and aether! The law and its justice may now be served in the Abyss, in the outer planes, the demi-elemental Planes and every single material plane. As of today, there is no way to escape the law!"

Dante took a bow. As he rose, he raised his arms again and cried, "Behold! The Inferno!"

Chapter 112

The recently cleaned pipe organs in the volcano throne room swelled in unison with the voices of the fully assembled D'Orc battalions at the conclusion of the oath taking.

> *United forever in comradeship and battle*
> *Our mighty Empire will ever endure.*
> *The Great Empire of Doom will live through the ages*
> *The dream of the people, their fortress secure.*
>
> *Long live our Mount Doom motherland*
> *Built by the people's mighty hand.*
> *Long live our people, united and free*
> *Strong in our comradeship tried by fire.*
> *Long may our crimson flag inspire*
> *Shining in glory for mortals to see.*
>
> *Through days dark and stormy where Lord Tommus leads us*
> *Our eyes see the bright fire of freedom above.*
> *And Tommus our leader, with faith in the people*
> *Inspires us to build up the land we love.*
>
> *Long live our Mount Doom motherland*
> *Built by the people's mighty hand.*
> *Long live our people, united and free*
> *Strong in our comradeship tried by fire.*
> *Long may our crimson flag inspire*
> *Shining in glory for mortals to see.*
>
> *We fight for the future, and shall destroy invaders*
> *And bring our homeland the laurels of fame.*
> *Our glory will live in the memory of mortals*
> *And all generations will honor her name.*
>
> *Long live our Mount Doom motherland*
> *Built by the people's mighty hand.*
> *Long live our people, united and free*
> *Strong in our comradeship tried by fire.*
> *Long may our crimson flag inspire*
> *Shining in glory for mortals to see.*

Reggie leaned forward and over to whisper in Tom's ear. "Does that music sound oddly like the anthem the sailors sang in *The Hunt for Red October?*"

Tom shrugged. It did sort of sound like the old Soviet anthem, but he was not an expert on empires that collapsed before he was born.

It did not matter. This was his home. His homeland, his people! The booming, very martial music was the perfect capstone on the last day of oaths. D'Orcs united and inspired once more for a bright future! They would take on the multiverse, right the wrongs of the past, and bring justice to the D'Orcs and the Orcs! No more would Lilith or the smugly arrogant Los Alfar be able to look down on their people!

Tom felt like his heart would burst with the pride and joy of the assembled and once more united D'Orcs and D'Wargs as well as their assembled allies. Truly a glorious moment that would remain in their memories for all eternity. Literally, for all of eternity. Immortality, fame, glory; it was theirs to claim! Tom let his breath out softly, realizing it had been stuck in his lungs; he had been inhaling the smell of the moment and had forgotten to let it go. At long last, or well, after forty days, he had a purpose, a place. For the first time since Lenamare had dragged him away from his past life, he could see a future for himself.

~

"Quite a day," Antefalken said to Drag-Krallnom, watching the assembled battalions beside him.

"Truly, bard. I confess, I did not think this day would ever come."

"You know that I am going to have to get you to tell me the real story of what happened four thousand years ago. I know the Balladae Orcusae, but I want to compose a new, accurate song to commemorate it properly."

Drag-Krallnom snorted. "It would be good to correct the propaganda that Lilith and her brood spews in the Abyss, and those vile alvar in Midgard."

"Are you saying that Lilith and the alvar are somehow in league with each other?" Antefalken asked in surprise.

"In no way that we can prove," replied Darg-Krallnom. However, Lilith has plagued us for millennia here and the Los Alfar have done the same in Midgard. It all goes back to tensions left unresolved at Ragnarök. Lilith, and for that matter, many others in multiple worlds, felt those issues were resolved in Etterdam with the treacherous defeat of Orcus. However, as was prophesied, those issues are *not* resolved." He chuckled. "There shall be another reckoning, and this time, justice will prevail."

"Interesting," Antefalken mused. "This is all way before my time. Clearly, there is a lot that Lilith has never revealed to me."

"You have met Lilith then?" Darg-Krallnom asked suspiciously.

Antefalken chuckled. "I have. I am, or I suppose *was*, the preferred bard for the Courts." He shook his head. "But I am sure I am persona non grata now. She knows that I am, and have been for some time, in Tom's camp. The Jilted Bride is a jealous mistress and will tolerate no infidelity." He paused and then added, "In other words, I am not going back to the Courts unless it is flying in formation with a D'Orc army." They both chuckled.

"The Jilted Bride?" Darg-Krallnom asked.

"Yes. I advise not using that name outside of Doom. She hates that title more than any other."

"Why? I do not know that name for her."

"A very, very long time ago, well before Doom was built, she was the intended of a man named Adam. She thought they were in love." Antefalken shrugged, "Old story; he ran off with another woman named Eve to bear children and live a mortal life."

"A mortal life?"

"As she tells it, there were four of them: Adam, Lilith, Sammael and Eve. Adam and Lilith were intended for each other, and Sammael and Eve were also intended for each other. However, long story short, Eve apparently ate some bad food and convinced Adam to do the same. Not sure if it was hallucinogenic or what, but the two ran off to become mortal and have babies." Antefalken shook his head. "I have no idea how much, if any, of that is true, but it's a version she tells, so it is possibly more accurate than any of the other stories. Of which there are many."

"So that is how she and Sammael got stuck together?" Darg-Krallnom asked.

"As she tells it."

Darg-Krallnom said, "Very well then. From now on, the Jilted Bride will be the official term for our enemy."

They watched as the D'Orcs began to file from the volcano basin, heading to the party. It was a good day.

~

Tom waited until the last of the D'Orcs had filed out of the throne room and then headed toward the master kitchen, where Zelda was working to get things out. As he crossed a ramp going down to other kitchens, he ran into Tizzy coming up the ramp.

"Tom!" Tizzy exclaimed happily.

"Tizzy!" Tom smiled at him.

"I've been looking for you," Tizzy said.

Tom stopped. "What's up?"

"There is a pile of mud in an alcove off my kitchen's main corridor that wants to talk to you," the octopod said.

"There is a what?" Tom asked, blinking.

"A pile of animated mud," Tizzy said.

"A pile of animated… mud?"

"Yes, you know—a mud golem."

Tom shook his head. "No I don't know. You are saying there is a mud golem down near your kitchen that wants to talk to me?" Tom looked at him askance. "Did you get too close to your oven's fires? You are not making much sense."

"It said that the shamans had promised to bring you to see it after you finished the oath taking."

"Uh, well, I have not seen them yet. I was going to meet with Zelda and then join them at the party," Tom said.

"Okay. Hate to think they were not keeping their promise to the mud golem."

Tom shook his head. Just when he thought the crazy was over for the day. "So do I need to talk to this mud golem?" He was tired, yet there was still a lot of work to do. He did not really have time for Tizzy's insanity.

"Yeah, I said I'd come get you. I'm not going to break a promise to a mud golem," Tizzy replied.

Tom tried to rub the bridge of his nose without gouging out his eyes with his claws. He sighed and shook his head. "Okay, lead on!"

Tizzy led him down the ramp to another level and then down a second corridor a short distance to another ramp down. They went down that ramp and headed toward what Tom recognized as the kitchen Tizzy and his demons were using. They turned and went down a side corridor a short ways until encountering an alcove with mud oozing out onto the corridor floor.

"Here we go." Tizzy gestured to what appeared to a mud statue of some sort of humanoid. The mud statue raised its right hand in a sort of wave greeting.

"Ahm puhleshed doe mheat u, Lorhd Dommush," the mud golem said.

Tom blinked. "I'm sorry, I don't quite understand…?"

The mud golem twisted its neck head towards Tizzy.

"Oh, sorry, I'll translate," said Tizzy. "It's speaking universal, but mud golems are not the best at pronouncing human words." He tilted his head. "Although they are much better at it than Denubians." The mud golem bobbed its neck/head up and down in agreement.

"So what did it say?"

"Oh, right. It said, 'I am pleased to meet you, Lord Tommus.' " Tizzy said.

"Can it understand me?" Tom asked. The mud golem nodded. Tom smiled. "Pleased to meet you… mud golem." Tom was not sure if mud golems had names.

"Whahaw. Mah nahmeesh dahmahreen," the mud golem said.

Tom glanced to Tizzy. Tizzy jumped. "Sorry, forgot. The mud golem laughed and said its name is Tamareen. Or is it Tamarin?" Tizzy asked the mud golem.

"Dahmahrine," the mud golem said.

"Tamarin, but pronouncing the 'i' more like a sort of 'ee' sound," Tizzy said.

"So, Tamarin… It is a pleasure to meet you. How can I help you?" Tom had no idea why a mud golem would want to talk with him, or…never mind. Tom reminded himself that asking too many questions just led to too many more.

"Wa wahn rhe-estahbish rehlaahshons wihdh Doohm."

"They want to re-establish relations with Mount Doom," Tizzy said.

The mud golem, Tamarin, nodded its neck/head.

"Okay, so mud golems had relations with Mount Doom in the old days and they want to re-establish them?" Tom supposed that made some sense. Most of Doom was underground, and now that it was raining, there was mud.

"Whahahw whahaw," the mud demon laughed, and Tizzy joined it.

"Okay, what's so funny?" Tom asked.

Tizzy shook his head. "You, that's pretty funny! Wanting to establish relationships with mud golems!"

"It just asked to do that! What's so funny?" Tom asked, annoyed.

"Mud golems are golems! They are automatons; robots would be the Earth equivalent. They are not sentient in and of themselves!" Tizzy said, still laughing.

"So the owner of the mud golem wants to re-establish relations?" Tom asked.

"Well, no," Tizzy said hesitantly, looking at the mud golem. "I assume that Tamarin is asking to re-establish relations with Mount Doom on behalf of hir people?" Tamarin nodded its neck/head.

"Tamarin's people?" Tom nodded, feeling they were getting somewhere finally.

"And who are Tamarin's people?" Tom asked.

Tizzy gave Tom a look like Tom was crazy. "Why the djinn, of course. I figured you knew that!" Tamarin nodded affirmatively.

"Djinn?" Tom shook his head. "You mean like genies?"

Tizzy twisted his lips a bit. "That is not their favorite term, but that is basically the common phrase for their race."

Tom shook his head. "So the race of genies—I'm sorry, djinn—want to have diplomatic relations with Mount Doom?"

"I think we've been making that pretty clear." Tizzy looked to Tamarin, who nodded.

"And the djinn had diplomatic relations with Orcus?" Tom asked.

"Indeed, although you do not want to use the word 'diplomatic'; that will cause a lot of problems. Think of it as a long and mutually beneficial partnership." Tizzy nodded, as did Tamarin.

"So, this is a good idea?" Tom asked Tizzy.

Tizzy shook his head. "Of course it is! No one in hir right mind would toss a bottle back in the sea or re-bury a lamp in the sand. That would be stupid. If the djinn want to do business with you, you take them up on it!"

Tom closed his eyes for a moment. "Okay, so what do we need to do to establish these relations?"

Tizzy looked to Tamarin. "Ahh neehd ahn ahngohr."

"Tamarin needs an anchor to this realm," Tizzy said.

"Okay, how do we find one of those?" Tom asked.

Tizzy shook his head. "An anchor is a person. Typically the king or prince of the realm."

"So me? I should be the anchor?" Tom asked.

"Exactly!" Tizzy said and Tamarin nodded.

"Okay, so how do I do that?" Tom asked.

Tamarin started speaking very rapidly to Tizzy. Tom could not even try to parse out what it said.

Tizzy nodded, seemingly having no problem understanding the mud golem. "You need to stick your hands into the mud golem's body and say 'I,' and then your true name, 'take you,' Tamarin's true name, 'to be my djinn.' And that's it.

"That's it?" Tom asked dubiously.

"Yep, and from the link that forms, Tamarin will choose a form from your mind that is most appropriate."

"Okay, so how do I know Tamarin's true name?" Tom asked.

"Tamarin will give it to you in your mind once you stick your hands in the golem," Tizzy said.

"Okay, then. Do we just do it now?" Tom asked. Tamarin nodded.

Tizzy said, "Yep."

"Okay, then," Tom said. He gently reached forward to touch the mud golem's torso. His claws met no real resistance as they slid into the mud golem's body. Once inside, Tamarin nodded. Tom could definitely feel something. With his demon sight, he could see Tamarin's aura and his own sort of intermingling at the mud golem's body. "I, Thomas Edward Perkinje, take you, Tamarines DarNathos Parfeuesnas Deblentre, as my djinn!"

Tom felt a rush very similar to the one he had felt with Vaselle and the shamans, as well to a lesser extent the D'Orcs. Sort of a brief joint possession of each other. He had to close his eyes at the world of colors, sounds, smells, emotions, tastes and other sensations that nearly overwhelmed him.

Tom opened his eyes, realizing they were closed. He blinked and looked to find a purplish bottle in his hands instead of a mud golem.

Tom looked at Tizzy. "Where did Tamarin go?"

Tizzy pointed to the bottle. "She's in the bottle now."

"*She* is in the bottle? Tamarin is a girl? Why did you keep calling her an it?" That seemed rude.

Tizzy shook his head. "Djinn don't have any sex. It makes no sense in their realms. When they anchor with someone on a material plane, or in this case, the Abyss, they take a form pleasing and comfortable to their new master."

"Master?" Tom asked dubiously.

"Sort of how the anchoring rules work. Very complex," Tizzy said, waving his upper hands dismissively.

"So Tamarin is in this rather large, purple bottle?" Tom asked.

"That is what I said."

"So how do I get her out?"

"Remove the cork and ask her to come out. However, you might want move out of the mud. I say that simply based on the sort of clothing djinn typically wear."

Tom sighed. "Okay, let's go back to the main corridor." The two walked back along the main corridor to the kitchen. Tom stopped and looked at the bottle. "Well, here we go!"

Tom pulled the rather large glass stopper from the bottle and said, "Tamarin, please come out!"

The bottle trembled and suddenly pink smoke started pouring out of the bottle. Tom suddenly had a bad feeling. If the djinn took an image from his mind…

The pink cloud grew to be about the size of a normal human and then moved beside Tom and Tizzy and hovered near the floor. The cloud began to reshape into a sort of hourglass form. The form bent over, and the next thing Tom knew, there was a very buxom, young, blonde, human woman in a pink harem outfit bowing before him.

"Master, I thank thee for releasing me from my bottle!" said Tamarin, smiling brightly and standing up straight.

Tom shook his head; there was no question of where Tamarin had gotten the image. The pink harem costume was quite revealing, but it covered her belly button. He really should not have watched so many old reruns on cable TV. Further, given the sort of problems Jeanie had caused Major Nelson, Tom was a bit worried as to what he was getting into.

~

DOF +10 DZ+40
Early 6th Period 16-07-440

Tom sat upon his short throne in the grand dining hall at the head table. Technically, this was only the second party he had ever been to, not counting any of his parent's parties. The last one had not ended so well. Or maybe it had. He now had a pretty cool volcano to live in, an army of super-warriors, and now a genie!

Tamarin had slid a stool up to his right, between him and Darg-Krallnom. Zelda was to his left. She had looked at their newest guest rather suspiciously at first, as had Darg-Krallnom. However, Darg-Krallnom noted the purple bottle Tom was carrying and nodded. When Tamarin had whispered something in Darg-Krallnom's ear, the D'Orc commander had laughed uproariously and slapped the table.

Tom had had so much to do, that he'd had little time to talk to Tamarin, just the time he could make between various stops on his rounds. She seemed fine with this, though, and said they could speak in more detail later. Her principal objective of anchoring had now been achieved.

Tom tried to focus on the music. The Doom Metal was pretty cool. He hoped that they were just rusty with their instruments and were not actually trying to get such an extreme, hard-core industrial sound. He supposed x-glargh would make the hard banging, clanking and shrill strings sound better. However, he would work at enjoying it sober, or as sober as possible. The D'Orcs were enjoying it, anyway, and that was what was important.

There was a clashing and banging off to his right. He looked; it was Reggie and Phaestus trying to get down a stairway out of the dining room. *How had the two of them gotten so drunk so quickly?* Tom wondered. Everyone was drinking now, but the pair must have started early. He shook his head in amusement. He looked for Rupert and Fer-Rog, hoping they were not drinking. He had no idea what the drinking age was in the Abyss. It probably did not come up that often, as almost everyone besides him and Rupert were vastly older than twenty-one. But ten-year-olds should not be drinking. Although, to be fair, at first Tom had planned on drinking even though he was under age, but then he had started worrying about an attack and decided to go light on the x-based beverages. He would do a few over the night, but he would try to stick to the non-x stuff. He had never had a hangover and this did not seem like a good time to start.

After a few moments, he spotted Rupert and Fer-Rog sitting over in a corner, talking and laughing. They did not appear to have any beverages with them. They were safely munching on a giant plate of cookies. Tom smiled, thinking about the fun they were probably having. When he had been ten, he and his only friend used to like to pig out on Oreos. At least Rupert might be able to have a minimally normal childhood here.

Thinking about childhood and drinking, Tom suddenly counted on his fingers. He was not really sure how long he'd been a demon. Those long periods sitting in his cave had been rather a blur, but it had to be getting close to his seventeenth birthday. When he had died, it had been less than seven weeks until his birthday. He chuckled, shaking his head. Getting his own Doompire for a birthday present was pretty cool. If only he had a candle, he could stick it in a cookie and light it.

"I think things are going well, My Lord!" Zelda yelled from her seat to his left. The song the band was playing was particularly loud at the moment.

"You did a great job, Zelda!" Tom smiled at her.

"Thank you, My Lord. I am so honored to have been able to arrange this celebration!" She grinned.

Tom reached into the Rod of Tommus to check system power levels. Things were charging quite well now, better than before. He needed to get this place self-sustaining. It was getting exhausting to feed it and deal with everything. He guessed it was a good tired, but if he stopped to think too much, he would have to curl up in a ball. He was riding a tiger at the moment; he had to hang on tight.

~

"What are you doing?" Farsooth GoreTusk asked Beya Fei Geist and Ragala-nargoloth as they stood at the buffet; they appeared to be trying to stuff cookies into their belt sacks.

"Have you tried these cookies?" Beya asked, looking up and back at him.

"No, why?"

"Try one!" Raga-nargoloth shoved one in his mouth. She clamped her hand over his mouth. "Don't let any of the crumbs fall out; you will want every one of them."

Farsooth chewed on the cookie, swallowed a few times and licked the crumbs from his teeth. When he could speak, he asked, "Why did you do that?"

"How did you like the cookie?" Beya asked.

Farsooth shrugged. "Fine, I guess; I am not big on sweets."

Ragala-nargoloth shook her head as if she was talking to an idiot. "Did you notice nothing interesting? The flavor of the cookie?"

Farsooth sucked on a few more crumbs from between his teeth. "Oatmeal. Hmm. There is a slightly odd taste to it. Is it the butter? Odd butter."

Beya closed her eyes and shook her head. "Yes, it is odd butter. Do you not recognize the taste? If not, you will after a few deminutes."

Farsooth shook his head, puzzled, and then his eyes went wide. "Is that the taste of—"

"Demon weed!" Ragala-nargoloth blurted loudly but quickly quieted down. "It's got demon weed in it!"

"Who the hell wastes demon weed in a cookie?" Farsooth asked incredulously. "You do that and everyone will start spirit walking. We don't need half the party out on the astral plane!"

"I think demons have a different sense of humor than orcs," Beya shook her head.

"So what are you doing?" Farsooth asked again.

"We are stocking up to take some home with us. I don't know about Romdan, but in Ithgar and Etterdam, this stuff is extremely hard to get."

Farsooth raised his eyebrows. "Good idea." He pulled out an empty bag from his belt pouch. "Someone should tell Tal Gor!"

"After we get our share, after we get our share!" Ragala-nargoloth said with a laugh.

Chapter 113

"So, Murgatroy has now been overrun by a new batch of alvar, dwarves and aetós?" Moradel asked Stevos, shaking his head.

"This seems to be escalating very quickly," Sentir Fallon said. "Do we know who these people are?"

Stevos shrugged. "Apparently there are some very powerful alvar with them. People who are rumored to be close to the Principality."

"Then I would guess that servants of Nét are involved," Sentir said.

"Who is Nét?" Hilda asked.

"Nét is the El'adasir god of war. The alvaren god of war," Beragamos said.

"They really did not like Orcus," Sentir Fallon said. "Even a small possibility of Orcus returning would put them on a warpath."

"Could there be conflicts of interest here?" Moradel asked.

"I would seriously hope not. That would be extremely difficult," Sentir said. "I worked with them a bit in Etterdam; they are not the most pleasant people."

"But don't elves move on really slow timeframes? Their elders sit around and contemplate things for years before doing anything," Hilda asked, thinking of stories she had heard.

"It's certain they have already done a few centuries of deliberations regarding Orcus and the D'Orcs. If Orcus is back, it is doubtful they will feel a large need to deliberate," Sentir said.

"I am thinking we may need to return to Murgatroy in the morning," Beragamos said to Hilda.

Moradel looked at him oddly. "What do you mean, 'we'?"

Beragamos smiled. "Things are escalating here, too, I fear. I have had to step up my role and have just spent the day in Freehold. I interviewed Ruiden, met Master Trisfelt and the wizards Lenamare and Jehenna." He shook his head. "Remembering Hilda's multiple engagements with them, I would now be tempted to canonize her again, if that were possible." Hilda chuckled as Beragamos smiled at her.

"In fact, I had to physically incarnate to get through the wards," Beragamos said.

"So now you are undercover as well?" Moradel asked, puzzled.

"I fear so; I am Gamos, Hilda's grandfather. Also an animage." Beragamos apparently noted Moradel's concern. "I realize I should have mentioned this before, since Astlan is in your charge; however, I had some pressure from above and felt it necessary to move immediately." Everyone in the room knew that if Beragamos was receiving pressure from above; there was only one above that he would be talking about. Moradel would just have to adjust to his boss's micromanaging his assignment.

"I am due at the Hall of Justice shortly after Astlanian dawn, so I am thinking I should be back in Freehold by mid-morning, and we can then go to Murgatroy and investigate a bit more," Beragamos said to Hilda.

~

Exador was leaning back in his favorite lounge chair, his feet propped up on the black leather topped ottoman, a very large raw beef sirloin steak covering his eyes. He kept the chair here in the best climate-controlled room in his Court penthouse. He had received the lounge chair and ottoman as a gift a bit over half a century ago from its designer, a man named Eames, and his wife in return for ensuring the chair's commercial success. His music system was currently playing some very relaxing trans-neo-classical chill from somewhere in Visteroth; he had forgotten the planet's name.

He had been in a very serious funk since his forcible return to the Abyss with a pile of meteors crushed on top of him. He had had to dig his way out of a 300-meter-deep crater that had been backfilled by crushed asteroids and some molten metals. His head still hurt from that first wallop; hence the cold steak.

There was a knock on the outer sliding glass door. He lifted the steak to peer through the dual glass doors that served as an airlock to the sky deck. Bess and Ramses were there. He would have shaken his head but it still hurt too much. He waved his hand to unlock the outer doors, allowing them into the airlock, and then when they were both inside, he unlocked the inner door.

"Now that's what I call airtight!" Bess said to Exador before realizing he had a raw steak on his face.

"Where have you been? You missed our last meeting!" Ramses complained, having not yet seen Exador's face. "And did you know they put the wards back up around Freehold?"

"I am guessing he knows." Bess pointed to Exador's meat-covered face as he continued to ignore his guests.

"What happened to you?" Ramses asked.

Exador groaned in a tired, worn-out and only moderately theatrically manner. "I have noticed the wards. And in case it is not obvious, there is no real need to waste time convincing them we are human. That opportunity has flown," he said from under the steak.

"You look like a pile of dung flattened by a giant. What happened?" Ramses asked.

"Talarius, the knight who was abducted, has a walking, talking sword. It is trying to locate and rescue Talarius and in the due course of its investigation, it outed me as a demon in front of a majority of the Council."

"How could it do that?" Bess asked, puzzled.

"Well, it claims to glow in the presence of demons, and it was glowing near me. It would not leave me alone, so I tossed it across the room. It then clove me in two, and I got pissed. Council got involved, including my traitorous sycophant Randolf, and well, let us just say we are no longer welcome there."

"So how are we going to get the book?" Bess asked.

"This will severely complicate things," Ramses observed.

Exador pulled the meat up and away from his face, resting it on his forehead. He looked at his allies. "Actually, things are much simpler now; there is nothing left to hide. The gloves are coming off. We are going to seize the book from Lenamare and the Council even if we have to flatten Freehold to do it."

~

DOF+11 Mount Doom Dawn

Tom strode down the extremely quiet halls of Mount Doom. All the D'Orcs had loosened up considerably later in the evening. The D'Orcs and the few demons had all gone through a lot of x-glargh and x-other beverages, and Tizzy's cookies had been a particular hit for some reason.

By the earliest hours of the morning, nearly everyone had been completely wasted and were sharing stories about how horrendous and awful Lilith was. They even had a new title for her: "The Jilted Bride." Antefalken had shared it with people. Apparently, it was the worst possible insult for her. At one point when Tizzy had come to bring up more cookies, he happened to mention that Mount Doom was the only place in the Abyss where one could get away with insulting Lilith without fear of repercussion. Everywhere else, her spies would find out and one was likely simply to disappear for several centuries or more.

Overall, it was a good party and now the entire palace was quiet. The only sounds were those of the poor grunts who had to wake to take over at the shift change at dawn. They would certainly have a bad case of x-glarghvost; with luck, they had limited their intake enough to be alert this morning.

Tom entered Tizzy's kitchen, where Tizzy and one other demon were washing bowls and large metal trays. "You still here?" Tom asked. He was surprised at the demon's tenacity in the face of baking cookies. It had been a huge effort and Tizzy had really came through and kept his word.

"Just finishing up; my other assistants started eating the cookies as we baked them and then passed out, so I sent them to bed." Tizzy shook his head, wiping down a large bowl with two of his hands and arranging cooking utensils in a crock on the counter with the other two. "Reliable help is so hard to get in the Abyss."

Tizzy suddenly looked at him, puzzled. "You seem very sober. Did you not drink?"

Tom grinned. "Not much; I alternated between glargh and x-glargh. I was too paranoid about which of my enemies might want to do a surprise attack while all my people were getting wasted."

Tizzy grinned brightly. "So, finally thinking like a demon lord!"

Tom grinned at Tizzy and said "Yes, and I need your help."

Tizzy paused and grinned more malevolently. "Ye-eh-ss?" he drawled like a third-rate spy movie villain.

Tom shook his head. Just when he thought the demon was turning sane. "You have a link to Gastropé, yes? He summoned you to fight liches."

Tizzy shrugged. "Yep. You need some liches?"

"No, thanks. I sort of screwed up and forgot to set up return gateways for the humans and orcs," Tom said.

"Hmm, that could be a problem. Maybe they should just stay here?" Tizzy suggested.

"Or maybe you could have Gastropé help the two of us open a gateway to Astlan and we can send the Astlanians through it," Tom suggested.

"And then we get to eat the others?" Tizzy asked hopefully.

"No. They are my people; I can't very well and go around eating my own people!" Tom exclaimed.

"You really have not met Lilith, have you?" Tizzy asked.

"No. And at the moment I don't want to. The other shamans are going to be trickier, however; from what I have read and heard, travel between the various planes of Midgard is easier than coming and going from the Abyss," Tom said.

Tizzy shrugged with his upper shoulders. "I guess. Never really tried it. I always hub out of the Abyss. Not by choice, of course. My accursed masters are the ones booking the tickets. However, that is the advantage of living on a hub plane: direct routes to everywhere. Whether you want to go there or not." Tizzy grimaced, apparently remembering some of his trips to visit accursed masters.

"Well, I figure that once we are in Astlan, Damien will know someone who can travel between the material planes," Tom said.

Tizzy shrugged. "Probably. Did you ask him?"

"He's asleep."

"Which is where I want to be! This place is really wears one out," Tizzy said. "I've been *baking* all night." He shook his head. "This place encourages bad habits." He pulled his pipe from behind him suddenly and lit up.

"So, can you check with Gastropé?" Tom asked. "I assume he's going to want some time to get somewhere private."

"Sure, he owes me one. When do you want to do it?" Tizzy asked.

"Well, everyone needs to get up yet, so maybe early afternoon in Astlan?"

Tizzy frowned. "I had planned to be out of it by then; I guess I could nap now, then open the link, you do your hijacking thing and then I continue my siesta."

"That works." Tom was a bit surprised that Tizzy did not want to go back to Astlan and torment Gastropé and Jenn.

~

Finding a private room for lunch in Murgatroy proved extremely vexing. It would have been quite nice to rent out a small back room of a tavern for lunch so that everyone could talk privately. However, that had not proven possible, so they had gathered food and drink at the market and one of the taverns and gone on a picnic. They had debated going into the woods, but Teragdor had suggested heading to a small copse on the plain, out past the wargtown. The forest on the other side of town was too likely to contain hidden listeners.

They were a rather odd lot that certainly would have attracted eavesdroppers: Stevos, herself and her aging grandfather, all of whom were well dressed by local standards, along with a half-orc priest of Tiernon and an ambulatory sword. Interestingly enough, the people of Murgatroy seemed less bothered by a walking, talking sword than those in Freehold. Either that or they were simply used to minding their own business.

Ruiden had insisted on coming along. When they had returned to the hotel and told Ruiden and Danyel that the two of them were going to Murgatroy, Ruiden wanted to know why. Explaining their reasons led the sword to the conclusion that Murgatroy was the last place the demon that had captured Talarius had been; thus, he needed to investigate.

It was, surprisingly, a decent picnic. The weather was nice, they had brought a good-sized blanket to sit on, and Hilda had managed to locate a few bottles of passable wine. The only slightly awkward thing was the way Teragdor kept looking at Beragamos. The awestruck look was amusing at first, but after a while, it started to seem a bit gauche. Although, to be fair to the young lad, he was a lowly itinerant priest stuck in the middle of a place worse than nowhere, and he had probably had to fight his way through incredible amounts of prejudice, as well as actual judgement, to get ordained. Yet, here he was, having lunch with two saints, a sword golem and a legendary figure who actually spoke directly with their god, Tiernon, on a daily basis. Not even the Thaddeus Barolos, the High Pontificate of Tiernon in Astlan, sitting on his holy throne Justicia could make such a claim. It was doubtful the man had even met a saint in the flesh, let alone a Supreme Archon.

Hilda shook her head. When had she become so jaded?

~

Gastropé pushed the plate towards the center of the table. The local tavern meal had been decent enough by his old standards; unfortunately, he had been completely spoiled on the food on the Nimbus, at the Grove and the alvaren food. He glanced at the candle clock on the left wall of the tavern. He would need to leave soon in order to get to the secure spot he had staked out after Tizzy had contacted him.

The request, while objectively rather odd, was subjectively quite reasonable in the world he currently found himself in. Tom had some people in the Abyss who needed to get back to Astlan and they needed a gateway. Only a few months ago, this would have terrified him on so many levels, but today it seemed like a completely reasonable request.

Gastropé had to chuckle at himself. Ever since the storm lich battle, he had pretended to others on the ship that traveling through the Abyss was old hat for him. Apparently it was, because this just seemed so routine at this point.

"I have to run a small errand," Gastropé told Jenn.

"What? Where?" Jenn asked, setting her iced tea down.

"Just have a small favor I have to return. I will meet you out at the investigation site by the wargtown."

"Do you want me to go with you?" Jenn asked.

Gastropé forced a smile. "Nah, it's no big deal, and if we both show up late, people will wonder where we are. You go and let them know I'll be there in no more than half an hour."

Jenn shrugged. "Okay. Have fun returning a favor or whatever." She shook her head, apparently displeased by his rather vague answer. However, he was positive she would not want to know about this.

Gastropé got to the location he had staked out, figuratively. It was about a ten-minute walk from the north gate, over a hill and near a small copse of trees. You could not see the town gates from here. He quickly gathered some branches and cleared the ground for a small fire. He lit the fire and chanted the spell for summoning Tizzy, linking the spell through their binding.

"*Greetings, accursed master. What may I do for you?*" Tizzy asked in his head. The octopod was standing in what looked like a stable of some sort. Rather odd, Gastropé thought; he had not known there were stables in the Abyss. Previously he had been buried in lava and called it a spa treatment; now he was in a stable?

"*You asked me to call you now,*" Gastropé replied; had the demon forgotten already?

"*Oh, yeah. For Tom. That's why I am here with these guys. Sorry, I just finished baking for two days straight and probably need to go take a nap!*"

Gastropé blinked; the demon making even less sense than normal. Baking? Was that some sort of spa treatment in the Abyss? "Wait. I thought you said you never needed to sleep —that demons did not sleep?" Gastropé asked.

"That was before we were Doomed. Getting Doomed makes you sleepy!" Tizzy nodded to someone Gastropé could not see. "See, Rupert agrees!"

"Rupert is there? Is he coming through? Jenn will be thrilled!" Gastropé said. Tizzy peered off screen for a bit. "He says not today, but he and Fer-Rog want to come through soon."

"Who is Fer-Rog?" Gastropé asked.

"They're schoolmates, training together," Tizzy said after a few seconds.

"Rupert is going to school? In the Abyss?" This really made no sense. "Do they have demon schools or something?"

"That would be interesting! I wonder what punishments would await those who tried to play hooky!" Tizzy grinned. "Nah, it's combat training."

"Combat training?" Now Gastropé was really confused.

"Anyway, Tom wants to open the gateway now, and I need to get some rest. Handing you over!" Tizzy shouted. Suddenly Tom was on the other end of the link.

"Hey, Gastropé, good to see you." Tom came into focus and Gastropé suddenly realized he was looking at Edwyrd. "I'm coming in as Edwyrd, since Damien and I have some work to do."

"Damien?" Gastropé shook his head. "What? Damien is there?"

"Yes, as is Vaselle and the rest. As soon as we come through, we will do introductions."

"Uhm, okay… what do I need to do?"

"Not much, I can feel your summoning for Tizzy; let me work with that for a moment." Edwyrd seemed to be concentrating on something and suddenly the flames leaped higher than one would have thought possible.

"Where are you, by the way?" Edwyrd asked.

"A place called Murgatroy." Gastropé said. "It is south and east of—"

"What a weird coincidence!" Edwyrd interrupted. "That will be great for Tal Gor. It's close to our allies there."

"Wait, what?" Gastropé asked. "What are you talking about? You know where Murgatroy is?" He was suddenly quite nervous.

"Sure, Tal Gor was there shopping just the other day with the rest of his clan and some of my people!" Edwyrd said even as the hole in reality split the bonfire in two.

"You were here the other day?" Gastropé asked aloud, even as he felt a cold dread coming over him.

Edwyrd jumped through the hole in the flames, carrying a very large staff of some sort. That was new. He then reached through and helped a young wizard, maybe six or seven years older than himself, step through. Following him came Damien, and then Antefalken after the councilor.

"Actually, I was only out by the wargtown," Edwyrd continued. "I just opened the portal to haul the supplies through." He turned toward the fire and said, "Good news, Tal Gor! We are coming out in Murgatroy, so you will be within flying distance of your tribe's campsite."

"Excellent!" An orc suddenly stepped through the portal.

Gastropé felt like he was going into shock. He was sure the blood had drained from his face.

Suddenly there was a terrible hissing and spitting noise and someone cursed. "Then get your lazy hind end through the portal!"

Gastropé blinked as some sort of nightmare from the Abyss angrily stomped through the portal. He stepped back awkwardly, narrowly avoiding tripping on the long grass. This thing was huge! At first, it sort of looked like a cross between a wolf and a bear, a seriously ugly crossbreed. But it had wings! *What was this monster?*

Edwyrd noticed his fear and said, "Don't worry, Gastropé. This is Schwarzenfürze, Tal Gor's D'Warg. She won't hurt you." Edwyrd grinned at him.

"D'Warg, as in Demon Warg? Like as in a D'Orc warg?" Gastropé asked.

It was now Edwyrd's turn to blink in surprise. "Wow, I am impressed. Very few people remember anything about the D'Orcs or Mount Doom!" He was grinning from ear to ear and chuckling. "You continue to amaze me, Gastropé!"

"How…? What…?" Gastropé was having trouble thinking or speaking.

"Long story. We'll have plenty of time to go over it. Short part is, I screwed up on making plans for returning my guests home after the party, and that's why we needed your help!"

"Party?" Gastropé was not following this. Or was he? He was seriously terrified that he was following all of this way more than he wanted to.

Edwyrd nodded, even as another older, female orc in ornate clothing stepped through the portal. "Yeah, that's why my people were here shopping. They were picking up supplies for the party after the swearing-in ceremony!"

Another orc, this one male, stepped through the portal; he too was dressed ornately, like the other two orcs.

"Ceremony?" Gastropé somehow managed to spit out.

"Yeah. I just took over this place called Mount Doom." Edwyrd waved the large staff around. It appeared have a metal demon head at the top. "Came with a whole bunch of mighty warriors, D'Orcs. Anyway, we had a swearing-in ceremony for them to pledge their loyalty to me."

"Ohh-kay," was all Gastropé could manage before he felt the ground suddenly attack him.

~

Jenn was waiting in line to fill a bucket of water from the wargtown well when an orc behind her bellowed out, "Hilda! You have returned! It is my turn to buy you a drink!" Her first thought was that it was odd to hear an orc speak perfect trade tongue. All the orcs she had spoken to sounded very brutish and barbaric, so it was strange to hear one speak without an accent. The second thing was the name "Hilda," particularly in the context of drinking.

The next voice left Jenn blinking furiously.

"Toothsetter!" Hilda—Trisfelt's Hilda—said. "Good to see you again! I have an errand to run yet, but I will be back a bit later and we can drink!"

Jenn turned to see Hilda, the same Hilda from Freehold, standing not ten feet away from her. She was carrying a picnic basket and was with a group of humans. Or humans and a relatively good-looking, skinny orc. On third thought, humans, skinny orc and a metal something.

"Hilda? What are you doing here?" Jenn asked, startled.

Hilda glanced at her, and then glanced again. "Jenn? What are you doing here?" Hilda was clearly as startled to see her as Jenn was to see Hilda.

The metal creature with Hilda was behaving very strangely. "I can sense him. There is a portal!" Suddenly the metal man-thing took off running extremely fast towards the north.

"What the...?" Jenn asked, looking after the charging metal creature. Hilda and the rest of her party were also watching in shock as the metal creature ran off to the north.

~

Edwyrd helped Gastropé get back to his feet. Gastropé looked around to realize there were now four oddly dressed orcs in the copse along with Damien, Vaselle, Antefalken and the D'Warg.

Gastropé shook his head. "I am not sure if I heard what I thought I heard," he mumbled.

Edwyrd chuckled. "What did you think you heard?"

"I swear you said that you just took over Mount Doom, the seat of the demon Orcus," Gastropé said.

Edwyrd made an odd expression with his mouth and bobbed his head up and down a few times.

"Yes, that is what he said," one of the orcs agreed. "Lord Tommus is the long-prophesied reincarnation of the Great Orcus!"

"You see, he carries the Rod of Tommus, formerly called the Wand of Orcus," one of the female orcs said.

It was very odd how these orcs spoke perfect trade, was about all Gastropé could think.

As Gastropé tried to collect his wits for his next question, an odd noise came from the south and east and an even odder voice shouted, "Do not close that portal!"

A metal man or something—a golem?—ran into the copse, heading straight for the portal. The odd metal creature suddenly stopped and stared at Edwyrd. Edwyrd, for once, appeared to be in as much surprise as Gastropé.

"If you have harmed so much as a hair, you will pay for all eternity, demon!" the metal creature announced sternly in a very loud voice before it turned and jumped through the still-open portal into the Abyss.

"What the hell was that?" the large male orc asked.

"I have no idea." Edwyrd shook his head and stared worriedly through the portal.

Chapter 114

Talarius took a drink of water from his Flask of Holy Refreshment, washing down his cold roast ox sandwich. They really could use some condiments, or at least some cheese, the knight reflected. He, Boggy and Reggie were in the main dining hall, breaking their fast. Talarius had his helm sitting on the table beside him as he savored this simple return to old habits.

It was odd how much a few pints of beer and several glasses of wine after one's first meal in a week could relax one. He had slept better last night than he had in a long time. The dining room was still being cooled, so it would have only been uncomfortably warm if he had not been in his armor. As it was, he was fine with his helmet off, as he'd been last night during the party.

Across the table, the incubus was shoveling leftovers into his maw at a prodigious rate. Talarius frowned. "For someone who does not need to eat, you seem to be starving," Talarius remarked.

Reggie paused, looking up to grin at the knight. "Phaestus and I seriously over-cookied last night. I have a badass case of the munchies!"

"I see," Talarius said, not really understanding the demon at all. He was beginning to suspect that demons could not help themselves in regards to speaking in riddles and convoluted language. Very similar to Oorstemothians in that respect.

"I'm surprised your new best mate isn't down here noshing as well," Boggy observed.

"He had to go roust Völund. The smith got pretty drunk last night," Reggie said. "They should be here shortly."

A loud clanging and clattering noise came from one of the entry corridors to their right. Suddenly a heavily armored individual came charging into the dining hall. "Talarius!" The armored man—no, a man made out of metal—shouted. Talarius sprang up, grabbing for his helm in shock, preparing for the metal creature's attack.

"At last! I have found you!" the metal man shouted.

Talarius blinked. This creature was quite odd. As it came to a halt, he realized it was some form of exquisitely crafted metal golem with very sharp edges.

"Who are you?" Talarius asked in surprise. Boggy and Reggie were staring at it as well.

The metal golem looked puzzled, almost hurt. "It is I, Ruiden!"

It was Talarius's turn to blink. "Ruiden? My sword?"

"Of course! Don't you recognize me?" The golem held out a hand, palm forward.

Talarius gingerly reached out with his ungloved hand and put his palm on the golem's hand. The knight blinked and shook his head, feeling the familiar link he'd had to Ruiden ever since he had first found the sword. He sat, or rather almost fell, back onto the bench in shock.

"But how…? What? What happened to you?" Talarius gestured up and down. This was impossible. How could his sword be running around as a metal golem?

The sword seemed to grin. "I got fed up with the Rod and their failure to relocate you, so I changed my form so that I could find you myself!"

"You changed your form?" Talarius shook his head. "I didn't know you could do that."

Ruiden shrugged. "Well, I didn't know I could either, until I tried."

"Abyssal dung bats, my head hurts!" someone harrumphed from a different corridor. It took Talarius a moment to realize it was Völund, the smith. He turned his head to see the two smiths come around a corner into an entrance way to the dining hall.

"That's why you should have done cookies rather than booze!" Phaestus said, leading the smith into the dining hall. "We'll put some food in your stomach and you'll feel better."

The two walked up to the table. As they approached, Phaestus blinked and stared at Ruiden, his eyes wandering over the sword's form in obvious appreciation. Völund simply nodded at those gathered. "Boggy, incubus, knight, Ruiden," the smith said, leaning against their table.

"Father?" Ruiden asked in shock.

"Ruiden?" Phaestus asked Völund, looking at him.

" 'Father'?" Talarius asked, looking back and forth between his sword and the smith.

"What are you doing here, father?" the sword asked, appearing to be in shock. If that was possible for a sword.

"Trying to recover from a hangover," Völund said, grabbing a small loaf of bread. He licked his lips with his tongue. "We got any water?"

Talarius handed the smith his flask; the smith nodded thanks and took a huge swig of icy-cold water. His eyes widened in surprise at the flask. "Hmm, I need to get me one of these!"

"Father?" Ruiden prompted again.

"Why do you keep calling him 'father'?" Talarius asked Ruiden.

The sword looked at him, still seemingly shocked. "Because he forged me!"

Talarius blinked and shook his head in surprise; he turned to the smith. "You forged Ruiden?"

Völund shrugged and said, "Yep." He tore off a big chunk of bread with his teeth.

"But what are you doing here in the Abyss?" Ruiden asked, clearly disturbed to find his maker hanging out in the Abyss.

Völund looked at the sword in puzzlement. "I live here."

"You live here? Since when?" Ruiden asked.

"Since before I made you," Völund said. He took another long drink from the flask before holding it a bit away from his face to stare at it. "Really, I want to get one of these."

"Before I was forged? But... but..." Ruiden was at a loss for what to say next.

"Are you saying you forged Ruiden in the Abyss?" Talarius asked the smith.

Völund shrugged. "Yep, in my smithy downstairs."

"But... I was forged to kill demons!" Ruiden protested.

Völund tilted his head from side to side slightly. "Yep."

"So why would you forge a demon-slaying sword in the Abyss?" Ruiden asked loudly, clearly disturbed.

Völund shrugged. "Where better? Sort of gets to the heart of the matter; fight fire with fire, all that sort of drivel."

"But you live surrounded by demons!" Ruiden gestured to Boggy and Reggie.

Völund grimaced. "No, technically I live surrounded by D'Orcs. Present company and a few others excepted." He gestured to Boggy and Reggie.

"Smith," Talarius interrupted. "I think Ruiden's point is this: D'Orcs or demons, why would you forge a demon-slaying sword?"

"Well, he can slay other things too. I didn't actually start out planning to make a demon-slaying sword; it just sort of worked out that way." The smith shrugged again and grabbed a cold spare rib to chew on.

"What do you mean 'worked out that way'?" Ruiden asked.

Talarius was a bit worried; he had never seen his sword so distressed. If he did not know better, he would think it was having some sort of existential crisis.

"Well, I was really pissed with Lilith and her minions at the time. They'd just permanently killed a lot of close friends of mine, not to mention my host and benefactor." Völund took another drink of water before continuing. "So I guess I sort of impressed my anger and fury towards her and the Courts into you as I made you." The smith shrugged. "I guess in some ways I created you as an instrument of my vengeance."

Phaestus nodded. "That makes a lot of sense."

"But—" Ruiden began, but was interrupted.

Whirrrr-RRAAAARRRRR-RAAAAHHHHRRRRR came the gut-wrenching wail of the dreaded Klaxon of Doom. Talarius, Boggy and Reggie jumped up from the table, nearly upsetting it.

"What in the Abyss is that?" Talarius shouted over the roar.

Völund sighed and handed the knight his flask back. "Trouble."

Tom was still grinning at Gastropé's rather typical shocked reaction at their first attempts to explain what was going on when a horrible, gut-wrenching wailing came from the portal. Everyone stared into the hole as the painful noise droned on.

"Is someone torturing a Ban Sidhe in there?" Ragala-nargoloth asked, covering her ears.

Tom followed his link to the command center. Vargg Agnoth was on duty. Suddenly, unconsciously on Tom's part, the gateway shifted to the command center. Those standing in Astlan were suddenly peering through the portal directly into the command center.

"What is going on?" Tom shouted through the portal.

"Radar has detected a large incoming force from Doom's Redoubt!" Vargg yelled back. "A very large force, easily twice as big as what we believed they had available."

Tom clenched his teeth. He had been worrying about this exact situation—everyone hung over and passed out—and now the enemy was attacking! "Crap!" He looked to his shamans and wizards. "I have to return. You guys stay here; it will be far safer here."

"Commander!" shouted some D'Orc that Tom did not immediately recognize. Darth Venstradt, he believed. "We are detecting signs of a Chaos Maelstrom!"

Vargg Agnoth cursed loudly, using some word that Tom did not recognize.

"What's a Chaos Maelstrom?" Tom asked.

Vargg turned to stare at Tom, his face a very unusual pale shade of green. If Tom did not know that D'Orcs were incapable of fear, he would have sworn the commander was giving him a look of terror. "It means Lilith is sending in the Knights of Chaos!"

"Unholy flatulent monkeys of despair!" Antefalken moaned and rolled his head.

"What in the Abyss are Knights of Chaos?" Tom asked.

"They are enforcers, mercenaries, freelance knights. They are not demons, but something else, something worse, from the other end of the multiverse," Antefalken said. "In legends they were occasionally employed by the Court to deal with rogue archdemons or rogue princes." He shuddered. "I thought they were mere legend; they haven't been deployed since the Great Demon Wars."

"So, what? The extra troops are all Knights of Chaos?" Tom asked.

Vargg Agnoth made a very odd sound on the other side of the gateway.

Antefalken's eyes popped open wide. "Concordenax forbid!" he exclaimed, his voice shaking slightly. "One Knight of Chaos is nearly a match for an archdemon!"

"Ouch! How many do we think she'll send?" Tom asked.

"It takes at least thirteen to form a Maelstrom," Vargg said. "And this looks like a big one."

"Shit," Tom sighed, feeling his stomach twist into knots.

~

Völund reached into a vest pocket and pulled out a small hand mirror. He tapped on it a couple of times, shouting "Command Center!" After a few seconds, someone apparently answered, as Völund shouted "What's with the damn racket?" into the thing. He put the mirror to his ear to hear better, and then pulled it back to look in. "Then we're going to need the heavy artillery. Phaestus and I will get on it!" he shouted and then put the mirror back in his pocket.

"What is it?" Phaestus yelled.

"Two thousand plus demons from Doom's Redoubt and a Chaos Maelstrom," Völund yelled back.

"A Chaos Maelstrom?" Phaestus shouted over the klaxons, looking at Völund in shock.

"A Chaos Maelstrom?" Talarius and Ruiden said in unison, looking at each other.

"Yes!" Talarius slammed his right fist into his left palm as the knight and his sword grinned like maniacs at each other.

"What's a Chaos Maelstrom?" Reggie asked.

"It's a dimensional rift, or disruption in reality that Knights of Chaos use to travel the planes," Phaestus yelled over the klaxons.

"Knights of Chaos?" Boggy and Reggie yelled, both looking puzzled.

"A very bad thing!" Völund yelled.

Talarius turned to smile broadly at Reggie and Boggy. "Knights of Chaos are absolutely the most supremely EVIL creatures in the multiverse!" The knight shouted excitedly, shaking his fist before suddenly getting quite sober and grimacing apologetically as he realized whom he was speaking to. "Sorry! No offense intended…" He gestured towards the two demons. "I mean you two *are* extremely evil but…"

Boggy nodded. "No offense taken. I'm okay with being only moderately evil."

Reggie nodded as well and said, "Yeah, we're good—er, okay."

Talarius nodded his thanks to the two demons for understanding that he had not intended to impugn their eviltude.

"This is the opportunity of a lifetime," Talarius said, looking to Ruiden. "We must prepare! Are you stuck like that or can you change back?"

"I can change back, I think. I hope," Ruiden said rather uncertainly; it was hard to hear the sword over the klaxons.

Phaestus jumped up and shouted to Völund, "You head to the tech armory to start getting the heavy artillery online. I'll join you shortly."

"Why not come now?" Völund asked.

"Knights of Chaos? Do you think my wife would ever forgive me if I did not tell her about this? Her reaction will be about the same as those two." He gestured towards Talarius and Ruiden, shaking his head ruefully.

~

Not knowing what else to do and not wanting to be in the way in the command center, Reggie and Boggy followed Phaestus.

"So you're going to contact your wife?" Reggie asked Phaestus over the roar of the klaxons.

Phaestus nodded and yelled back, "Yes. I'll also open a gateway for her."

"Where is she at?" Boggy yelled.

"She should be in Astlan."

"So that's where you live normally?" Reggie asked.

"Recently, yes. It's where she and I have spent much of the last few hundred years. We have homes and I have workshops in several different worlds," Phaestus replied at the top of his lungs. "Of course, now that Doom is back online, I will probably move a lot of my work back here. The resources are so much better here." Phaestus grinned at them. "And other than the occasional invading demon army and Chaos Maelstrom, it's much more secure." The smith chuckled. "Actually, in fifty-two thousand years there was only one breach; admittedly a very big one. However, both Völund and I were off plane at the time, or things might have gone differently." Phaestus frowned at the memory.

"That was a very big mistake. All four key players gone at the same time. One we shall not repeat," the smith said inaudibly under the wail of the klaxons.

"So where are we opening this gate?" Boggy yelled as he followed the limping man down the hallways.

"The portal room!" Phaestus shouted.

"Where is the portal room?" Reggie asked. He did not remember any portal room.

"It's off the Temple of Doom!" Phaestus shouted back.

Reggie's eyebrows furrowed. He did not remember any portal room near the temple. He had not been there very often, but he thought he would have noticed it.

The three of them entered the temple and Phaestus headed to the wall behind the altar. The smith quickly began poking wall stones in some predetermined manner, and suddenly a doorway appeared in the formerly blank wall.

"Whoa! That's new!" Reggie exclaimed.

Phaestus grinned at him. "No, it's actually very old, but you have to know it's here." He led the way into another room of roughly the same size. The temple had been lit by a few magical braziers, but this room was dark until Phaestus waved his hands along the side walls, lighting the braziers in the room.

The first thing Reggie noted was that the room had a lot of cobwebs. These were the first cobwebs he had seen in the Abyss. "Are there spiders here? I've not seen any spiders in the Abyss before," Reggie said.

"Nor have I!" Boggy shouted in puzzled agreement.

"They aren't spider webs. They are D'Rachnid webs!" Phaestus pointed toward a very heavily cobwebbed corner between two columns. Reggie blinked to see the reddish light from the braziers reflecting off a couple of pairs of large, red orbs.

"D'Rachnid webs?" Boggy asked nervously.

"Yeah. Think of them like the D'Orc equivalent of arachnids. Extremely poisonous bite to pretty much every living creature. Their saliva is acidic; hence all the pockmarks on the floor." He gestured to the large number of tiny pits in the floors.

"So are we in danger?" Reggie asked loudly.

"Nah!" Phaestus shook his head. "They know me, they trust me. They are also linked to Mount Doom, so anyone linked to Tommus is safe, unless he doesn't want them to be." He turned to grin at the two demons. "They are here as a welcoming committee in the highly unlikely event someone manages to open the World Gate from some other side. Or more specifically, someone we don't like opens the gate. I use them in most of my gate rooms."

Phaestus walked to the center of the room, where a large stone tray sat on a smaller stone pedestal. The stone tray had a large array of different-colored crystals packed into it. The crystals were tightly arranged in a twelve-by-twelve array. There appeared to be a good-sized handprint indention on a smaller stone pad at the base of the crystals.

The array looked somewhat familiar, but Reggie cold not place it. He looked up from the array to the back wall of the chamber and blinked. There was a large set of concentric metal rings standing up against the wall. The rings were freestanding and carved with various runic symbols at various intervals around each one. The rings were supported by a large stand that held them at their base. A ramp allowed one to walk up smoothly to the top of the innermost ring. A large indicator that seemed to be made of the same colored metal as the base capped the top of the two rings. The indicator had a pointer to a symbol on the inner ring, and an opening to display the rune selected on the outer ring.

The rings looked even more familiar to Reggie than the tray of crystals. But it was different enough that he couldn't quite place where he'd seen something like this. "So is that the World Gate?" he asked.

"It is," Phaestus replied over the klaxons. He was busy rearranging the crystals in the array. Apparently they were removable and could be turned to different orientations so that different facets of any one crystal could connect with different facets of other crystals. "I need to concentrate for a few minutes," the smith warned.

It took Phaestus a few minutes to get all the crystals arranged as he wished, but finally he seemed satisfied. He placed his right hand in the hand-shaped indentation below the tray. Suddenly there was a large screeching sound as metal that had not moved in nearly four thousand years began to move again.

Reggie looked up to see the two concentric rings rotating in opposite directions. The two rings spun around at different rates and then stopped briefly. As they stopped, a rune on the top ring lit within the indicator, as did the rune the indicator pointed to in the lower ring. After a brief pause, the rings started rotating again in the opposite directions, again at different rates of rotation so that they completed different numbers of rotations per ring before stopping on a new set of two runes.

Reggie suddenly realized it was like a double-combination lock. There was an inner combination lock that had to go around so many times to land on a specific rune, and the outer combination lock had to rotate the opposite way some other number of times to land on a different rune, the two runes matching up at the same time. Reggie shook his head trying to conceive of how many combinations there could be with all the various runes and different numbers of rations of the two rings.

Boggy and Reggie were mesmerized as the rotation continued for what seemed like several minutes. The screeching of the metal had been replaced by a deep humming, almost roaring noise and a very physical, bass-like throbbing of the air and stone of the room.

Finally, the rings came to a final set of runes and Phaestus removed his palm. Golden light flooded the chamber as a highly reflective pool of liquid gold appeared inside the two rings, perpendicular to the floor. Suddenly it was as if a giant stone had splashed into the center of the golden pool as the reflective liquid seemed to splash inward in a giant spike, with a surrounding counter ring splash coming back into the room. The roaring turned to a giant whistling and then died down into a sustained throbbing beneath the roar of the klaxons as the reflective pool became somewhat quiescent. Small waves rippled in the golden pool of light within the rings.

"A Star Gate?" Reggie had suddenly realized what the rings reminded him of.

"No, a World Gate; Star Gates are much simpler technology. Star Gates are basically very high-powered, long-distance Runic Gateways. A World Gate, on the other hand, can literally go anywhere in the multiverse where another World Gate is. Any distance in space, any distance in time, any distance in inter-planar space." Phaestus grinned at them. "It can also connect to a Star Gate, of course, but it has to provide the power to keep the link open. A simple Star Gate can't manage that; it can only act as a destination endpoint for a World Gate."

"Blimey! You built this?" Boggy asked, impressed.

Phaestus shrugged. "Völund and I built this one. However, the technology was a joint venture by us, the Altrusian engineers who built the boom tunnels, and a few others."

"Tizzy said that Sleestak wizards built the boom tunnels," Reggie said. Boggy nodded.

Phaestus snorted in humor. "That's what he calls them. And in some sense that is true. The Altrusians are the ancestors and descendants of the Sleestaks."

"How can they be both?" Boggy asked, puzzled.

"Altrusians are temporally cyclical," Phaestus said. "Meaning they exist at multiple points in time simultaneously in the past and the future. Not unlike the Mobius Mage, only on a much larger scale."

"The Mobius Mage?" Reggie asked.

"You don't want to know. He's a pain in the ass." Phaestus shook his head. "With luck, we will never need to discuss him—or rather, I guess, *it*—again." Phaestus gestured to the World Gate.

"We should go through. Remember, we are about to be under attack from Knights of Chaos. If my wife misses that, things will be much worse than they are now." Phaestus paused as he walked around the control stones. "At least for me."

Phaestus moved towards the World Gate and motioned for the others to follow him. He walked up the ramp to the golden pool and walked through. Boggy gave Reggie an uncertain look; Reggie shrugged and stepped through as well. Boggy followed.

The world seemed to stretch, twist, reform. Reggie thought he might throw up, but as suddenly as the disorientation began, it seemed to end and he found himself on a ramp leading down into a very crowded workshop. He looked behind him and as expected, there was another World Gate with a golden liquid center, through which Boggy walked.

The best thing about the new location was the quiet. They could no longer hear the wail of the klaxons. "Whew. That's a relief!" Boggy said, touching his ears. Phaestus grinned.

"So we are in Astlan?" Reggie asked.

Phaestus twisted his head around in a sort of wobbly motion. "Not exactly. We are on Uropia, the closer of the two moons of Astlan."

Reggie's eyes popped wide. "Your wife lives on the moon?"

"Well, one of the two moons. As the population grows, we will extend onto the other moon, Anuropia." Phaestus then made a shushing motion with his fingers.

"Your presence here is a bit awkward, so we need to stay low-key. We did not come through the proper channels, and if certain individuals find out I have a back door that bypasses our normal security, I'll have a lot of explaining to do. Sekhmekt, my wife, knows about the World Gate, but very few others do." Phaestus looked towards the door. "I am hoping she doesn't have any visitors here in our villa at the moment."

He gestured for them to follow him around a few tables and counters with a wide plethora of odd-looking instruments, tools and half-finished projects. He leaned up against the door to the workshop and seemed to concentrate on something, as if listening. He finally nodded.

"She's in the den, and only our household servants are here." He opened the door and gestured for them to follow him. The three left the workshop and proceeded down a large marble corridor with several good-sized columns all inlaid with gold, silver and other odd, gemstone-like tracings. Reggie felt like he was in a museum or a very fancy government building.

Phaestus led them to a doorway with a large red curtain, which he divided and said "Knock, Knock!" as he stuck his head through.

From the other side of the curtain a very deep, yet still feminine voice exclaimed, "pêTah! You are back from Mount Doom already?"

Phaestus moved into the room. "I am, my darling, and I have a couple of friends with me!"

"Well, show them in!" the woman's voice said.

"Reggie, Boggy?" Phaestus called. The two demons went into the room. Reggie shook his head in surprise; the room was not what he was expecting. It was luxuriously decorated with rugs, carpets, ferns and all manner of fine furniture. It resembled nothing so much as a very high-end Victorian hunting den or lounge. However, rather than having a lion's head on a wall, there was a twelve-foot-tall, extremely muscular yet voluptuous, human woman with the head of a lioness standing before a large chair.

"Boggy, Reggie, this is my wife, Sekhmekt," Phaestus announced proudly, gesturing at each of them as he introduced them.

Reggie heard Boggy murmur behind him, "Wow, lucky bloke—seriously married up!"

Sekhmekt raised one eyebrow in surprise at the sight of the two demons. "To what do we owe this honor?"

Phaestus grinned. "Mount Doom is under attack!" he said almost gleefully.

The lioness scrunched her eyebrows in puzzlement. "You are not one to shy from battle, particularly when it involves one of your creations."

"No," Phaestus said with a chuckle. "I had to come get you!"

"Why?" The lioness seemed puzzled.

"Lilith is sending two thousand plus demons..." Phaestus said, and Sekhmekt shrugged, not that concerned, "...and a Chaos Maelstrom!"

The lioness's brow relaxed as her eyes went wide. "A large one?"

Phaestus nodded. "A large one!"

"Oh, my beloved pêTah! You are the sweetest husband a woman could ever desire!" She clapped her hands. "I am so excited! How much time do I have? I need to summon some troops!"

"They are on radar, outside the DoomNet at the moment; we have a few hours at most. We also need to coordinate and plan with the others," Phaestus explained.

Sekhmekt shook her head in dismay and puzzlement. "What? Was this some sort of sneak attack?"

Phaestus nodded. "Yes, remember—huge party, Tizzy baked cookies, lots of x-glargh, half the fortress is still passed out."

Sekhmekt stroked her chin. "Well, one cannot fault Lilith's timing, then." She sighed. "Well, we'll just have to make do." She chuckled. "If nothing else, it means more for me!"

Sekhmekt turned to stare at the wall over a large mantled fireplace and shook her head sadly. "Unfortunately, Knights of Chaos vanish like demons after you slay them, albeit a bit more violently. I'd love to mount one of their heads above the fireplace!"

~

"I will zoom in a bit," Horken said, adjusting some dials on his terminal as they peered at the computer screen showing the radar images of the advancing army. "This mass here is what we believe to be the demon army from Doom's Redoubt, plus their reinforcements."

Tom nodded at Horken's explanation.

Vargg Agnoth spoke up. "They have not had over one or two thousand demons there for several centuries. It appears that she sent in about the same number of demons as reinforcements."

"Is there any way to determine how strong they are?" Tom asked.

Arg-nargoloth, standing beside him, said, "Not until they are on the DoomNet. At that point, the main table"—he gestured to the 3D mapping table in the other room—"should be able to gauge them."

"How long did you say that was?" Tom asked. He had been told before, but the klaxon had been so loud that he'd had trouble hearing it. Once they had been sure all the commanders were awake, they had turned off the klaxons and let the commanders take care of rousting any still-glarghvost-passed-out D'Orcs.

"About half a period. Once on the DoomNet, they have about another half period until they reach an entrance," Vargg said. Tom quickly calculated that to be about two hours for each leg.

"From past experience, they will probably try for multiple entrances. We are sending reinforcements to the most likely entrances first," Darg-Krallnom said.

"The knights?" Tom asked.

"Let me pan over here," Horken said, spinning a trackball in front of him.

"See that dead zone?" asked Zog Darthelm, the commander in charge of the TCC, pointing to an unlit region that Horken had moved over. "We know from deep space experience that this sort of blackness typically indicates a Chaos Maelstrom. The maelstrom has very distinctive effect on most all tech scanning systems."

"You've encountered Knights of Chaos in space?" Tom asked.

"Not me, personally, but there have been many reports from starship shamans describing this effect. It's been well documented. Naturally, these were the shamans' last reports; so follow-up was always difficult."

"And we are sure it's not a glitch with the radar system? We just brought it up the other day," Tom asked.

"Glitches don't usually move," Horken observed.

"And the movement is tracking with the demon horde," Zog Darthelm added.

"Same speed?" Tom asked.

"Roughly," Horken said.

"Hello!" Phaestus called to them from the command center.

Tom looked towards the smith and was surprised to see a very large anthrolioness in very ornate plate armor standing behind him. Tom nodded to the others in the TCC as he moved to join Phaestus in the other room.

"Hello?" Tom asked, looking at the lioness, who was his own height and size.

"Tommus, this is my wife Sekhmekt!" Phaestus said.

Tom shook his head slightly in surprise. "I'm sorry, I hadn't realized you were married."

"Seems to surprise a lot of people," Phaestus said as Sekhmekt stuck out a hand for Tom to shake.

"Glad to meet you, Sekhmekt!" Tom said, shaking her hand.

The lioness's expression was hard to read, but she seemed quite happy. "Honor to be here. My husband tells me you have a Chaos Maelstrom heading your way?"

"We do. I take it you are familiar with them?" Tom asked.

The lioness nodded. "Indeed, they are worthy opponents in battle. Not very nice opponents, but worthy. I do not get that many opportunities to battle them. At least not in the last hundred thousand years."

Tom nodded, trying to keep a neutral expression at the idea that this woman was at least a hundred thousand years old. "Well, we would really appreciate your help," he told her.

"I only regret the short notice; I was only able to summon half a dozen of my most experienced warriors," Sekhmekt said.

"They are waiting in the dining hall at the moment," Phaestus said. "They are still adjusting their barding; we really scrambled."

"Barding?" Tom asked, puzzled.

Sekhmekt grinned, or so Tom thought. "They are sphinxes."

"Wow, I've never met a sphinx before," Tom said.

"They are truly the best guards in the multiverse," Sekhmekt said. "Nothing gets past them."

"And to be clear, they won't be asking any riddles today," Phaestus said. "They'll just be killing knights, and any of Lilith's demons that get in the way." He chuckled.

"Excuse me!" Talarius shouted from the doorway to the main corridor. He had needed to shout over all the various discussions going on in the command center, which was rather packed.

"Yes, Talarius?" Tom asked.

"Has anyone seen Völund?" The knight gestured behind him to the weird metal being that had dived into Tom's portal from Astlan. Tom shook his head. He had completely forgotten about that invader. "We are having difficulty getting Ruiden to shift back to his regular form," Talarius said.

Tom closed his eyes in a slow blink and looked back at the knight, trying to understand what the man was saying and why now, in the middle of preparing for battle. "I am not following you. Who is this Ruiden? I believe he threatened me earlier?"

"He's my sword; you remember, the one I chopped you to bits with? He turned himself into a golem to search for me; and now he has found me. So we are trying to get him back into sword form so we can go battle Knights of Chaos," Talarius said matter-of-factly.

"What is a knight of Tiernon doing here?" Sekhmekt demanded after turning around and seeing the knight. She made a motion to grasp the sword on her back.

Phaestus reached out and grabbed her sword arm. "Relax, he's Lord Tommus's hostage and is bound by the Oaths of Hostage."

"Hostage?" The lioness turned to look at Tom curiously. "Are you the demon that stole mana from Tiernon?"

Tom inhaled. "Yes, that would be me."

"Hah!" Sekhmekt clapped him on the shoulder. "Well met indeed! Bess has been quite preoccupied by you lately. She will be glad to know you are the Master of Mount Doom!" She shook her head. "So much makes sense now."

"Well… great!" Tom really had no idea what to say; he turned his attention back to Talarius.

"So why do you need Völund?" Tom asked wearily.

"As I said—to help get Ruiden back into sword form!" Talarius said, sounding exasperated.

"How can he help?" Tom asked patiently.

"He's my father!" the sword said from behind Talarius.

Tom restrained himself from shaking his head in surprise; he would end up getting dizzy if he kept doing that. "Your father?"

"Völund forged Ruiden," Phaestus explained.

"Seriously?" Tom looked to Phaestus.

"Yep, apparently to help vent his anger at Orcus's death." Phaestus shrugged. "Which is why Ruiden likes to slay demons so much."

"That makes sense," Sekhmekt nodded thoughtfully. "Vengeance is usually the best way to get a good forging. I mean, it's no real substitute for a good, final forge quenching in the blood of newborns, but it's a good third or fourth."

Phaestus sighed, shaking his head, looking up at his wife. "How many times have I told you those are just old wives' tales! There is no basis for quenching a blade in newborn blood. Seriously, the metal doesn't care if the blood is from a newborn or an old man."

"Are you calling me an old wife?" Sekhmekt stared down at her husband.

"You know that joke is getting old." Phaestus stared back at her, undeterred.

"Okay." Tom looked at Talarius. "Zog Darthelm in the TCC will know where Völund is. He's working on bringing up some heavy artillery."

Phaestus gestured to Talarius and Ruiden. "Come with me, I need to find him to determine if we are going to get the high-tech stuff ready in time." The smith headed towards the TCC.

Sekhmekt nodded to the mapping table. "Great table! Let's talk strategy and tactics! War is something of a specialty of mine."

~

Tom's body sat on his throne in the center of the volcano, his right arm gripping the Rod of Tommus in its throne holder. His mind, however, was running through the Doomplex and the DoomNet. Lilith's forces would be shortly crossing the border to the land connected to the DoomNet.

The D'Orcs were quickly armoring and organizing into their ranks and companies. At first the D'Orcs had grumbled, annoyed to be awoken from their glarghvost-induced slumber, but when they'd learned of the size of the demon army and the fact that a Chaos Maelstrom was on its way, they'd perked up with excitement. Arg-nargoloth had told Tom that for D'Orcs, the best cure for glarghvost was blood. Mayhem, the act of hacking an opponent limb from limb, was the perfect activity to clear away the cobwebs of the mind.

Fer-Rog and Rupert were complete sleepyheads this morning; Zelda had sent them along with Reggie to bard the D'Wargs. It would be a new experience for them, but a great learning exercise. Antefalken had returned with him, having borrowed Damien's scrying ball to record the battle. There was no way the bard was going to miss out on such an epic battle.

Tom wished he felt as confident as Antefalken did. Actually, Antefalken had not been so enthusiastic at first, but after meeting Sekhmekt, he had really perked up. Clearly, the bard was aware of Sekhmekt's prowess in battle; he presumed she must be famous or something. She was impressive, Tom had to admit, as were her sphinxes.

She had brought six very large sphinxes with her. The sphinxes were more than proportional to Sekhmekt and himself and were all of the winged variety. With their golden plate and great helms, they were a truly magnificent presence.

All of his commanders were preparing, distributing the battle plans they had devised over the map table. While they did this, it was Tom's task to prepare the battlefield. After coordinating with Völund, Phaestus had returned and given him some instructions on optimizing the battlefield.

According to Phaestus, since they had begun building the fortress over fifty thousand years ago, the volcano had never actually had a full Plinian eruption from the main cone, where his throne was. This was principally because that would be a rather destructive event for the fortress. Thus, to contain excess heat buildup, there were multiple smaller vents along the sides of the volcano and across the DoomNet. These consisted of both smaller parasitic cones and fumaroles. The goal for right now would be to bring the volcano up to full power and begin filling the channels to these vents.

In particular, they needed to channel the volcanic pressure to the vents on the side of the mountain near the invaders and release pyroclastic flows. These flows, Phaestus explained, were fluidized mixtures of solid and semi-solid fragments of rock, along with extremely hot expanding gases that would flow down the flanks of the volcano. They would move very much like a snow avalanche down the mountain, but at hurricane-force speed. According to Phaestus, the heated gases and fluidized earth would move at speeds of thirty leagues per hour or more, burying everything in their path.

Tom figured this should slow the invaders down; at least, once they were far enough in that they couldn't quickly retreat off the DoomNet. Once the elemental forces were channeled onto the plane and through the volcano, they became a force of nature and would not stop at the border of the DoomNet, but he did not want to leave anything to chance.

In order to accomplish this, he needed to open up the portals to Earth, Air and Fire located in the volcano's magma chamber, located beyond their current level. The magma chamber below him right now was essentially a giant, elemental soup pot where he needed to boil these three elements and let them overflow the sides of the mountain and down onto the invaders.

As he delved into the magma chambers with his mind, it rapidly became clear that this would be a tricky exercise that would require a fair amount of skill on his part. He really did not want this mess coming up and flooding his new house. So it was worth taking the time to get it right.

In the meantime, since he was opening the Fire and Air portals, he split their output and channeled them up the main cone and into the Water and Air portals above Doom, which he was also cranking open. The pyroclastic flows might move like a hurricane, but he wanted to dump a traditional hurricane on the invaders as well. Given that the DoomNet contained an electrical network, if he could manage to lower the electric potential on the ground, he should be able to pull storm lightning to the ground. They would not be directed attacks, but they would be disheartening and annoying.

If Lilith wanted to attack him with no actual provocation with the terror of a Chaos Maelstrom, then he would unleash the full power of Doom upon her forces. In some ways, it was a bit odd that someone as old and as experienced as Lilith would be foolish enough to attack a volcano.

~

"I don't know how Bess and her people stand this place," Sekhmekt complained to her husband as he worked underneath a large cannon in one of the machine shops. She was stretching and doing yoga to be ready for battle.

"You get used to it," Phaestus said from under the large metal gun housing. "You know I like volcanos."

Sekhmekt shook her head. "Yes, I know, I get it. Vulcan, volcano, you've been making the same joke for thousands of years now. However, I am not talking about Mount Doom. I'm talking about the Abyss, about being cut off from the pools!"

Phaestus chuckled under the gun. "So you're feeling naked reduced to only the mana you can store on your person?"

Sekhmekt nodded. "This is about the only place in the multiverse where I can't touch my god pool or the pantheon pools. I don't see how you do it."

"You do realize that the vast majority of individuals in the multiverse don't have access to super-high-powered mana pools and anima jars? That the overwhelming majority of life in the multiverse has nothing more than their own reserves to work with?" Phaestus asked.

"Yes, but I am not one of the vast unwashed masses. I'm a goddess, for my sake!" Sekhmekt complained.

"Uh huh, and as such, naked as you might now be, you still have more reserves than the other 99.99 percent of life in the multiverse," Phaestus pointed out.

"I don't seem to recall too many objections on your part when we all signed up for this latest venture to try and get us back on our feet, to boost ourselves back up from the 0.01 percent to the 0.001 percent of life in the multiverse!" Sekhmekt retorted.

"That's because sometimes agreeing with all of you is easier than arguing with you!" Phaestus groused. "Now, I need to concentrate on this cannon. In case you have not noticed, I am literally 'under the gun' to get this done."

"Very well, ptooey on you, pêTah!" She gave him a friendly snarl that he could not see under the gun.

Chapter 115

"This weather really sucks!" Lesteroth yelled to his nearest companion, Bellyachus.

"You think?" Bellyachus yelled back. "I'm kind of glad to have weather for a change. It's been a very long time since I've had any."

"Yes, but it's getting very hard to fly with these winds! They keep getting worse," Lesteroth complained.

"You in a hurry to get chopped to pieces?" Bellyachus yelled back.

"No, but I'm not sure about working my ass off to fly into battle as cannon fodder for the Knights of Chaos!" Lesteroth complained.

"Better that than relaxing your way to Lilith's dungeon!" Bellyachus shouted.

Lesteroth cursed, using an extremely unprintable epithet. "Now it's also getting hard to see through this rain! It has really picked up in the last several deminutes," Lesteroth complained.

"Why are you doing all the complaining? I'm the one called Bellyachus —I should be doing the belly aching!" Bellyachus said.

"You weren't doing your job!" Lesteroth grinned over to his buddy.

CRACK!

A bolt of lightning came down just to their left about a hundred feet away.

"Unholy bat dung!" Bellyachus screamed. "That was fragging close! Are we under attack?"

"No idea!" Lesteroth yelled back.

They flew on for a bit as the winds continued to grow stronger.

Finally, Bellyachus spoke up again. "You know how soldiers going into battle are always saying 'Today is a good day to die?' or something like that?" Bellyachus shouted.

"Yes," Lesteroth returned. "My favorite is 'Tonight we dine in hell!' " They both laughed at that one.

"We've had a lot of meals down here!" Bellyachus yelled back.

"We have!" Lesteroth shouted back.

"Well, so, I know I'm supposed to say stuff like that, and yeah, I'm like forty-two hundred plus years old, but today is *not* a good day to die!" Bellyachus shouted.

"Don't worry!" Lesteroth said, grinning. "You'll get over it!"

"Ours is but to do or die!" the two shouted together while laughing ruefully.

"Radar shows that the army has slowed and appears to be on the ground," Horken reported from the TCC. "I would have to guess this is due to the wind speed. We are measuring sustained wind speeds of nearly 30 leagues per hour."

Tom, standing at the 3D map board in the Command Center, replied, "Excellent! Those are hurricane-class winds, and I haven't even started venting the volcano!"

"Affirmative," Horken agreed. "We have them on the ground. We are also recording significant lightning strikes in the area. No direct hits so far, but there are plenty of close calls. At least for the demons. Really hard to see through the Maelstrom."

"So, they continue on foot," Arg-nargoloth stated. Since they were now on the rune network of the complex, the board could map their progress. "The Maelstrom has slowed as well; however, I am not sure if that's due to the weather or simply keeping pace with the grounded demons."

"Either way, for the demons, that's somewhat impressive," Darg-Krallnom said.

"Or stupid." Vargg Agnoth chuckled.

"I would go with desperate," Antefalken said.

Tom looked at him. "What do you mean, 'desperate'?"

"I mean Lilith." Antefalken shook his head. "Given the relatively short notice, the logistics of getting here, and most important, the very serious risk of using Knights of Chaos, I suspect she is feeling a bit desperate."

Arg-nargoloth nodded in agreement. "She has never used Knights of Chaos against us here; not since the defeat, and never before."

"We think she used them in Etterdam against Orcus. That is the most likely explanation for all the permanent casualties we had," Vargg said. Tom looked at him curiously.

Vargg shrugged. "Knights of Chaos can kill demons permanently if they get a good strike in. At least against lesser demons."

"So, as planned, we keep the D'Orcs focused on the demon army. Tommus, myself, Talarius, the sphinxes and Morok's regiment will focus on the Knights of Chaos," Sekhmekt said.

"Targeting them inside the Maelstrom will be difficult," Zog Dethelm said.

Sekhmekt grimaced. "We will need to work to separate the knights, break up the Maelstrom."

Zog nodded. "I think that is critical. The Maelstrom also acts as a shield to deflect attacks. As best as we can measure, it acts as some sort of dimensionally phased shield."

"So back to Lilith," Tom said, changing the topic. "You said she's desperate?" He looked to Antefalken.

"She doesn't normally strike first. For some reason, she's not trying to negotiate with you or trying to trick you. She is coming at you with as much as she can muster on short notice. This isn't her style."

"If she doesn't take Lord Tommus now, she may have to wait another twenty thousand plus years," Darg-Krallnom suddenly spoke up. Antefalken looked at him curiously. "After a few failed attempts early on once she discovered Doom, she never attacked the fortress again. She realized quickly that when fully powered and with someone who knows how to use the wand—sorry, rod—Mount Doom is essentially impenetrable by a force of any size."

"That is why she waited until almost all of our forces were in Etterdam. Even so, we still do not completely understand how she managed all of what she did. Even with Sentir Fallon, it had to have required a lot of luck," Arg-nargoloth said.

"So she needs to take out Mount Doom before Lord Tommus can fully control it," Sekhmekt commented. "It makes sense, but it is risky; if she is once again working with those treacherous Etonians, they could be pushing her."

Tom said nothing, thinking about what was being said. He suddenly remembered something Antefalken said. "What did you mean about the serious risks of using Knights of Chaos?"

Sekhmekt snorted. "You are right, bard!" She shook her head. "I really hadn't thought on that."

Antefalken nodded. "Knights of Chaos are agents of change, insurrection, anarchy and destabilization. Typically one would unleash them to overthrow the forces of law and order, to destabilize a situation."

"Using them to preserve the status quo is actually a very perverse use for them," Sekhmekt agreed.

"Hmm. Therefore, if Lilith sees me as a threat to her and the current status quo that she established after Etterdam, then technically, I am the source of change. The knights should be on my side!" Tom exclaimed.

"One would think; but they are mercurial by definition. It depends perhaps on a larger scale than what we can currently see. They may have other reasons to agree to help her that create more chaos elsewhere in the multiverse," Sekhmekt said.

"Or she could be bluffing. Playing a game to bring them into play. When she last used them she was trying to destroy the status quo. She was trying to establish a new paradigm without Lord Orcus," Darg-Krallnom said.

"So perhaps they don't know that the landscape has changed." Antefalken nodded his head in agreement.

Tom suddenly stared upward for a moment and then looked around the map table, grinning. "Good news! My kettle is finally at boiling point!" Tom raised his arms with the Rod of Tommus in his right hand. "Doom is at hand!"

Suddenly the ground shook with deafening thunder. The heat level in the room seemed to go up by an amount easily noticeable even to demons. Red spots suddenly appeared on the 3D map as the vents of Doom began erupting. Huge roiling clouds of greyish ash and smoke with highlights of both lightning and fiery magma could be seen sweeping down towards the invading army.

"Now, we bury them!" Tom shouted in glee.

"This is just too old school," Bellyachus complained to Lesteroth as they marched through the wind, rain and steam. Steam. Steam was the worst visibility problem on the ground. The ground was still hot enough that a fair amount of steam was being generated as the rain hit it. It made the landscape seem foggy. Or maybe it *was* fog; Lesteroth had no idea. He had not seen either since becoming a demon.

"This is hell!" Lesteroth yelled in reply.

"No, it's the Abyss!" Bellyachus laughed at the old joke.

"Seriously, does Darflow even know where we are? If we are on track? I can't see a thing!" Lesteroth yelled.

"Well, he is a greater demon; they get paid to know that sort of thing!" Bellyachus shouted back.

"Wait! He's getting paid?" Lesteroth returned with another of their favorite jokes.

"This is a miserable way to go into battle!" Talgorf yelled, coming up between them.

"The good thing is…" Lesteroth paused to make sure the other two could both hear him yelling. "They won't be trying to oppose us on open ground!"

"That had been my fear with the new management! I was afraid we'd never make the tunnels!" Talgorf yelled. "Once we are in the tunnels, though, it should be much more like the old days!"

"Yeah, no way they would come out to fight in this weather!" Bellyachus yelled back. His voice suddenly sounded quite loud as the blowing wind died very quickly. The rain intensity also let up considerably. It was still very windy, and it was still raining, which was simply unnatural in the Abyss.

"What happened?" Lesteroth asked and then the world lurched.

"What the Abyss?" Bellyachus exclaimed as another rumble occurred, shaking them where they stood.

"An Abyssquake?" Talgorf asked. "I've never heard of such a thing!"

Suddenly their conversation was washed out by a large explosion, followed by a roar that didn't seem to end. Lesteroth was pointing forward and to their left, where a giant, greyish black plume of smoke and ash was skyrocketing upward. Bellyachus grabbed Lesteroth's arm and dragged him to the right, where another large plume was roaring upward as if in stereo. The ground began to shake even worse as the wind returned to a ferocious speed.

Bellyachus could see Lesteroth mouthing something like "What the hell?" even as he stared over the demon's head at the rapidly onrushing greyish black cloud thousands of feet high with streaks of red fire and flashes of lightning rushing towards them like a tidal wave.

Bellyachus's last thought before being engulfed was that it looked like a giant wall of doom. The irony was not lost on him.

~

"Whoa!" Zelda exclaimed, looking at the empty grey plain where the invading demons had just been buried by the eruption.

"Such mastery!" Tamarin exclaimed from her vantage point up near the ceiling, where she was floating cross-legged. She clapped her hands enthusiastically. The djinn had wandered up to the command center a short while ago and was trying to stay out from underfoot. However, the explosive use of para-elemental forces was something she obviously enjoyed.

"That is going to take them some time to dig out of!" Arg-nargoloth laughed and high-fived Darg-Krallnom.

"We need to get troops out there to chop them to pieces as they come out!" Vargg said.

"Give the order!" Tom told Vargg. "What about the knights?"

"There!" Sekhmekt pointed to the area where the knights had been, which was now also covered by the eruption avalanche. An eruption which continued to drop ash, dirt and magma on the ground, albeit at a slightly slower pace. As they watched on the map, a distortion appeared in the region where the knights had been. The blackish distortion seemed to be growing, like a bubble forming on the surface of a liquid.

"It looks like they are floating to the top," Arg-nargoloth said.

"Are you two ready?" Tom asked Sekhmekt and Talarius.

"Yes," Talarius said, patting the hilt of Ruiden, once more a sword and on his back.

"Yes. The sphinxes are in position at the exit," Sekhmekt said. "Grab my hands and I'll teleport us there."

Tom nodded. He looked at Vargg, Zelda and Zog and said, "You three have the conn." He turned to Darg-Krallnom and Arg-nargoloth. "As planned, you come with us and join your troops from there." The two D'Orc commanders nodded.

Talarius, Tom, Darg-Krallnom and Arg-nargoloth all joined hands with Sekhmekt, as did Antefalken, who had his scrying ball ready.

"To victory!" Sekhmekt shouted; the others, including all the D'Orcs in the command centers, repeated the cheer. The leaders vanished and flashes of light suddenly appeared on the map table, indicating their presence at the two exits from Mount Doom on the map.

~

Tom flew towards the Maelstrom with Talarius flying to his left and Sekhmekt to his right. The sphinxes fanned out in an array behind them. Behind the sphinxes came the twelfth regiment led by Morok Deathstealer, two hundred D'Orcs strong in heavy mech suits, and a wide assortment of fully charged high-tech weapons of various types.

In person the Maelstrom, which by now had almost finished emerging from the newest layer of ash and magma, appeared to be an amorphous blob of shiny blackness. One could see movement inside the blob, barely, but it was hard to decide how many Knights of Chaos were in there, and how much of the space consumed by the giant blob was space between the knights.

The blob was large enough to contain at least a few dozen knights and mounts around the size of Tom or Sekhmekt, assuming the knights actually were humanoid, which Tom was not sure of. He had just assumed they looked like knights.

"Getting through the Maelstrom could be tricky," Morok said dispassionately, coming up beside Tom.

"It's a very nasty gravitational force-field sort of thing," Sekhmekt said. "As I mentioned in the prep, we can try the portable gravity cannons on them first."

Their unit was now about a thousand feet from the giant Maelstrom blob. "The key point is that we need to break the Maelstrom and force the knights to emerge," Sekhmekt said.

Tom nodded. "As planned, let's start with our two portable gravity cannons and then, while those recharge, we will hit them with the BFG 40K's, and then riddle the thing with our blasters as the plasma from the BFGs play out over the Maelstrom."

Tom looked over at the four D'Orcs with the two gravity cannons. "Let me know if you can lock on the Maelstrom with your instruments." He looked at the BFG and blaster troops. "Same with you guys; I want to take down the visibility levels so they can't hit us with any ranged weaponry."

CRRAAACCKKKK!!!

Even as Tom spoke, a bolt of black lightning came arcing through the air, only to be deflected by Sekhmekt leaping forward and batting it away with a large, round shield that shone as bright as the noonday sun, causing Tom and the D'Orcs to shield their eyes. Where in the Abyss the disk had come from was a total mystery, but it was now on her left forearm. The black lightning bounced harmlessly off it into the ground.

CRRAAACCKKKK!!!

Sekhmekt leaped, spinning in the air to deflect another bolt.

CRRAAACCKKKK!!!

The lioness spun again and nearly somersaulted to intercept another black bolt.

CRRAAACCKKKK!!!

CRRAAACCKKKK!!!

CRRAAACCKKKK!!!

CRRAAACCKKKK!!!

Tom blinked at the dizzying speed with which the lioness leaped and spun through the air, catching and deflecting each bolt of inky blackness.

"Target acquired!" the gravity cannoneers yelled.

"Affirmative!" yelled the various rifle groups.

Tom raised the Rod of Tommus above his head and summoned the power of Doom. A shudder shook the ground.

CRRAAACCKKKK!!! The lioness leaped again.

ZZZZzzztttt!! Crash! Normal lightning came from the sky, crashing against the Maelstrom as Tom created a large negative electrical potential below it.

Suddenly a grey cloud of ash, soot, rain and mud came raining down as hurricane-force winds began to buffet the region once more. The D'Orcs engaged their suits' gravlocks to keep their position. Suddenly a thundering blackness came from in front of Tom as the first gravity cannon fired. A giant concussion rocked them as the gravity wave hit the Maelstrom as fast as the blackness that ate the very light around it appeared. *ZZZZzzztttt!! Crash! ZZZZzzztttt!! Crash!* Flashes of Tom's weather lightning lit the darkness. The light in the region came back to grey and then went black again as the second gravity cannon fired and instantly struck the Maelstrom.

ZZHHHHOHHSSSHTTTT—ZZZSSSSTTTTTHHHSSSSZZZ! A purplish-green ball of superheated charged gas shot from the first BFG 40K plasma rifle to strike the Maelstrom, spreading out in a fiery, sparkling burst of electricity and luminescent gas against the inky Maelstrom bubble.

ZZHsshhZZZSSHHOHHSSSHTTTT—
ZZZSSSSTTTTTHHHzzzooohhHHTchchSSSSZZZ! went the second plasma ball, this one orange, red and white as it struck the Maelstrom.

ZZZZzzztttt!! Crash! More of Tom's lightning bounced off the Maelstrom.

CRRAAACCKKKK!!! Came what Tom assumed was another black lightning bolt, followed by a brilliant flash of blinding light from Sekhmekt's shield as the bolt bounced into the ground.

CRRAAACCKKKK!!!   *ZZHHHHSSSHoohhhssZZTTTT—*
ZZZSSSSTTTTTHooohhHHssHHSSSSZZZ!

CRRAAACCKKKK!!! ZZZZzzztttt!! Crash!

KABOOM! KABOOM! KABOOM! The thunder of the blaster rifles shook Tom's eardrums. *ZZZZzzztttt!! Crash!*

Tom shook his head. It was hard to see with his eyes, but he could sense the Maelstrom's darkness on the DoomNet grid. Things were looking rather at a standstill. He reached with his mind towards the nearest magma flow and started pulling it through the ground towards the Maelstrom.

ZZZZzzztttt!! Crash! Came his automated lighting.

ZZHHHHOHHSSSHTTTT—ZZZSSSSTTTTTHHHSSSSZZZ!   Plasma rippled through the grayish darkness. *KABOOM! ZZHHHHOHHSSSHTTTT—ZZZSSSSTTTTTHHHSSSSZZZ! KABOOM! ZZZZzzztttt!! KABOOM!*

This was going to take several minutes. He sent a signal through his links to Morok and the D'Orcs around them to keep firing to keep the knights distracted. Blackness hit them all again as the first gravity cannon fired again. In the distant light of the plasma coruscating over the Maelstrom after the blackness cleared, there did seem to be some changes to the shape of the Maelstrom bubble. He was not sure if that was from damage or from the knights shifting around inside.

ZZZZzzztttt!! Crash!

CRRAAACCKKKK!!!

ZZHHHHOHHSSSHTTTT—ZZZSSSSTTTTTHHHSSSSZZZ!

Tom kept his concentration on channeling magma and superheated gas below the ground. He needed to burst open a giant pyroclastic gusher directly under the Maelstrom. Tom closed his eyes to increase the power and speed of the flow. He could feel the ground around them shaking as he forced the flow, pulling tremendous energy from the Fire portal as well as huge amounts of fluidic material from the Earth portal.

ZZZZzzztttt!! Crash!

ZZHHHHSSSHsshhhhssZZTTTT—ZZZSSSSTTTTTHHHssHHSSSSZZZ KABOOM!

KABOOM! CRRAAACCKKKK!!! KABOOM! Even with his eyes closed, he could   feel   the   flashing   light   of   Sekhmekt's   sun   shield. *ZZHHHHSSSHsshhhhssZZTTTT—ZZZSSSSTTTTTHHHssHHSSSSZZZ!*

Tom imagined he could feel mental sweat on his brow as he struggled to pull the elements together, along with gushers of air. He needed more mental hands than Tizzy had real hands! It was the high air pressure driving the fluid-like earth and magma through the ground. The superheated gas was dissolving the solid ground before it, tunneling towards the Maelstrom.

ZZZZzzztttt!! Crash! KABOOM! KABOOM! KABOOM!

There! "Aim higher!" Tom yelled at the top of his lungs as he finally released the pyroclastic flow beneath the Maelstrom. He was about to erupt a small volcano under the maelstrom. *WHOOOOMM!!!!!* The fluid earth shot thunderously skywards, taking the maelstrom blob with it.

Inky blackness and a large *thud* followed as the first gravity cannon's tracking system followed the maelstrom up and blasted it; almost simultaneously, the second gravity cannon fired at a slightly different angle. The blasters and BFGs followed suit.

Suddenly, giant armored horses and eight-to-ten-foot-tall knights in purplish-black plate armor were falling through the sky and smashing against the ground! They'd broken the maelstrom!

Sekhmekt leapt to the front of their unit and drew a huge breath despite the rainy gray sludge permeating the atmosphere. "*RRROOOOOOOOOOOOAAAAAAAAAAAARRRRRRRRRRRRRRRR!!!!!!*"

Tom cringed and covered his ears at the loudest, most terrifying lion roar he could possibly have imagined. A roar that unleashed what could only be described as a truly hellish blast of incredibly superheated air. Even behind her, the backdraft made Tom feel like a human who had stuck his head in a furnace. How hot could her breath be if he, a demon, thought the heat was scorching? His face felt like it was blistering in the heat!

As the roar ended, Tom stared ahead. Light ash rather than sludge fell quickly to the ground, the rain in the air had completely vaporized and the muddy ground was now parched, actually burnt and cracked as far as Tom could see, which was several leagues.

There were numerous large horse skeletons now dotting the scorched plane, barding falling from the bleached bones. A plain drier than anything else he had ever seen in the Abyss —which was really saying something. The Knights of Chaos were mostly kneeling on the ground, crouched behind sandblasted shields.

"Wow! Now *that* is a true scorched-earth strategy!" Talarius whispered.

"Unholy terror," Morok agreed, breaking the stunned silence. Drops of rain finally started falling again; apparently, the roar had dried up the atmosphere quite effectively if the rain had taken this long to return.

Sekhmekt turned and grinned at them. She coughed a bit and licked her lips. "The Roar of the Lioness." She chuckled. "I haven't had an opportunity to do that since I created the deserts of Egypt!"

"Yeah, well, remind me not to ask you to blow out the birthday candles on my cake." Tom shook his head and grinned at the lioness.

The knights were climbing to their feet and getting into formation. "It appears to be time to get back to work," Morok said, pointing to the knights.

Talarius rotated to face the knights. "Charge!" he shouted, rocketing off towards the Knights of Chaos. The sphinxes leaped over the D'Orcs who had moved in front of them to attack the Maelstrom, and charged the knights.

"AAAAIIIIIGGHHHHAAAIIIIAAAHHH!!!" Sekhmekt let out a terrifying battle scream, although it was quite restrained compared to her roar, and charged the knights.

Tom laughed and slowed the production of new ash and sludge, thus turning the atmosphere completely back to rain. "Twelfth Regiment, fire at open targets at will!" he screamed. Morok laughed insanely beside him as the two charged the knights, who were scrambling to regain their footing on the dust, now returning to its former slippery mush state.

"Fafnir's beard!" Lesteroth shouted to Bellyachus beside him. Both demons stared down at their blistered and burnt skin. "What in the most infernal depths of this damnable place was that?"

The D'Orc he had been fighting had also paused; he, too, was looking severely burnt. "Dung crabs! In six thousand years in the Abyss, I've never felt anything that hot!" The D'Orc said.

He, Lesteroth, Bellyachus and another nearby D'Orc who had been in the process of ripping Bellyachus's right arm off for the third time, looked towards the source of the loud roar.

They had to use their demon sight to peer through the slowly resuming rain to where a giant anthrolioness with a shield as bright as Fierd, a knight of Tiernon, a tall pale D'Orc, and the Demon Lord Tommus, trailed by six giant sphinxes and a D'Orc regiment, were charging towards a formation of Knights of Chaos, who were now on foot.

"Now that is a sight you do not see every day!" Bellyachus exclaimed.

Lesteroth blinked a couple of times. "Is that Sekhmekt?" he asked in awe.

"Yes, the wife of Phaestus," The D'Orc said, ignoring the smaller invading enemy beside him for the moment.

"Wife of Hephaestus? Also known as pêTah?" Lesteroth asked.

"Yeah. Hephaestus is the smith's real name. Don't know about the pêTah part," the D'Orc said as the battle between the knights and Lord Tommus's forces began.

"Shit! She's the Nyjyr Ennead Goddess of War!" Lesteroth exclaimed.

"A goddess?" Bellyachus stared at Lesteroth; the two D'Orcs did the same.

"Yes, an honest-to-herself goddess!" Lesteroth screeched, raising his arms above his head. "Her husband, pêTah, is also known as Hephaestus, God of the Dwarves, and as Vulcan, God of Fire and the Forge."

"Shit," Bellyachus moaned.

The first D'Orc chuckled. "Phaestus is up in the turrets getting more heavy artillery ready to slaughter you guys!" the second D'Orc chuckled as well.

"More heavy artillery?" Bellyachus moaned.

"We are seriously on the wrong side!" Lesteroth whined.

"Why are you standing there?" a large D'Orc yelled, strolling over to them. He had Talgorf under one arm and was twisting the smaller demon's head around in circles, turning the poor fellow's neck into a corkscrew. Talgorf gave Lesteroth and Bellyachus a very pained stare.

The second D'Orc answered, "We're watching that battle while letting our burns regenerate. This little fellow says that Phaestus's wife, Sekhmekt, is a goddess!"

"A goddess?" The newest D'Orc said. "Hmm. I had heard rumors that Phaestus was some sort of dwarven deity, so I suppose that makes sense. Still doesn't explain how he got such a hot wife."

"You aren't kidding on the hot; did you get burnt by that giant blast of wind?" the first D'Orc asked the D'Orc twisting Talgorf's head around and around.

"Yeah, was that from her?" the D'Orc asked. "Pretty nasty; I haven't had blisters in at least five thousand years!" He shook his head in admiration.

The first D'Orc nodded and looked back at Lesteroth. "So are you ready for me to resume slaughtering you?"

"Yeah, feeling a bit better now. But I am going to put up a fight!" Lesteroth replied, once more belligerent.

"Yeah, you can try!" the D'Orc grinned, chuckling.

~

Talarius swung Ruiden in an upward sweeping motion to slice at the Knight of Chaos's shoulder joint. This thing's armor was seriously impenetrable, even by his own standards. The joints in the armor were extremely tight, making finding an opening very difficult. Add to that the knight's shield work, which was quite impressive, and Talarius was beginning to get a bit concerned. He wished he had his shield to parry the other creature's shield and keep it out of the way; unfortunately, that was still in Astlan.

Interestingly, the Knight's larger size was playing to Talarius's advantage; his smaller size combined with the enhancements provided by his Girdle of Grace was allowing him to dodge in and out. To be fair, it was being unencumbered with a shield that allowed him to do this.

Talarius dodged under the Knight's shield, parrying its blade with Ruiden as his left hand shot outward, grasping his Rod of Holy Lightning. He jammed it directly into the Knight's crotch and fired point-blank. *Krssshhhhhh!!!! ZZZZszzsssttt!!!* The holy lightning coruscated over the Knight's purplish-black armor. Talarius jumped back slightly while the Knight of Chaos was momentarily paralyzed by the electricity zapping through its armor.

Talarius brought Ruiden down, the sword assisting with an otherwise impossible move that rotated the blade into position so that he could now sweep upward into the joint between the metal codpiece and the knight's right leg. This scored a solid hit, wedging Ruiden temporarily in place. Talarius used the wedged sword to pull himself down and through the larger knight's legs, twisting Ruiden in the joint.

He switched out his Rod of Holy Lightning for one of his daggers in his left hand, and coming between the creature's legs, he jammed the dagger into the back of its right knee joint, wedging the dagger deeply into place. Talarius's left hand came up so he could hold Ruiden with both hands and pull the sword free of the

Knight's thigh joint. Using the sword to leverage his forward momentum up and into a spin, he pulled Ruiden free.

Spinning in midair and using his Sash of Heavenly Flight to increase his altitude, he brought Ruiden around in a two-handed slash at the back of the Knight's neck. He felt Ruiden shift in his hand as the sword more tightly aimed its blow to one of the small cracks in the Knight's neck armor.

He managed a solid hit on the neck before the Knight's head and neck twisted enough that Ruiden was forced out of the crack. Still in the air, Talarius tossed Ruiden upward and pulled his Rod of Smiting from its secure hidden location, activating it to expand the head and increase the length and weight, Talarius grasped it in both hands and brought it crashing down upon the Knight's head with a loud *CRUNCH!*

Talarius swapped the Rod of Smiting to his right hand, allowing it to shrink to a single-handed mace as Ruiden came back down, twisting in midair to land hilt-first in his left hand. He would parry the Knight of Chaos with his left hand and smite it with his right, at least for a bit. It was important to shake things up and keep one's opponent off guard. This was most likely going to be a very long fight!

~

CRUNCH! came the sound of one of the now even more gigantic and suddenly stone sphinxes as it stomped a Knight of Chaos under its forepaw. Tom shook his head as he swung the Rod of Tommus at the head of his Knight. Those sphinxes were something else!

As the sphinxes had charged into battle, they had begun to expand in size. At the start, their human heads on top of their lion's bodies had been eye level with himself and Sekhmekt; by the time they reached the Knights of Chaos they had almost tripled in size, and they kept on growing.

As if that hadn't been interesting enough, when they struck against a Knight of Chaos, they could either rake it with their huge claws—talons, really—or they could turn themselves or various body parts to stone. When they turned themselves to stone, their huge paws and legs would act like giant columns of marble coming down to crush whatever was underneath them; specifically, in this case, a Knight of Chaos.

Amazingly enough, the Knights being squashed by the now fifty-foot-tall sphinxes were managing to get back up, albeit in a very dazed and wobbly manner. Tom shook his head. If he had thought Talarius was tough to battle, he had been mistaken. The armor on the Knights of Chaos was nearly impenetrable; his claws raked uselessly along it and the joints were much more tightly sealed than Talarius's had been. He was not actually sure how the Knights were moving with such tight joints, yet they were. To be fair to Talarius, however, the Knights were neither as dexterous nor as agile as Talarius. Not by a long shot. They were, of course, far faster and more fluid than any human in such armor could be, but not as fluid as Talarius.

"Shit!" Tom yelled as the knight's blade sliced completely through his left arm. He flashed it back together again. The knight had stepped back a bit after slicing his arm, presumably to avoid being smashed by the Rod of Tommus. Tom used this to his advantage, leaping forward and planting the sharp spike of the Rod into the ground and using it as a pivot point for a flying dropkick with both hooves into the Knight of Chaos's chest. He winced as the sharp edge of the knight's shield sliced into his shins. That hurt!

Tom exhaled; these things were tough! By his count, there were twenty-three of them. He had one of them, Talarius had another; Sekhmekt was fighting two at once somehow and seemed to be winning. That woman was truly impressive; he was damn glad she was on his side.

Morok had been a bit of surprise; the D'Orc commander had waded in with only a short rod in one hand. Tom had been worried until he'd heard a somehow-familiar *sshhZZZZDDDTT* sound and a reddish black beam of light about five feet long had appeared from the end of the D'Orc's short rod. The D'Orc commander was using a light saber!

Tom had shaken his head. That thing was seriously impressive. It was the one sword they had that was capable of damaging the armor worn by the Knights of Chaos. It could not slice through it in one blow, at least not so far, but it was melting tracks in the armor. Tom had to chuckle. Morok Deathstealer was one of the odd-looking bald, pale D'Orcs from Visteroth; if the D'Orc had worn robes and not had wings, he would have looked very much like a Sith Lord. He certainly fought like one.

Each of the six sphinxes was tackling two knights apiece. The knights did not seem to be having any more luck damaging the sphinxes than he and Talarius were having damaging the Knights of Chaos. The remaining six Knights were being kept busy by the D'Orcs.

Unfortunately, the knights appeared to be too small and fast to be easily targeted by the gravity cannons, at least not without hitting their own people; however, in a few instances, they had been able to zap knights with the BFGs; and the blaster rifles seemed to work quite well. There were two D'Orcs with odder-looking rifles who were having luck vaporizing various knight body parts and limbs with some sort of Star Trek "phaser"-like effect; unfortunately, like demons, the knights were able to regrow those limbs. It would probably require a full body hit to take a knight down with the "phaser" rifles or whatever they were, and the knights were just too nimble for that so far.

~

Talarius was losing track of time. This was a battle of endurance in the truest sense. He spun, parrying the knight's blade with Ruiden and smashing his Rod of Smiting into the dagger still wedged in the back of the knight's knee; the knight stumbled. Talarius quickly swapped out the Rod of Smiting for the Rod of Holy Lightning and jabbed the lightning rod into the small crack in the armor plates near kidney level. He released the lightning, causing the knight to go rigid for a few moments.

Talarius was not sure how many charges he had left in the Rod of Holy Lightning. It was effective in stalling the knight long enough for him to fly up and try to wedge the small hole he had managed to open in the crack of the knight's neck armor a bit wider. He had no idea of the number of rounds he'd taken trying to accomplish this. He'd taken every opportunity, when flipping overhead and to the back of the knight, to try and wedge the tight crack wider. Talarius knew from long experience that either the neck or the underarm was the best place to try to pierce the plate mail for a killing strike. Normally the neck would be the harder spot of the two, but given the size difference and the fact that he could fly, the neck was easier than dealing with the knight's sword or shield.

He felt bad for flying when the Knight of Chaos was grounded, but he was seriously overmatched and as he had noted to Boggy and Reggie, Knights of Chaos were truly the most evil creatures known to the Rod. Although probably a small distinction when compared, say, to Lilith. Demons at least had some rules and laws. Knights of Chaos were agents of pure anarchy and annihilation. While demons did want to control the multiverse and make everyone in it miserable, Knights of Chaos simply wanted everyone and thing dead and miserable.

There! His final wedging may have given him a large enough point in which to plunge Ruiden on his next pass. It was going to require a rather tricky setup. He began a series of parries and stabs at the knight to distract the knight from his true intention. He wanted the knight to focus on other areas, as well as luring it into deeper attacks against himself.

In order to lure the Knight of Chaos, Talarius allowed himself to start slowing down, as if winded and worn. Which admittedly, he was, but nowhere near enough to actually show in his fighting. He needed to simulate weariness to trick the Knight of Chaos into being more aggressive, less defensive, to draw the knight out.

It took several more minutes but at last, Talarius saw his opportunity. The Knight of Chaos lunged for him, and Talarius fell back in disarray, as if falling over backwards. Instead, he did a backflip while storing his Rod; on coming up, he launched himself into the air using the sash even as he took Ruiden in both hands and came down feet first onto the knight's shoulder, Ruiden aimed down between his legs.

The sword twisted in his grip, positioning itself for maximum effect, and then down they came. It really was an awkward angle; if not for his extensive training with the sash and Ruiden's self-direction, it would have been impossible. He willed the sash to accelerate at maximum downward speed onto the Knight of Chaos.

Down! In! Ruiden entered the narrow slit, splitting it open wider and wider. *Success!* The sword plunged deeply into the knight's chest cavity, right where the heart should be.

VOOOOOOMMMMMMMMMM!!! There was a tremendous explosion.

Pain! Screaming pain! Horrendous pain!

Talarius was not sure whether that was him or Ruiden. When the sword had plunged into the knight, something, a vast gusher of raw energy, had come blasting out of it, reaching upward and scorching him and Ruiden. His armor was glowing as bright as Sekhmekt's shield as its protective rituals kicked into full gear. He could feel the mana pool on the chain around his neck heat up as mana was funneled to his armor.

This really, really hurts! Ruiden shouted in his head.

I know! But I take the pain as a sign of great gain! Talarius shouted back to Ruiden. Suddenly the pain stopped as the giant blast of energy that had shot up from the knight ended. Talarius fell to the ground, exhausted, his armor still glowing brightly in the aftermath of the Knight of Chaos exploding.

"Whoo hoo! Great job, Talarius!"

Talarius looked up to see Tom shouting at him and giving him a huge thumbs-up. The Knight of Chaos behind Tom suddenly cleaved the demon in two with his sword. Before the demon's two halves could fall, the Lord of Mount Doom flashed to flame and turned to continue battling his own Knight of Chaos.

VOOOOOOMMMMMMMMMM!!!!!

Talarius looked over to where the creepy-looking D'Orc commander with the sword of blood-red light had just exploded his own Knight of Chaos. This blast was coming from the center of the knight's chest. The knights all had giant emblems of eight pointed stars on their chests; the D'Orc had somehow pierced the knight's breastplate right in the center of the symbol. The D'Orc commander was grimacing and holding his sword before him, trying to deflect the insane blast of energy coming from the hole in the Knight of Chaos, even as Talarius often used Ruiden to split fire.

Talarius was impressed. Having felt the blast of a dying Knight of Chaos, he doubted he could have done a split shielding on that energy blast.

CRUNCH! FFFOOOOOMMSSHHHHHH!!!! came a sound from his right, and then a loud, catlike yowl of pain that actually hurt his eardrums. He looked to see one of the sphinxes lifting its paw off an exploded Knight of Chaos. The sphinx's paw was completely blackened and looked rather crumbly.

THUD! VOOOoommmmmpph!! Everything went pitch-black for a moment.

As the light came back, Talarius looked over to where that very weird sound had come from. Cheers rose from the D'Orc regiment. There was a crater where one of the knights had been; apparently, the rifle D'Orcs had managed to pin a knight down with crossfire so that the gravity cannon D'Orcs had managed to get a lock. The Knight of Chaos had tried to explode, but the gravity blast had swallowed the blast, or damped it. The air around the crater was glowing in a color similar to the knight explosions, but very subdued.

Talarius climbed back to his feet. He needed to pick a new knight, but hell and damnation, was he worn! He took a moment to drink some cooling water from his flask before trudging off after his next Knight of Chaos.

~

Tom shook his head. This was going to take forever. Fortunately, his allies were having some success. Talarius had gotten the first kill, and then Morok, then one of the sphinxes, and surprisingly, the D'Orcs had gotten one. That kill was a true testament to teamwork and coordination; he was so proud of his D'Orcs.

VOOOOOOMMMMMMMMM!!!!!

Tom glanced over to see a now headless Knight of Chaos with a giant jet of black energy shooting up into the sky where its head had been. Sekhmekt had killed one of her two knights. Tom grimaced; they were all here defending his new house, and everyone else was finishing off their knights faster than he was. He was just not having any luck. He had tried pretty much every trick he had used against Talarius, but the Knight of Chaos was much larger, almost his own size, and even more invulnerable. Bashing it with the Rod of Tommus seemed to work the best, but he was not making any dents in the armor.

He needed to fight smarter, not harder. The only problem was, he had no idea what "smarter" might be. He stared at the knight in front of him as they exchanged blows. Its armor had a glowing, reddish-black set of eight arrows radiating from a central point towards each of the eight cardinal directions. The symbol of Chaos in the world of the Eternal Champion.

For the knight's sake, he hoped Michael Moorcock or his publisher had not trademarked that symbol, or the knights would have Big Publishing coming after them. Of course, while that would be bad, it would not be as bad as putting a giant, stylized "S" inside a diamond on one's chest. That would have set Warner Bros. on a warpath, and Tom was pretty sure their lawyers were meaner than a Knight of Chaos.

Given all the crazy stuff that he had seen the last few months, there probably was a universe in which people flew through the air in blue and red tights. In which case, maybe the Multiversal Trademark ^{MTM} would reside with the real Man of Steel, if there was one.

Of course, even the term *multiverse* might be copyrighted by Michael Moorcock, who had invented it. Hmm, if he was going to set himself up as a "dark lord," he had probably better make sure he was not going to violate any copyright or trademark laws. Of course, the coop had already been flown on his new house. It was probably only a matter of days before he was swarmed by hobbits (©JRR Tolkien) with lawsuits.

"Ouch!" Tom shouted as he was split in two horizontally. He flashed himself whole. He needed to stop this internal monologue or he would lose this battle. That was a known problem for dark lords: they always had to have these infernally long monologues that ended up costing them the victory.

"Ouch!" *Crap!* He had done it again.

Think, Tom! These things were agents of chaos, whatever that was. Chaos was disorder, it was entropy, it was change, and it was energy. Certainly, the exploding knights released a lot of wild, crazy-looking black energy. The blasts had even looked chaotic; giant vents that spewed out of the hole in the knight in all directions. Very much like a regenerating Time Lord, only more evil-looking.

So if these things were chaos, raw entropy, then what would stop them? *Order.* That was the obvious answer. If you impose order on chaos, it loses its power. In physics, or at least in science fiction, unordered states had more entropy, more energy. They were hot. The opposite of a highly chaotic or entropic state was a perfectly ordered state. That only happened at absolute zero. At absolute zero, all the electrons were in their lowest energy state. All the uncertainty as to their position and momentum was resolved at that point. The entropy, the chaos was gone.

Tom paused to think about this. "Ouch!" he yelled as his leg was chopped off. He re-formed. If this logic held, then he had been going about this all wrong. Fire, like the volcano and its eruptions, increased temperature, increased entropy and energy. He needed to freeze the crap out of these things; then they would lose their energy, their entropy, their chaos. It would be hard to be an Agent of Chaos without any chaos! But how could he freeze these guys? He had fed the volcano by sucking Fire through the Fire portals, when what he really needed now was cold. How did he get cold?

CRUNCH! FFFOOOOOMMSSHHHHHH!!!! Another sphinx smooshed a knight.

Well, he could do cold fire. He had cold runes all over the place. How did they work? Tom had to think on what those runes were actually doing. It took a few moments because he was in the middle of battle, but he suddenly realized what had once been obvious to him: the cold runes were sucking Fire out of the rooms! They were returning Fire to the elemental plane of Fire. In fact, that was really what his cold fire was: it was anti-fire, negative fire.

That was the key: he needed to reverse the fire portals. Suck the heat out of these guys. Tom grinned. His Rod was directly connected to the Fire portal. He just needed to return Fire to its place of origin. He needed to concentrate. He shifted to his fire form, which he supposed was ironic. Turning into a living flame in order to figure out how to extinguish fire?

The knight took several swipes, rather ineffectively. Tom winced; the knight's sword had started glowing differently. It was figuring out how to hurt his fire form. Fair enough; Tom almost had it. He concentrated on the Rod of Tommus and the Fire portal. He became one with the Fire, one with the portal. Yes, that was it.

Tom rematerialized and grinned at his knight. He swung the Rod of Tommus at it, imagining the Rod as the hose of a vacuum cleaner. He fully channeled the Fire portal, willing it to return Fire from the knight back to the elemental plane of Fire.

Wham! The Rod struck like a mace once more, but with far more impact. Ice crackled across the knight's armor. Tom grabbed the Rod of Tommus like a baseball bat, willing it to suck as much Fire as it possibly could, and struck again. *Wham! Wham! Wham! Wham!* He completely ignored the knight's strikes against him. He let himself be hit, he took the damage. He wanted only to concentrate on sucking all the energy from the knight.

With each blow, he imagined the electrons orbiting the knight's atoms relaxing, going to a lower, colder energy state. *Wham! Wham!* The knight's armor was turning a dull gray all over. No more purple blackness. It was taking him a while to get the hang of this reverse Fire. It was different from cold fire, but not that different, if he really delved into the mechanics of each.

Wham! Wham! CRRRAAAAAACCCCKKKKKKKK!!!!!

The knight suddenly shattered like an ice sculpture. No giant gusher of energy, no explosion—it just shattered and then vanished. "BWAH HAH!" Tom shouted at the top of his lungs. He plunged the bottom tip of the Rod of Tommus into the ground and reached to the magma tunnels, to the DoomNet. While the others continued to battle the knights, Tom focused on pulling flame through the DoomNet to the Fire portal. He focused on the cold rune, imagining it traveling through the DoomNet. Tom began chanting the cold rune over and over at the top of his lungs.

A deep chill suddenly fell over the battlefield as the temperature began dropping fast. As he gained confidence in removing Fire, he upped the mana-draining net. He was going to suck any excess mana away from his enemies as well. He needed all energy to go. Anything the knights could use to focus chaos.

If he was doing things correctly, the DoomNet would not only be draining excess mana that was generated or released, it would be draining Fire. Actually, it should be draining fire even more effectively, since it would suck up all the Fire that was present in the region. That meant it should be draining the knights of Fire. He himself was actually getting cold. Given that he was a demon, he should not feel normal cold any more than he felt heat. He was therefore reasonably certain the reverse portal was actively draining Fire and energy. Draining chaos.

The rain that had been falling suddenly turned to sleet and then to snow.

"Holy shit!" he heard a D'Orc yell. "It's snowing in the Abyss!"

There, finally. Tom had the portal completely reversed. By default, it would have drained Fire from the entire DoomNet, but he worked feverishly to restructure it. He wanted to focus the Fire drain to this region so that it would drain faster.

~

Lesteroth's current D'Orc stopped ripping his right wing off in order to try and grab the snow that had started falling. Lesteroth used the brief lull to reseat his wing. *Ouch!* That hurt, but it would regenerate faster this way.

Lesteroth glanced down to see Talgorf sticking his tongue out, trying to catch snow on it. His D'Orc had also stopped squashing the smaller demon under his hoof to stare at the snow. All around them, D'Orcs and demons were stopping in amazement at the snow and the rapidly increasing cold.

It was suddenly a very cold day in the Abyss. Everyone knew to expect amazing things when the Abyss finally froze over. Of course, no one actually thought that would happen, but it seemed to be what was going on. Lesteroth laughed, looking at the snow.

"Wah hhabbaahnning?" came Bellyachus's voice from a few feet over. "Asz gold!"

Lesteroth wondered why the demon's voice was so muffled, but looking over, he quickly understood. Bellyachus's D'Orc had shoved the demon's head up his own butt. It looked to be a very uncomfortable position for Bellyachus, but it did explain why his voice was muffled and why he couldn't see what was going on.

VOOOOOOMMMMMMMMM!!!!!

Sekhmekt killed her second knight, but no explosion happened this time.

"That is pretty impressive," Lesteroth said.

His D'Orc tormentor nodded in shared amazement before hugging himself. "It's damn cold here," he complained. Lesteroth had to agree even as the snow turned to painful shards of ice, slicing at his skin.

~

VOOOOOOMMMMMMMMMM!!!!!

Morok killed another knight. It was getting easier as the temperature dropped. It had to be far below freezing at this point.

Tom charged one of the knights being shot at by the D'Orcs. He came up on the knight and smashed at it using the Rod and both hands.

Wham! Wham! Wham! Wham! Wham! Wham! Wham! CRRRAAAAAACCCCKKKKKKKK!!!!!

CRUNCH! FFFOOOoommmshhh!!!! A sphinx squashed another knight.

The knights were slowing down quickly in the cold. Tom had no idea how cold it was, but if he were to guess based on the previous cooling rate, it was probably closing in on one hundred degrees below zero Celsius; as cold now as it had previously been hot.

THUD! Voomphsss… Everything went pitch-black for a moment. The gravity cannon had taken another knight.

Wham!   Wham!   Wham!   Wham!   Wham! CRRRAAAAAACCCCKKKKKKKK!!!!! Tom took out another knight. The more he did this, the better he was getting, or maybe it was the ambient cold.

Wham! Wham! Wham! CRRRAAAAAACCCCKKKKKKKK!!!!!

CRUNCH! CRACKLE! CRACKLE! The sphinx' stomping was getting better. The knights were losing their energy to fight.

Foom! Talarius killed another knight.

Foom…Foom… Sekhmekt killed another knight, quickly followed by Morok. Only five more to go.

CRUNCH! Crackle. Another sphinx.

CRUNCH! Three left.

CRUNCH! Two.

CRACKLE! The final knight fell to Talarius and Ruiden.

Lacuna

Arg-nargoloth made his way down the dark corridor. He was tired; he'd been up since the start of the party, staying sober and alert. He had been heading to bed when the klaxons had gone off. Then chaos, planning and rousing his troops. Then the battle.

The fact that they had buried the demon army and forced them to dig themselves out had given them a huge advantage. They had been able to get into position above most of the demons before they finished digging their way out of the ground. At that point, between fourteen hundred D'Orcs and seven hundred D'Wargs, it had been more of a fun afternoon of glorious mayhem than a full battle.

At least, until the Knights of Chaos had started popping; at that point both demons and D'Orcs had slowed down to watch. It was so fascinating and the demons so beaten that the D'Orcs had only perfunctorily maimed and tortured them, the majority of their attention on the battle with the Knights of Chaos.

Of course, once Lord Tommus had started the freezing thing and draining all the mana, regeneration had slowed to almost a halt and they all became frozen and exhausted quickly. And then it was clean-up. He'd done what was absolutely necessary, but then left things to the more rested D'Orcs. Including Darg-Krallnom. The other commanders could assist Lord Tommus in dealing with the defeated demons. As far as he knew, none had died permanently, yet. Lord Tommus would decide which of the enemy would be allowed to regenerate, return to Lilith or otherwise be disposed of.

Arg-nargoloth was too beat to care. For now he was making his way towards one of the kitchens to see what food and x-glargh might be left from the party. He was not hungry, having eaten during the party. He was, however, ready to relax with some x-glargh. He had been sober for way too long. And after this battle, he deserved some x-glargh before it was all swallowed up in the victory celebration.

As he entered the nearly empty kitchen, where they had stored the extra barrels of x-glargh, he spotted a suspicious figure heading down a seldom-used and unlit cross corridor that led to an old storage room. That suspicious figure was quite distinct, as was the smell still present in the cross corridor. He grinned malevolently and went after the suspicious figure.

Arg-nargoloth had not followed this winding passage in many a century. There had not been any real need for going into this storage room. Until the recent hunting trips, there had been nothing in the room.

He entered the room to see Tisdale leaning against a barrel of something. "You!" Arg-nargoloth snarled loudly.

"Me," Tizzy stated nonchalantly.

"Trickster!"

"Two-bit thug!"

They glared at each other in the dark for some time.

"Hah!" Arg-nargoloth shouted.

Tizzy chuckled.

"You win!"

"I do." Tizzy grinned despotically.

"You know, I never believed you," Arg-nargoloth stated.

"Very few did."

"I thought you were simply spinning a fable to give people hope."

Tizzy shrugged. "It did for some, yes?"

Arg-nargoloth sighed. "Yes, but not for enough. We lost so many."

"I am sorry for that. Things took longer than expected."

"And yet, you did it, and yesterday—the very day of his death!" The D'Orc commander shook his head in disbelief. "And then today? The Jilted Bride seeks to take us unaware and we see the full power of Doom restored!" Arg-nargoloth chuckled and grinned with joy and admiration.

"I had my doubts on the final timing. Afraid we might not finish the swearing in by the end of sixth period. Prophecies are such a bitch."

"But the attack today didn't bother you?" Arg-nargoloth asked.

"It gave me pause, but I trust him." Tizzy shrugged. "He's a good lad." He gave Arg-nargoloth a wicked grin. "Plus, once I felt the World Gate open, I knew Sekhmekt would be coming."

Arg-nargoloth chuckled. "She is good in battle. We should have involved her more the last time around."

"Hindsight." Tizzy shrugged.

The two stood there in silence for a moment before Arg-nargoloth said, "I should have trusted you."

"Yeah, but again, not many do," Tizzy said.

"I am not sure anyone does!" Arg-nargoloth said, laughing.

Tizzy shrugged and pulled his pipe out of the air with one hand and a foot-long, rolled-up, stuffed paper with another. "D'Orc doobie?"

Arg-nargoloth chuckled and reached for the doobie. "Abyss, you do not know how I have missed this. You were always the best demon weed dealer in the multiverse!"

Tizzy flicked his thumb and offered Arg-nargoloth a light. The D'Orc commander inhaled, bringing the flame into the doobie.

Tizzy lit his own pipe and inhaled deeply as well. "To be honest," he said, pausing in his smoking, "I don't have a whole lot of competition."

"True!" Arg-nargoloth shook his head. "I still cannot get over your doing it!"

Tizzy tilted his head and grinned. "I wrote it down." The demon took a quick hit off his pipe. "As it is written, so it shall be done!" he intoned solemnly before bursting into a giggle.

Arg-nargoloth burst out laughing as well. "You and that damn book of yours! You were always running around scribbling all sorts of nonsense in it!" Tizzy shrugged.

Arg-nargoloth paused in thought for a moment. "You know," the D'Orc said, "this time around, I have not seen you scribbling in it. Where is it?"

Tizzy stopped inhaling to think. He grimaced as if trying to remember something, started to say something and stopped as if to think some more. He tilted his head. "You know, I am not sure. I haven't seen it in some time."

Tizzy squinted in thought and finally shrugged and said, "I must have misplaced it somewhere."

Arg-nargoloth frowned. "Couldn't that be a problem?"

Tizzy shrugged. "It's bound to show up at some point. It always does."

Arg-nargoloth shrugged as well. "Yeah. Well, as I recall, it was rather tricky to open." Tizzy nodded.

Arg-nargoloth inhaled deeply, feeling the demon weed penetrating his lungs and nasal cavities. It felt so good to finally relax like this after four thousand years of misery.

In the dark room, Arg-nargoloth could just make out the white of Tizzy's toothy grin lit by the embers in his pipe bowl, which nicely matched the burning red coals of the demon's eyes.

The Demons of Astlan will continue in *Apostles of Doom*

Appendix: Clerics: Priests, Monks, Nuns and Holy Warriors

The term "cleric" is used to describe members of a religious order who serve a god. Specifically, these are members who have taken vows and are bound to a deity, as opposed to those who are simply worshipers or members of lay associations.

The most widely known clerics are a deity's priests; however, most religions have other more secular members who are also pledged to the deity. These members may have different skill sets, functions and may or may not be mana wielders. Those who are mana wielders channel mana in the same way as priests; the primary difference is that they typically don't conduct worship rituals and collect mana from worshipers.

Listed below are the most common clerical types. The exact names may vary from religion to religion, and not all religions have all positions; some may have more.

Priests: Priests are the principal agents of the deities on Astlan. They conduct worship and collect offerings of mana, animus and money from worshipers. They also provide healing, religious instruction, mentoring, care and other services as required.

Monks: Monks are typically male members of the religion who have taken vows of loyalty and are linked to the deity; they are not, however, typically illuminaries. Illuminaries are people who collect and funnel mana and animus upstream to a deity. Monks are often craftsmen for the church. They can be clerks, scholars, sages, and in some religions, warriors.

Nuns: Nuns are typically female members of the religion who have taken vows of loyalty and are linked to the deity. Like monks, they are not typically illuminaries. In many religions, nuns perform healing and caretaking roles at the instruction of the priests. Like monks, they may also be craftsmen, clerks, scholars and sages, and again like monks, warriors in some religions.

Holy Warriors: Holy warriors are military units of churches. Not all churches have armies, but if they do, this is how they are typically classified. Vows and linkage to the deity depend on religion and level. In some cases, no particular vow is needed and the soldiers are simply in the employ of the church, although typically they are also worshipers. Higher-rank soldiers typically have greater devotion and have vows and linkages, and are thus true clerics as well as soldiers.

Holy Knights: Holy Knights are knights who may or may not be of noble birth. Holy Knights are formally invested by a high-ranking member of the priesthood (typically higher than a priest). Depending on the knight, the religion and their rank, knights may or may not channel mana from the deity. If they do, their rituals and chants are generally of a martial nature for either offensive or defensive purposes when fighting the enemies of the church.

Appendix: The Church of Tiernon

The Church of Tiernon is the official representative organization of the Etonian god Tiernon. It is based in Justicia in New Eton. The church's highest authority is the high pontificate, who resides at the Supreme Temple in Justicia. The current high pontificate is Thaddeus Barolos. The high pontificate is assisted by High Chamberlain Mericas and both his own and the high chamberlain's staff of functionaries.

The arch-diocese is the council of eight arch-diocates, each of whom are designated with full responsibility for a region of Astlan. They are the church's highest authority in their domain. The arch-diocese is also the body from which a new high pontificate is selected upon the death of the previous high pontificate.

In addition to the formal priesthood, the Church of Tiernon has three other organizations:

The Brothers of Tiernon are monks who provide administrative and personal services to the priesthood. They also operate monasteries that provide instruction and training both to other clerics and to worshipers. These monasteries also provide hostel services to clerics of Tiernon in their travels, and produce goods and services for use within the church.

The Sisters of Tiernon are nuns who specialize primarily in education, particularly that of children, healing, counseling and shelter for worshipers, as well as providing crafts and services for the church.

The Rod of Tiernon is probably the best-known organ of Tiernon in Astlan outside of the priesthood. In some regions, it is more well known, and often confused with, the priesthood. The Rod is the military arm of the church and is responsible for the safety and security of all church members and property. They are also the front line in exploration and conversion for the church. The often work closely with the Rangers of Torean and the Seafarers of Namora to expand the reach of all Etonian religions.

Below is a table listing the major ranks within the Church of Tiernon and the names, domains and seats of power for the senior members of the religion.

		Church of Tiernon		
Rank	Title	Domain	Location	Name
1	High Pontifcate	Astlan	Justicia	Thaddeus Barolos
2	High Chamberlain	Astlan	Justicia	Mericas
3	Arch-Diocate	New Etonia	Justicia	Tremane
	Arch-Diocate	Eastern Free Eton/ NW Norelon	Tiern Anon	Iskarus
	Arch-Diocate	Etonia/Southern Eton	Seren	Rafaeon
	Arch-Diocate	Natoor	New Memphis	Aleana
	Arch-Diocate	Najaar	New Cairo	Hesforus
	Arch-Diocate	Cythanian Federation	Cythania	Migueras
	Arch-Diocate	The UF, Murgandy, Ferundy, Naajar	Murgatroy	Daeon
	Arch-Diocate	Cal Crestor	Crestor City	Xerphaeon
4	Diocate	Regions of Primary Domains	Multiple	There are 45 Diocates, approx 4-6 per Arch-Diocate
5	High Priest	Temples	Large Cities	Head of a Temple
6	High Chaplain	Large Chapel	Med. Cities, Temple overflow	Head of a Chapel
7	Priest	Temples, Churches, Itenerant		
8	Deacon			

Brothers of Tiernon				
Rank	Title	Domain	Location	Name
1				
2				
3	Patriarch	Astlan	Justicia	Baronan
4	Arch-Montassary	New Etonia	Justica	Yenov
	Arch-Montassary	Eastern Free Eton/NW Norelon	Dale Anon	Vistrus
	Arch-Montassary	Etonia/Southern Eton	Rasparta	Kleeghon
	Arch-Montassary	Natoor	New Memphis	Thas Anoor
	Arch-Montassary	Najaar	New Cairo	Ptha Eron
	Arch-Montassary	Cythanian Federation	Dobai	Stephos
	Arch-Montassary	The UF, Murgandy,Ferundy,Noajar	Murgatory	Feron
	Arch-Montassary	Cal Crestor	Cal Edon	Markus
5	Father			
6	Chaplain			
7	Brother			
8	Novitiate			

Sisters of Tiernon				
Rank	Title	Domain	Location	Name
1				
2				
3	Matriarch	Astlan		Seralina
4	High Abbess	New Etonia	Justicia	Mariana
	High Abbess	Eastern Free Eton/NW Norelon	Kestral Anon	Sarah
	High Abbess	Etonia/Southern Eton	Soriel	Jane Margot
	High Abbess	Natoor	New Memphis	Lavalla
	High Abbess	Najaar	New Cairo	Osira Bet
	High Abbess	Cythanian Federation	Madai	Sophias
	High Abbess	The UF, Murgandy,Ferundy,Noajar	Murgator	Esther
	High Abbess	Cal Crestor	Cal Phedon	Jaena
5	Mother			
6	Chaplain			
7	Sister			
8	Novitiate			

Rod of Tiernon				
Rank	Title	Domain	Location	Name
1				
2	Arch-Vicar General	Astlan	Tiern Anon/Justicia	Barabus
3	Arch-Vicar	New Etonia	Justicia	Paranon
	Arch-Vicar	Etonia/Southern Eton	Soriel	Mararan
	Arch-Vicar	Natoor/Najaar	New Cairo	Oth-Manaan
	Arch-Vicar	Cythanian Federation	Cythania	Parafel
	Arch-Vicar		Cal Crestor	Nicademus
	Knight Rampant		Multiple	
4	Knight Paladin High Commander			
5	Knight Commander		Large Cities	
6	Esquire		Med. Cities, Temple overflow	
	Sergeant			
7	Corporal			
8	Squire Rod Member			

A short (adult human-size) demon rises to its full height and moves into a fighting stance. "At least this time I'll be able to put up a fight," he answers bravely to a question posed by the Knight Rampant, Talarius.

"I don't think it will be that much of a fight; I've taken your measure once before, demon," Talarius responds very seriously.

"Well, then," a voice booms down from above as a demon identical to the one on the ground, but easily twice as large, comes in for a landing between the knight and the smaller demon. "How about fighting an adult? Man to man, rather than slaughtering children for sport?"

Talarius steps back in surprise and shock as the twelve-foot tall demon lands. The entire circle of priests steps back, giving them more room, the priests behind the front row getting shoved violently back.

"What lies are you spewing, demon?" Talarius asks the greater demon.

"First, I thought you were a holy man, sworn to goodness? You sounded a bit smug and egotistical talking to the *[garbled]*. You know what they say: Pride goeth before the fall? Vanity is the root of all evil? And so on."

One can see the knight's eyes twitch within his helmet; the demon has hit a nerve.

"Second, *[garbled]* is just a child. I don't think it's very honorable for a great and glorious knight to go around killing children for sport, do you?"

"That is no child, it's a demon," Talarius tells the greater demon sternly, "and removing evil from this world is not a sport, it's a duty. A solemn duty."

The greater demon shakes his head as if in exasperation. "What, you think demons don't have children? You've seen his human form. That is what he really looks like; that is who he really is. And you killed him, in your own tent, for no reason other than he'd been flying overhead the night before."

"Lies, lies! He came with you through a portal to take over the world!" A high priest pushes his way forward to yell at the greater demon.

The greater demon looks with pity at the priest. "Verigas, you were meddling where you shouldn't have been. I needed a doorway to get my human charges back to Astlan; you simply provided that gateway. No one harmed you. We even arranged for you to escape. If we meant you harm, you wouldn't be here now."

"Liar! All demons lie. You seek to confuse us with your lies!" Verigas shouted.

"You are as crazy as those damn wizards, blinded by your own paranoia and fear. You can't even see the truth when it's presented to you because you are too wrapped up in silly superstitions and prejudices," the greater demon retorts.

"Enough chatter, demon!" Talarius shouts. "You simply seek to delay us so that your compatriots can destroy us!"

"Destroy you?" The giant demon waves his arms around. "We—my compatriots as you call them and I—aren't the ones who were lying in ambush outside the city waiting for us to be driven out against our will where you could begin slaughtering us!" He raises his arms above his head in frustration. "You have seriously got to be kidding me. It is you who seek to destroy us; we are simply trying to get out of Freehold, thanks to a spell cast by wizards. The only people getting killed are demons! Look around!" He waves his arms more vigorously.

"Your words are ever so cunning. Greater demons are 'greater' not just for their size but for their cunning and deceptiveness."

"Dude," the demon says, "—and I say that in most laid back way I can— you are seriously tripping! I don't have to be cunning or deceptive; you guys are falling all over yourselves with your own paranoia and self-deceptions."

"Why do you prevaricate? Let's have this out," Talarius demands.

The demon sighs. "So you want to fight me?" The knight tilts his head in agreement. "Very well: here's the deal. We fight, just you and me, no one else. If you win, you guys get to continue on with what you were doing before I arrived. If I win, you and the Rod stop attacking the demons and let them go their own way in peace. Agreed?"

Talarius's eyes narrow in calculation for a moment and then he finally nods and says, "Agreed."

The greater demon nods and gestures for everyone to step back. The priests surrounding them do so, as do the three demons standing behind him. The demon looks around the circle as if judging whether or not they can be trusted to keep their word. He blinks staring at the surrounding army, almost as if puzzled and distracted by something.

Swooshhh-thud! "Agghhh!" the demon roars as Talarius's sword rips into his side. The demon looks down at his side, where there is a huge gash and blood oozing out. He shakes his head and flashes to flame, suddenly re-forming without the wound. One can hear a few gasps from the crowd as the demon easily heals itself.

The demon turns his attention back to the knight just as his sword comes slashing towards him. The demon blocks it with his hand and curses as the blade bites deeply into his hand. He turns his hand to flame and then re-forms it.

The knight is winding up for another huge slash, so the demon quickly spins and gives the knight a standing back kick in the gut at full strength, grimacing on impact.

The knight goes flying backwards, smashing to the ground on his buttocks. He springs back up like a gymnast, almost as if he wasn't covered head to toe in heavy metal.

Talarius advances, this time with shield ready to deflect a kick. The demon changes fighting stances. The knight's left side is protected by the shield while the right hand holds the sword. As the knight moves in, raising his arm to slash, the demon moves quickly to the knight's right side and performs a whirling back kick to the knight's right flank, roaring loudly. A brilliant flash of red light strikes the knight along with the demon's hoof.

Talarius goes flying forward and to the left, off balance, taken by surprise. His sword coincidentally slashes the demon's forearm, slicing deeply, but the demon flash-heals it almost without a thought. The knight regains his balance quickly, clearly breathing harder.

The knight moves in again, whirls and slides down low under the demon's legs, twisting somehow to bring his very pointy spiked boot right up into the demon's monstrously oversized testicles. The demon howls in agony; his tail slashes down like a razor, raking with a nasty shriek across the knight's armor.

As the sharp spade squeals across the armor, lightning coruscates over the surface of the armor, released from the demon's tail spade. The demon completes his action, pulling away from the knight and crouching, protecting his testicles. In doing so, his tail leaves the knight and the electricity stopped.

"That was rather a low blow, knight!" the demon growls at Talarius.

"It pays to protect the family jewels, fiend!" Talarius glares back at him.

The knight moves in for another slice; the demon blocks with his arm and tries a forward kick. The blade slams tightly into his forearm, lodging in the bone. The demon's kick bounces off the knight's shield.

The demon flashes to fire, releasing the sword, and starts a new spinning back kick between sword and shield while in fire mode, solidifying as his foot slides through the opening. *Wham!* The knight goes flying backwards, shield and sword spreading wide. The demon seizes the moment; scrambling forward and using his wings, he pounces on the knight with a hard, open-handed punch to the solar plexus, clearly intending his claws to gouge through the armor. Again, that huge screeching noise as the demon's claws slide and scrape along the armor!

The knight struggles to curl himself together and eject the demon. The demon, whose left hand is drawn back, brings it forward in an open-handed thrust at the shoulder joint of the knight, a region protected only by chain mail.

This time the demon strikes home, hard. His nails cannot quite seem to pierce the chainmail, but the blunt force causes a cracking noise and a screech from Talarius. The knight's sword flashes through the air, slicing through the demon's wing. The demon screams in anger and pain and flashes to flame.

During the few seconds it takes to do that, the knight dives through the demon's flame form and regains his feet. Once solid, the demon starts to rise and

Talarius takes the opportunity to slice the demon's tail off. It falls flat on the ground, twitching. The demon flashes to flame again and then back.

While this has been happening, the priests of Tiernon have begun chanting in unison, and a gold circle forms around the greater demon and, in fact, the entire area of combat.

The demon begins repositioning itself as Talarius removes his hand from his shoulder, where he apparently had been using a healing ritual to fix his most recent wounds.

The knight gets back into fighting position, as does the demon. The knight thrusts forward suddenly; however, the demon was prepared and side steps, grabbing the knight's sword arm with both hands and lifting. The knight is over six feet tall, but the demon nearly twelve, so in many ways it is like an adult battling a child. The demon lifts the knight up and over his own shoulder, spinning and then slamming the knight as hard as he can into the ground.

The knight had managed to slash the demon's side deeply with his sword during this, and his shield had smashed the demon's head, but the knight seems to have gotten the worst of the deal.

The knight is on the ground, winded and wounded. For some odd reason, the demon steps back and waits for the knight to slowly climb to his feet. As the knight stands, one can hear him chanting something and suddenly golden light washes over the knight. Now his armor seems to glow more brightly, and he stands straighter.

The knight tilts his head forward, glaring at the demon in anger. He shouts something in a strange language and charges, point first. The demon steps aside, apparently intending to repeat his last maneuver, but suddenly the knight stops, spins and seems to shimmer. His blade whisks around, seeming to turn to pure light and extending beyond its normal reach to slice through both the demon's thighs! The demon screams as it crashes to the ground, its bat-like wings fluttering frantically but unable to catch him before he falls. He bursts into flame again and swats the knight hard with his flaming hand. Talarius ducks, but is still grazed by the fire.

The demon assumes a fighting stance and begins fist-punching the air, pointing at Talarius. As his hand reaches out, blasts of fire leap from the demon's fist to strike the knight. The knight deflects the blasts with his shield. The demon rises into the air and fires straight down; still the knight deflects the blasts. Fireballs ricochet into the surrounding priests to loud howls of pain, and the priests quickly begin patting the flames out on their compatriots.

The demon moves in closer and the knight slashes at him. The sword moves through the flames slowly and jerkily and the demon roars in pain, clearly surprised that the knight can wound him.

The demon lands and suddenly launches a solid, continuous blast of flame at the knight, as if unleashing a portal to the Plane of Fire. Instead of raising his shield to defend, the knight simply brings his sword forward, clasping it with both hands, the shield hanging unused on his left forearm.

The flames are being parted by the sword; parted and swept aside like water before the bow of a ship. The blasts are redirected to the surrounding crowd, scorching several before they are able to raise magic shields to protect themselves.

Suddenly the demon's flame turned a mixture of white with blue streaks of lightning. The knight shuddered under the new assault and began mouthing some ritual. The cold fire began to close in on the knight. The demon's body was now cold fire with blasts of lightning from it. However, there is a steady seepage of flame from the demon to the ring surrounding the combat. It appears that the priests are siphoning off the demon's energy.

The demon suddenly seems to realize what is happening and becomes even angrier, but it does him no good, for suddenly archers of the Rod begin shooting magical arrows at him. As each arrow strikes the demon, a burst of golden yellow light, like a tiny star, appears for a few seconds.

The demon's flames begin to flicker. Suddenly the torrent of cold fire and electricity ceases as the icy demon leaps spinning into the air, materializing as he lands behind the knight. Immediately he grabs the knight's legs and jerks them out from under him, pulling the knight upside down as the demon stands. The demon handles the knight as if he were but a rag doll, smashing him face first into the ground. He then pulls the knight's legs apart and kicks him right in the crotch— payback from before.

The demon picks the knight up and smashes him into the ground again, the knight twisting feverishly to escape the demon's grasp. The demon lifts and smashes the knight into the ground yet again, then he drives the edge of his hoof in between the knight's thigh plates and calf plates until a crunching sound is heard. The demon pulls back, twisting and lifting the knight, bringing him up and over his own shoulders and head, and then smashing the knight down on his back.

The arrows had stopped after the demon had moved to the other side of the knight and materialized; at this point the Rod starts firing again. Several other priests had begun chanting loudly. As the demon begins picking the knight up for another smashing, a dark mist grows around the two of them, the knight's armor suddenly turns white hot in appearance, and the demon begins sweating blood. The arrows continue to rain through the mist, and scorch marks are appearing on the demon's hide wherever they strike.

The demon's bloody palms have made the knight slippery and the demon loses his hold as Talarius scrambles free. As the knight regains his footing, he brings his sword around and slices through the demon's left ankle, chopping his hoof off.

The demon teeters, trying to right himself with his wings, but is obviously getting tired. A priest hurries to Talarius's side and begins casting healing spells. The demon launches itself into the air to fly over to the knight and priest, but a yellow glowing mist, different from before, envelops him, slowing his progress and dragging him back down towards the ground.

The knight climbs to his feet and slashes at the demon's other leg, slicing through it at knee level. The demon is extremely wobbly and blinking furiously.

"Prepare for the final rites," Talarius orders. "Have you got the others secured?" he asks his people even as he moves in for the kill, swinging his blade and lopping off the demon's left arm. The demon wobbles in the air, looking as if it might crash at any moment. In the background, a glowing yellow magical net has engulfed the other demons with the greater demon.

"This will be the final death for all of them," a priest shouts towards those casting the net.

Talarius moves in and slashes off one of the demon's wings, bringing the demon to the ground. The demon's one remaining arm waves uselessly in front of him, one moment clawing at the ground and the next waving feebly back and forth in the air. A sight that would have brought the bravest warrior to pity if this had been a fellow mortal.

Talarius ignores the demon writhing on the ground as one group of priests surrounds him to apply healing rituals and another group begins assembling the necessary implements for killing all the demons permanently.

The priests aiding Talarius are finished, and the knight stands and strides over to the pathetic, flailing demon on the ground. "So, demon. You are defeated, and now you and your immediate compatriots will face true death."

"You cheated," the demon croaks.

"There is no such thing as cheating when fighting Evil." The knight takes his helmet off. He almost looks sad as he stares down at the demon.

"So you say. I disagree," the greater demon says quite clearly. The demon is smoldering a bit now. He lets out a loud sigh and suddenly there is nothing but glowing ashes on the ground.

"Curses!" the knight yells. "He fled back to the Abyss!" He turns back to the group of priests who had been preparing the ritual. "How are the preparations going?"

"Are you sure you want to do this?" a man who appeared to be a general asked. "This is the sort of thing that can have unintended repercussions."

The knight sighs. "I understand, Barabus, but these demons are clearly the root of the problem we and the Sky Fleet have been pursuing, and we need to deal with them once and for all."

"Do you not want to question them?" Barabus asked.

"What good is questioning demons?" Talarius asked. "We'll get better results from their human henchmen." Barabus was nodding as a senior priest nearby suddenly threw up.

"Are you okay?" Barabus asks. The man is quite pale and shaking his head no, gasping and too weak to speak. Another high priest suddenly turns pale and falls on the ground, vomiting. Then another, and then a fourth high priest.

"What the hell is going on?" Talarius demands, looking around. "Verigas? What's wrong?"

The high priest named Verigas, the whiny one from the beginning of the scene, is very rigid and silent, seemingly locked in some sort of internal struggle. After what seemed like an interminable time with everyone staring at the high priest, he seems to wake from his trance and turns to face Talarius.

"Well, knight, you said that in the battle with Evil, there is no such thing as cheating."

Talarius looks at the priest strangely, clearly sensing something is not right.

"So I've decided to pull out all the stops," the priest says.

"Verigas, what the hell are you talking about?" Barabus asks the high priest.

Verigas smiles a rather wicked-looking smile. "What makes you think I'm Verigas? Where are your paranoid conspiracy theories now, when you need them? You've really pissed me off, Talarius. You cheated. You have no honor, no integrity."

"Oh, shit," Talarius says, the blood draining from his face.

Suddenly the embers where the greater demon had fallen burst into flame. A whirlwind of embers and smoke rise into the air over the site of the fallen demon. Suddenly the smoke and embers join into flame, growing and growing. The knight and priests stare as the flames grow and meld themselves into a humanoid form—a large humanoid form.

The high priest Verigas lets out a shriek and falls to the ground, collapsing in a heap like a discarded marionette. No one moves to attend him.

The flames grow to twelve feet tall and then solidify in the form of the demon who had just been defeated.

"I'm afraid you won't get rid of me that easy, Talarius." The demon grins.

"So you're back?" Talarius asks, putting his helmet back on.

"Yes, I am, and you cheated." The demon shakes his head. "Seems to me that violates the Knight's Code of Ethics?"

The knight winces slightly this time and sighs. "As I've said, there can be no mercy in fighting Evil."

"I suppose, then, that it's a matter of how, or who, you define as Evil," the demon states. "Personally, I'm getting tired of being called Evil when there are plenty of other people around behaving far more dishonorably and despicably than me."

The knight gets a steely look in his eyes. "Enough of your prevarication, demon. I've slain you once; I'll do it again."

"Not if I cheat first," the demon said in a tired and resigned voice. "Fire!" He yells, and suddenly large numbers of archers among the Rod raise their bows and begin raining arrows upon Talarius.

Talarius falls to his knees, crouching and covering himself with his shield as best he can, trying to minimize the exposed parts of his body. Taking advantage of the knight's embattled state, the demon rises into the air and flies over to the net where the other demons are contained. He quickly rips it to shreds, yelling something that is hard to hear over the shrieks of the terrified priests.

The demon returns to his position near the knight. The rain of arrows is receding as other members of the Rod managed to subdue their possessed compatriots. The possessed Rod members fight viciously, almost desperately.

The demon comes up behind the knight as he starts coming out of his crouch. The demon grabs him by the legs and begins thrashing him all over again, this time watching out for any priests that might try to help the knight.

He smashes the knight into the ground about a dozen times, kicking him as hard as he can in between turns of slamming him into the ground. Periodically he stops and jabs with his claws between the joints to try and do damage; then he smashes the knight a few more times. This goes on for several minutes as the disorganized Rod and priests fight amongst each other, and the other demons, holding a defensive ring, slash any priest or Rod member who comes near.

Eventually, after what must seem a merciless eternity to him, the knight calls out, "Enough! Stop, please." The demon stops.

The knight crawls to his knees, then tosses his sword and shield away. He takes his helmet off and puts it under his arm. "I surrender; you have defeated me, demon!" he shouts. It certainly looks that way; the knight is black and blue all over his head, he has blood running out of his nose, several cracked teeth and various head injuries.

"Kill me now and be done with it, oh vile demon! Know that you have beaten Talarius," the knight sobs, tears running down his cheeks. The demon shakes his head at the knight and then suddenly seems to shrink in on himself, even as his skin color fades from red to pink. An average-looking young man not much younger than Talarius suddenly stands where the demon had been.

The naked man walks toward the kneeling knight. "I don't want to kill you, Talarius." The young man looks almost sorrowful, as if he pities the knight. "I do not hate you, nor do I wish to destroy you. I only want to protect my friends and my people." The man-demon stares down at the knight. "I am not different, nor are they"—he waves towards the other demons—"from any other man. All we want is to live our lives, the same as you."

The knight looks at him suspiciously and skeptically.

"Killing you would only perpetuate this stupidity. It needs to end. This whole Astlan-demon thing needs to end. We have to start somewhere; why not here?"

The knight shakes his head. "I don't know. You make no sense, demon."

"Talarius, you don't have to change your opinion now. I don't expect that. I am going to simply spare your life today so that you might, possibly, start to think that not everything you've grown up believing is true." The demon makes a questioning gesture with his hands. "Okay?"

The knight hangs his head. "Okay," he whispers.

The naked man-demon smiles and puts his hand down on the knight's shoulder. The knight lunges upward. A large, shiny, black metal blade suddenly appears in his hand, and he stabs into the side of the demon. The demon lets loose a scream of pain and then bends over.

"The Holy Dagger of Tiernon!" Talarius raises his arm, showing off a black metallic dagger on a switchblade mechanism on his forearm. "It is instant, permanent death for Evil!"

The demon bends over in agony, twitching. For some reason he is unable or unwilling to flash to fire to heal itself. In the man-demon's abdomen, a large, almost glowing black wound can be seen with tendrils of inky blackness radiating from the wound.

The demon groans again; however, this time it is a very different groan than the moans of agony he'd been uttering. Suddenly a crystal-white sparkle of light appears in the middle of the wound and begins digging away and dissolving the inky black tendrils. The man-demon grabs the wound, tilting his head upward as if relishing the healing power of the light. The man-demon stands up straight, his clasped fingers no longer able to conceal the glowing golden whiteness within them.

"Talarius?" the man-demon says, smiling. The knight turns from receiving his cheers. His face goes cold when he sees the glowing white light at the man-demon's midsection. The demon pulls his hands back to reveal the wound, glowing with brilliant white light and healing quickly. "Do you recognize the aura of that light? What magic it is that heals me?"

The knight is staring at the demon's midsection in shock. The man-demon turns to face Barabus and the fancy priest beside him. They turn pale. He rotates back to face the still-shocked knight.

Trivially, the man-demon reaches out and snaps the dagger from the knight's wrist. The knight just jerks in response, too shocked to react. The demon seems to stare at the dagger, and the inky-black color of the metal begins to fade to a solid grey and then to a silverfish color, and finally the blade is glowing with a pale white light.

The demon tosses it over towards the feet of Barabus and the other priest. Talarius stares at it dumbly.

The demon returns his gaze to the knight. "One question, Talarius. When I was blasting you with fire, you deflected it with your sword, but wasn't the air super-hot? How did you stand that?"

The knight is still in shock. Seemingly without thinking, he mumbles, "The armor keeps me safe in any environment."

"Good, that's what I had hoped." The demon looks over to his friends. "<*garbled*> get ready to play catch." He gestures to the ground at Talarius's feet, and the other demons nod.

A spark of fire suddenly appears between Talarius's feet, and then it is a flame. Before the knight has time to realize what is happening, the fire has turned into a ring that is expanding between his feet. A hole opens in the center of the ring, growing wider. There appears to be empty space below; well, empty except for a few balls of fire.

"Talarius?" The knight looks at the man-demon. "Time for a vacation! Off you go—into the Abyss!" With that, the hole widens and Talarius falls through it, screaming. The demon gestures to his friends. "Make sure he doesn't hit the ground!" The miniature version of the greater demon laughs and dives head first through the hole; the others, grinning widely, follow. The demon begins rotating and waving his hands over the priests and Rod members, particularly in those regions where he had possessed the most.

He then turns to Barabus and the other high priest and says, "Don't worry; I'll try to keep him safe."

The two priests seem to have no idea what he means; they simply stare at him in even greater shock. Getting no response from the two, the naked, human-looking demon grins and steps over the gaping hole to hell and lets himself fall through into the Abyss.

The hole shrinks and closes behind the demon, leaving the Rod members gaping. After a few moments of silence, the sound of battle can be heard as soldiers who had stopped to watch resume clearing the area of demons. The balling goes dark.

Deities are primordial forces in the cosmos. They are the puppet masters that all mortals jump to. Their abilities cannot be measured in any rational manner, unlike demons or angels. They can be ranked against each other, but even so, those rankings are based upon mortal perceptions and may be grossly inaccurate.

The deities exist in the Planes of the Gods. This is a loose term for any region of the multiverse beyond the Astral Plane that is not the Abyss or the Elemental Planes and is not any of the Planes of Men. These planes, in many ways, are extensions of their inhabitants and creators. The physical laws on each of these planes are dictated solely by the will of the deity or deities inhabiting it. Thus, they vary greatly amongst themselves, and several even vary from whim to whim of the local deities. There is no guarantee that any of the tenets of magic, animus, or anything else will apply on any of these planes.

While many large regions of these planes have been set aside for the followers (deceased and otherwise) of various deities, other regions are completely hostile to mortal life. Normal, unprotected animus cannot survive in many of these regions: the magical and animatic forces are simply too great.

Many religions try to place the deities in their pantheons in specific hierarchies. In general, this system rates the deities of a specific pantheon by a class system, similar to avatars and others. The important thing to remember, however, is that this is not the same level system used for demons or avatars. Deities have no levels measurable in mortal terms. This is, further, a relative rating of deities within a pantheon. A class VI deity in a minor pantheon, in objective power, may only be able to shape the course of time as much as a class II deity in a major pantheon.

In general, the power of a particular pantheon, and its ability to control events on the Planes of Men, is usually (but not always) commensurate with the number of worshippers on that plane. Deities within pantheons are usually very busy struggling between themselves for domination and usually will not pay too much attention to things beyond the realms of their worshippers on the Planes of Men. Thus, most friction between deities comes from within a pantheon.

Pantheons, however, do not live in a vacuum. There are quite obviously other pantheons competing for control of the same nearly infinite number of (in)finite planes of men. One might presume that there is enough space to go around, but apparently not. In addition to rivalries within pantheons, there can also be rivalry between pantheons.

It is only within these horrifying times of struggle that one can make judgements on the powers of specific deities relative to those in other pantheons. Even so, it is nearly impossible to do, since so much of the battle is truly beyond mortal ken. Further, such battles are also usually indirect, played out by mortals acting as the pieces in a game of chess (in the same manner deities in a pantheon might struggle, only on a more epic scale). Often, such titanic struggles may destroy entire nations (and/or banish or slay pantheons) or even entire planes.

Even in non-epic struggles, in everyday business, few deities get too involved. Except for certain very independent-minded deities, very few will ever engage directly with any opponent, or even work directly on the Planes of Men. Almost all prefer to work through mortal agents, with free will providing the randomness that makes the game exciting for the deities.

Agents of the gods, those magical beings variously called saints, angels, or avatars, along with mortal agents used by prophecy or chance, are for our purposes simply referred to as avatars.

Avatars

Avatars are the agents of the gods. They are servants who are assigned to a wide variety of tasks and act as the emissaries and agents of the gods upon the Planes of Men and other planes. The term *avatar* is actually a generic term referring to a wide variety of beings. Avatars include angelic beings, saints, occasionally mortals, and even physical manifestations of the gods themselves. As with many things in dealing with the gods, avatars can be difficult to quantify or categorize. Nonetheless, mortals still try.

Angels are perhaps the most categorized of all avatars. There exists a hierarchy of angels which seems to transcend the different pantheons. While not all pantheons have angels (and often, if they do, they will be called something else), most do have at least a few. Not all pantheons that have angels have angels of all classes. Some may only have one or two angels in the entire pantheon. Finally, often it is not apparent to the average worshipper if a particular divine servant is an angel or something else. For the purposes of this treatise, all avatars that are not saints, mortals, or deific incarnations (gods in physical form) are considered angels.

Angels are immortal, eternal beings (although in principle, they can be slain) like the gods themselves, but created by the gods. Angels are primarily beings of spirit who are capable of assuming physical form. Various religions have, in fact, commented on the noted similarity between angels and demons. In fact, there is a great deal of similarity, even in terms of mortal descriptions of these beings. Heretical individuals might even go so far as to suggest that the principal difference between demons and angels is that angels are in the service of the gods and demons are not. Obviously, however, there is much more to it than that. Angels are generally benevolent towards mortals (at least towards those of their deity's faith) and most reports indicate that they are beings of great beauty and magnificence. The obvious counter to this is that the angels of the darker gods are not necessarily beautiful, and are certainly every bit as dangerous as any demon. The angels of a particular pantheon always mimic the ways of their masters.

Angels have been classified by many religions and many sects within religions. An objective classification scheme for angels is much more difficult than with demons (partly due to the fact that wizards have been highly adamant about their schemes and most religions simply follow along). The names of the classes of angels is even more varied. However, in general, most religions will agree in principle to a classification scheme of between seven and nine levels of hierarchy in the angelic structure. Nine often seems to work best to meet observables (specifically, to iron out inter-pantheon conflicts). However, seven has the benefit of being symmetric to the demonic hierarchy. The names of the hierarchies are still pretty much open to debate. Two example classification schemes found on several planes are shown below, along with the well-known Etonian scheme for both angels and saints:

Priority	Jeromic	Gregorian	Etonian	Class	Etonian Saints	Demons
1	Seraphim	Seraphim	Supreme Archon	VI	Hand of God	Demon Prince
2	Cherubim	Cherubim	Attendant Archon	V	Prophet	Arch Demon
3	Powers	Thrones	Greater Archon	IV	Greater Saint	Greater Demon
4	Dominations	Dominations	Archon	III	Saint	Major Demon
5	Thrones	Principalities	Lesser Archon	II	Lesser Saint	Fiend
6	Archangels	Powers	Minor Archon	I	Minor Saint	Imps
7	Angels	Virtues		I		Sprites
8		Archangels		I		Shadows
9		Angels				

A great deal of differences between classification schemes has to do with simply rearranging the order of the lower ranks. The problems often come from the fact that specific angels are known to be (or have been at one time) in specific groups, and since very seldom are there multiple angels together at the same time, judging relative power is difficult. A heretic might be tempted to say that there is often a case of "my angel is bigger than your angel" going on in these schemes.

What is known is that the members of the foremost rank, the seraphim, are indisputably the most powerful. The individual seraphim are, in turn, the leaders of the various other ranks of angels and thus also have dual classification in some schemes (in this case, a power level classification scheme breaks down). Further, it is clear that the seraphim are nearly as powerful as some of the more major gods, and certainly as powerful as the lesser gods. In most pantheons, the seraphim are acknowledged to have taken part in the creation of the multiverse.

If one were to persist in trying to gauge or classify angels in a power level scheme (which time and time again has proved fraught with problems), one might like to heretically compare power levels to those of the demons (strictly in theory, of course). The seraphim are thought to be on the level of the demon princes. Many blasphemous rumors insinuate that the Concordenax was actually a renegade seraphim, who thought himself more of a god than a seraphim. Following this, to use the Jeromic system, the cherubim would be roughly equivalent in power to class V demons, and so on down to the minor angels. Again, it must be stressed, this association is tenuous at best because even the weakest of angels is more than a match for the weakest of demons (or so many like to believe).

While it is extremely difficult to classify angels, it is even more difficult to classify saints. *Saint* is a generic term used only in this treatise to refer to a divine servant of mortal origin. Saints are unquestionably beings who were once mortal (or quasi-immortal like the Sidhe) and who have, by the grace of their deity, somehow transcended this state. The powers and abilities of such individuals seem to be highly random, and vary not only from pantheon to pantheon, but also from saint to saint.

Some saints have the ear of their deity; others are little more than errand boys. What exactly their powers and abilities are is highly varied and spans the entire spectrum of existence. In some cases, the sainted being has actually gone on to become a deity in his or her own right (usually of lesser stature) within the pantheon. Relationships between saints and angels is not predictable and must be determined on a case-by-case basis. Blasphemous speculators have speculated that much of a saint's relative power is related more to politics and the favor of the deity than to absolute raw power.

Another form of avatar is the mortal agent. Sometimes, deities will use their followers (or annoyingly, innocent bystanders) as instruments of change or action. These individuals are often no more than pawns, but can go on to become very powerful and influential individuals if their deity wills and things work. Otherwise they usually end up as a Blessed Martyr to the Cause (read: dead). While some mortal avatars can go on to become saints, it is generally not the preferred way of doing things, because the gods do not usually consult with the mortal in question.

The final form of avatar is that of the deific incarnation. On extremely rare occasions, deities will embody themselves upon the Planes of Men to enact their plans. These individuals are extremely powerful, as they are gods and are only moderately hampered by physical form. This "hands-on approach" is very rare and generally only used in either very grave situations (like the end of the multiverse or pantheon) or by the more quirky (no blasphemy intended) or individualistic deities.

There are a great many pantheons of gods in Astlan. For the sake of reference, we list the major deities of the two largest active pantheons among humans, The Etonians and The Narveson, which began on Eton and Norelon respectively. We also provide the principal deities of the hybrid races along with a great number of Sidhe, simply known as the Gods of the Grove.

We also list a few known deities from (mostly) forgotten pantheons: the "Old Ones," who have a few cult members hidden around, and the Nyjyr Ennead, a pantheon driven from Astlan by the Etonians. Very brief mention is made of an alvaren pantheon, the El'adasir, simply because their principal deity is mentioned by the alfar; however, very little is known about the religion outside alvaren realms.

The Etonians

The Etonians originated primarily in Eton. While missionaries expanded their circle outside of Eton for years, it was not until the Cult of Tiernon in AC -1288 began expanding into Norelon that they attained a sizable presence outside of Eton. This incursion earned them and their followers the wrath of the Narveson, who had held sway upon Norelon.

The Etonians, and the Rod of Tiernon in particular, played a critical role in the overthrow of the Anilords. As a result of this, the Etonians gained a substantial foothold in Norelon as the Narveson were displaced with the Anilords.

The Five Major Gods are all siblings, brothers and sisters. Their mother is commonly believed to have been the Goddess Danu of the El'adasir pantheon. Their father's name, Aetherus All Father, is considered to have been the original creator of the multiverse. However, he seems to have vanished and is rarely mentioned in any of the Etonian religious texts.

The Lesser Gods tend to be the children of the Major Gods and typically represent different aspects under their parent.

Hendel: God of Healing (Element of Earth)

Hendel is the Etonian god of health and healing. He is particularly popular with thaumaturges, alchemists, chemists. Hendel's Supreme Temple is in Hendel's Hearth on the west coast of Eton.

Krinna: Goddess of the Wind and Sky (Element of Air)

Krinna is the Etonian goddess of the Sky, Wind and Air. She is the goddess of Enchantment, Seduction, Bewitchment and Flight. Krinna's Supreme Temple is in Krinna's Reach on the west coast of Eton.

Namora: Goddess of the Sea (Element of Water)

Namora, the Etonian Goddess of the Sea, is worshiped by all sailors, particularly adventurers and merchants, fishermen and naturally, sorcerers.

Namora's largest temple and the center of her worship is on the island of Namora off the west coast of Eton. The entire island is dedicated to her service.

Tiernon: God of Justice and War (Element of Fire)

Tiernon is the best known of the Etonians Gods outside of Eton and is widely worshiped by warriors and nobility. He is the God of Justice and War and is dedicated to the elimination of Evil (with a capital E). Justicia is the seat of Tiernon's power in Astlan. It is located in western Eton.

Torean: God of Valor and Exploration (Element of Spirit)

Torean is the second most popular Etonian outside of Eton. He is the god of adventurers, exploration, combat and glory. Torean's Fast is the seat of Torean's supreme temple and the starting point for all great adventures and exploration.

The Narveson

The Narveson are the old gods of Norelon. In particular, they were the gods of the Anilords. With the overthrow of the Anilords, the Narveson have lost a sizeable number of followers in favor of the Etonians, who were instrumental in overthrowing the Anilords.

Drott Kmon: God of Law and Order

Drott Kmon and his cult had a very awkward relationship during the age of the Anilords. He was officially a patron of the Anilord regime, yet often seen as in opposition to the corruption found within the ranks of the Anilords. He is still popular with traditionalists. Neither he nor his adherents get along well with Zbibik and his worshipers.

Illania: Goddess of Magic

Illania was extremely popular with the Anilords and their adherents; however, her cult managed to survive relatively well by embracing wizardry quickly after the fall of the Anilords. She is also a strong patron of craft and professional women.

Maera: Goddess of Nature and Healing

Maera is still quite popular with peasants, farmers and thaumaturgists.

Soth Ammon: God of Life and Death

Soth Ammon is the Narveson god of birth, life and death. In more recent years he has become more associated with death and the underworld, primarily due to the pantheon's affiliation with the Anilords.

Teth Ammon: Goddess of Destiny

Wife of Soth Ammon. It is said that it is Teth who instructs her husband on who lives and who dies, based on thread lines within her giant loom.

Zbibk: God of Change, Chaos, Anarchy

Zbibk was very popular during the war against the Anilords (he was opposed to them) and is still popular among any rebel groups. He is also very popular among a number of non-human races, Orcs and Jotun in particular.

The El'adasir

The El'adasir are the gods of the Los Alfar. Very little is known about these gods outside of alvaren realms, as the Los Alfar keep their religious beliefs quite private. The best known deity is Danu, the Mother Goddess of Nature.

Danu the All Mother: Goddess of Creation and Nature

Mother Astlan, Earth Mother, the principal oneness of nature and life.

Nét: God of War

Nét is the El'Adasir God of War, has at times been a prominent and well known figure even to alvaran allies and enemies. However, in recent times little has been heard of him in Astlan or the localverse; this is most likely because the Los Alfar have not been engaged in any large scale warfare in the last few thousand years.

The Gods of the Grove

The Gods of the Grove are the primary protectors of the Grove. Outside of the Grove, they are not currently widely worshiped by urban humans or farmers. However, they are very popular among woodsmen, hunters, rangers and scouts, as well as shepherds throughout Astlan. They are extremely popular with many of the hybrid races as well as a sizable number of Sidhe.

The pantheon has a relatively ribald nature and is frowned upon among knowledgeable elites who consider the practices of their followers to be very animalistic, primitive and too overtly sexual.

Nearly all the gods are intimately associated with nature, the seasons, life, death, rebirth and fecundity. The major deities all have deep affiliations with fertility, sexuality, passion, and uninhibited behavior.

Artemis Agrotera: Goddess of the Hunt, The Divine Archer, Goddess of the Wilderness, Chastity, Birth, Protector of Women

Artemis is the female counterpart to Cernunos. They are joint consorts and represent male and female sexuality as well as the circle of life, death and rebirth. She is typically portrayed as a woman ranger with a large bow and quiver of arrows.

Cernunos: The Horned God, Master of the Wild Hunt, God of the Circle of Life

Cernunos is typically portrayed as a horned humanoid with, at a minimum, the horns of a stag, often the head of a stag, and occasionally also the hooves of a stag. He is known to be the consort of Artemis Agrotera.

Dionysus: God of the Harvest, Lord of the Feast, God of the Grape, The Story Teller and Patron of Theater, a.k.a Bacchus

Dionysius is the god of celebration, the successful harvest, wine, feasting, joy and drunken madness.

Dis Pater: God of Fertile Riches, the Element of Earth, Minerals, Death and the Afterlife and Underworld

Also known simply as Dis. A god of death and the underworld, but not a particularly dark god. Rather, a god who represents a return to the source of life, the richness of the soil and later rebirth and renewal.

Pæles, Goddess of Justice and the Rule of Law, Patroness of Heroes, Goddess of War.

Pæles is the goddess of wisdom, strategy and adventure. She is the patron of heroic endeavors and a champion of justice and the rule of law.

Pan: God of the Wild, Master of the Music of Life, God of the Pipes, Shepherd of the Flock, Virility and Male Sexuality

Pan is the nearly exclusive god of the satyrs and fauns. He is also worshiped by nymphs and many of the forest and pasture-dwelling Sidhe. He is portrayed as a large satyr and is known for playing multiple pipe instruments. He is the patron of shepherds and their flocks, and all grazing animals.

The Nyjyr Ennead

The Nyjyr Ennead are a now nearly forgotten pantheon on Astlan. However, unlike the Old Ones, the demise of the Nyjyr Ennead happened much more recently, within the last twelve hundred years.

They Nyjyr Ennead had held great sway on the continents of Natoor and Najaar. When the Etonians began expanding under the commands of Torean and Tiernon, the Nyjyr Ennead put up a much more directed and bitter fight than the Narveson. In particular, the Nyjyr Ennead had no connections to the Anilords and had much greater popularity among the residents of the two continents.

As a consequence, they and their followers were able to strongly resist the Etonians, which led to widespread conflict across the two continents, with the Etonians eventually emerging victorious and then proceeding to convert (or eradicate) worshipers of the Nyjyr Ennead. Thus, within a few hundred years the worship of this pantheon was effectively eliminated and the pantheon forced out of Astlan.

The proscription against worshiping the Nyjyr Ennead has been very effective, as has the destruction of holy documents and articles, and very little is still known of the pantheon or its rites. What did prove much harder to eradicate were the rather incredible feats of engineering their worshipers created. Large, pyramid-shaped temples and tombs can still be found throughout the two continents.

Anup: Protector of Graves. (Element of Earth)

Anup was the Lord of the Underworld, Master of the Dead.

Astet: Goddess of Magic, Motherhood and the Air

Astet is the goddess of magic and the patron of mothers, birth and childcare. She is also the Queen of the Air and a great enchantress.

Atum-Fierd: The God of Fierd (Element of Fire)

God of Light, Fire and the warmth of Fierd, often assumed to be the leader of the pantheon.

Bastet: Defender of Home (Element of Earth)

Bastet was the goddess of house and home, and of the people. She was often portrayed as being a hybrid human and cat, typically with the head of a cat and a body covered in deep black fur.

Nefer-Tum: God of Healing, Beauty and the Sea (Element of Water)

Nefer-Tum is a beautiful young lad of typically human form. He is known for his incredible beauty, his kind nature, his love of the sea and seafaring, as well as his powers of Seeing. He is the son of pêTah and Sekhmekt and completes the Ennead Triad (with his parents).

Sekhmekt: Goddess of Healing, Goddess of Hunting (Elements of Earth and Fire)

Sekhmekt is typically portrayed as a woman with the head of a lioness with a head of golden fur and paws for feet. Wife of pêTah, mother of Nefer-Tum.

pêTah: God of Craftsmen and Architects; a principal God of the Modgriensofarthgonosefren (as Hephaestus) (Element of Earth)

Also known as pi-Tah and Hephaestus. He is the god of jewelers, artists, craftsmen and is (or was) one the favored gods of the Modgriensofarthgonosefren. Rumor has it that worship of Tah under the aspect of Hephaestus continues to this day among the Modgriensofarthgonosefren. Husband of Sakhmekt, father of Nefer-Tum.

Usiris: God of Resurrection and Rebirth (Element of Spirit)

A powerful god representing the apex of the Circle of Life.

The Old Ones

"The Old Ones" is not the actual name of this pantheon; rather it is the vernacular term for these ancient gods of both Eton and Norelon. The last temple to these gods was built outside Gizzor Del and is known as the Cathedral of Pynrex. Most of what is know about them comes from long-ago excavations.

There are some sages and bards who know the tales of the last three high priests, Arand, Estenthor and Galgoren, who built the cathedral, but even so, these last priests were but a revival of a long-lost religion.

The two best-known gods are Sezenon and Mendenon. Mendenon was "Mother Earth" and Sezenon was "Father Sky." Because of these references, in particular to the term "earth"—one of the elements and also the ground/soil—it is believed the old ones were a purely elemental pantheon representing the five elements.

Hierelen: God of Conjury and Pyromancy (Element of Fire)

Also known as Hierelegon.

Mendonon: God of Mercy and Forgiveness (Element of Earth)

Not much is known of Mendonon other than his name.

Sezenon: God of Leadership (Element of Air)

The ruler of the pantheon of these gods.

Mana wielders (and animus wielders) are specially trained (or talented) people who are able to tap into mana and use it to do physical things. Different types of mana wielders access mana in different ways. All mana wielders are able to accumulate and contain larger levels of mana than normal people, due to their training and ability.

Wizards: Wizards tap directly into the raw elemental mana of the universe. They draw the mana directly from the elements and their surroundings and use it for their own purposes. Different specialists are more easily able to tap mana from different elements (necromancers are sometimes an exception). Wizards manipulate mana through the use of spells. Spells are pattern frameworks to contain, direct and control the flow and processing of mana. With the exceptions of conjurors and necromancers, wizards deal very little with animus itself, generally dealing only with mana.

Clerics: Clerics are mana wielders who do not draw their mana directly from nature at all. Rather, clerics tap into the vast streams of mana being channeled to their gods. The ordination process for a priest is the ceremony in which they are attuned to the mana stream flowing to their deity, and the deity allows them to utilize this power to perform "miracles" in the deity's name. Thus, clerics are actually using mana that is already "processed" by living beings (this type of mana is sometimes referred to as spirit mana, not to be confused with the element of Spirit). Clerics generally only deal with animus in the highly organized state, with living spirit entities as a whole, and not with the smaller details that animages and animistic druids do.

Druids: Druids are similar to clerics in that they normally use processed mana, but rather than drawing their mana from worshippers, they typically draw their mana from the plants and animals around them. There are three types of druids: hermetic, shamanistic and animistic. The different classifications are based upon the methods they use to channel mana. Druids generally use the excess mana that is naturally radiated away by living creatures, the principal exception being the sacrificial ceremonies performed by hermetic druids, where they take both animus and mana. Further, some druids are also capable of using raw elemental mana like a wizard, but do this less often, as it is more taxing and difficult for them. Like animages, druids also tend to work with animus a great deal. Animistic druids deal with animus in a manner similar to animages; hermetic druids deal with it more like wizards do (or don't), and shamanistic druids treat it in ways not unlike the cleric.

Animages: Animages tend to defy easy classification. They are actually quite different than the other mana wielders. In some ways, one might consider the animage to be the purest form of mana and animus wielder. Animages make use of animus directly. They generally use the natural affinity of animus to animus to link their animus to that of others. This linking is what allows animages to read minds and do similar mental tricks. Other animages use animus to manipulate mana directly, without the use of spells. Since animages use mana through the manipulation of animus, they can manipulate the various elemental forces.

Necromancers: Technically speaking, a necromancer is just another type of wizard, and they do function that way. However, in addition, the very nature of the necromancer is such that they also utilize "spirit mana" and are in contact with animus quite often. Necromancers often "harvest" mana from unwilling victims for their own purposes (as do "evil clerics"). Necromancers often use fear and other strong emotions to help them collect mana from others. Because they understand the effect of emotions and how they help to radiate mana, necromancers often try very hard to control their emotions, and thus often come off as being cold. Necromancers by definition are specialists in reanimating things that have died and chaining spirits to the earth in mana bodies or otherwise. Most creatures such as liches were once necromancers who decided they didn't want to leave and thus cast great spells and collected a lot of mana from others just for this purpose.

Conjurers: Conjurers are wizards, and they use mana like any other wizard. The reason they deserve special mention is because what they do with this mana is different. Conjurers exploit the natural affinity for animus and mana. They use mana to contact and summon specific concentrations of animus (e.g., spirit-type beings, demons, ghosts, etc.) Normally animus attracts mana; in this case, conjurers use mana to attract or pull animus.

Bards: While not normally considered spell weavers, legend dictates that some bards can use the power of music and song to cast spells. This is an alternate form of wizardry that is not well advertised. There are very few such bards and schools for them are rare, but they do exist.

Others: Certain foreign individuals with skills in the martial arts seem to be able to perform magical or nearly magical feats. These feats are generally forms of animastery, similar to the work of some animages.

Mana pools and anima jars are special arcane devices that allow the storage of mana and animus, respectively. Wizards, clerics, druids, and animages all may create these devices subject to the limitations of the spells or disciplines that govern the creation of mana pools and anima jars.

In general, mana pools are constructed from the highest quality gemstones. Anima jars are usually, but not always, finely wrought crystalline containers that may be sealed. The amount of mana or animus that may be stored depends upon the material from which the device is made, the abilities of the creator of the object, and the limitations of the spell or discipline used to create the device.

In all cases, the mana or animus stored in these devices may only be accessed through the use of mana and animus links (respectively). In the case of professions such as wizards, where such fine distinctions are not made on links, a simple object link is sufficient.

Mana pools and anima jars are extremely useful devices that allow mana and animus wielders to greatly extend their power. Any mana wielder may use any mana pool or anima jar made by others, as long as no current link to an owner exists. If such a link already exists, and if the individual desiring to use the mana pool or anima jar is capable, he or she may attempt to break the pre-existing link. However, the destruction (or even willful release by the owner) of the link destroys the anima jar or mana pool.

One of the first things attempted by overly ambitious mana wielders when mana pools and anima jars were first discovered was to try and use multiple pools at one time. Unfortunately, this tragic experiment met with great disaster and resulted in what was posthumously named Michael's First and Last Law of Animagic Containers. The law states that the animagic feedback through linked animagic pools is proportional to the square of the number of pools.

More simply speaking, using multiple mana pools or multiple anima jars in series (or parallel) is extremely dangerous. Using one of each is no problem, as anima jars and mana pools do not resonate, nor do they add to each other's feedback. Specifically, whenever a mana wielder attempts to use multiple mana pools or multiple anima jars, there is a chance of magical fumbling skyrockets in proportion to the number of mana pools *or* anima jars linked to the wielder (note that jars do not create feedback with pools; pools resonate only with pools, and jars with jars). This applies to all classes; the chance of a resonance feedback scales in proportion to the number of pools or jars in the link.

Thus, for safety reasons, very few mana wielders ever employ more than one mana pool at a time. The only known exception to this is the spell Mana Wheel, where somehow the creator of the spell got around this limitation. The details of this breaking of Michael's First and Last Law of Animagic Containers has puzzled more than a few hundred magical theorists. The best guess is that somehow, the very mana-draining nature of the spell keeps the feedback minimized.

One common confusion is that mages often tend to have multiple mana pools on them. However, generally only one or maybe two pools are for the wizard's own personal use. Most of the other mana pools have links to other magic items on the mage's person. While typically an arcane device that uses a mana pool would have its own mana pool, sometimes that item is too small to mount a gem of the correct size, so the creator may have created two matching pieces of jewelry, say a ring and pendant, where the actual mana pool for the ring was in the pendant, or perhaps someone later reworked the ring to add an extra mana pool. There are many possibilities.

Timekeeping in the Abyss, and most of the locations in the localverse, are imprecise. Aside from the cost of accurate timekeeping devices, there are few official authorities. Typically, the ruler of each region dictates the hours of the day in their region. In most cases, local scholars base the time of day on observations of Fierd and the moons. These scholars are then charged with synchronizing the sometimes-faulty timekeeping devices.

The most obvious effect of this is that there is essentially no synchronization of time between kingdoms. Most mana users who have an interest in interregional trade typically have a table of offsets so that they can coordinate communication via mirrors or other long-distance communication devices. The same is true for interdimensional traders, where time can be even trickier since different worlds may not only have a different breakdown of time, but often have different periods of rotation, and thus different day lengths.

The Abyss is even stranger, since it doesn't have days. As far as anyone has been able to determine, the Abyss is flat, and probably infinite, or at least very large. No known entity has found and reported an edge, nor has anyone managed to circumscribe a spherical Abyss, despite journeys lasting centuries to millennia by intrepid explorers.

Further evidence of the Abyss's flatness or extremely large spherical nature was provided during the construction of the boom tunnels. Throughout the breadth and scope of the boom tunnel network, Altrusian engineers were unable to detect any sign of systemic curvature to the Abyss. While there were numerous elevation differences over the vast distances, there was no evidence of actual curvature.

Most demons that visit the localverse use Court Time, based on the artificial days of the Courts of Chaos. While there are other cities or regions in the Abyss that have their own time, most copy the conventions of the Courts.

Court Periods	Court Deminutes	Astlan Time	Earth Time
Period 1	000:111	0:00 to 3:33	0:00 to 4:00
Period 2	112:222	3:34 to 6:66	4:01 to 8:00
Period 3	223:333	6:67 to 9:99	8:01 to 12:00
Period 4	334:444	10:00 to 13:33	12:01 to 16:00
Period 5	445:555	13:34 to 16:66	16:01 to 20:00
Period 6	556:666	16:67 to 19:99	20:01 to 24:00

Appendix: Druids and Shamans

Druids, along with animages, are one of the most enigmatic professions in the world. Like the animage, part of this stems from the fact that the job specialization found within the profession can at times be so distinct as to make the specializations seem like completely different professions. Similar to animages, druids tend to guard rather closely the secrets of their power, making themselves seem more mysterious. This is different from clerics, who make no secret about where their power comes from, or wizards, who also make no secret of their craft; they simply charge a lot to teach people what they do. Finally, unlike the animage, a druid's sense of secrecy comes not so much from historical reasons, but rather from the fact that most druids are more concerned about the natural and spirit worlds than the worlds of men. Hence, druids tend to ignore the questions of men, trying to answer instead the questions of nature.

Specializations:

There are three distinct types of druids. All three types share the same method of collecting and utilizing mana, and all three effectively have the same goals in mind: that of understanding and preserving the natural world around them. The differences in the specializations come in the means to these goals and their training on how to observe the natural world.

All druids generally use processed mana, or spirit mana, that has been absorbed and collected by living things. They collect the excess mana radiated by the living world around them and channel it back into the world in a more constructive manner (in theory, at least). This is not a hard-and-fast rule, however. Because they use mana that has been processed by living creatures, they are similar to clerics, but they do not have the intermediate buffer of the deity, so their use of mana can be a bit more hazardous.

The different approaches for druidic lore are given below. These are only rough overviews of the different lores. These are broad patterns that often vary and even overlap in different places and cultures. Also, one should be aware that while the ultimate goals are the same, and that while in some cultural groups these traditions and methods may overlap and blend, mix, and match, there are also places in the world where the different traditions are vehemently opposed to one another. The most notable of these are conflicts between hermetic and animistic druids in some parts of the world.

Hermetic Lore: Hermetic druidism holds that the entire world, nature, and super-nature is a completely closed set. As such, it has limits and rules that can be understood and manipulated. Hermetic druids use ritualistic ceremonies, chants and complex dances to manipulate the natural world and influence the spirits that govern the day-to-day operation of nature.

Shamanistic Lore: Shamanistic druidism holds that the world is populated by vast numbers of powerful spirits and beings, humanoid-kind being only the smallest part. It is the harmonious interaction of all these beings, these flows of animus and spirit, that drive the world. All such spirits have knowledge and intelligence to at least some degree, and by interacting positively with these beings, the good of all can be served.

Animistic Lore: Animistic druidism holds that all of nature and super-nature is one. While on the surface, there is the appearance of separateness and individual free will among different beings and spirits, in reality all are part of a single entity. While at times, parts of the body may work in opposition to each other and sometimes even against the greater good of the whole, these are but temporary deviations. Animistic druids work at causing all parts of the Oneness to work together harmoniously for the greater good. Since animistic druids realize that all spirit, all animus, and even all matter and mana are one, they are able to manipulate all of these forms of the Oneness, much as they would their body. Consequently, the actual manipulation of mana and animus is very similar to that of animages.

Druidic Magic:

Druidic magic comes in three basic forms: spells, disciplines, and totem. Spells are divided into three basic types: ceremonies, chants and dances. Ceremonies are completely analogous to clerical rituals, and chants are analogous to clerical mantras. Mechanically speaking, dances are a combination of chants and ceremonies in the sense that their casting time is until something happens or until the spell caster gets tired and gives up.

Dances are used primarily to influence or entice spirits into doing what the caster desires (if one is a shaman—hermetics generally insist that dances are simply extremely complex patterns that are used to channel energy).

Disciplines work similar to animage disciplines and/or skills. As one progresses in knowledge of a discipline, one gains the ability to do greater and greater things with that discipline.

Totem is something very hard to explain to a non-shaman (or "non-totemed" individual of any sort). Mechanically, totem behaves something like a skill or discipline. It is, however, much more. Totem is a way of life, an outlook, and a guide and guardian all rolled into one. One important distinction is that one does not exactly direct or use totem. Instead, totem guides, directs, inspires, and assists the "totemed" individual. The whole point of the totem "skill" is actually learning to listen to one's totem. It is the ability to recognize, listen to, and understand one's totem that is measured and discussed as if it were a skill.

Totem
What is a Totem?

The first step (and also the last step) in the path to understanding nature and the world is to understand oneself. To understand oneself, one must know who one is in the world and where one is going. This first step is not easy, and, in fact, many spend their entire lives trying to do just this. In this endeavor, it is very useful to have a guide or guideline to follow. Such a guide is a totem. An individual's totem can explain a lot about who that person is, where he or she has been and where he or she will go. It is a summation of the individual's past and family's path and a guide pointing to the future. Simply recognizing one's totem is a major undertaking.

Recognizing One's Totem:

In order to recognize one's totem, one must typically study with a sentient teacher the nature of totems. A shaman is someone who has recognized their totem and tries to live by it.

Living By One's Totem

After discovering one's totem, the aspirant should have a better understanding of their nature and their outlook and motivation. This is generally useful in explaining why one feels a certain way or behaves in a certain manner.

Since the totem of an individual is directly indicative of his or her true nature, consistently not following the nature of totem, or fighting it, could be considered unwise and counterproductive from the point of view of personal growth. Any person who suppresses or denies his or her true nature is only doing self-harm.

Manifestations of Totem:

Totems manifest themselves in many ways. Totems are a reflection of who the person is and are at the same time a separate individual. Totems most often manifest themselves to the shaman as spirit-like beings in their visions and dreams, or as omens in the physical world.

Usually there is a specific spirit manifestation of the totem that the individual comes to associate with the totem. The level, nature, and frequency of the communication with this spirit manifestation is dependent on the nature of the totem and the skill level the shaman has in recognizing and understanding when the totem is trying to communicate.

Such manifestations are generally at the discretion of the totem. Naturally, the individual can seek out the totem's advice and the totem may or may not choose to give it, dependent on the nature of the totem, the skill level of the individual, and the need of the individual.

The totem may choose to manifest in dreams, hallucinations, or in the physical form of an animal of the totem's type, or simply in urges or compulsions as appropriate.

As examples, Bear is generally very blunt, direct, and to the point, but not overly explicit, generally being terse and without much patience. Rat tends to be secretive in giving information and may choose riddles or things of a similar nature. Owl, on the other hand, may get pedagogical to levels of detail undesired.

As the individual gains knowledge of his or her totem, he or she may even be able to assume attributes and the very form of the totem at will.